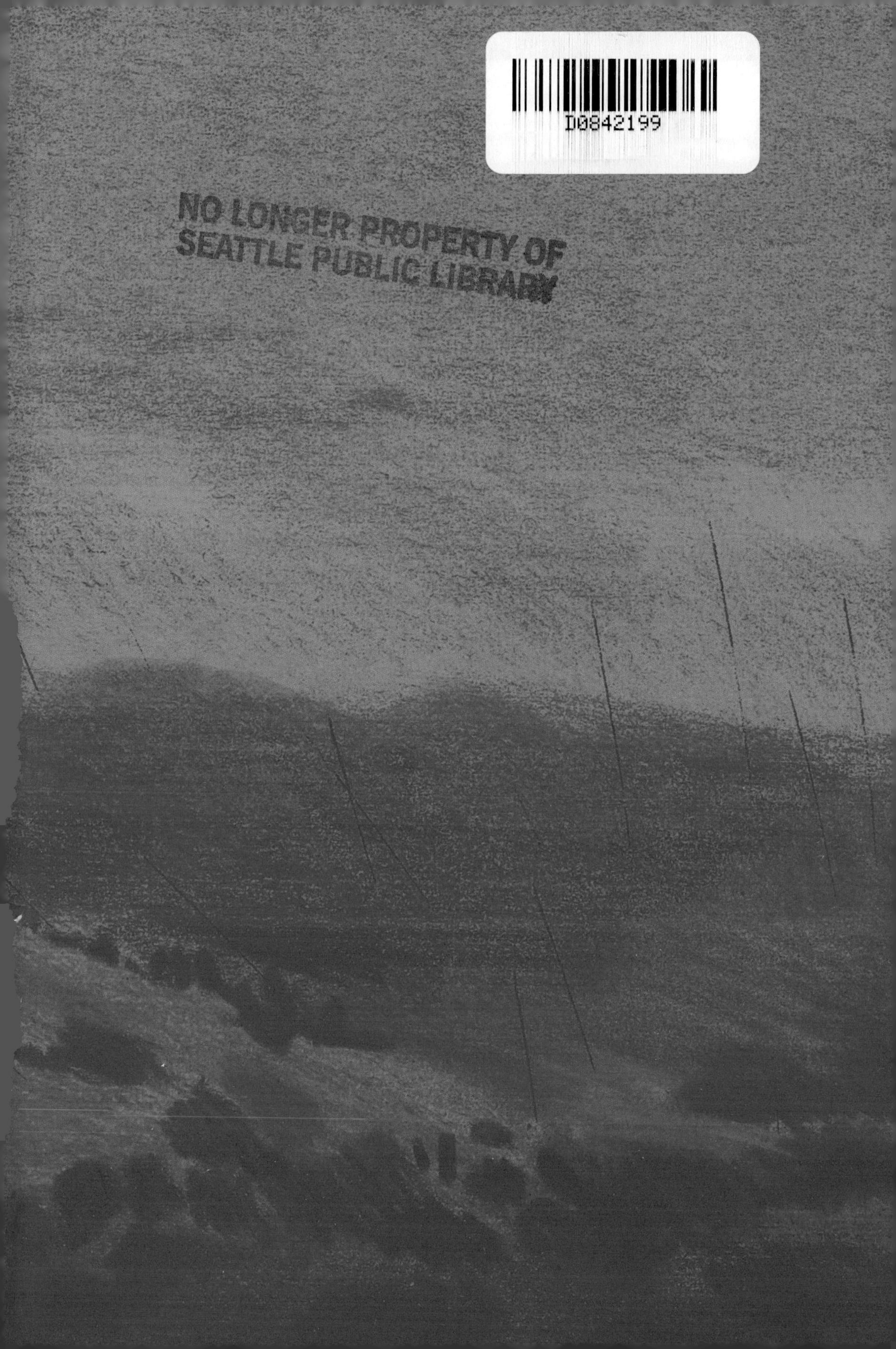

*Dedicated to Lidia.*
*A girl from the north.*
JUDITH

*Dedicated to all my Rosas.*
*To Sonia and M.J.*
*To Miguel, my angel writer.*
*To all the birds who became dogs.*
*To all the Jeremiases and Javiers.*
*To all mothers, my mother and*
*my son's mother.*
*To all children.*
*To my son.*
MARK

First published in English in 2019
by SelfMadeHero
139–141 Pancras Road
London NW1 1UN
www.selfmadehero.com

English translation © 2019 SelfMadeHero

Words by Mark Bellido
Art by Judith Vanistendael

Translated from Spanish by Erica Mena

Publishing Director: Emma Hayley
Sales & Marketing Manager: Sam Humphrey
Editorial & Production Manager: Guillaume Rater
Designer: Txabi Jones
UK Publicist: Paul Smith
With thanks to: Dan Lockwood

© 2016 Judith Vanistendael and Mark Bellido.
Originally published by De Bezige Big I Oog & Blik, Amsterdam.

A CIP record for this book is available from the British Library

ISBN: 978-1-910593-70-7

10 9 8 7 6 5 4 3 2 1

Printed and bound in Slovenia

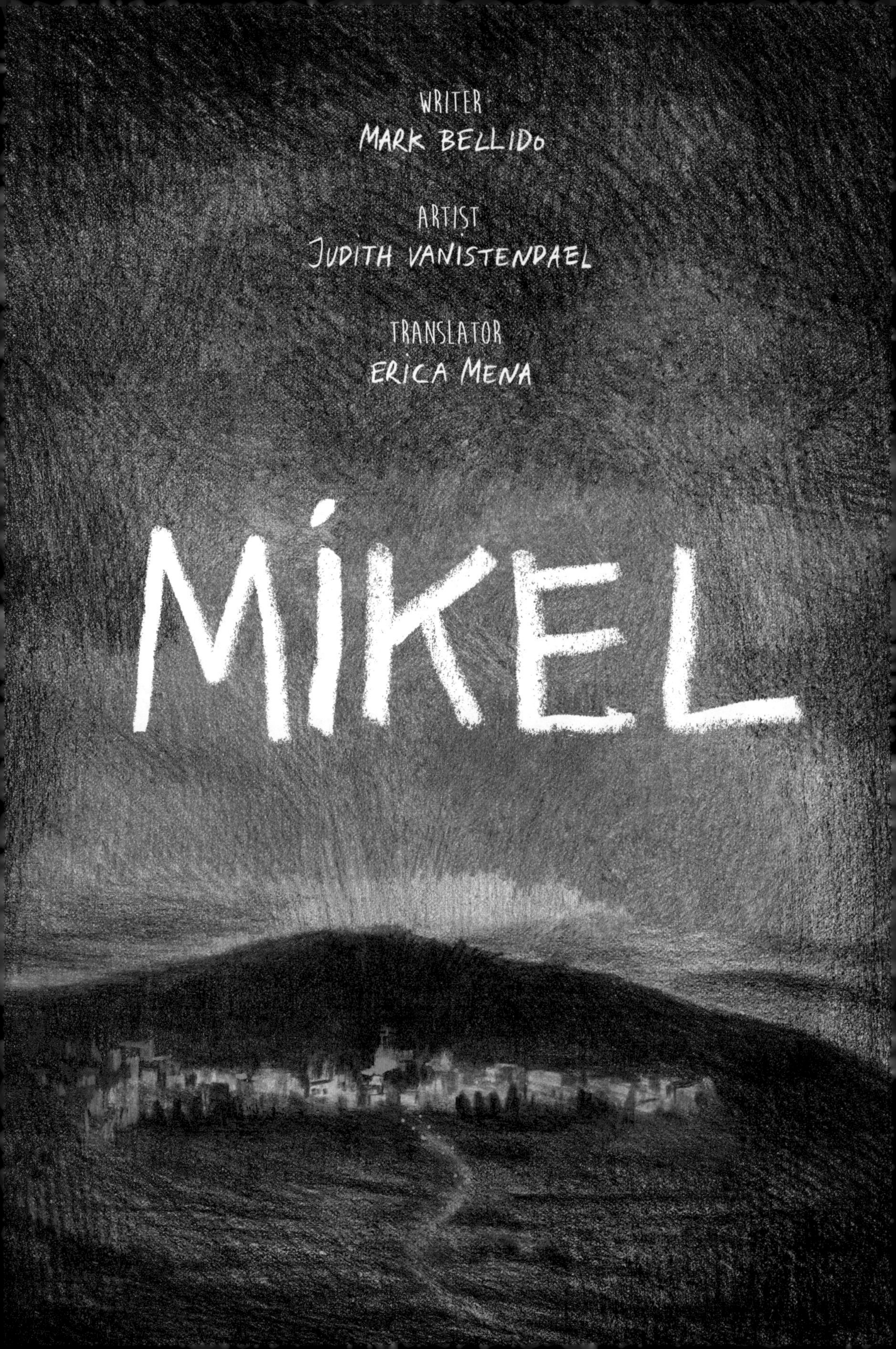
WRITER
MARK BELLIDO
ARTIST
JUDITH VANISTENDAEL
TRANSLATOR
ERICA MENA
MIKEL

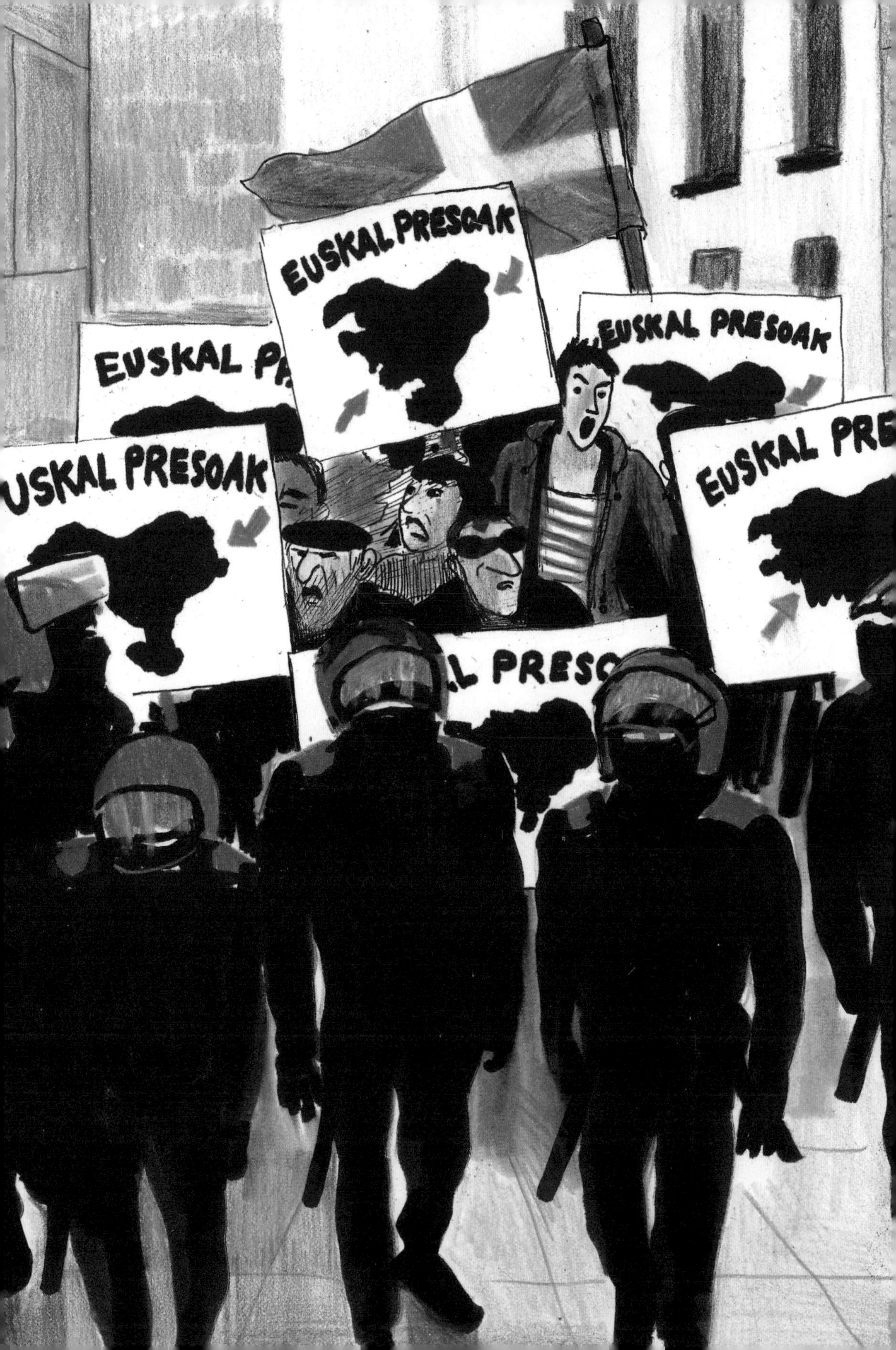
EUSKAL PRESOAK
EUSKAL P
EUSKAL PRESOAK
USKAL PRESOAK
EUSKAL PRE
L PRESO

On 20 October 2011, the separatist group Euskadi Ta Askatasuna (ETA) (Basque Country and Freedom) declared a permanent cessation to their armed struggle. To date, they have yet to lay down their arms... In the 52 years of ETA's existence, some 800 people died, and thousands of exiles were forced to flee the oppressive climate.

During the last 20 years of ETA activity, judges, academics, journalists, politicians, artists and officials - in total, over 1,000 Basque citizens - lived under the protection of private security personnel pejoratively called "txakurras" (dogs). These bodyguards - up to 3,000 of them in the darkest periods - came from all over, were poorly trained and were armed only with a pistol and 25 bullets.

THIS IS THE ALMOST-TRUE STORY OF ONE OF THEM.

"I DISAPPROVE OF WHAT
YOU SAY, BUT I WILL
DEFEND TO THE DEATH
YOUR RIGHT TO SAY IT."

**EVELYN BEATRICE HALL,**
*THE FRIENDS OF VOLTAIRE*

# PROLOGUE

## Today, 8 December 2010, Pamplona.

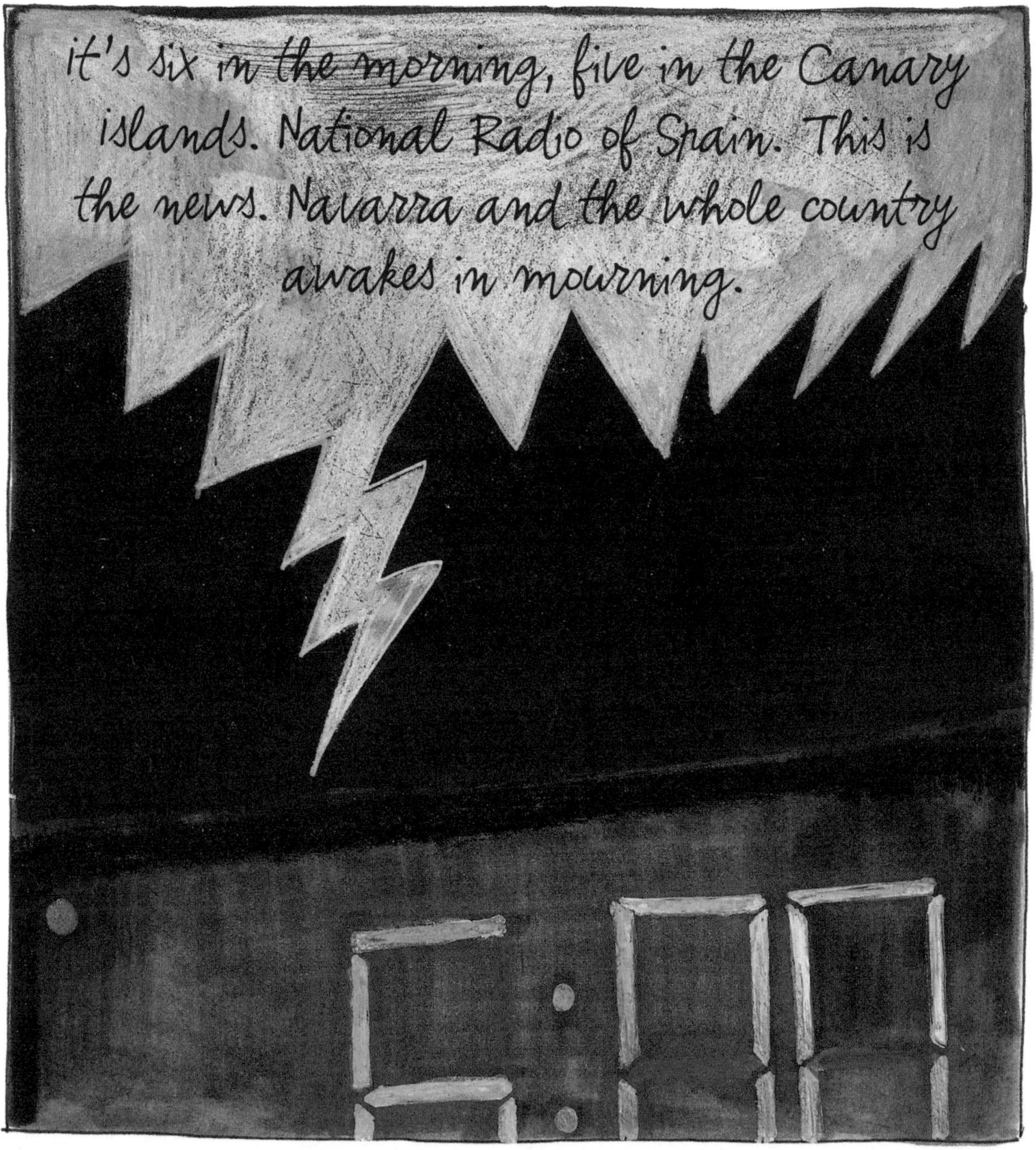
it's six in the morning, five in the Canary islands. National Radio of Spain. This is the news. Navarra and the whole country awakes in mourning.

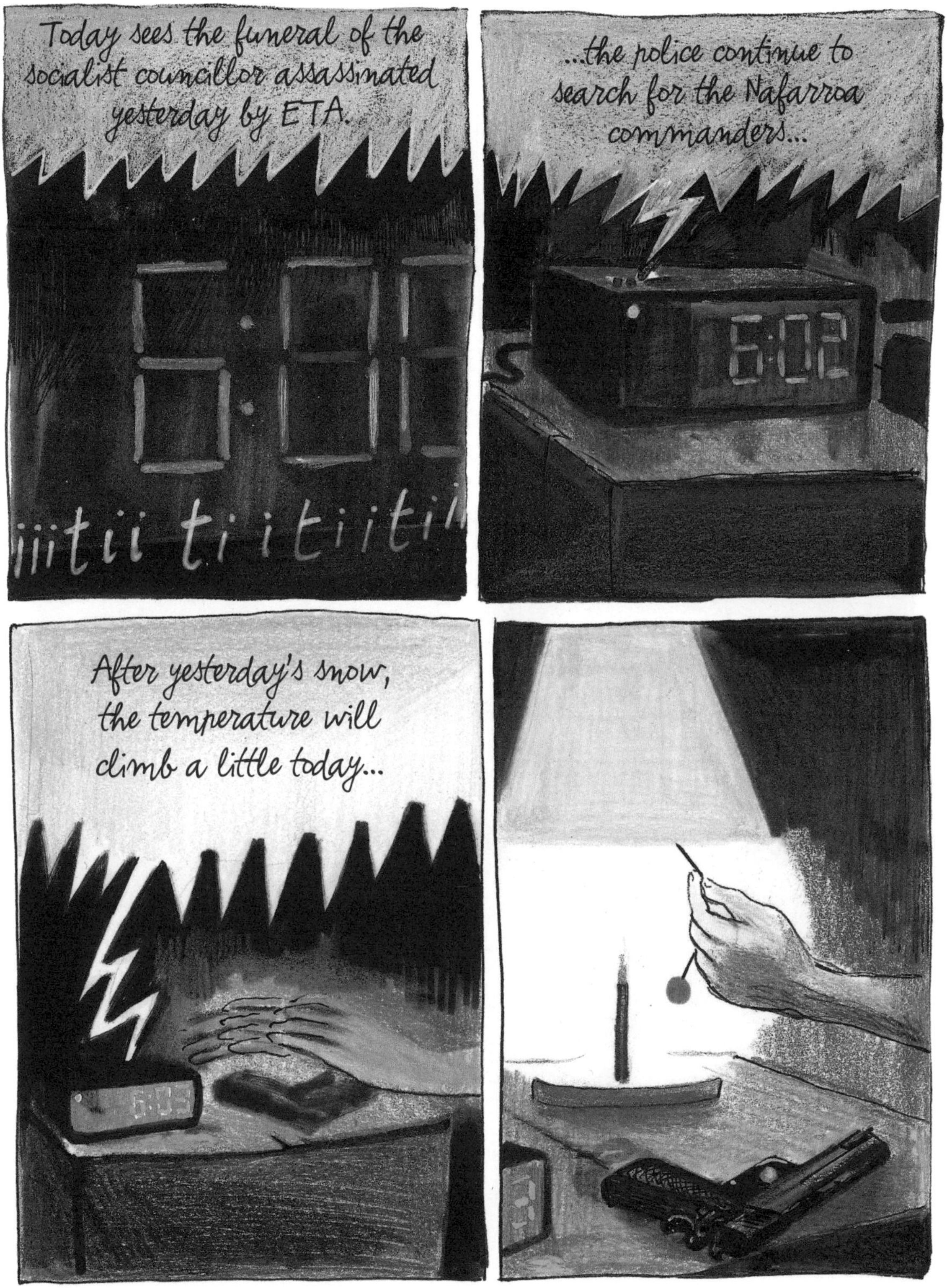
Today sees the funeral of the socialist councillor assassinated yesterday by ETA.
...the police continue to search for the Nafarroa commanders...
After yesterday's snow, the temperature will climb a little today...

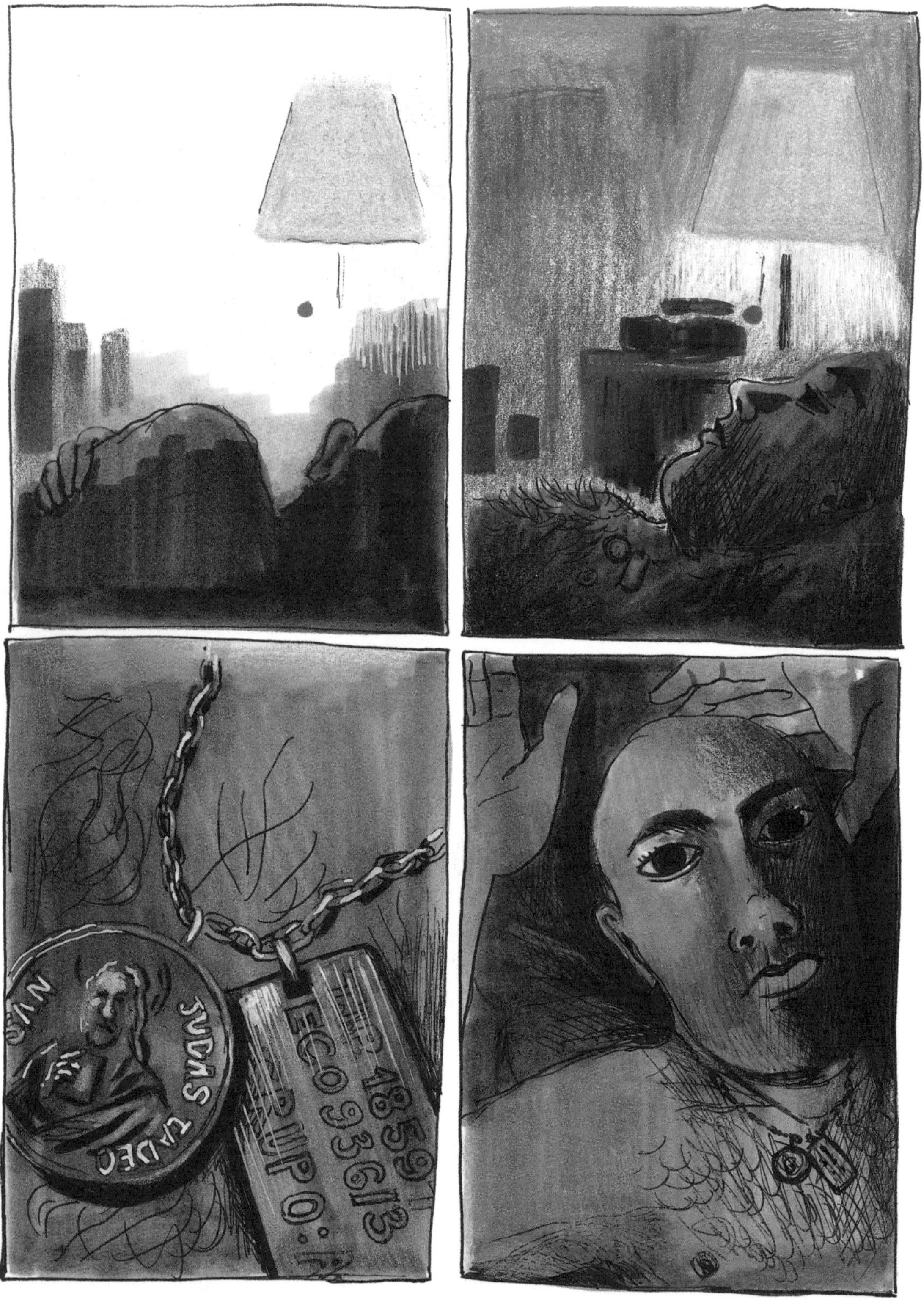

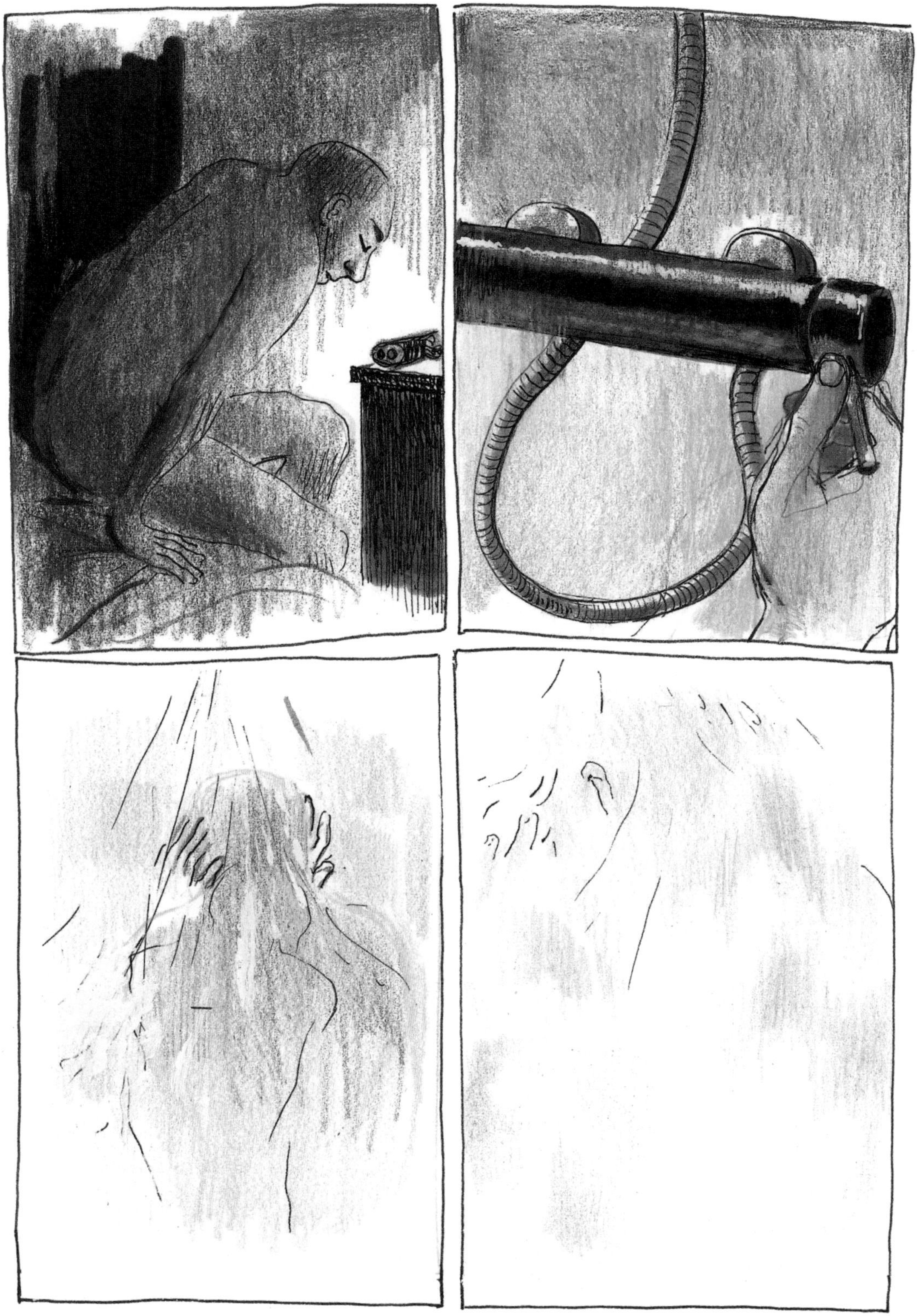

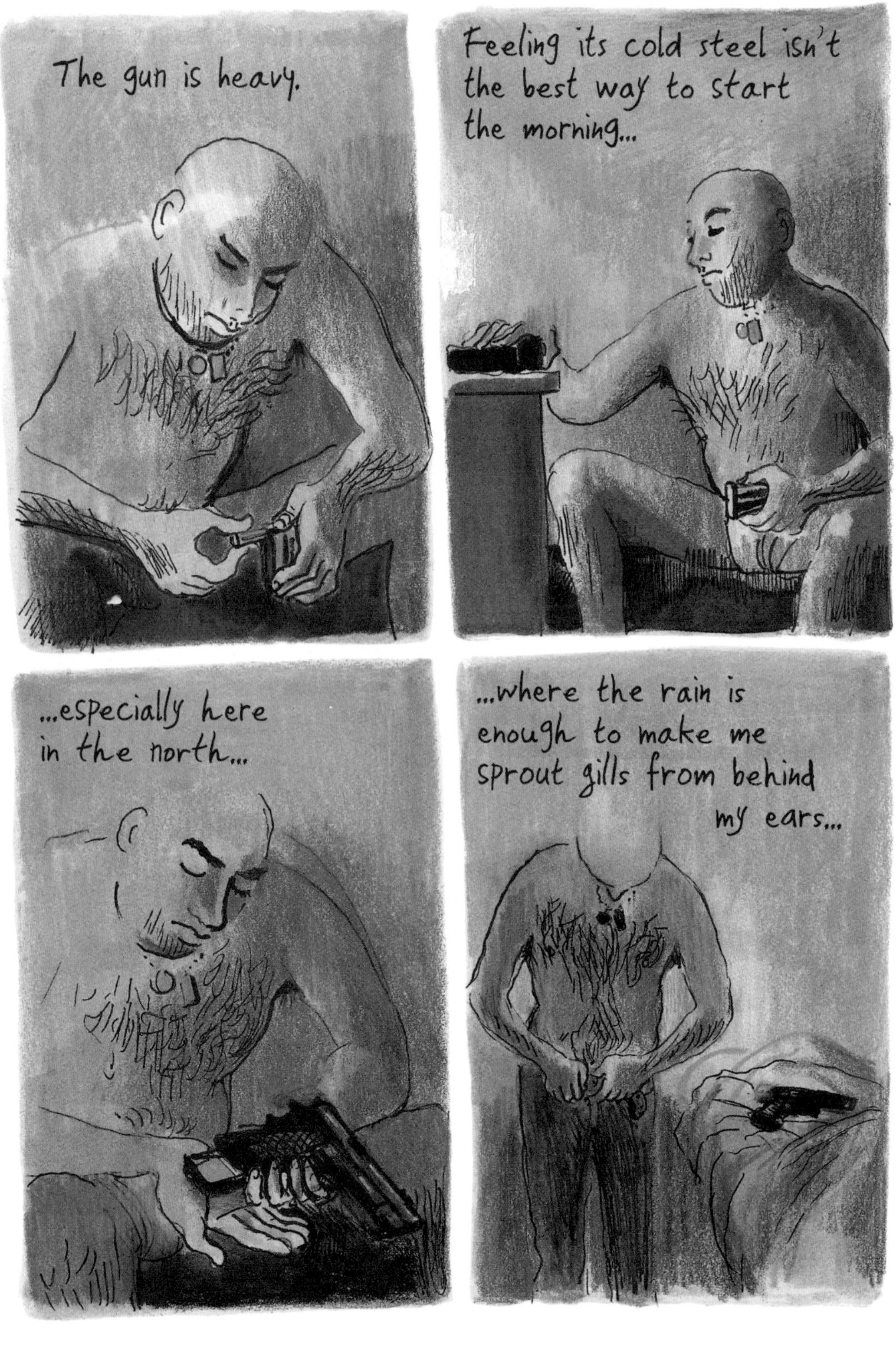
The gun is heavy.
Feeling its cold steel isn't the best way to start the morning...
...especially here in the north...
...where the rain is enough to make me sprout gills from behind my ears...

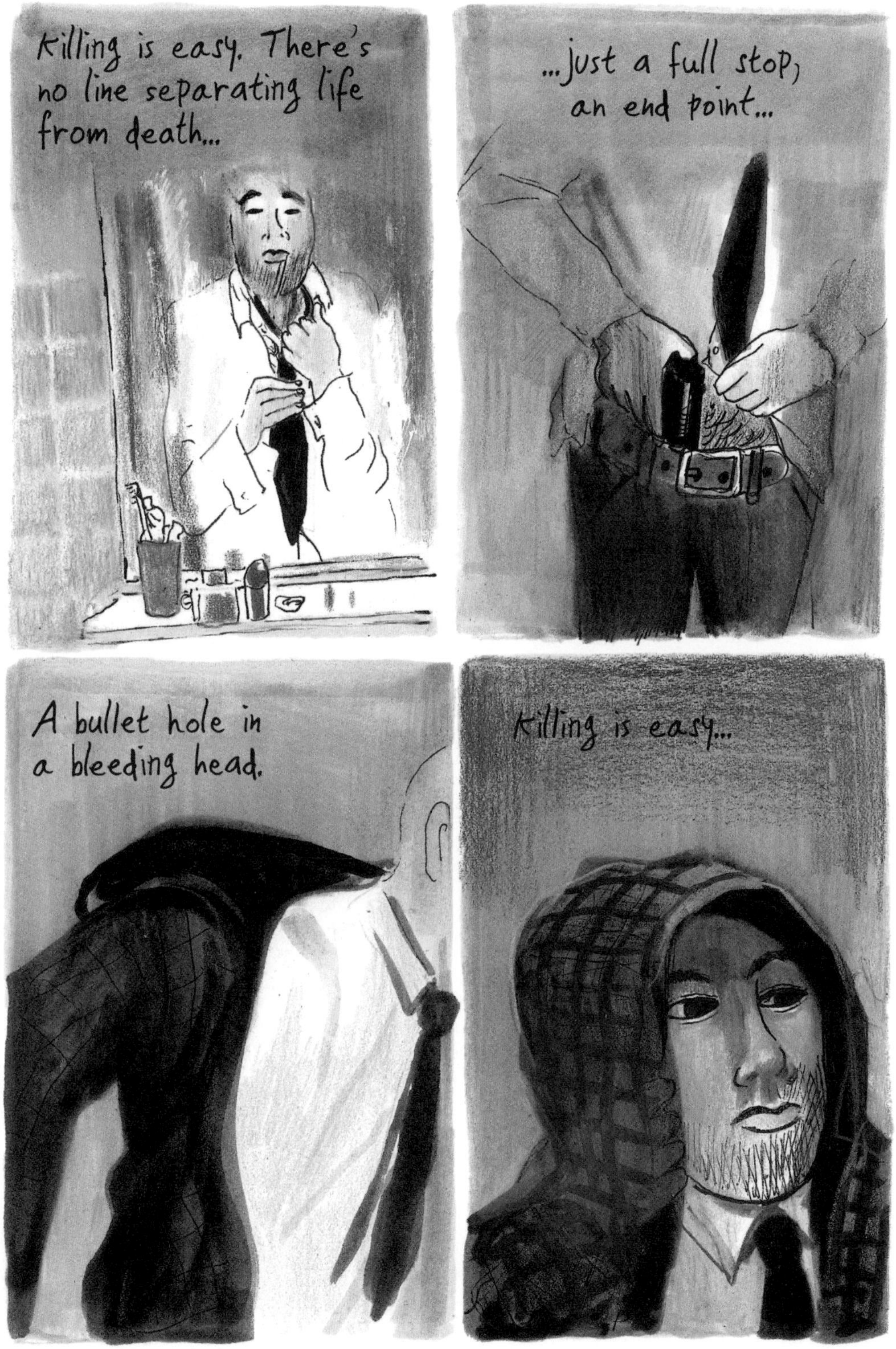
Killing is easy. There's no line separating life from death...
...just a full stop, an end point...
A bullet hole in a bleeding head.
Killing is easy...

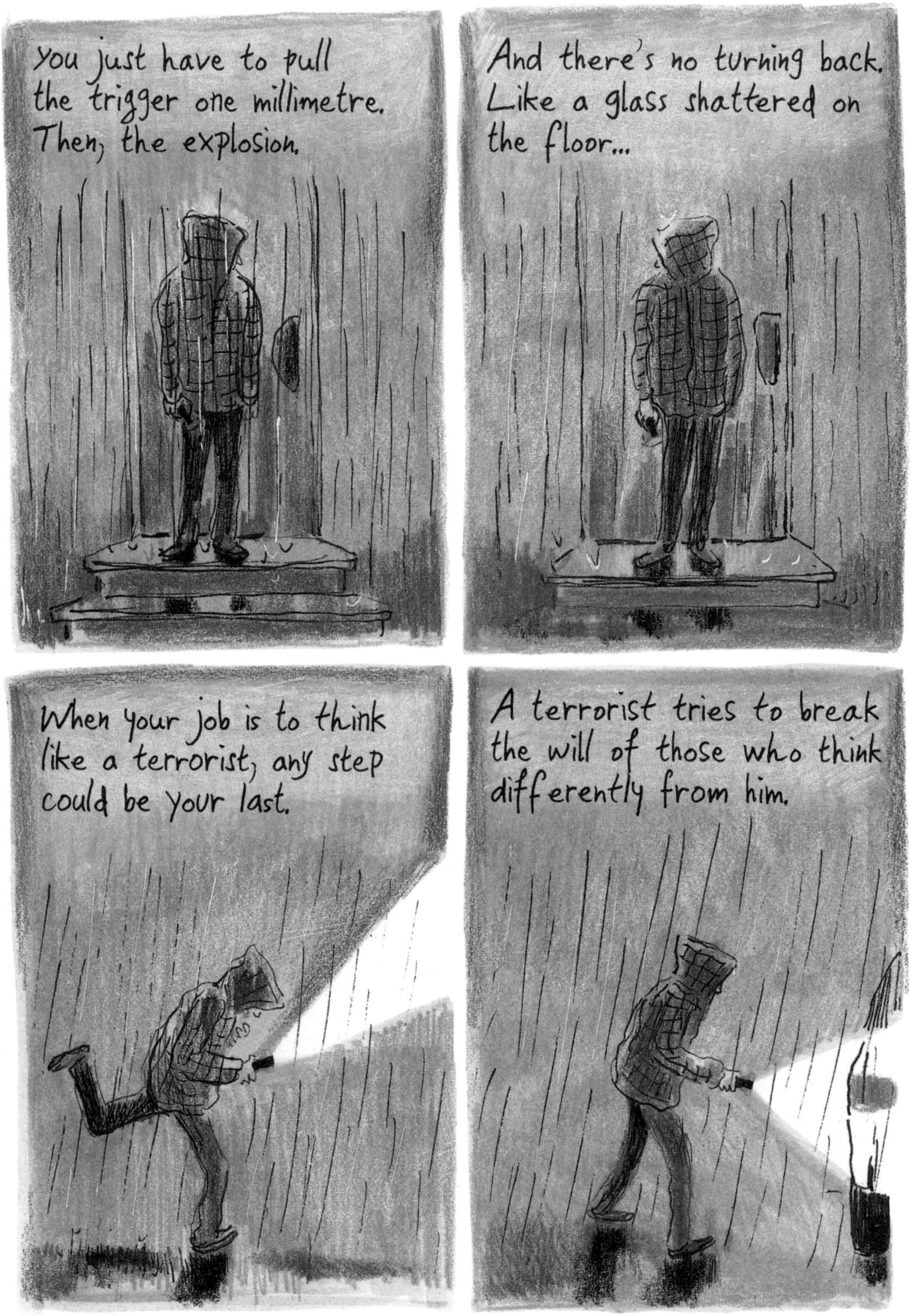
You just have to pull the trigger one millimetre. Then, the explosion.
And there's no turning back. Like a glass shattered on the floor...
When your job is to think like a terrorist, any step could be your last.
A terrorist tries to break the will of those who think differently from him.

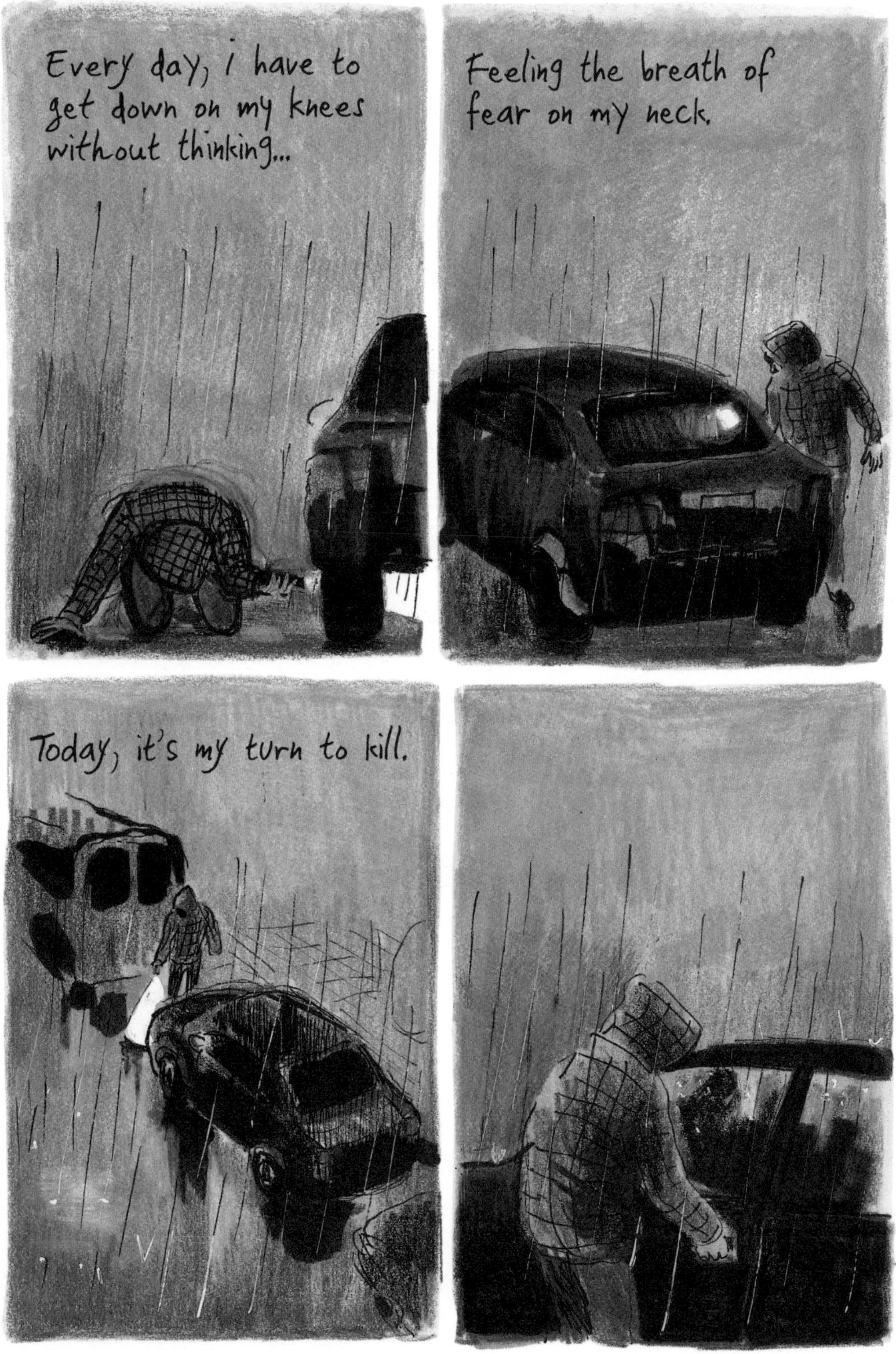
Every day, i have to get down on my knees without thinking...
Feeling the breath of fear on my neck.
Today, it's my turn to kill.

But i had another life,
before...

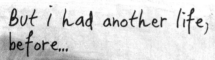

And it was nothing
like this.

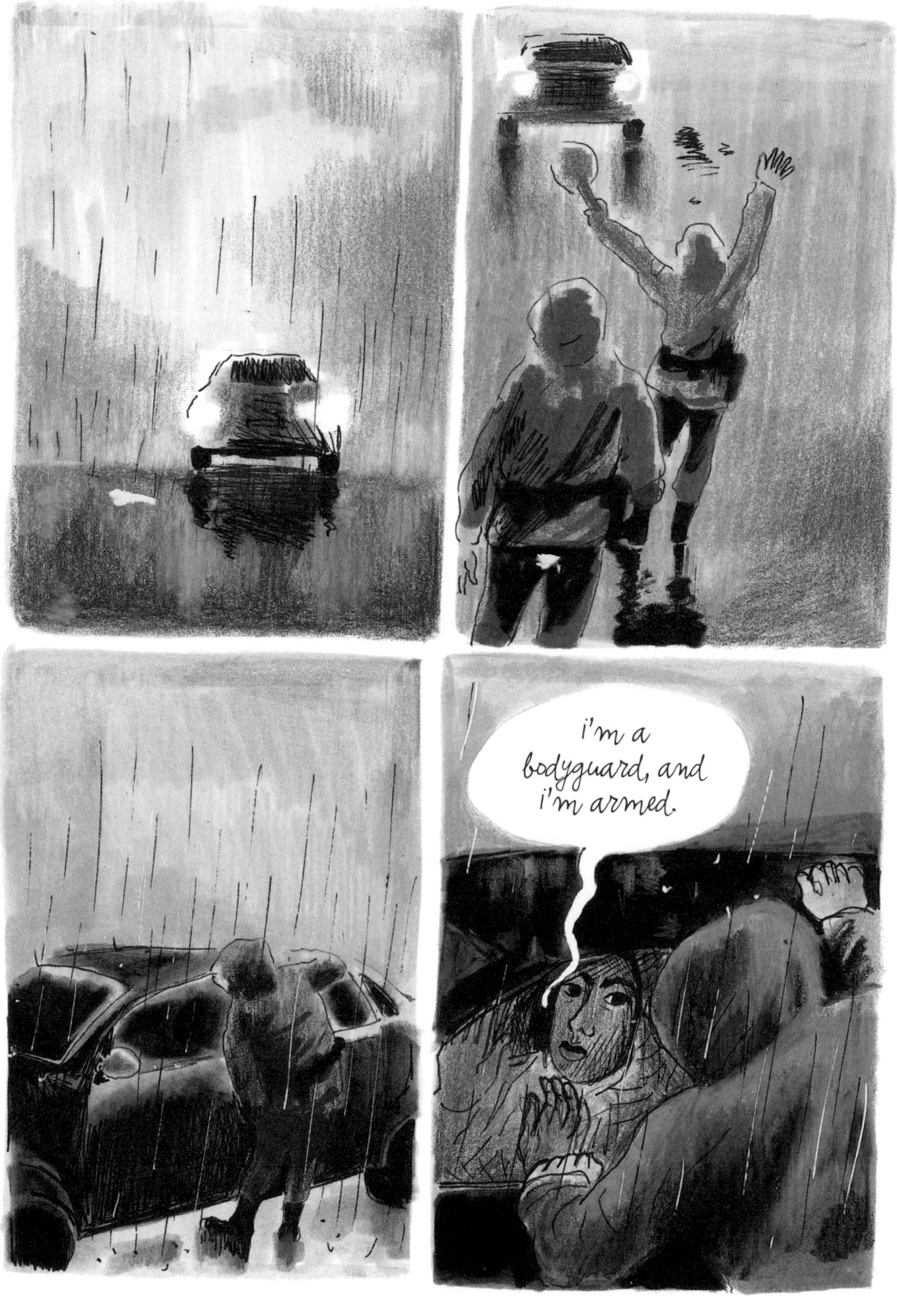
i'm a bodyguard, and i'm armed.

# MiQUEL

spring 2006. Costur, Castellón, Spain.

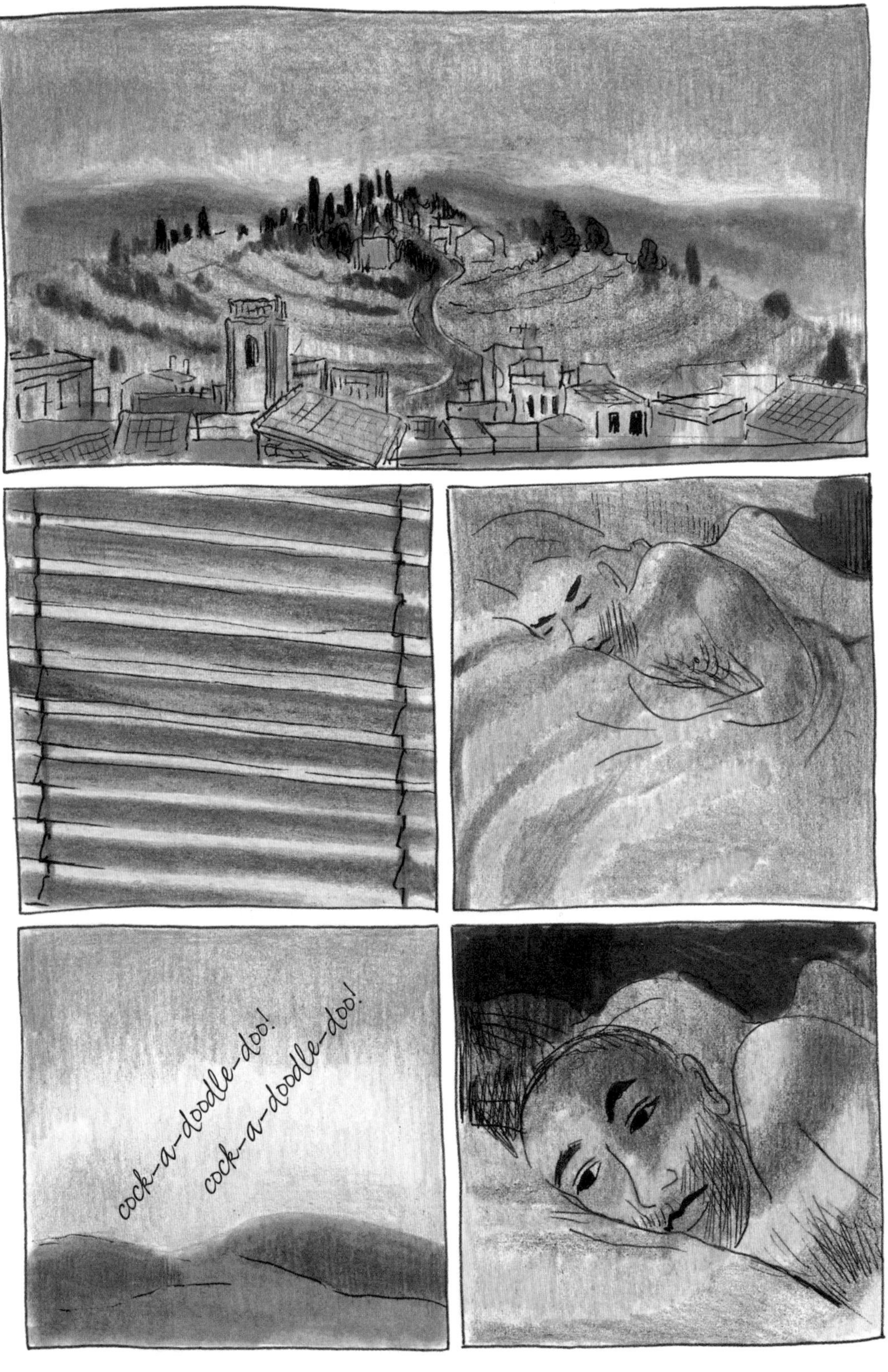
cock-a-doodle-doo!
cock-a-doodle-doo!

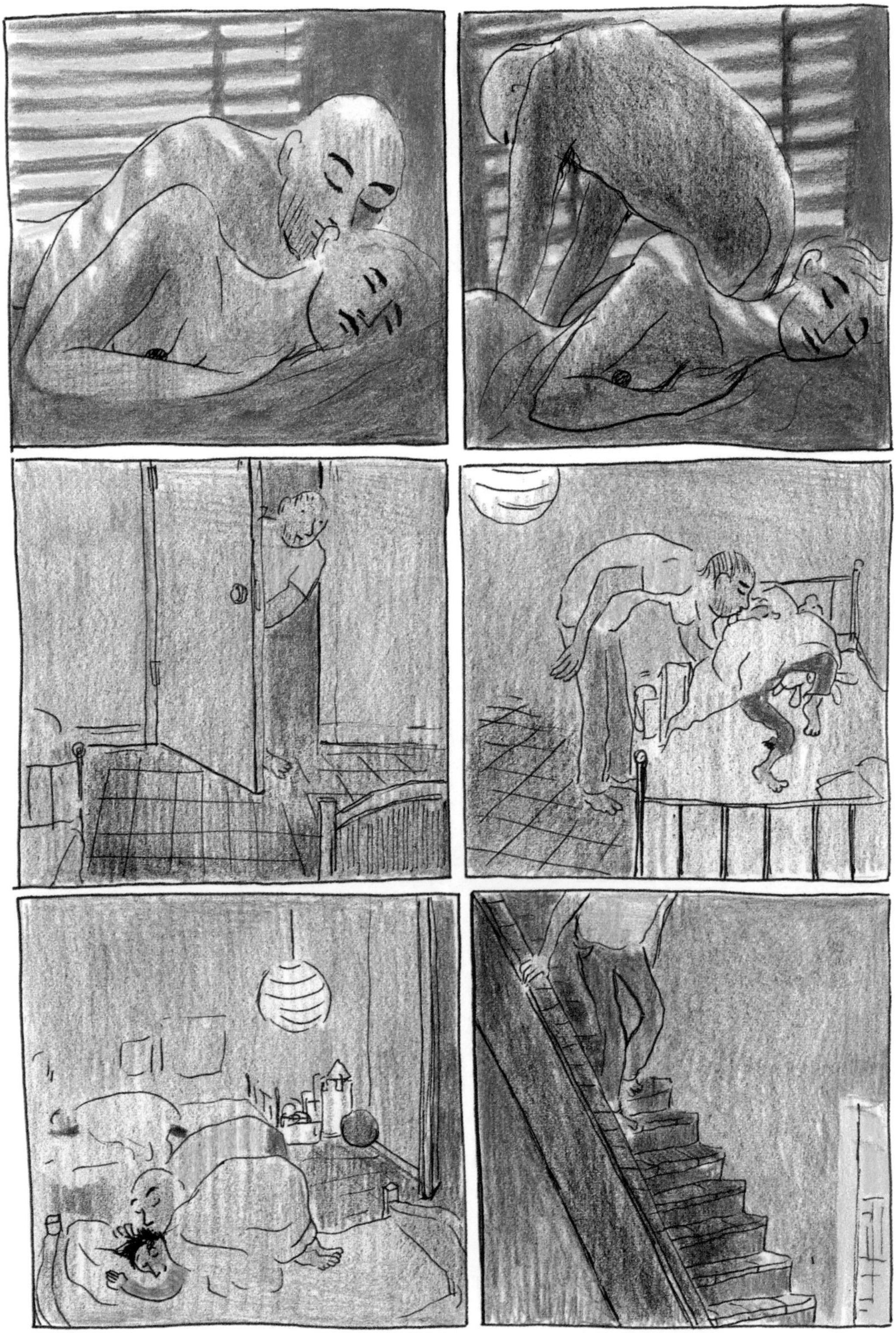

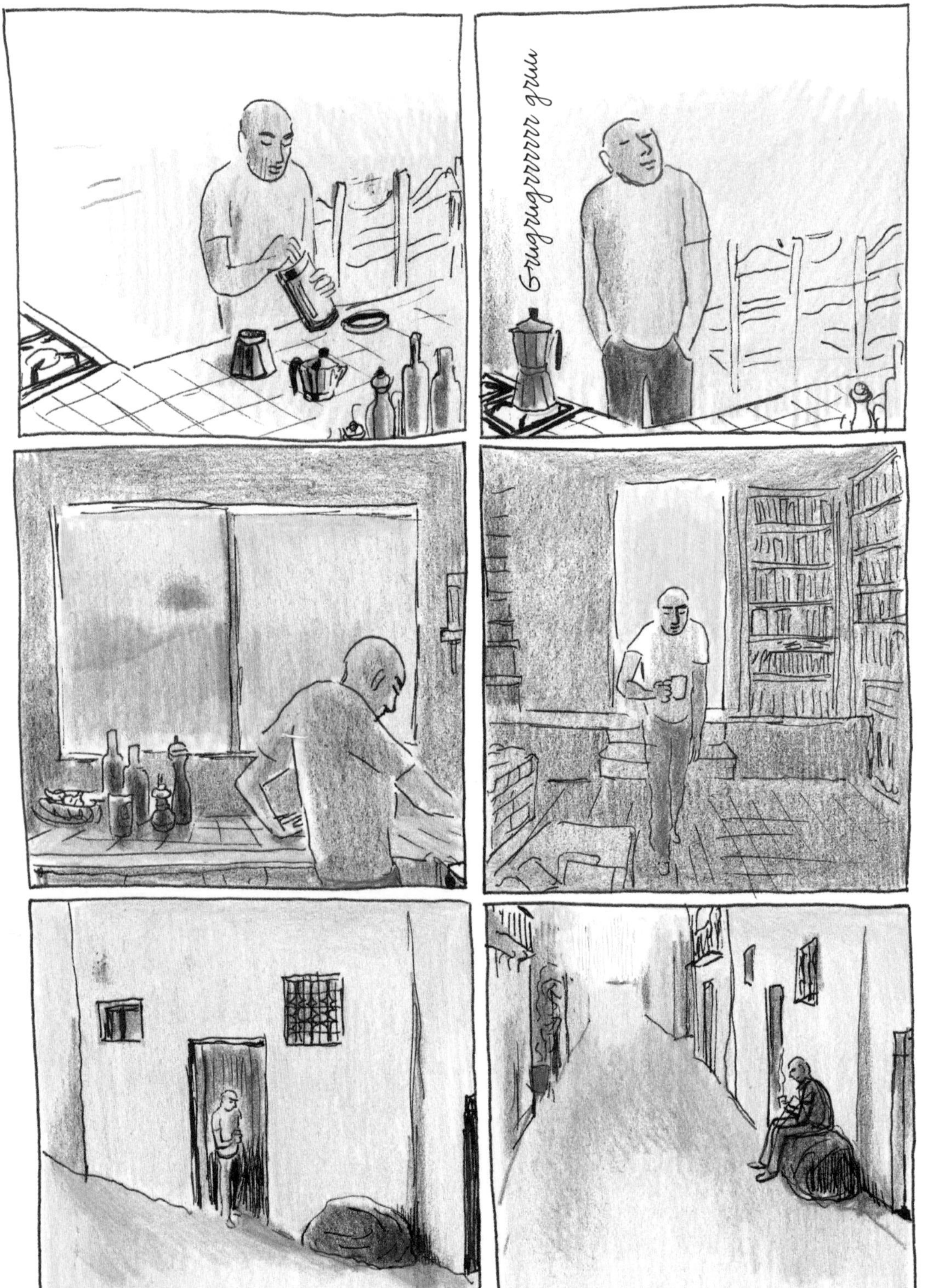
Grugrugrrrrrr gruu

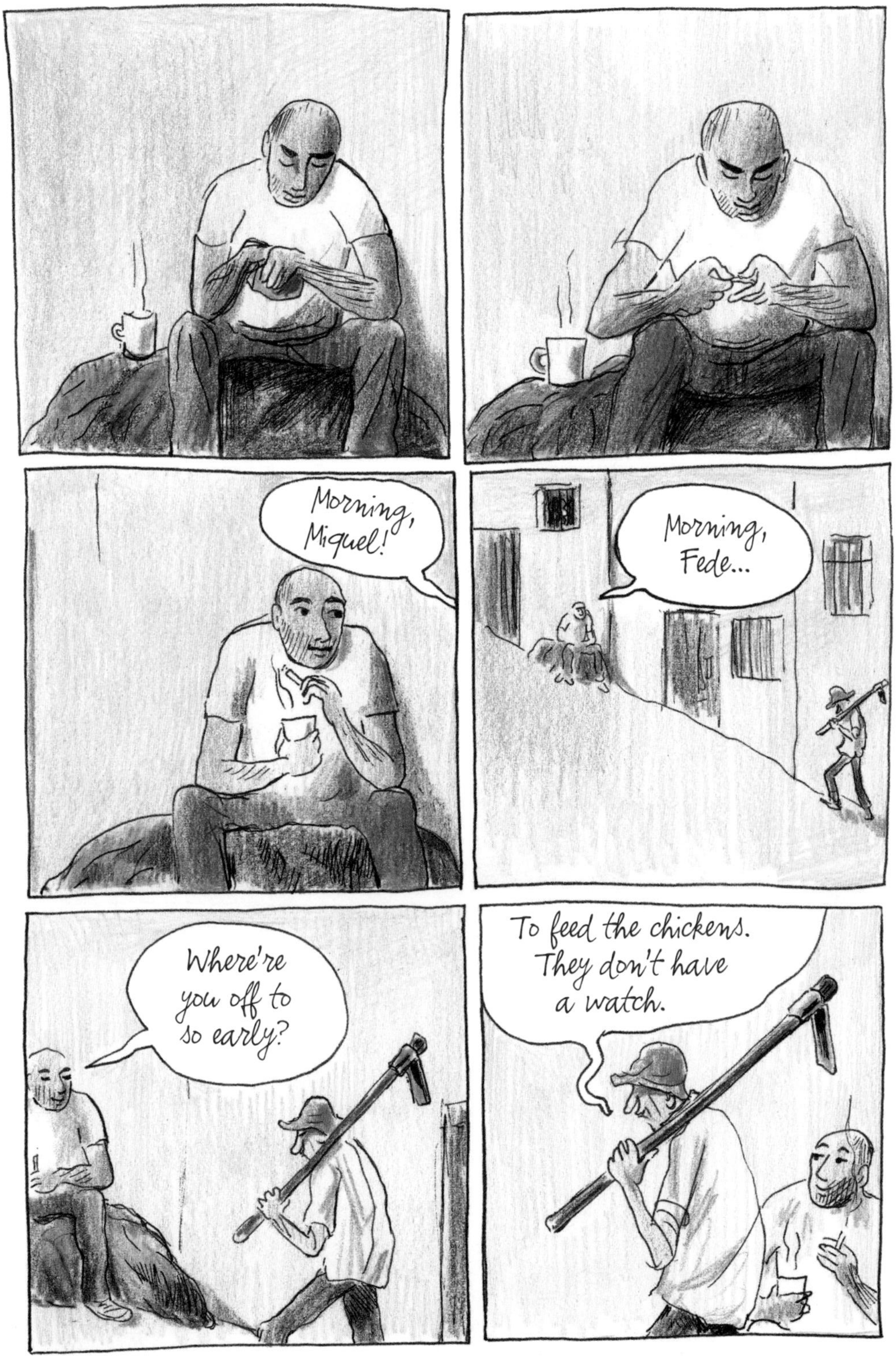
Morning, Miquel!
Morning, Fede...
Where're you off to so early?
To feed the chickens. They don't have a watch.

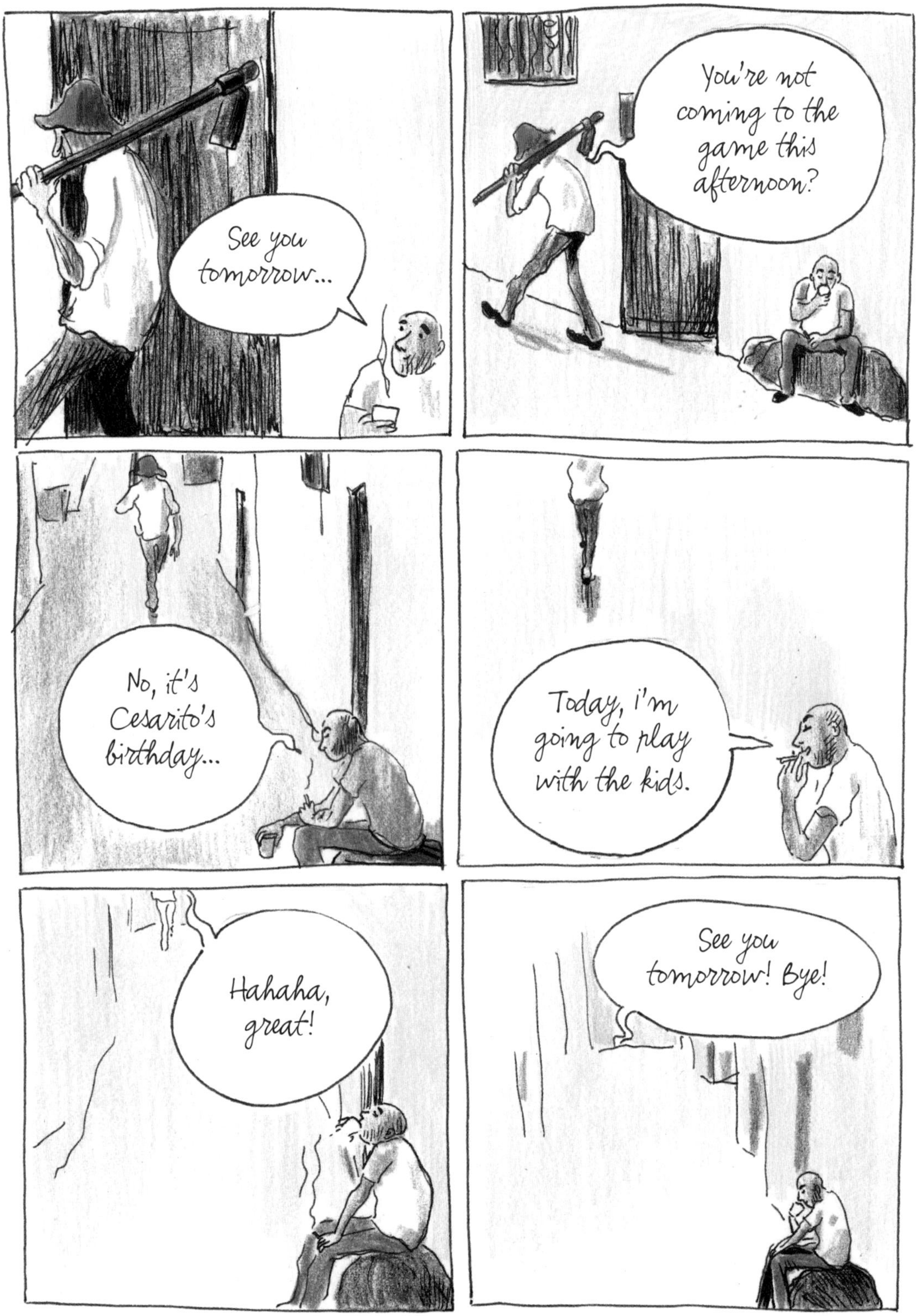
See you tomorrow...
You're not coming to the game this afternoon?
No, it's Cesarito's birthday...
Today, i'm going to play with the kids.
Hahaha, great!
See you tomorrow! Bye!

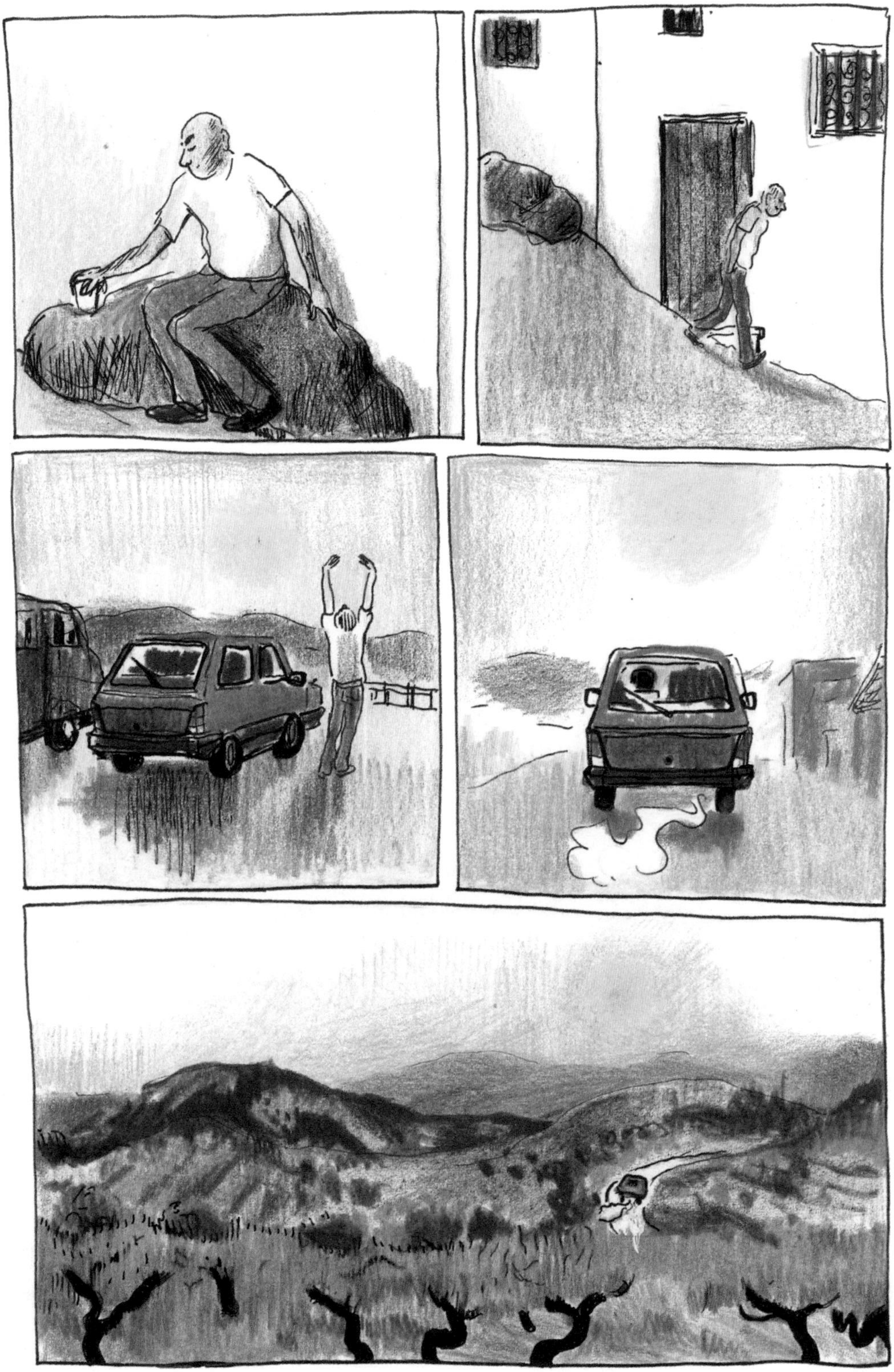

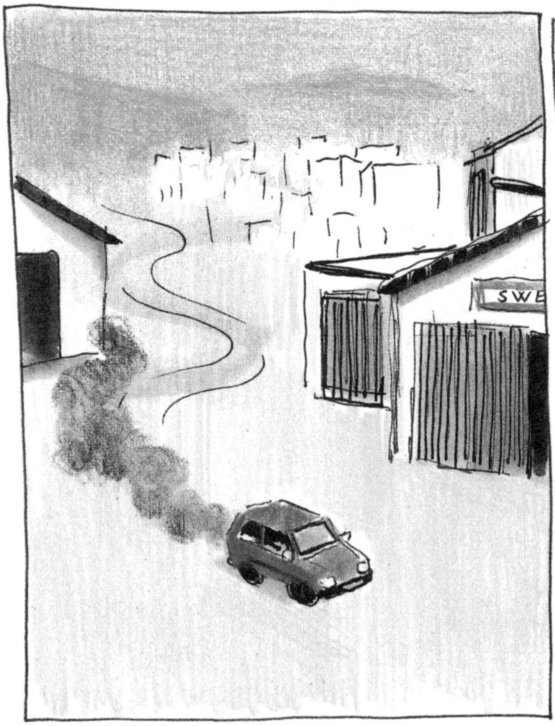
SWE

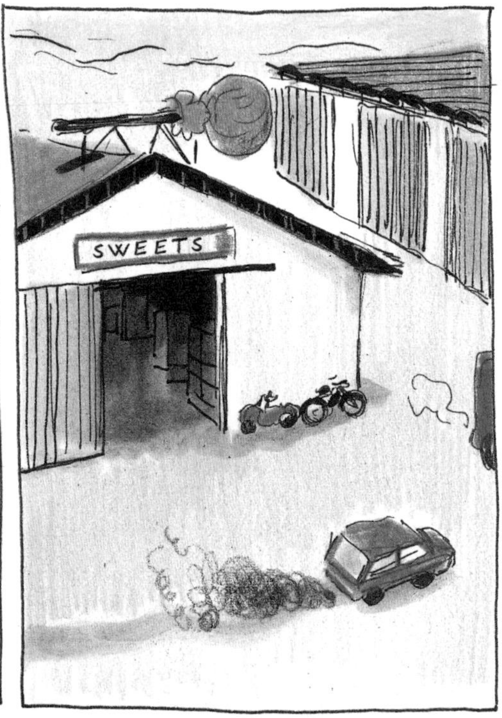
SWEETS

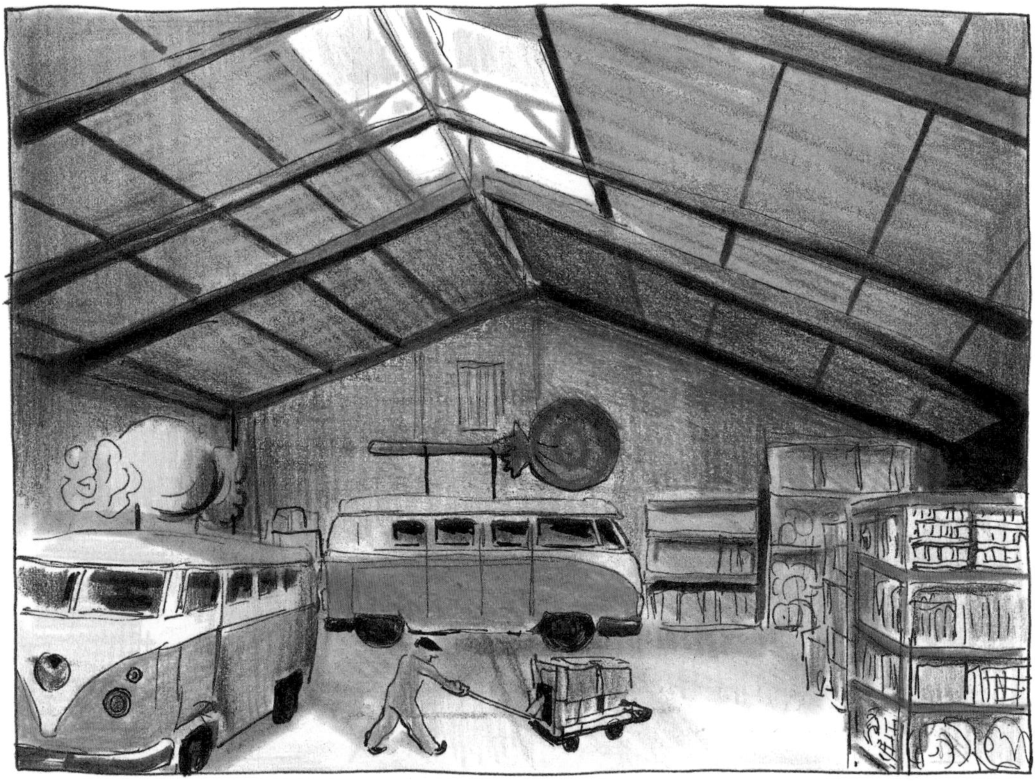

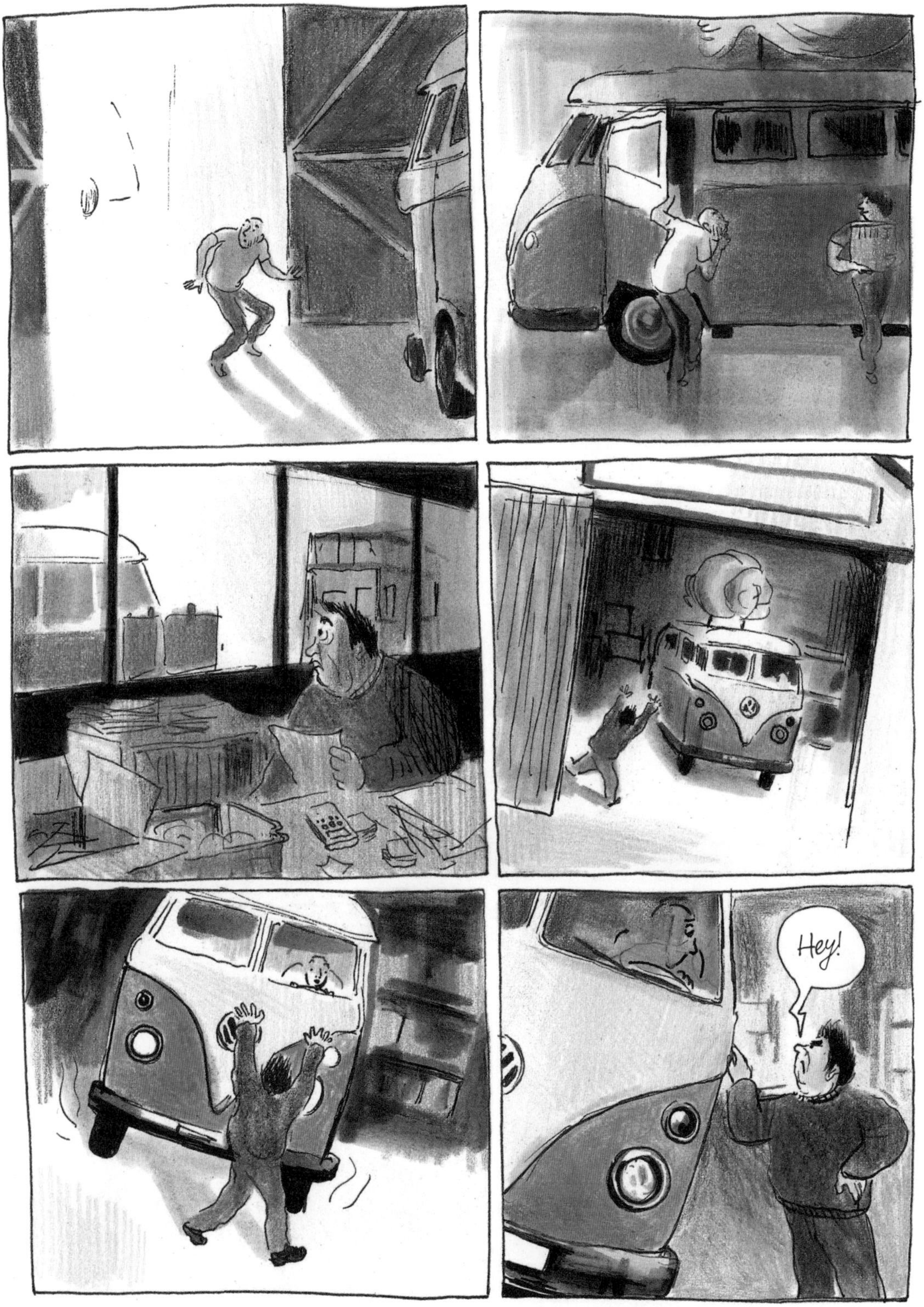
Hey!

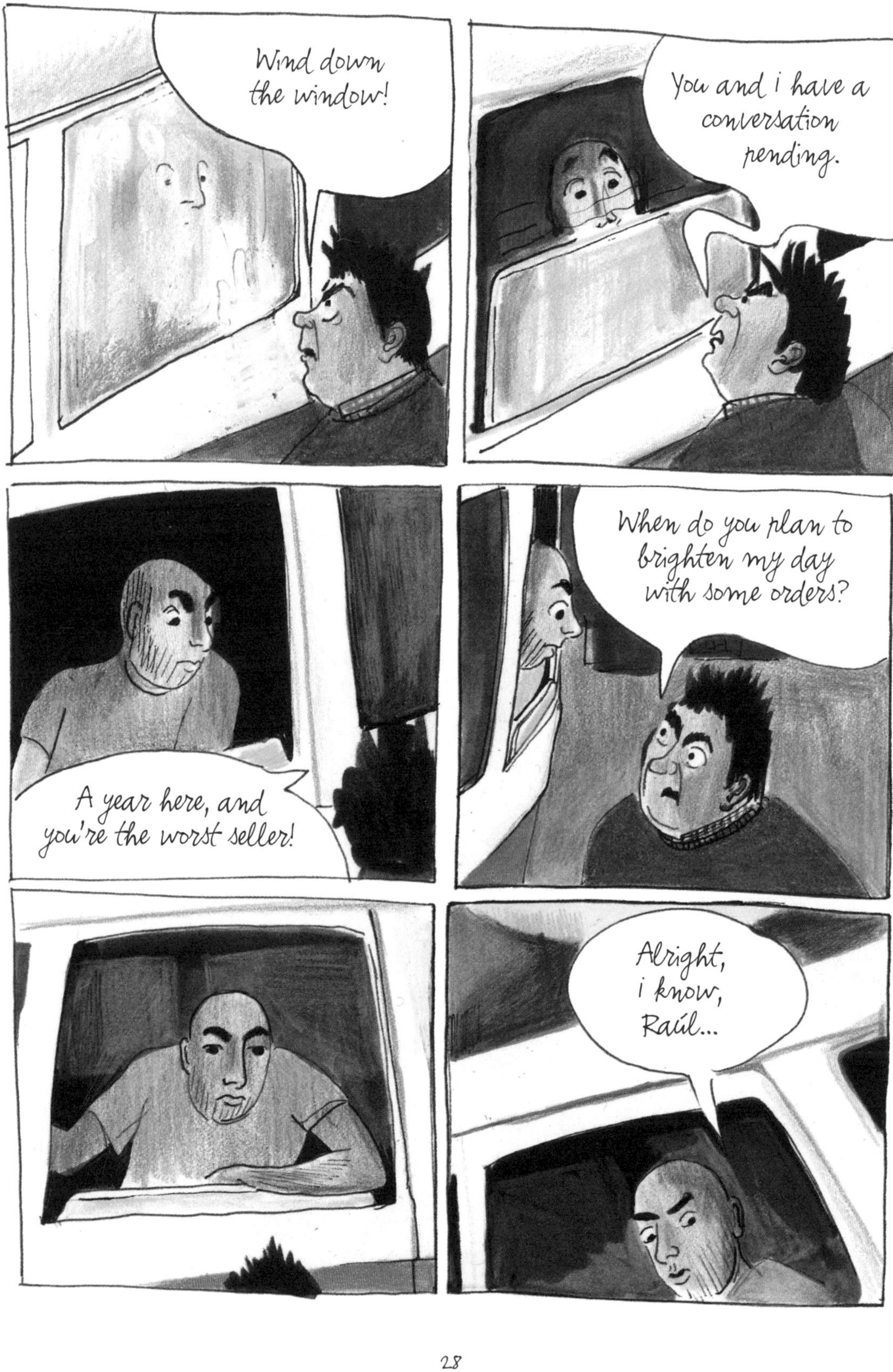
Wind down the window!
You and i have a conversation pending.
A year here, and you're the worst seller!
When do you plan to brighten my day with some orders?
Alright, i know, Raúl...

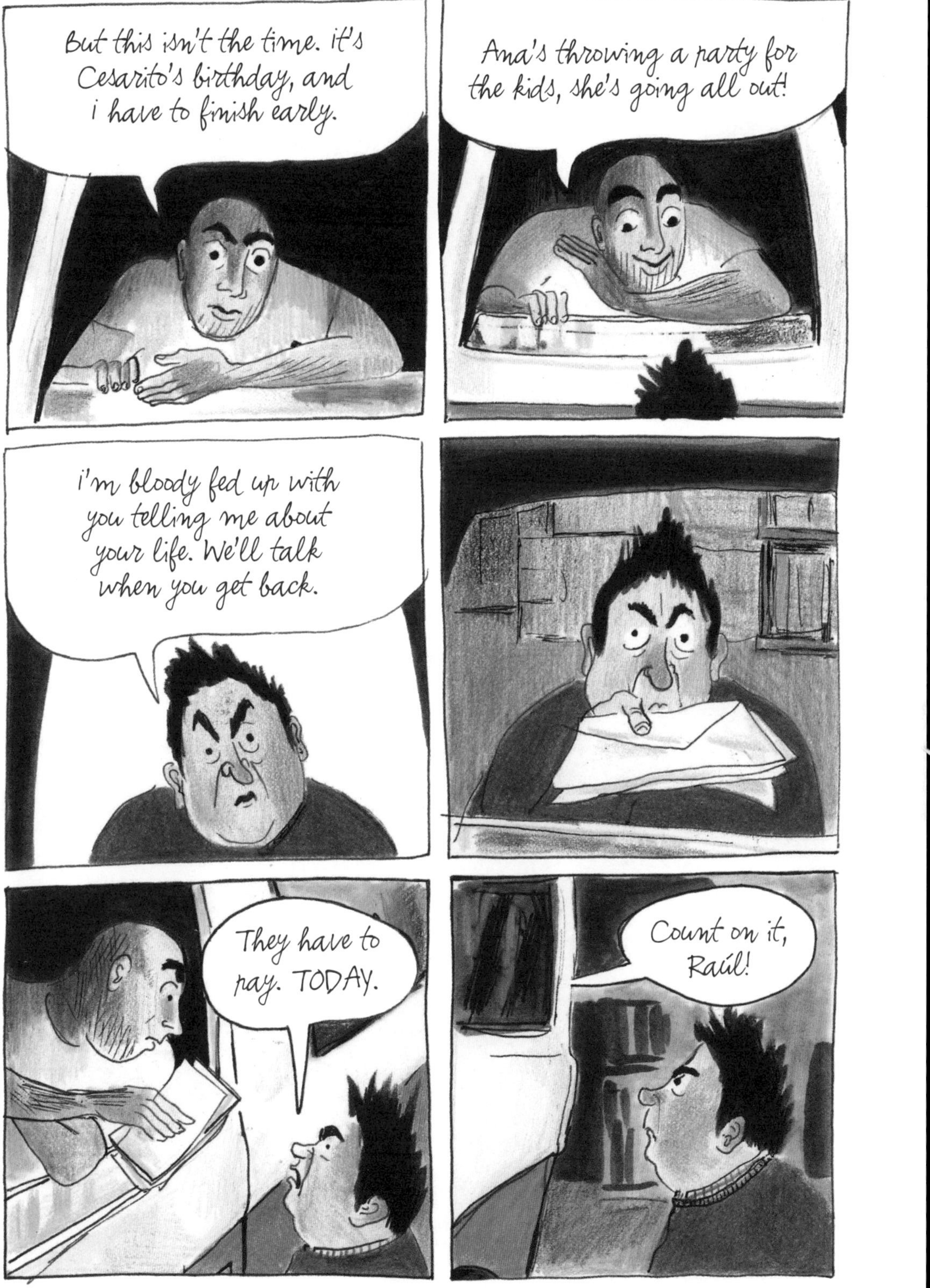

But this isn't the time. it's Cesarito's birthday, and i have to finish early.
Ana's throwing a party for the kids, she's going all out!
i'm bloody fed up with you telling me about your life. We'll talk when you get back.
They have to pay. TODAY.
Count on it, Raúl!

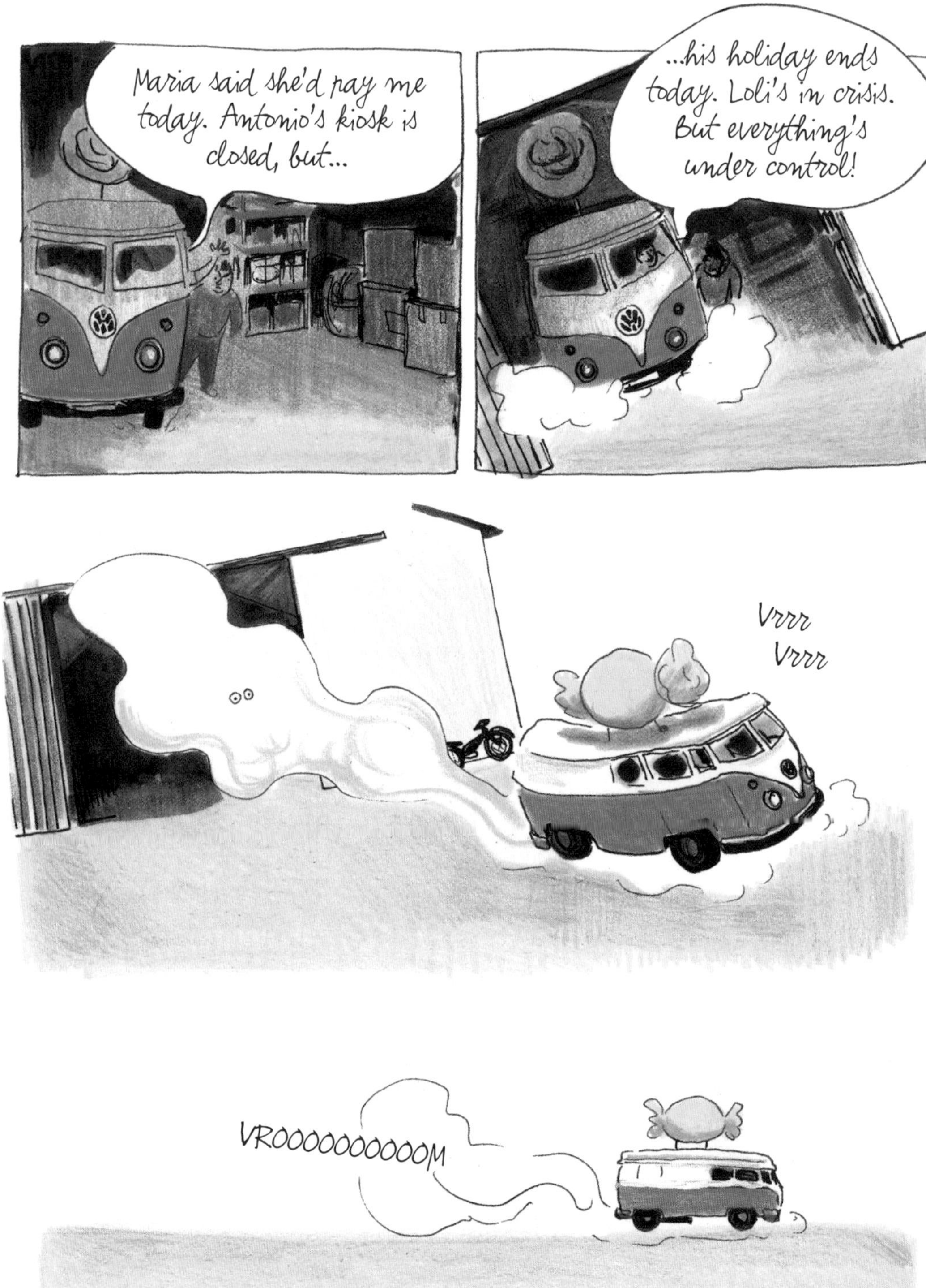
Maria said she'd pay me today. Antonio's kiosk is closed, but...
...his holiday ends today. Loli's in crisis. But everything's under control!
Vrrr Vrrr
VROOOOOOOOOOM

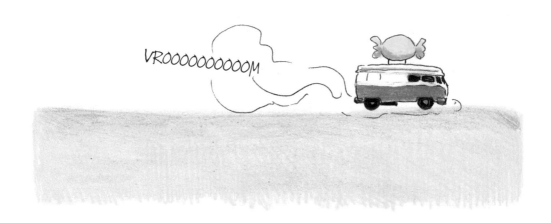

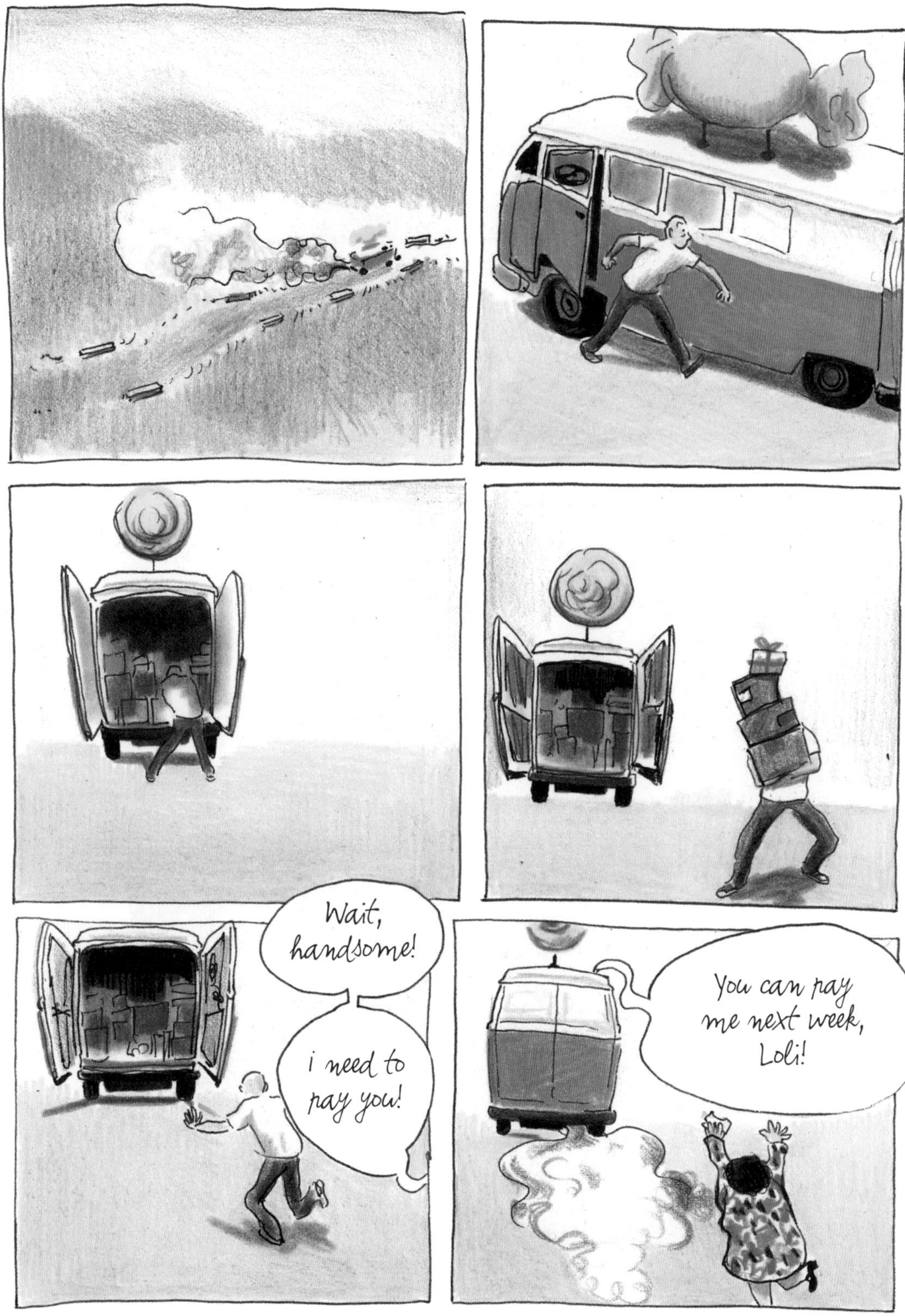
Wait, handsome!
i need to pay you!
You can pay me next week, Loli!

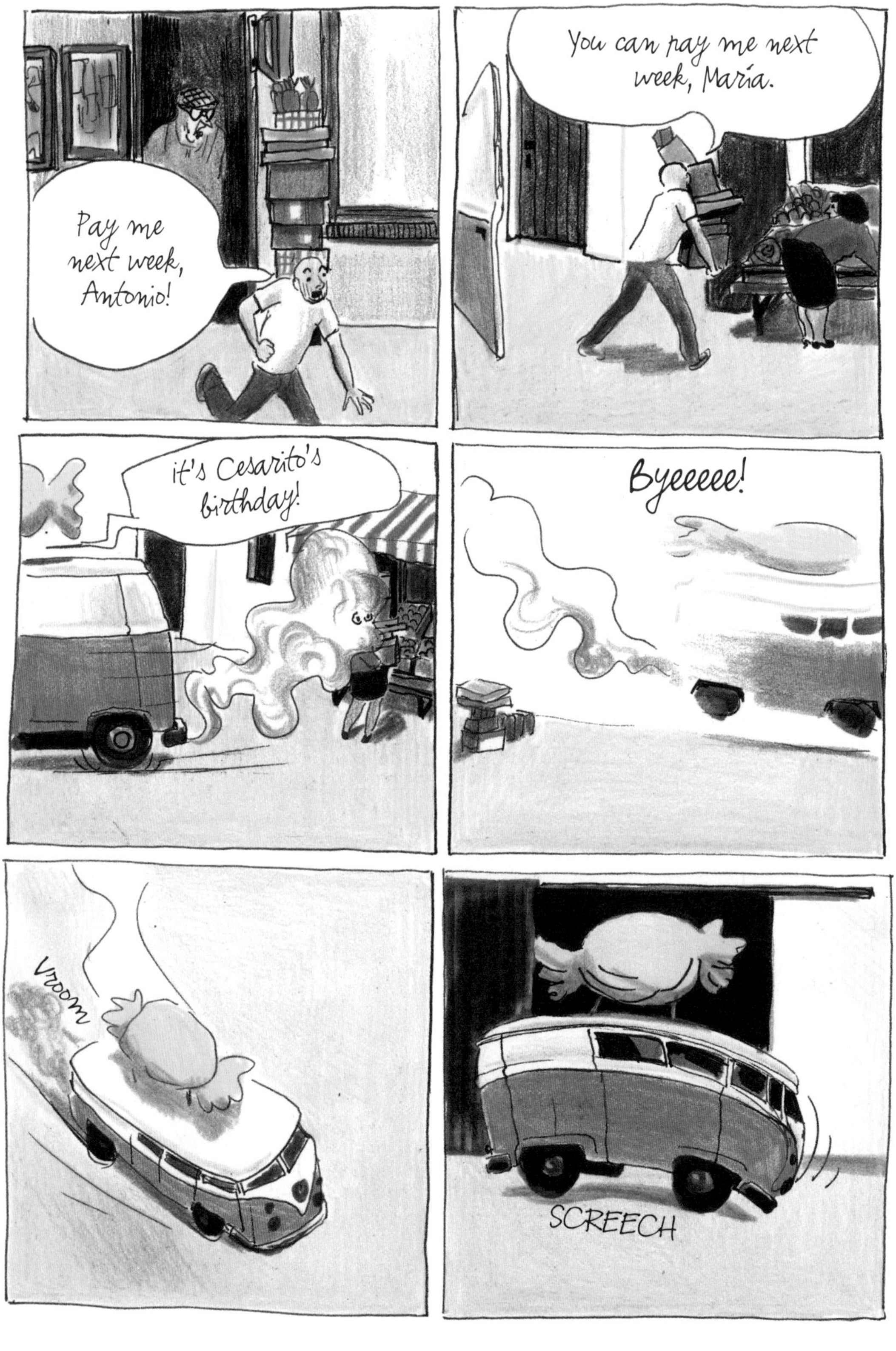
Pay me next week, Antonio!
You can pay me next week, Maria.
it's Cesarito's birthday!
Byeeeee!
Vroom
SCREECH

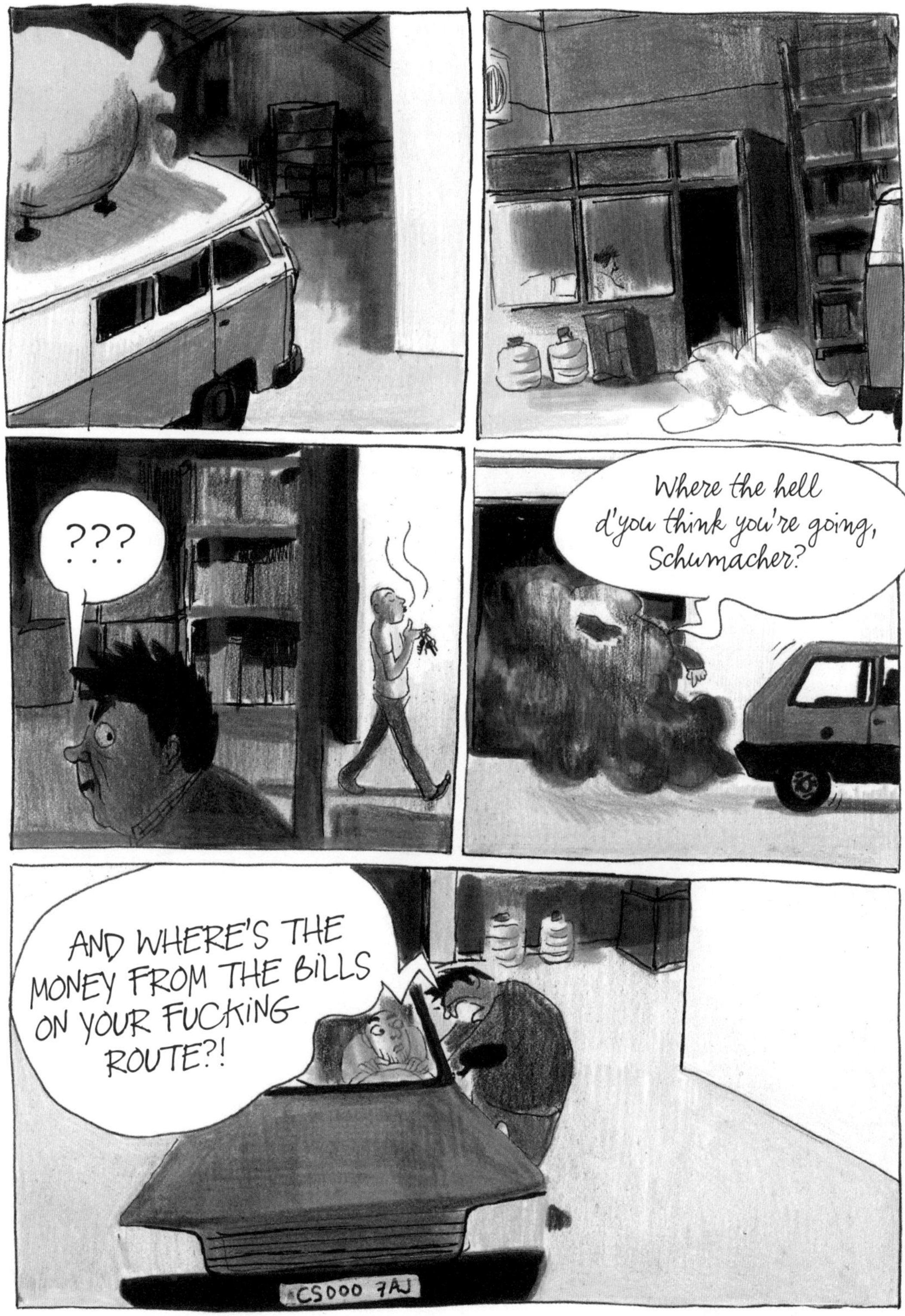
???
Where the hell d'you think you're going, Schumacher?
AND WHERE'S THE MONEY FROM THE BILLS ON YOUR FUCKING ROUTE?!
CS000 7AJ

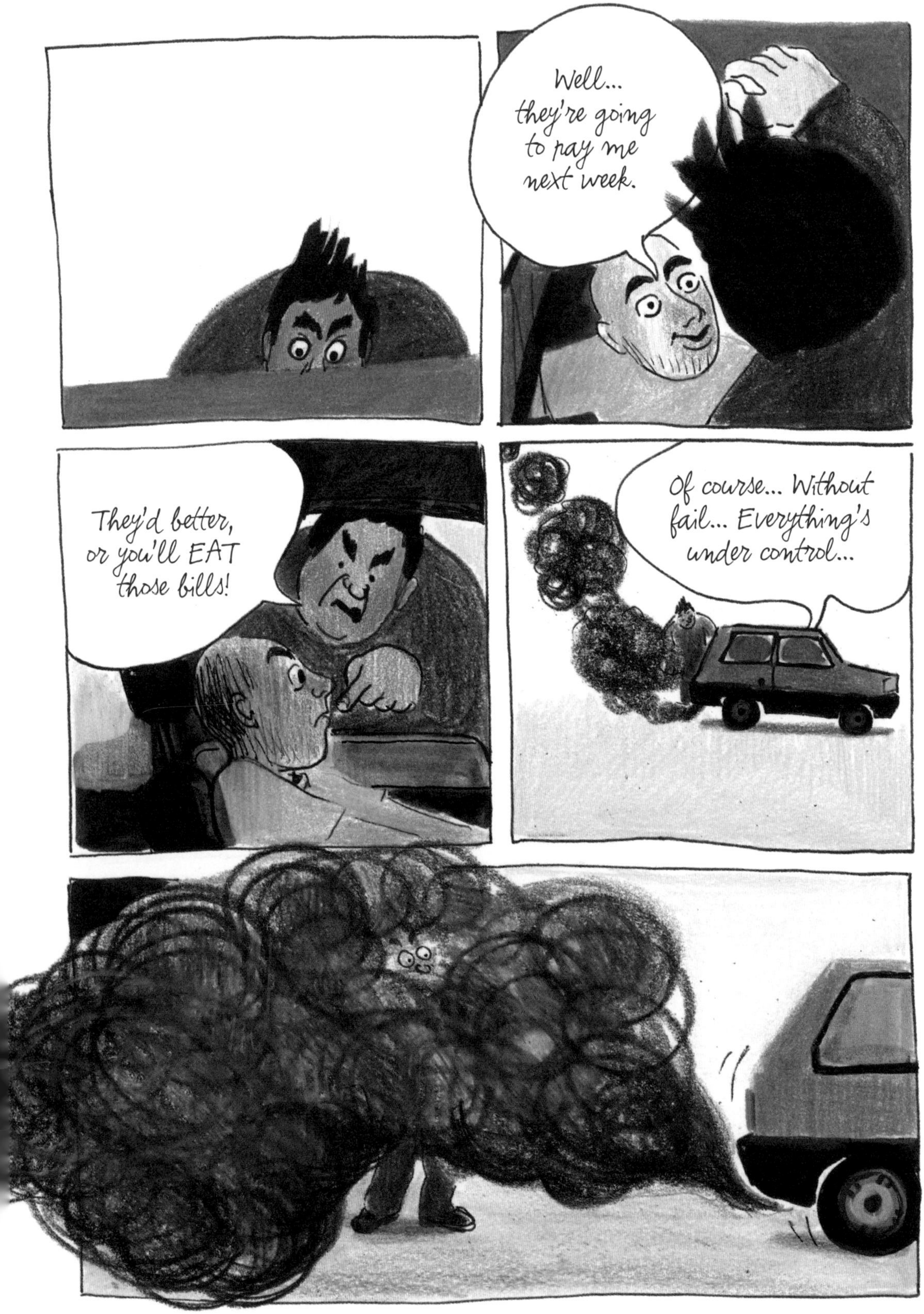
Well... they're going to pay me next week.
They'd better, or you'll EAT those bills!
Of course... Without fail... Everything's under control...

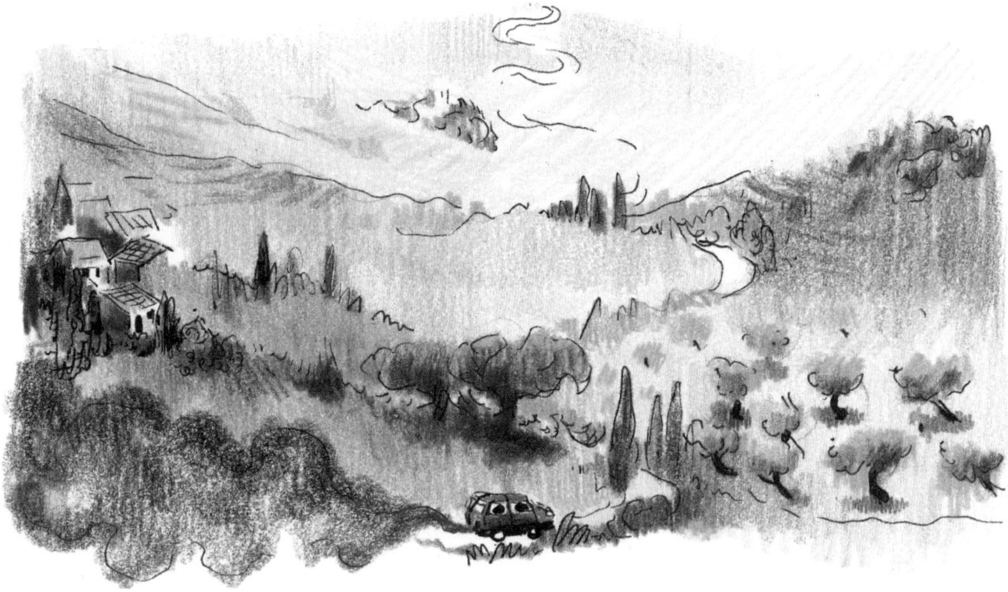

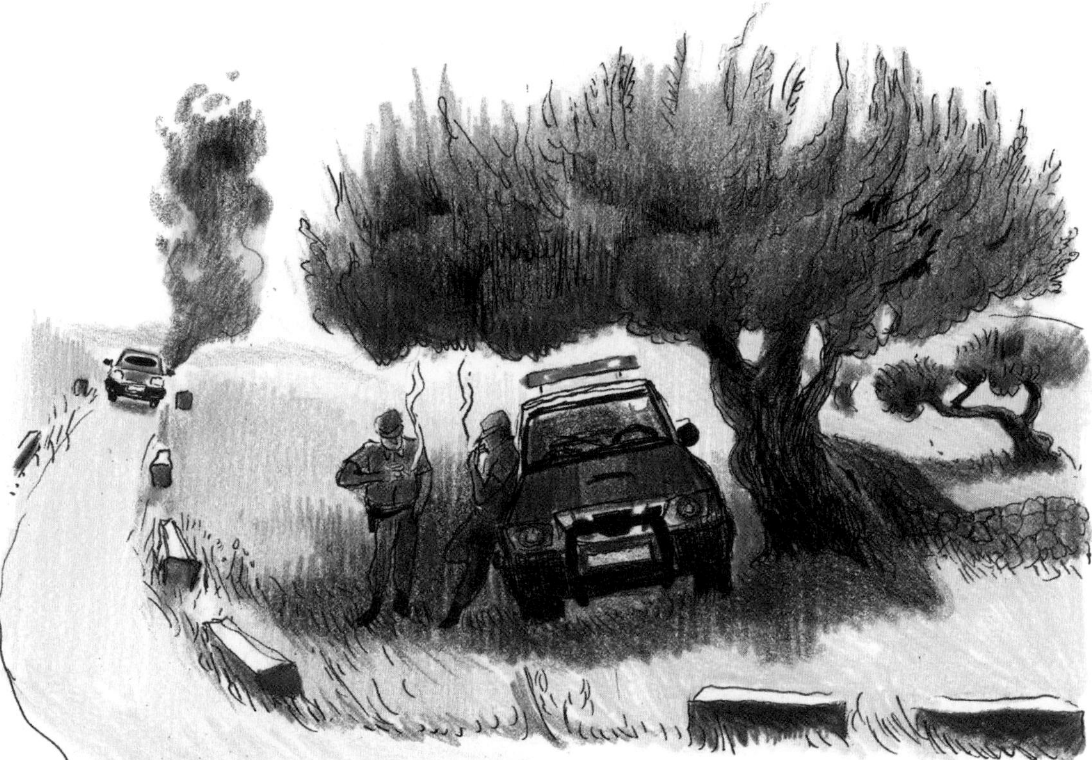

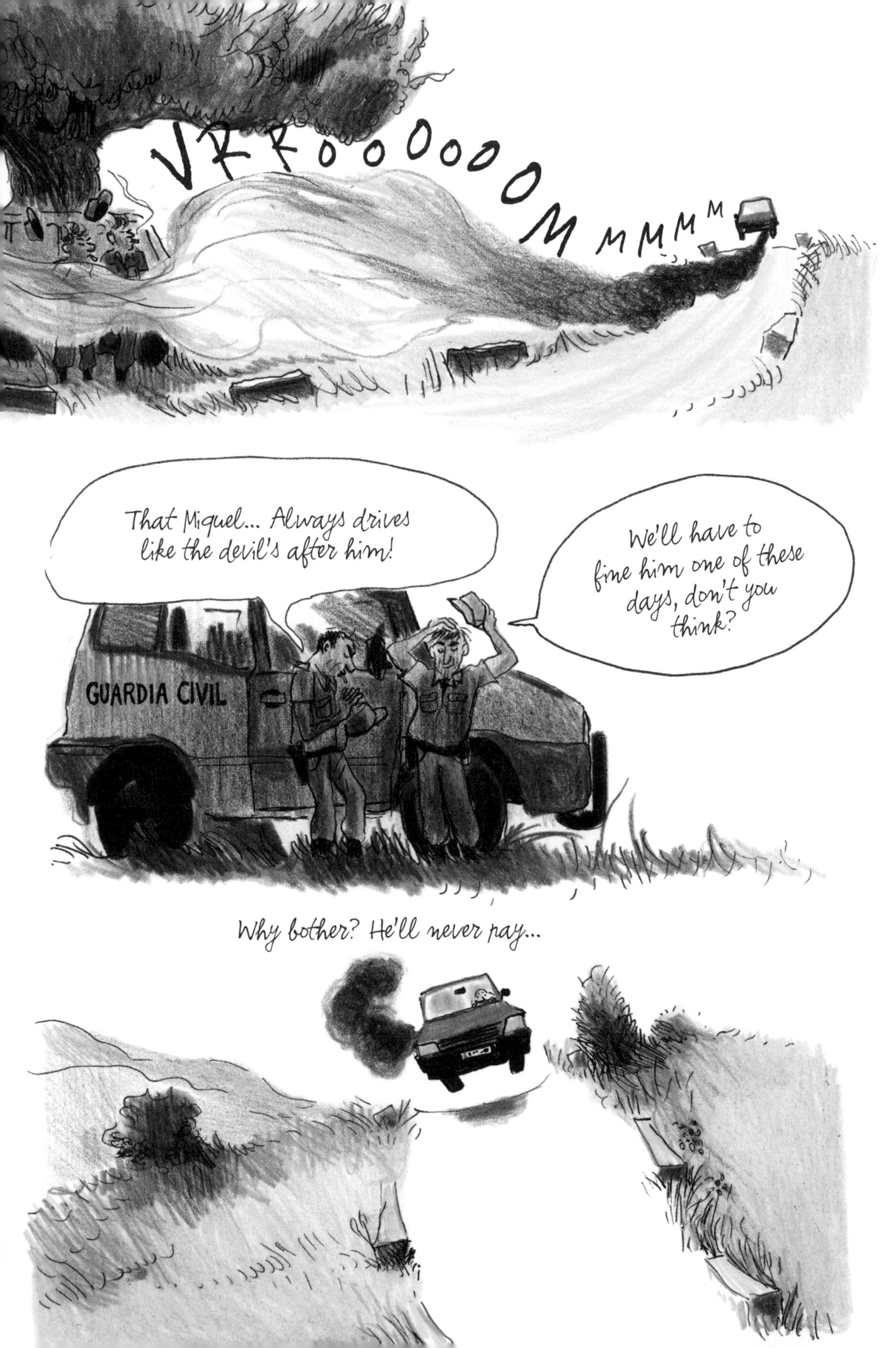
VRROOOOOOMMMMMM
That Miquel... Always drives like the devil's after him!
We'll have to fine him one of these days, don't you think?
GUARDIA CIVIL
Why bother? He'll never pay...

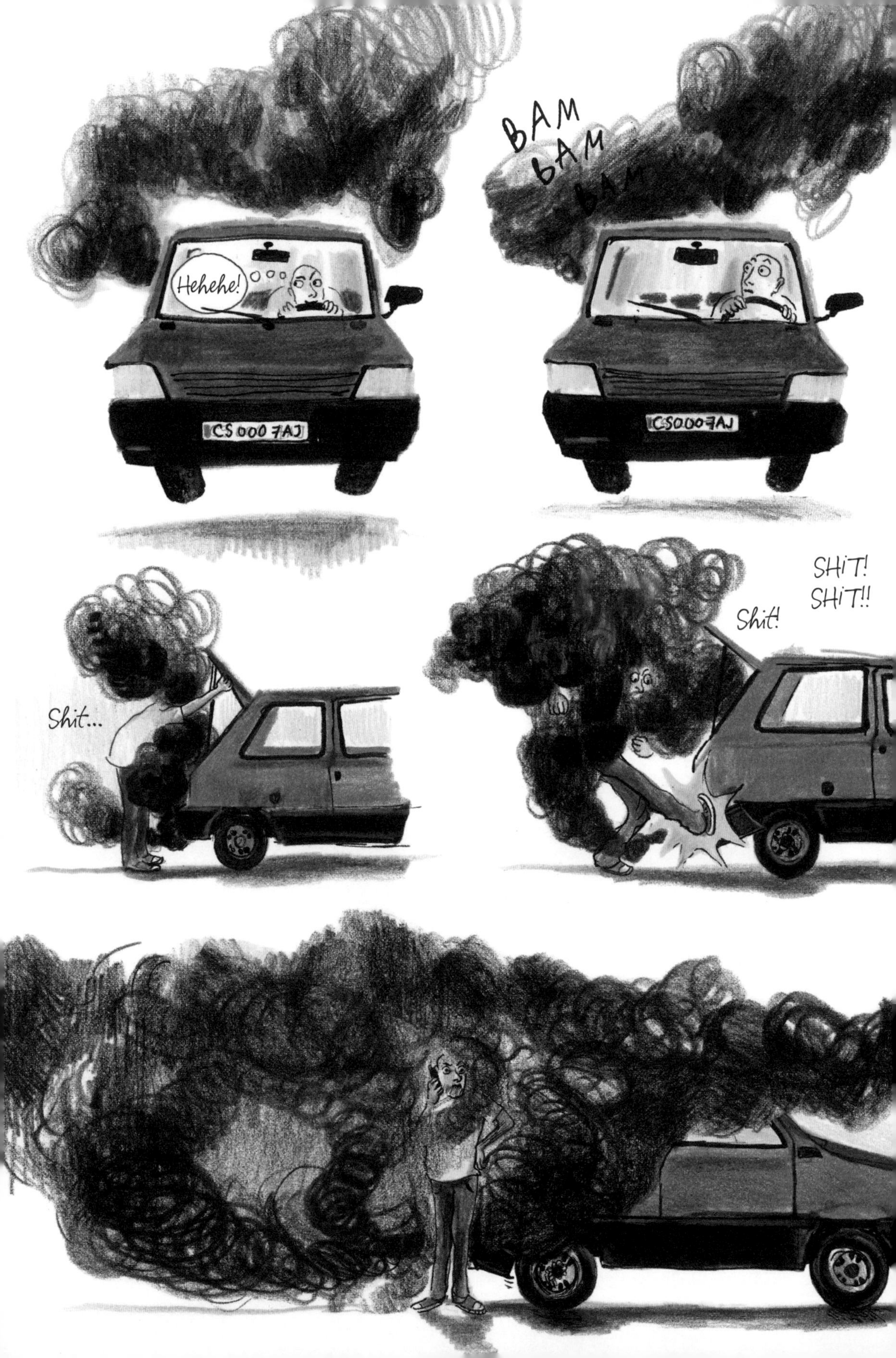

Hehehe!
CS 000 7AJ
BAM
BAM
CS0007AJ
Shit...
Shit!
SHIT!
SHIT!!

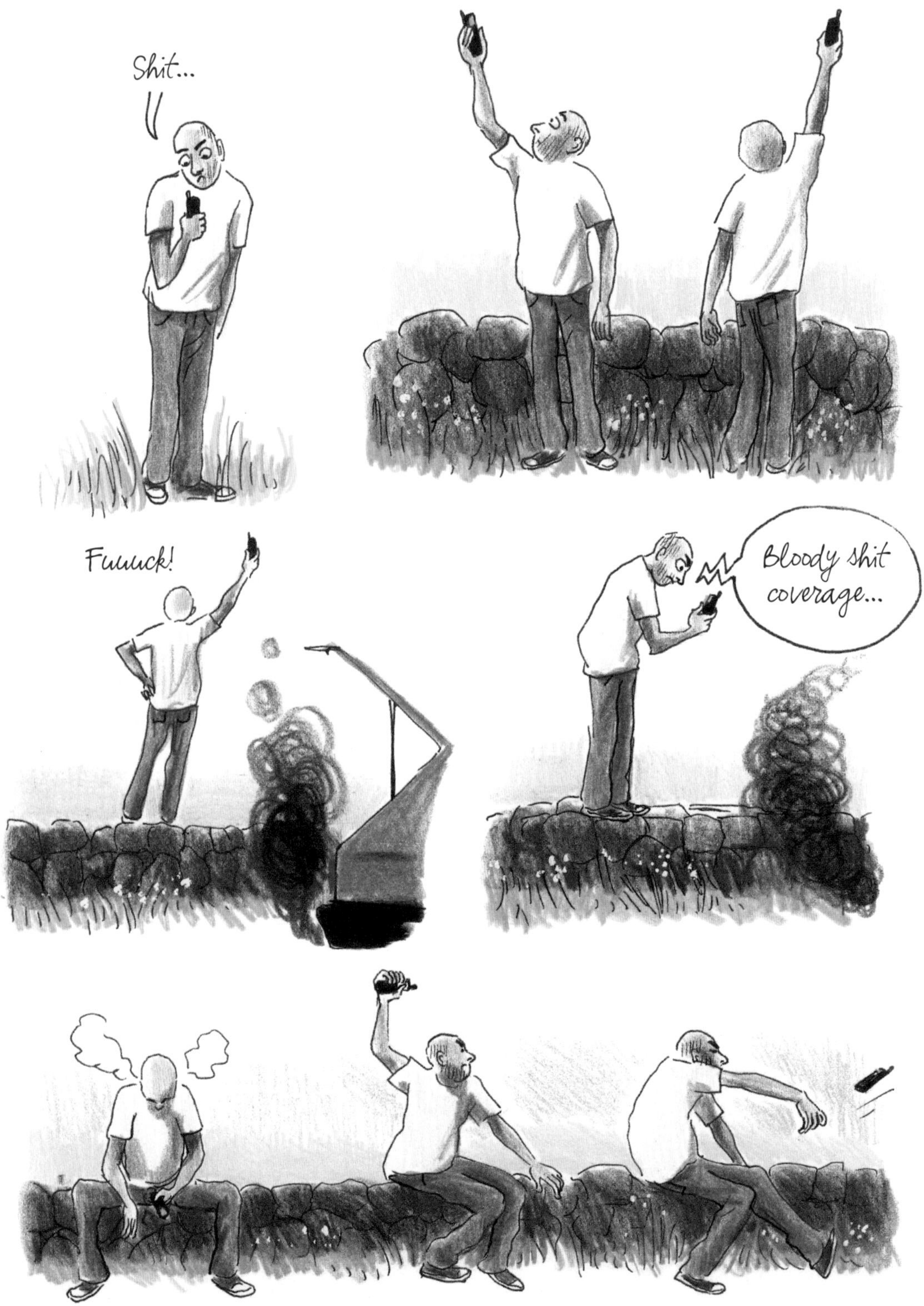
Shit...
Fuuuck!
Bloody shit coverage...

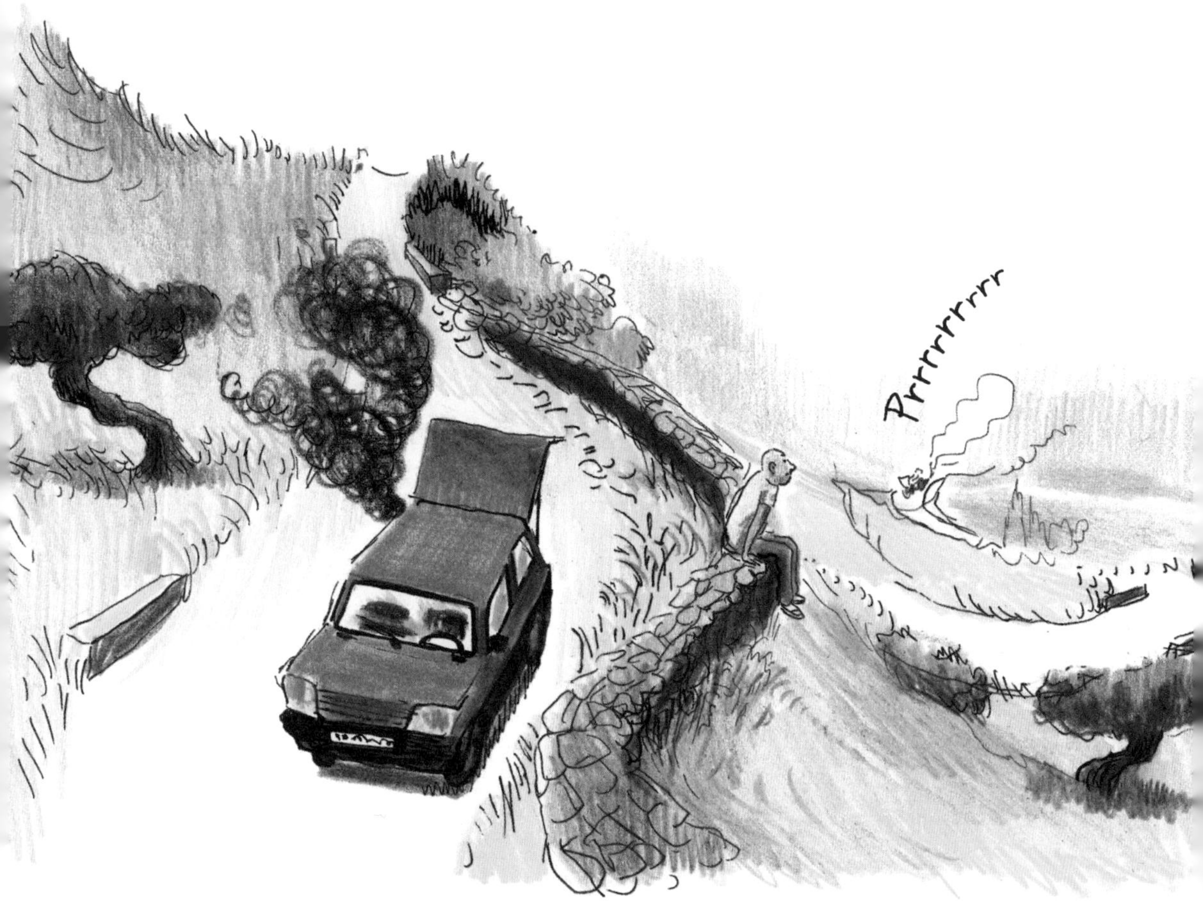
Prrrrrrrr

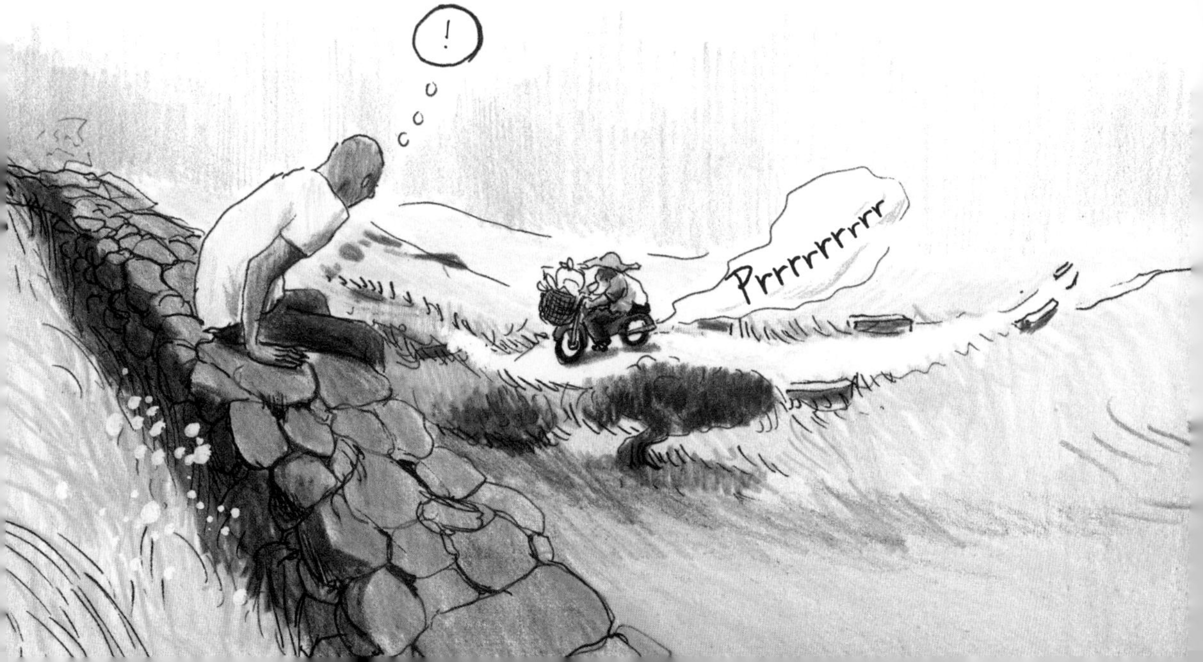
!
Prrrrrrrr

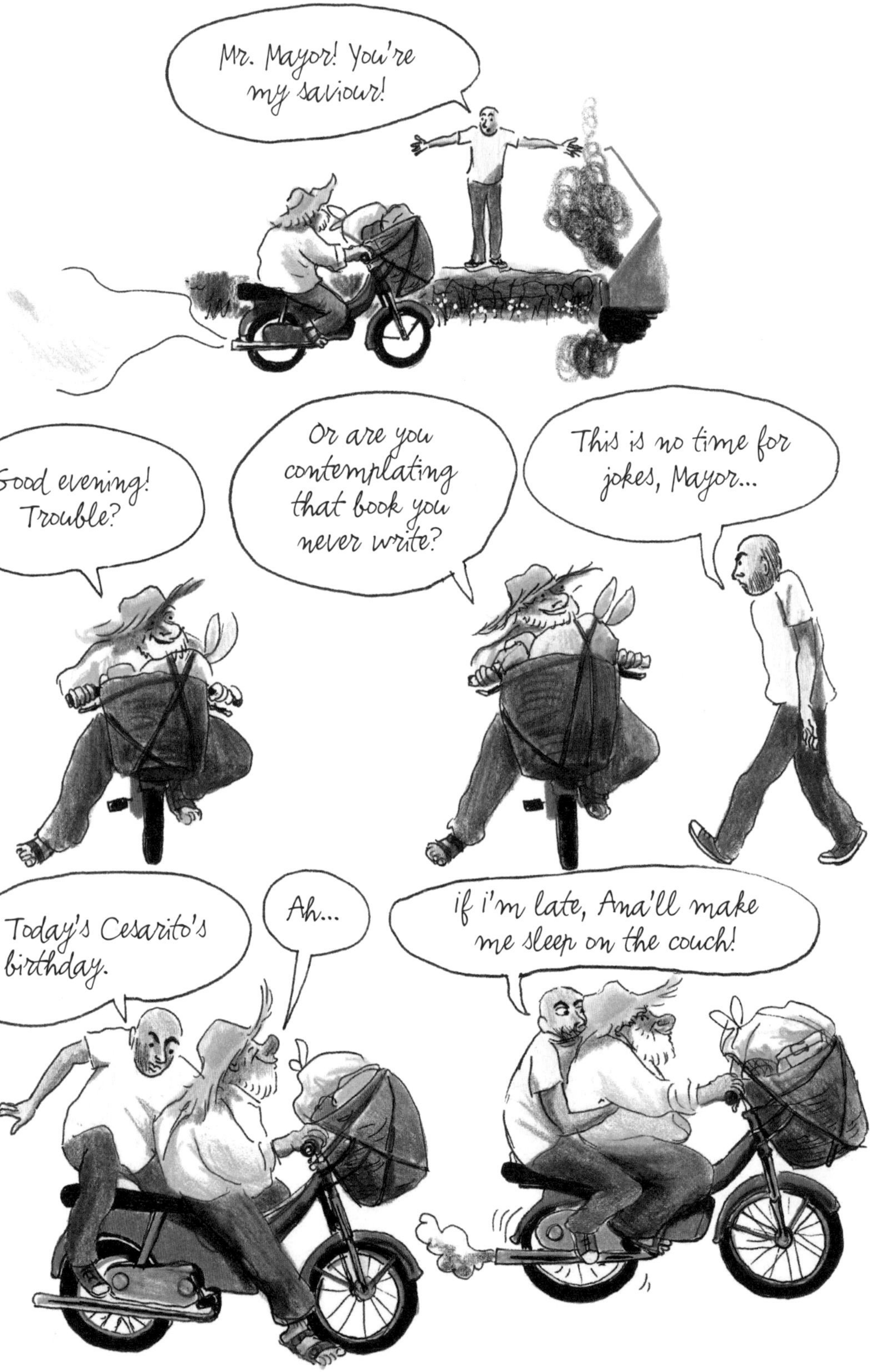
Mr. Mayor! You're my saviour!
Good evening! Trouble?
Or are you contemplating that book you never write?
This is no time for jokes, Mayor...
Today's Cesarito's birthday.
Ah...
if i'm late, Ana'll make me sleep on the couch!

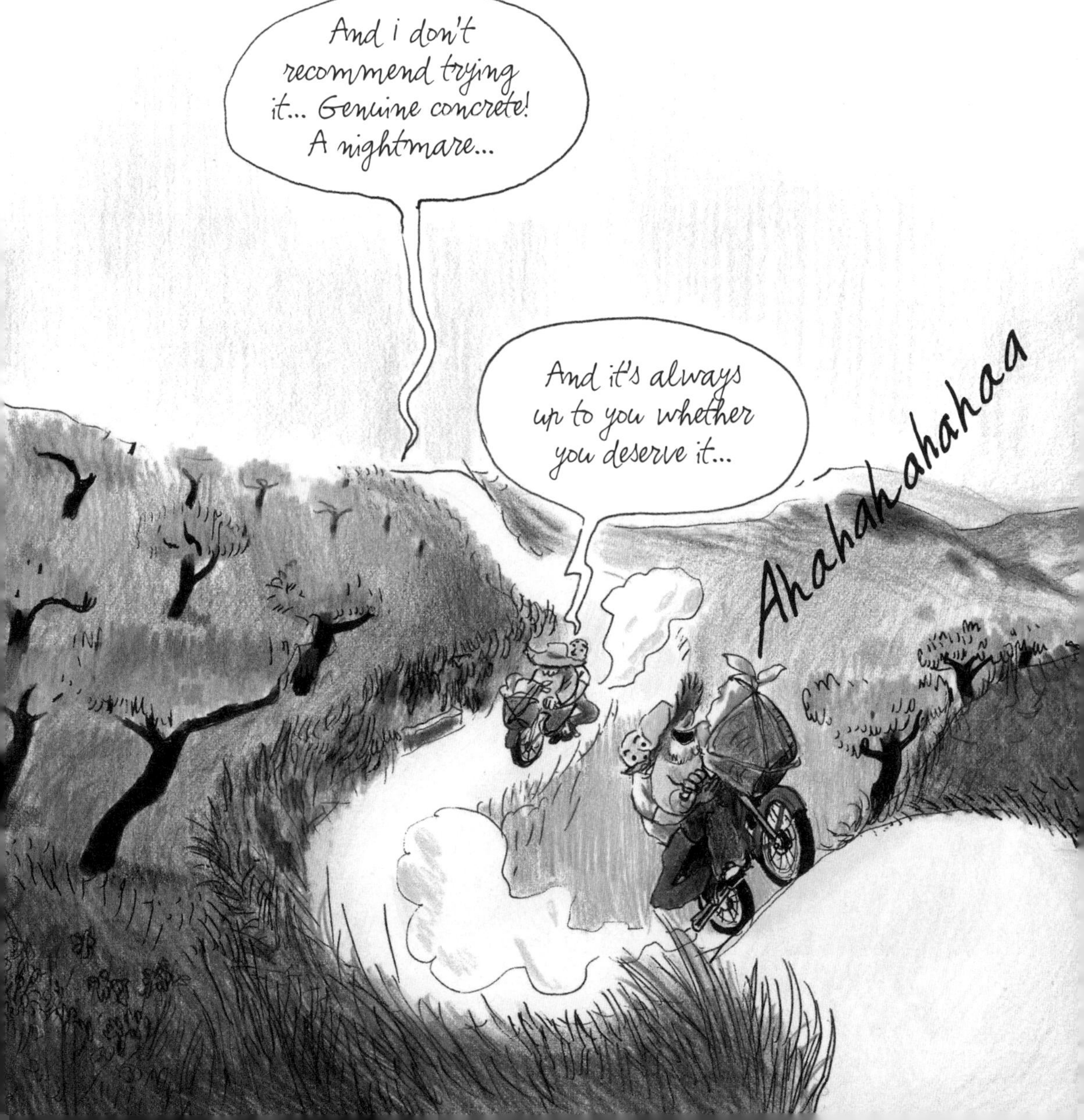
And i don't recommend trying it... Genuine concrete! A nightmare...
And it's always up to you whether you deserve it...
Ahahahahahaa

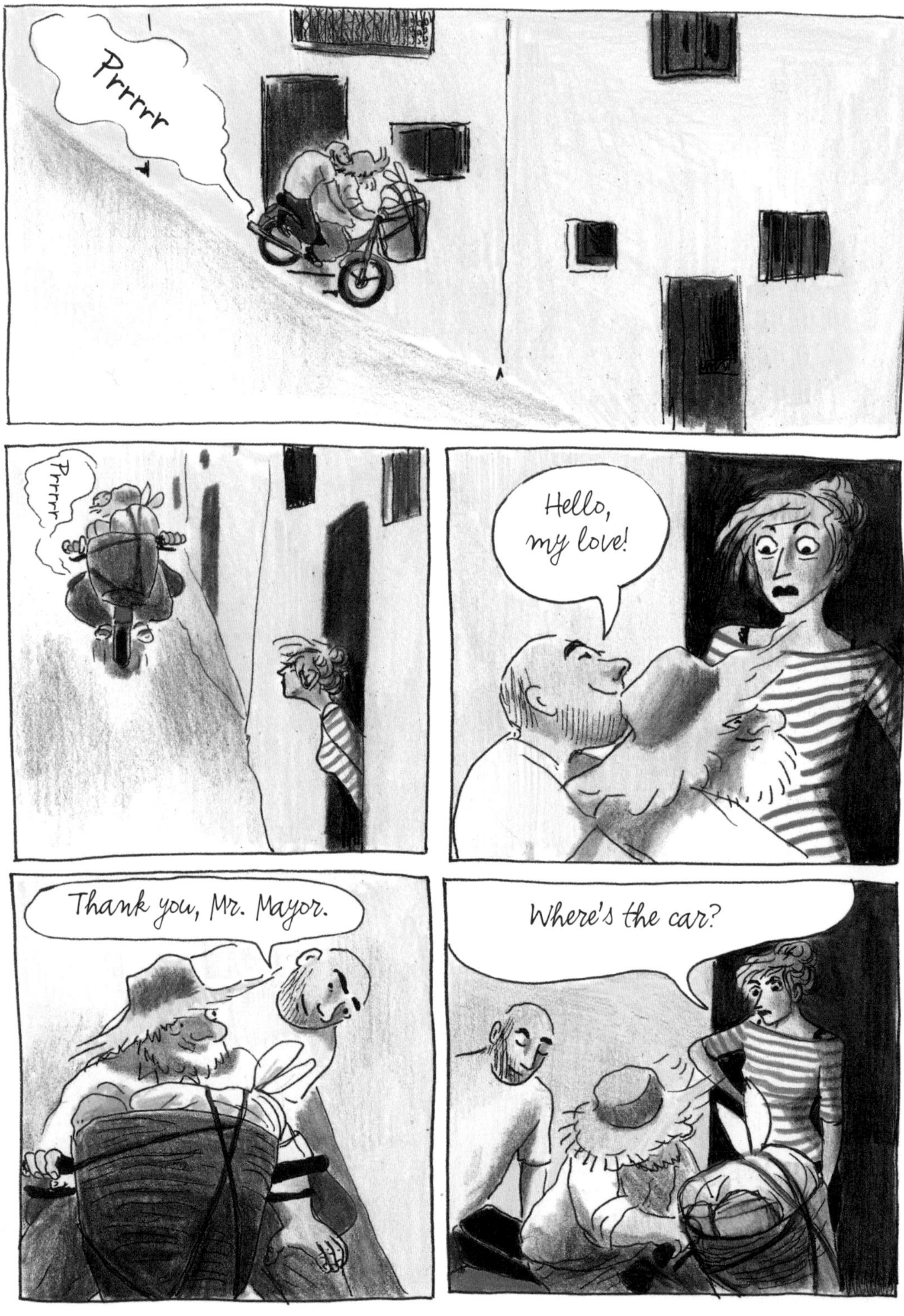
Prrrrr
Prrrrr
Hello, my love!
Thank you, Mr. Mayor.
Where's the car?

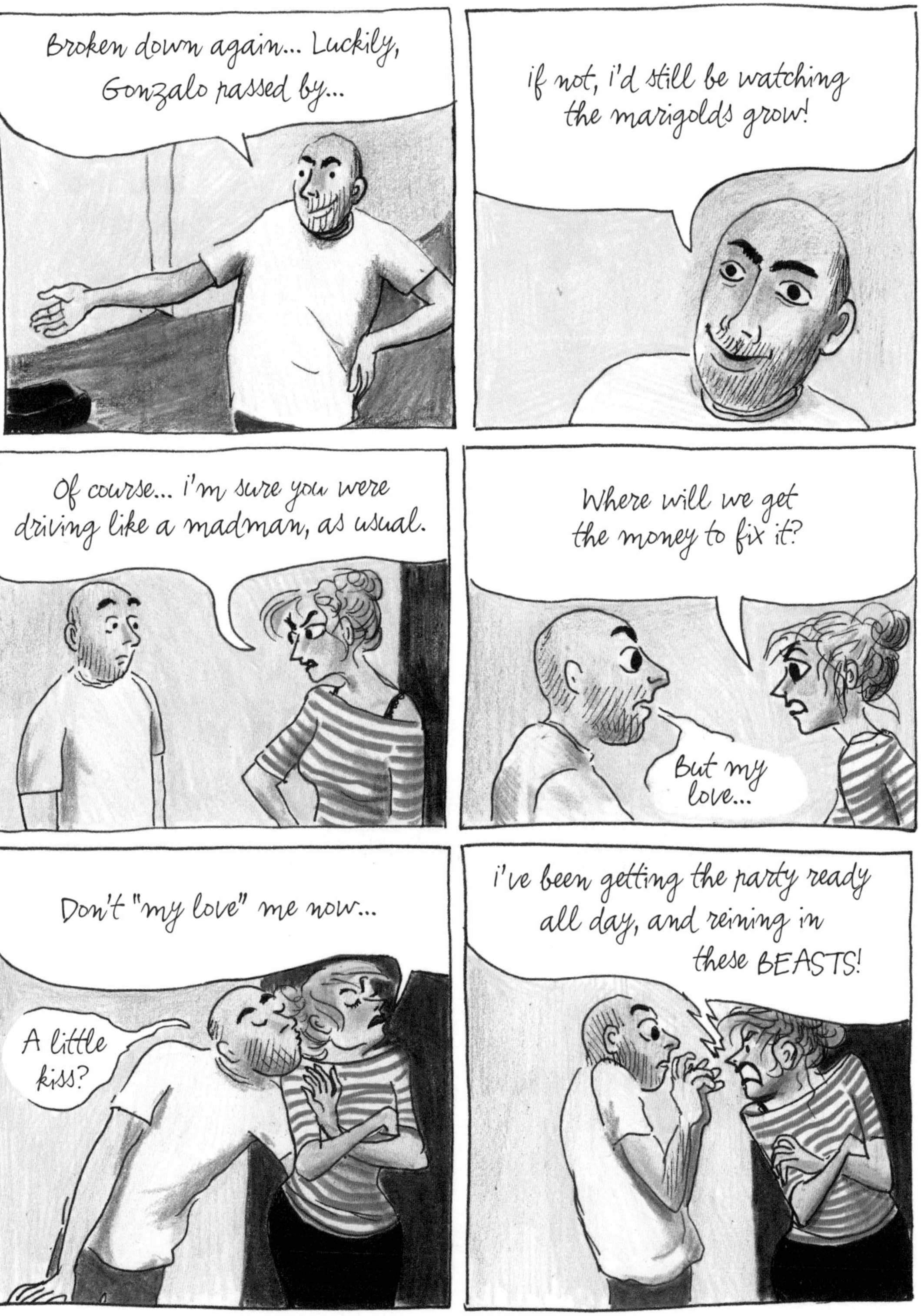
Broken down again... Luckily, Gonzalo passed by...
if not, i'd still be watching the marigolds grow!
Of course... i'm sure you were driving like a madman, as usual.
Where will we get the money to fix it?
But my love...
Don't "my love" me now...
A little kiss?
i've been getting the party ready all day, and reining in these BEASTS!

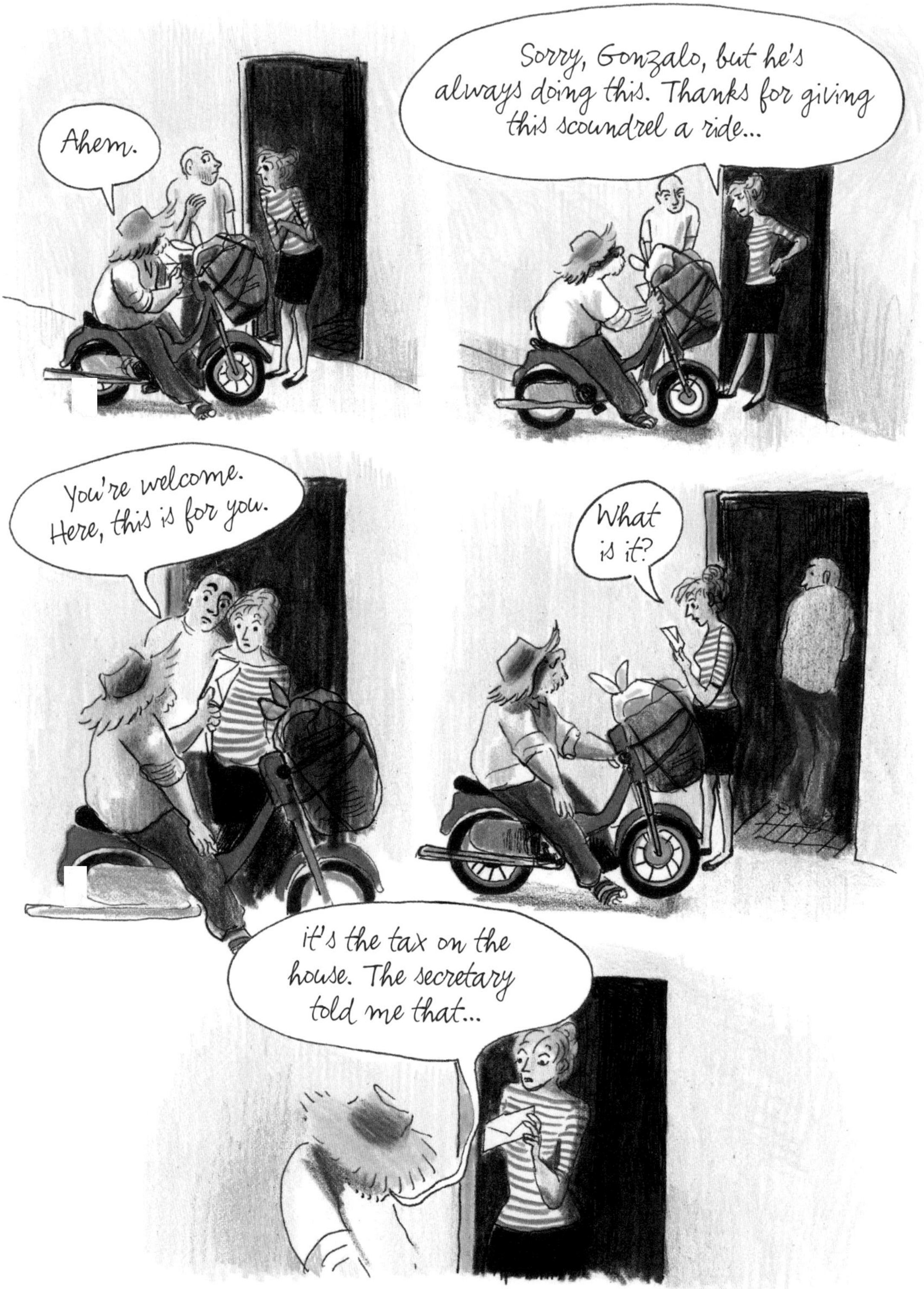
Ahem.
Sorry, Gonzalo, but he's always doing this. Thanks for giving this scoundrel a ride...
You're welcome. Here, this is for you.
What is it?
it's the tax on the house. The secretary told me that...

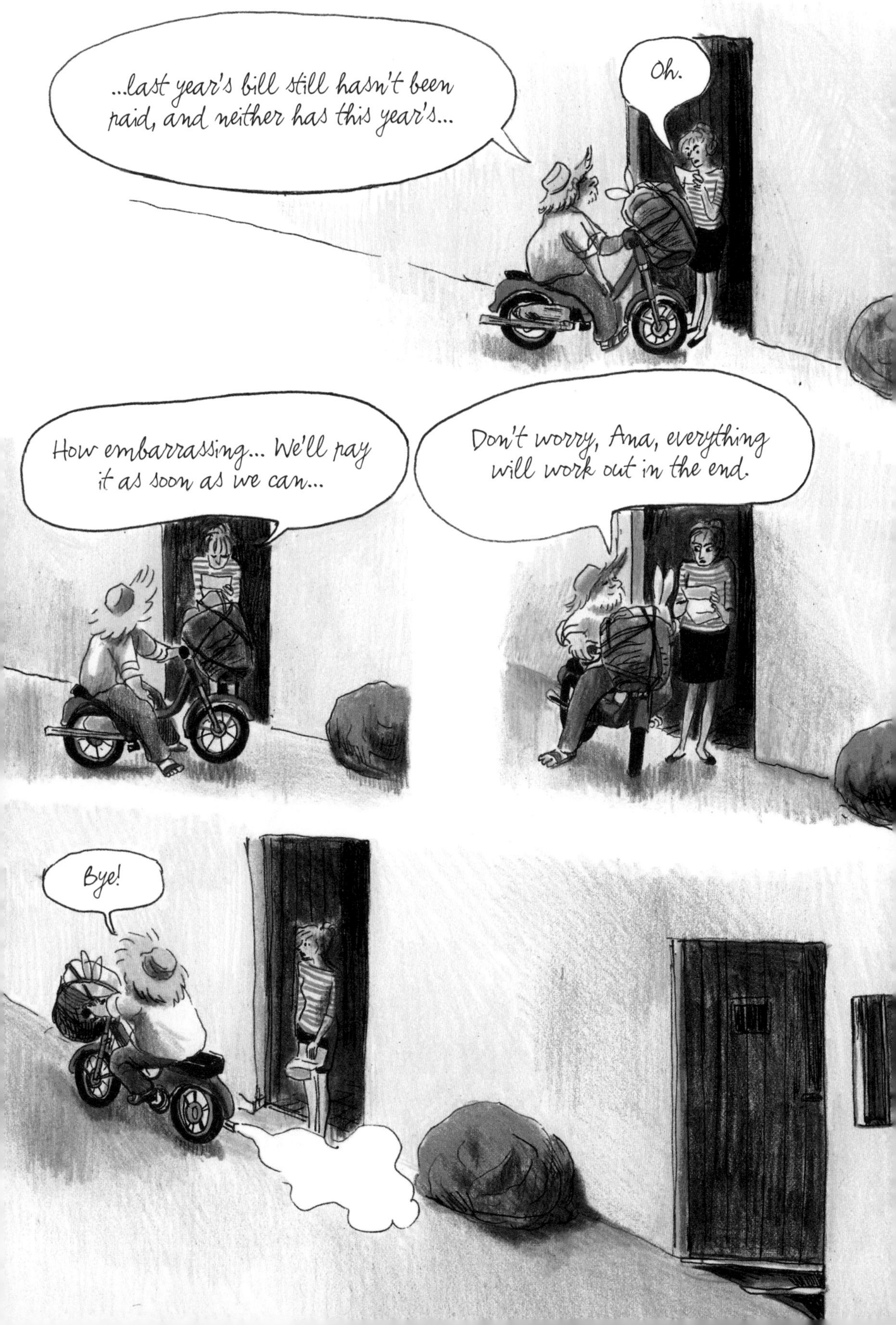
...last year's bill still hasn't been paid, and neither has this year's...
Oh.
How embarrassing... We'll pay it as soon as we can...
Don't worry, Ana, everything will work out in the end.
Bye!

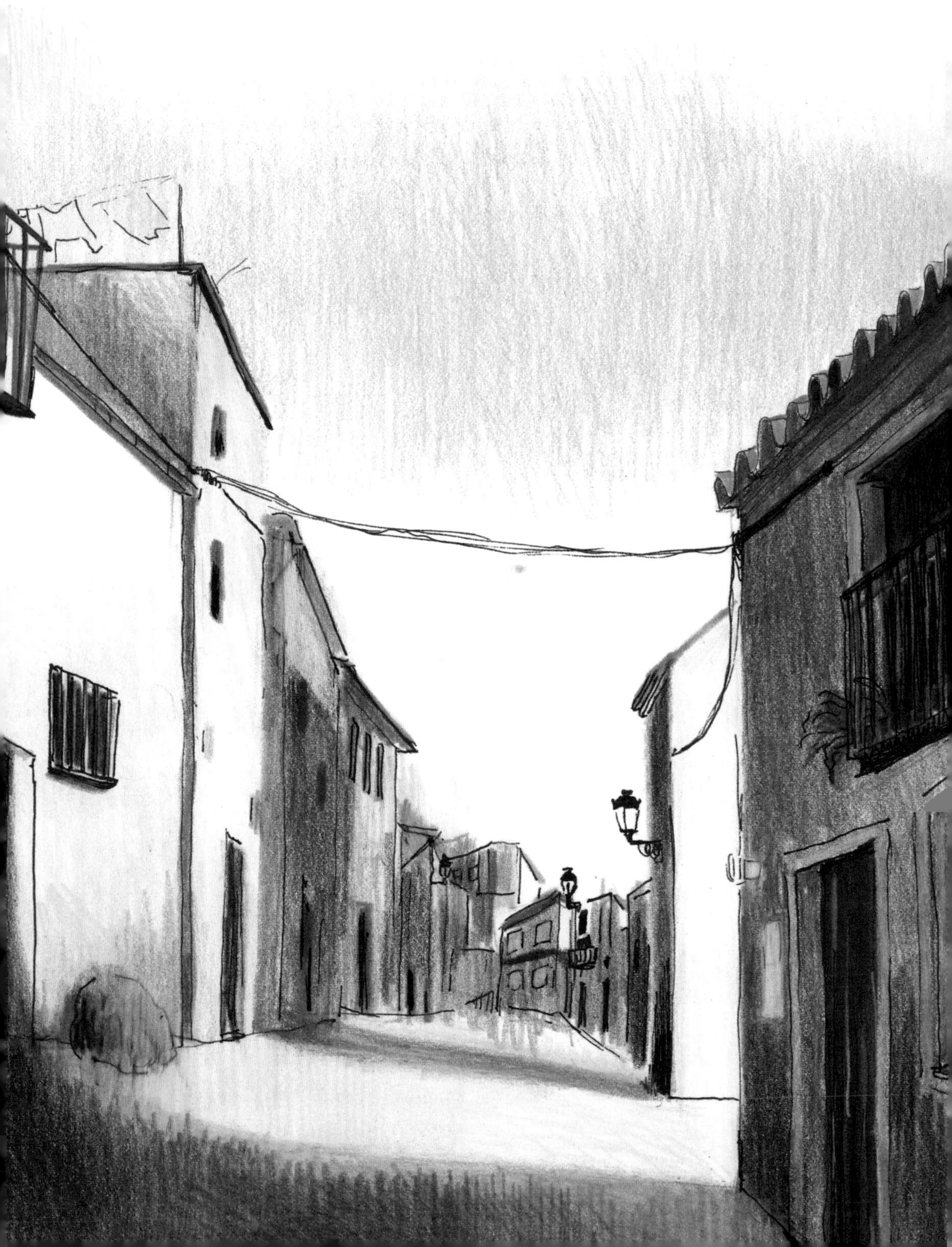

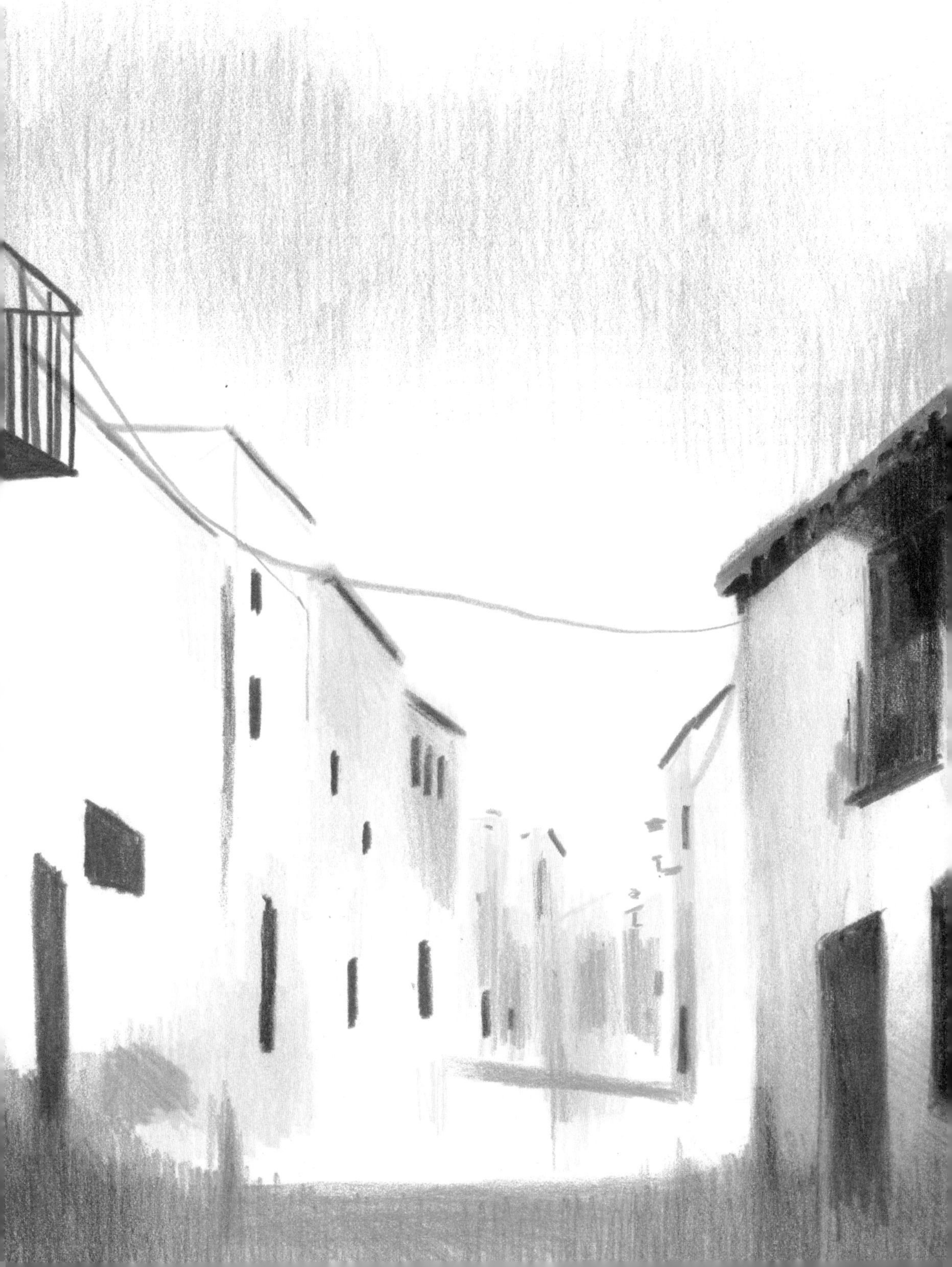

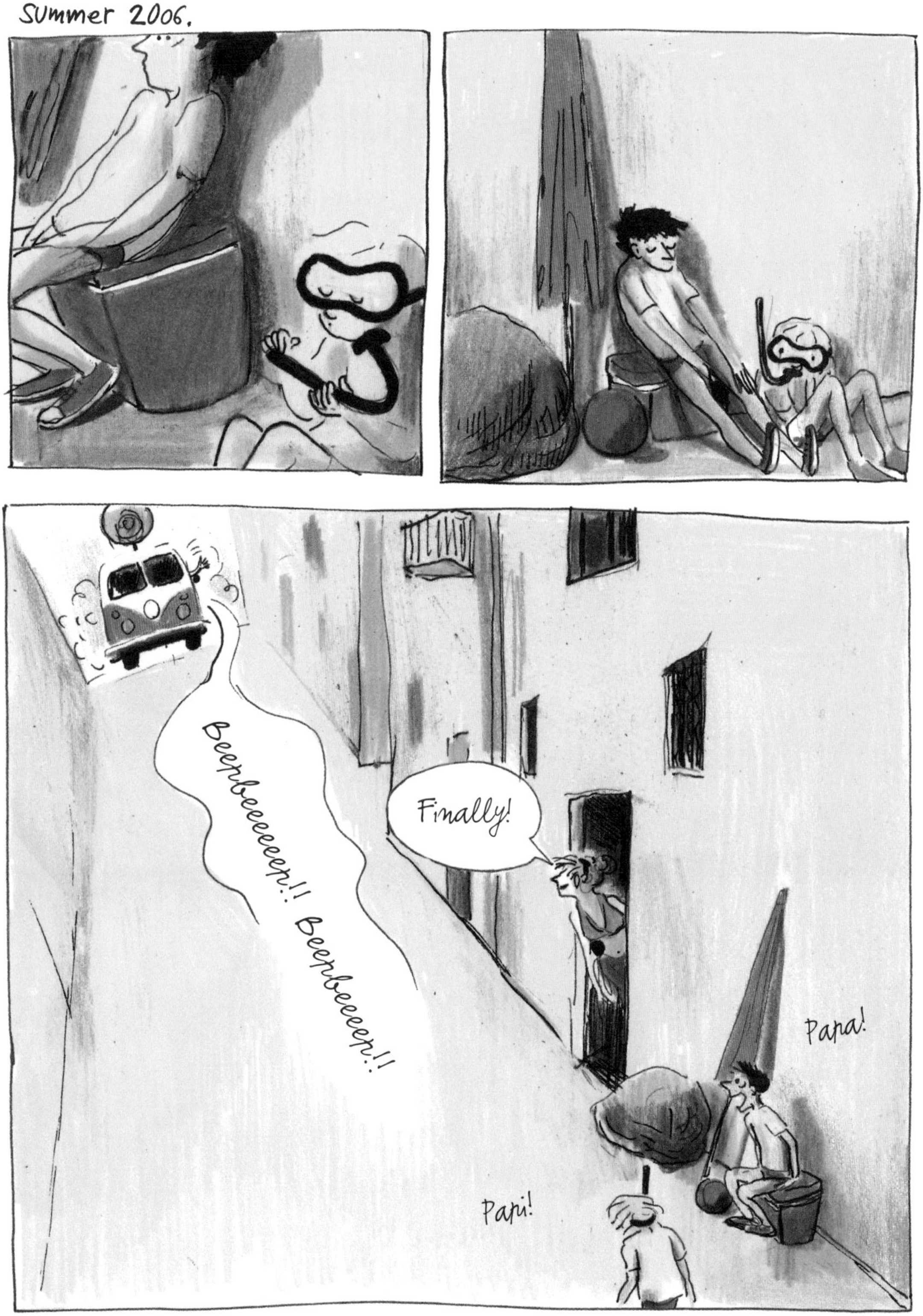
Summer 2006.
Beepbeeeeep!! Beepbeeeep!!
Finally!
Papa!
Papi!

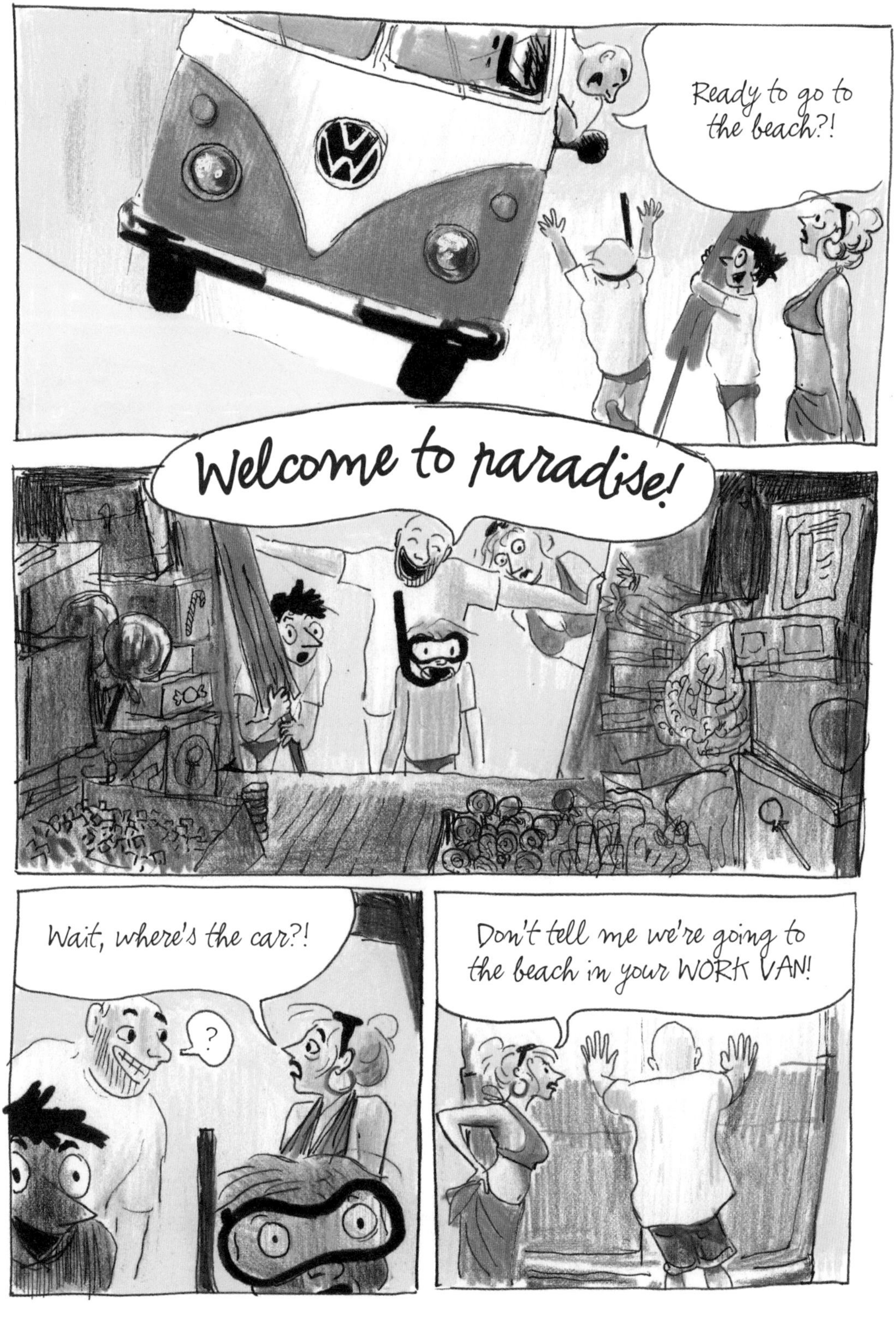
Ready to go to the beach?!
Welcome to paradise!
Wait, where's the car?!
?
Don't tell me we're going to the beach in your WORK VAN!

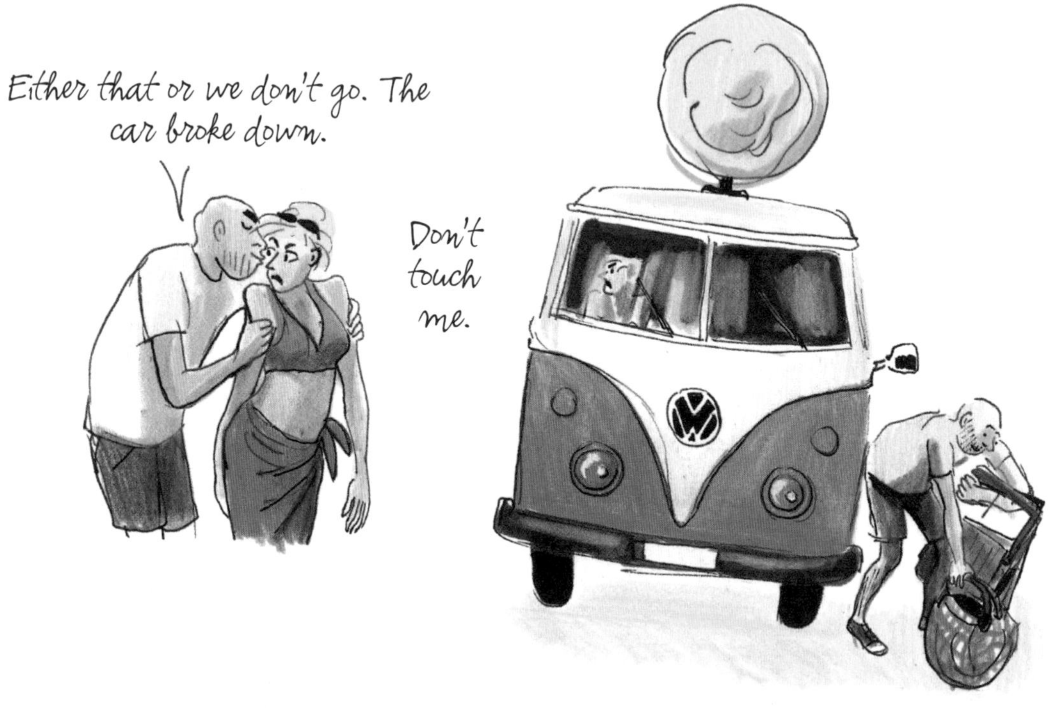
Either that or we don't go. The car broke down.
Don't touch me.

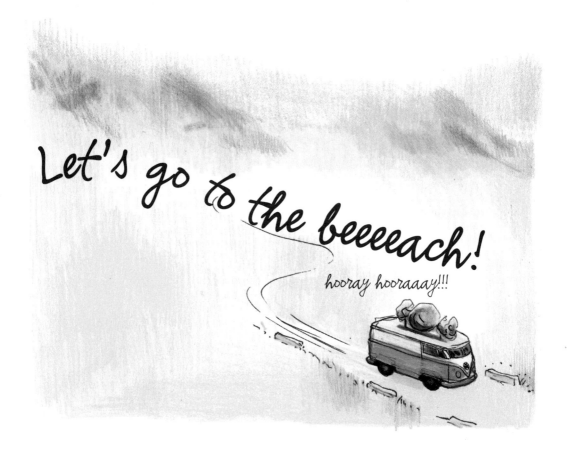

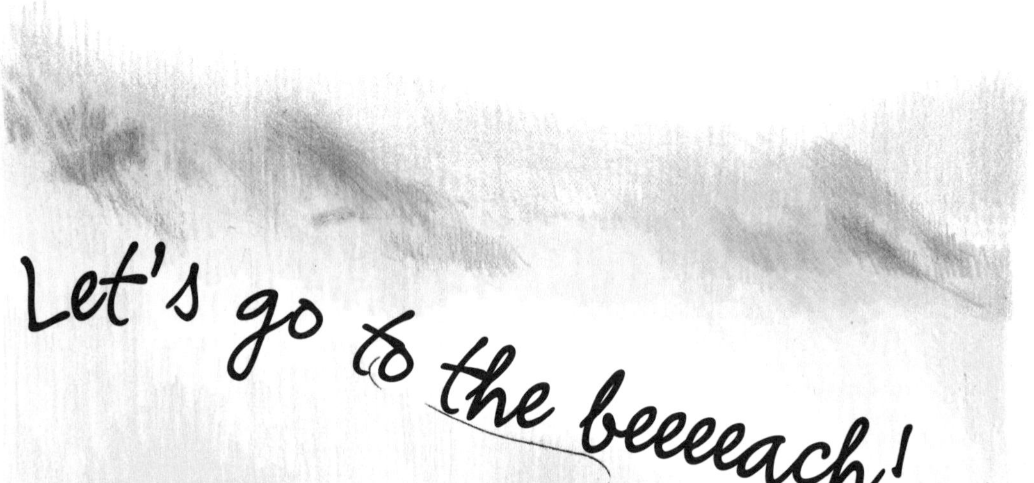
Let's go to the beeeeach!
hooray hooraaay!!!

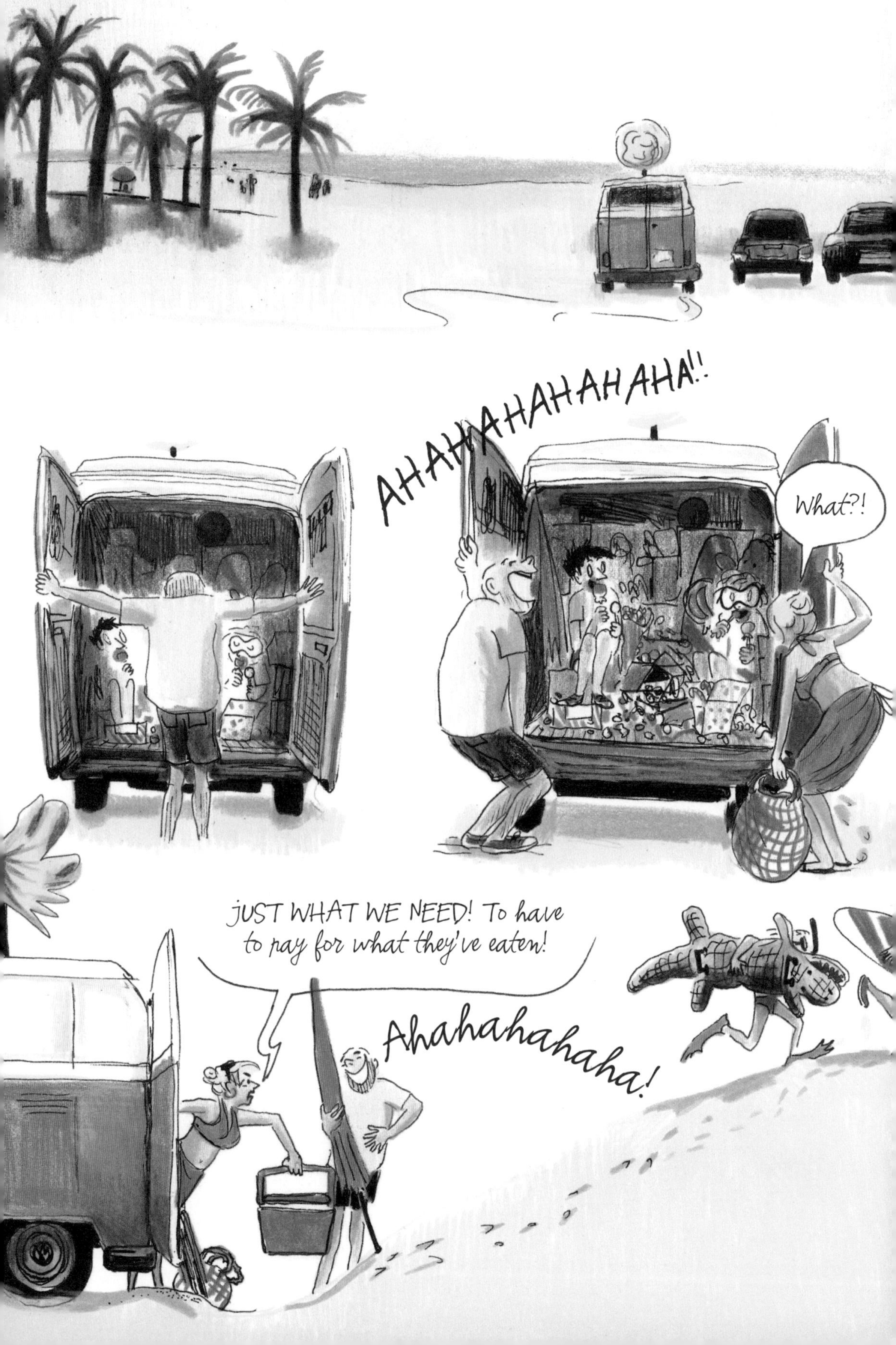
AHAHAHAHAHAHA!!
What?!
JUST WHAT WE NEED! To have to pay for what they've eaten!
Ahahahahahaha!

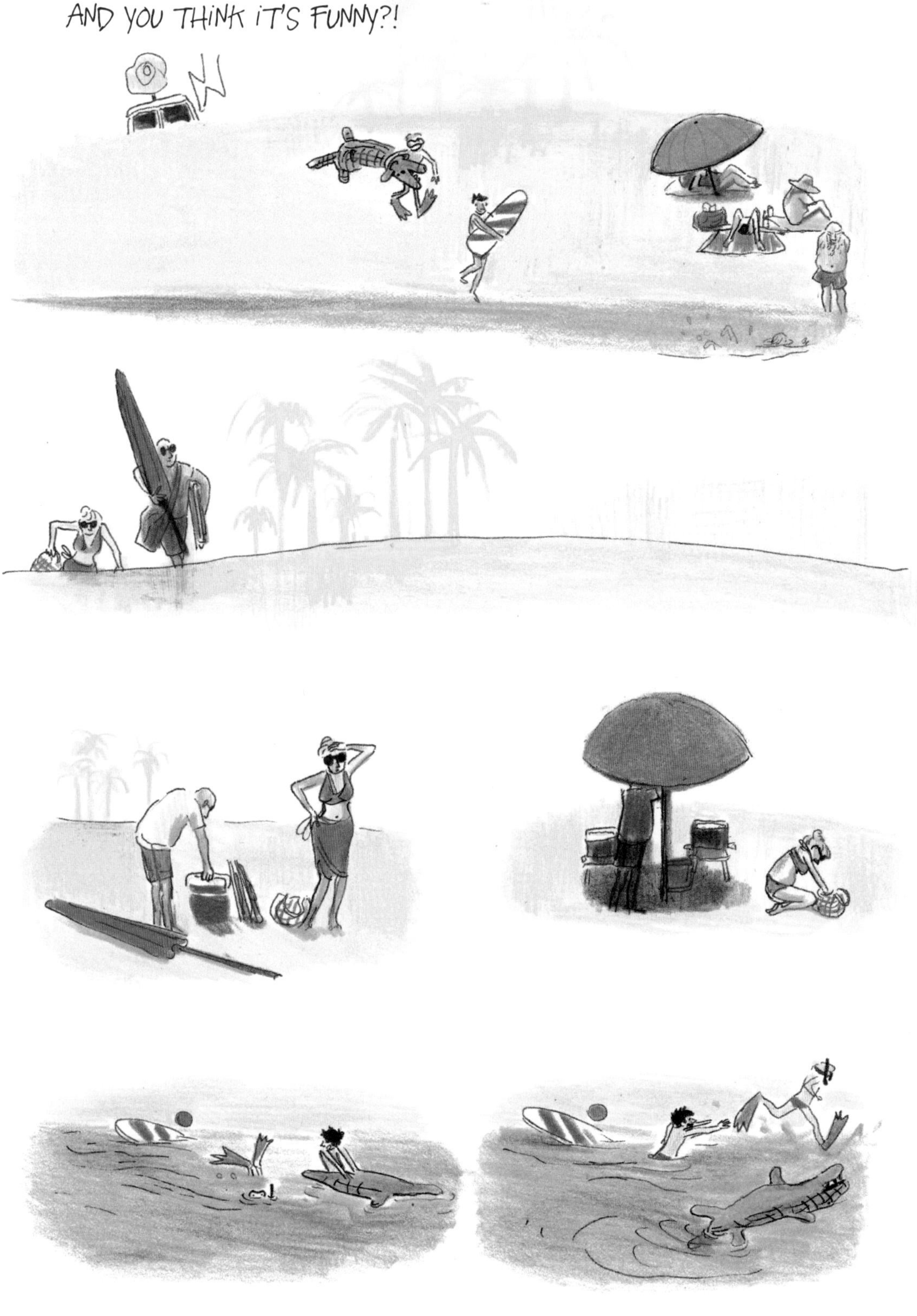
AND YOU THINK IT'S FUNNY?!

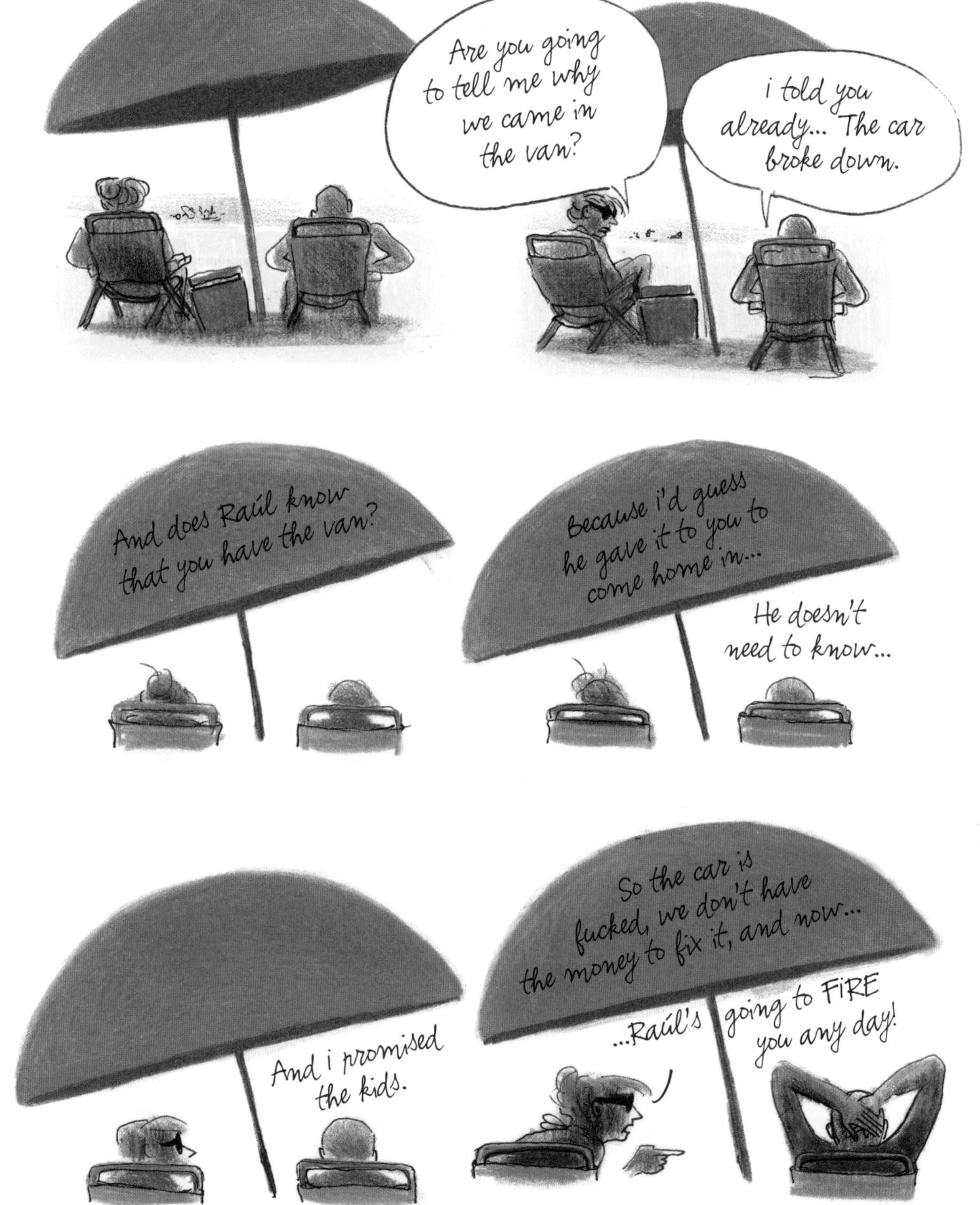
Are you going to tell me why we came in the van?
i told you already... The car broke down.
And does Raúl know that you have the van?
Because i'd guess he gave it to you to come home in...
He doesn't need to know...
And i promised the kids.
So the car is fucked, we don't have the money to fix it, and now...
...Raúl's going to FiRE you any day!

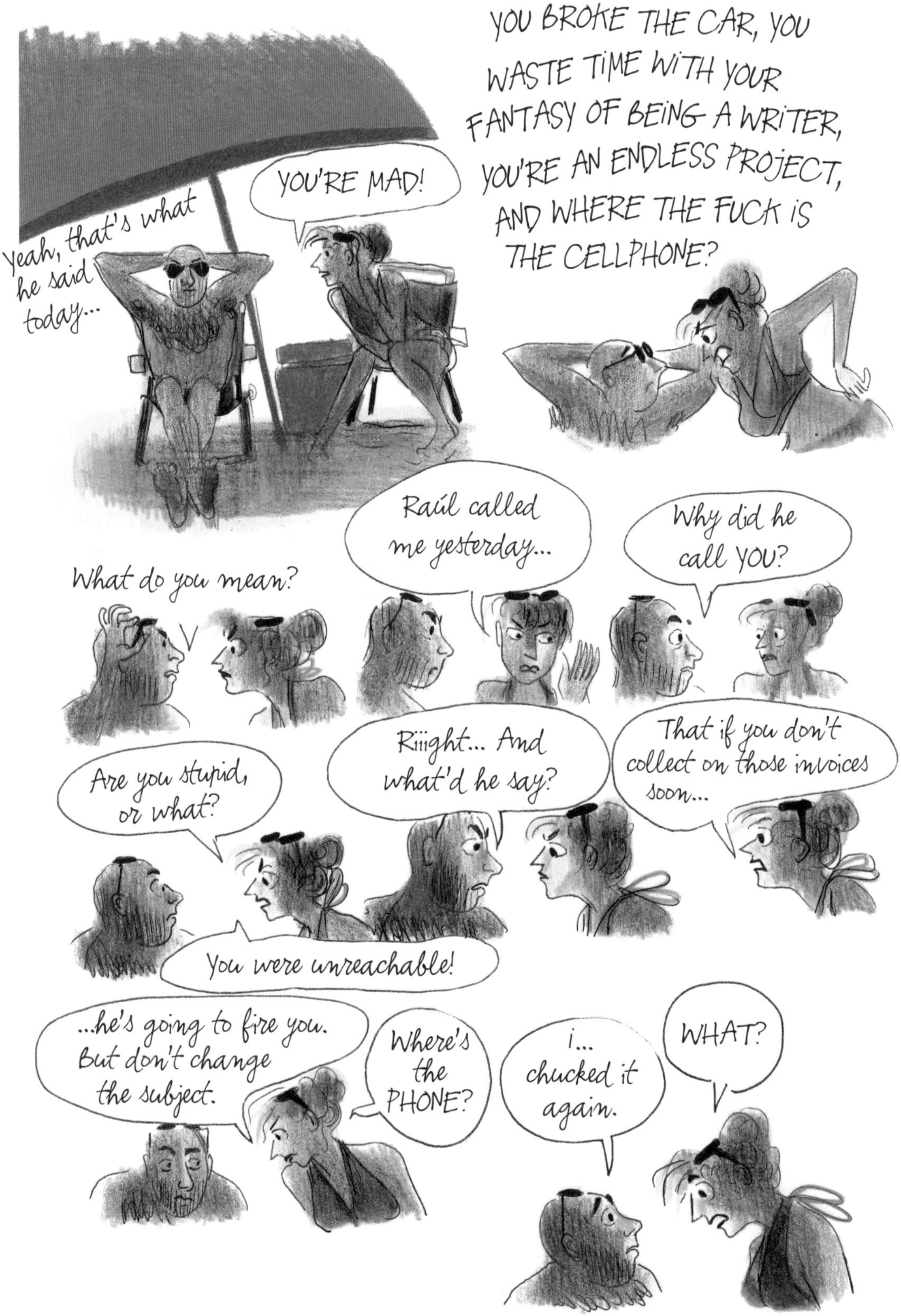
Yeah, that's what he said today...
YOU'RE MAD!
YOU BROKE THE CAR, YOU WASTE TIME WITH YOUR FANTASY OF BEING A WRITER, YOU'RE AN ENDLESS PROJECT, AND WHERE THE FUCK IS THE CELLPHONE?
What do you mean?
Raúl called me yesterday...
Why did he call YOU?
Are you stupid, or what?
You were unreachable!
Riiight... And what'd he say?
That if you don't collect on those invoices soon...
...he's going to fire you. But don't change the subject.
Where's the PHONE?
i... chucked it again.
WHAT?

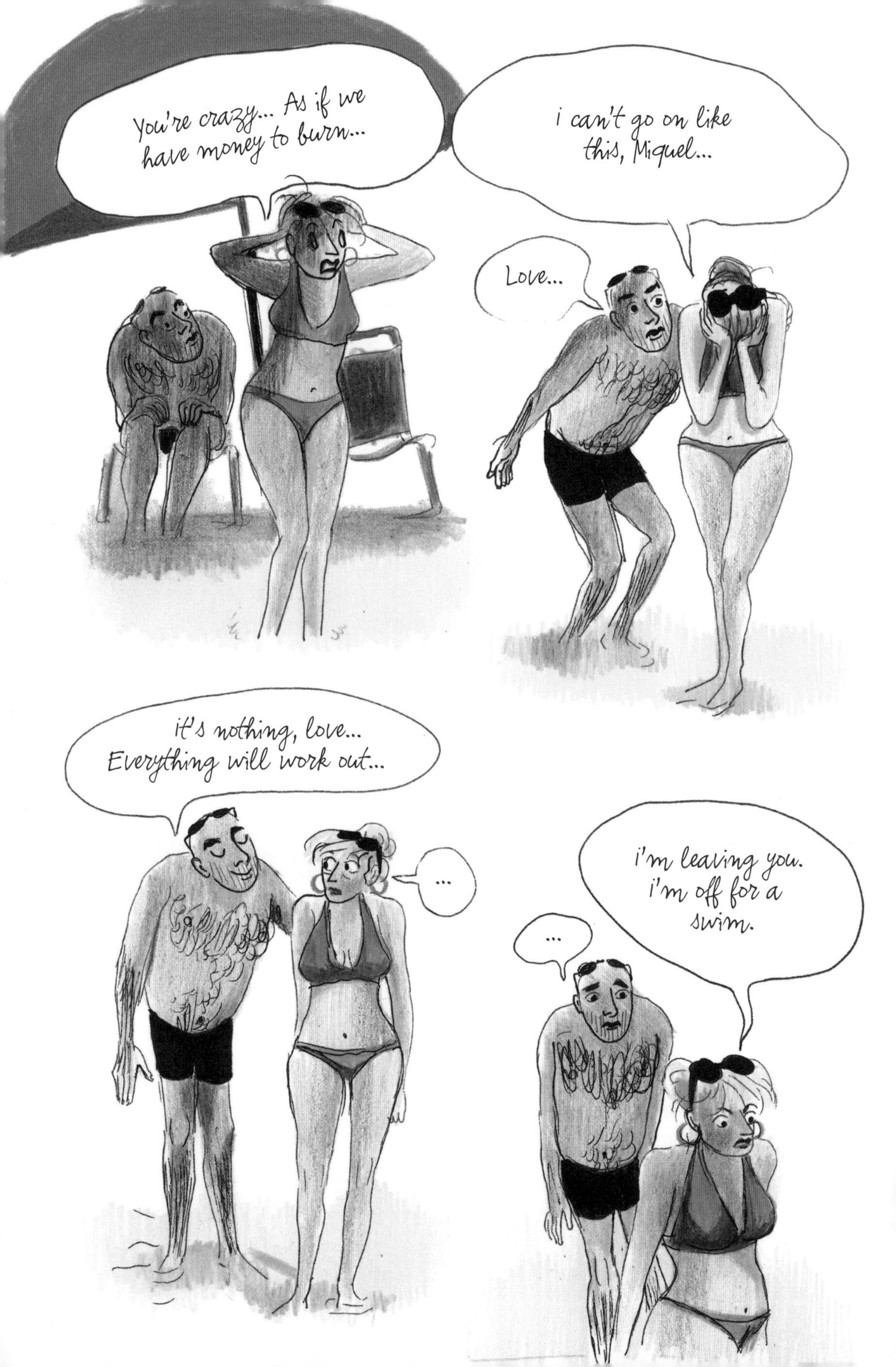
You're crazy... As if we have money to burn...
i can't go on like this, Miquel...
Love...
it's nothing, love... Everything will work out...
...
...
i'm leaving you. i'm off for a swim.

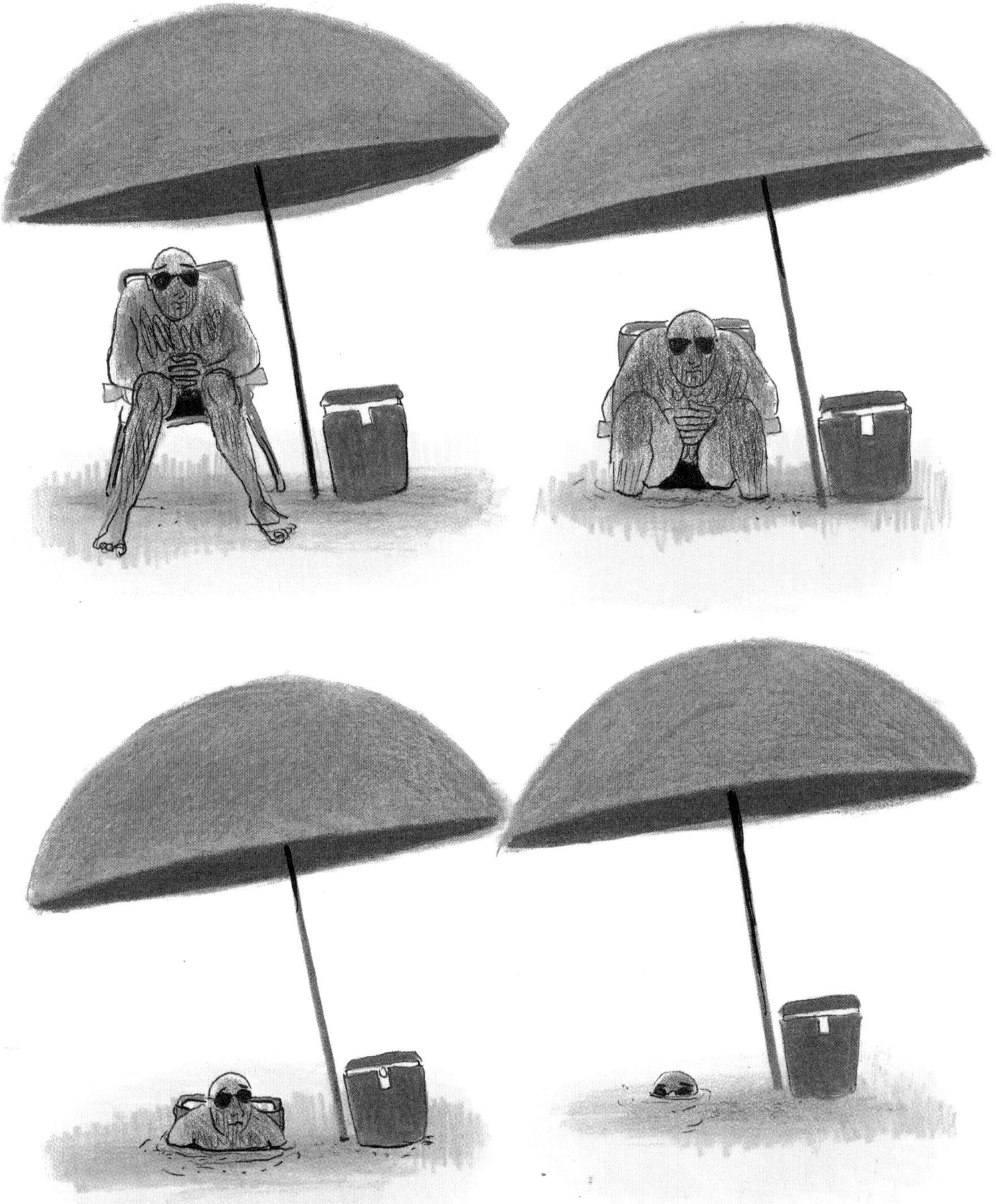

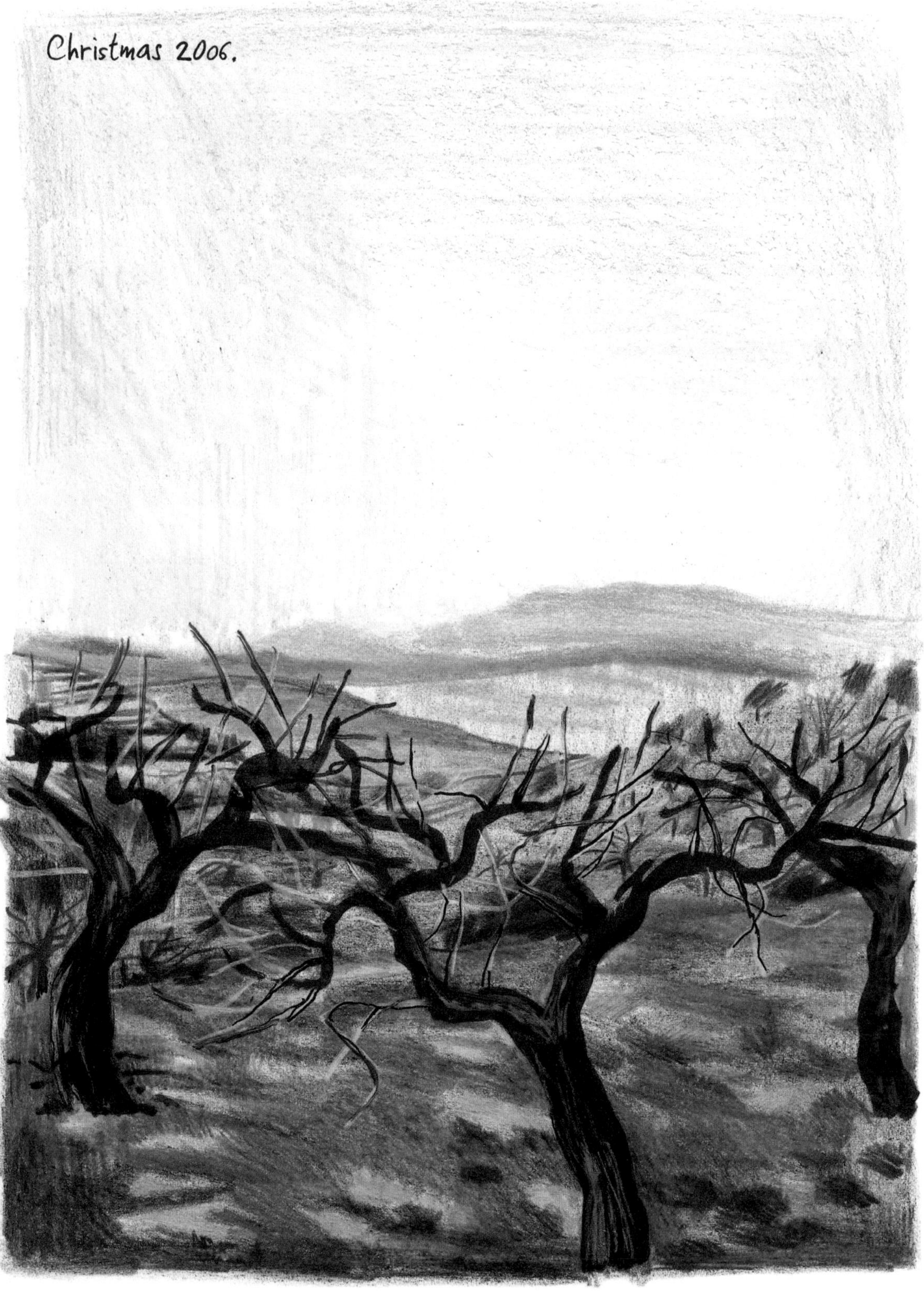
Christmas 2006.

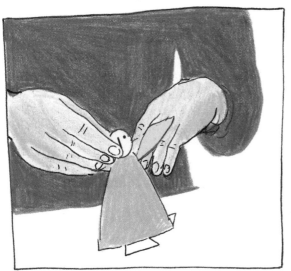

There! And now...

...we just have to wait until Christmas Eve when the baby Jesus is born.

And when'll you make him?

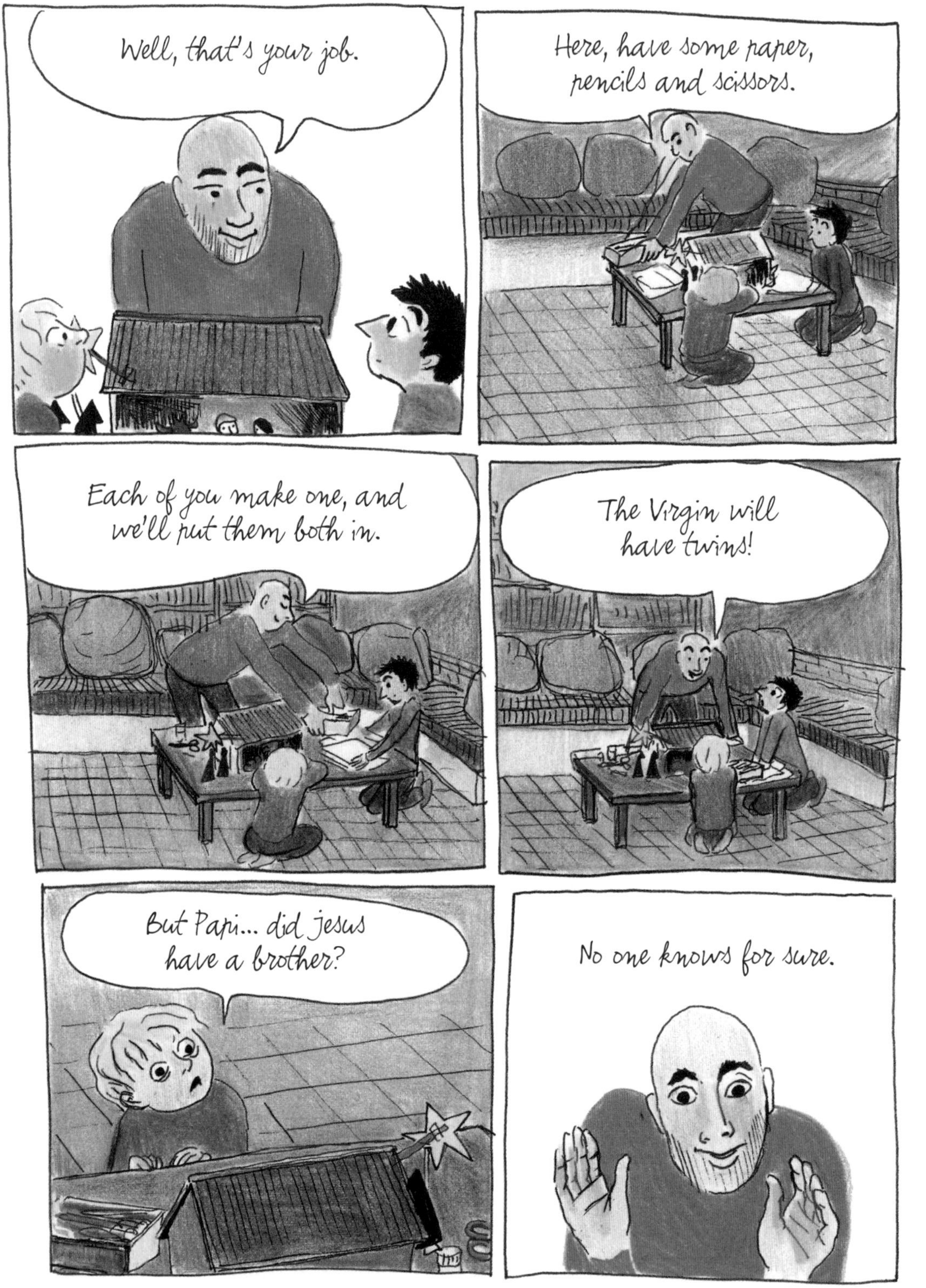
Well, that's your job.
Here, have some paper, pencils and scissors.
Each of you make one, and we'll put them both in.
The Virgin will have twins!
But Papi... did Jesus have a brother?
No one knows for sure.

But my grandma told me the true story of Christmas...

You can't tell anyone, because it's a secret, but jesus had a twin brother.

That's not true, Papi. They don't say that at school.

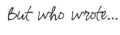

That's because jesus got all the attention.

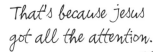

But who wrote...

...the story of jesus?

it was...

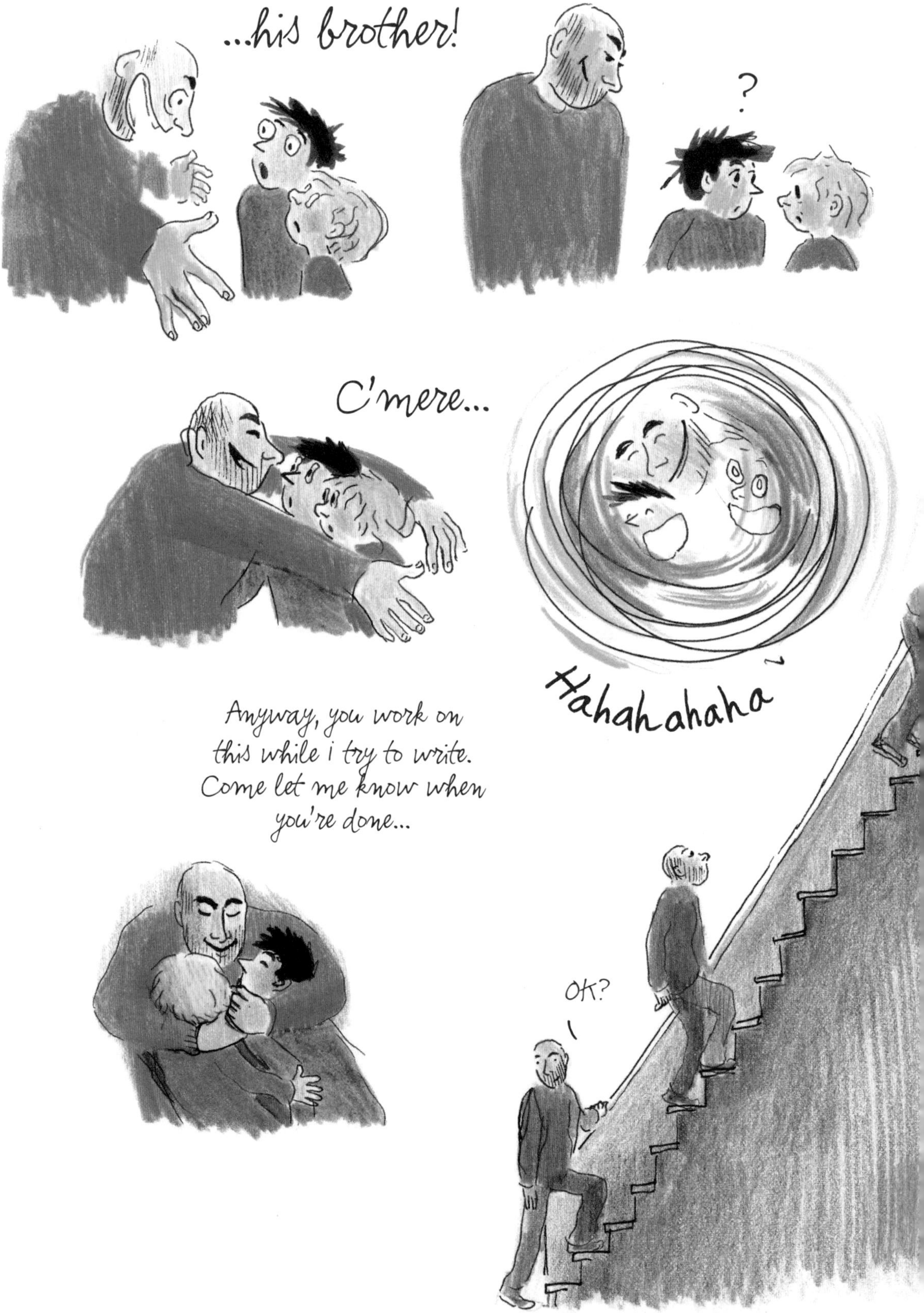
...his brother!
?
C'mere...
Hahahahaha
Anyway, you work on this while i try to write. Come let me know when you're done...
OK?

CANNON
CANNON FODDER

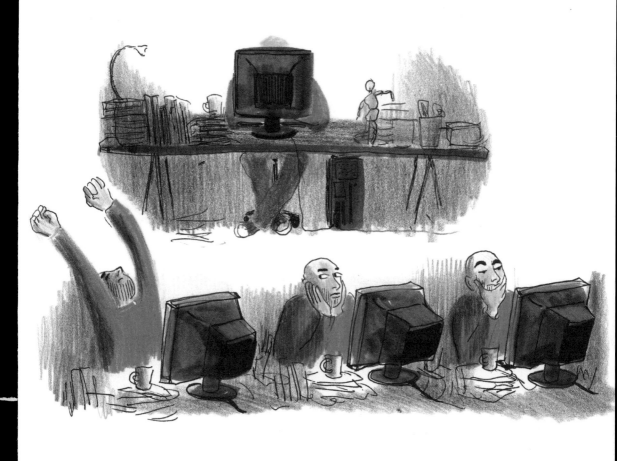

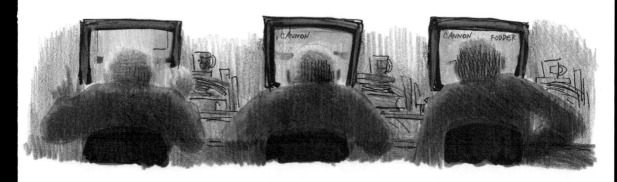

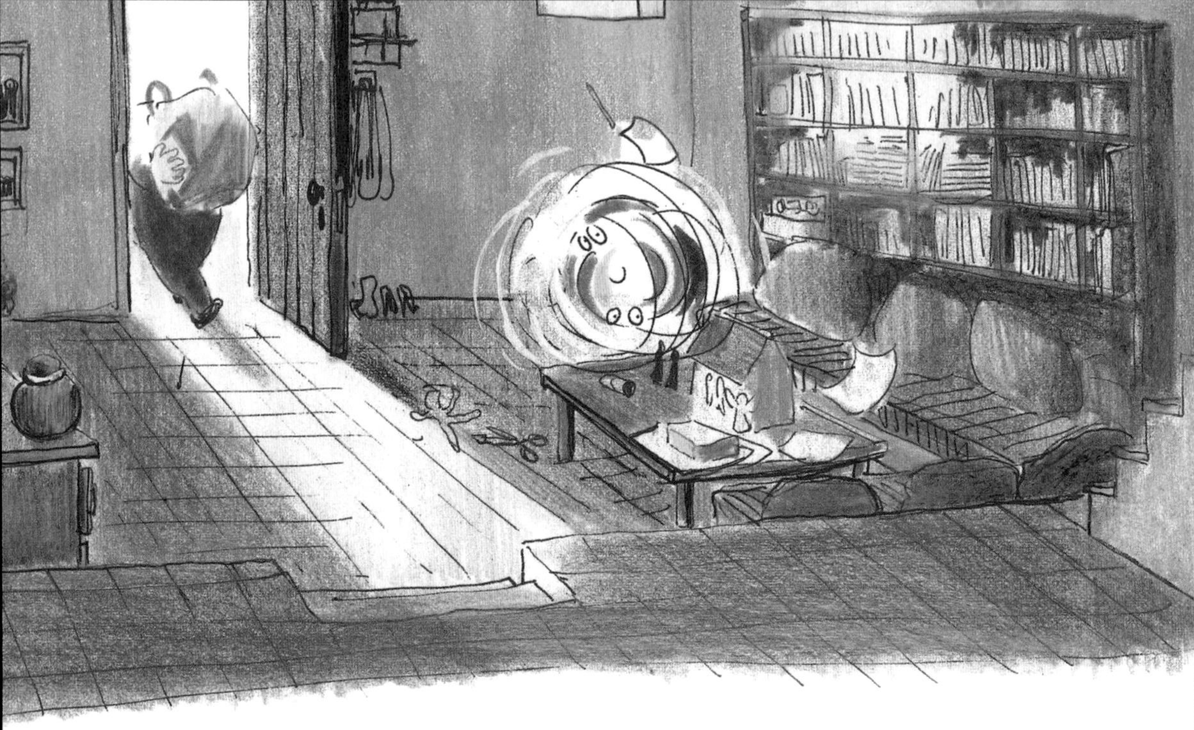

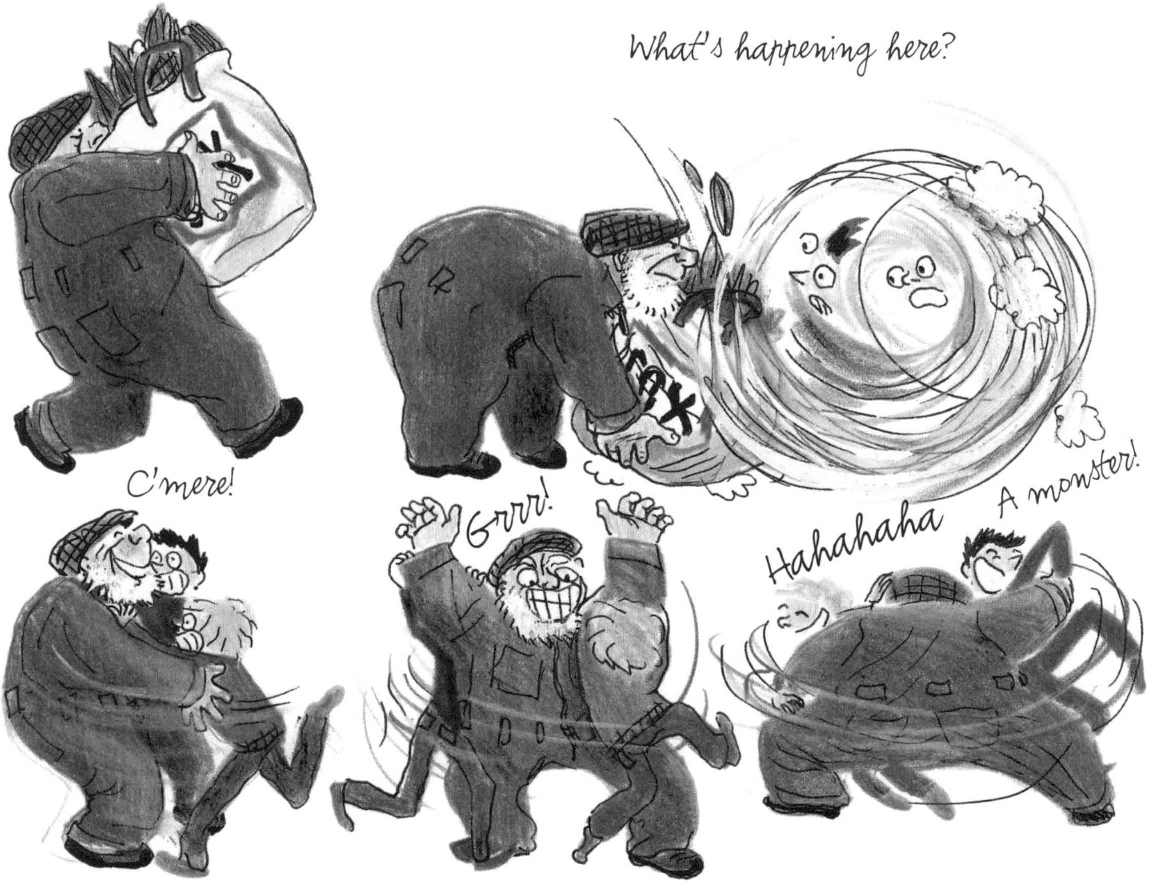
What's happening here?
C'mere!
Grrr!
Hahahaha
A monster!

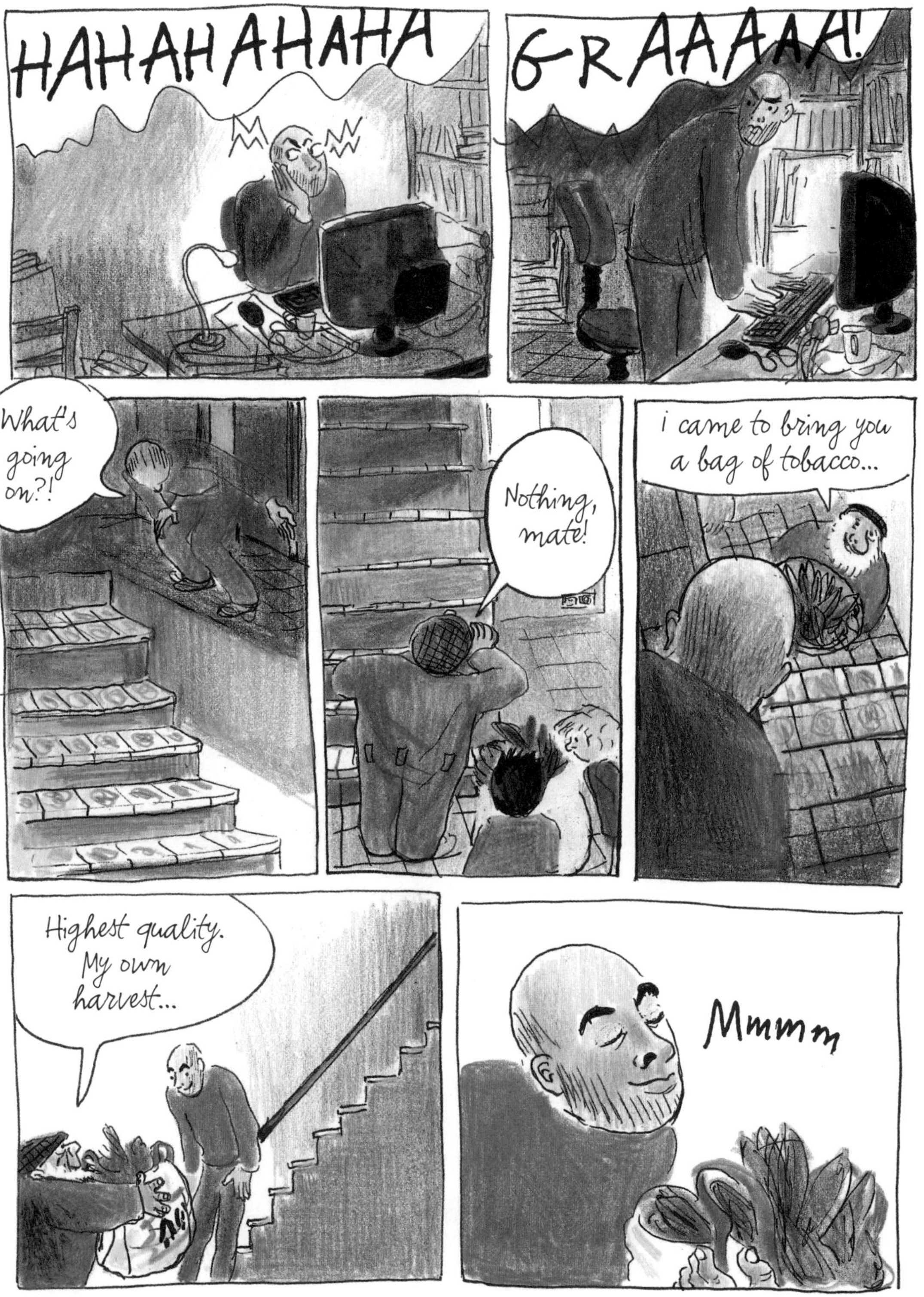
HAHAHAHAHA
GRAAAAA!
What's going on?!
Nothing, mate!
i came to bring you a bag of tobacco...
Highest quality. My own harvest...
Mmmm

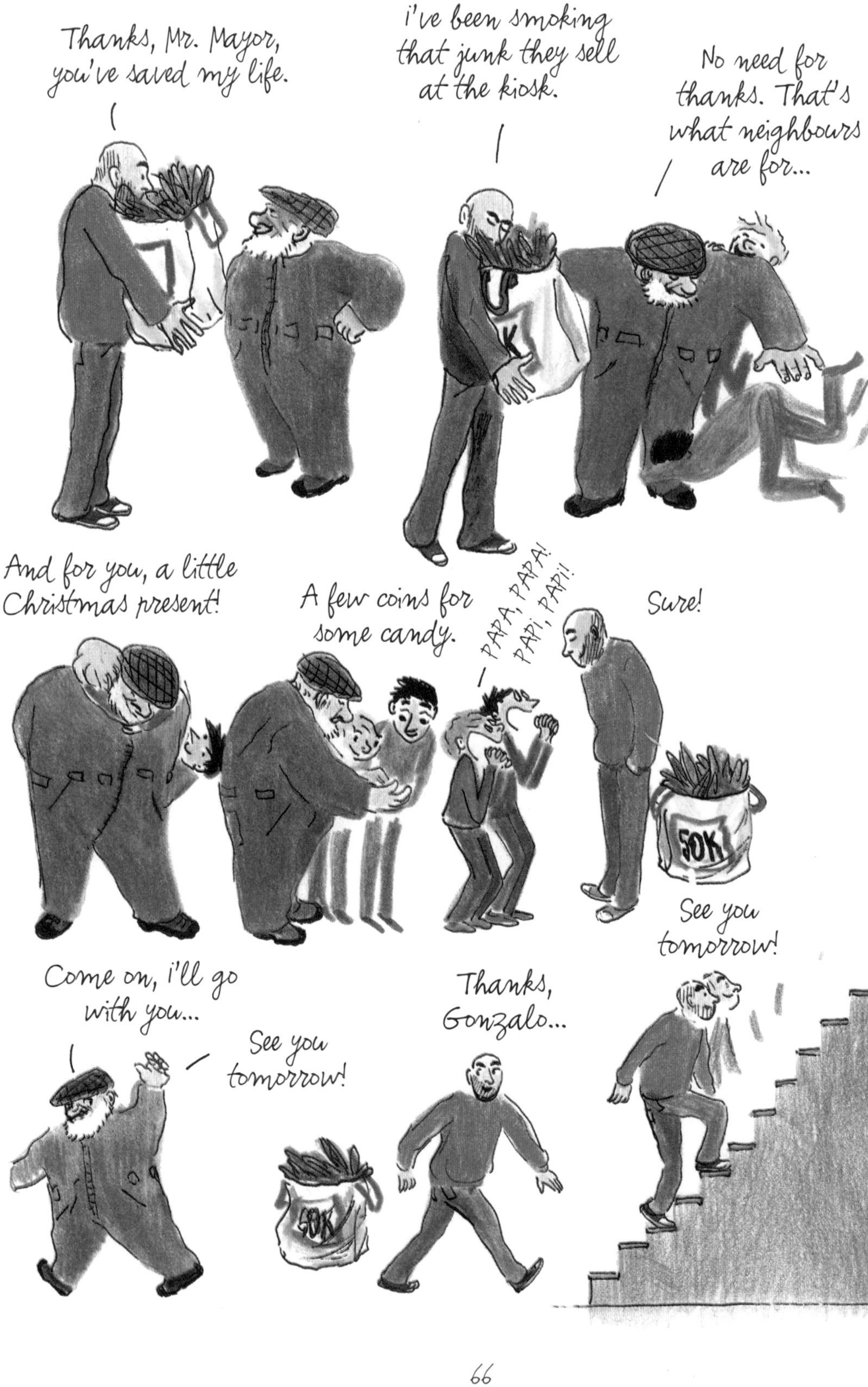
Thanks, Mr. Mayor, you've saved my life.
i've been smoking that junk they sell at the kiosk.
No need for thanks. That's what neighbours are for...
And for you, a little Christmas present!
A few coins for some candy.
PAPA, PAPA! PAPI, PAPI!
Sure!
SOK
Come on, i'll go with you...
See you tomorrow!
SOK
Thanks, Gonzalo...
See you tomorrow!

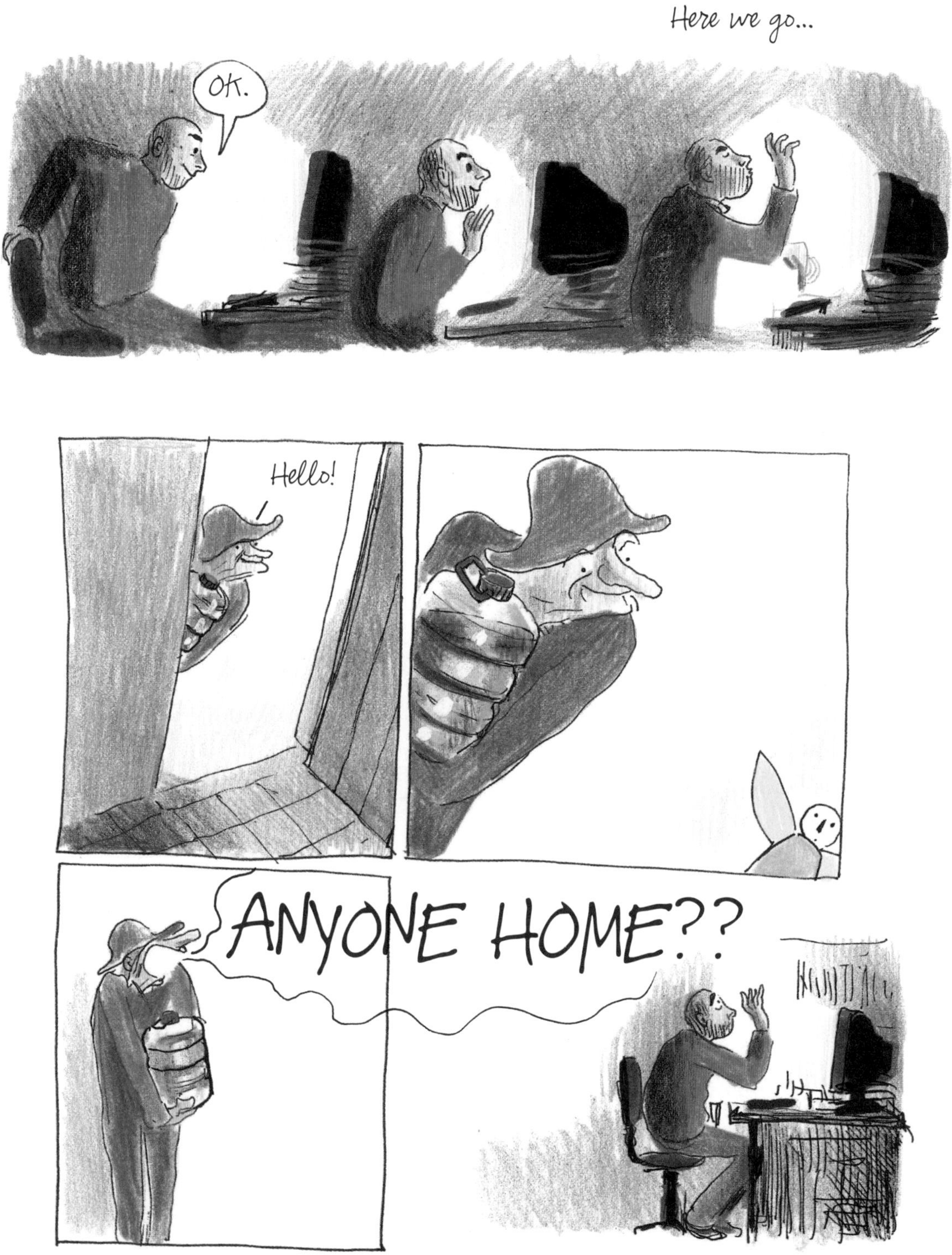
Here we go...
OK.
Hello!
ANYONE HOME??

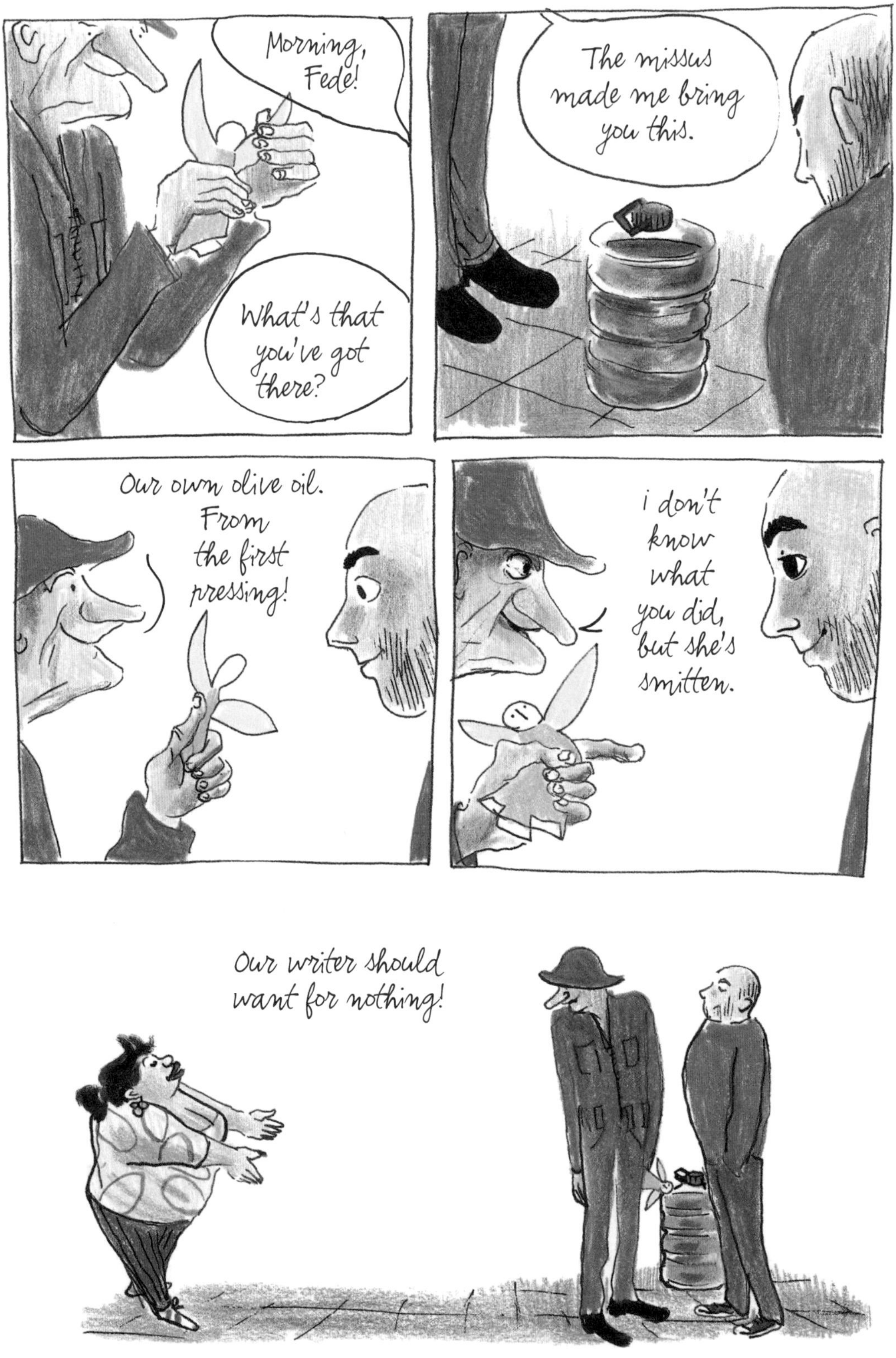
Morning, Fede!
What's that you've got there?
The missus made me bring you this.
Our own olive oil. From the first pressing!
i don't know what you did, but she's smitten.
Our writer should want for nothing!

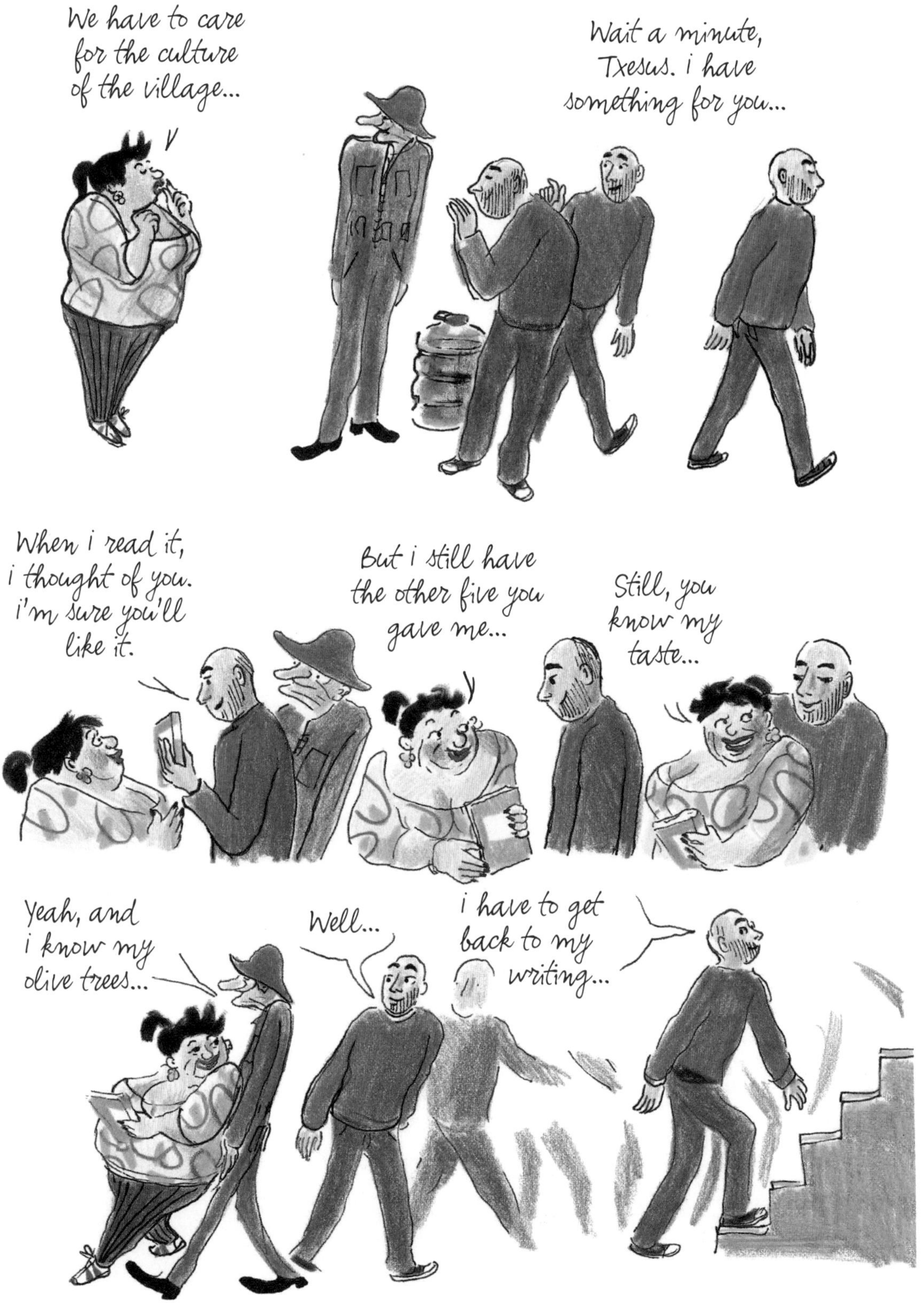
We have to care for the culture of the village...
Wait a minute, Txesus. i have something for you...
When i read it, i thought of you. i'm sure you'll like it.
But i still have the other five you gave me...
Still, you know my taste...
Yeah, and i know my olive trees...
Well...
i have to get back to my writing...

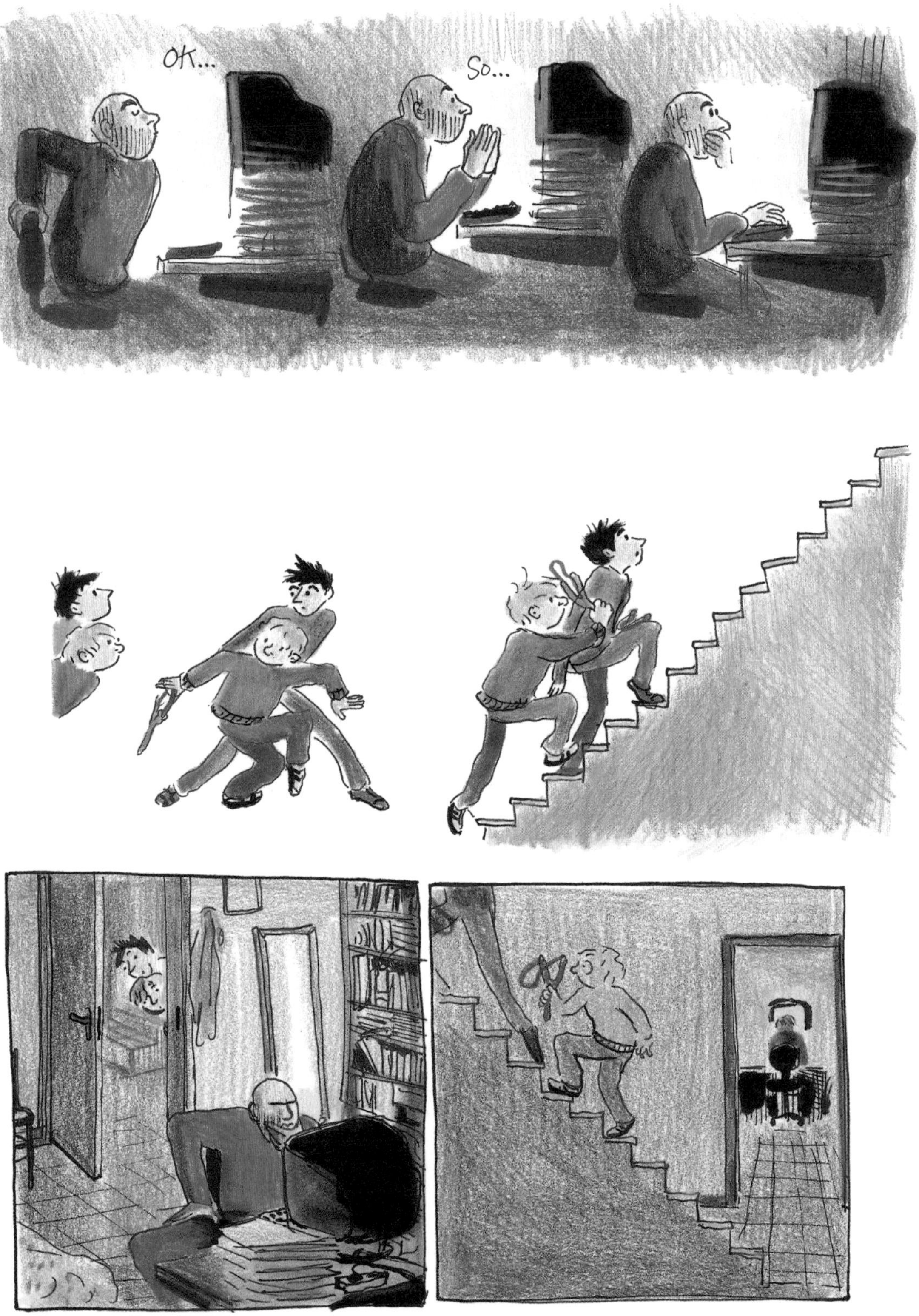
OK...
So...

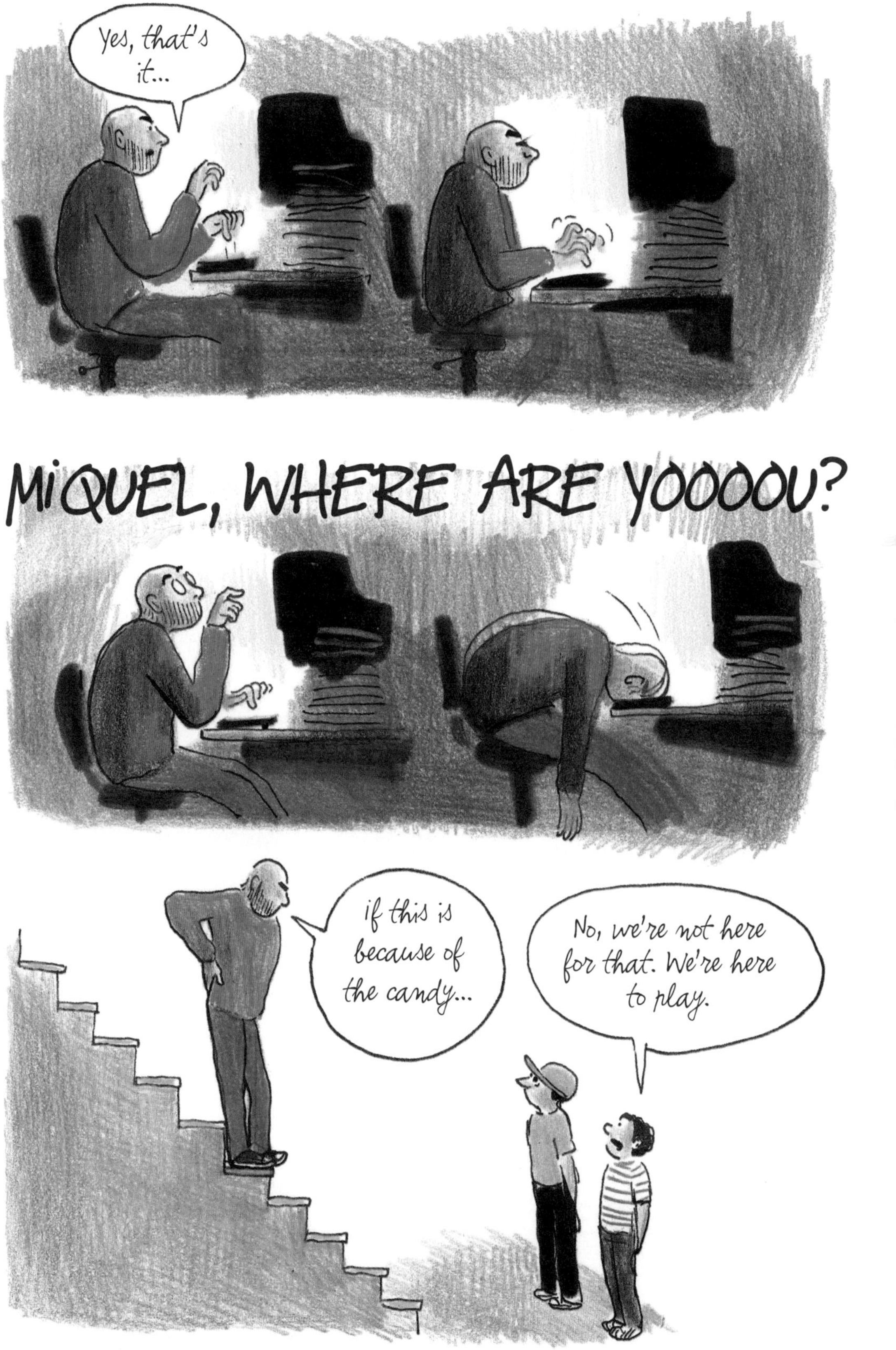
Yes, that's it...
MIQUEL, WHERE ARE YOOOOU?
if this is because of the candy...
No, we're not here for that. We're here to play.

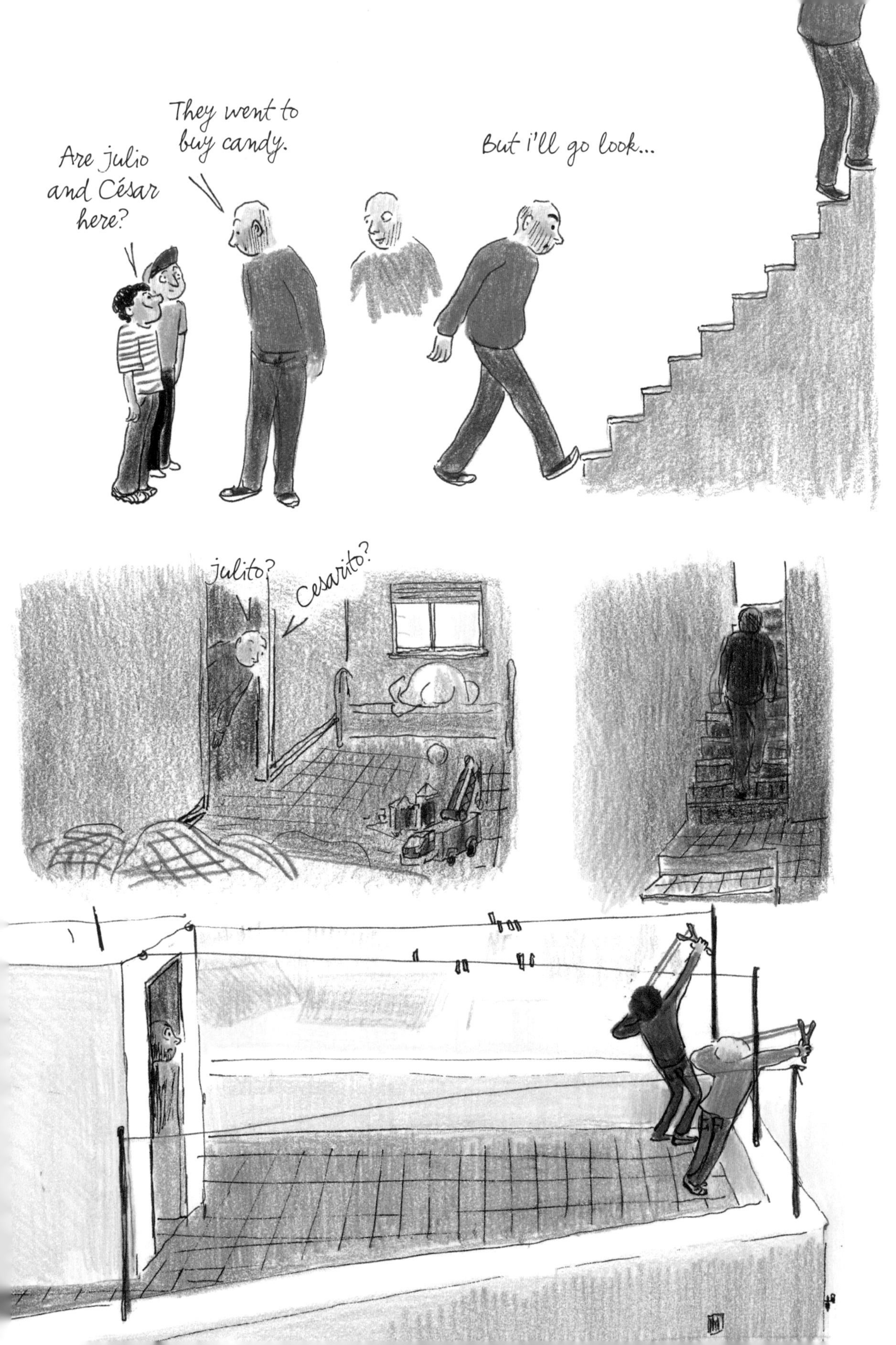
Are julio and César here?
They went to buy candy.
But i'll go look...
julito?
Cesarito?

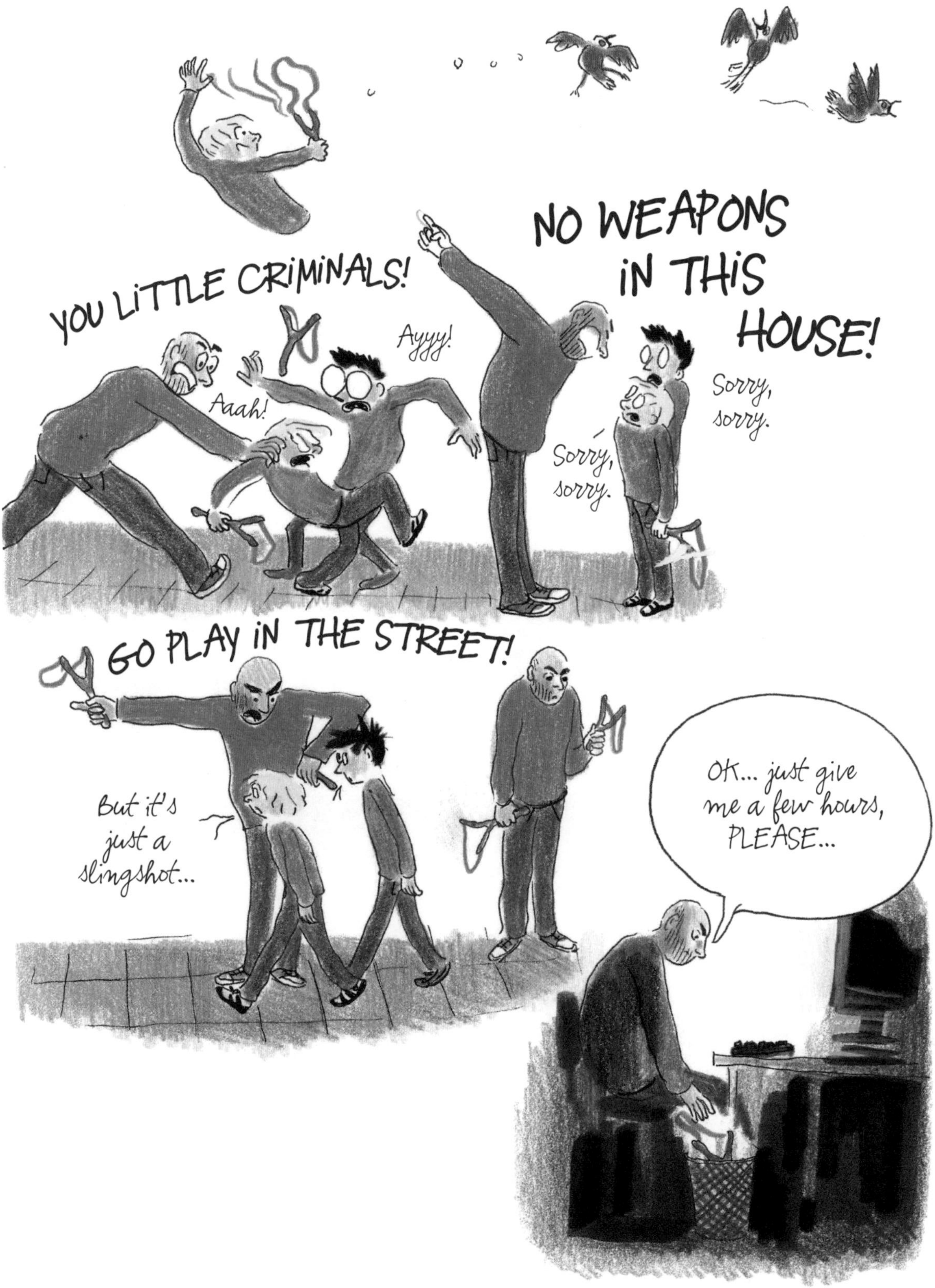
YOU LITTLE CRIMINALS!
Aaah!
Ayyy!
NO WEAPONS IN THIS HOUSE!
Sorry, sorry.
Sorry, sorry.
GO PLAY IN THE STREET!
But it's just a slingshot...
OK... just give me a few hours, PLEASE...

New Year's Eve, 2007.

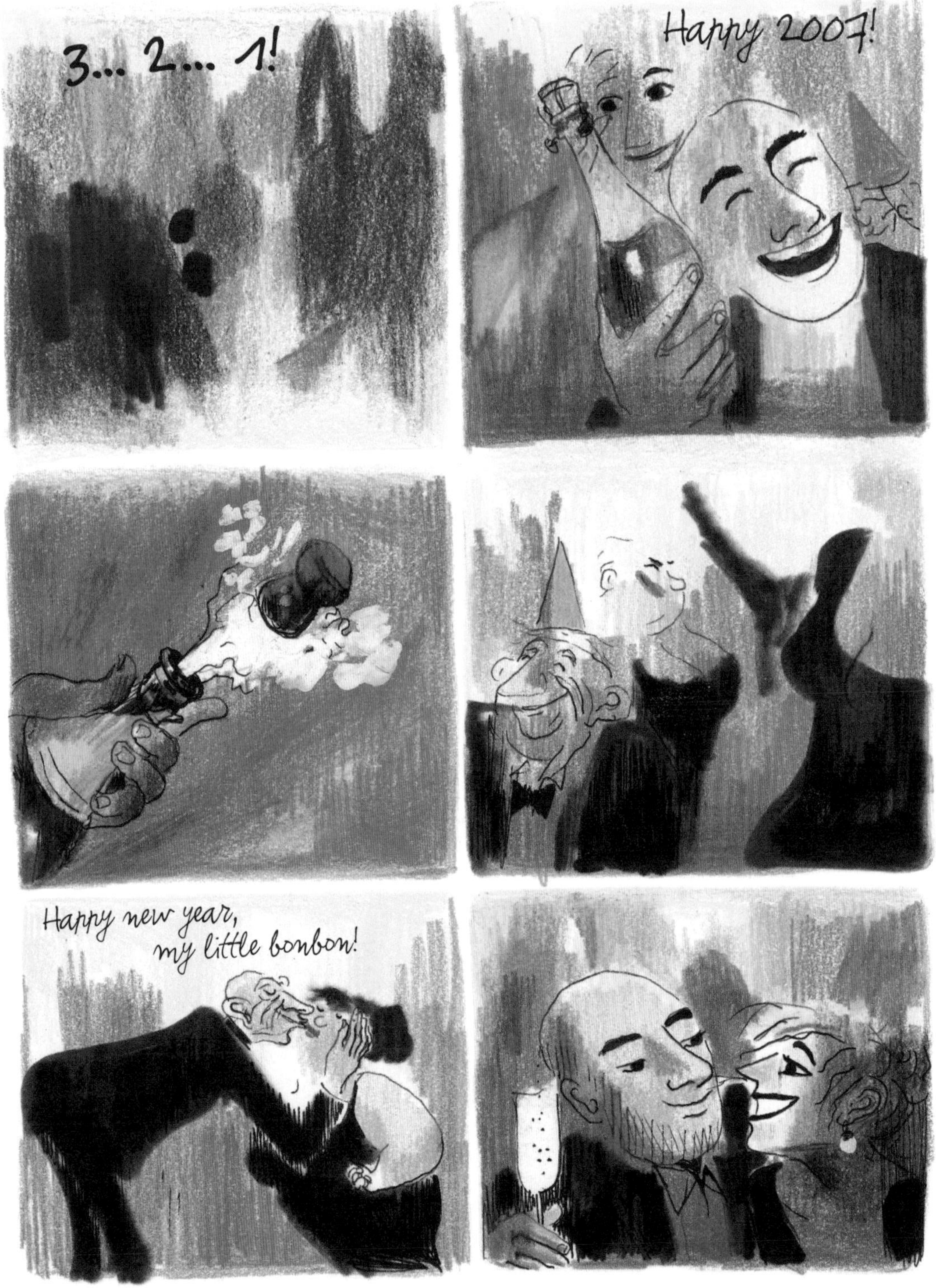
3... 2... 1!
Happy 2007!
Happy new year, my little bonbon!

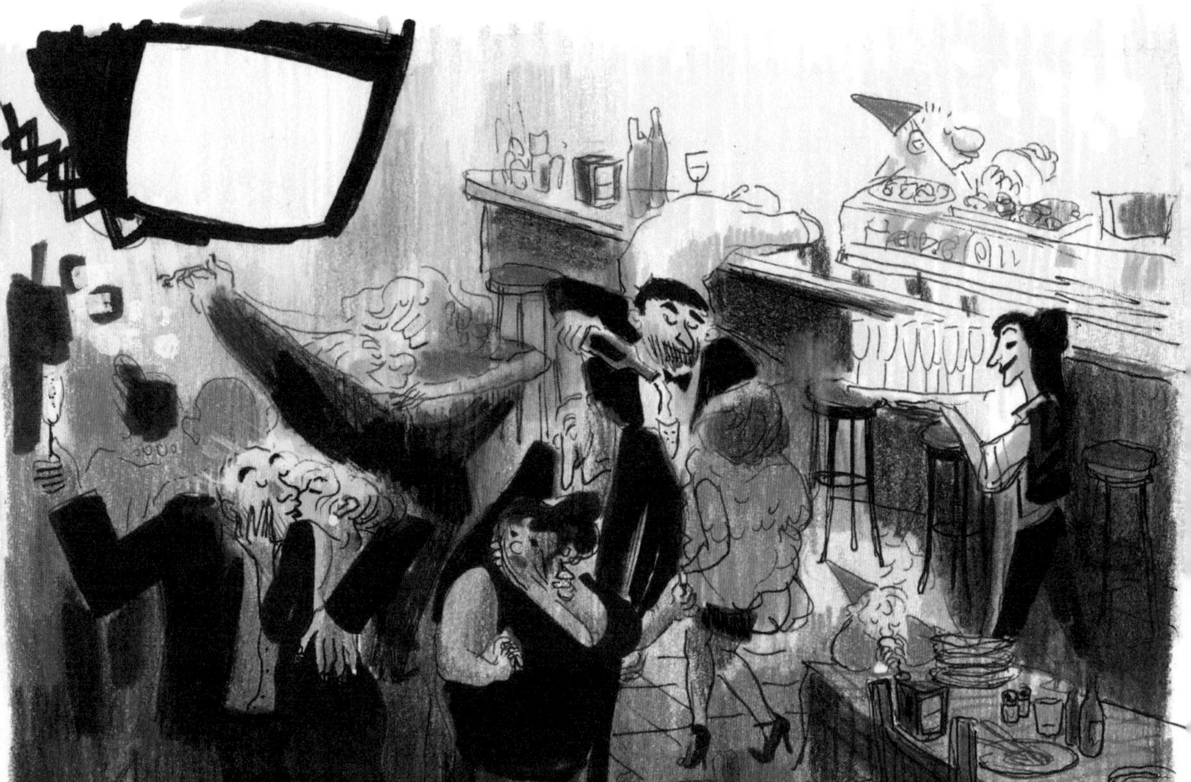

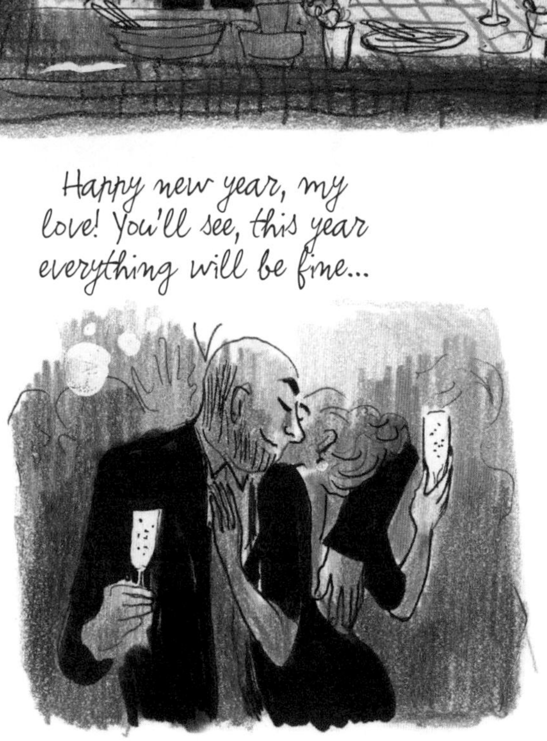
Happy new year, my love! You'll see, this year everything will be fine...

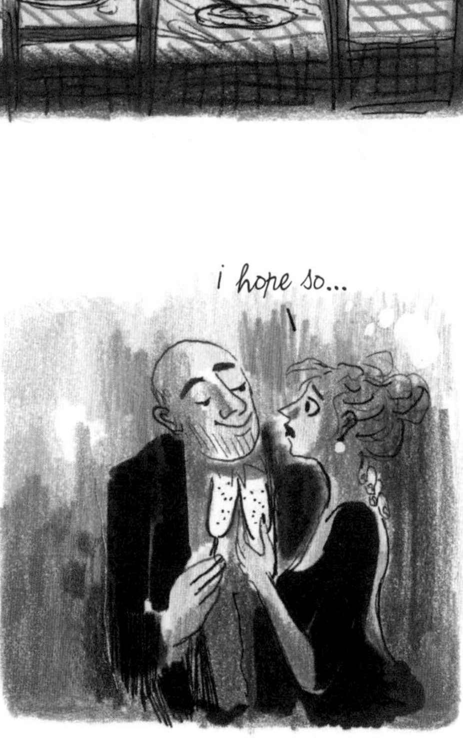
i hope so...

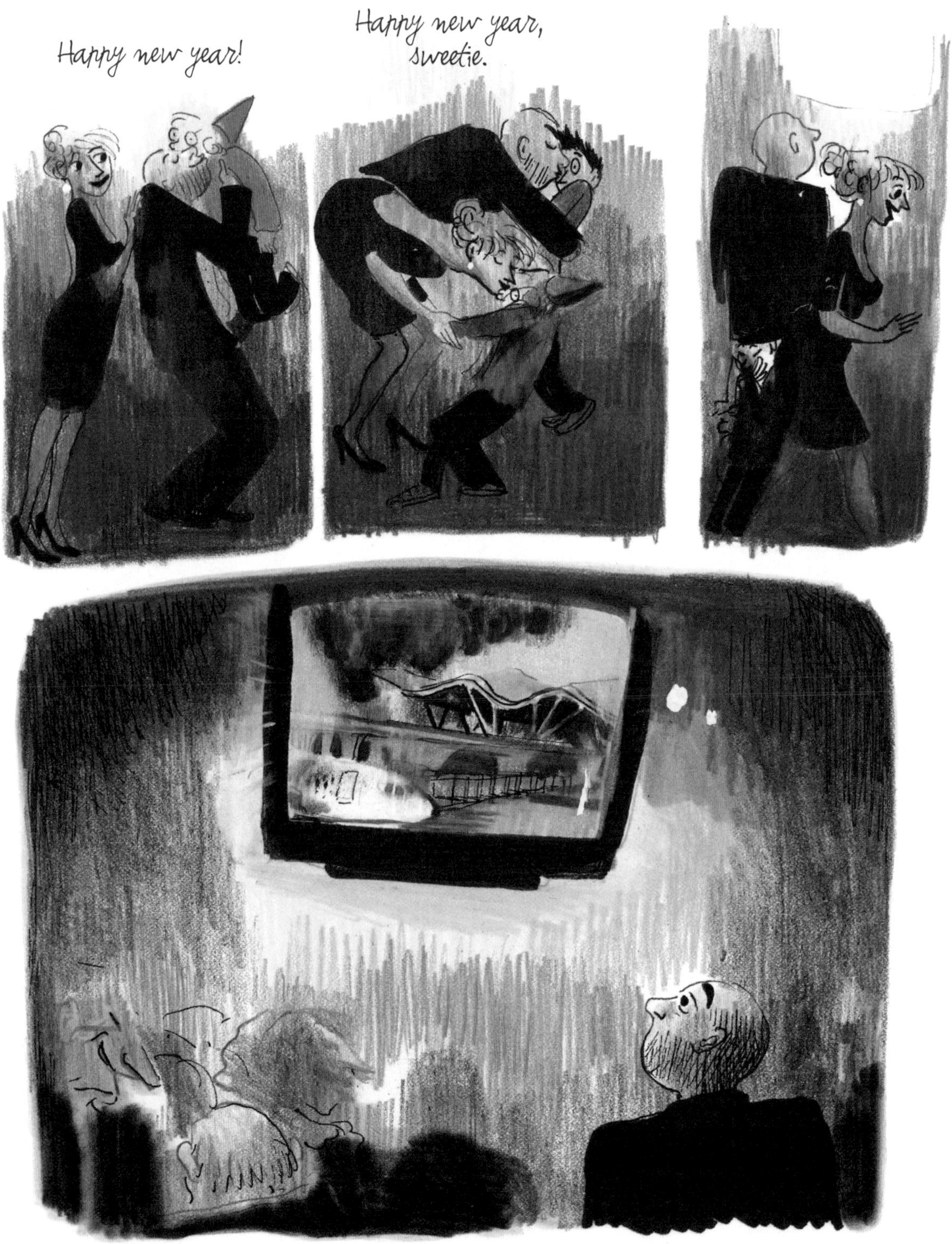
Happy new year!
Happy new year, sweetie.

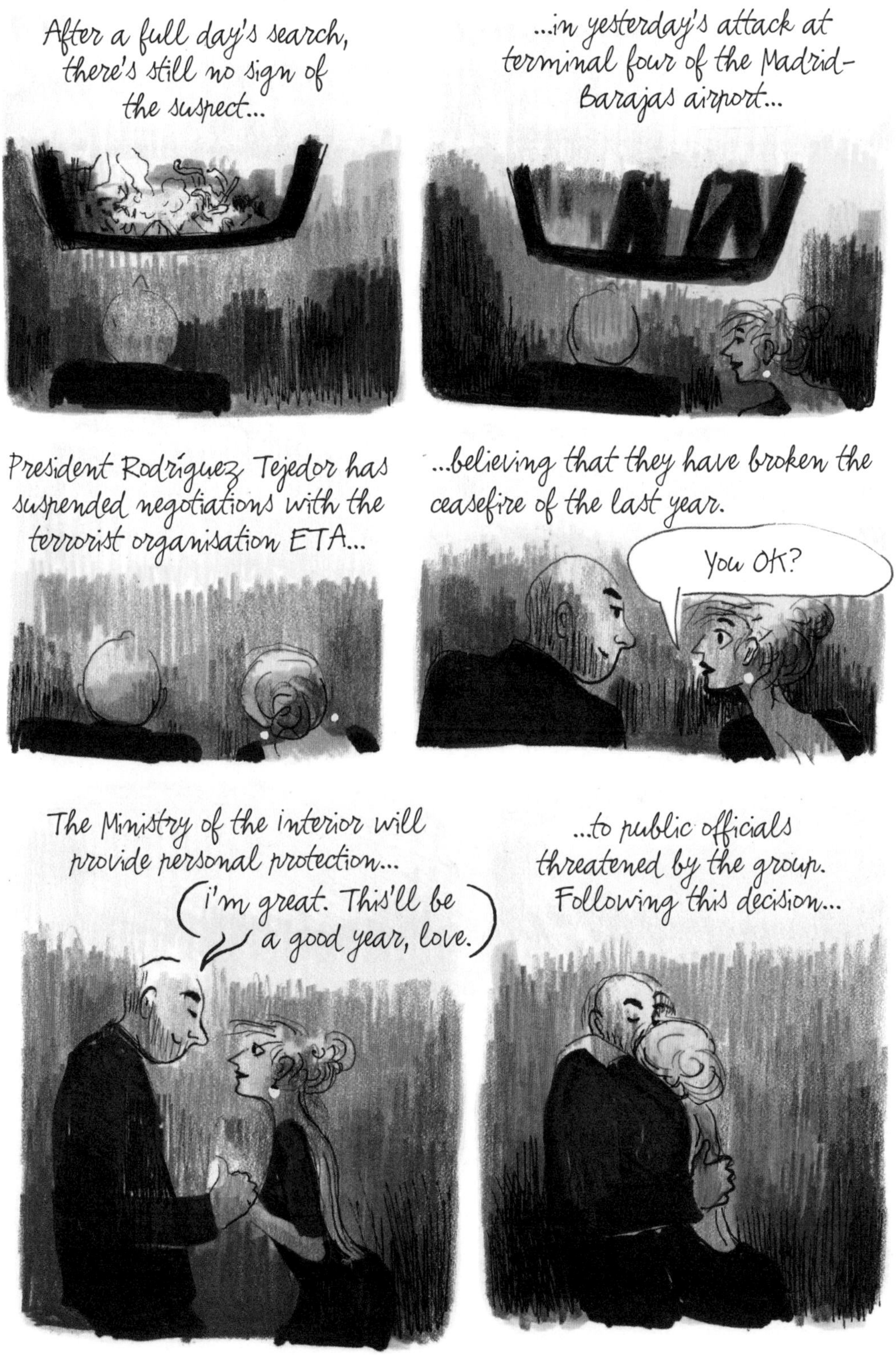
After a full day's search, there's still no sign of the suspect...
...in yesterday's attack at terminal four of the Madrid-Barajas airport...
President Rodríguez Tejedor has suspended negotiations with the terrorist organisation ETA...
...believing that they have broken the ceasefire of the last year.
You OK?
The Ministry of the interior will provide personal protection...
I'm great. This'll be a good year, love.
...to public officials threatened by the group. Following this decision...

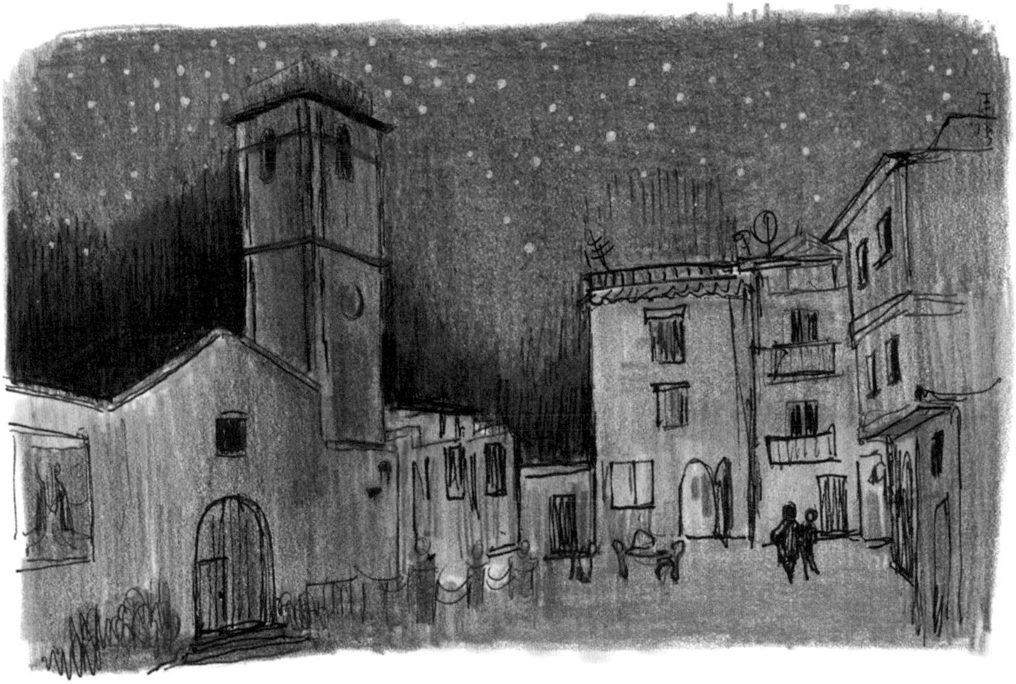

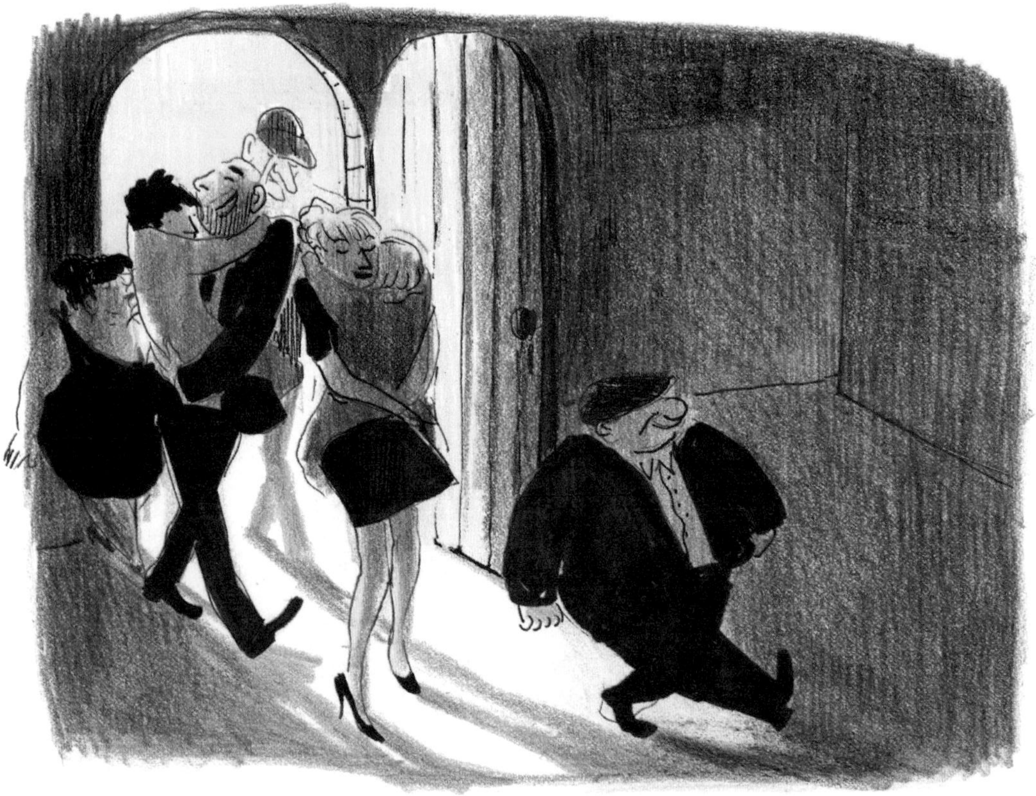

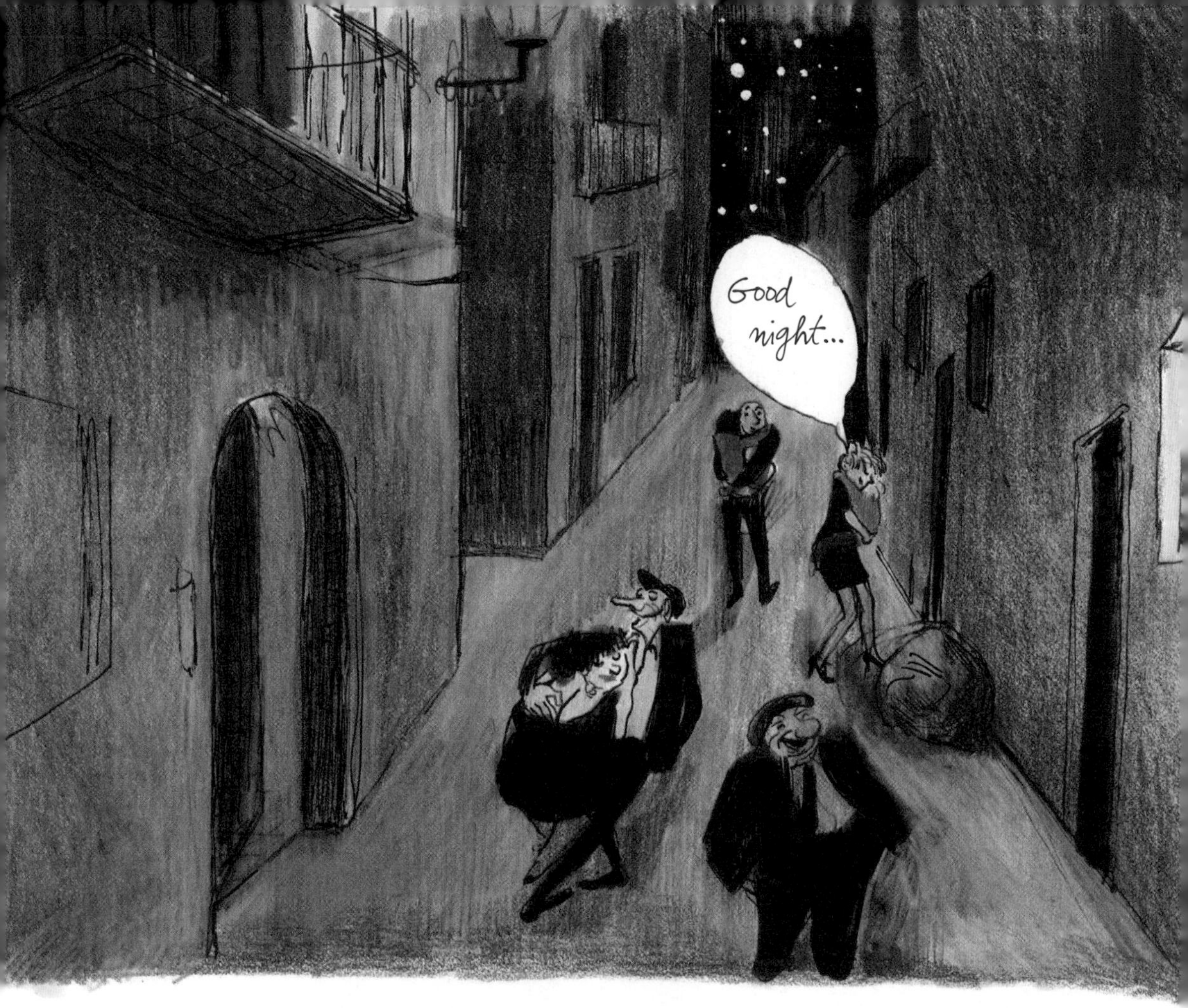
Good night...

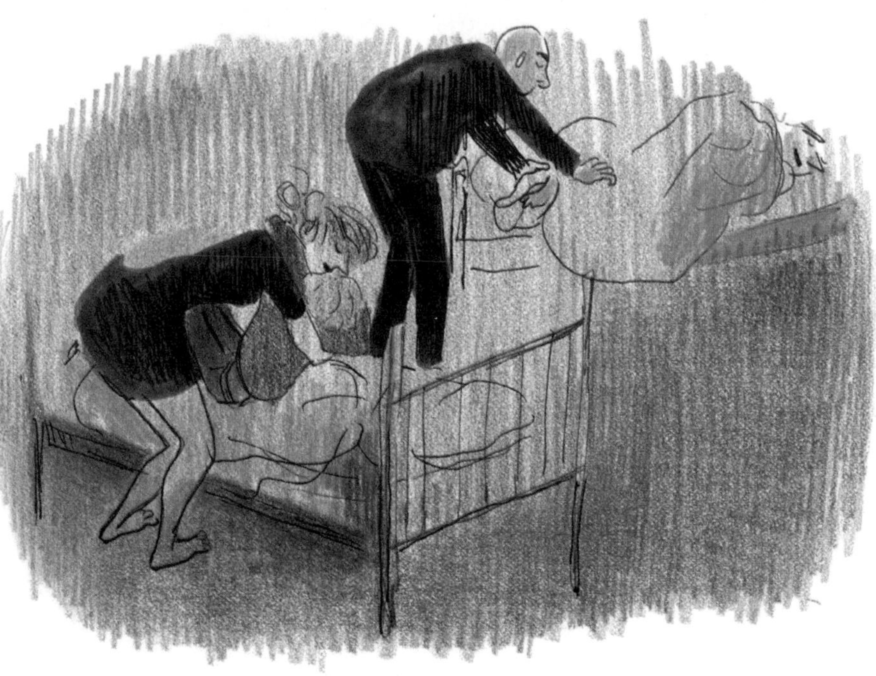

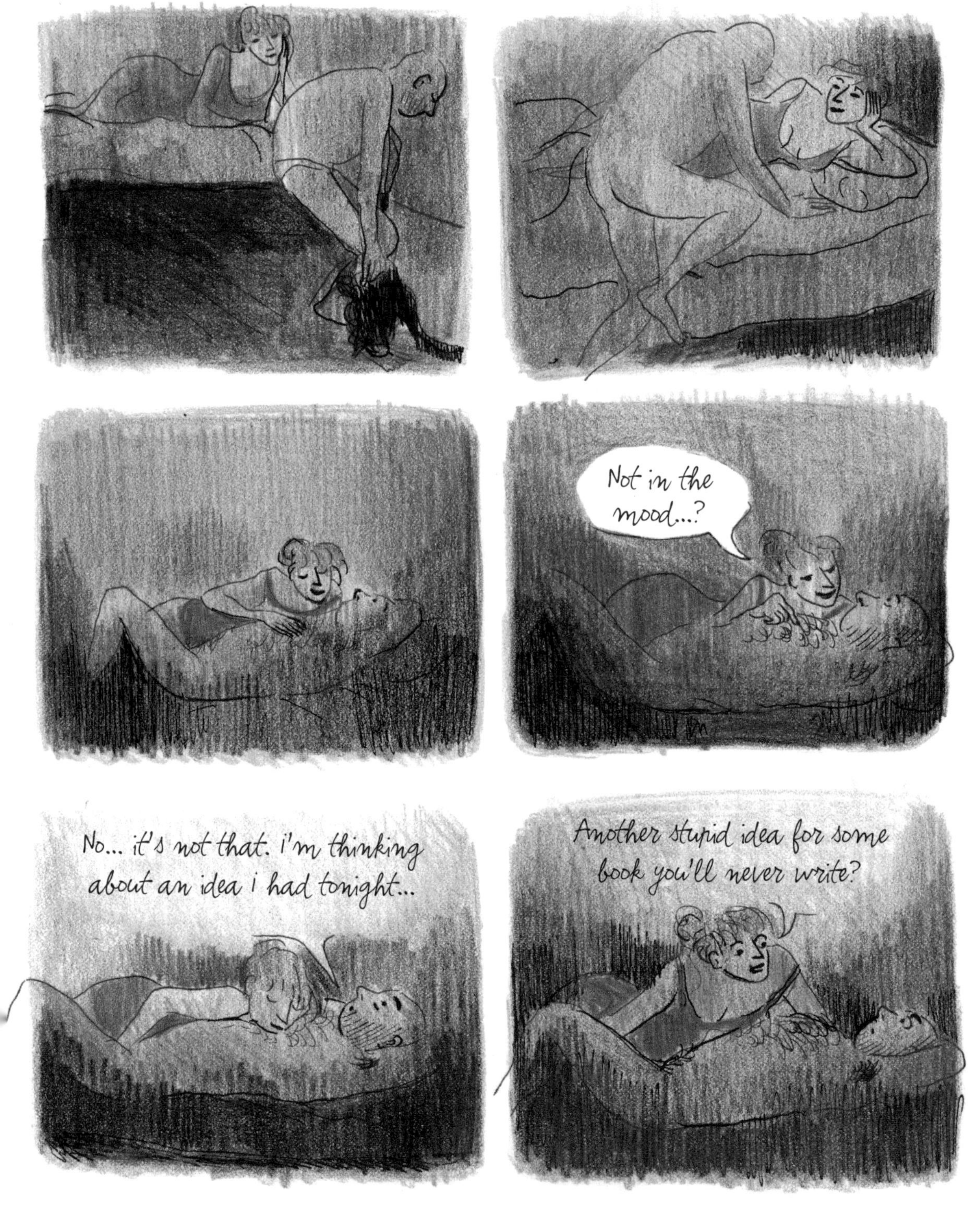
Not in the mood...?
No... it's not that. i'm thinking about an idea i had tonight...
Another stupid idea for some book you'll never write?

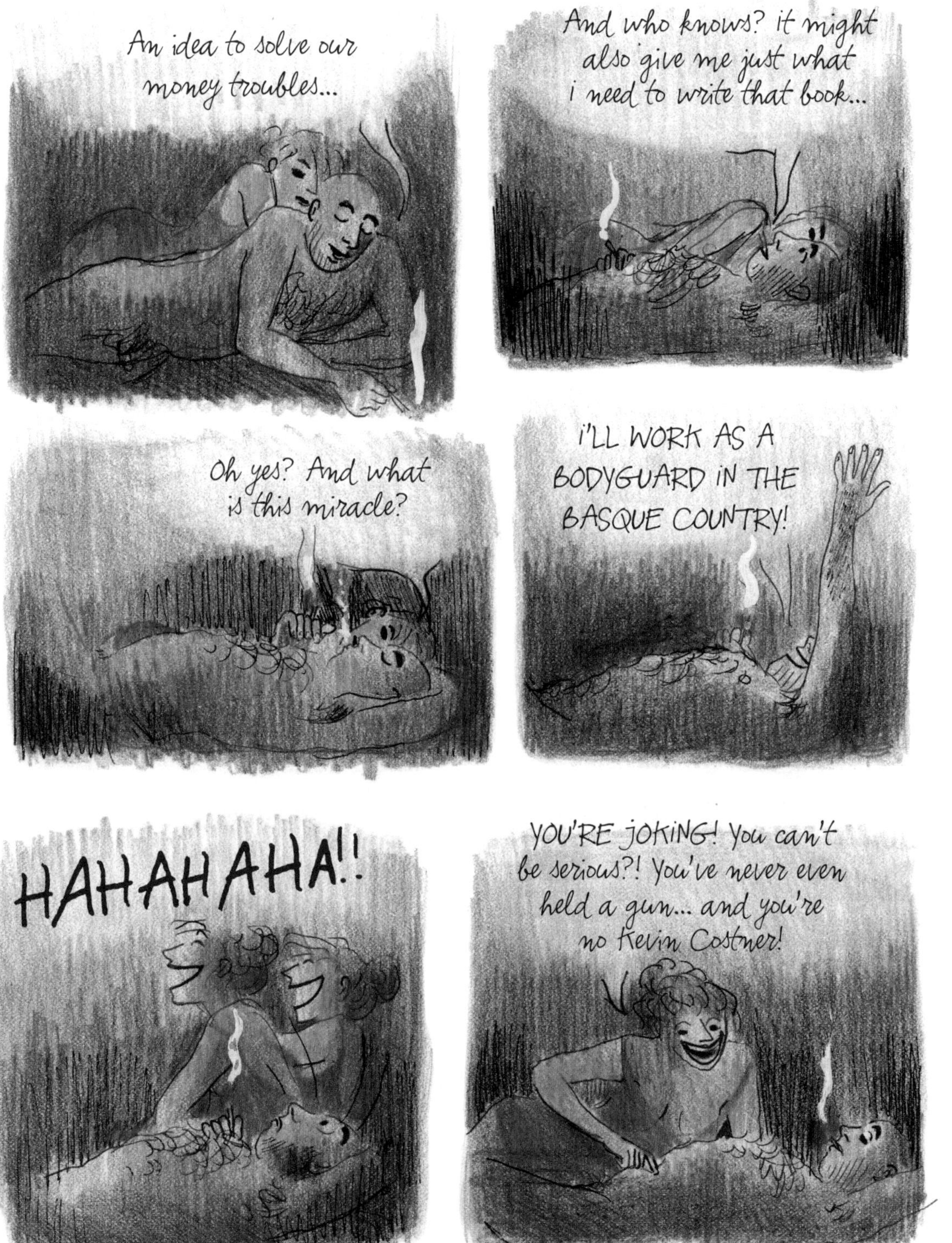
An idea to solve our money troubles...
And who knows? it might also give me just what i need to write that book...
Oh yes? And what is this miracle?
I'LL WORK AS A BODYGUARD IN THE BASQUE COUNTRY!
HAHAHAHA!!
YOU'RE JOKING! You can't be serious?! You've never even held a gun... and you're no Kevin Costner!

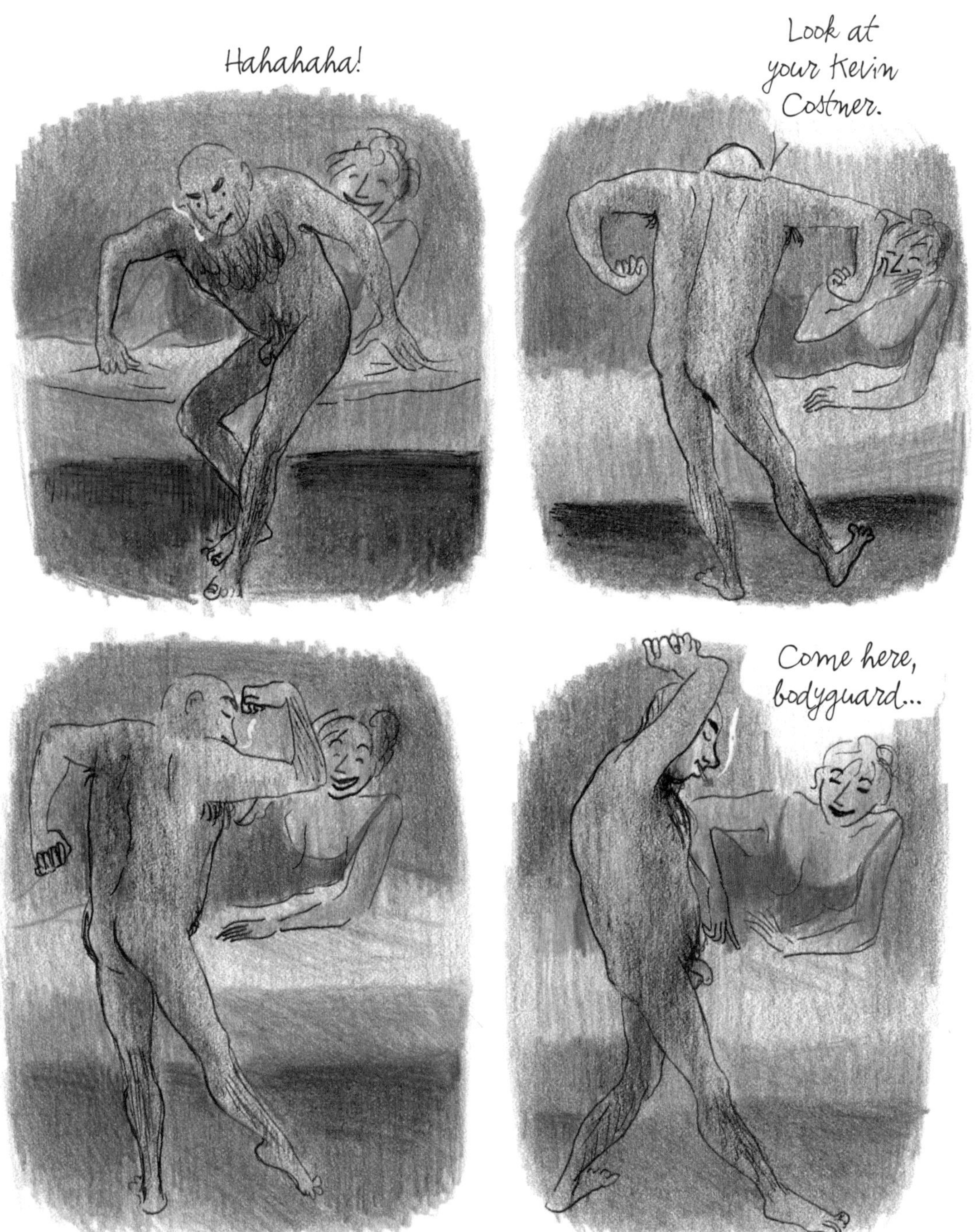
Hahahaha!
Look at your Kevin Costner.
Come here, bodyguard...

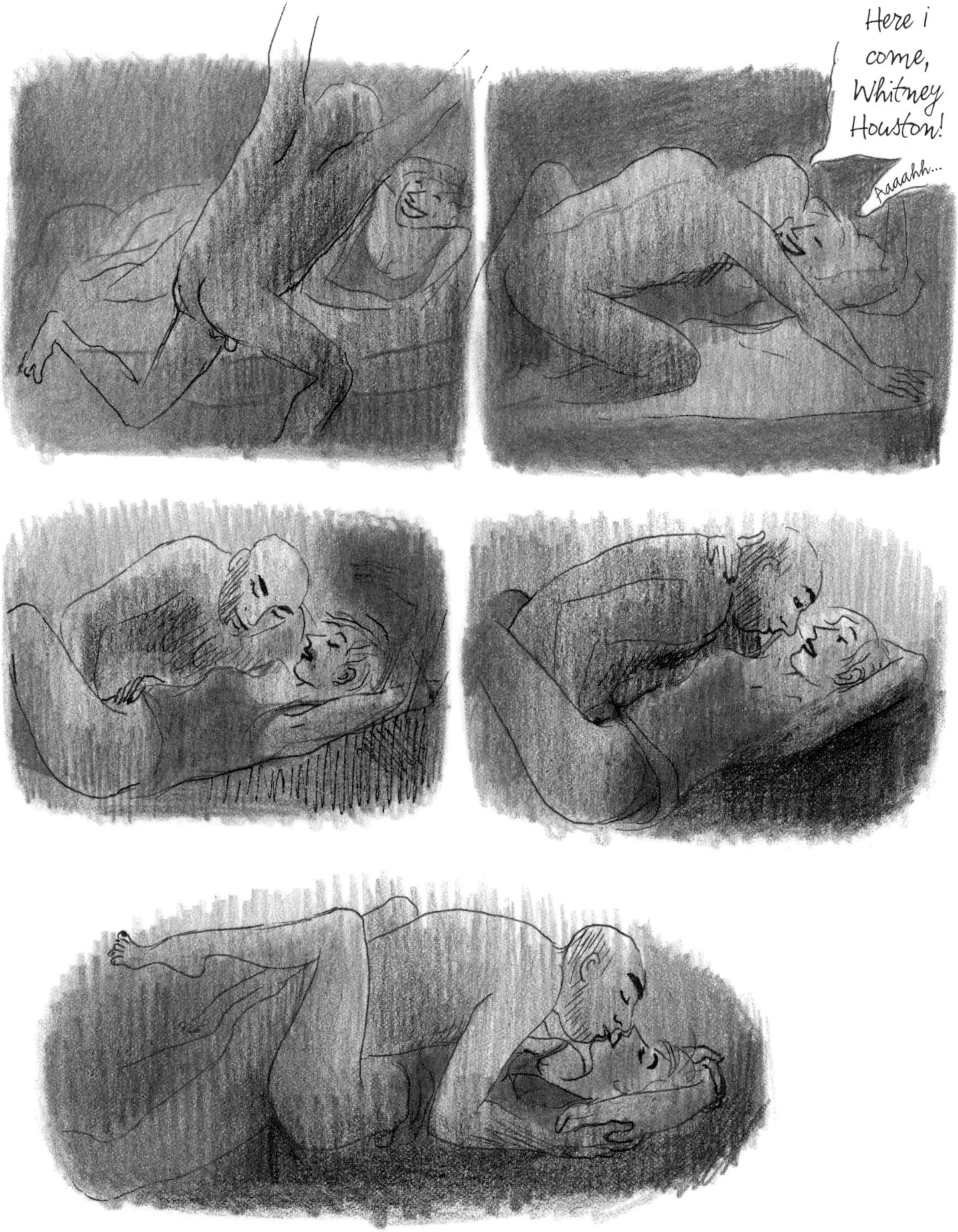
Here i come, Whitney Houston!
Aaaahh...

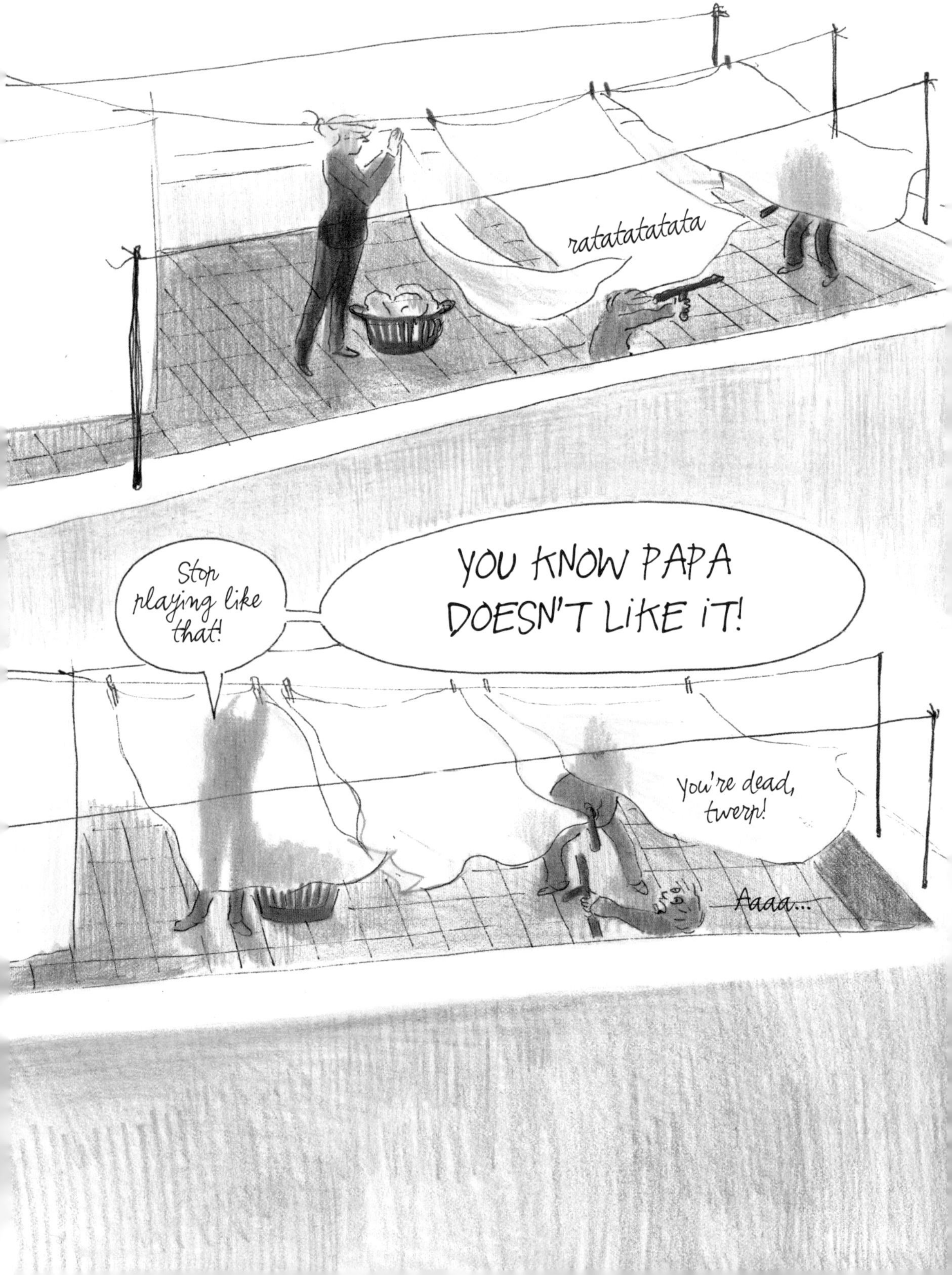
ratatatatatata
Stop playing like that!
YOU KNOW PAPA DOESN'T LIKE IT!
You're dead, twerp!
Aaaa...

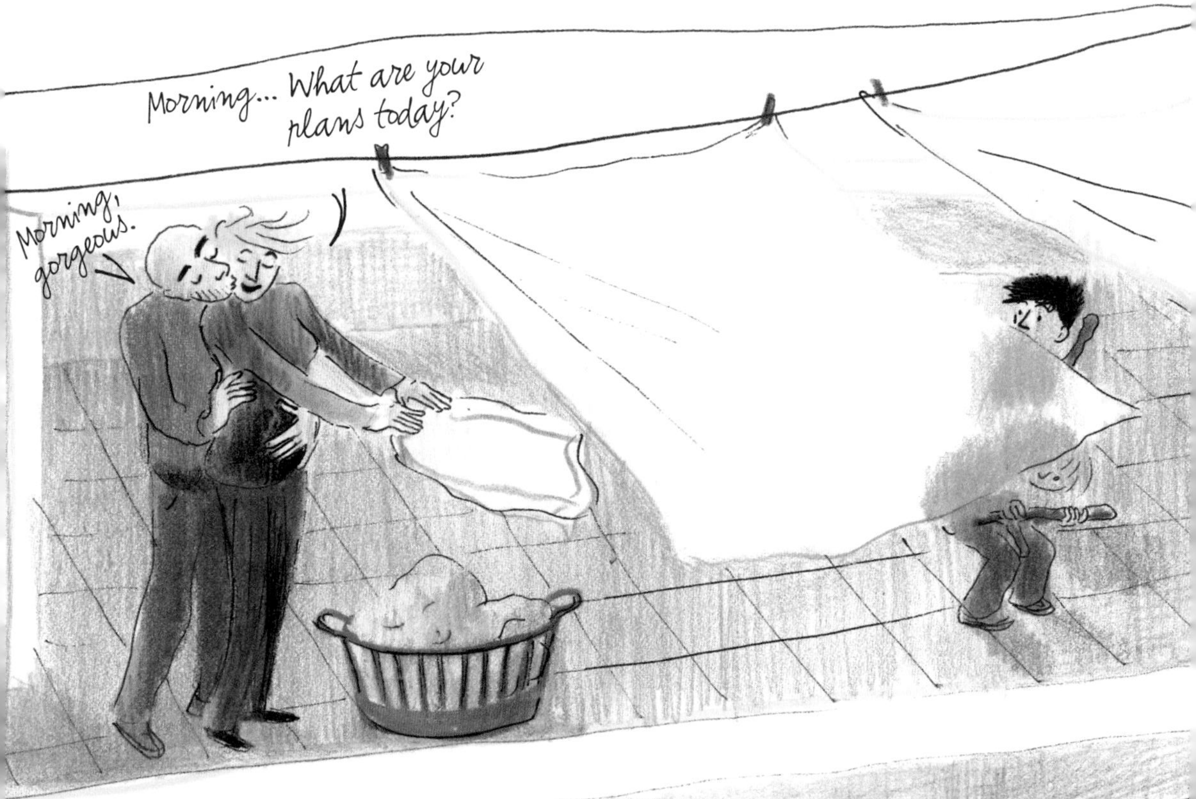
Morning, gorgeous.
Morning... What are your plans today?

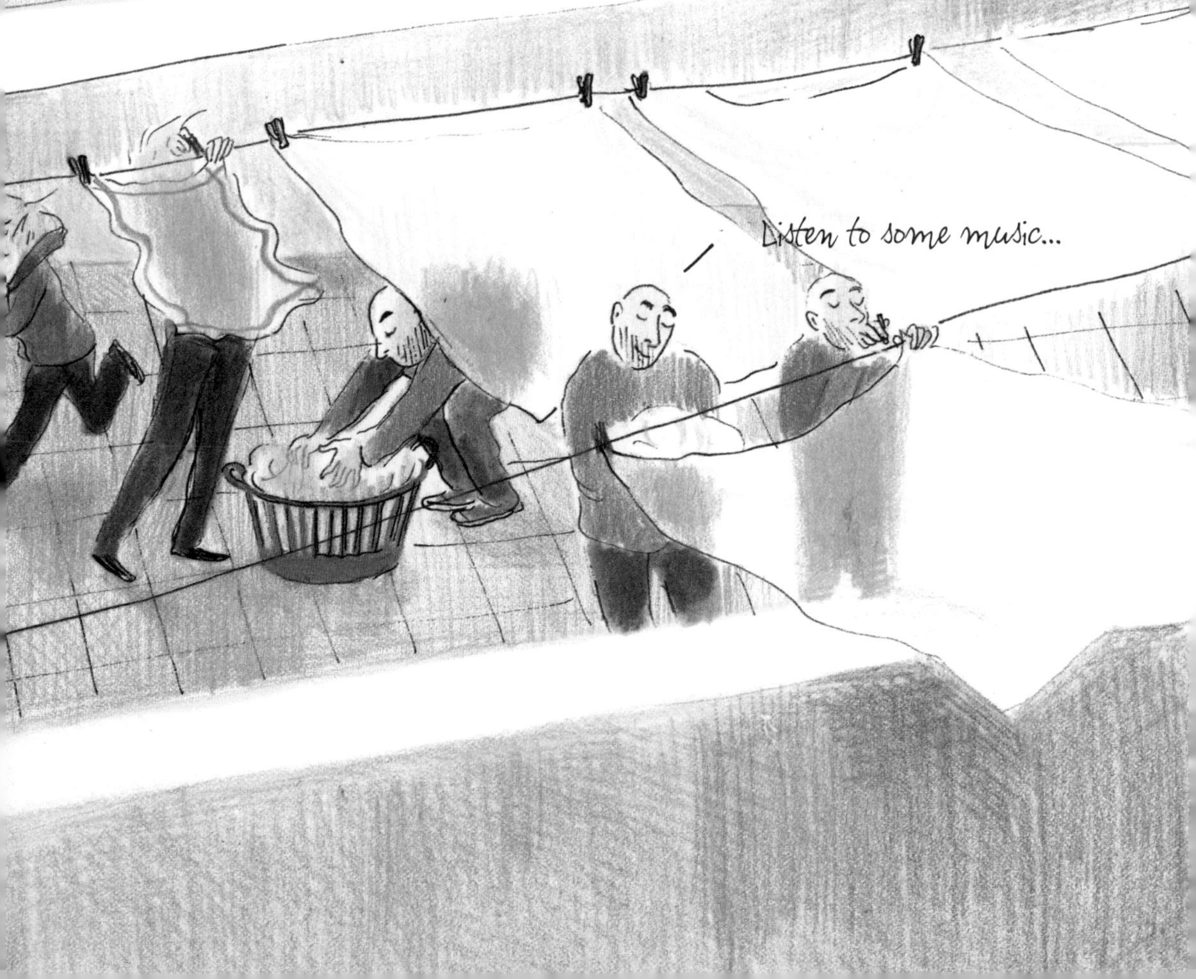
Listen to some music...

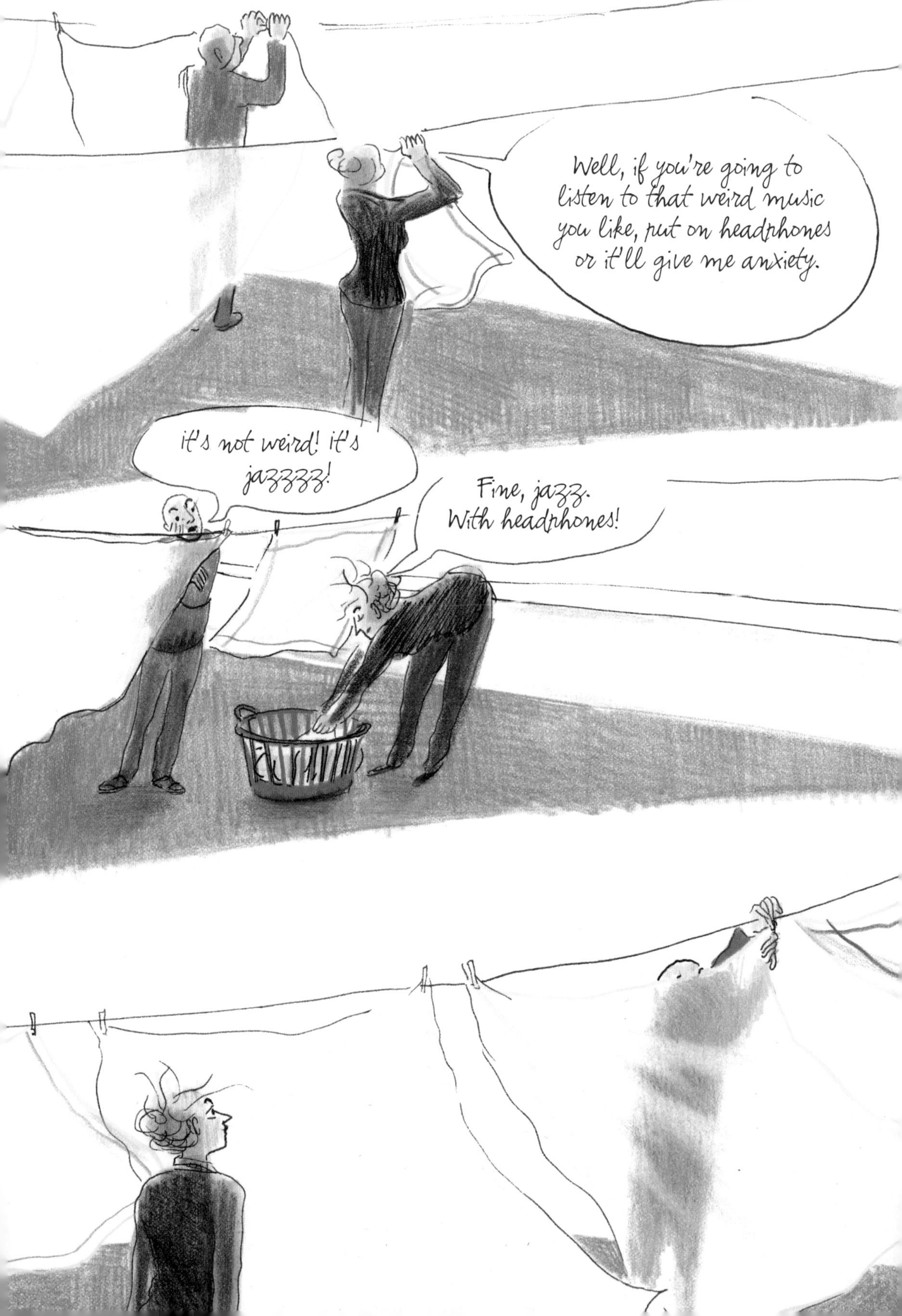
Well, if you're going to listen to that weird music you like, put on headphones or it'll give me anxiety.
it's not weird! it's jazzzzz!
Fine, jazz. With headphones!

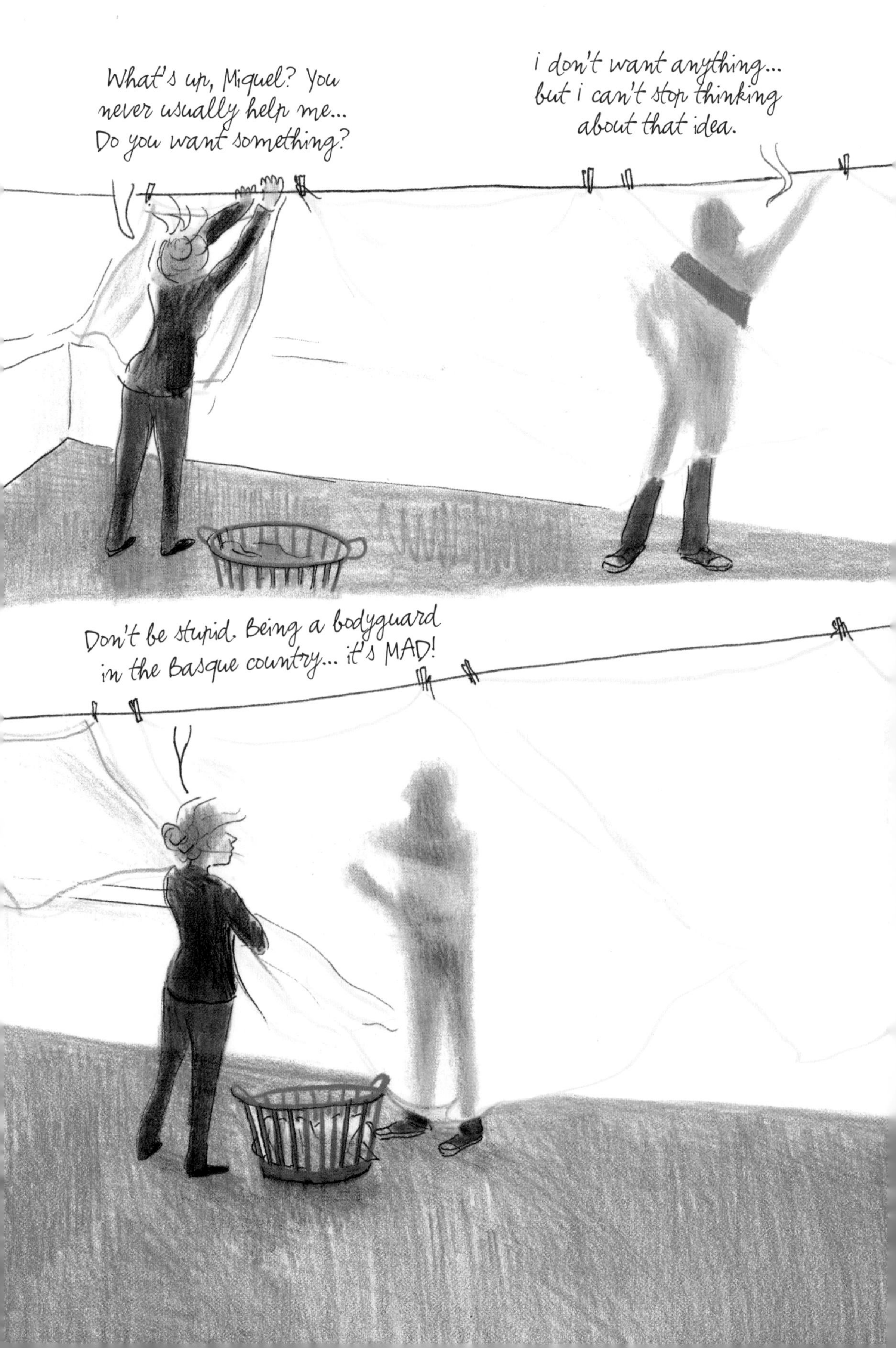
What's up, Miquel? You never usually help me... Do you want something?
i don't want anything... but i can't stop thinking about that idea.
Don't be stupid. Being a bodyguard in the Basque country... it's MAD!

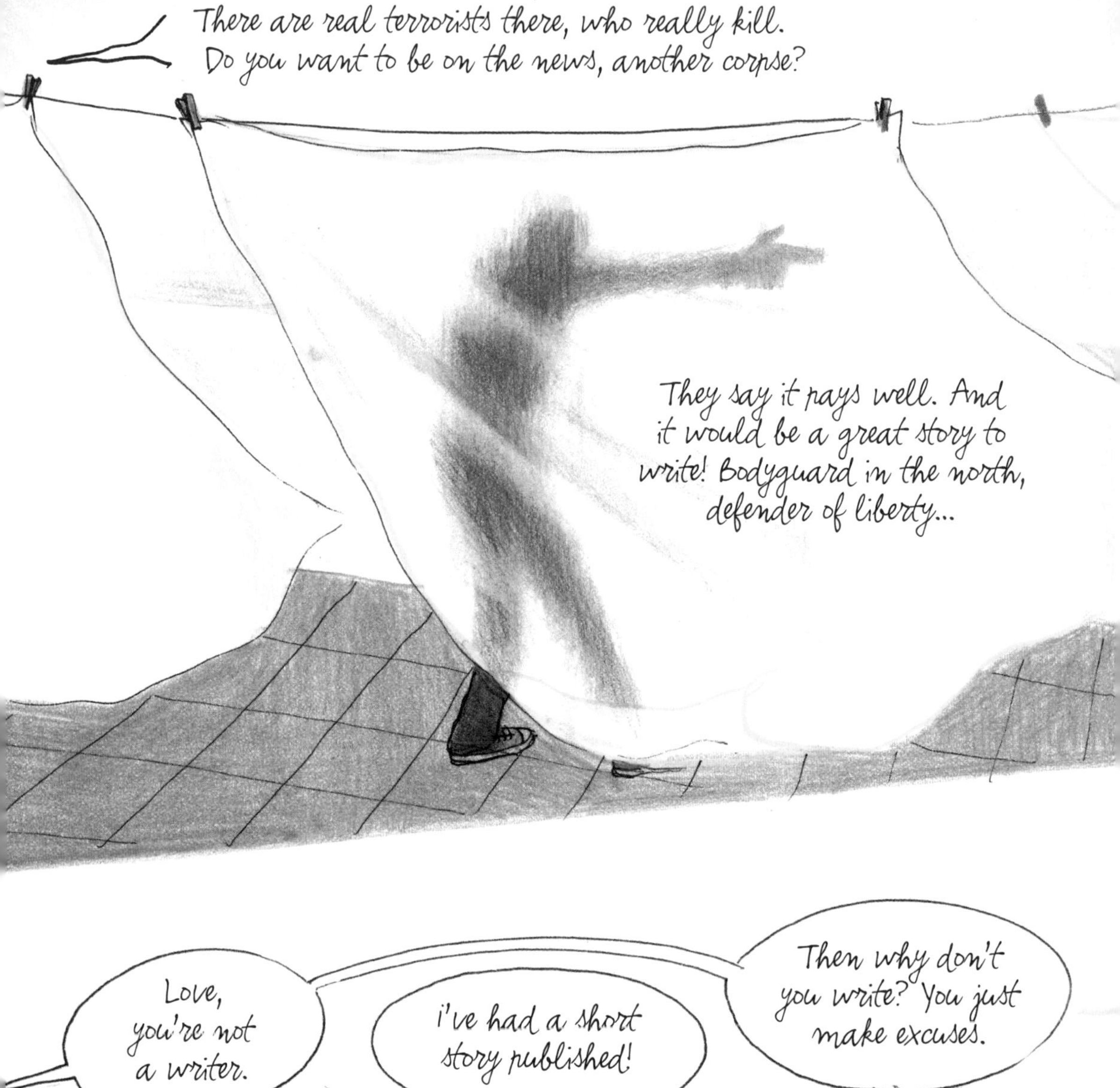
There are real terrorists there, who really kill. Do you want to be on the news, another corpse?
They say it pays well. And it would be a great story to write! Bodyguard in the north, defender of liberty...

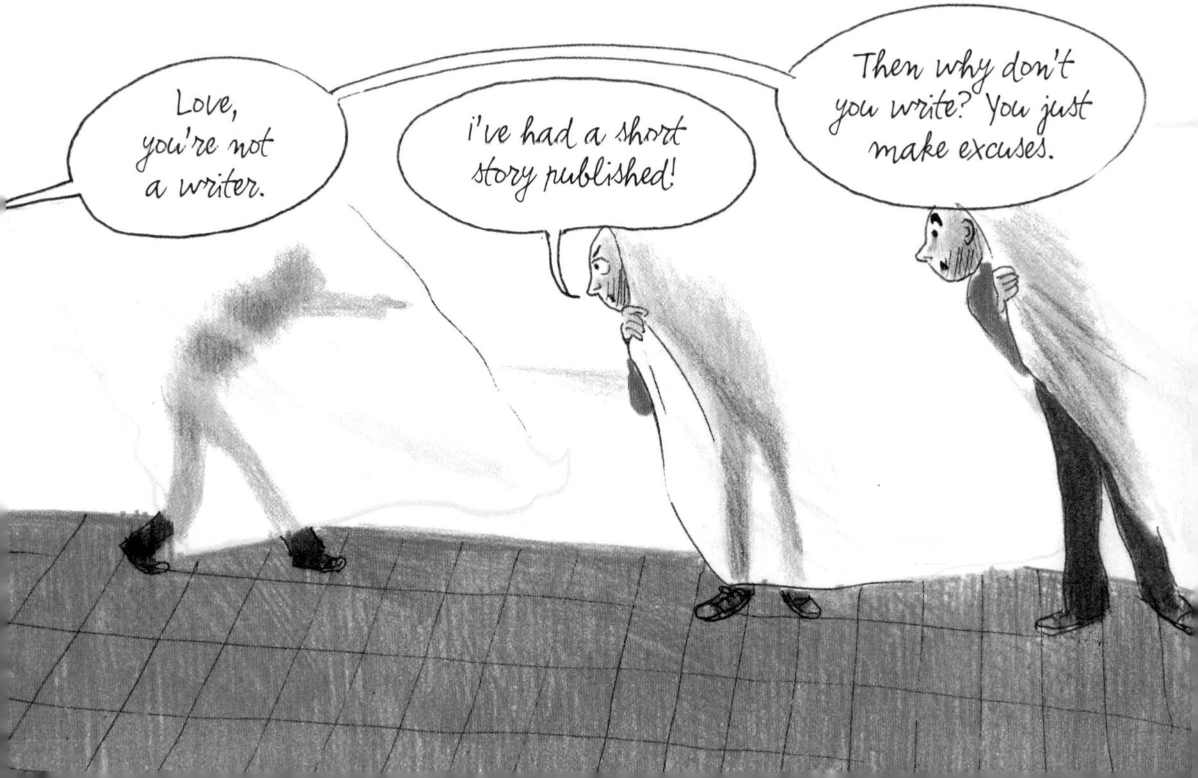
Love, you're not a writer.
i've had a short story published!
Then why don't you write? You just make excuses.

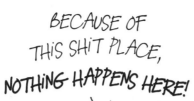

BECAUSE OF
THIS SHIT PLACE,
**NOTHING HAPPENS HERE!**

But... GUNS! TERRORISTS! CHASES! IT WOULD BE GREAT!

Don't be an idiot. Focus on selling sweets, and leave guns for the men.

i think you don't write because you're scared shitless. You're afraid your writing will be worthless, and you'll realise you're not what you thought you were... Take the bull by the horns, AND JUST WRITE!

Ana was right. if i wanted to write, i had to take the bull by the horns. i had to face my fears, look them straight in the eyes. Get away from the daily routine that had protected our lives. i had to jump. jump straight into the unknown in search of a good story to write...

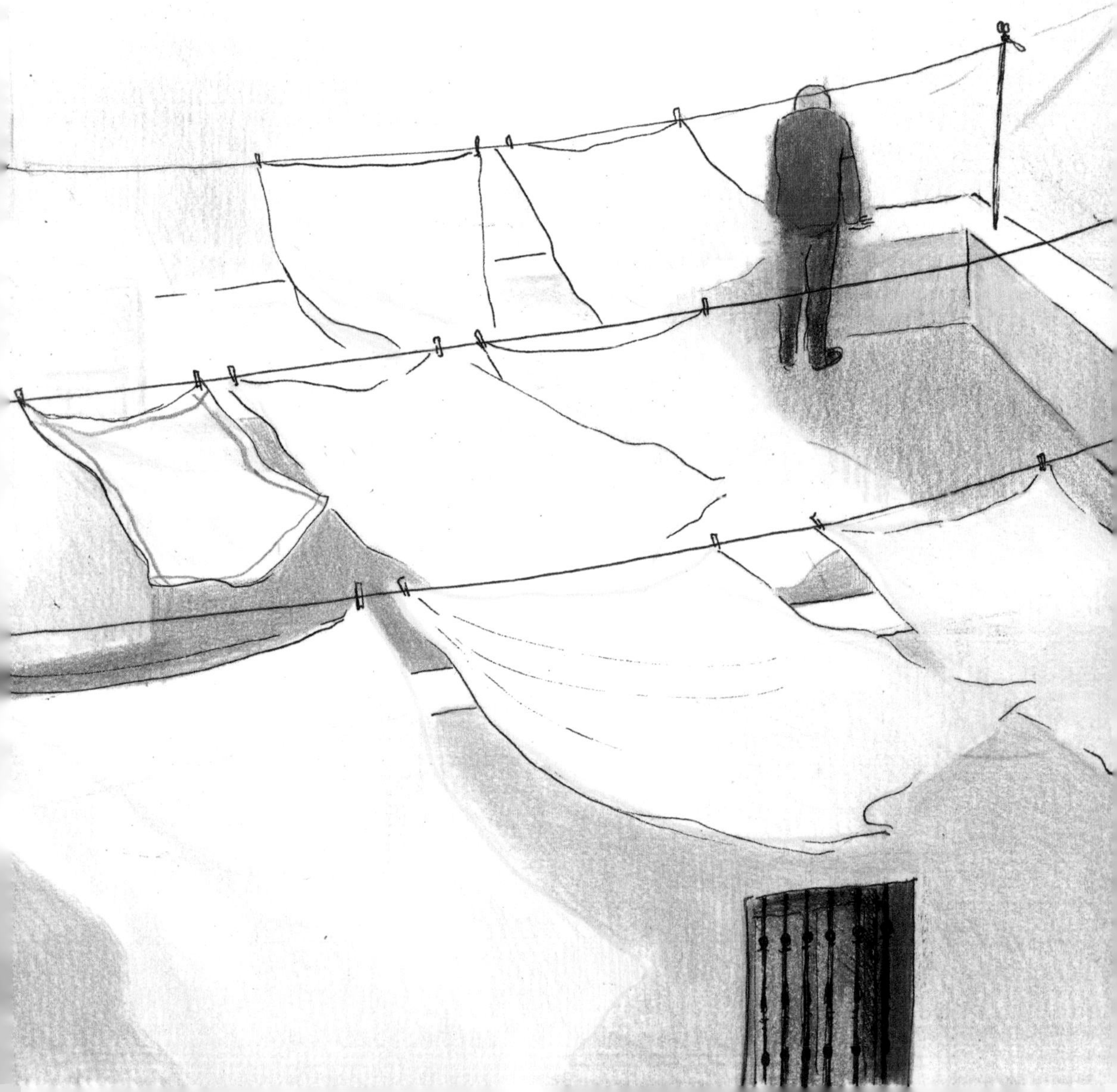

And so i did.

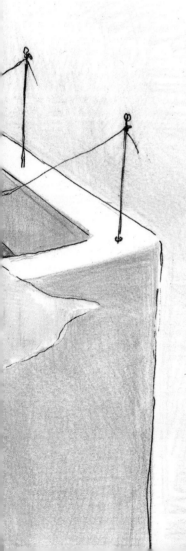

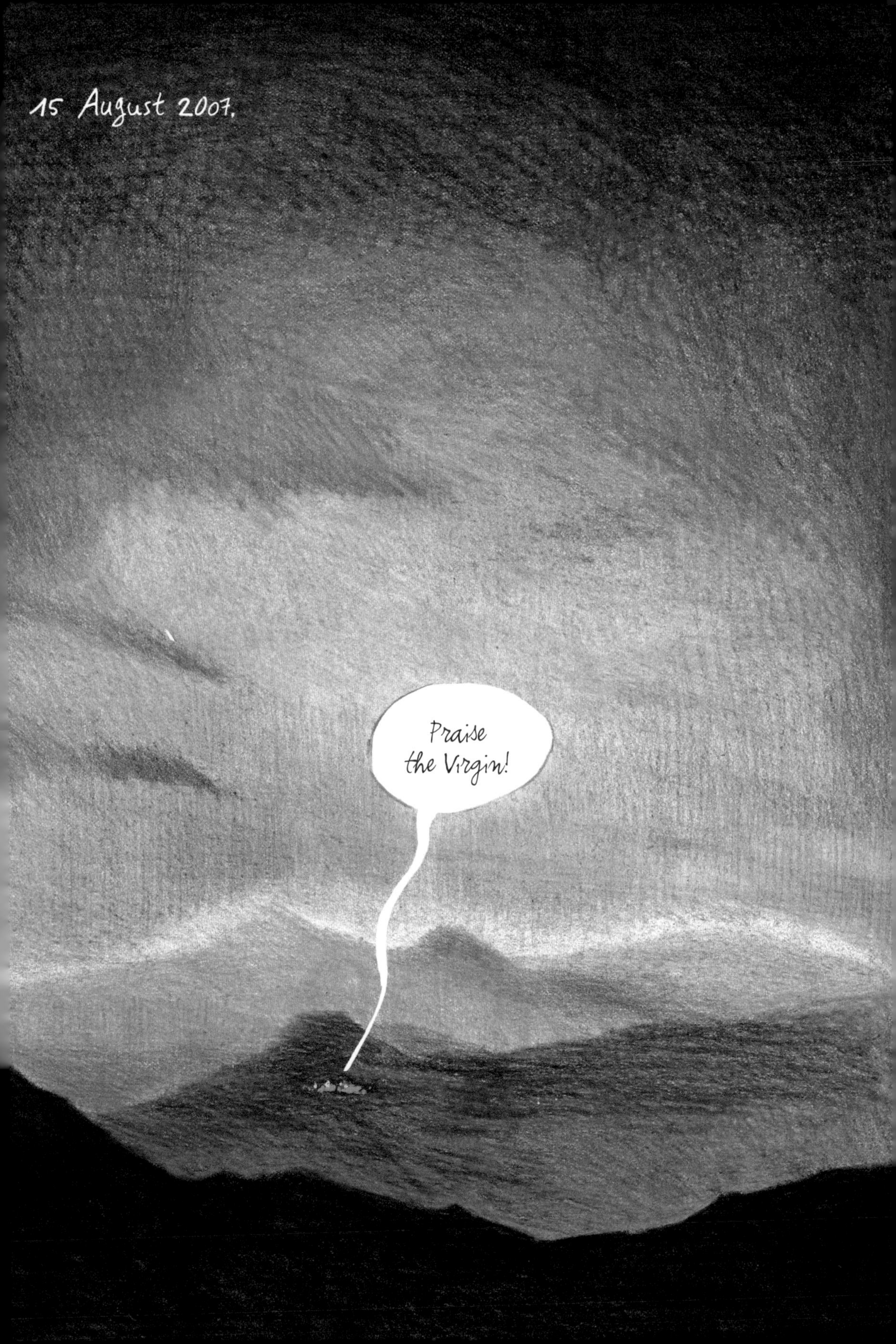
15 August 2007.
Praise the Virgin!

it's your day, Miquel!
This'll be the year!
Look at his eyes!
The beast can smell your fear!

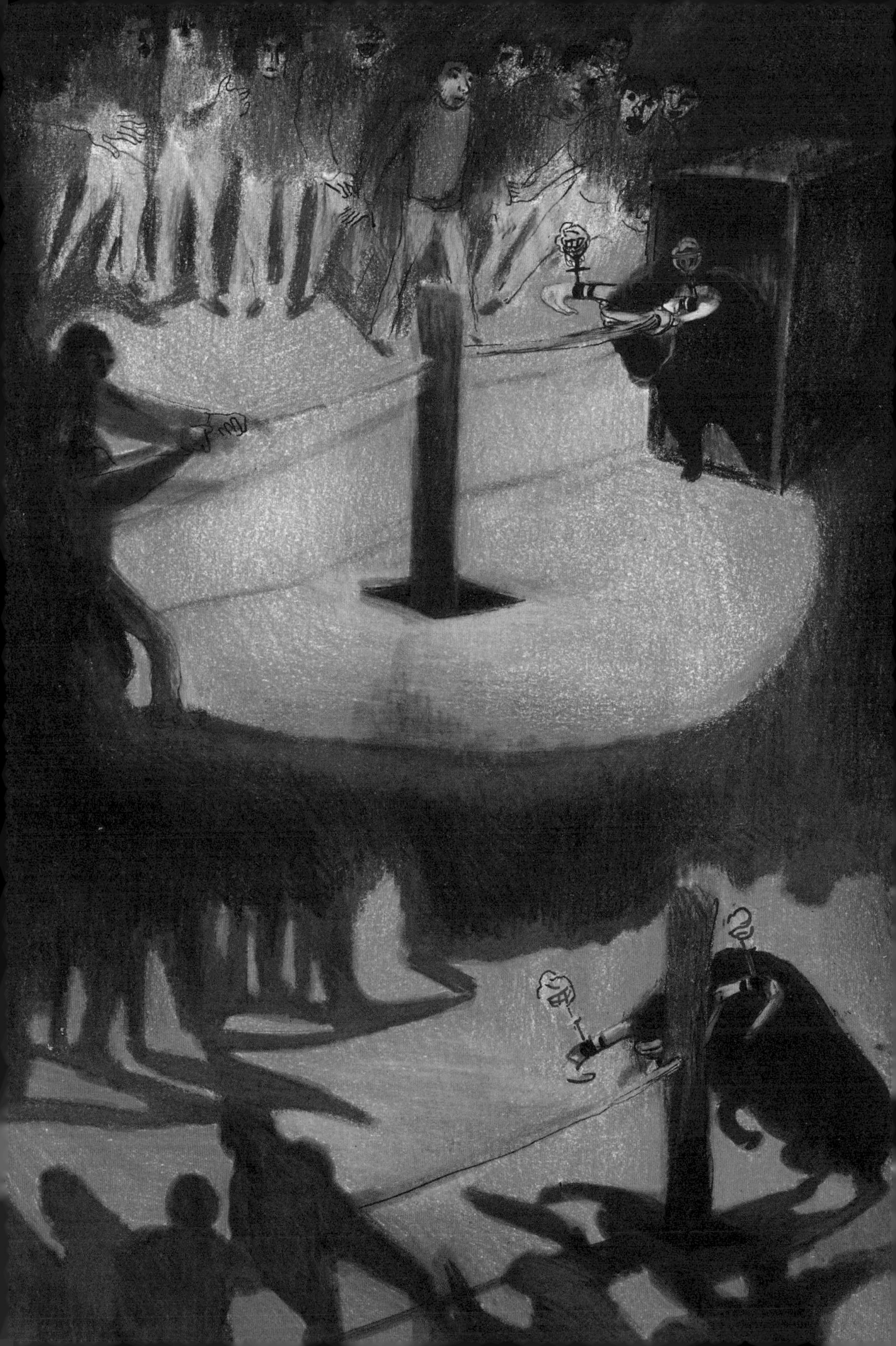

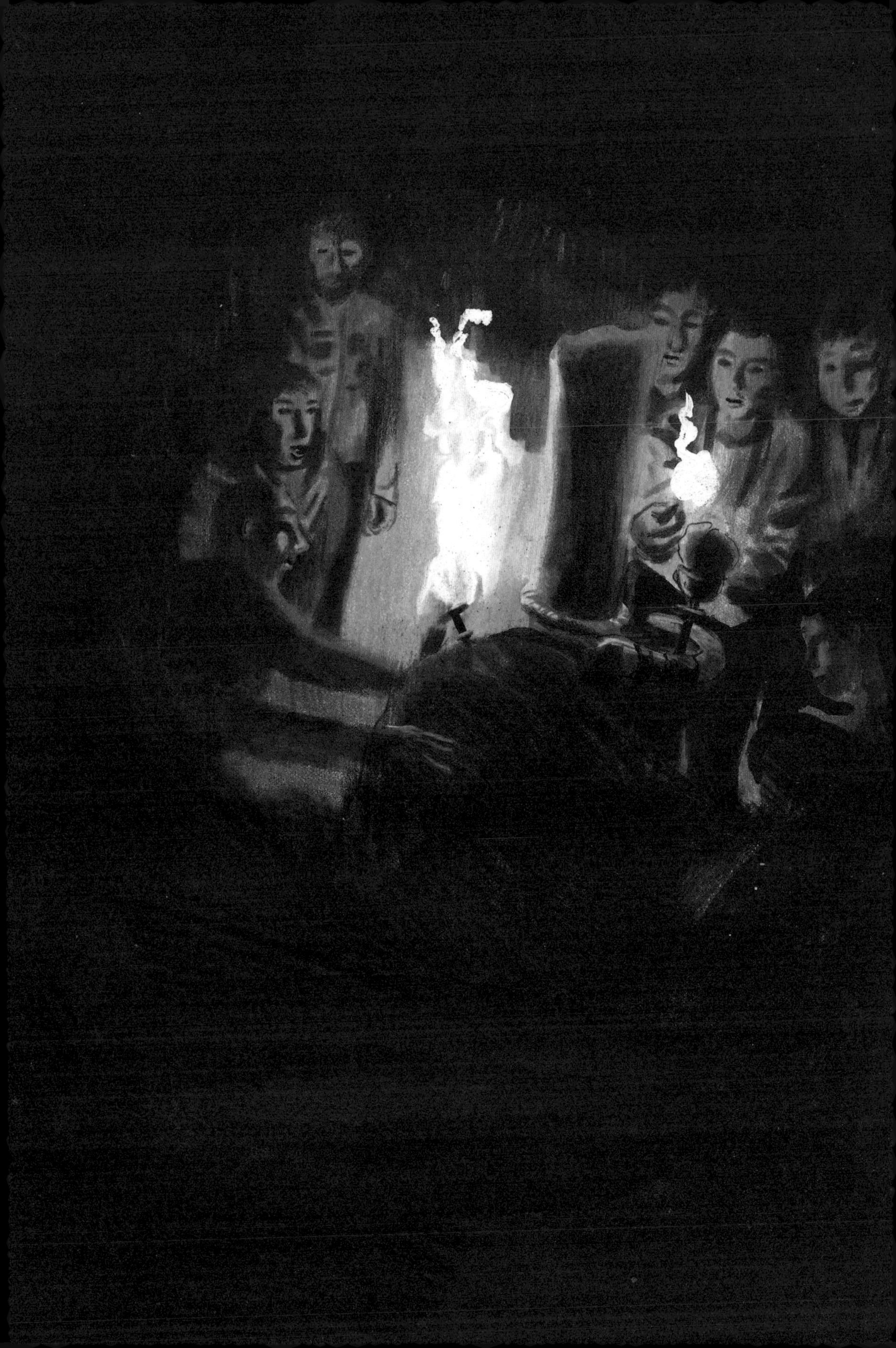

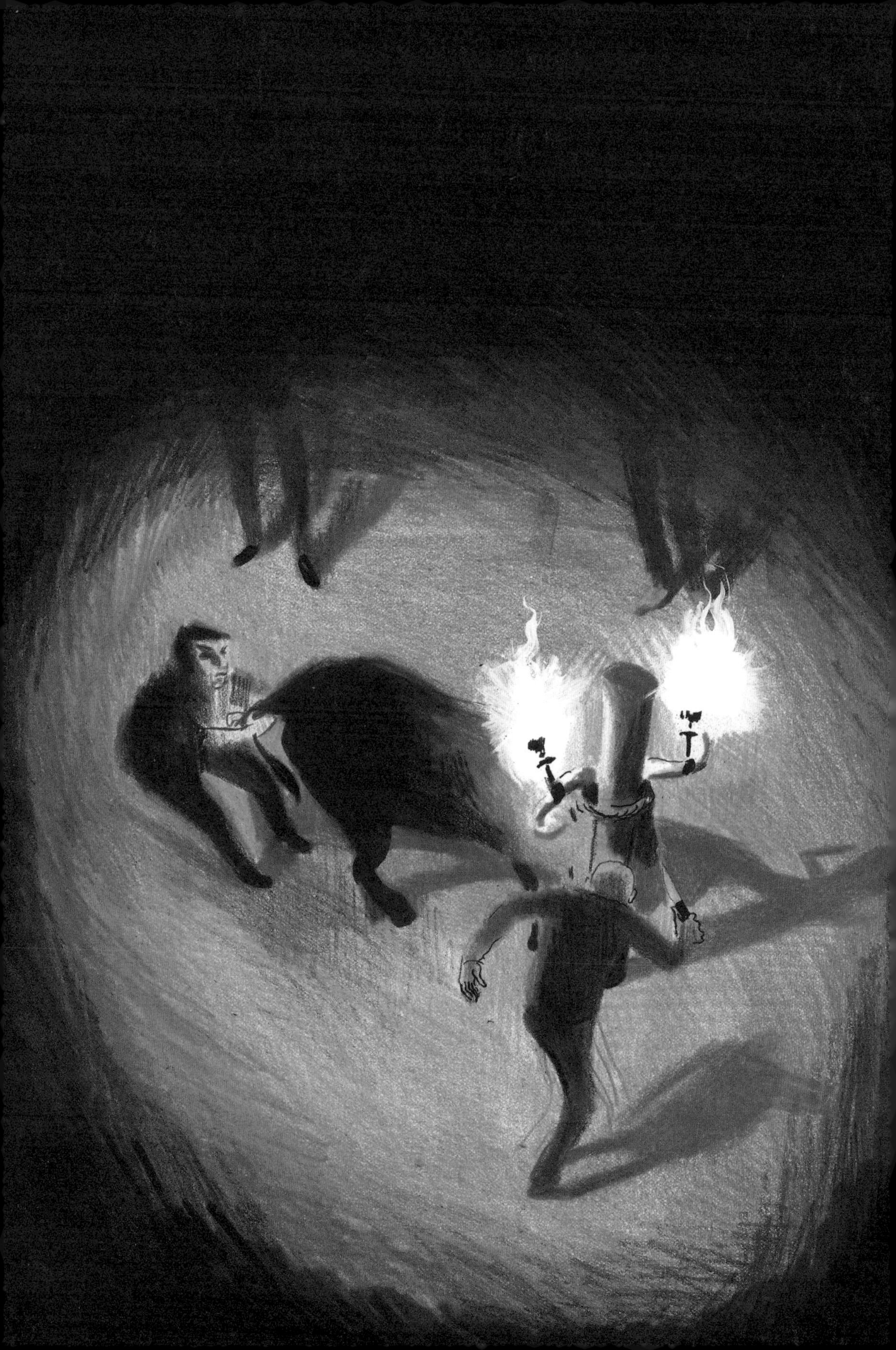

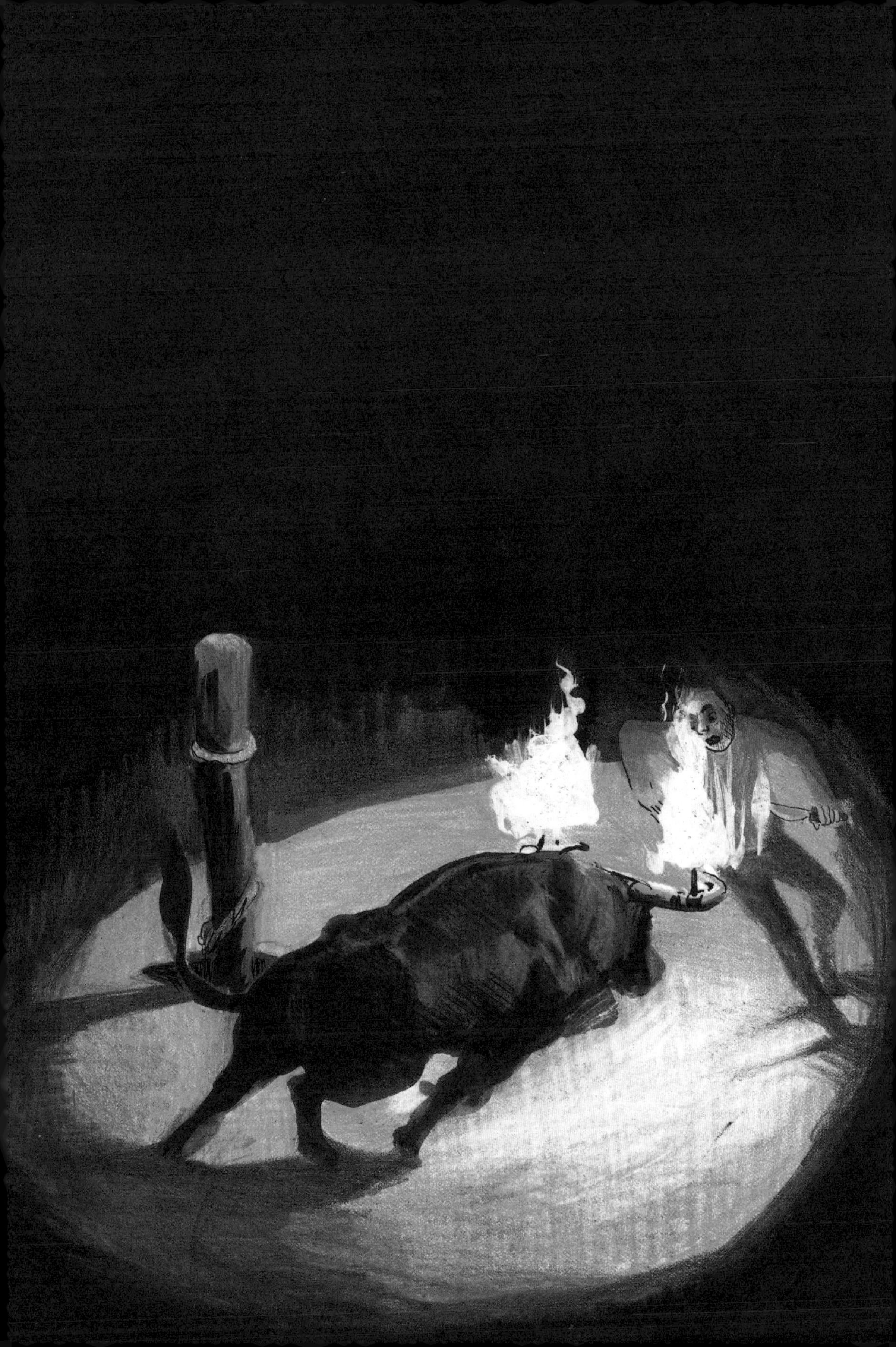

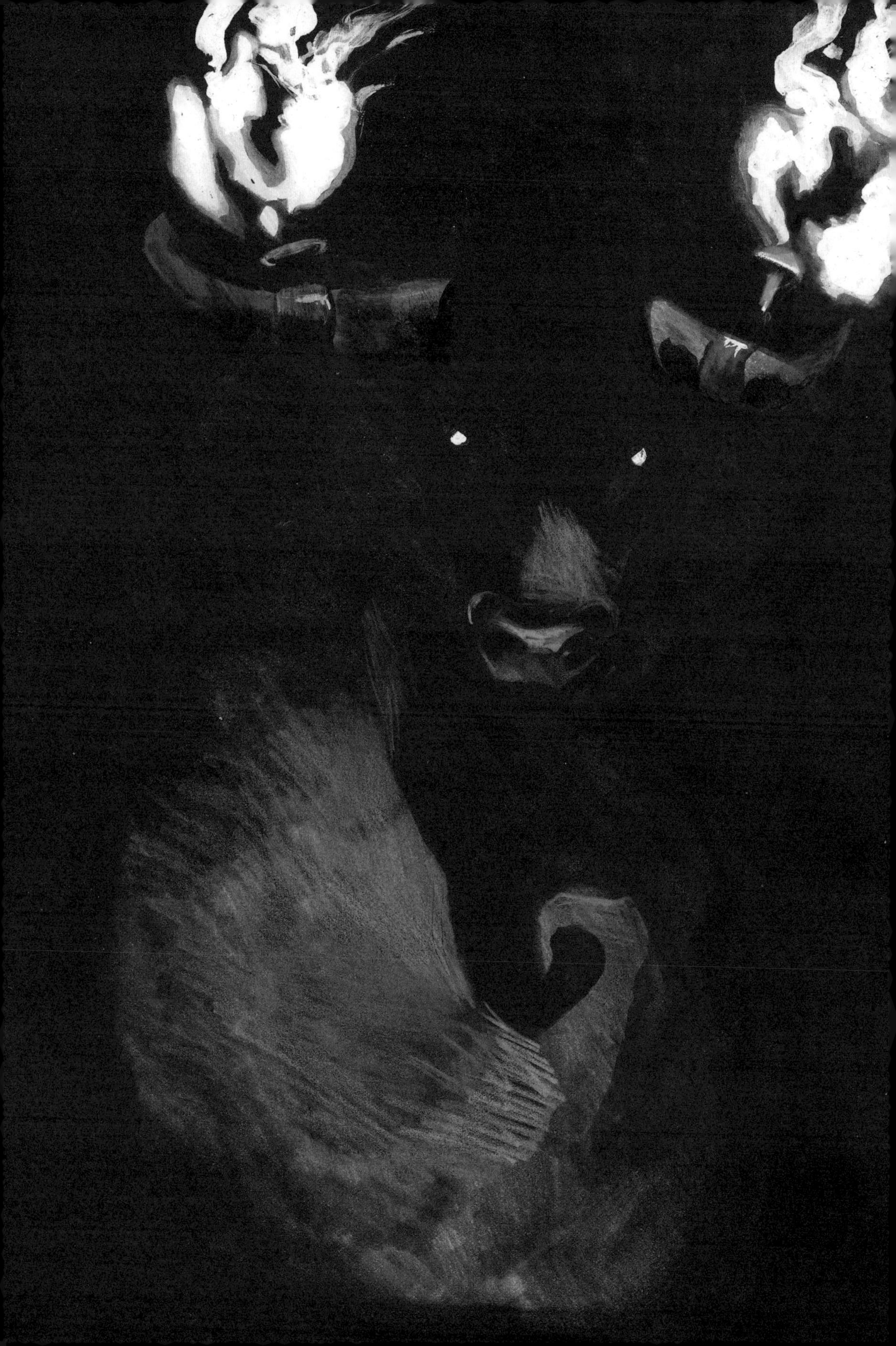

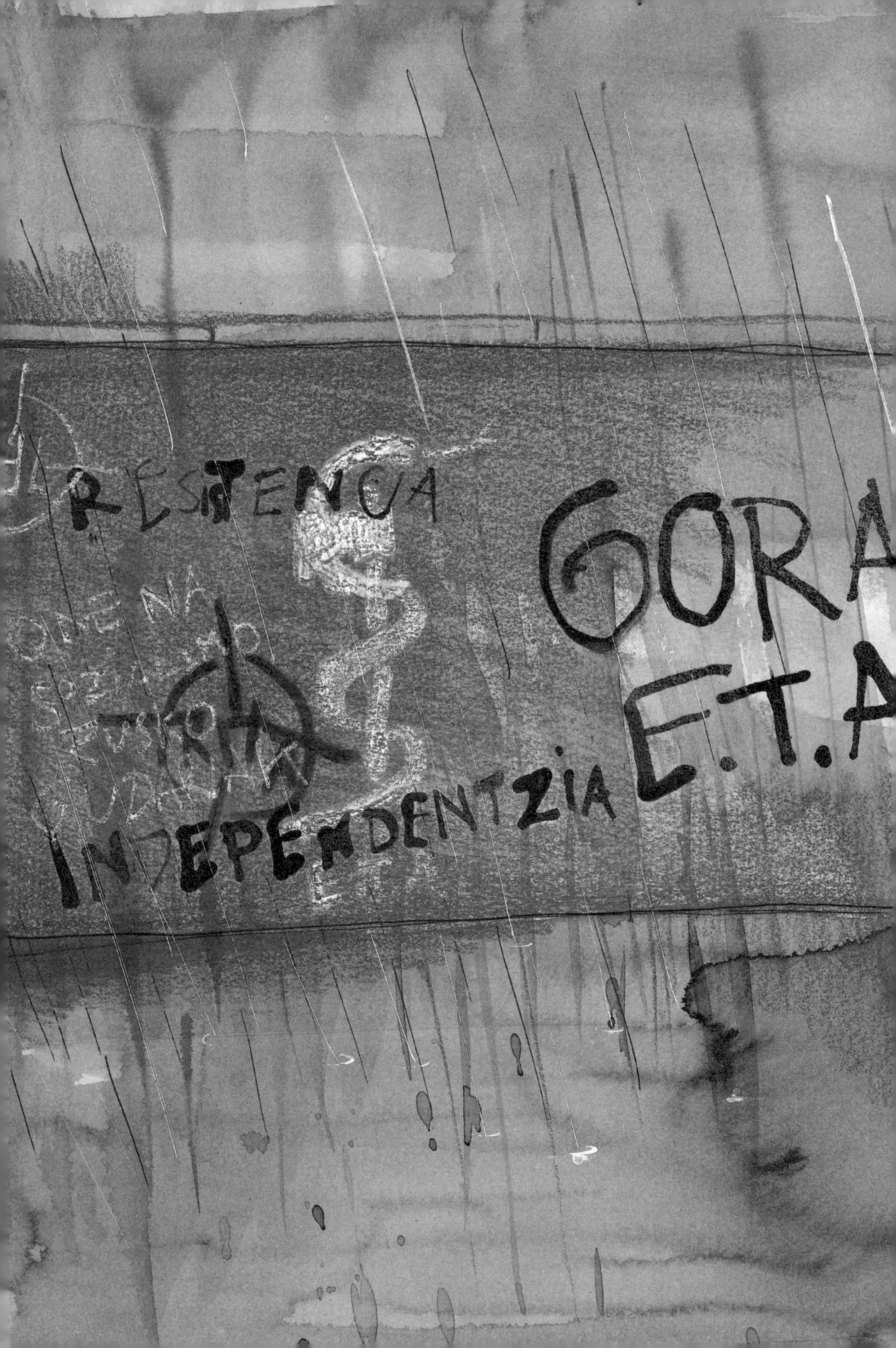
RESISTENCIA
INDEPENDENTZIA
GORA
E.T.A

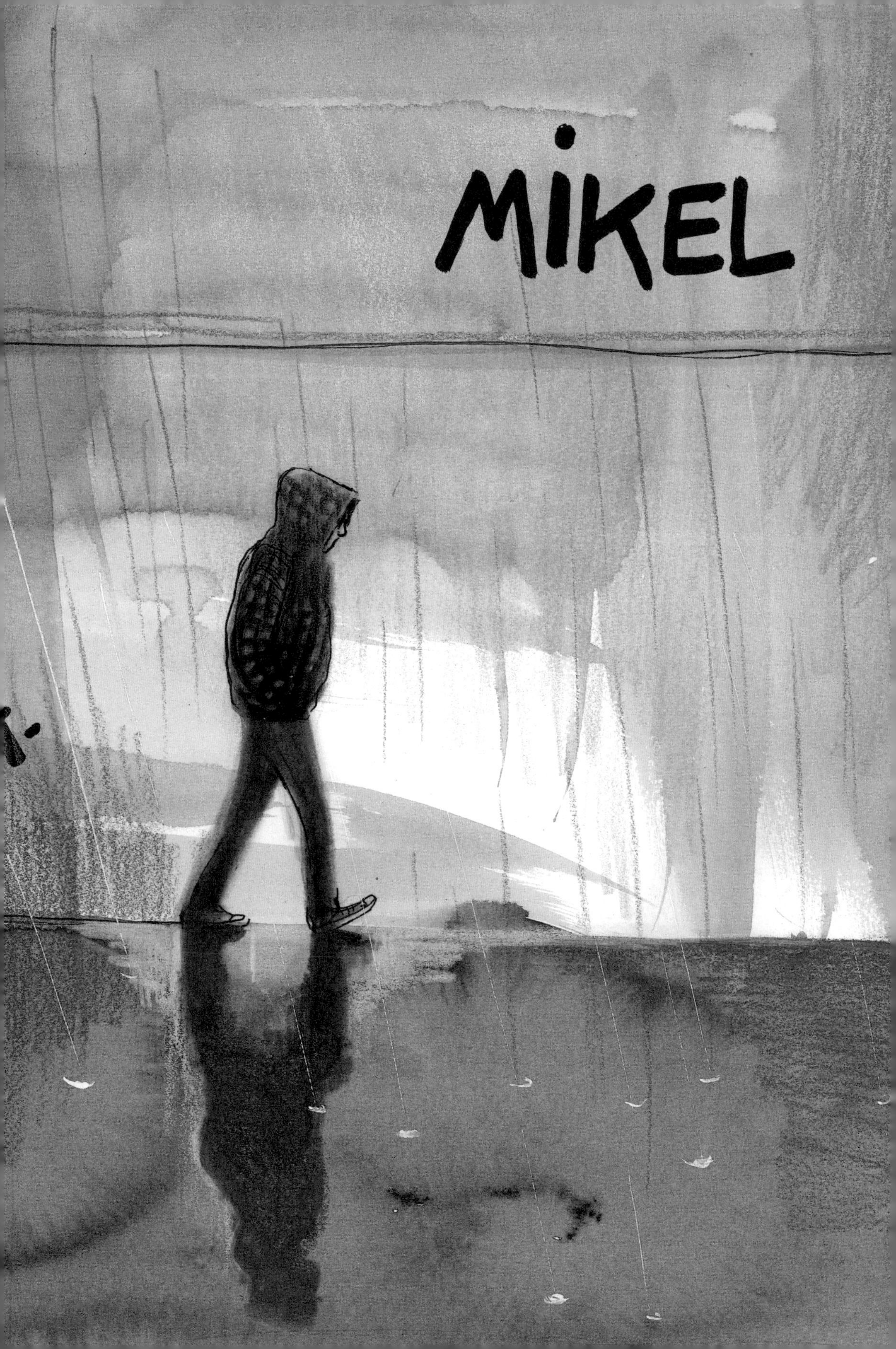
MIKEL

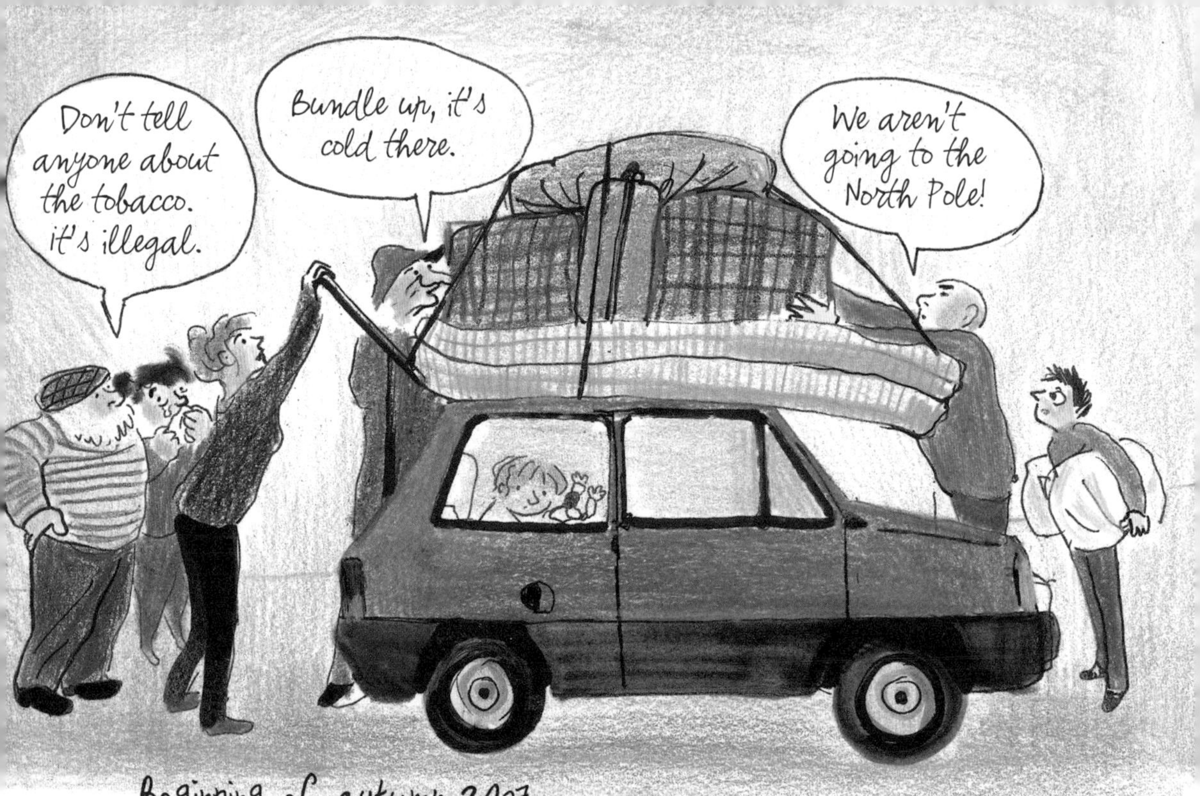
Don't tell anyone about the tobacco. it's illegal.
Bundle up, it's cold there.
We aren't going to the North Pole!

Beginning of autumn 2007.

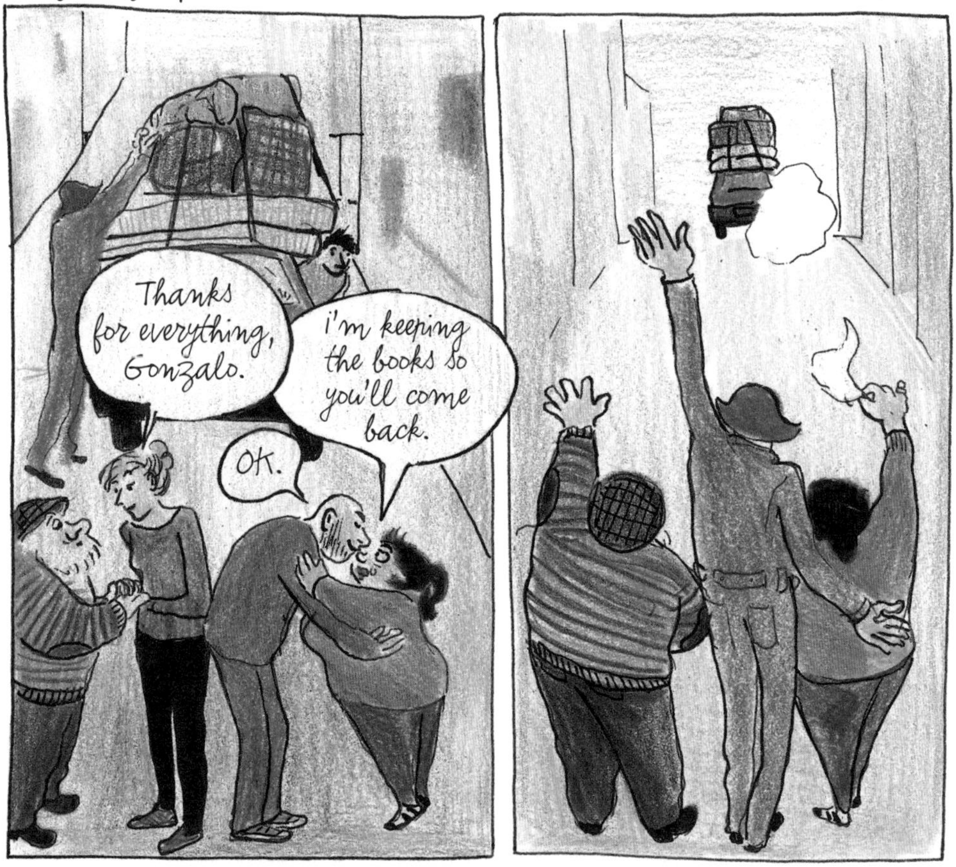
Thanks for everything, Gonzalo.
i'm keeping the books so you'll come back.
OK.

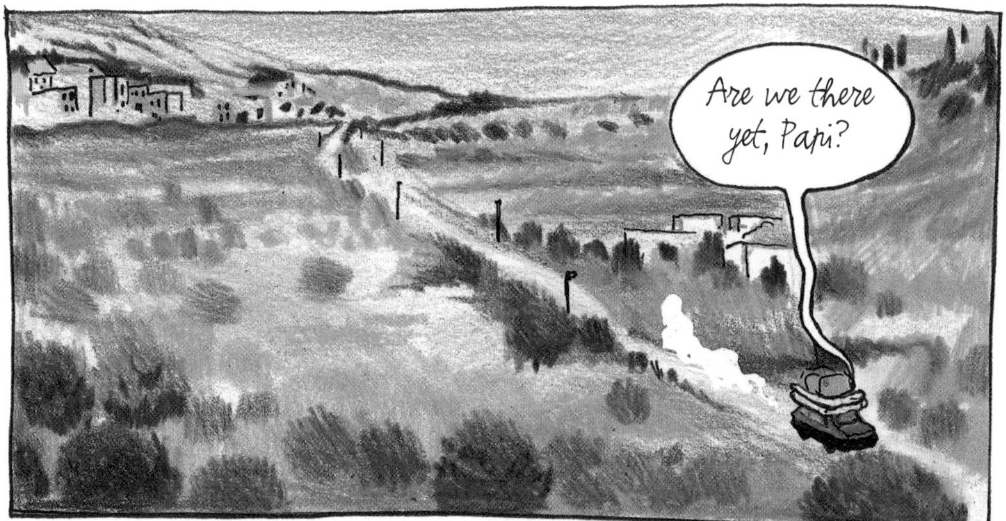
Are we there yet, Papi?

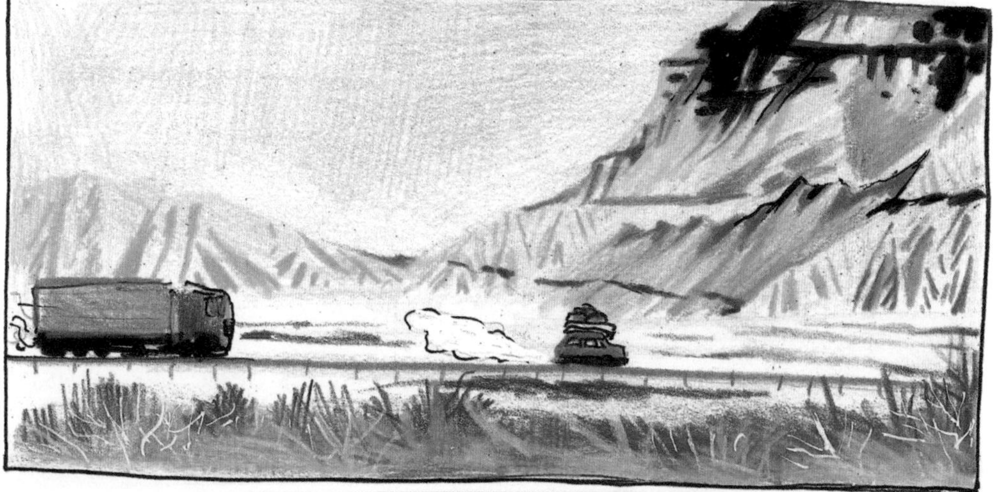

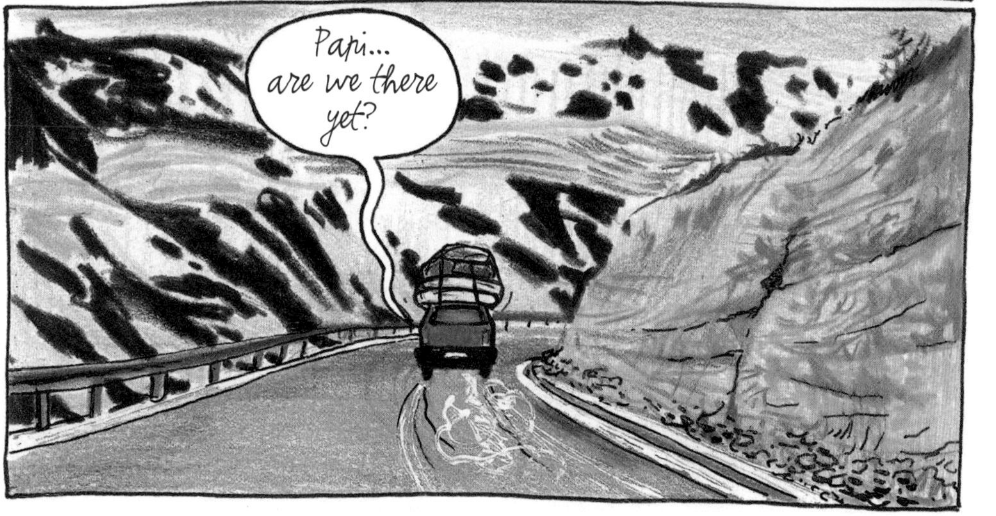
Papi... are we there yet?

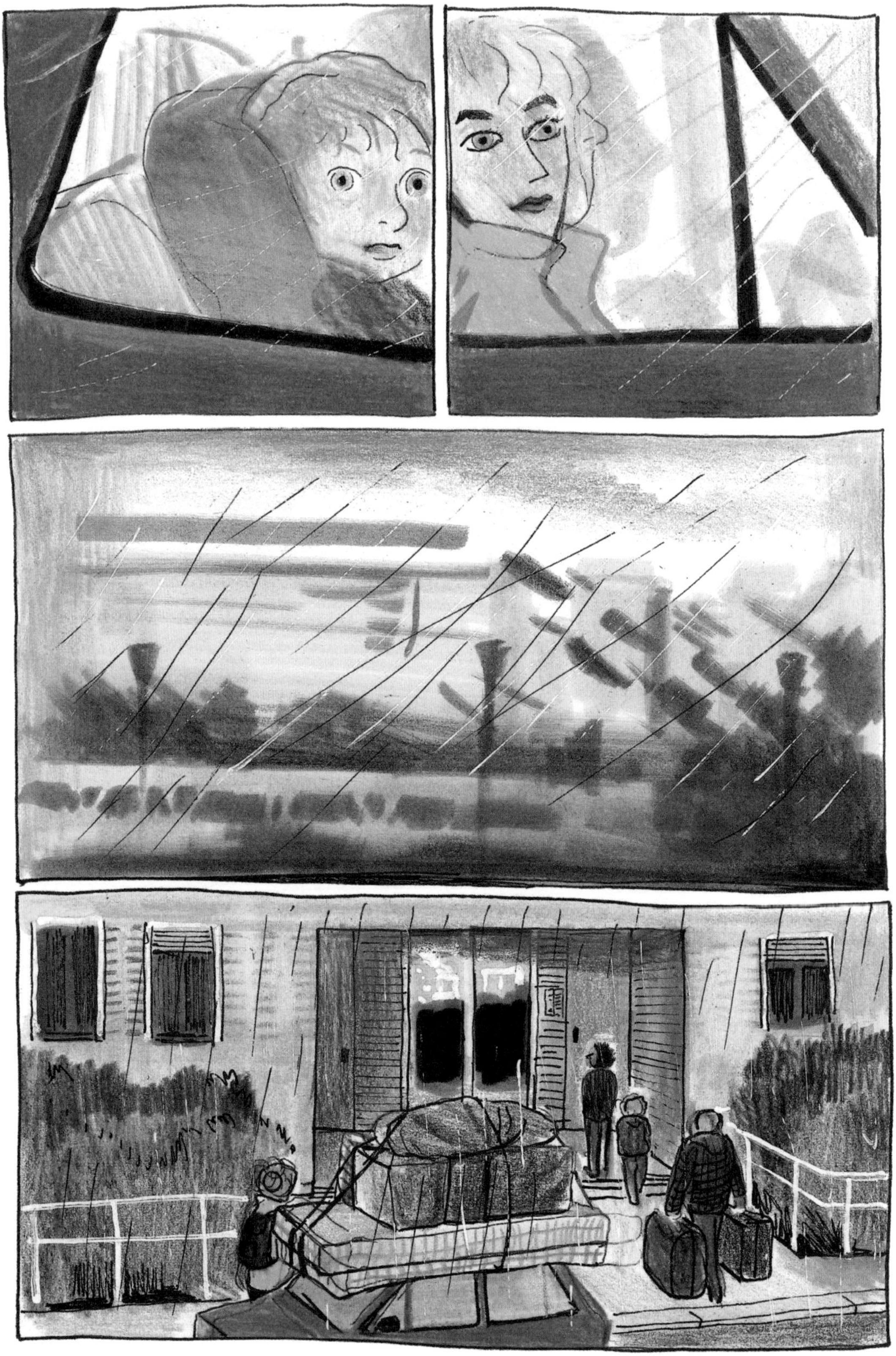

Pamplona. 17 September 2007. A new home.

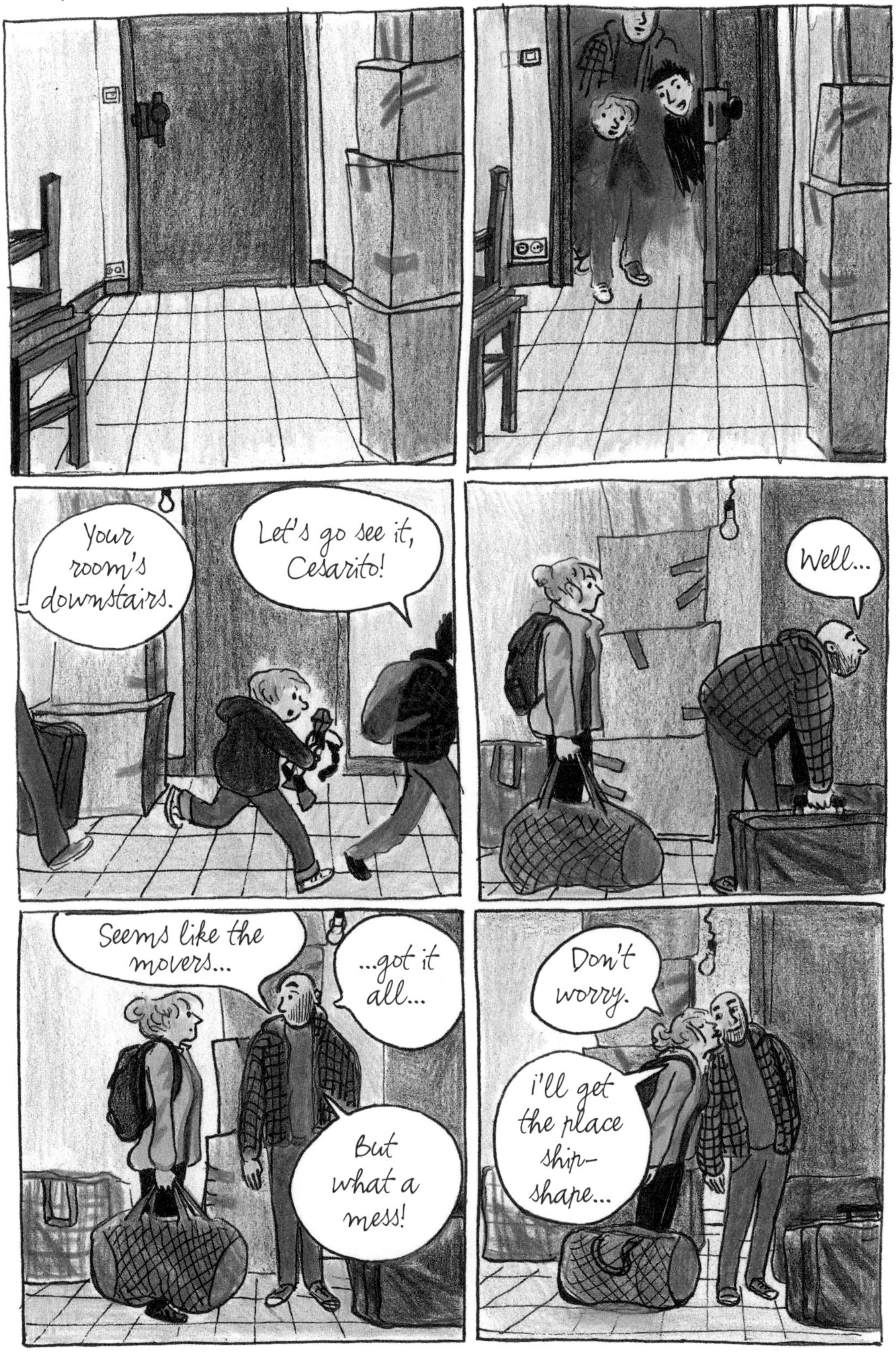
Your room's downstairs.
Let's go see it, Cesarito!
Well...
Seems like the movers...
...got it all...
But what a mess!
Don't worry.
i'll get the place ship-shape...

Downtown Pamplona.

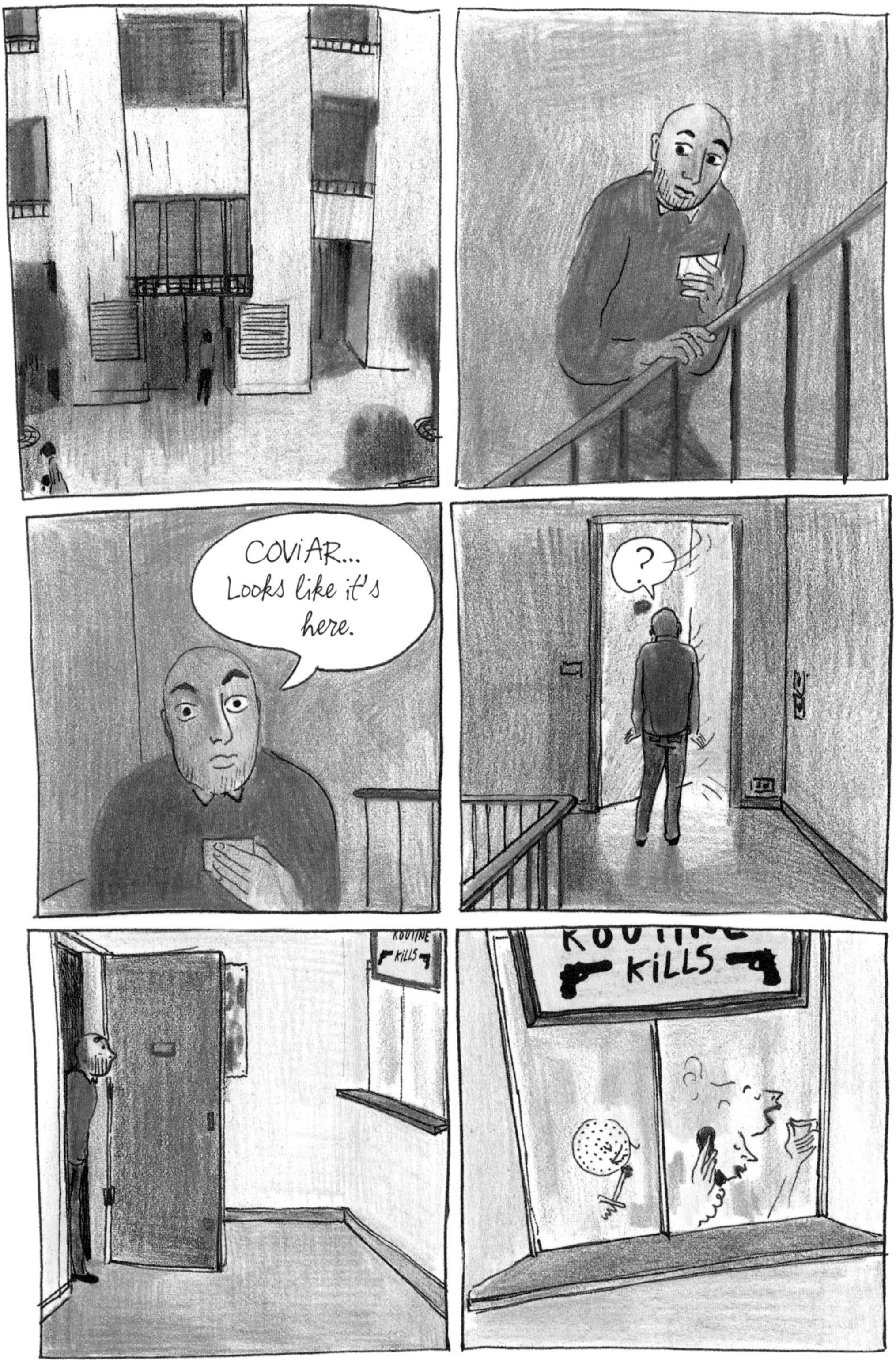
COVIAR...
Looks like it's
here.
?
ROUTINE
KILLS
KILLS

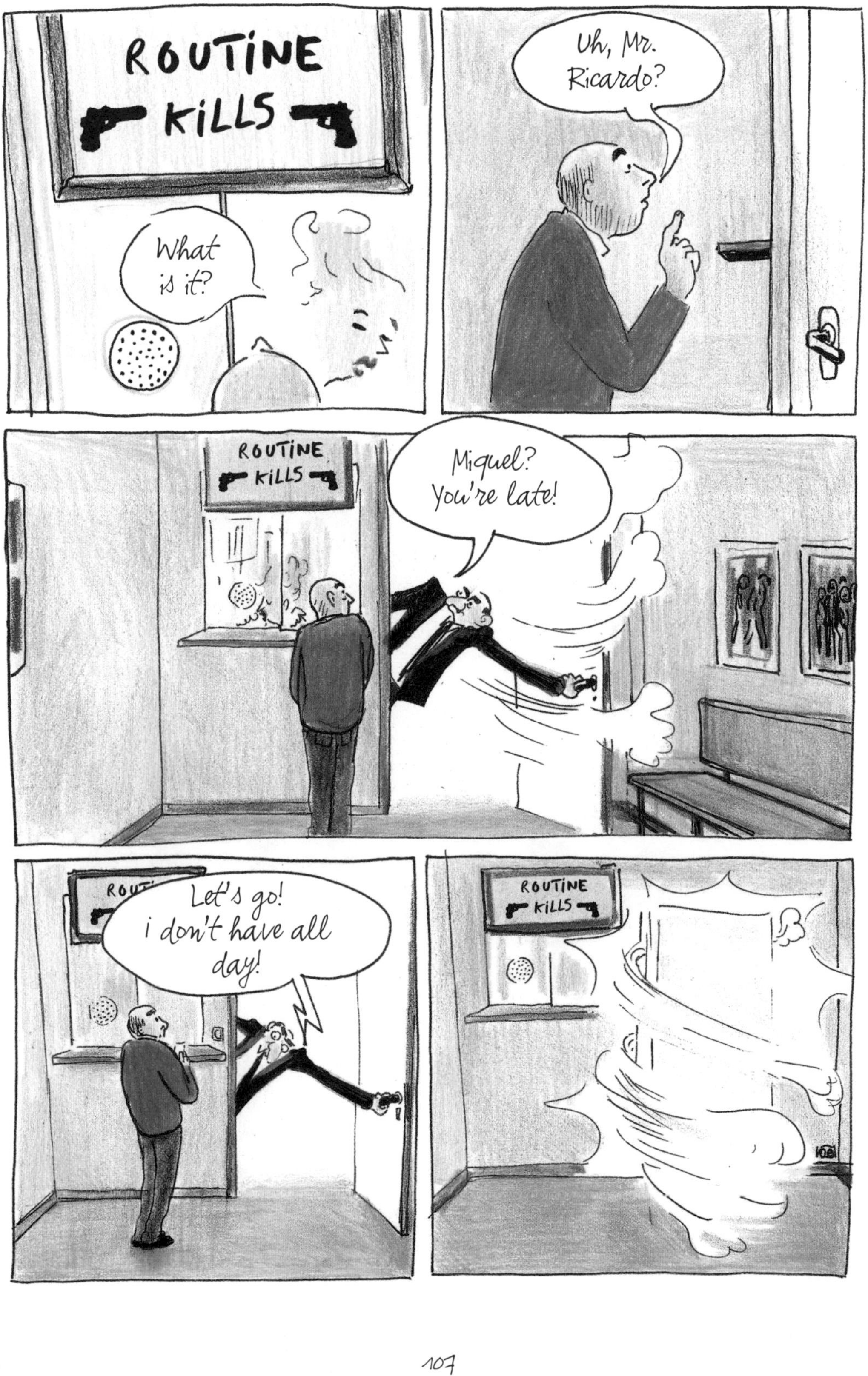
ROUTINE
KILLS
What is it?
Uh, Mr. Ricardo?
ROUTINE
KILLS
Miquel? You're late!
Let's go! i don't have all day!
ROUTINE
KILLS

Let's see. Married with two kids. And no military service?
Conscientious objector.
So what happened? You woke up one day and your conscience had changed?
i don't know what you're thinking...
But you'll spend more time with your gun than with your wife...
Doesn't matter...
Look, i'll be honest...
if it were up to me...
...you wouldn't have even made it through the front door, but...

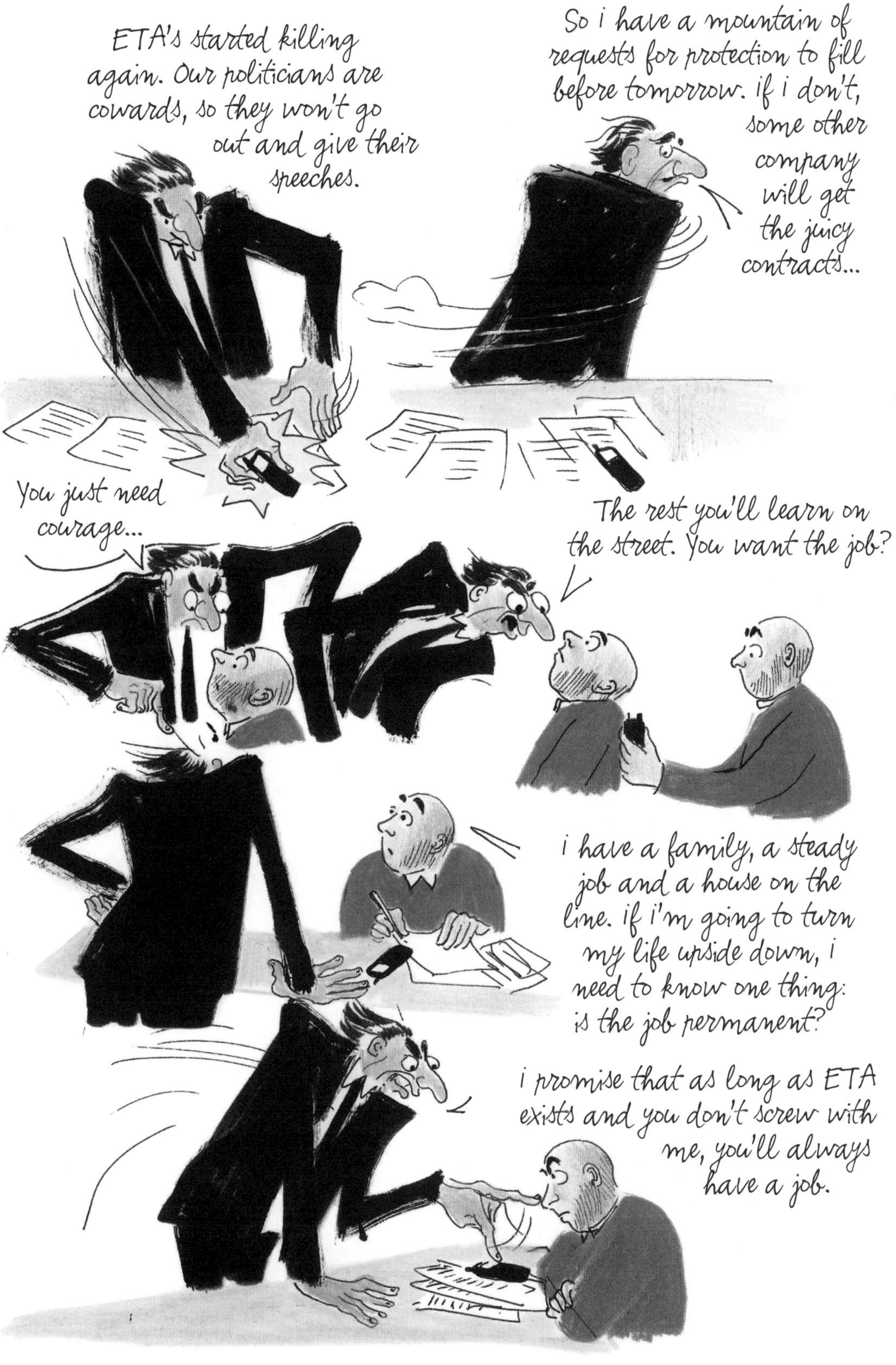
ETA's started killing again. Our politicians are cowards, so they won't go out and give their speeches.
So i have a mountain of requests for protection to fill before tomorrow. if i don't, some other company will get the juicy contracts...
You just need courage...
The rest you'll learn on the street. You want the job?
i have a family, a steady job and a house on the line. if i'm going to turn my life upside down, i need to know one thing: is the job permanent?
i promise that as long as ETA exists and you don't screw with me, you'll always have a job.

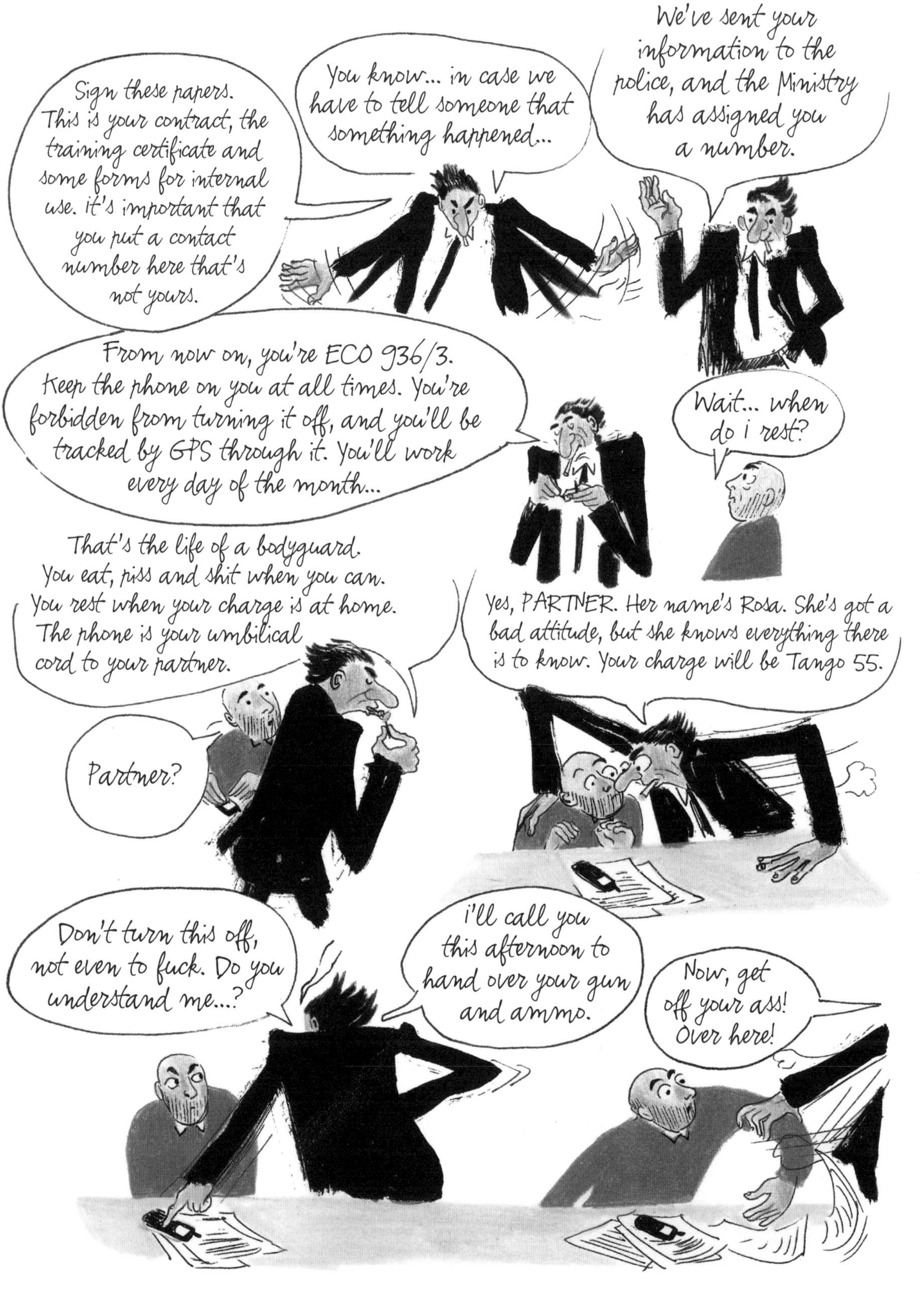
Sign these papers. This is your contract, the training certificate and some forms for internal use. It's important that you put a contact number here that's not yours.
You know... in case we have to tell someone that something happened...
We've sent your information to the police, and the Ministry has assigned you a number.
From now on, you're ECO 936/3. Keep the phone on you at all times. You're forbidden from turning it off, and you'll be tracked by GPS through it. You'll work every day of the month...
Wait... when do I rest?
That's the life of a bodyguard. You eat, piss and shit when you can. You rest when your charge is at home. The phone is your umbilical cord to your partner.
Partner?
Yes, PARTNER. Her name's Rosa. She's got a bad attitude, but she knows everything there is to know. Your charge will be Tango 55.
Don't turn this off, not even to fuck. Do you understand me...?
I'll call you this afternoon to hand over your gun and ammo.
Now, get off your ass! Over here!

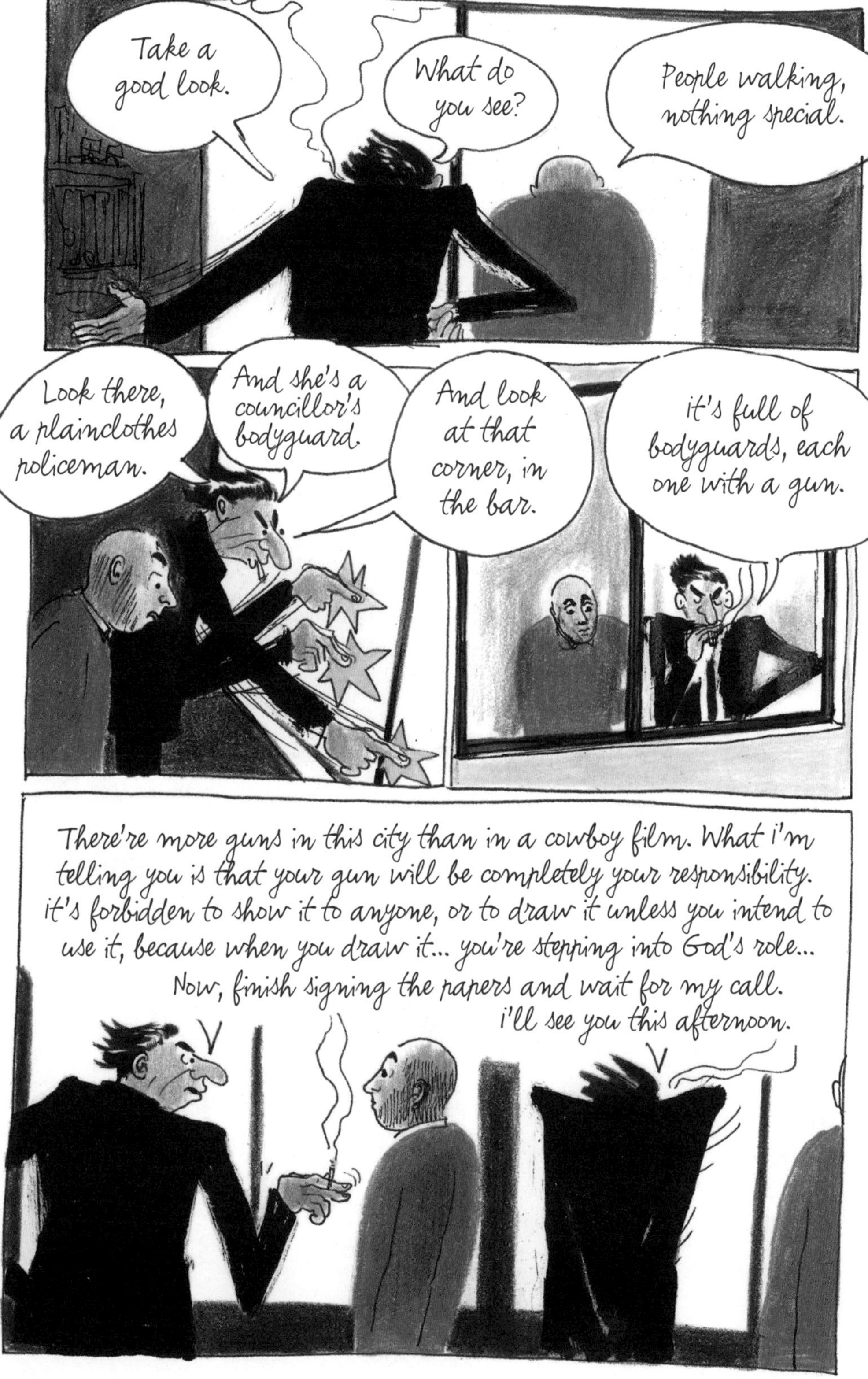

Take a good look.
What do you see?
People walking, nothing special.
Look there, a plainclothes policeman.
And she's a councillor's bodyguard.
And look at that corner, in the bar.
it's full of bodyguards, each one with a gun.
There're more guns in this city than in a cowboy film. What i'm telling you is that your gun will be completely your responsibility. it's forbidden to show it to anyone, or to draw it unless you intend to use it, because when you draw it... you're stepping into God's role... Now, finish signing the papers and wait for my call. i'll see you this afternoon.

so there i was, ready to trust a guy who looked like an undertaker and promised steady work as long as there were people dying... And that guy was about to give a 9mm semi-automatic Parabellum to a novice pacifist. The books were balanced. But i never should have trusted myself, because... what can you expect in a place where life is worth only the price of a bullet?

Walther PPK, like James Bond, and 25 bullets.

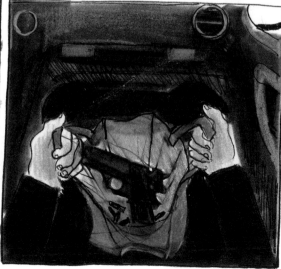

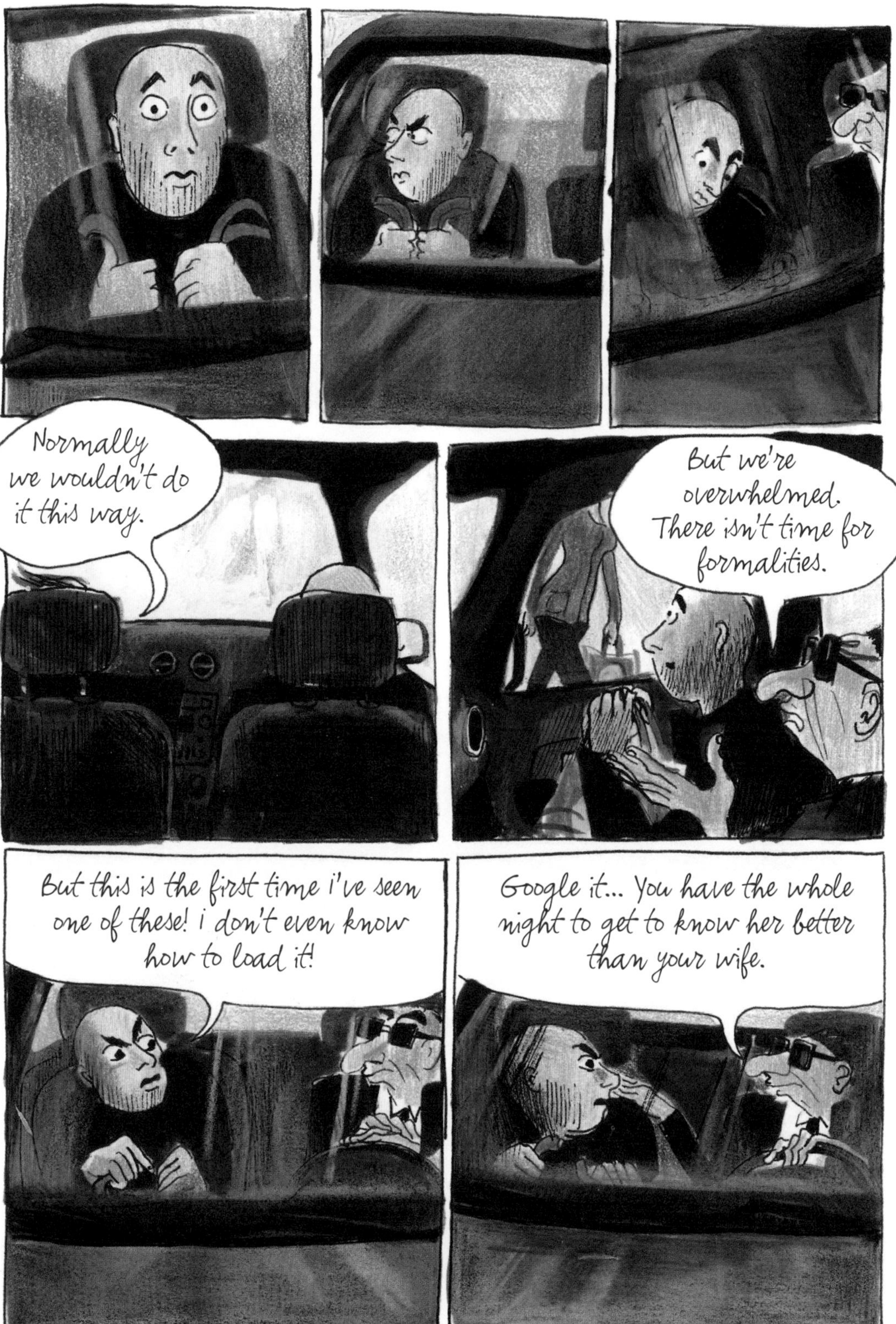
Normally we wouldn't do it this way.
But we're overwhelmed. There isn't time for formalities.
But this is the first time i've seen one of these! i don't even know how to load it!
Google it... You have the whole night to get to know her better than your wife.

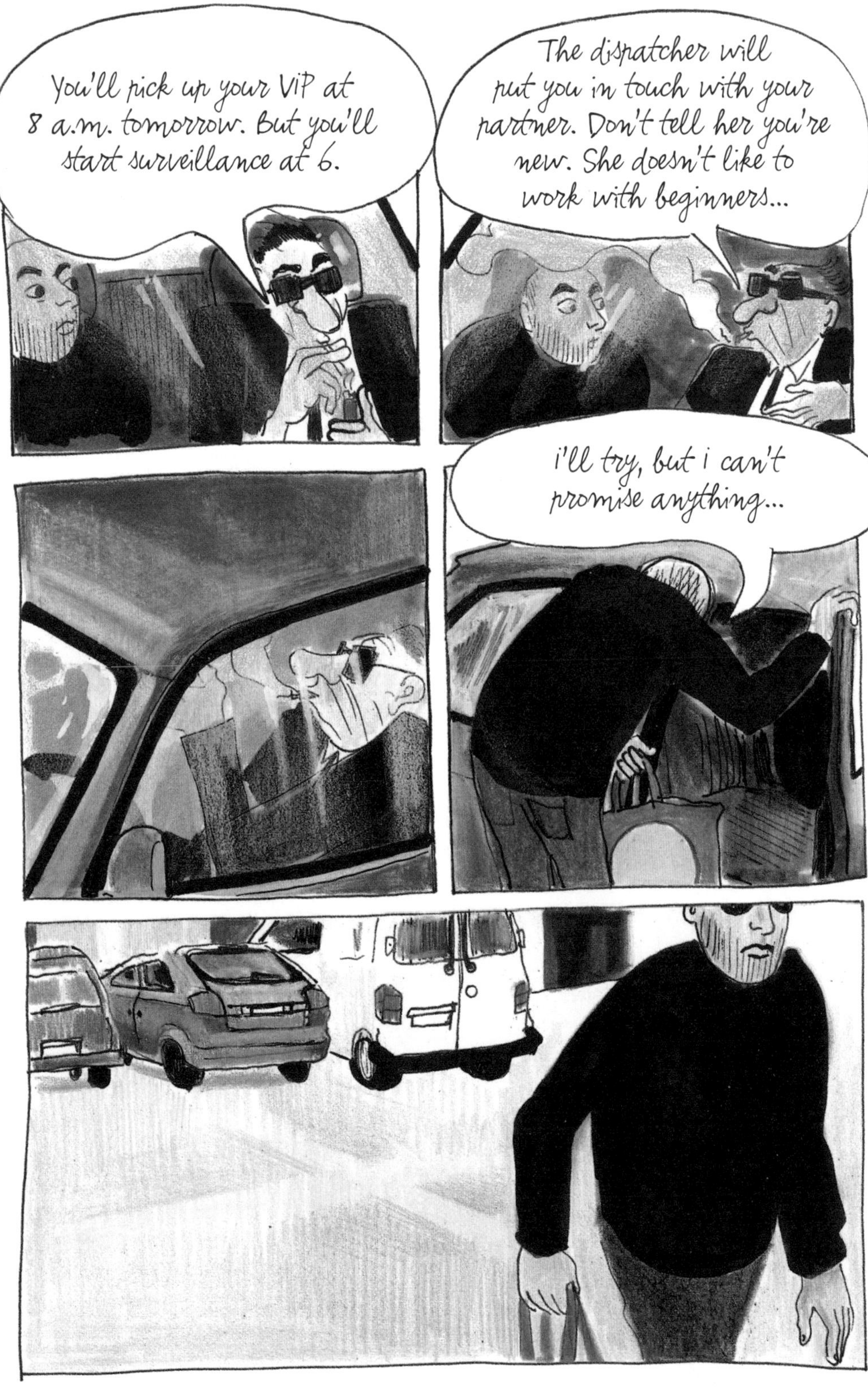
You'll pick up your ViP at 8 a.m. tomorrow. But you'll start surveillance at 6.
The dispatcher will put you in touch with your partner. Don't tell her you're new. She doesn't like to work with beginners...
i'll try, but i can't promise anything...

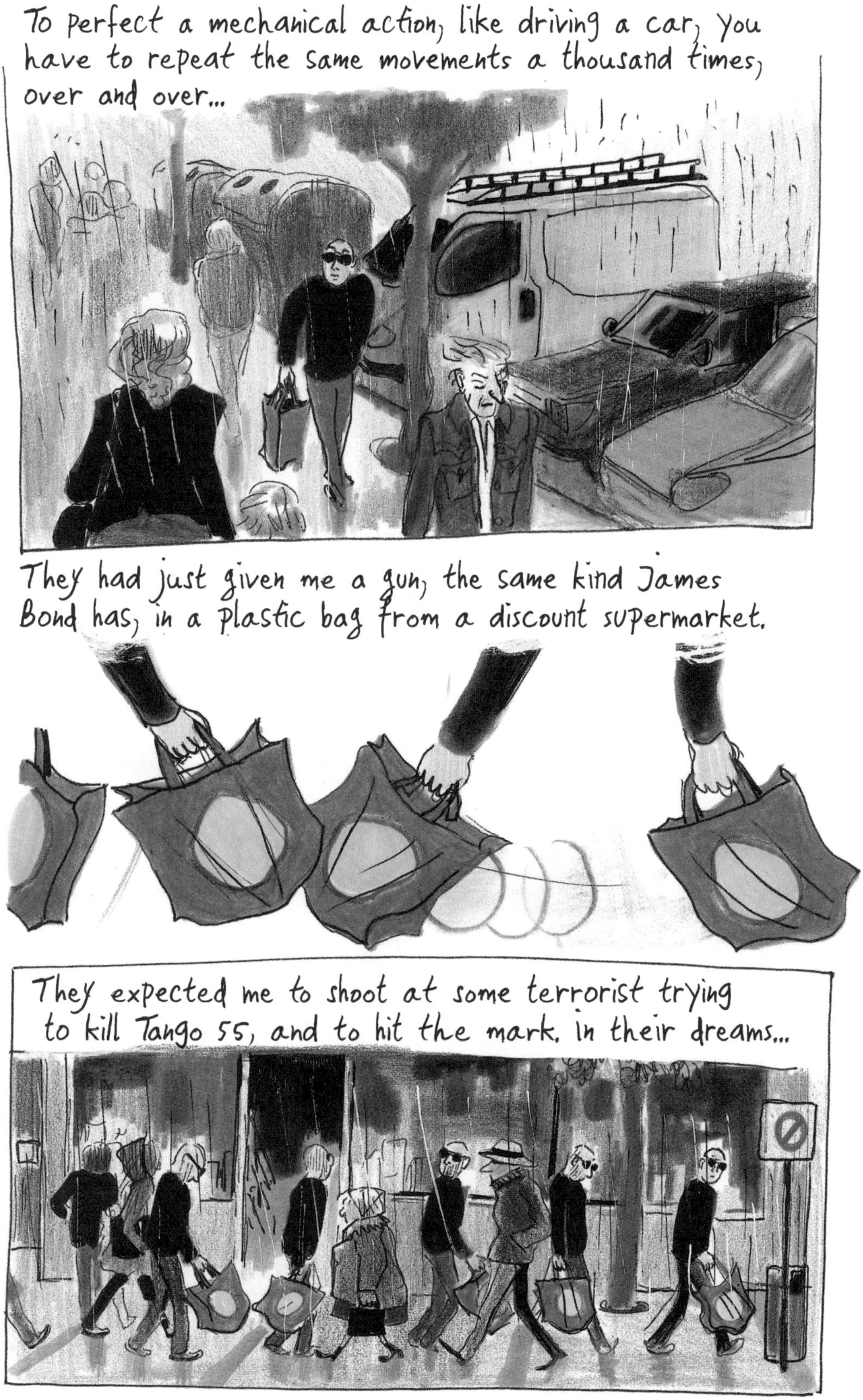
To perfect a mechanical action, like driving a car, you have to repeat the same movements a thousand times, over and over...
They had just given me a gun, the same kind James Bond has, in a plastic bag from a discount supermarket.
They expected me to shoot at some terrorist trying to kill Tango 55, and to hit the mark. In their dreams...

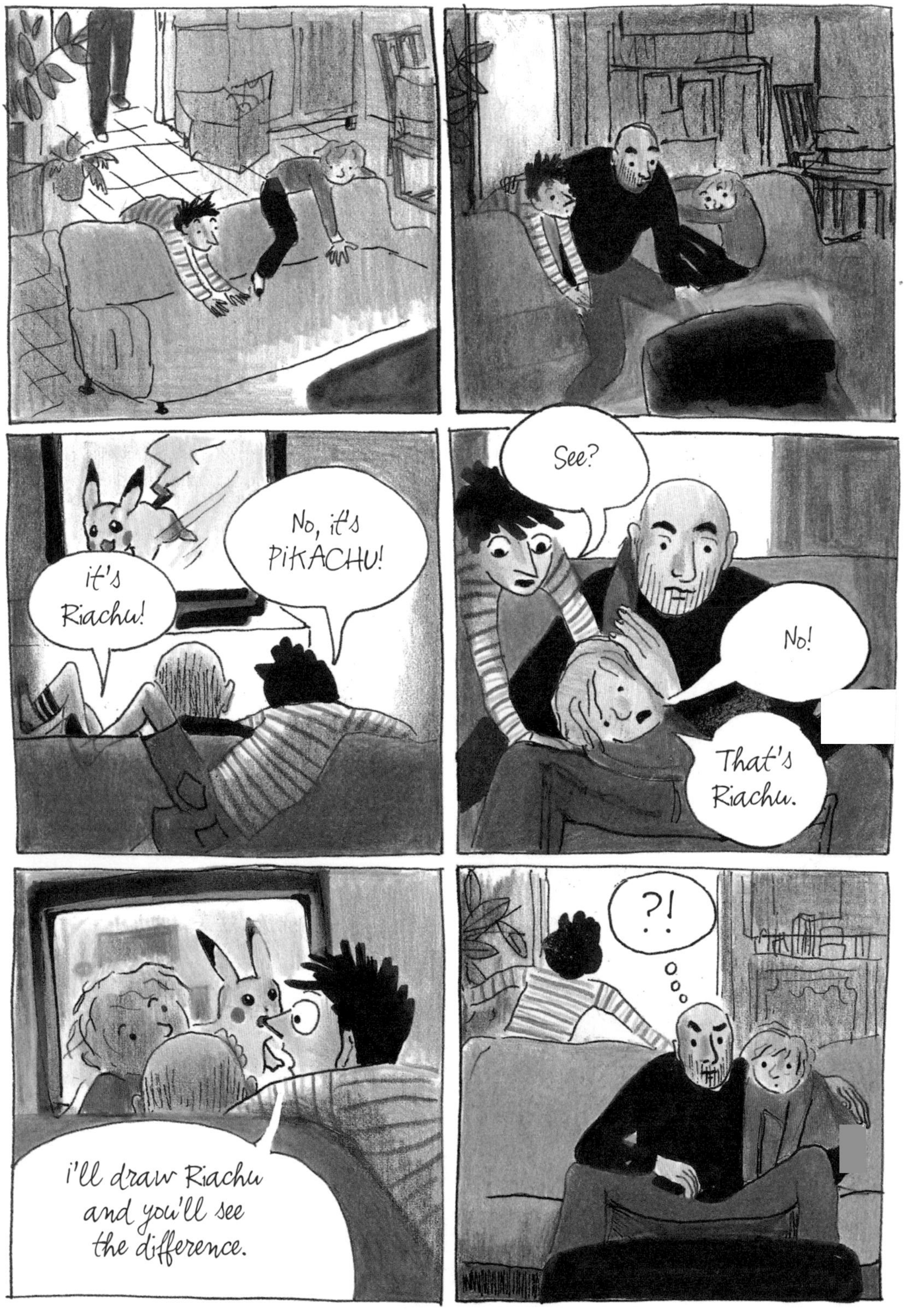
it's Riachu!
No, it's PIKACHU!
See?
No!
That's Riachu.
i'll draw Riachu and you'll see the difference.
?!

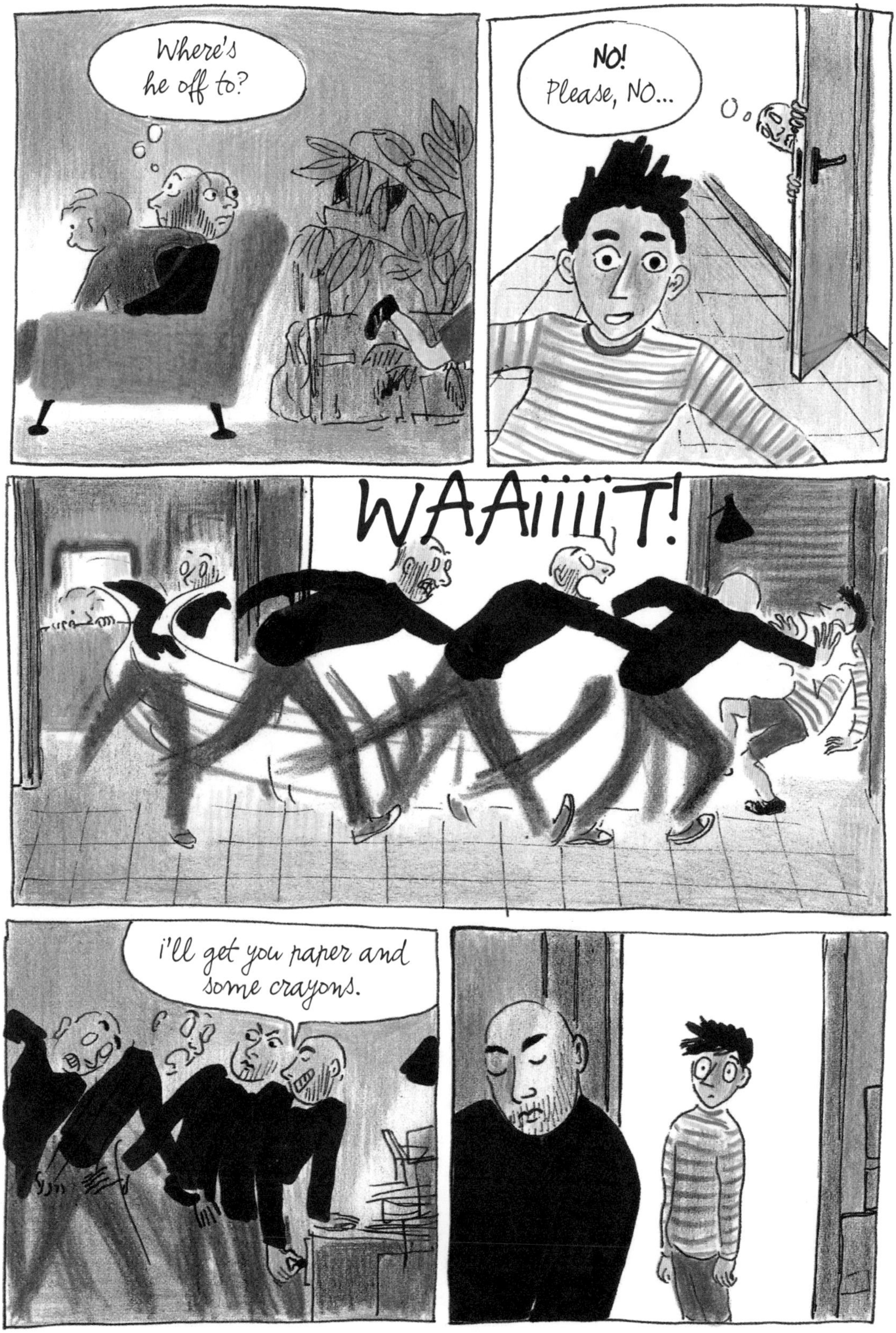
Where's he off to?
NO! Please, NO...
WAAiiiiT!
i'll get you paper and some crayons.

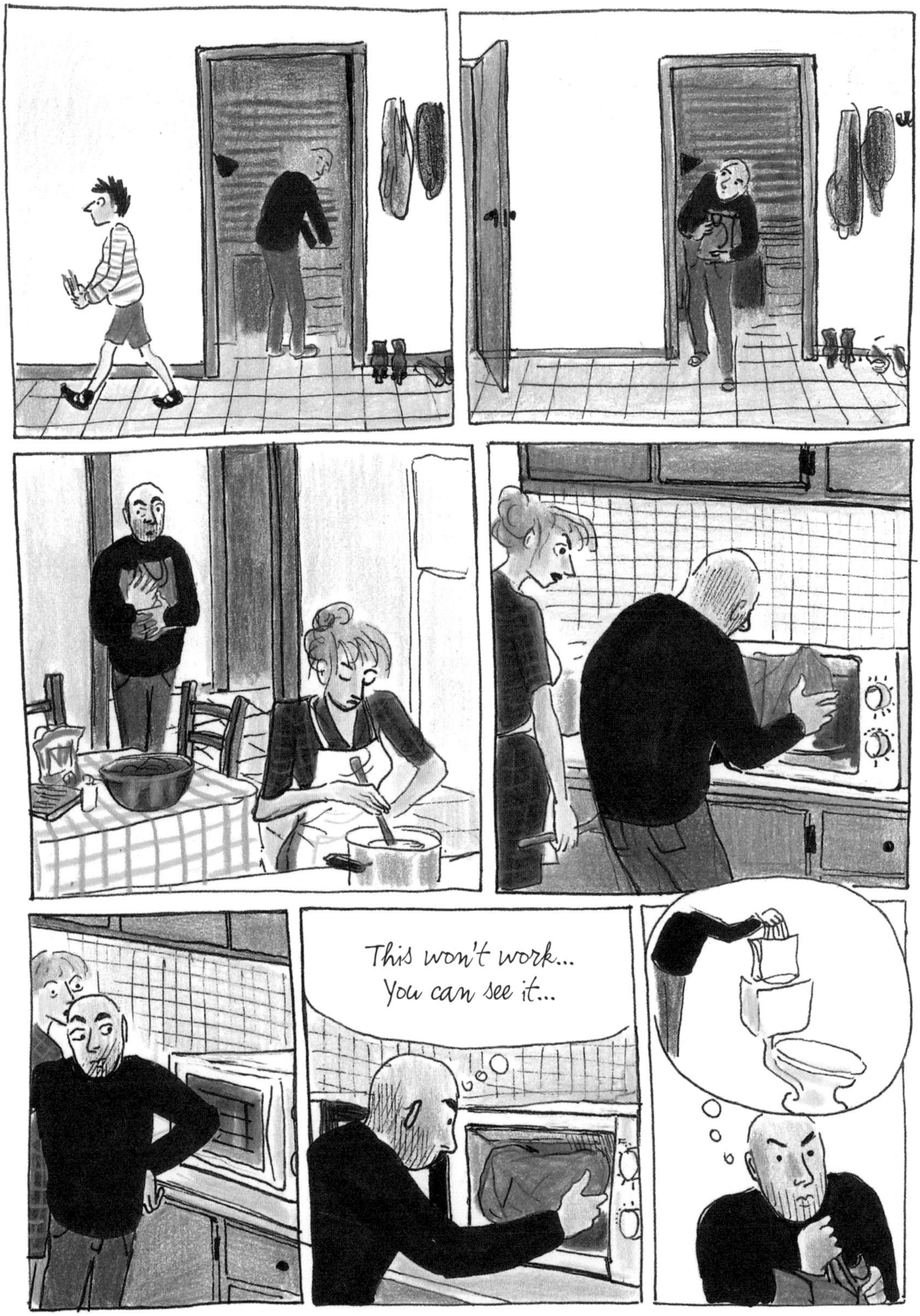
This won't work...
You can see it...

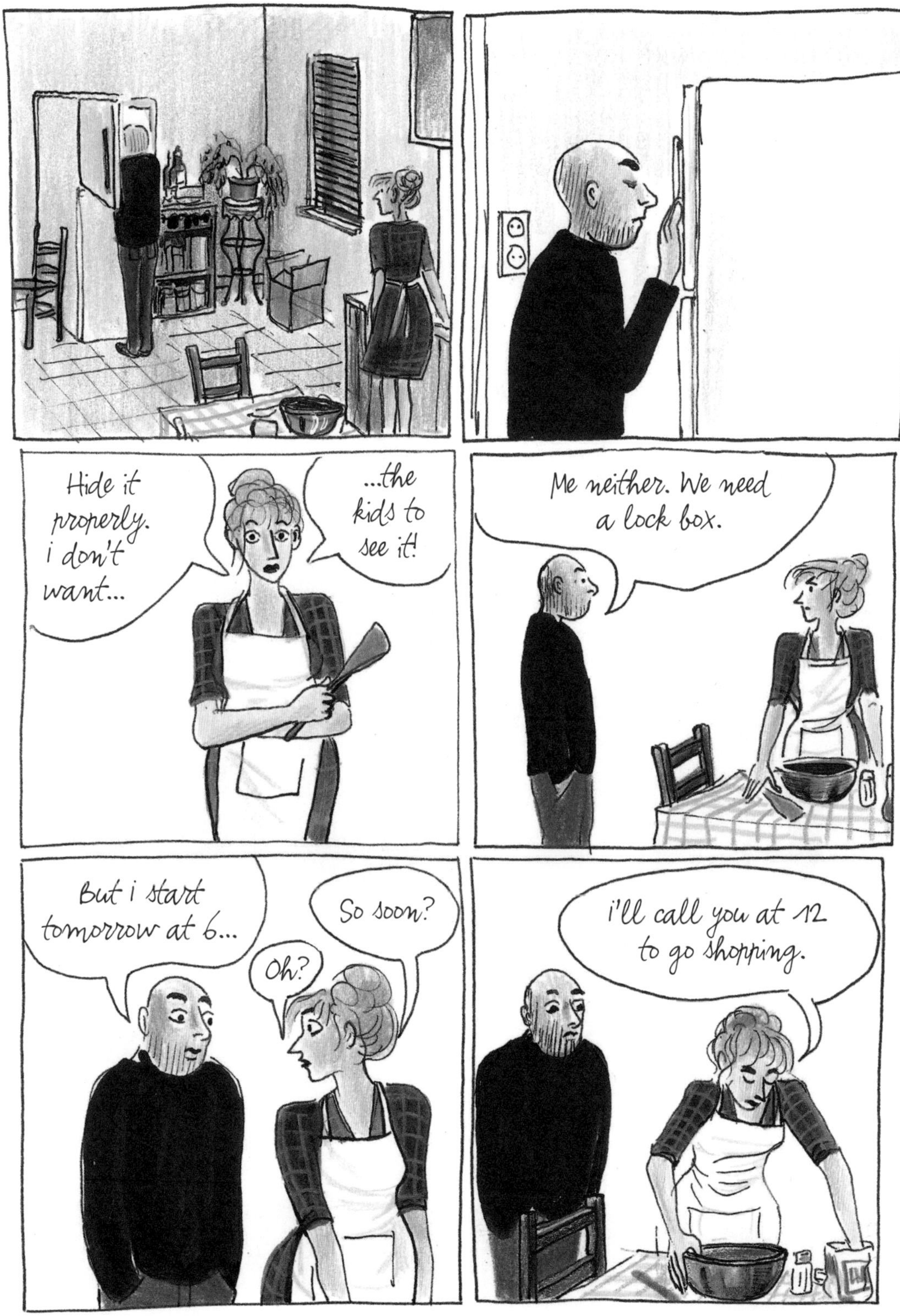
Hide it properly. i don't want...
...the kids to see it!
Me neither. We need a lock box.
But i start tomorrow at 6...
Oh?
So soon?
i'll call you at 12 to go shopping.

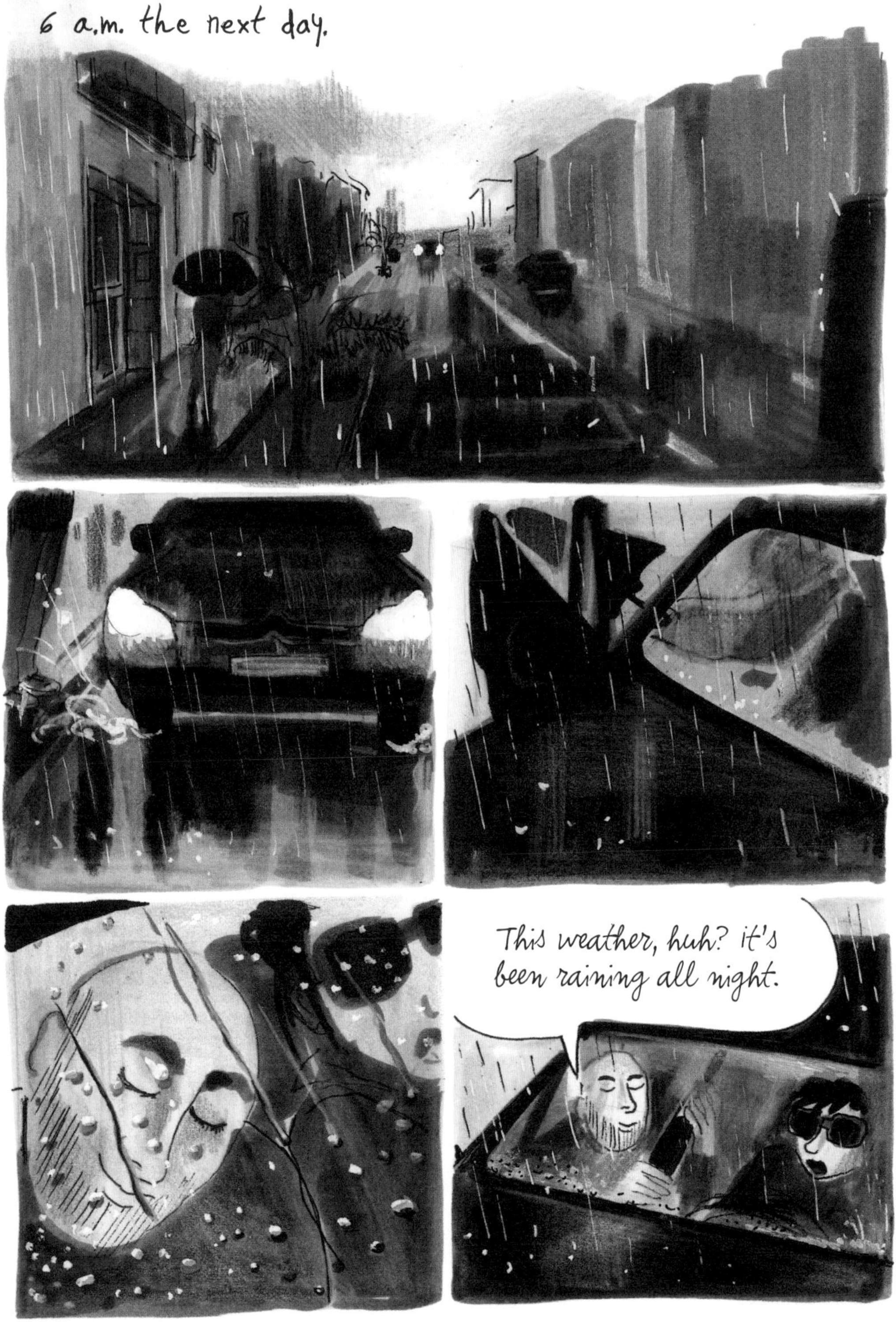
6 a.m. the next day.
This weather, huh? it's been raining all night.

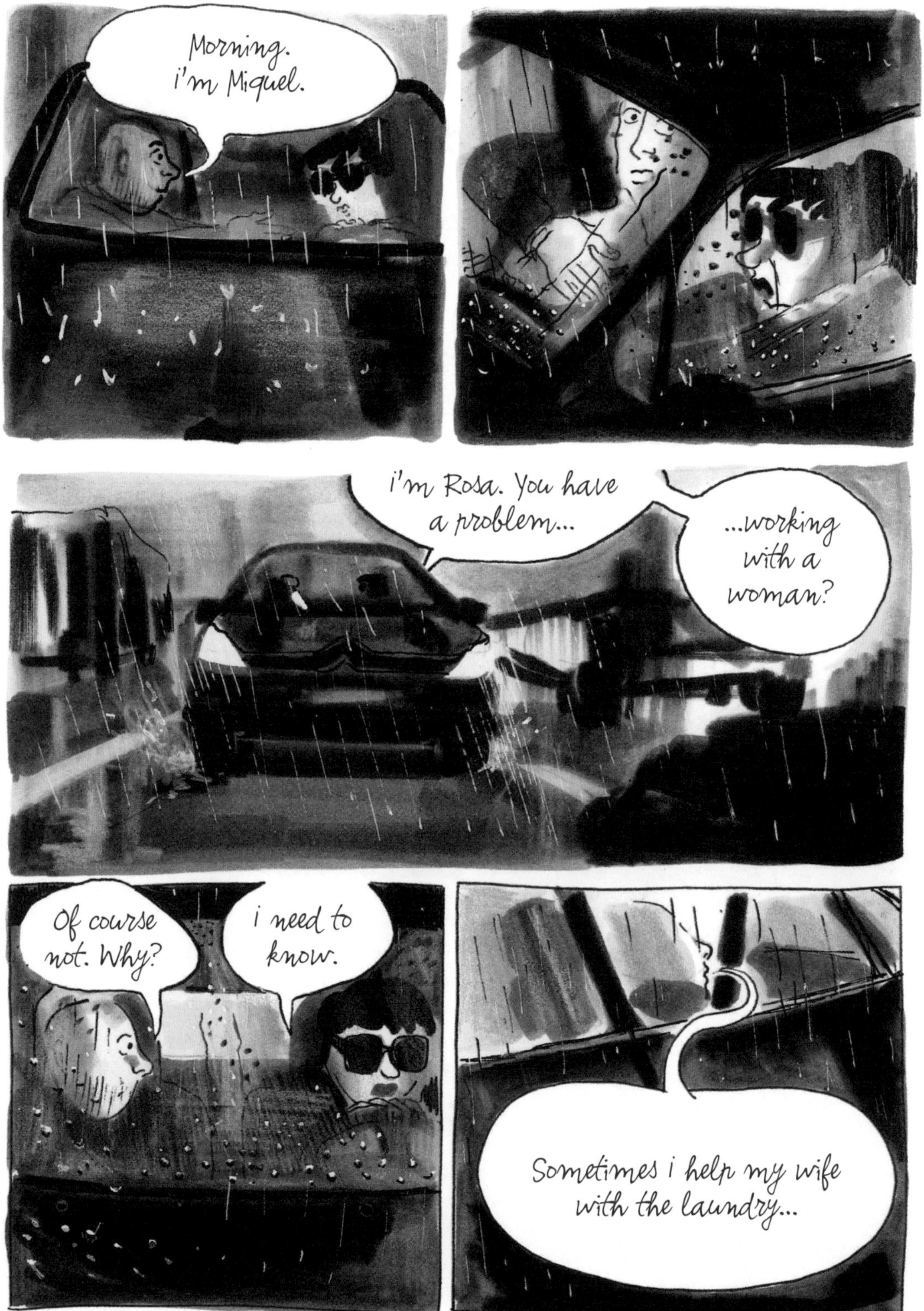
Morning. i'm Miquel.
i'm Rosa. You have a problem...
...working with a woman?
Of course not. Why?
i need to know.
Sometimes i help my wife with the laundry...

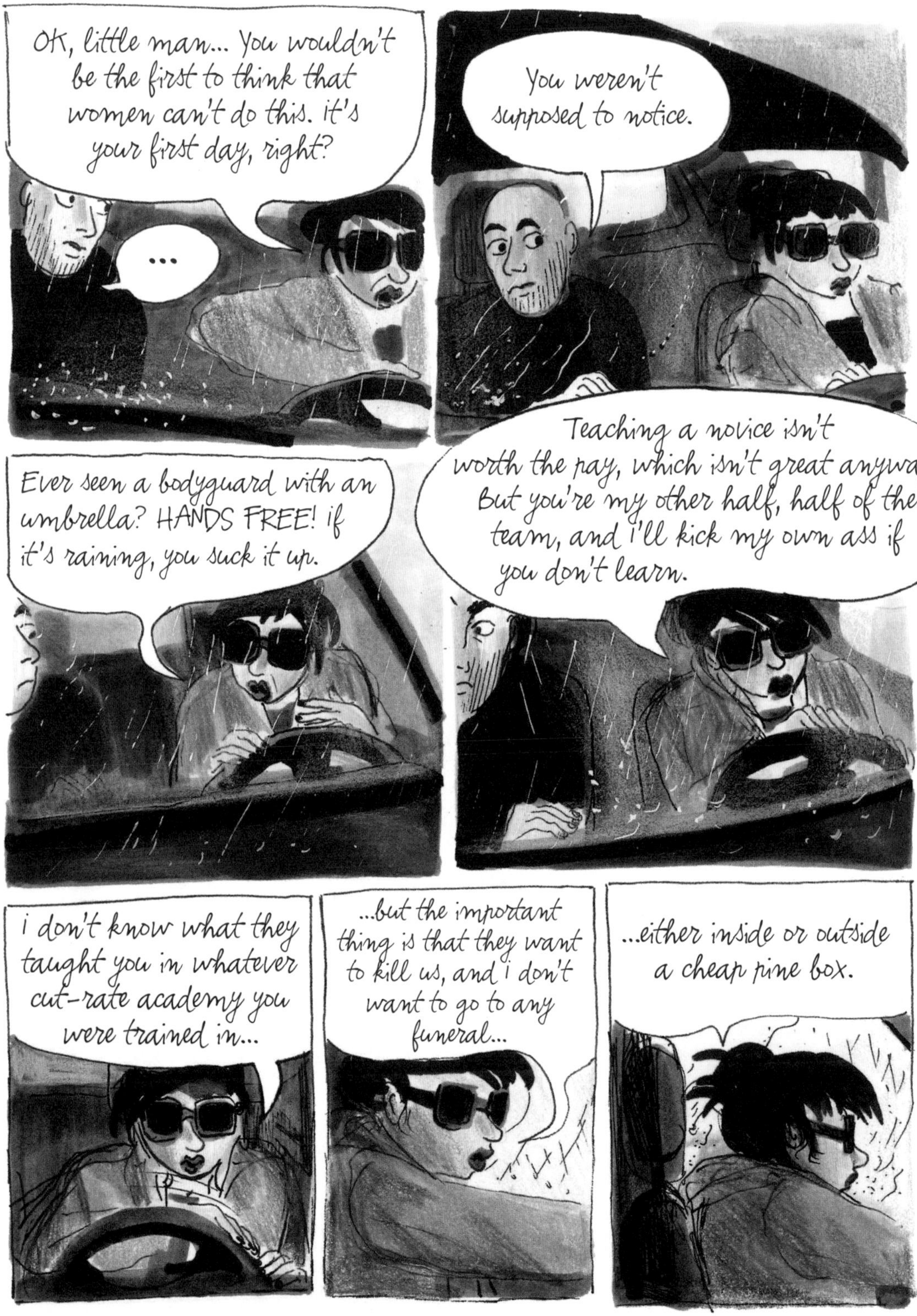
OK, little man... You wouldn't be the first to think that women can't do this. it's your first day, right?
...
You weren't supposed to notice.
Ever seen a bodyguard with an umbrella? HANDS FREE! if it's raining, you suck it up.
Teaching a novice isn't worth the pay, which isn't great anyway. But you're my other half, half of the team, and i'll kick my own ass if you don't learn.
i don't know what they taught you in whatever cut-rate academy you were trained in...
...but the important thing is that they want to kill us, and i don't want to go to any funeral...
...either inside or outside a cheap pine box.

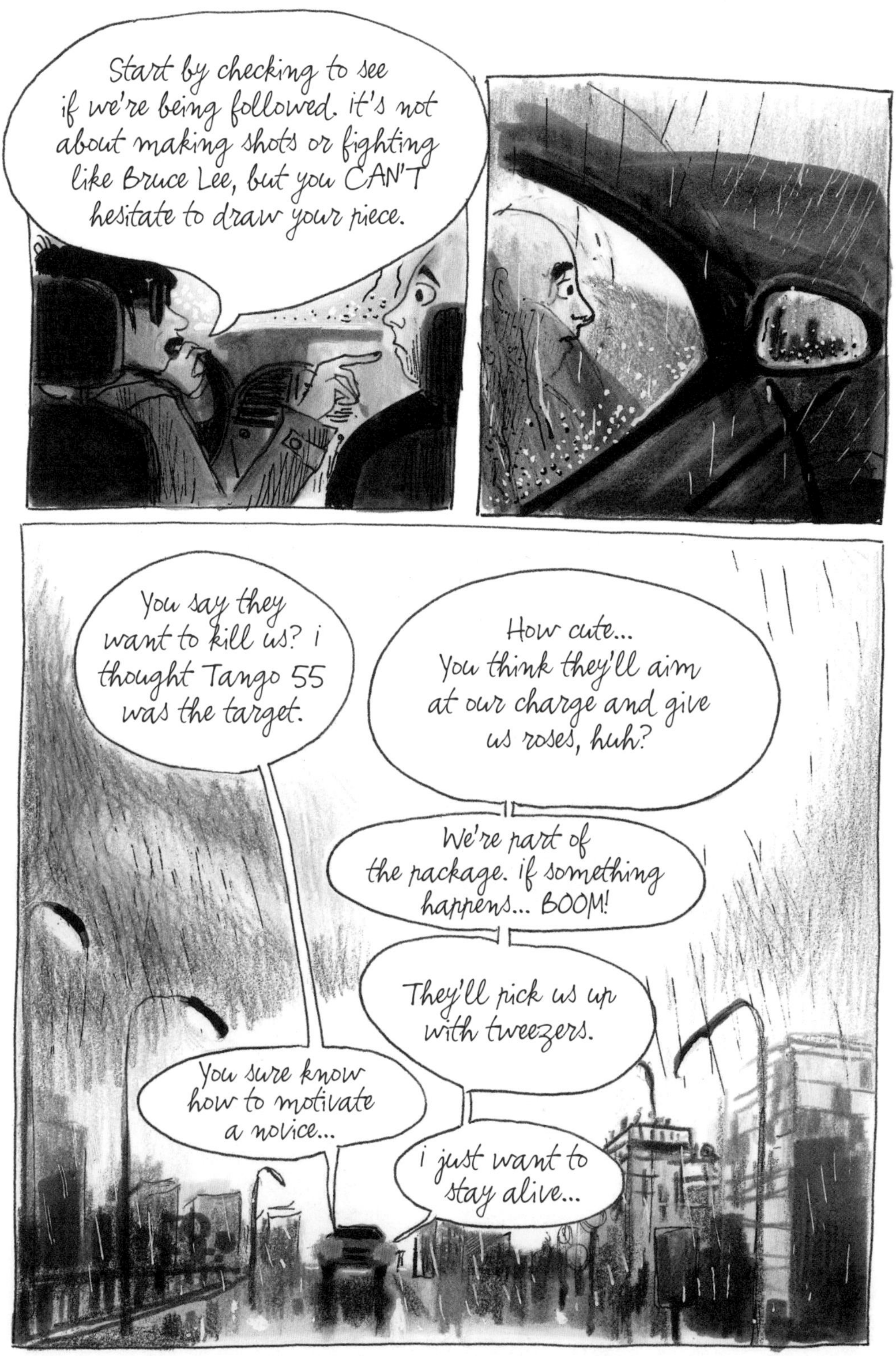
Start by checking to see if we're being followed. it's not about making shots or fighting like Bruce Lee, but you CAN'T hesitate to draw your piece.
You say they want to kill us? i thought Tango 55 was the target.
How cute... You think they'll aim at our charge and give us roses, huh?
We're part of the package. if something happens... BOOM!
They'll pick us up with tweezers.
You sure know how to motivate a novice...
i just want to stay alive...

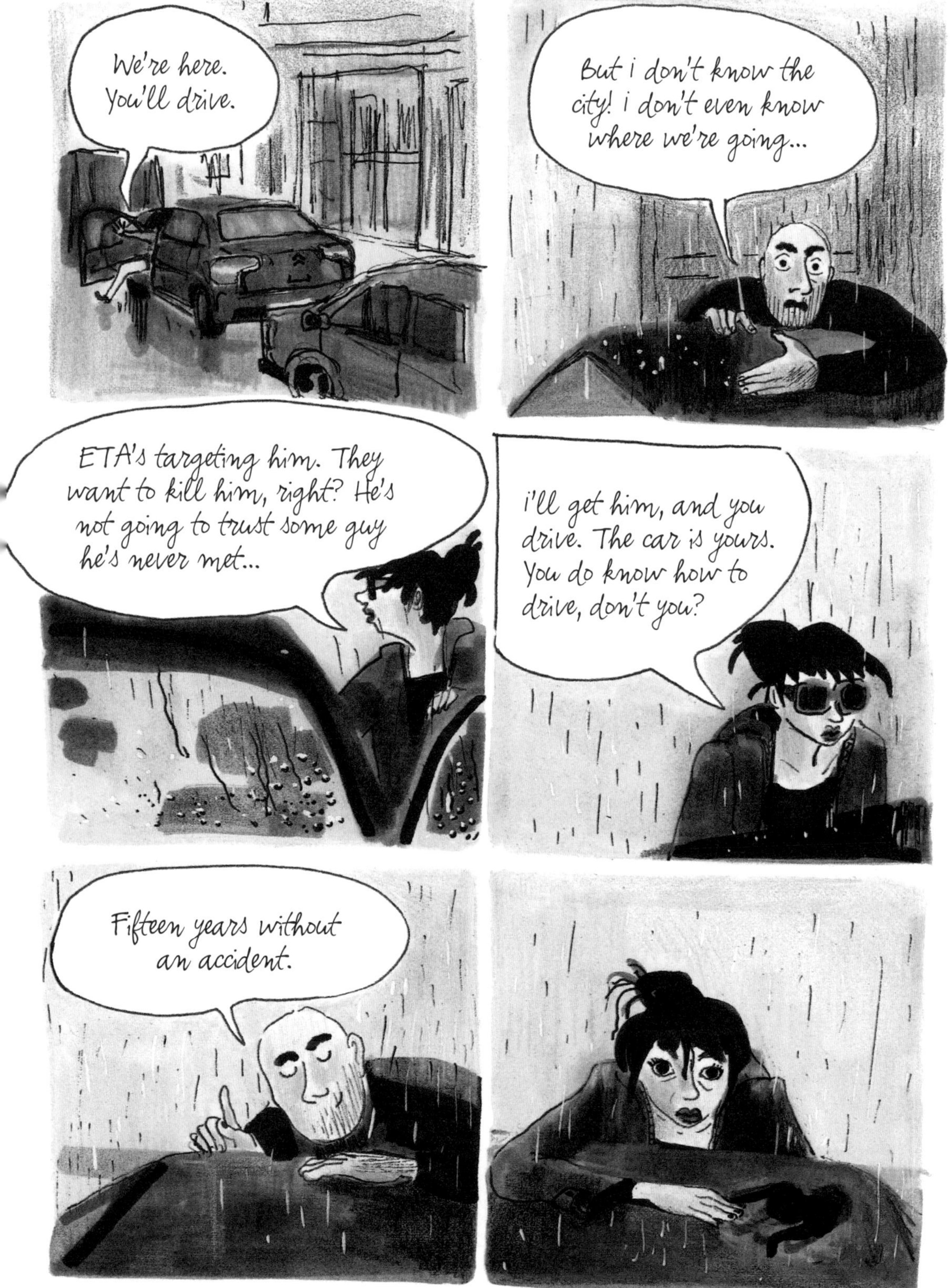
We're here. You'll drive.
But i don't know the city! i don't even know where we're going...
ETA's targeting him. They want to kill him, right? He's not going to trust some guy he's never met...
i'll get him, and you drive. The car is yours. You do know how to drive, don't you?
Fifteen years without an accident.

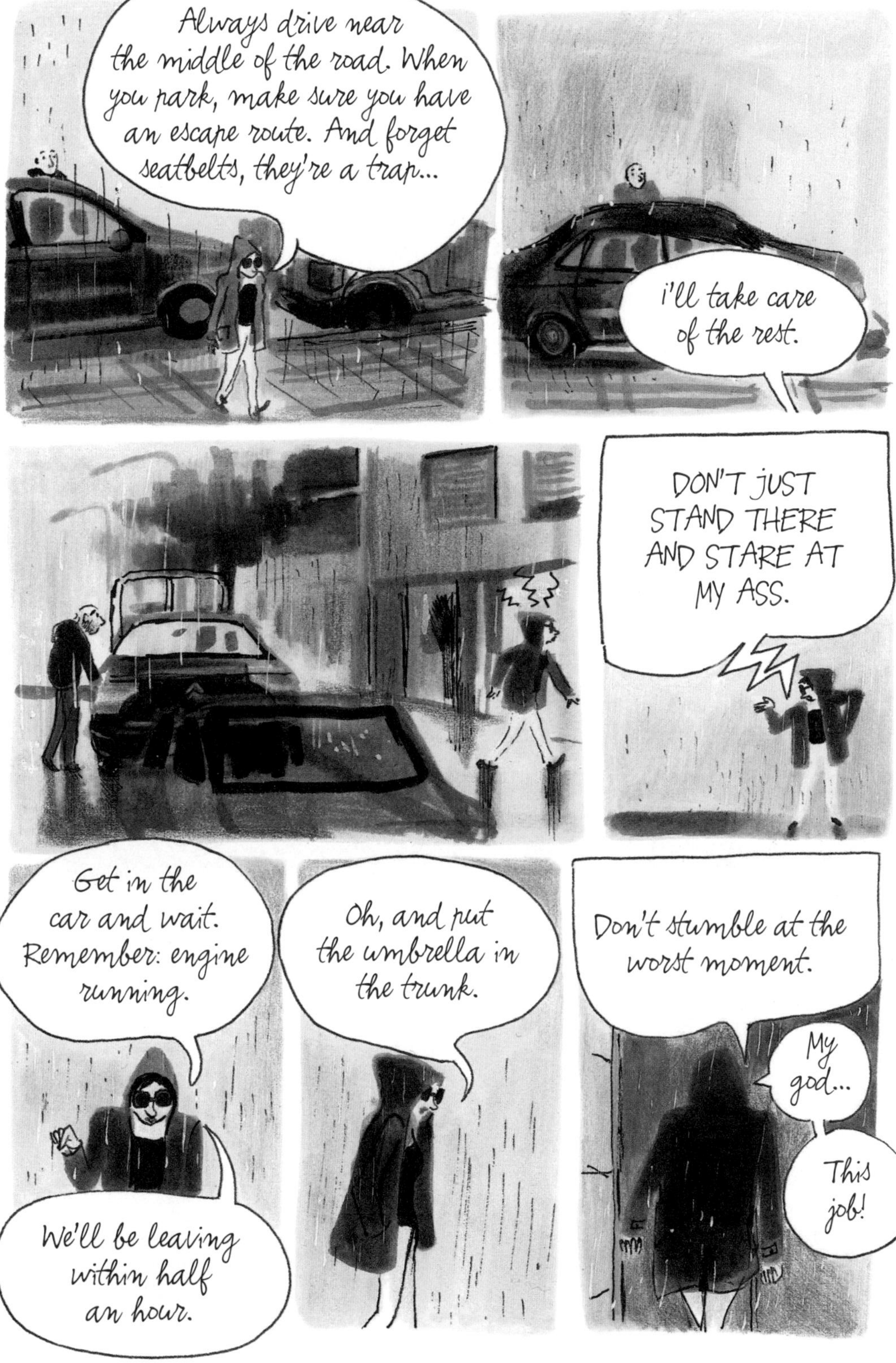
Always drive near the middle of the road. When you park, make sure you have an escape route. And forget seatbelts, they're a trap...
i'll take care of the rest.
DON'T JUST STAND THERE AND STARE AT MY ASS.
Get in the car and wait. Remember: engine running.
We'll be leaving within half an hour.
Oh, and put the umbrella in the trunk.
Don't stumble at the worst moment.
My god...
This job!

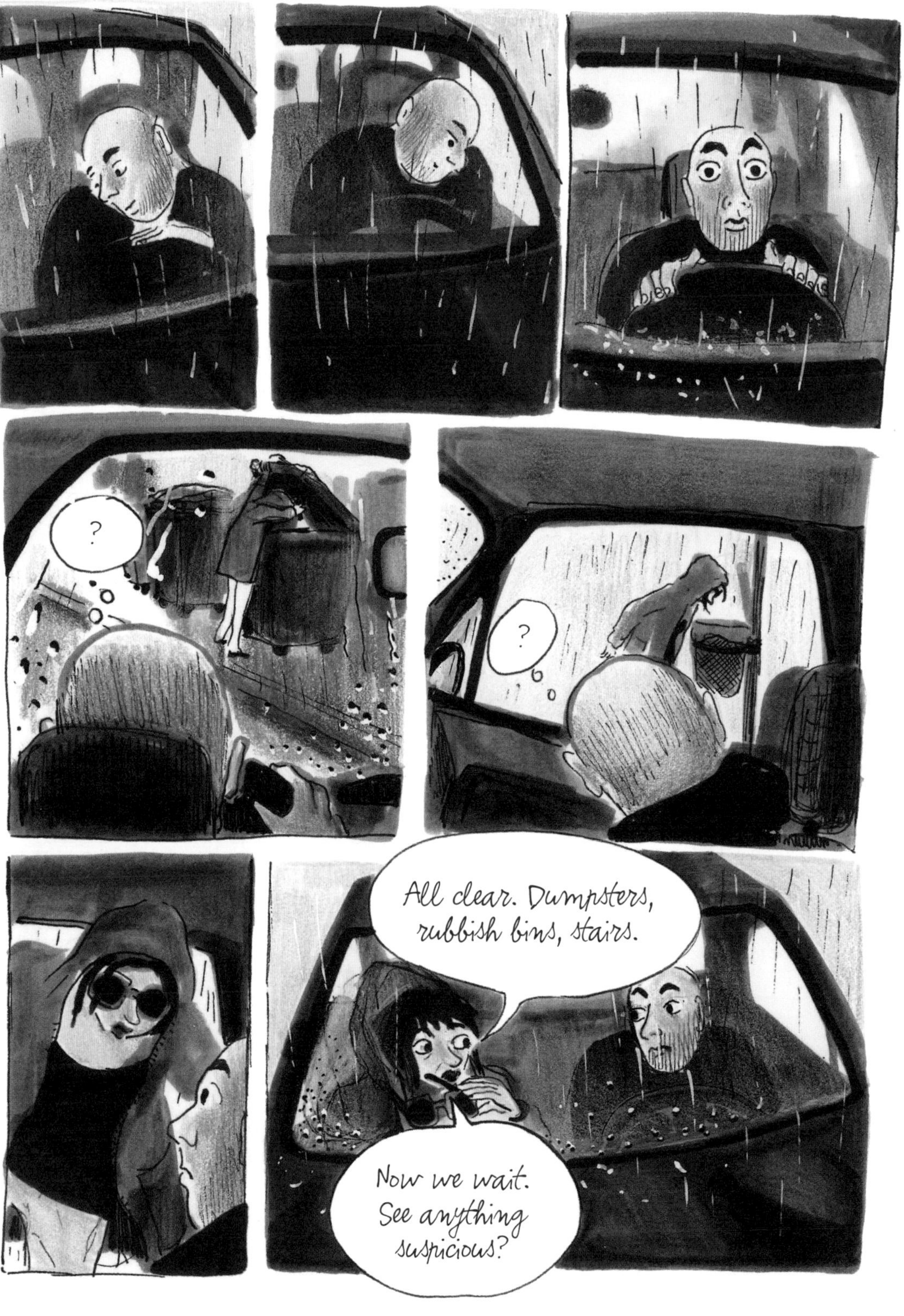
?
?
All clear. Dumpsters, rubbish bins, stairs.
Now we wait. See anything suspicious?

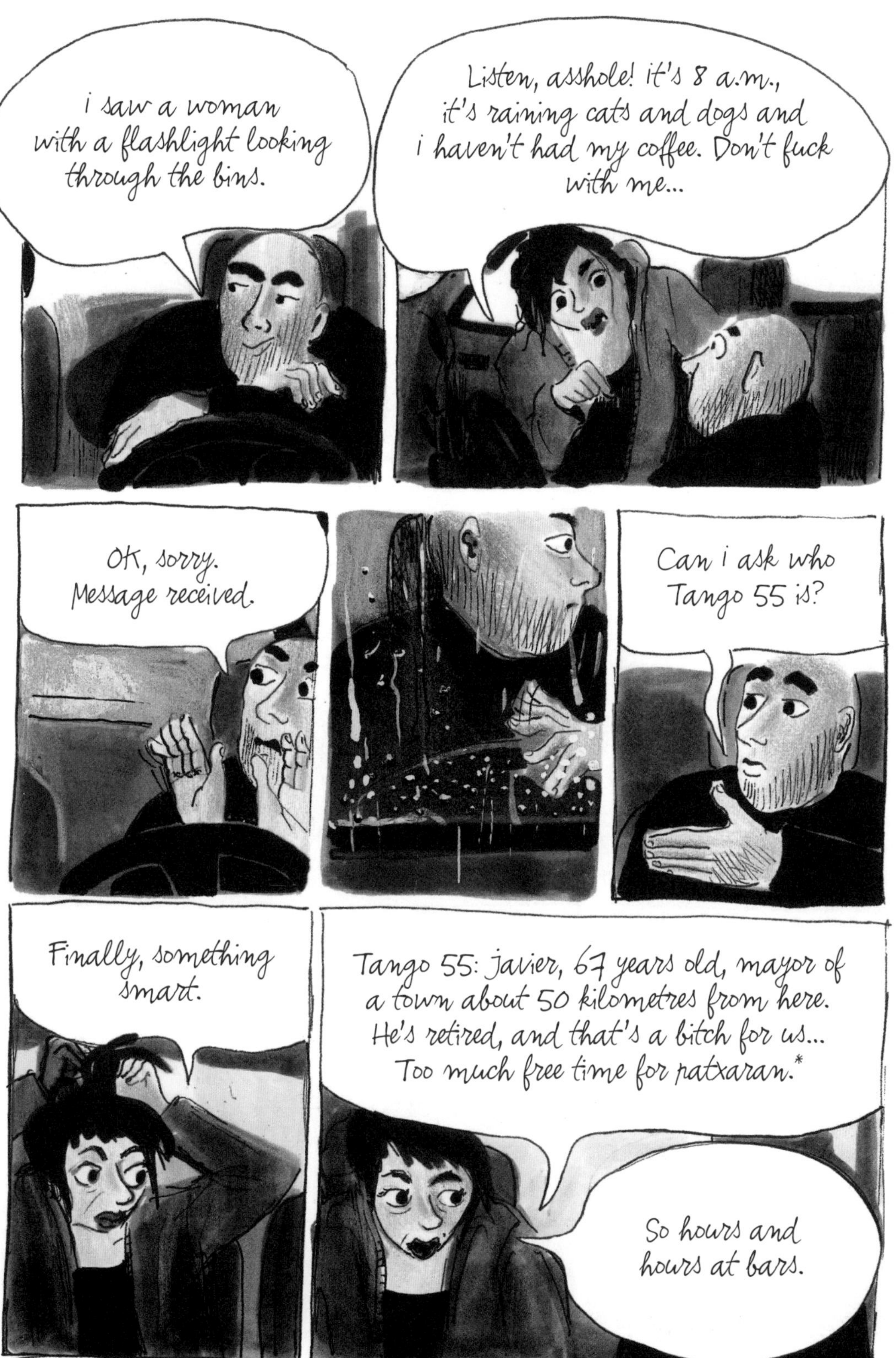
i saw a woman with a flashlight looking through the bins.
Listen, asshole! it's 8 a.m., it's raining cats and dogs and i haven't had my coffee. Don't fuck with me...
OK, sorry. Message received.
Can i ask who Tango 55 is?
Finally, something smart.
Tango 55: Javier, 67 years old, mayor of a town about 50 kilometres from here. He's retired, and that's a bitch for us... Too much free time for patxaran.*
So hours and hours at bars.

* Patxaran: sloe gin liquor.

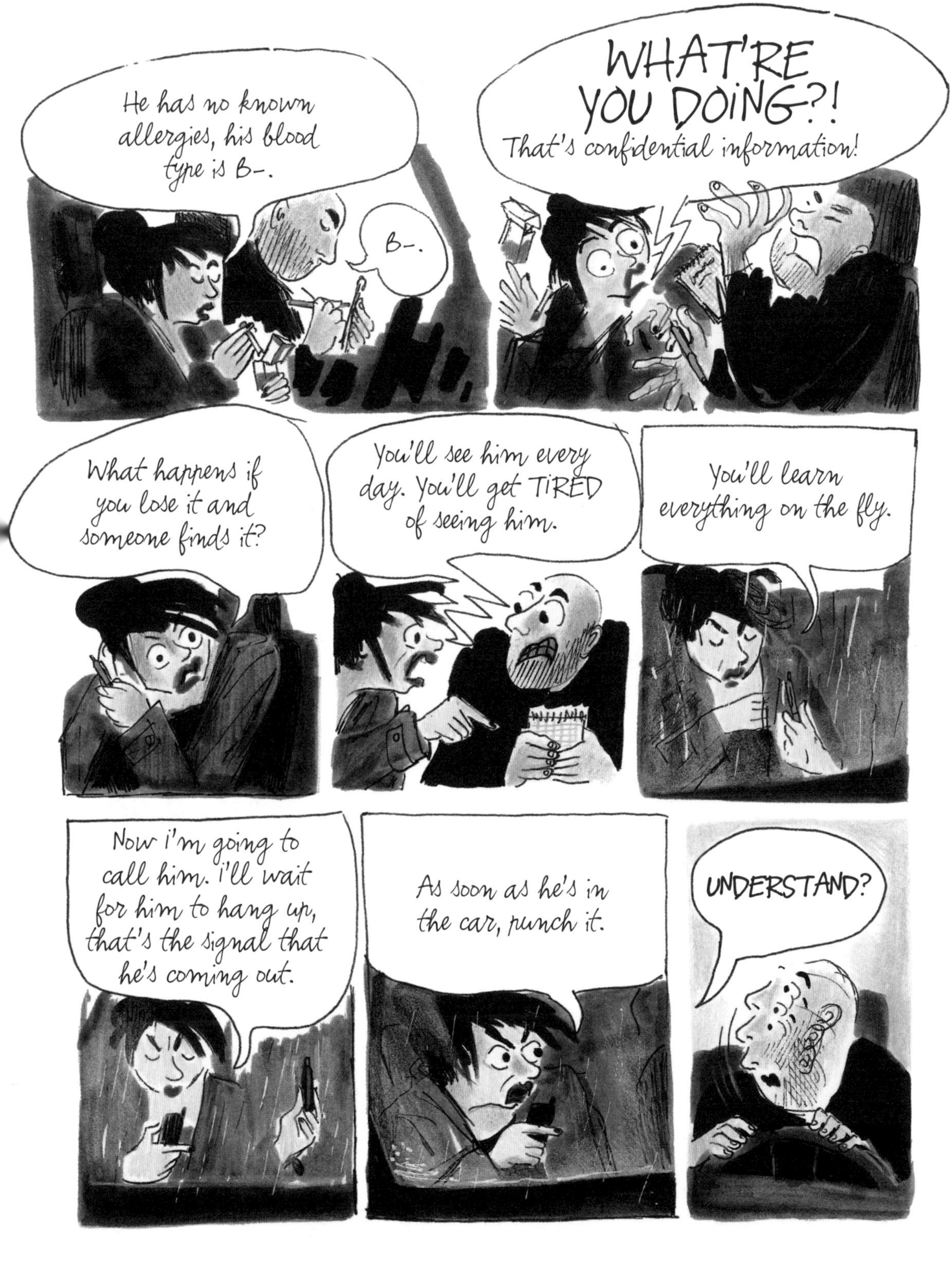
He has no known allergies, his blood type is B-.
B-.
WHAT'RE YOU DOING?!
That's confidential information!
What happens if you lose it and someone finds it?
You'll see him every day. You'll get TIRED of seeing him.
You'll learn everything on the fly.
Now i'm going to call him. i'll wait for him to hang up, that's the signal that he's coming out.
As soon as he's in the car, punch it.
UNDERSTAND?

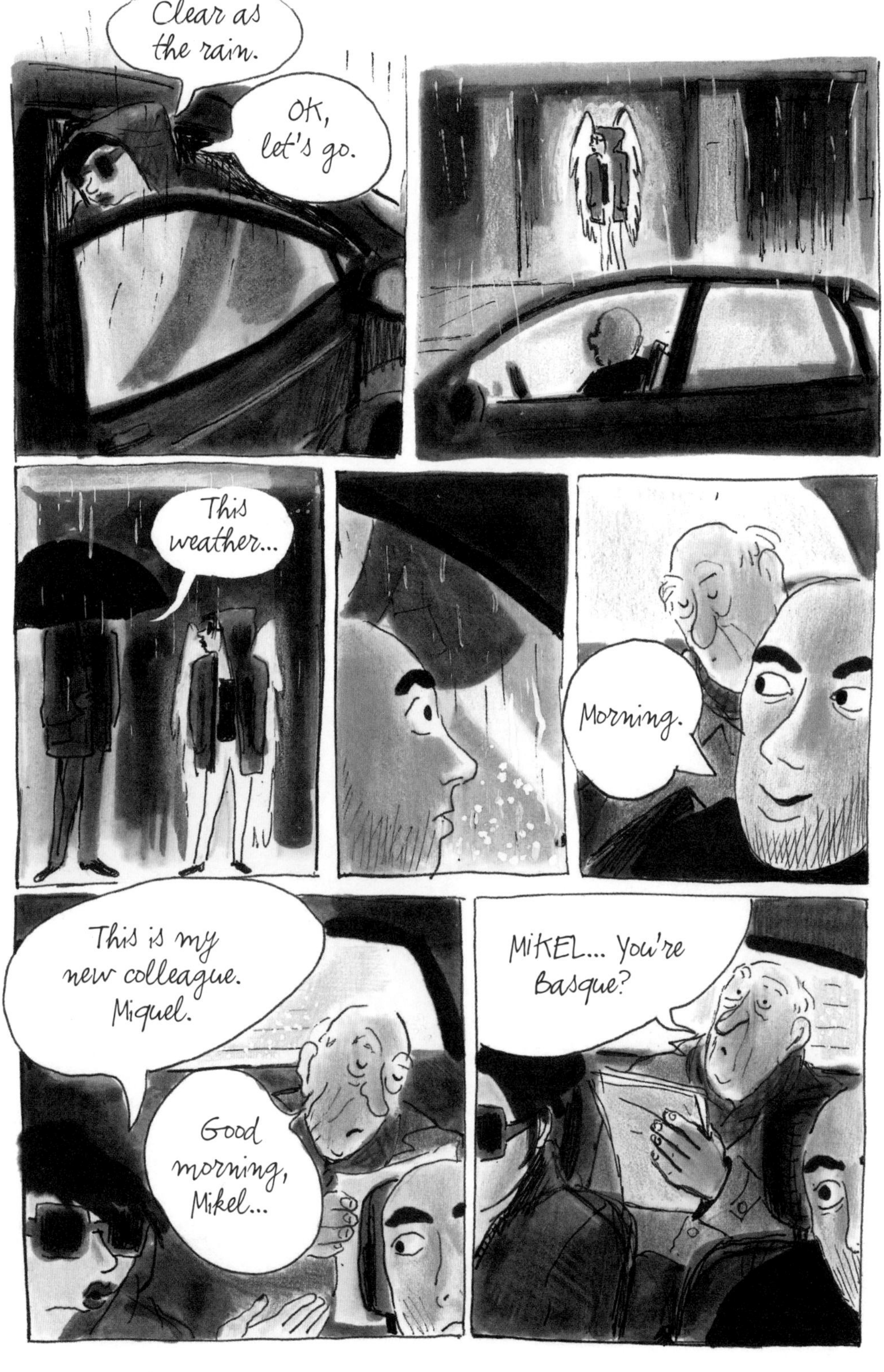
Clear as the rain.
OK, let's go.
This weather...
Morning.
This is my new colleague. Miquel.
Good morning, Mikel...
MIKEL... You're Basque?

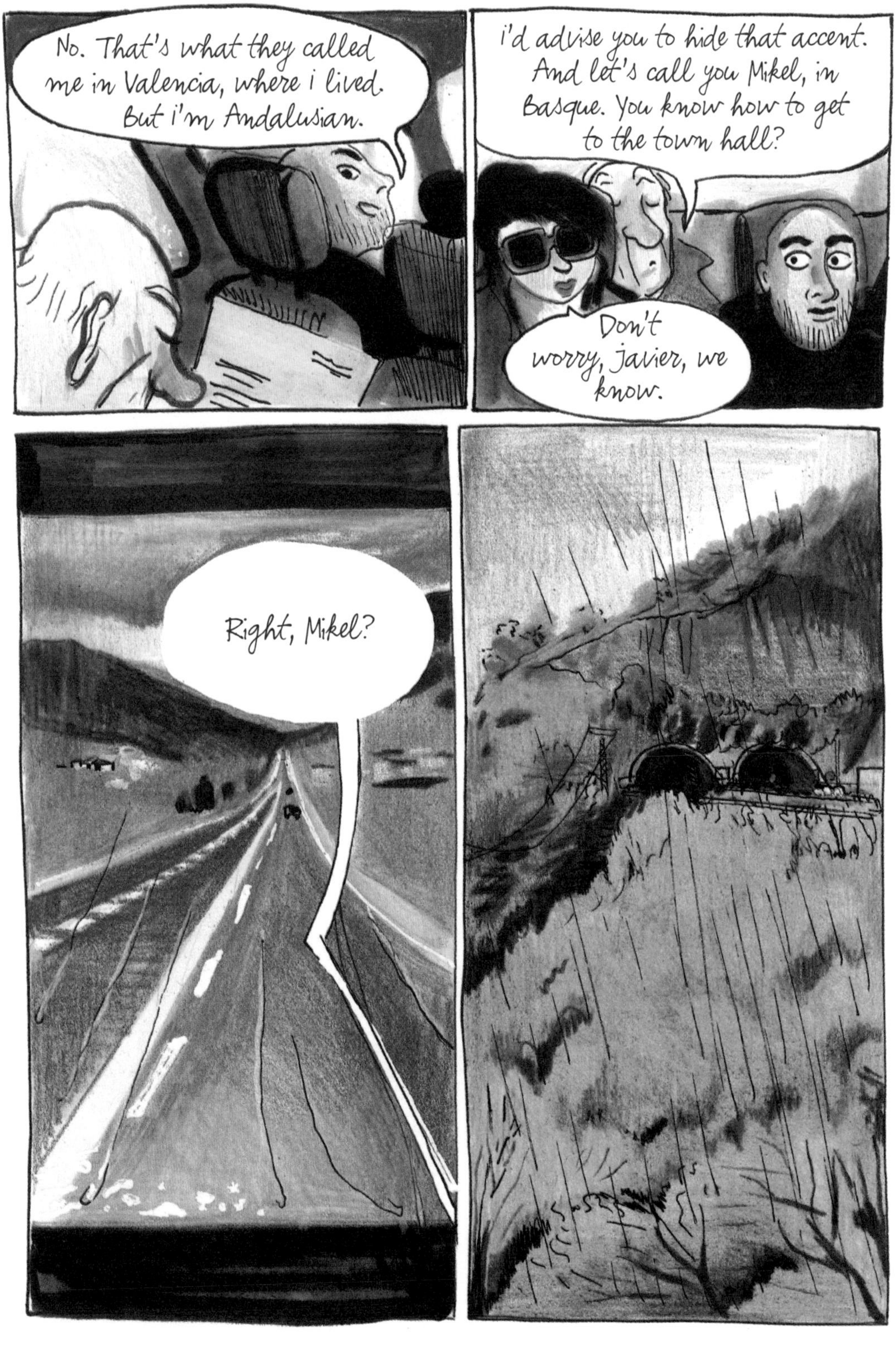
No. That's what they called me in Valencia, where i lived. But i'm Andalusian.
i'd advise you to hide that accent. And let's call you Mikel, in Basque. You know how to get to the town hall?
Don't worry, Javier, we know.
Right, Mikel?

Leitzaran, Navarra.

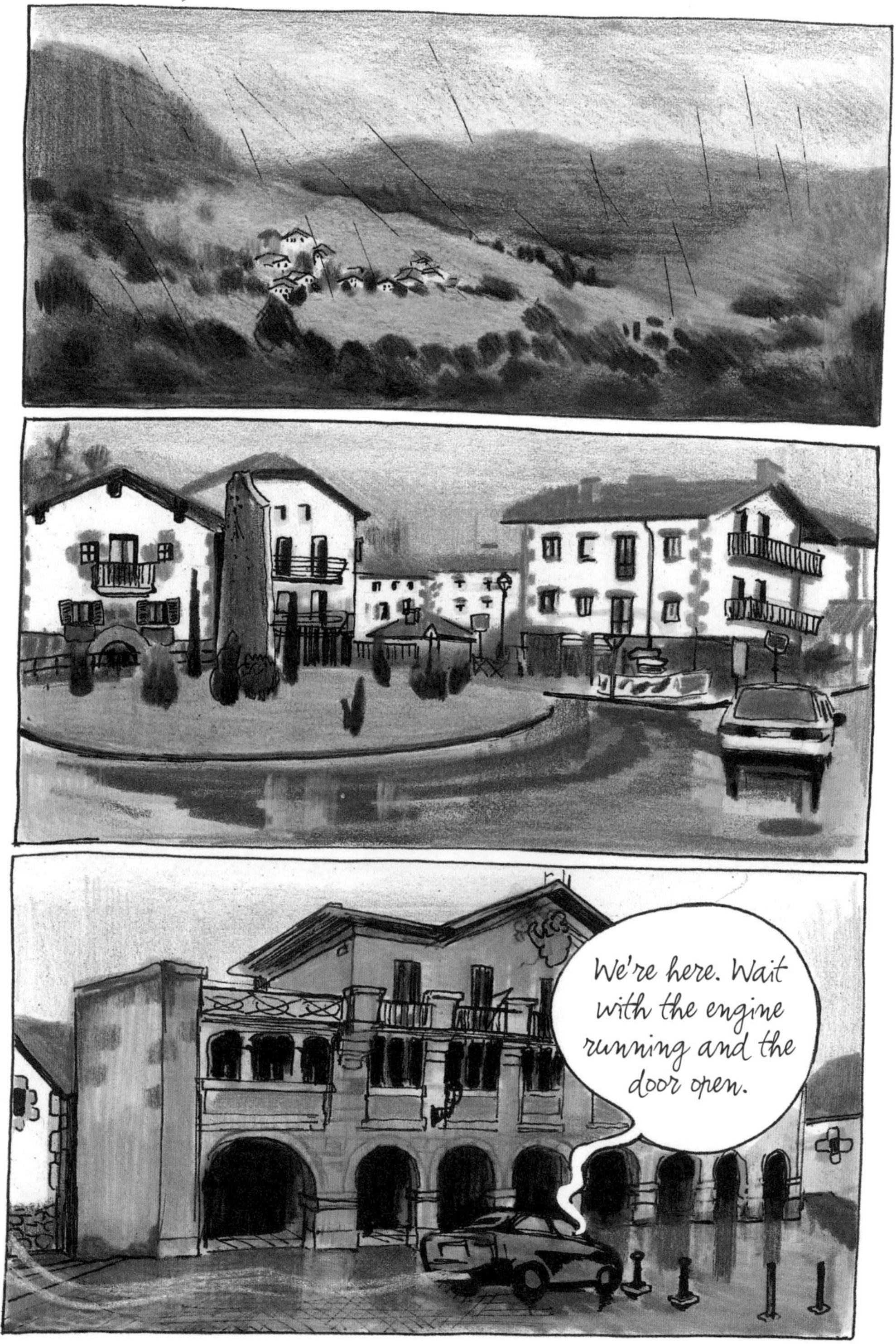
We're here. Wait with the engine running and the door open.

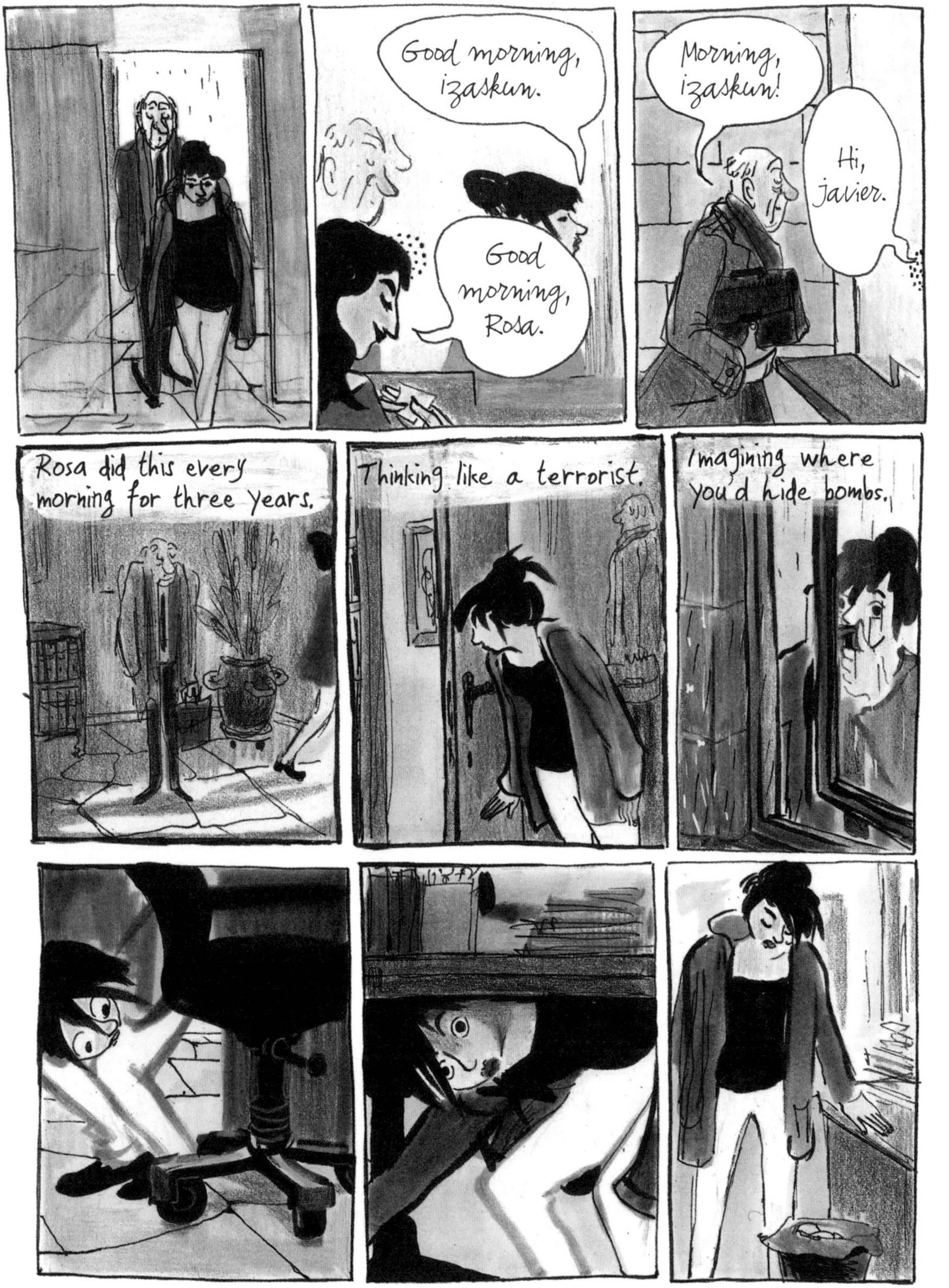
Good morning, izaskun.
Good morning, Rosa.
Morning, izaskun!
Hi, Javier.
Rosa did this every morning for three years.
Thinking like a terrorist.
Imagining where you'd hide bombs.

Everything's fine. What time will you be done, Javier?

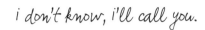

i don't know, i'll call you.

"As usual."

Today's mail.

All clean. Nothing explosive...

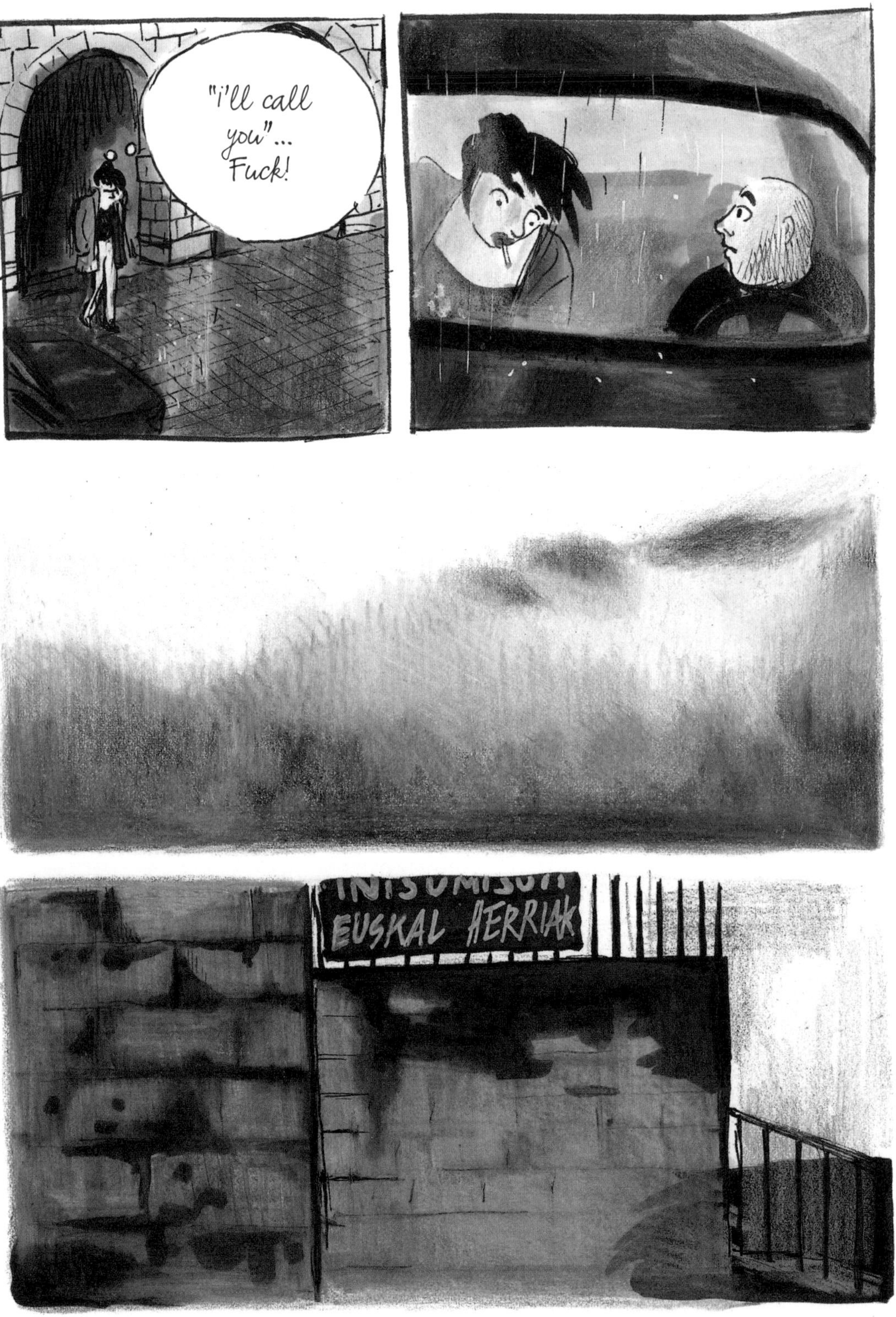
"i'll call you"... Fuck!
EUSKAL HERRIAK

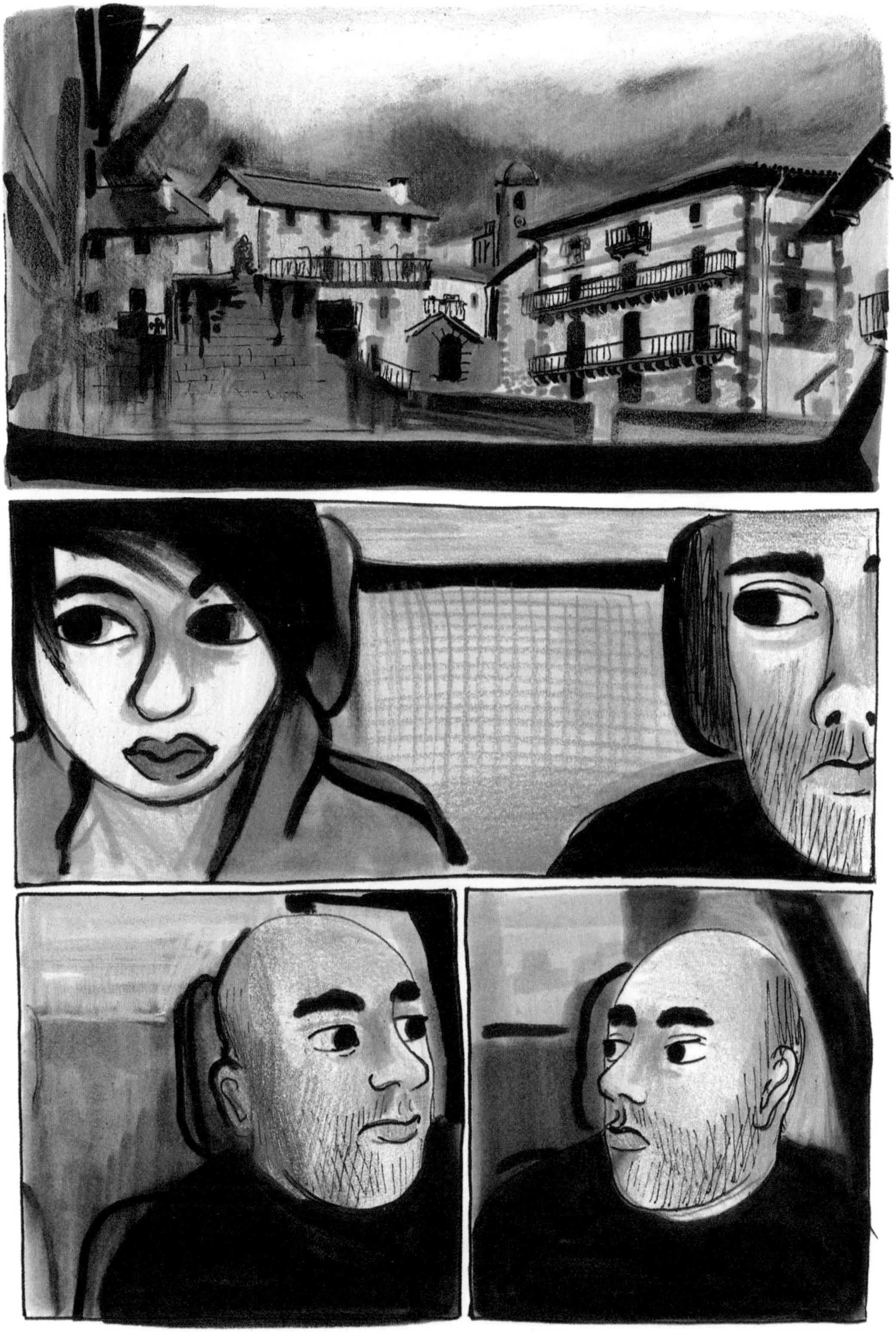

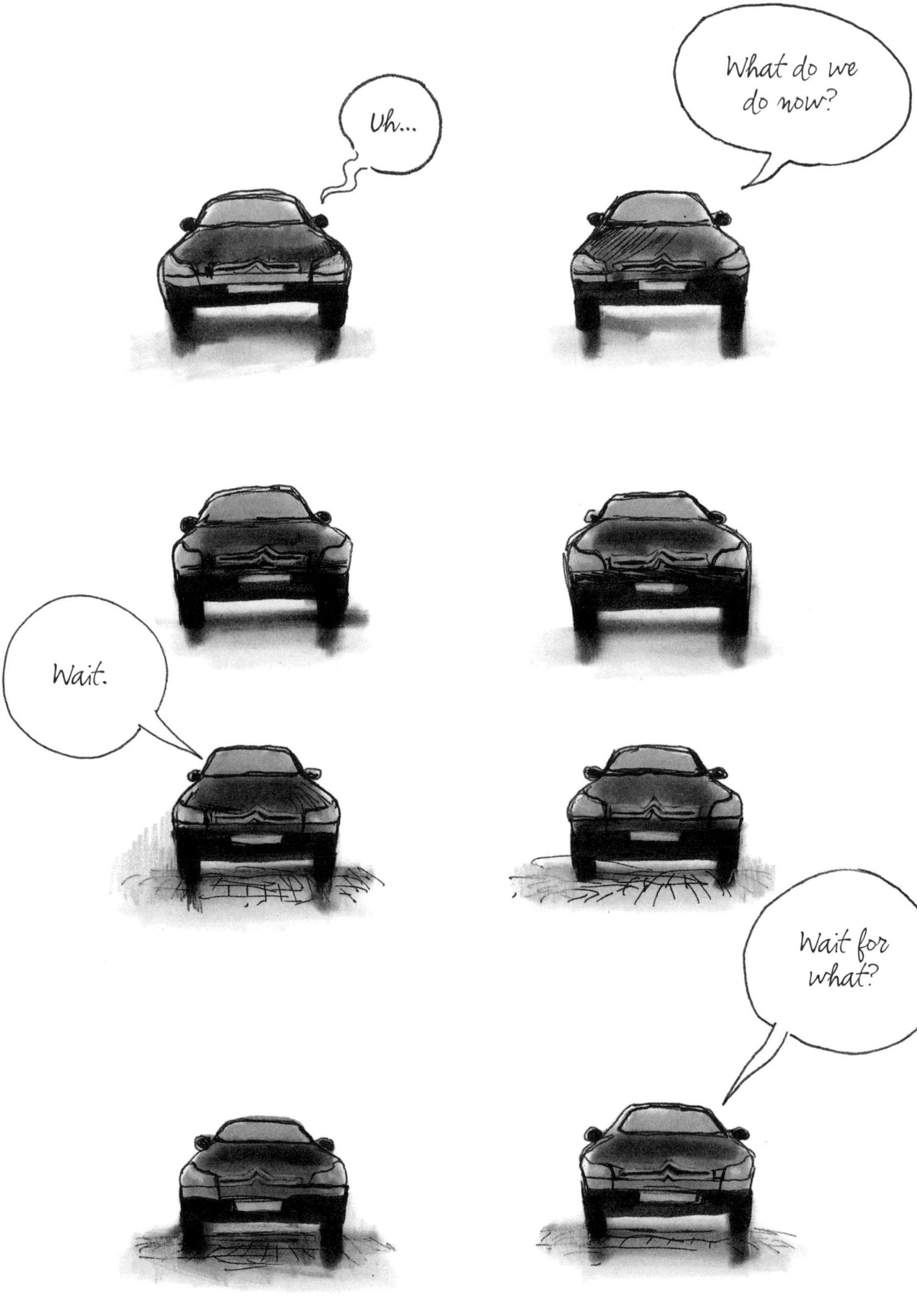
Uh...
What do we do now?
Wait.
Wait for what?

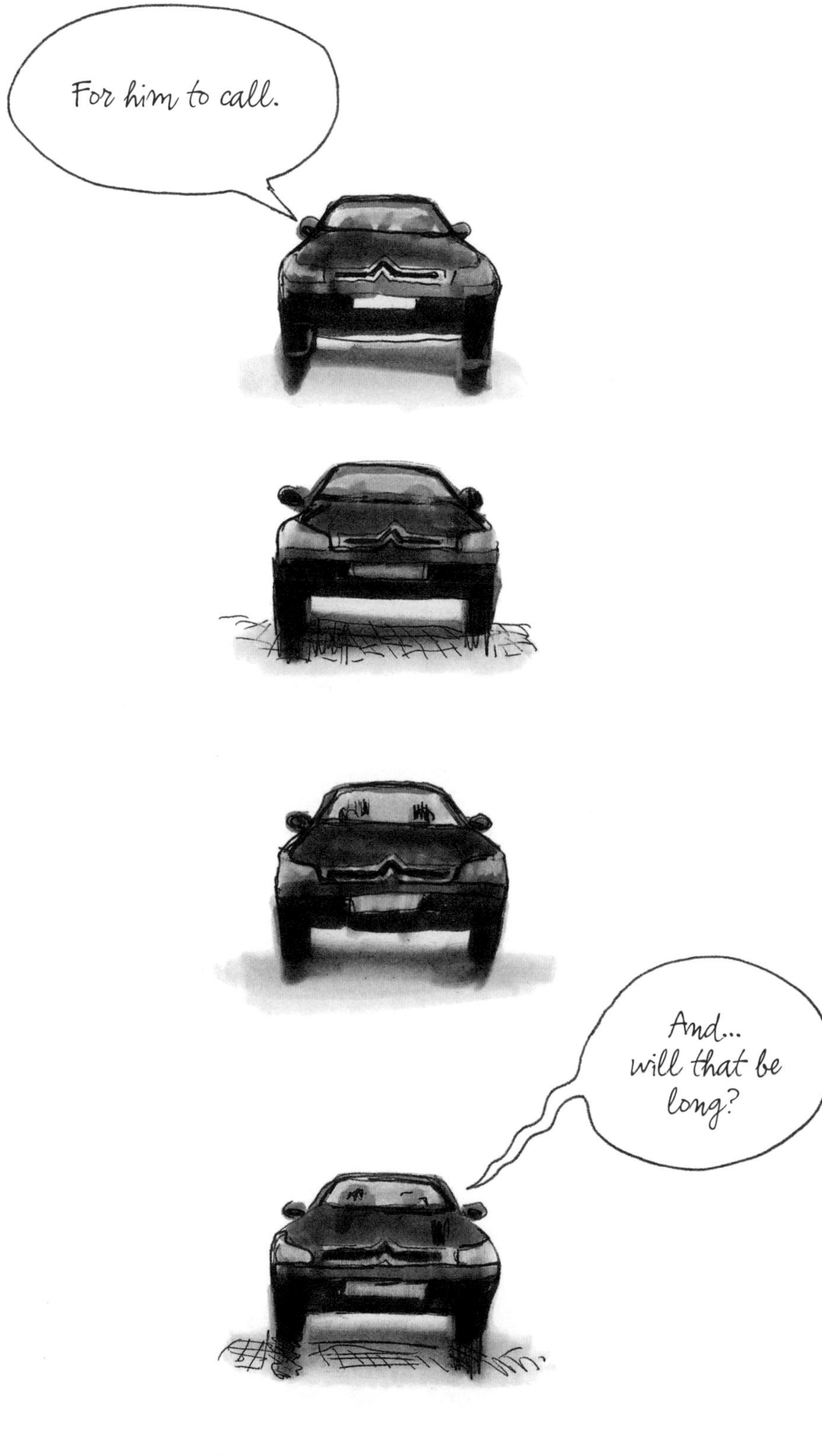
For him to call.
And... will that be long?

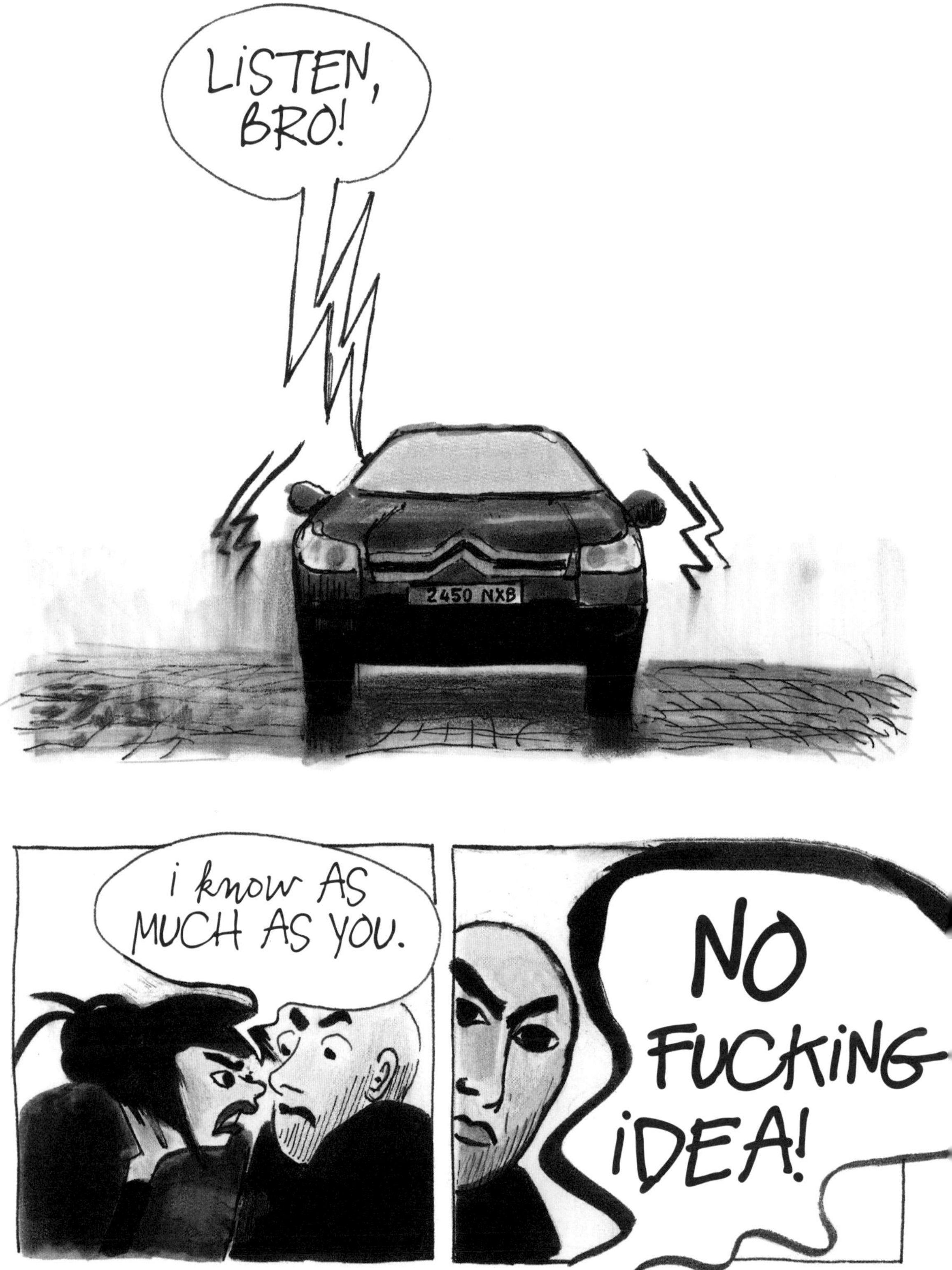
LiSTEN, BRO!
2450 NXB
i know AS MUCH AS YOU.
NO FUCKiNG iDEA!

Don't ever use that tone with me again.

And don't call me "BRO".

i'm your other half. That's what you said.

And if my questions bother you, FUCK OFF!

Ok, sorry, Mikel. i'm tired.

i'm sorry, i shouldn't have raised my voice.

i was just trying to figure out if I can go home to have lunch with my wife...

See my kids, read, write...

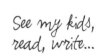

139

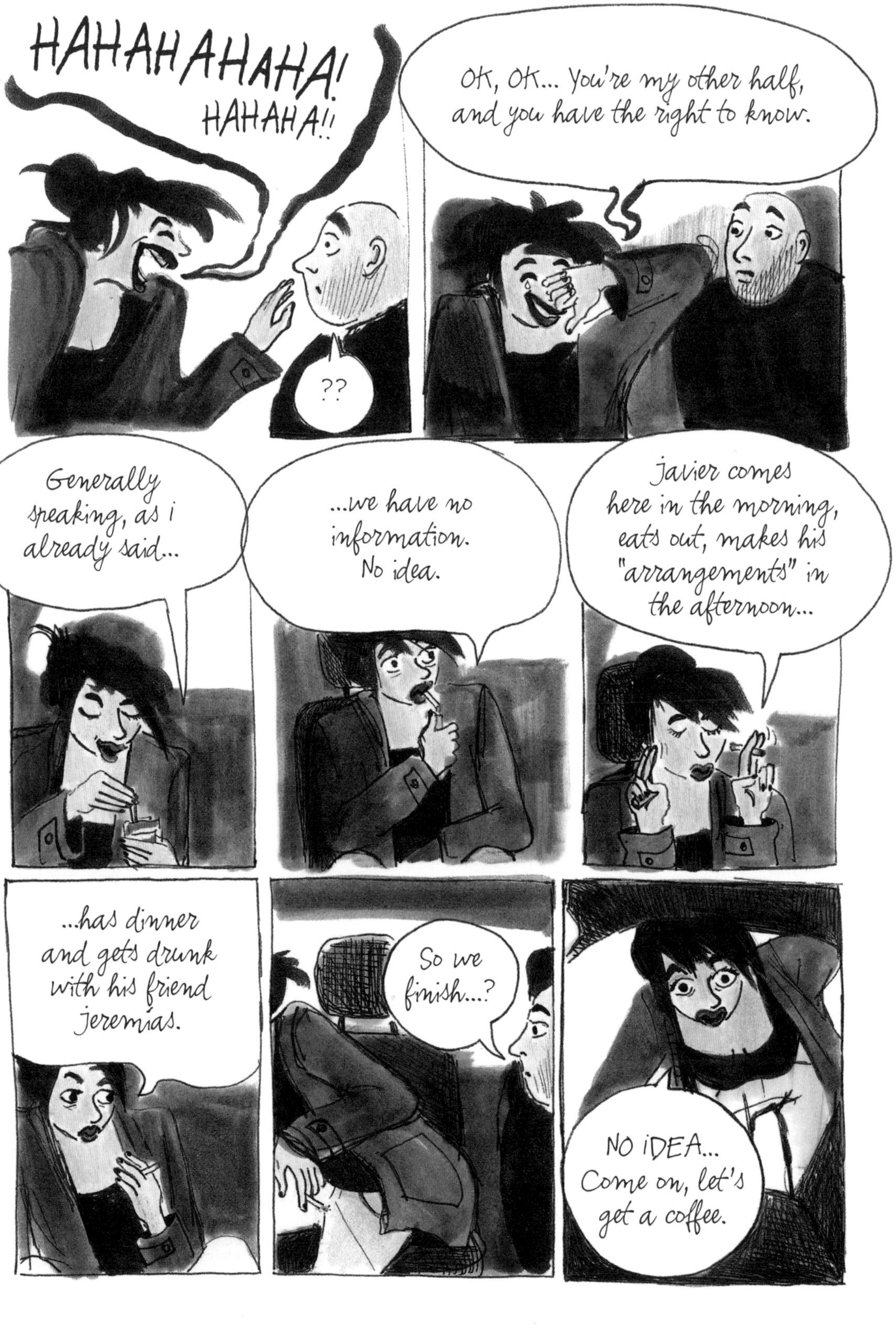
HAHAHAHAHA! HAHAHA!!
??
OK, OK... You're my other half, and you have the right to know.
Generally speaking, as i already said...
...we have no information. No idea.
Javier comes here in the morning, eats out, makes his "arrangements" in the afternoon...
...has dinner and gets drunk with his friend Jeremias.
So we finish...?
NO IDEA... Come on, let's get a coffee.

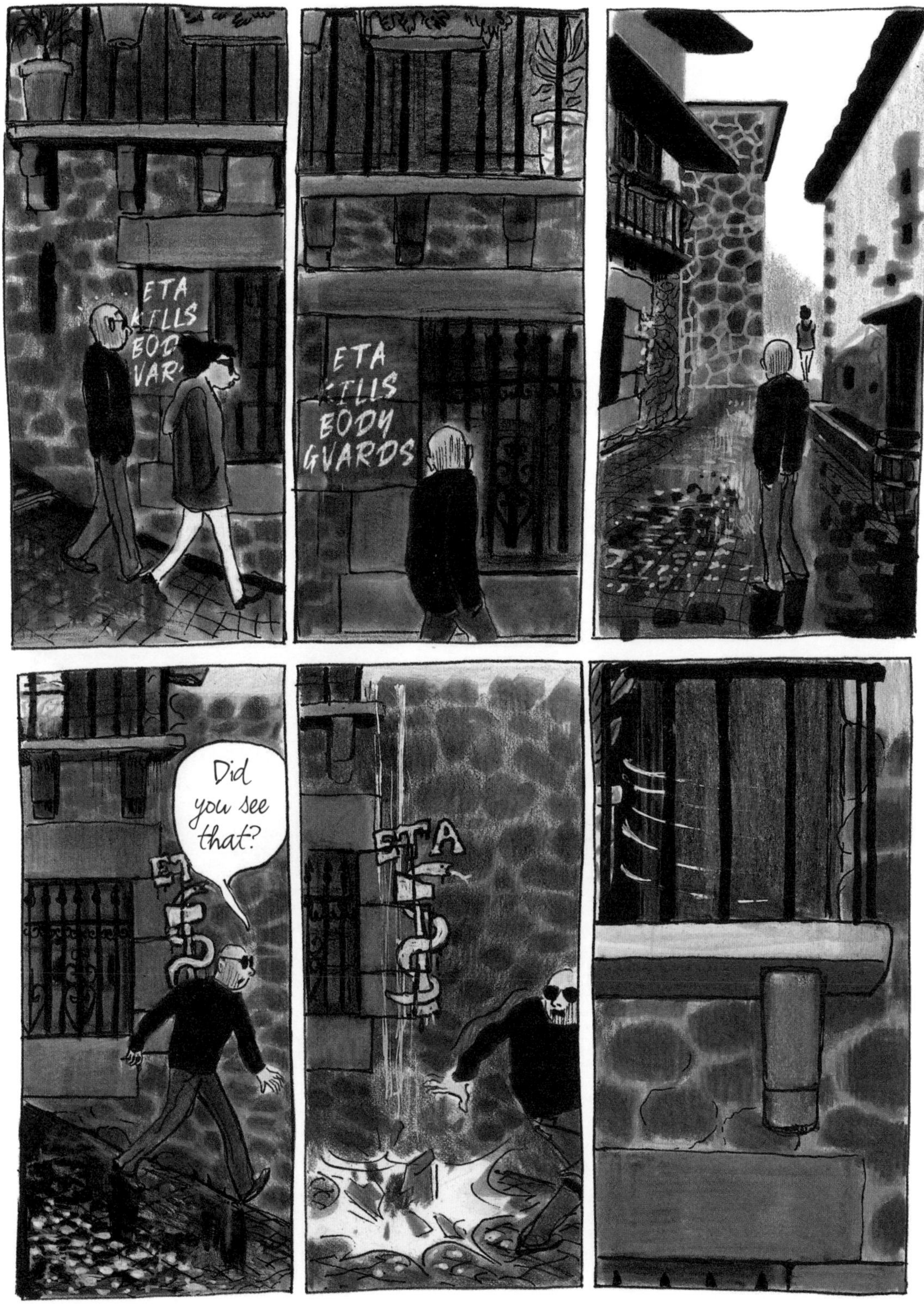
ETA KILLS BODY GUARDS
Did you see that?

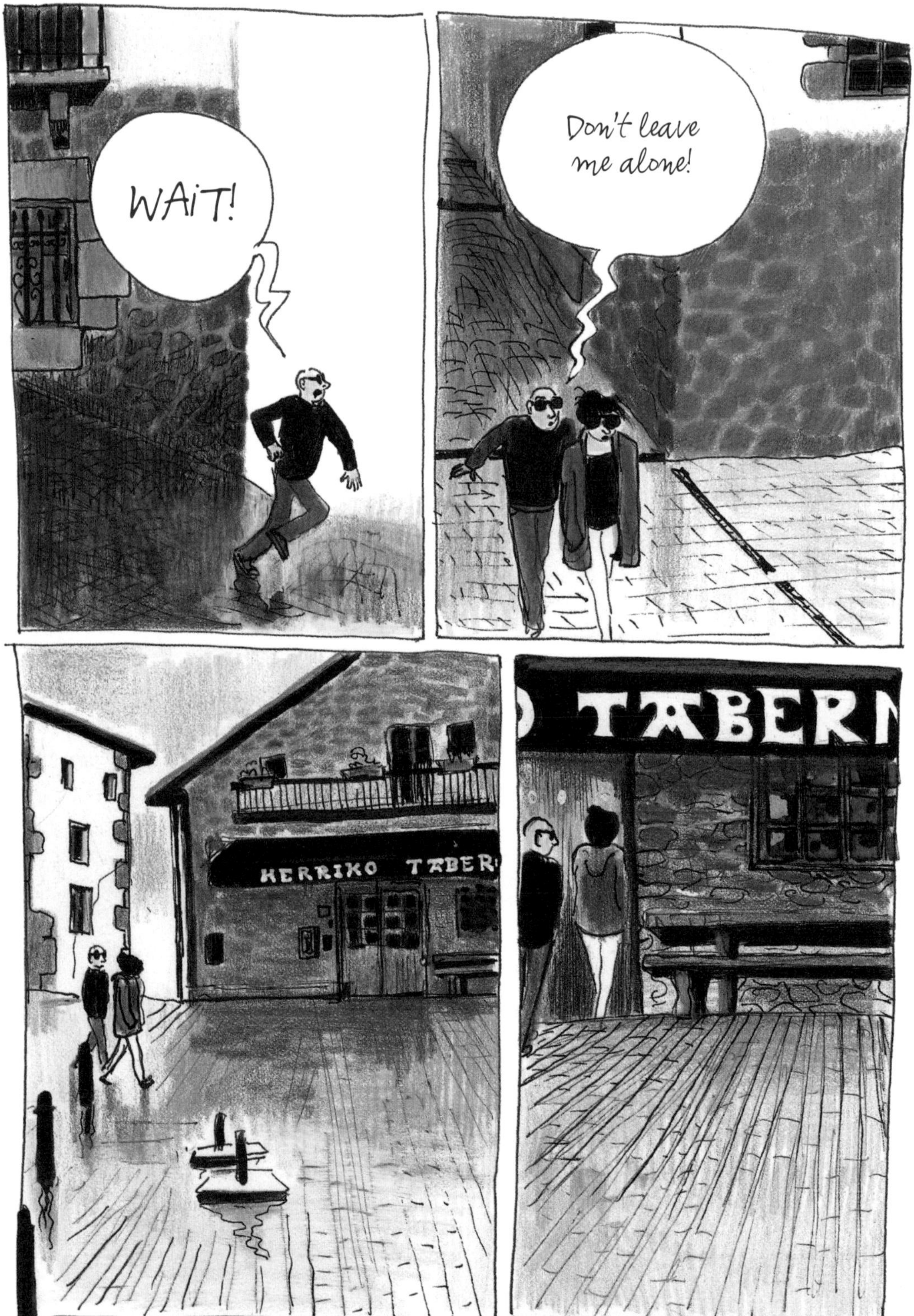
WAIT!
Don't leave me alone!
HERRIKO TABER
TABERN

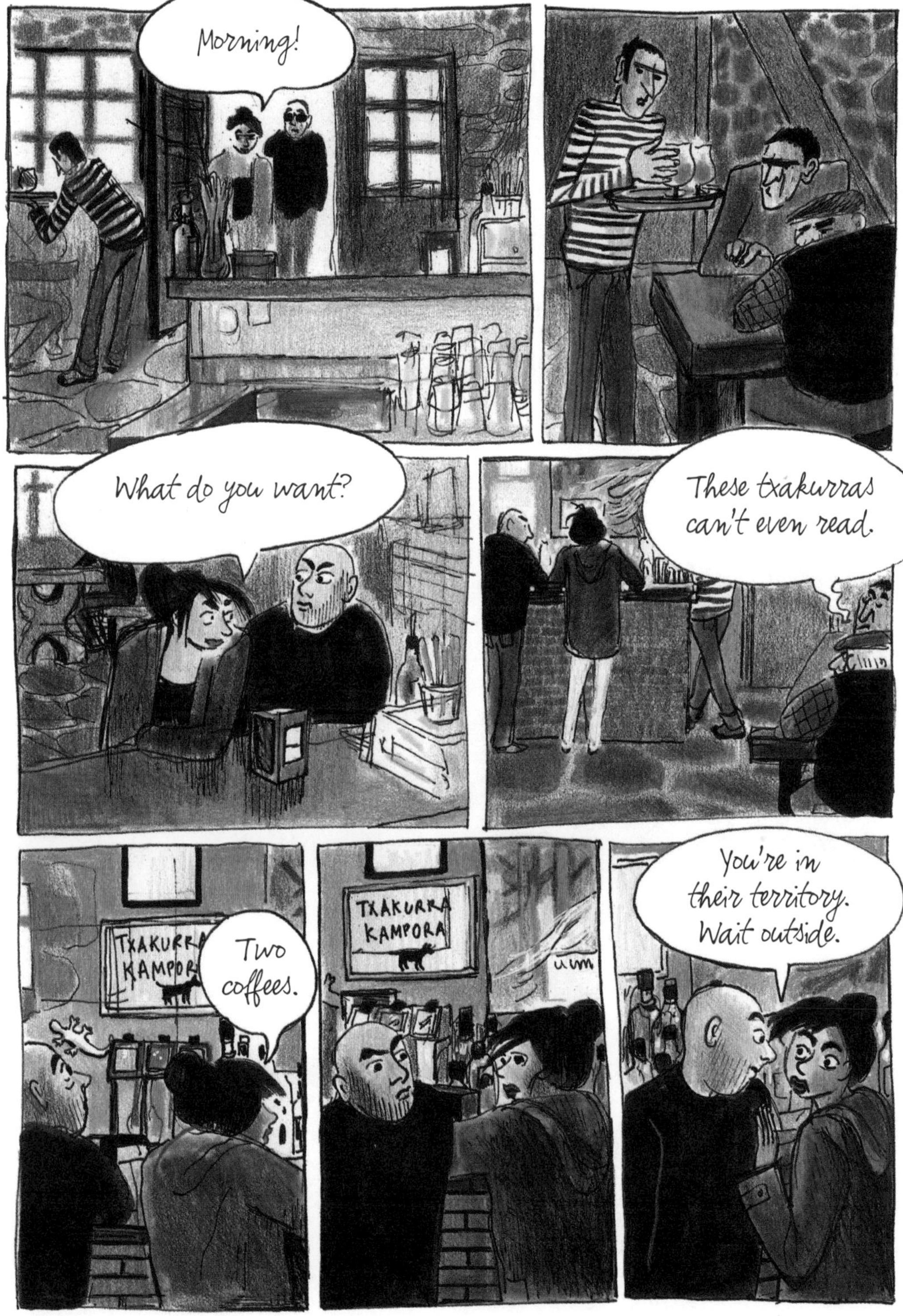
Morning!
What do you want?
These txakurras can't even read.
TXAKURRA KAMPORA
Two coffees.
TXAKURRA KAMPORA
You're in their territory. Wait outside.

Txakurra kampora: No dogs allowed.

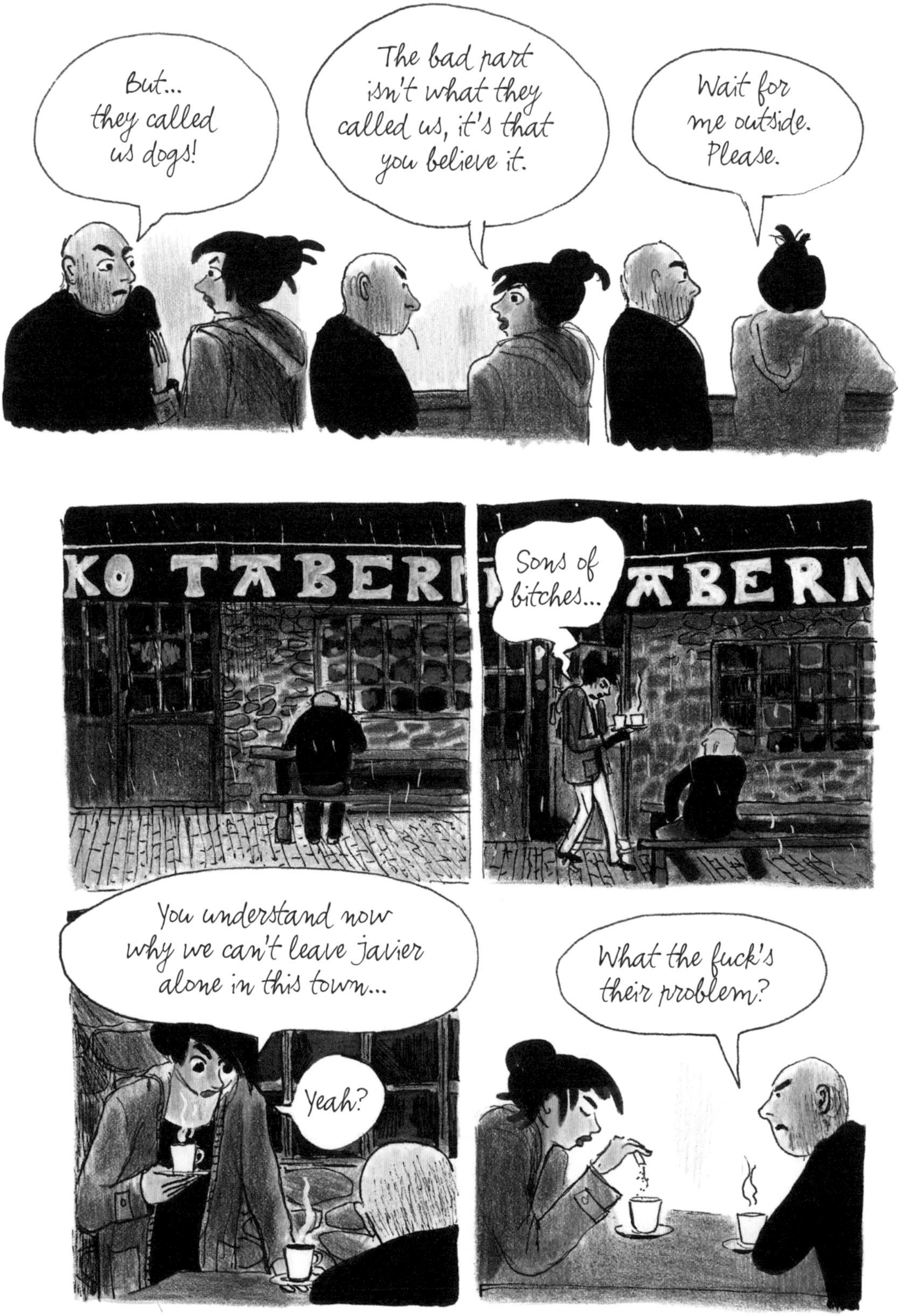
But... they called us dogs!
The bad part isn't what they called us, it's that you believe it.
Wait for me outside. Please.
KO TABERN
Sons of bitches...
TABERN
You understand now why we can't leave Javier alone in this town...
Yeah?
What the fuck's their problem?

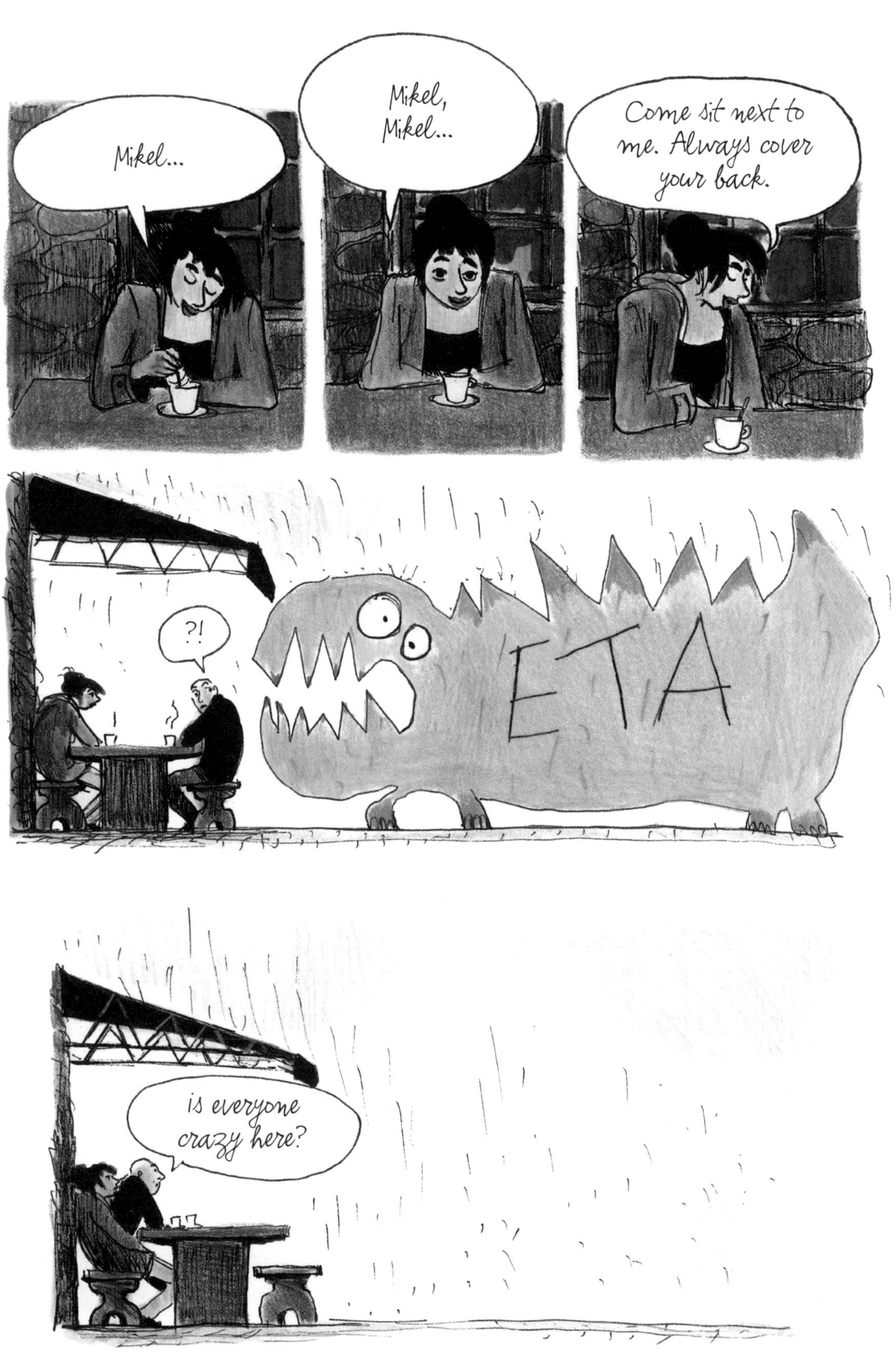
Mikel...
Mikel, Mikel...
Come sit next to me. Always cover your back.
?!
ETA
is everyone crazy here?

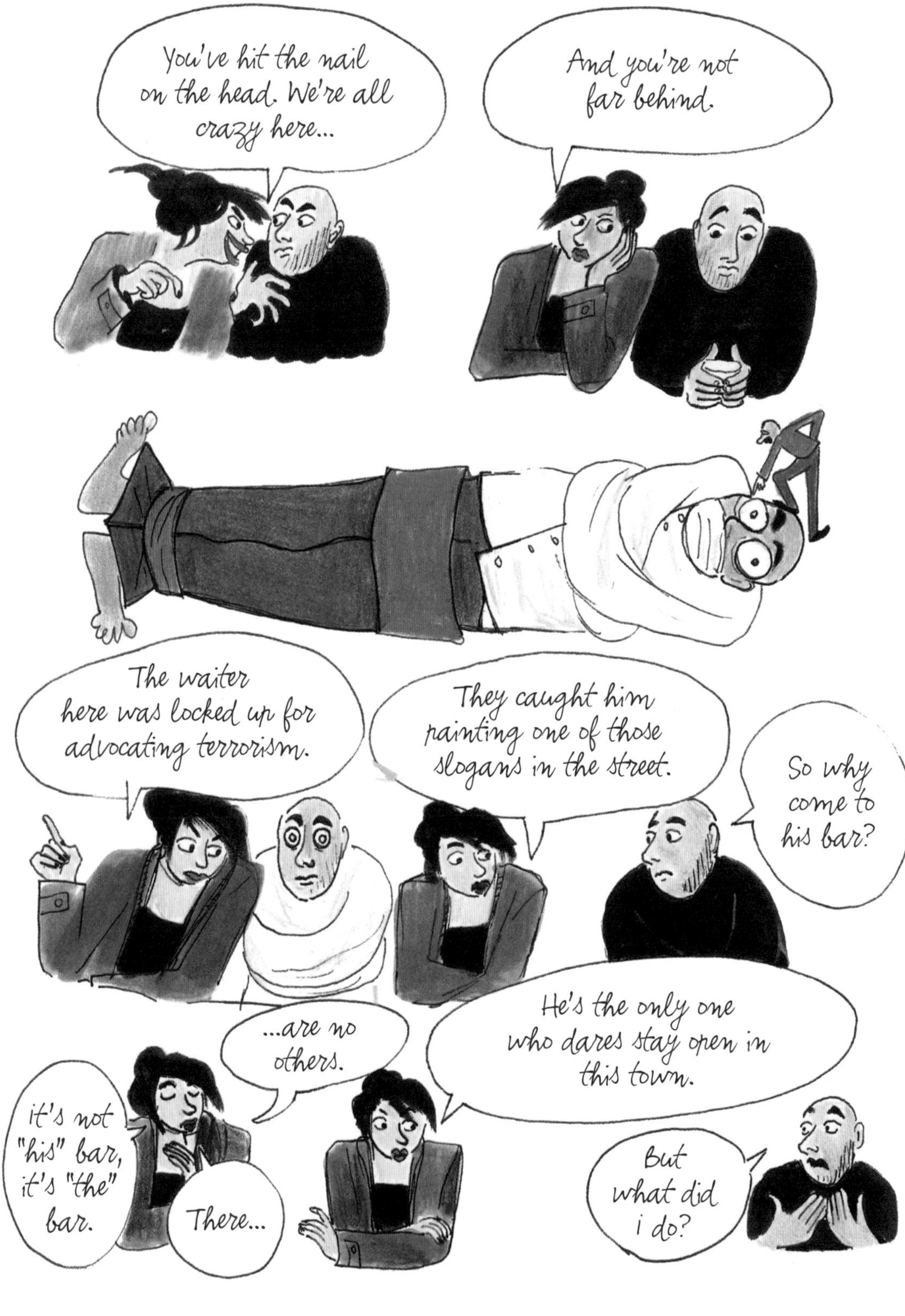
You've hit the nail on the head. We're all crazy here...
And you're not far behind.
The waiter here was locked up for advocating terrorism.
They caught him painting one of those slogans in the street.
So why come to his bar?
it's not "his" bar, it's "the" bar.
There...
...are no others.
He's the only one who dares stay open in this town.
But what did i do?

You're the mayor's txakurra...

And it was the mayor who turned him in.

The bad guys don't hide here.

They're proud of what they do...

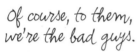

Of course, to them, we're the bad guys.

Another coffee?

Yeah.

How do you say "bathroom" in Basque?

Komunak...

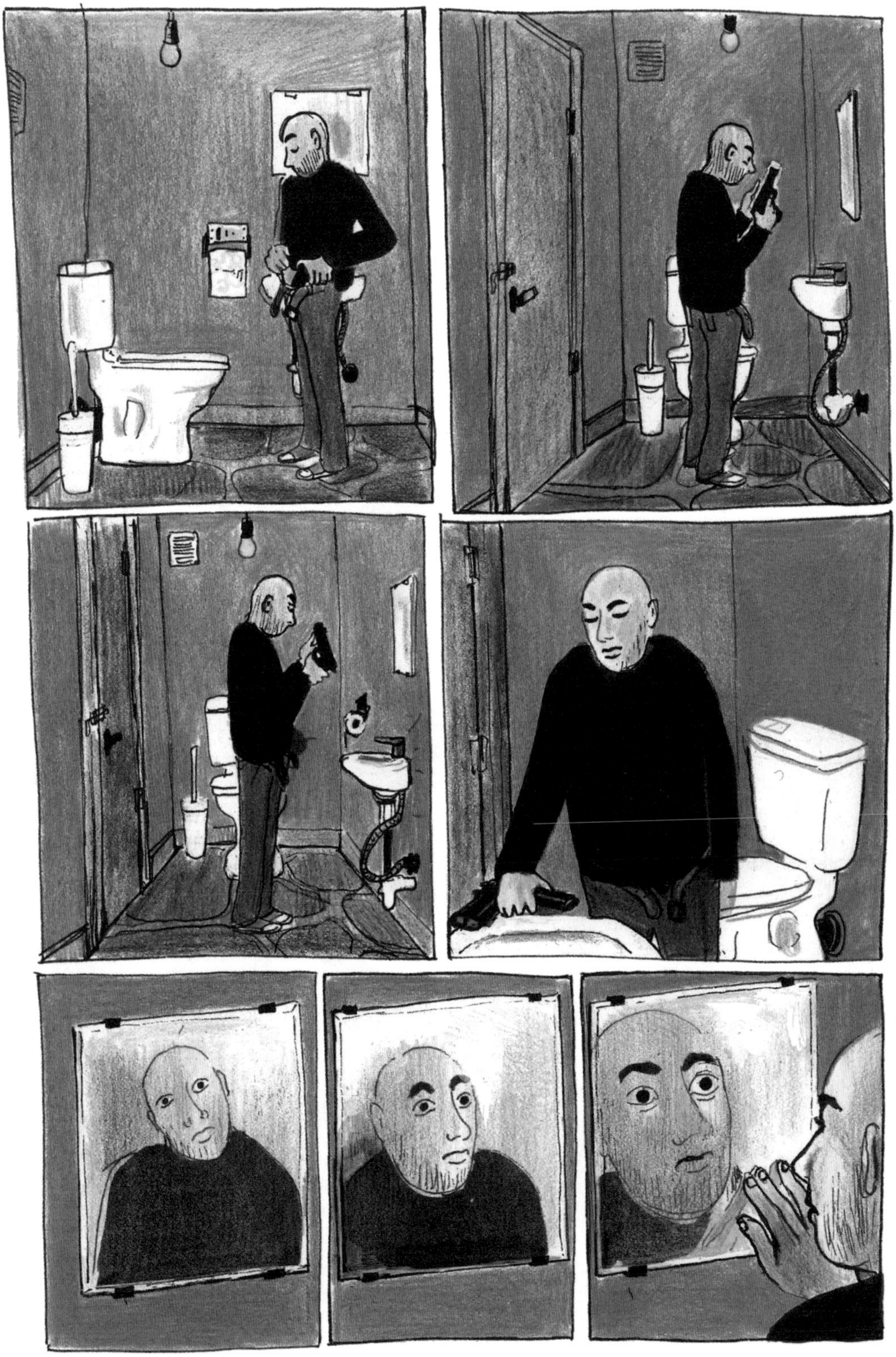

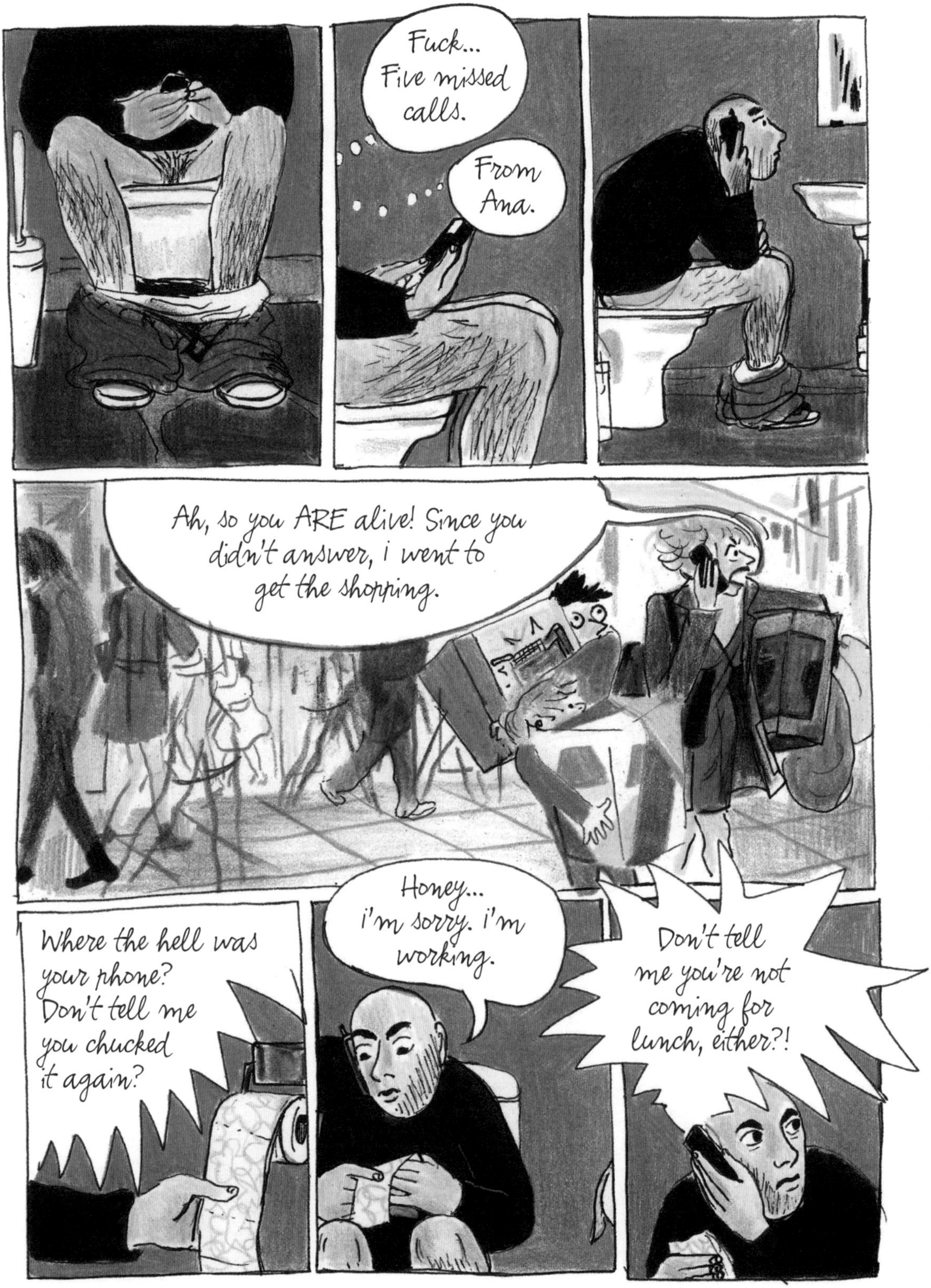
Fuck...
Five missed calls.
From Ana.
Ah, so you ARE alive! Since you didn't answer, i went to get the shopping.
Where the hell was your phone? Don't tell me you chucked it again?
Honey... i'm sorry. i'm working.
Don't tell me you're not coming for lunch, either?!

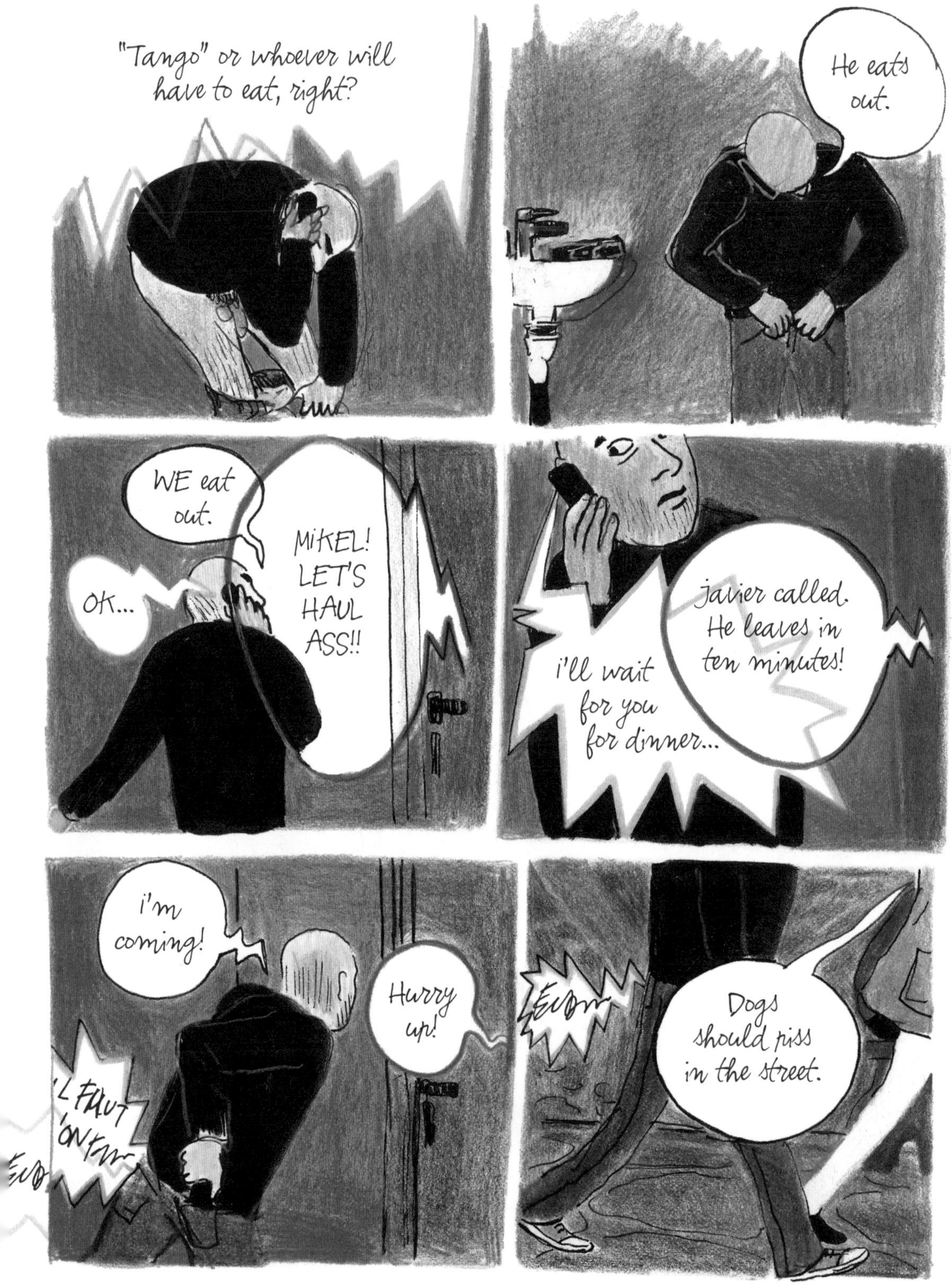
"Tango" or whoever will have to eat, right?
He eats out.
WE eat out.
MIKEL! LET'S HAUL ASS!!
OK...
Javier called. He leaves in ten minutes!
i'll wait for you for dinner...
i'm coming!
Hurry up!
Dogs should piss in the street.

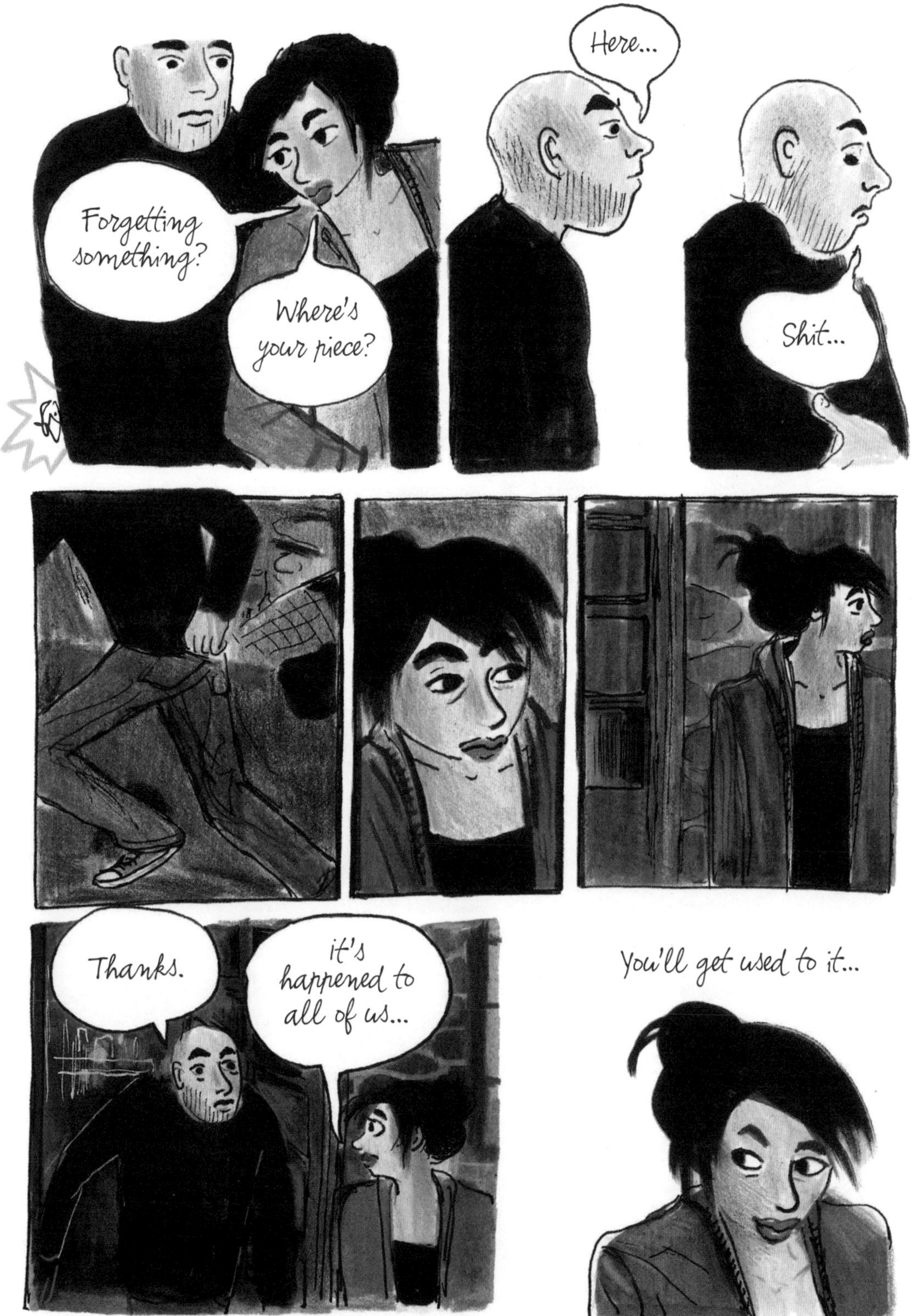
Forgetting something?
Where's your piece?
Here...
Shit...
Thanks.
it's happened to all of us...
You'll get used to it...

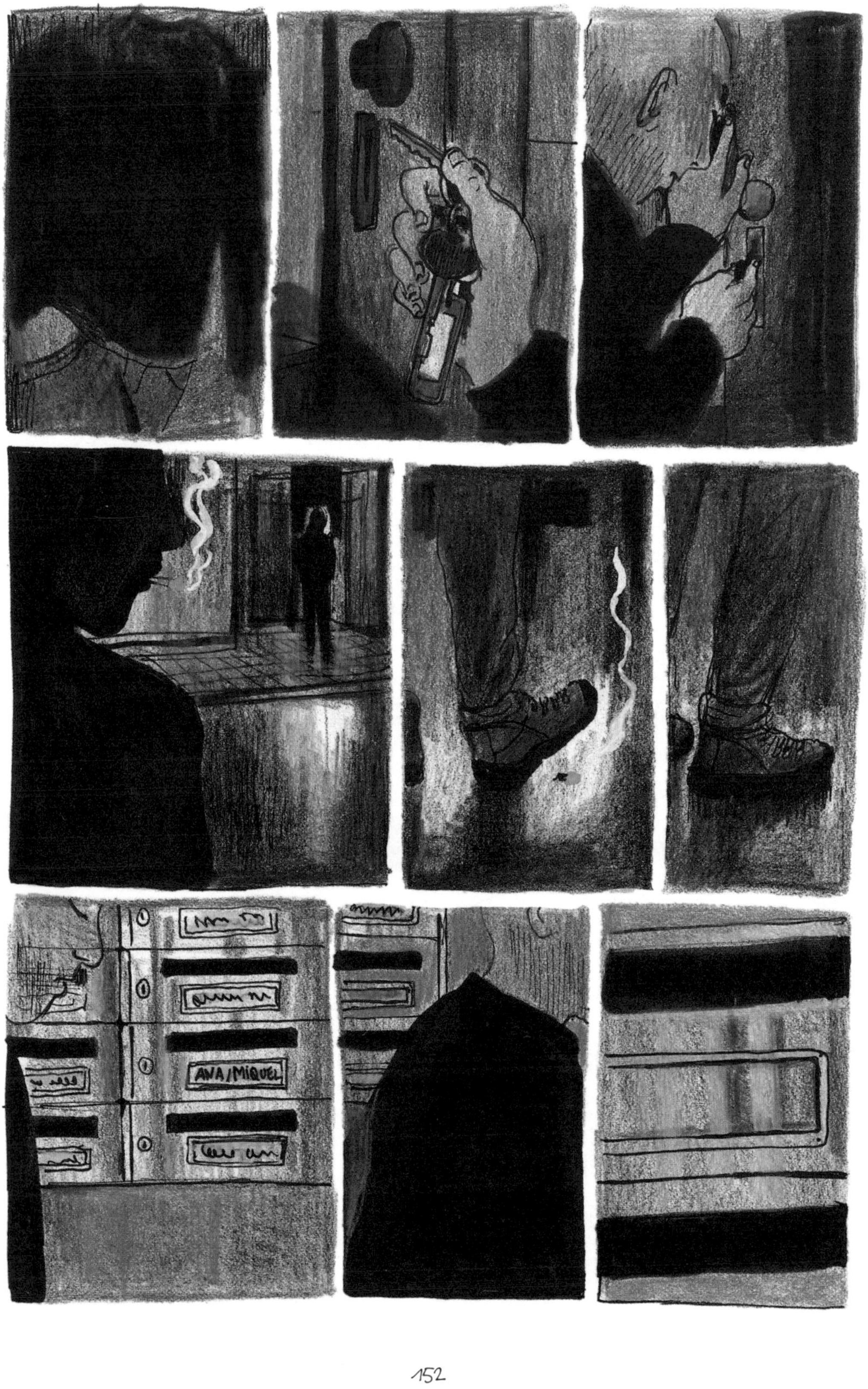
ANA/MIQUEL

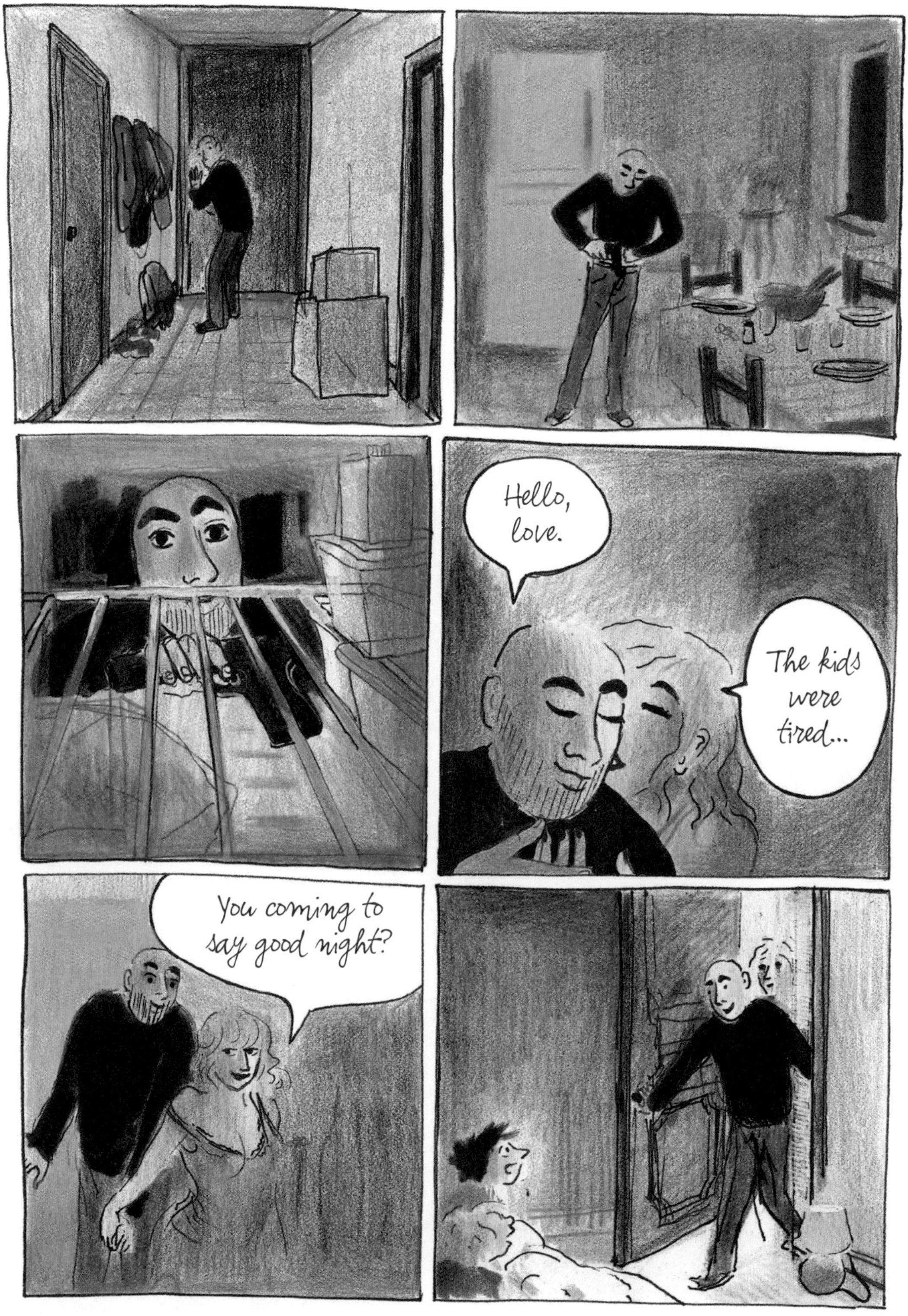
Hello, love.
The kids were tired...
You coming to say good night?

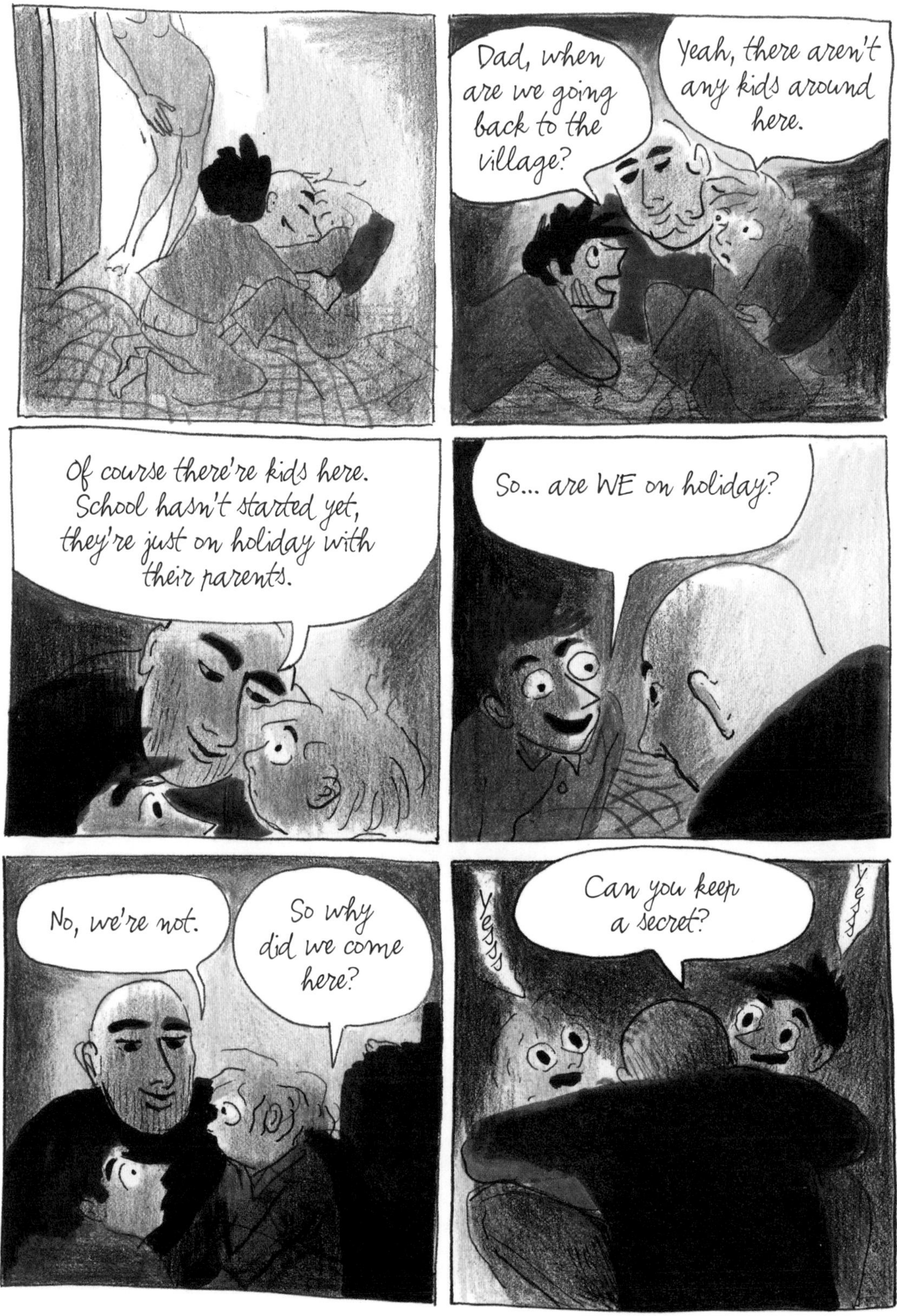
Dad, when are we going back to the village?
Yeah, there aren't any kids around here.
Of course there're kids here. School hasn't started yet, they're just on holiday with their parents.
So... are WE on holiday?
No, we're not.
So why did we come here?
Yesss
Can you keep a secret?
Yesss

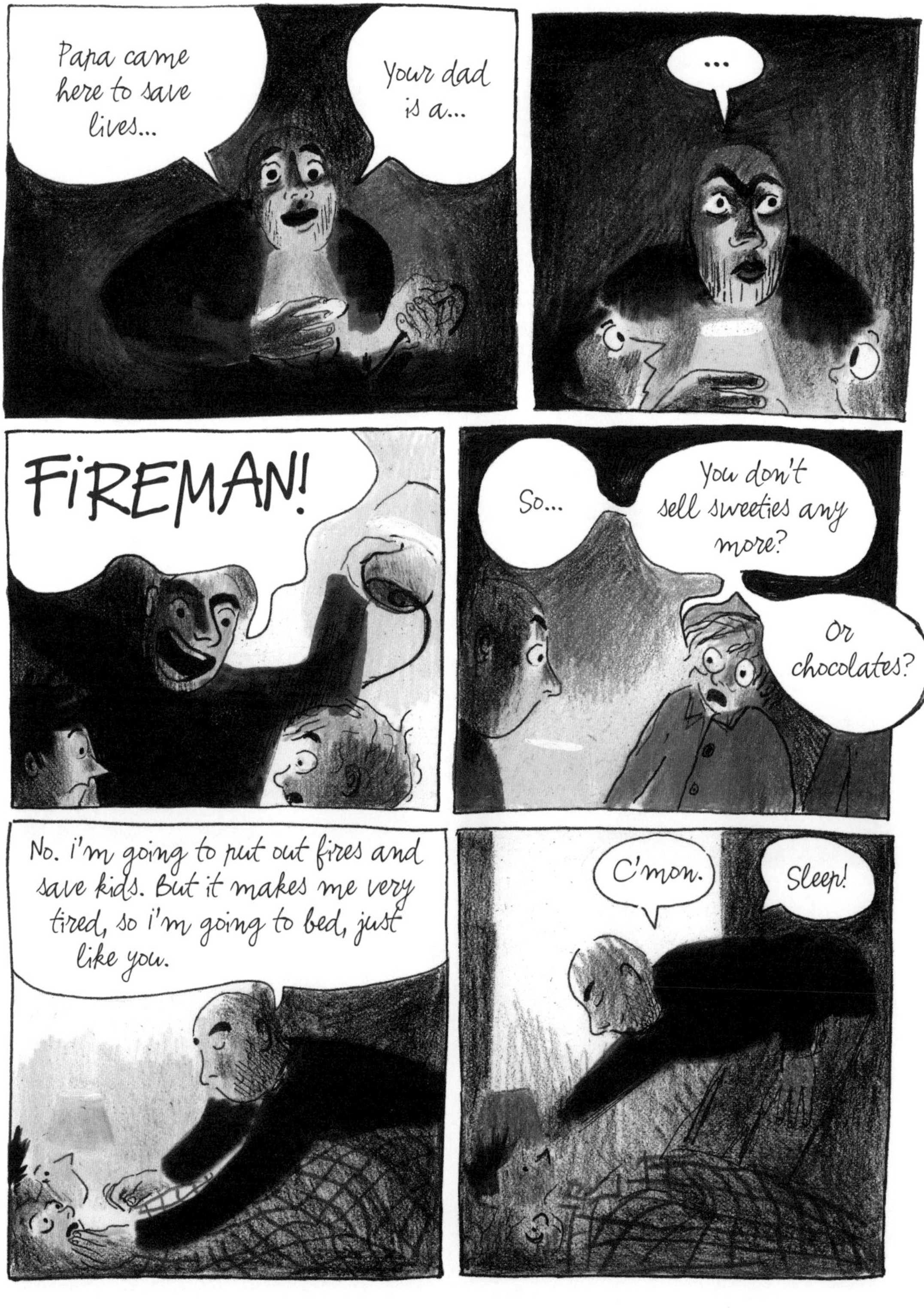
Papa came here to save lives...
Your dad is a...
...
FIREMAN!
So...
You don't sell sweeties any more?
Or chocolates?
No. i'm going to put out fires and save kids. But it makes me very tired, so i'm going to bed, just like you.
C'mon.
Sleep!

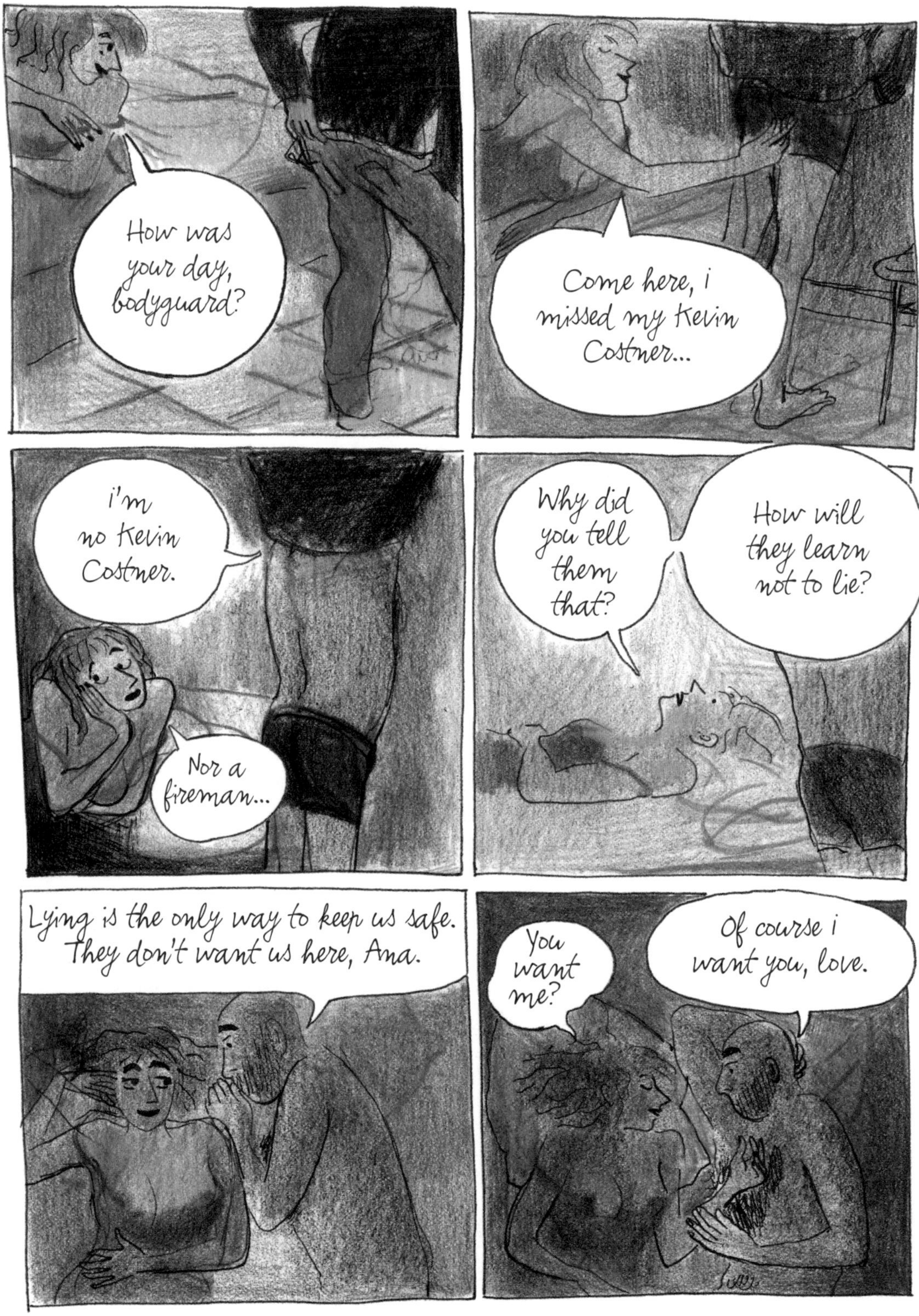
How was your day, bodyguard?
Come here, i missed my Kevin Costner...
i'm no Kevin Costner.
Nor a fireman...
Why did you tell them that?
How will they learn not to lie?
Lying is the only way to keep us safe. They don't want us here, Ana.
You want me?
Of course i want you, love.

What the hell's that smell?

Huh?

What?

is that perfume?

All those missed calls...

And you come home late...

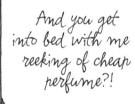
And you get into bed with me reeking of cheap perfume?!

DON'T YOU TOUCH ME!

Love...

157

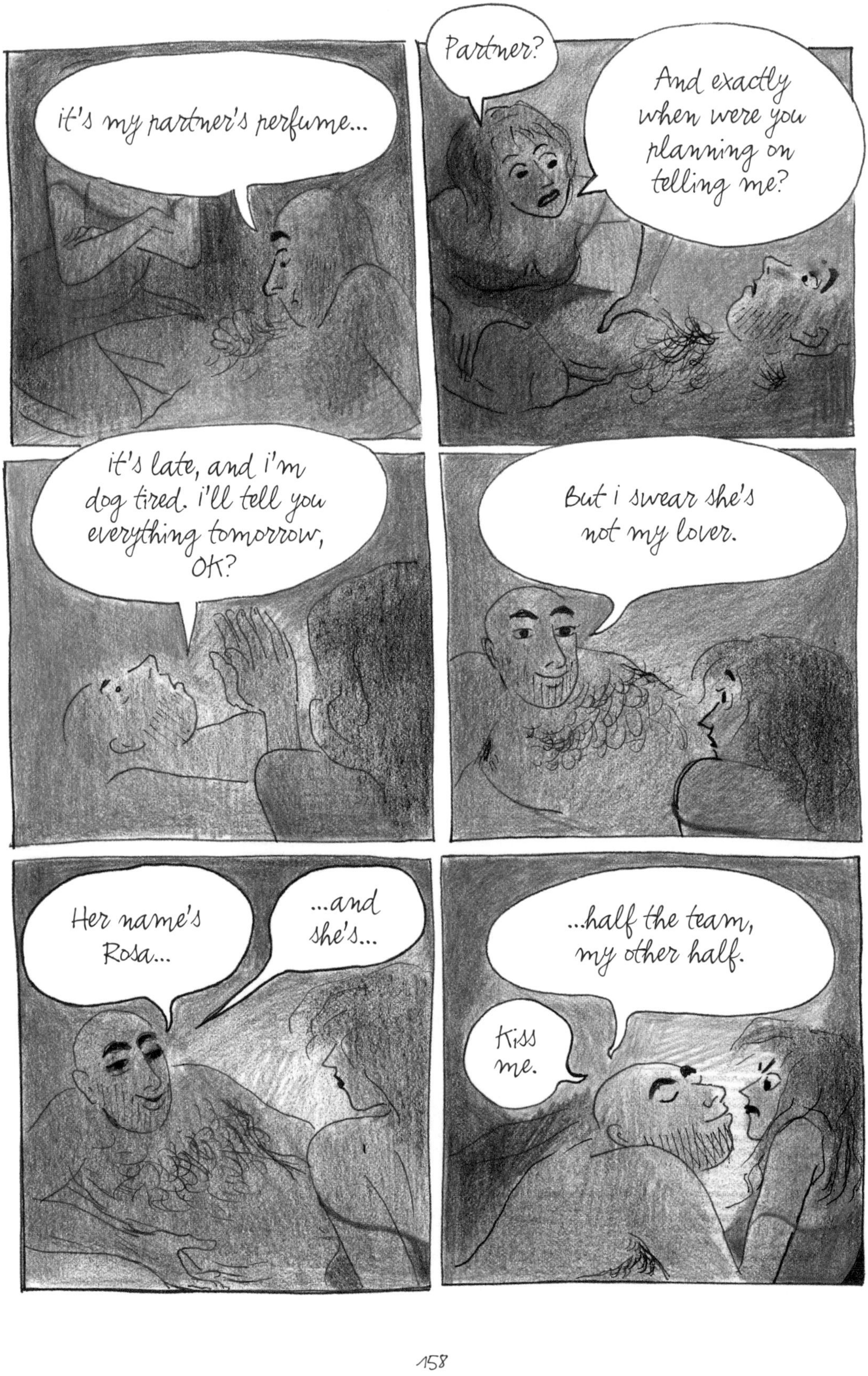
it's my partner's perfume...
Partner?
And exactly when were you planning on telling me?
it's late, and i'm dog tired. i'll tell you everything tomorrow, OK?
But i swear she's not my lover.
Her name's Rosa...
...and she's...
...half the team, my other half.
Kiss me.

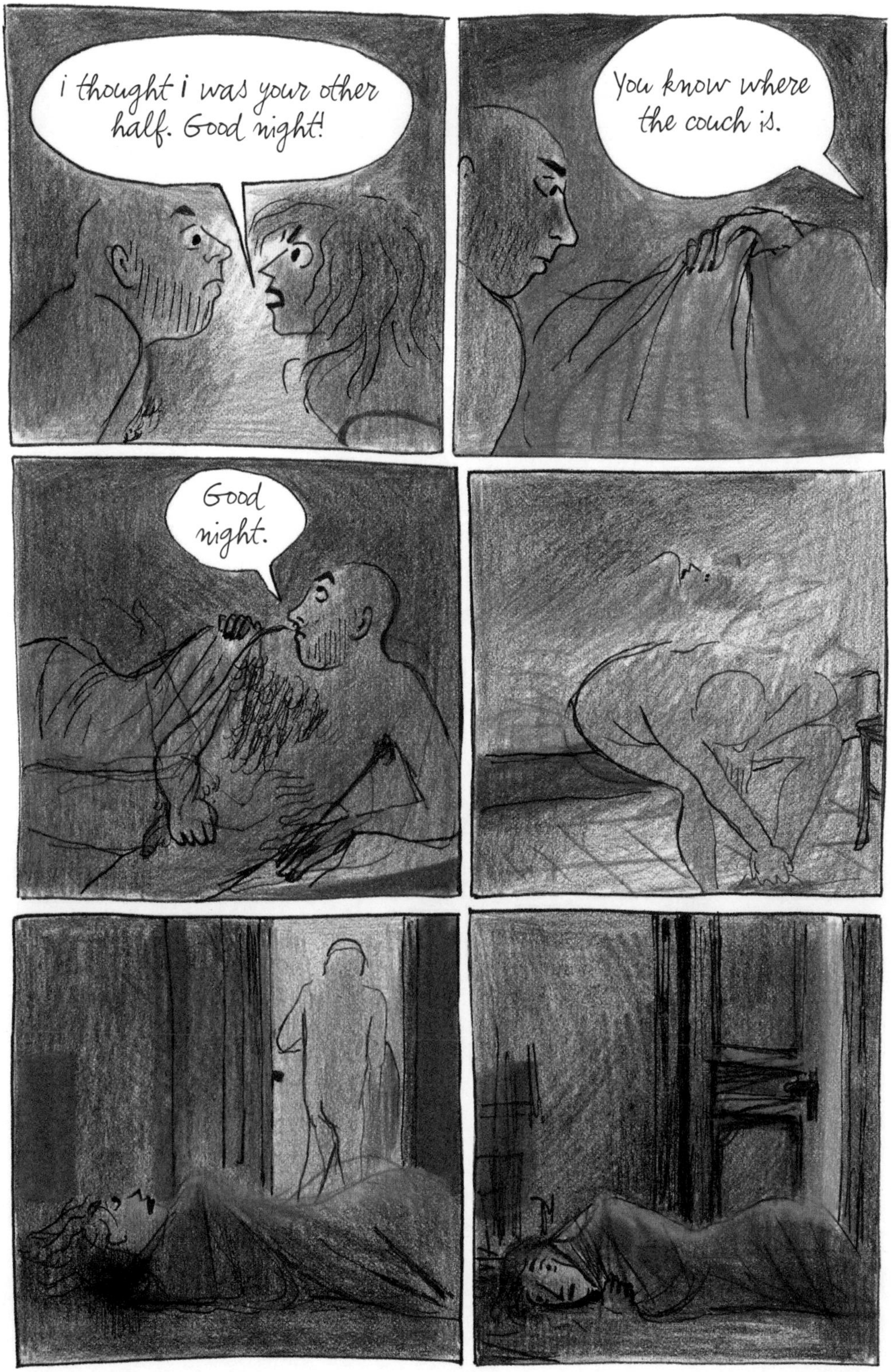
i thought i was your other half. Good night!
You know where the couch is.
Good night.

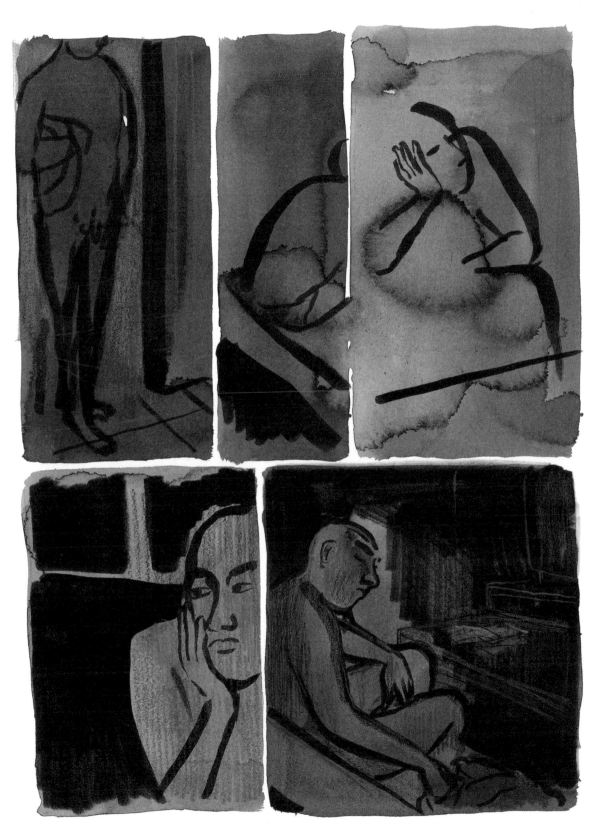

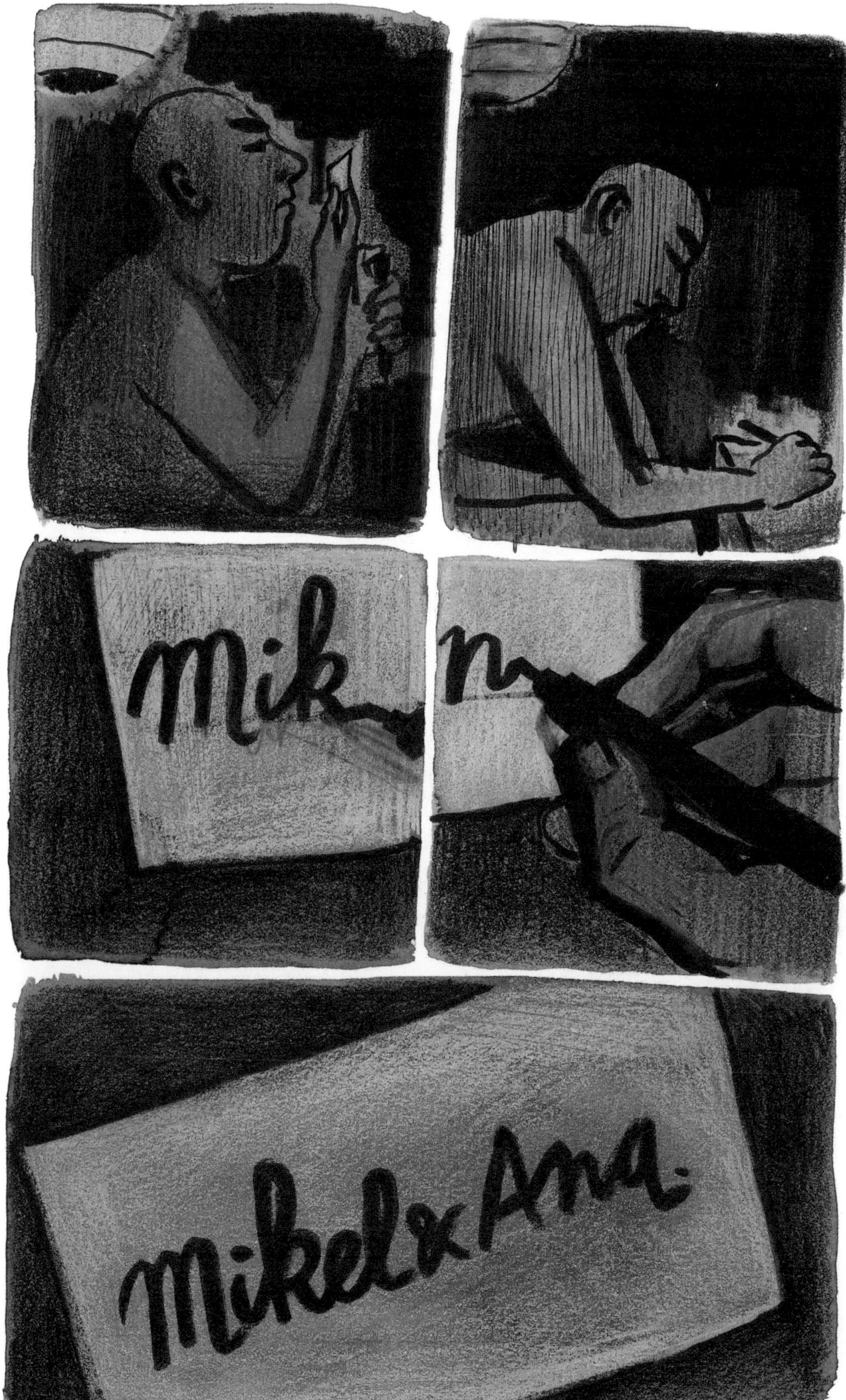
Mik
Mikel & Ana

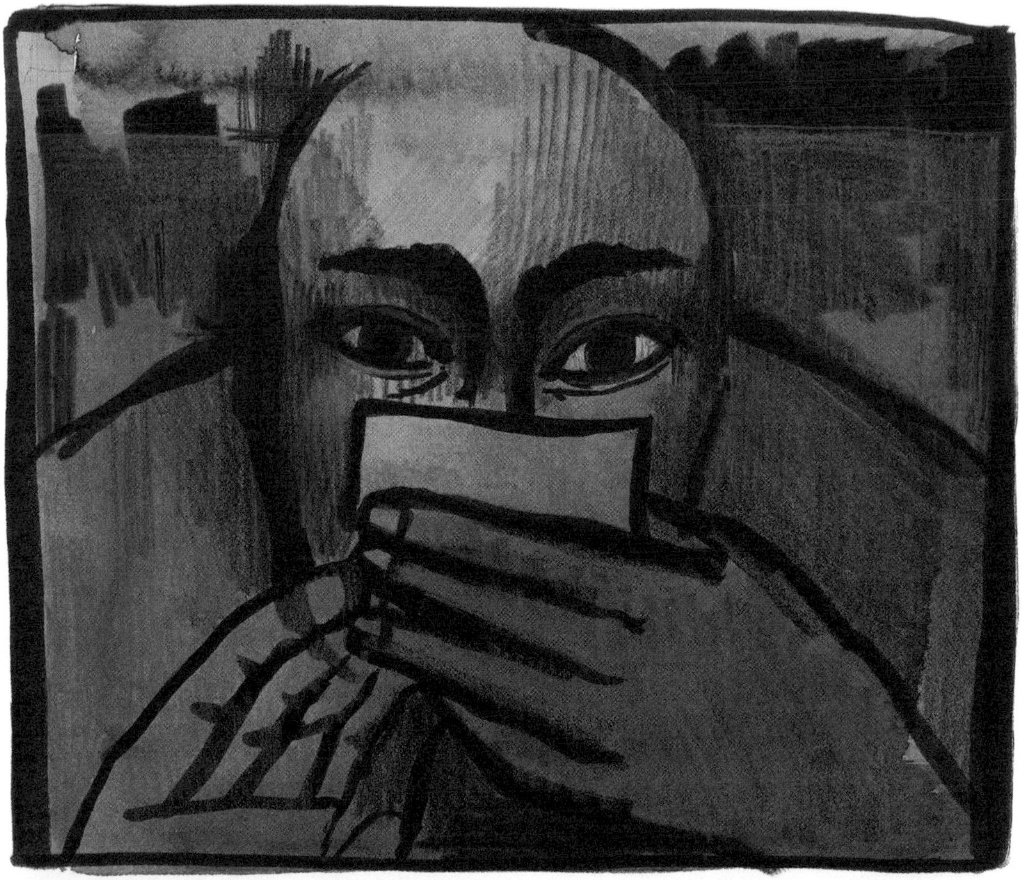

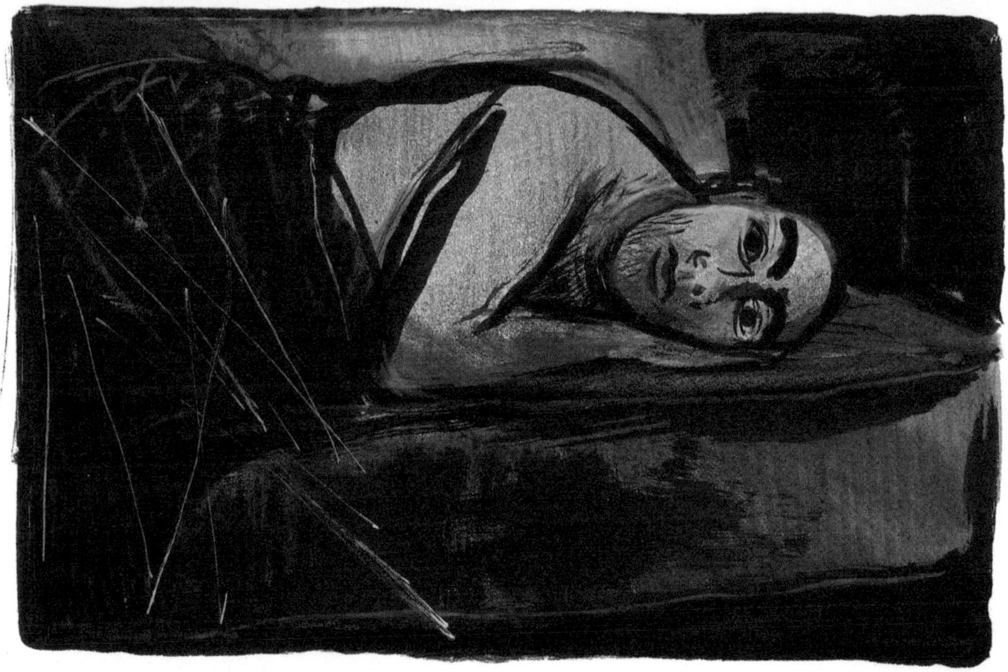

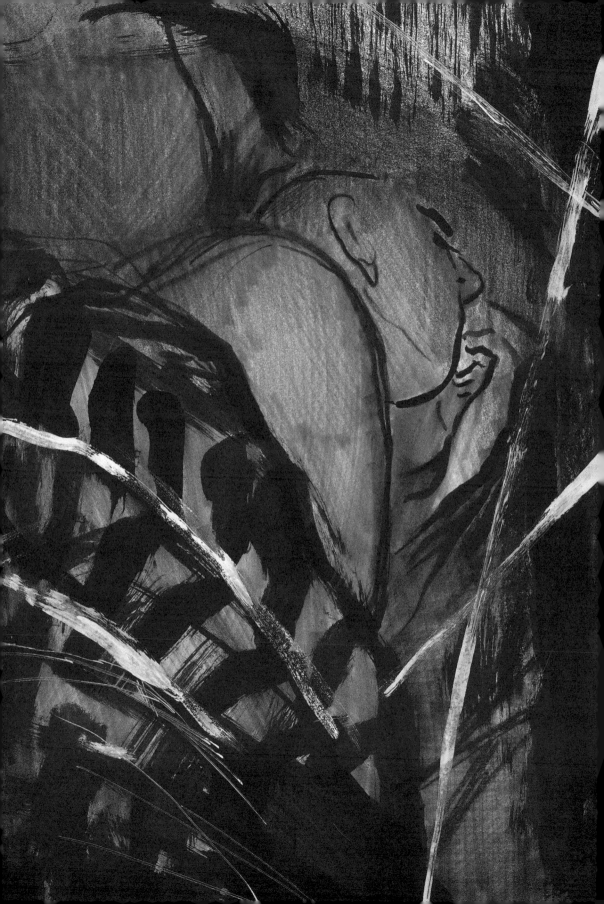

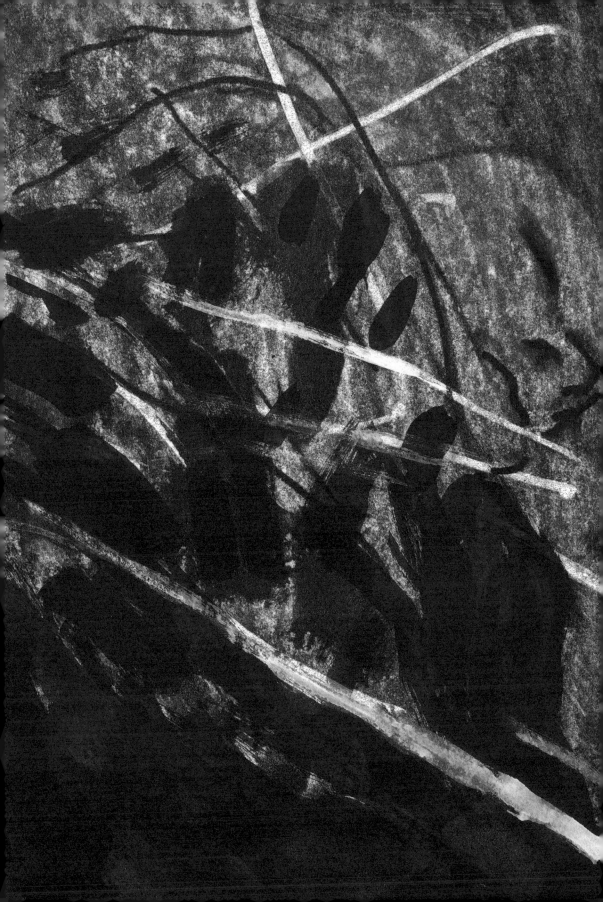

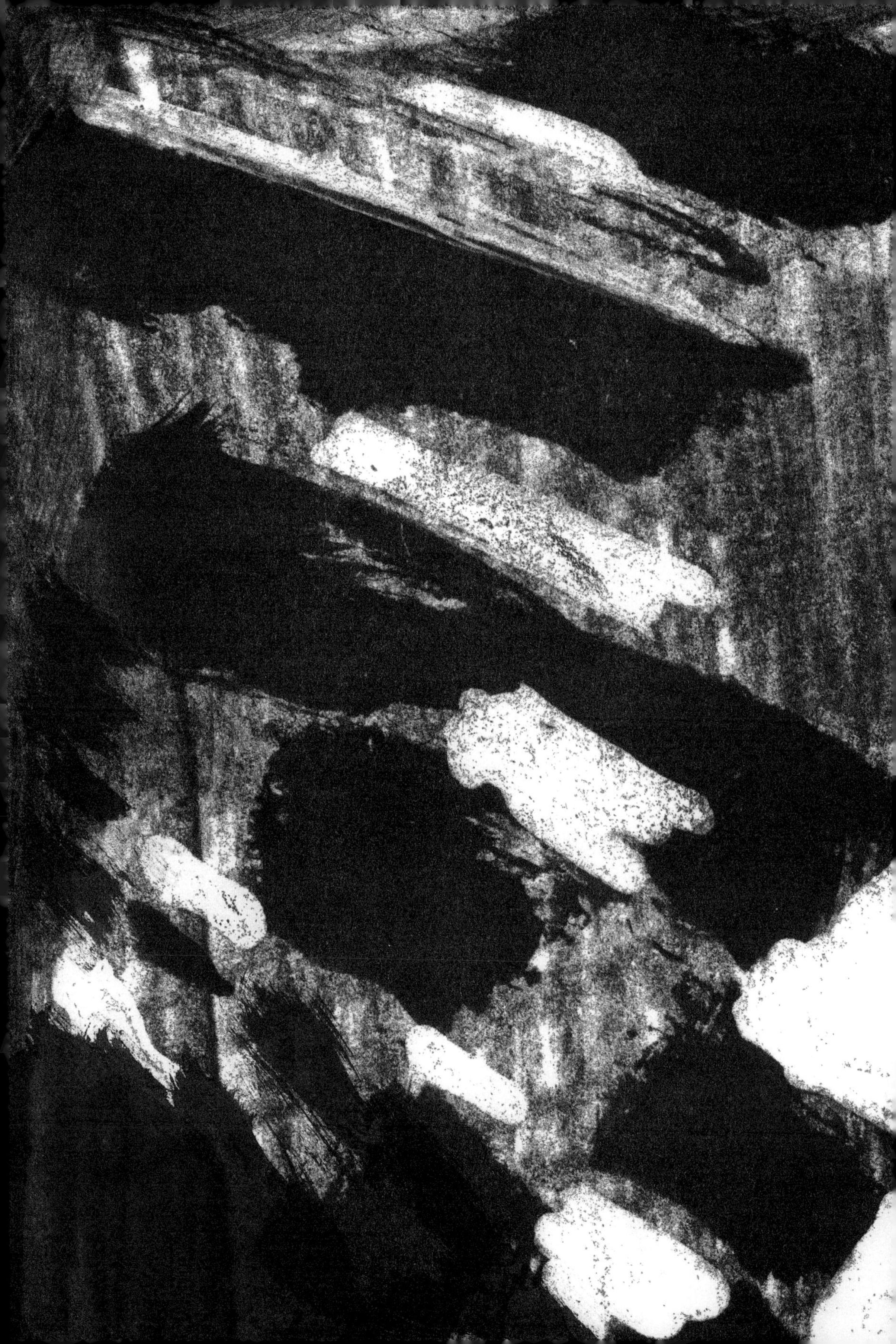

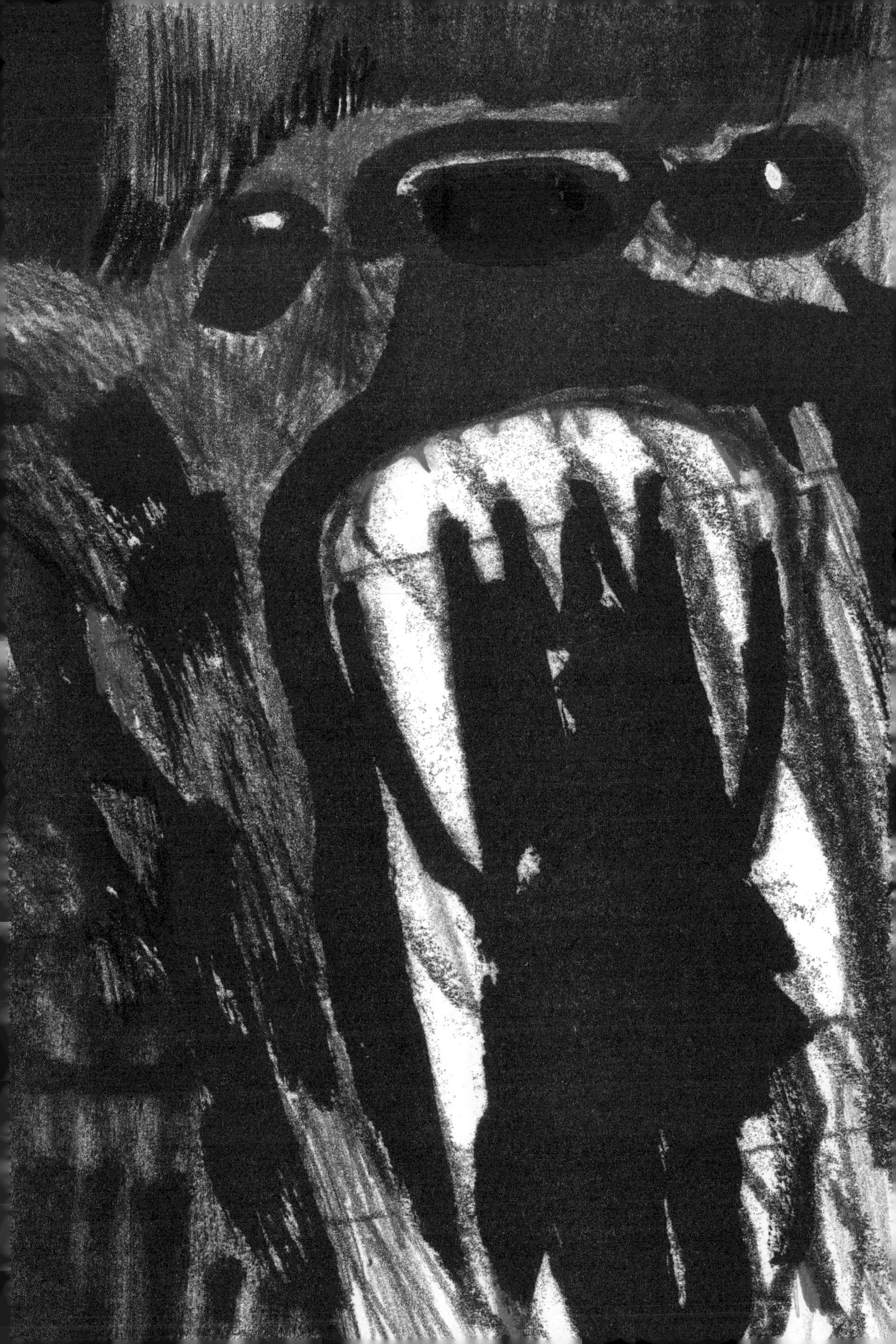

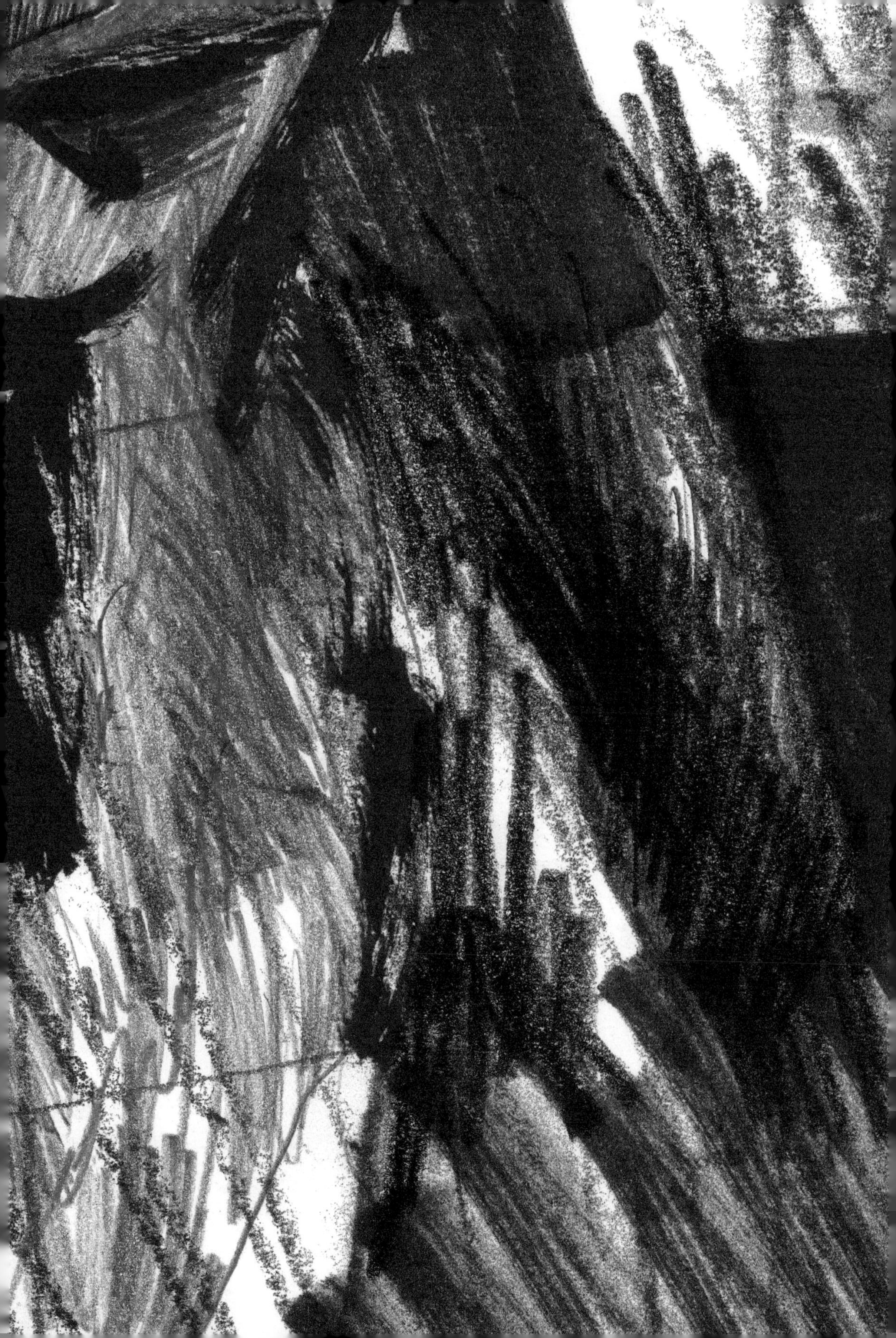

Three months later. UPN* Party Headquarters, Pamplona.

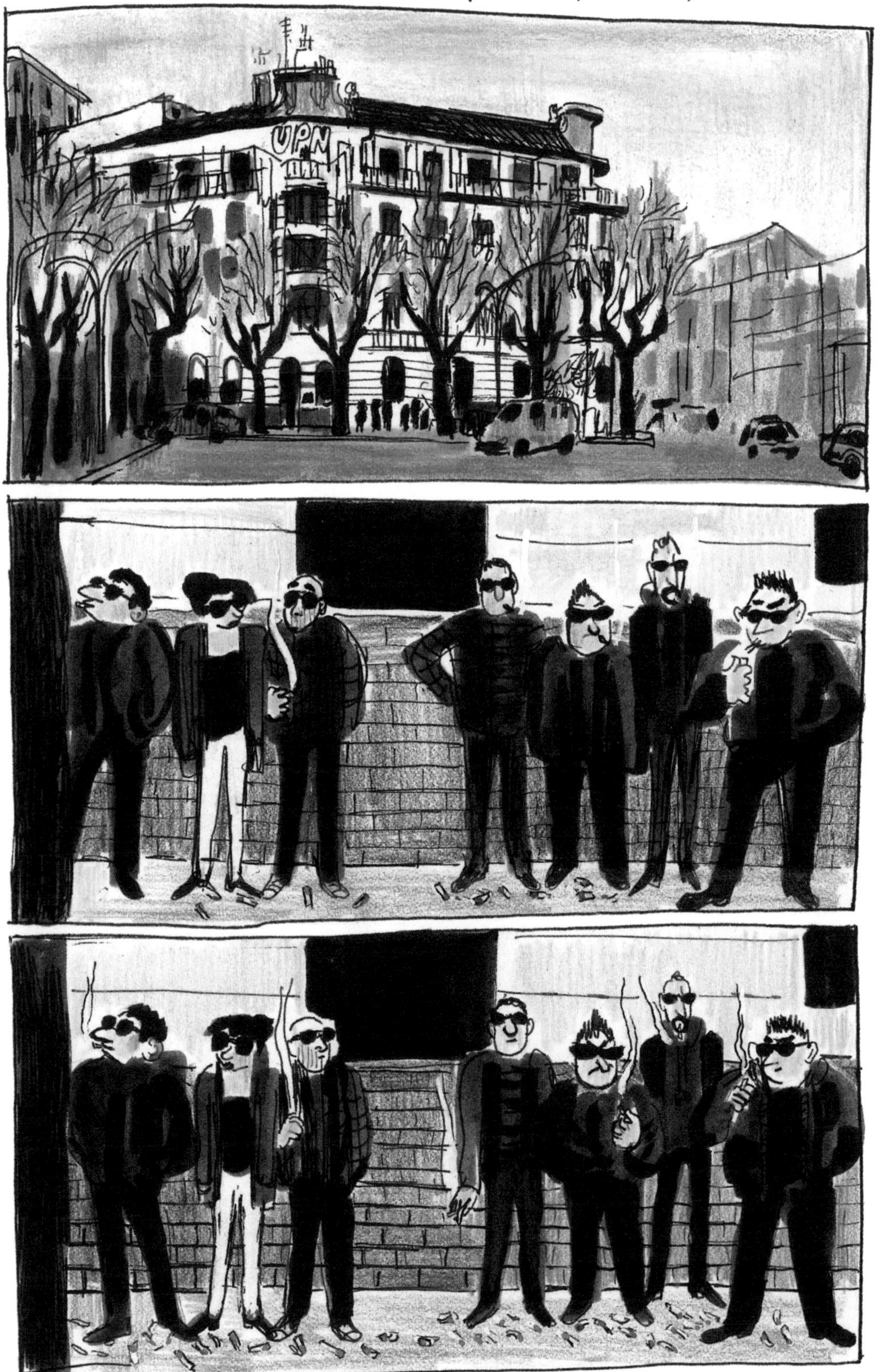
UPN

* Union of the Navarrese People, a party opposed to Basque independence.

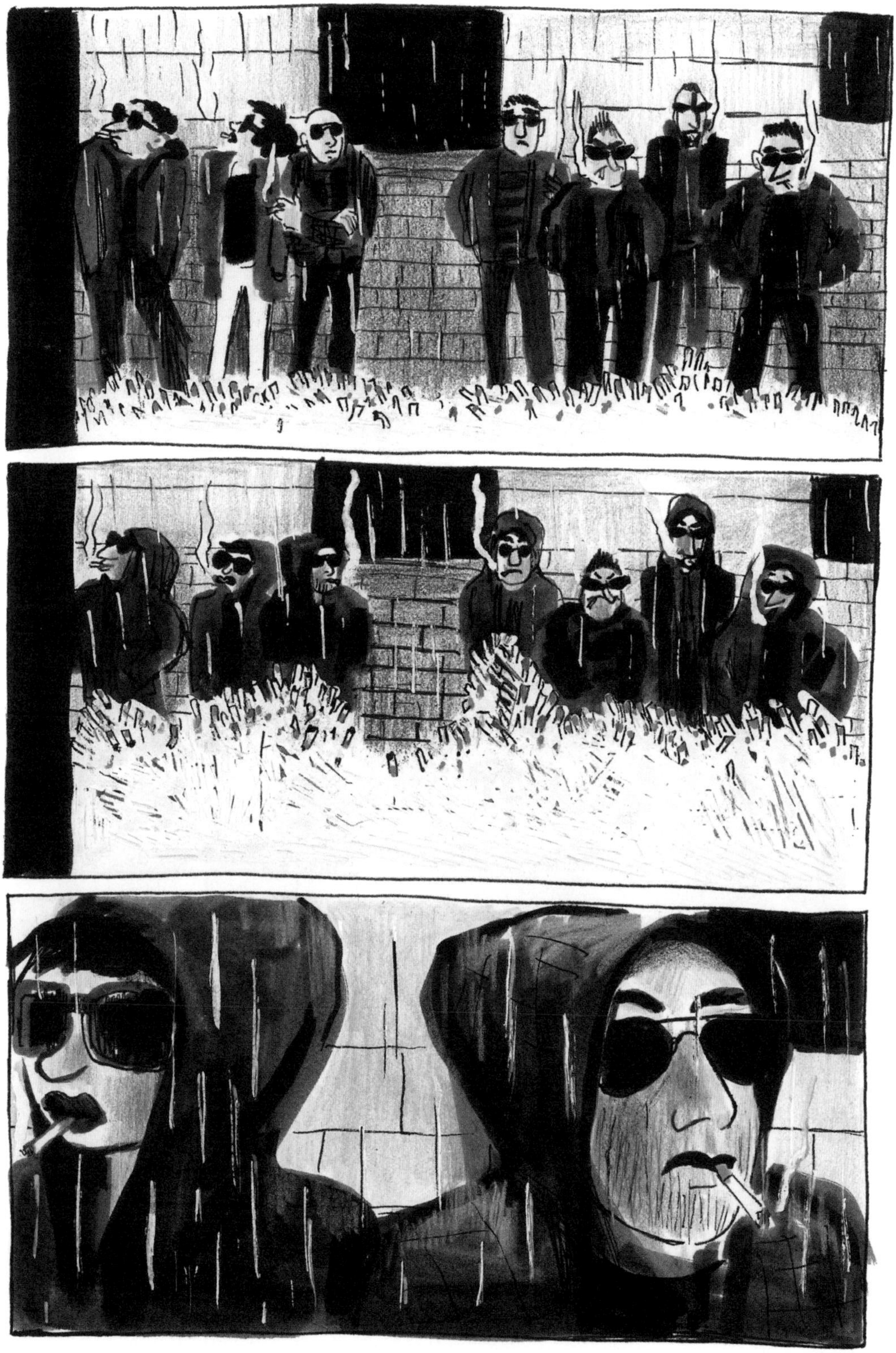

An afternoon near the end of 2007.

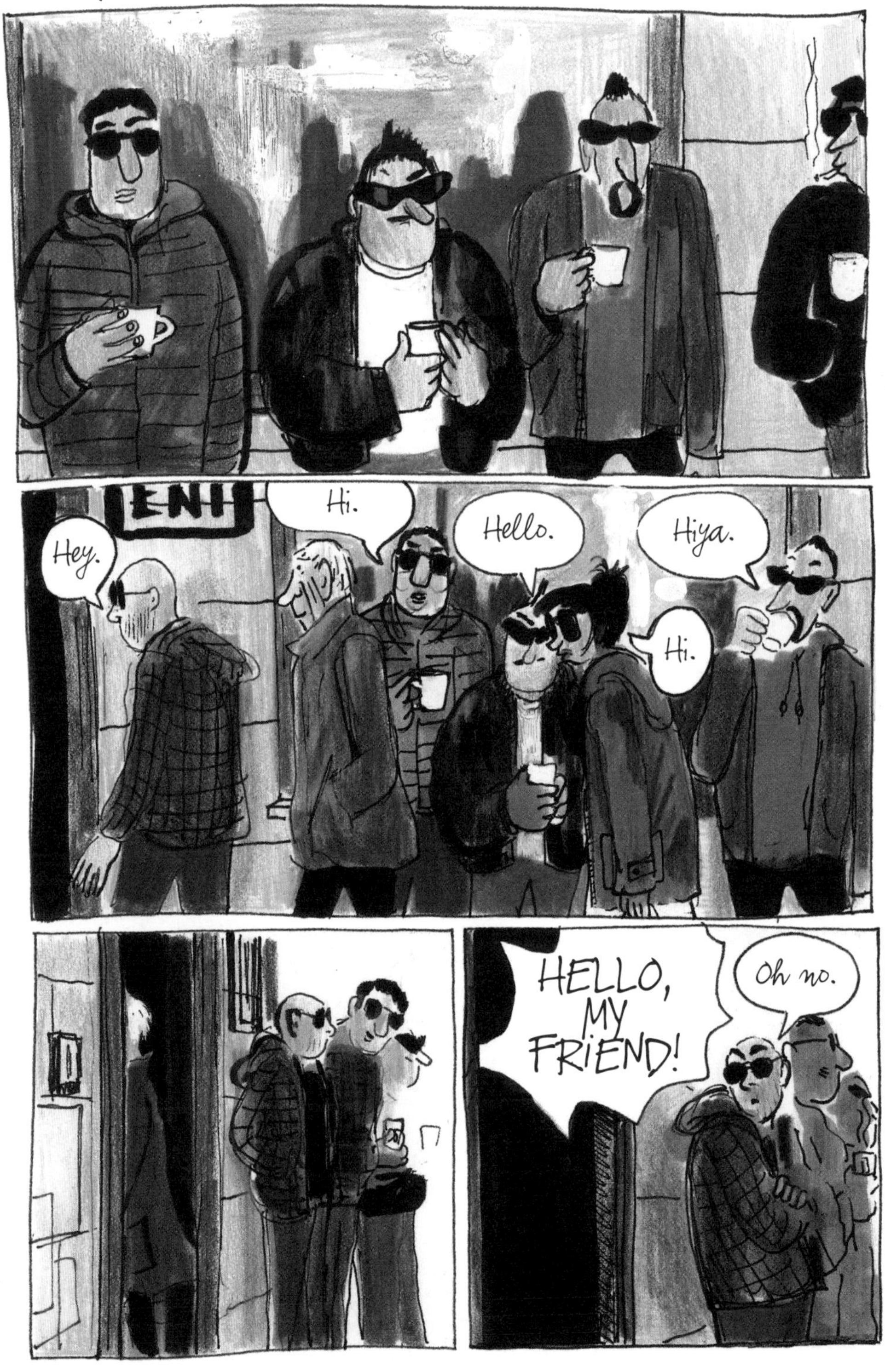
ENI
Hey.
Hi.
Hello.
Hiya.
Hi.
HELLO, MY FRIEND!
Oh no.

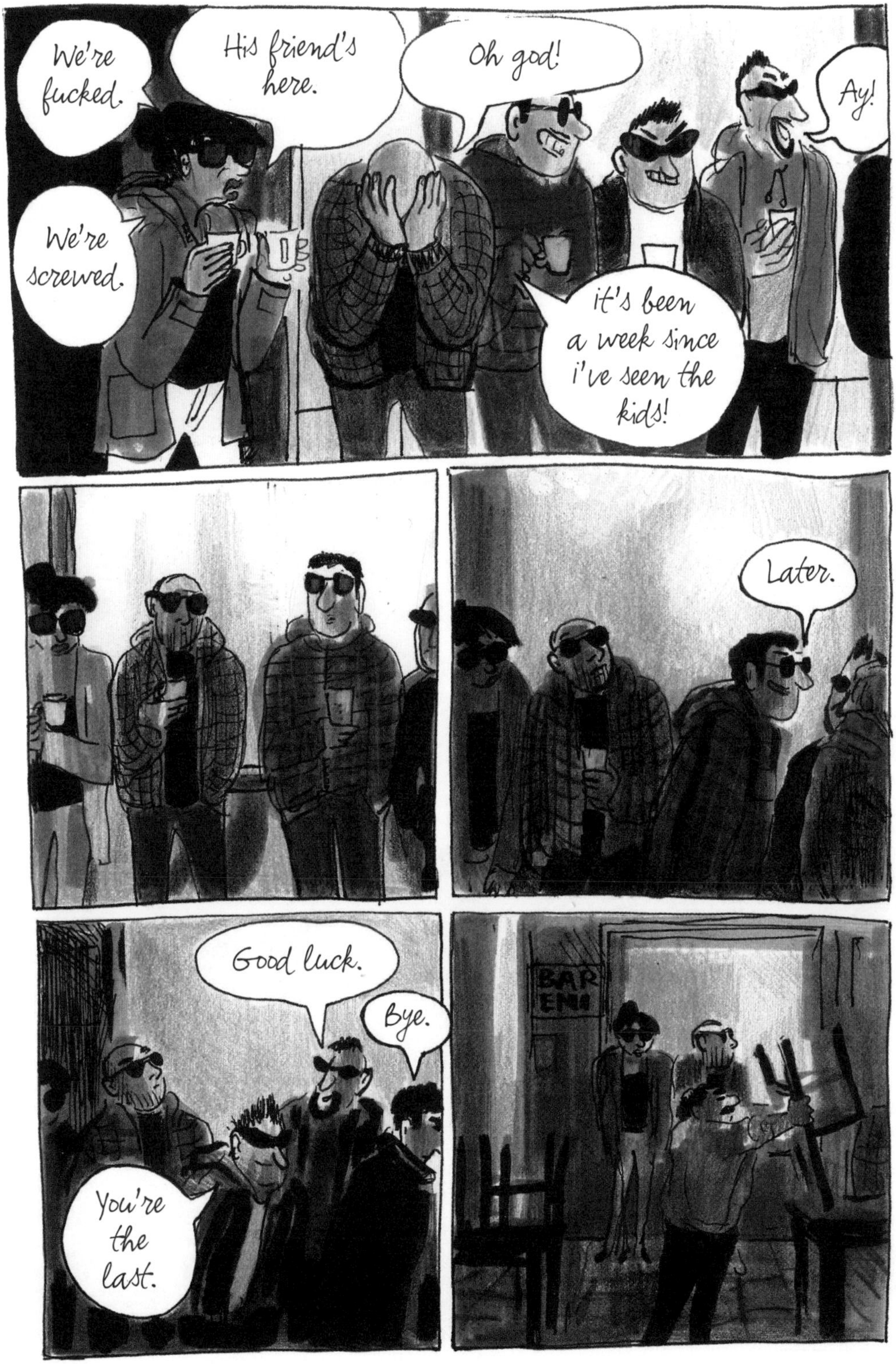
We're fucked.
His friend's here.
Oh god!
Ay!
We're screwed.
it's been a week since i've seen the kids!
Later.
Good luck.
Bye.
You're the last.
BAR ENI

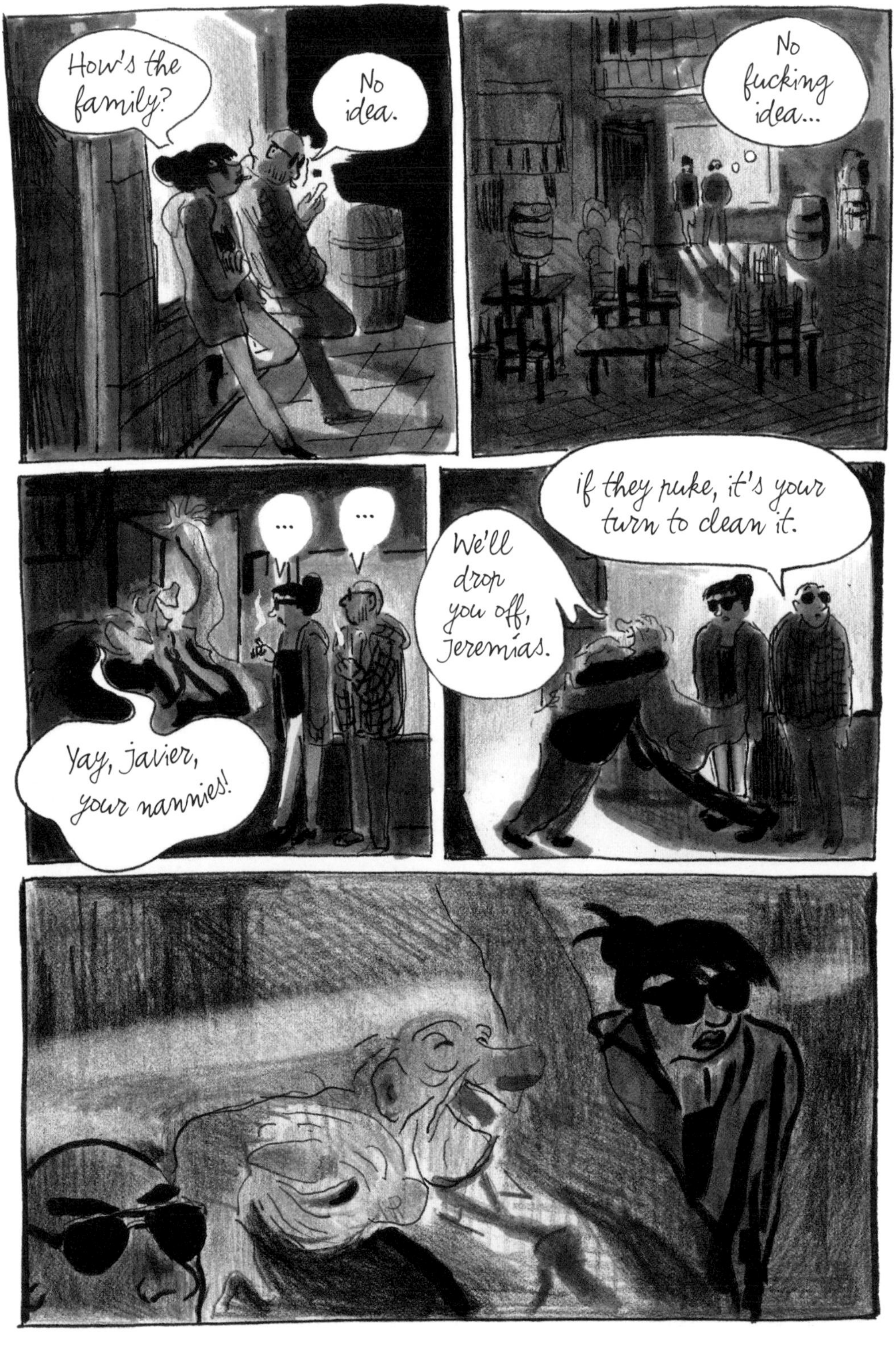
How's the family?
No idea.
No fucking idea...
...
...
Yay, Javier, your nannies!
We'll drop you off, Jeremías.
if they puke, it's your turn to clean it.

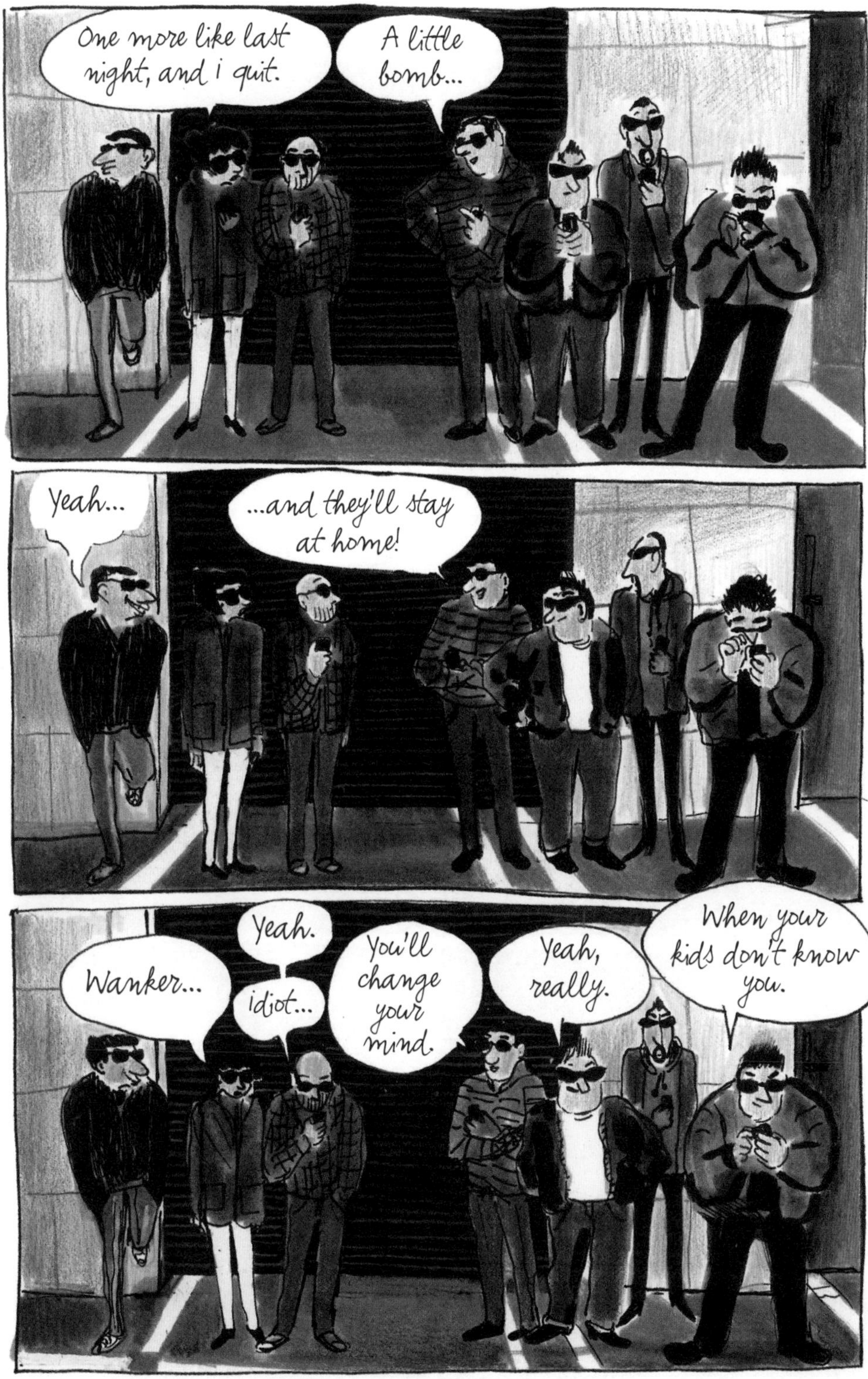
One more like last night, and i quit.
A little bomb...
Yeah...
...and they'll stay at home!
Wanker...
Yeah.
idiot...
You'll change your mind.
Yeah, really.
When your kids don't know you.

A month later.

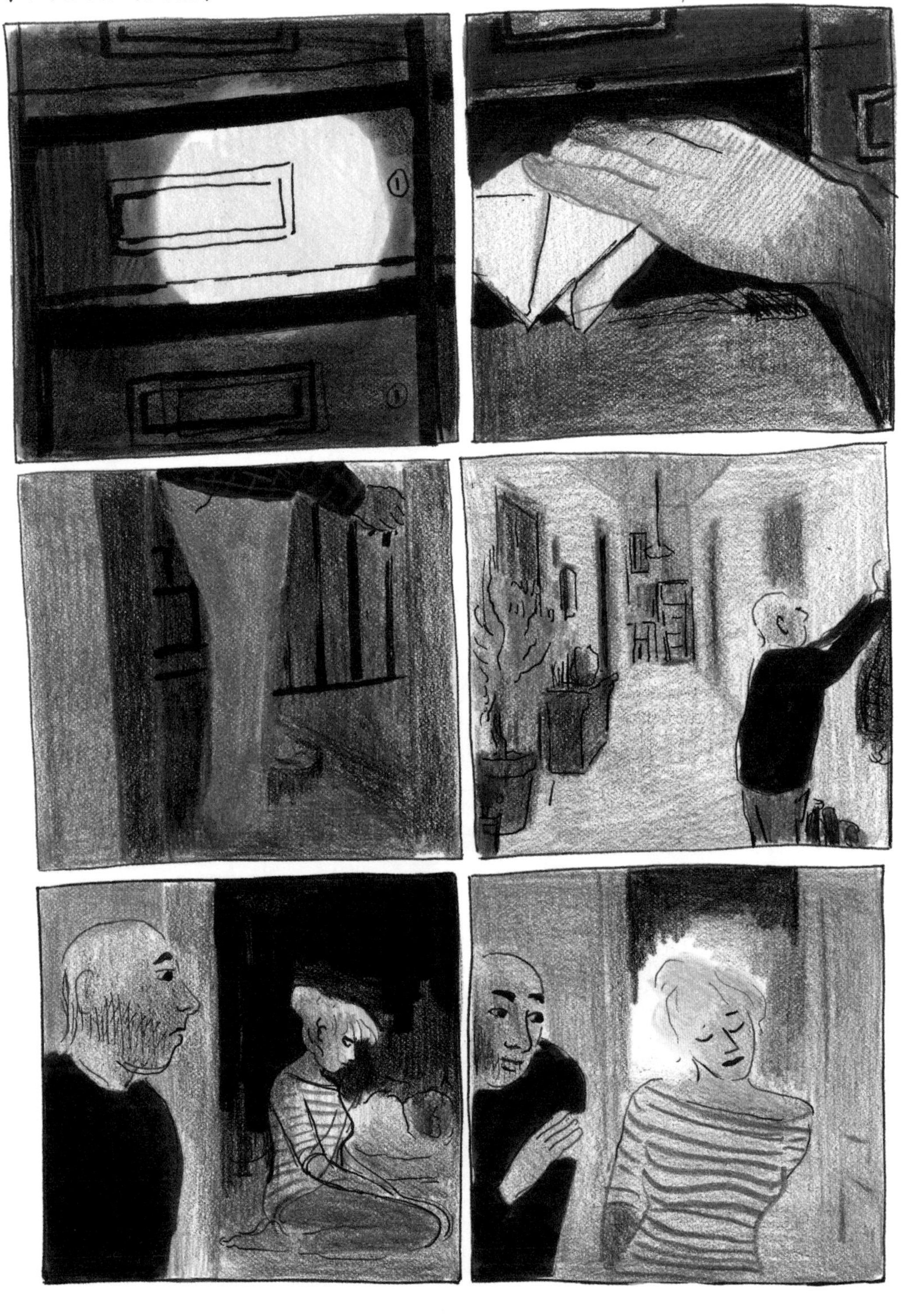

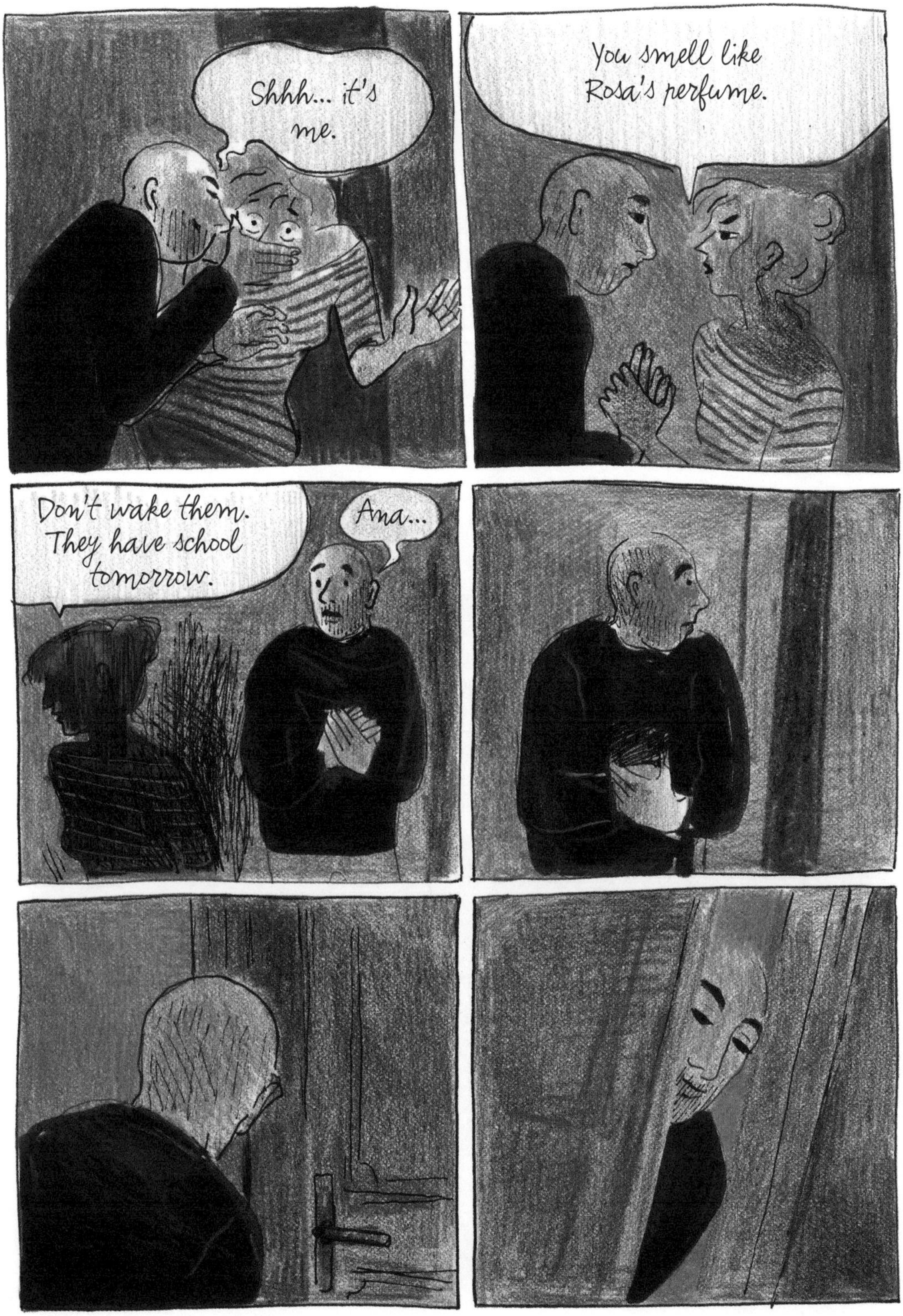
Shhh... it's me.
You smell like Rosa's perfume.
Don't wake them. They have school tomorrow.
Ana...

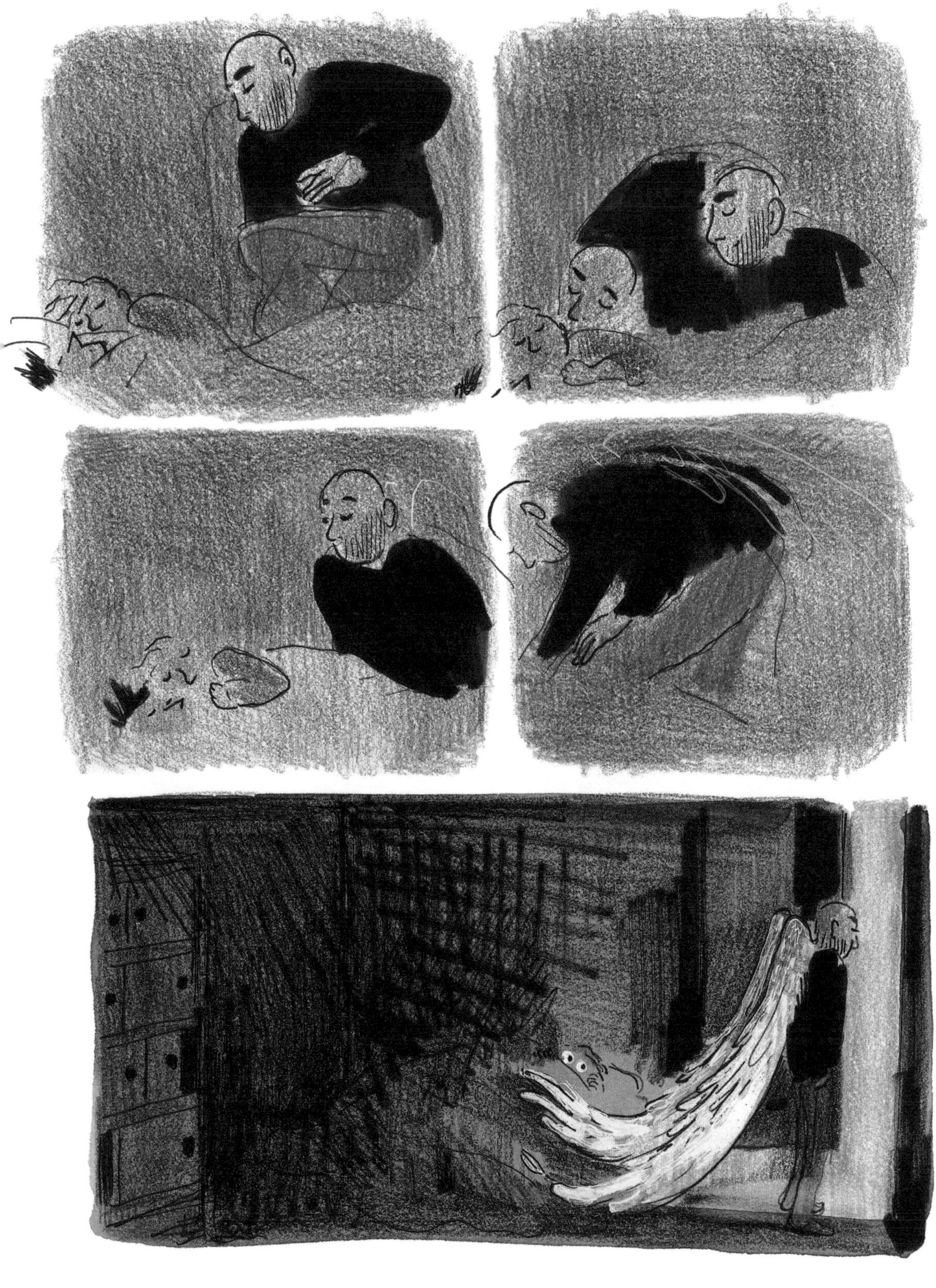

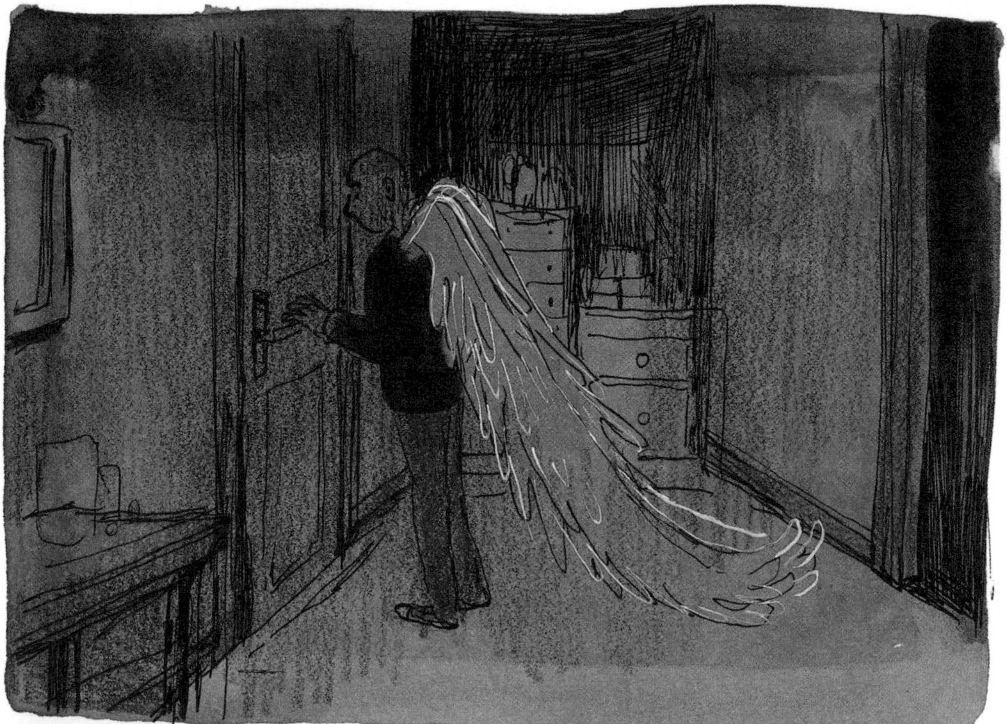

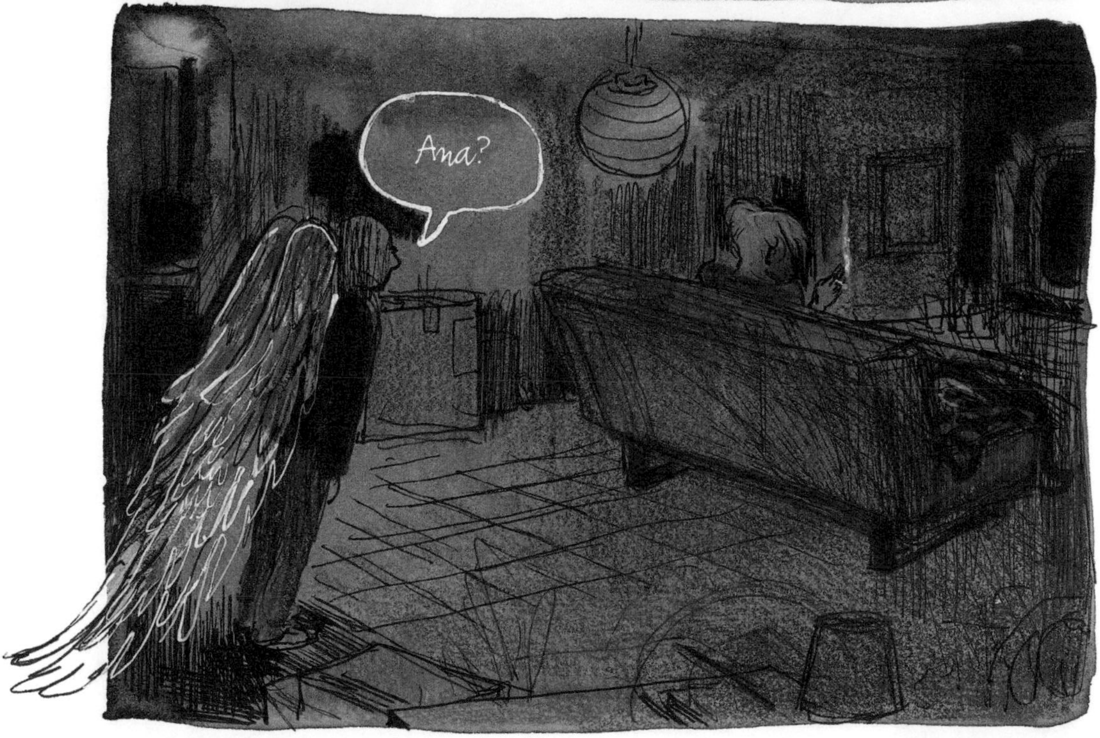
Ana?

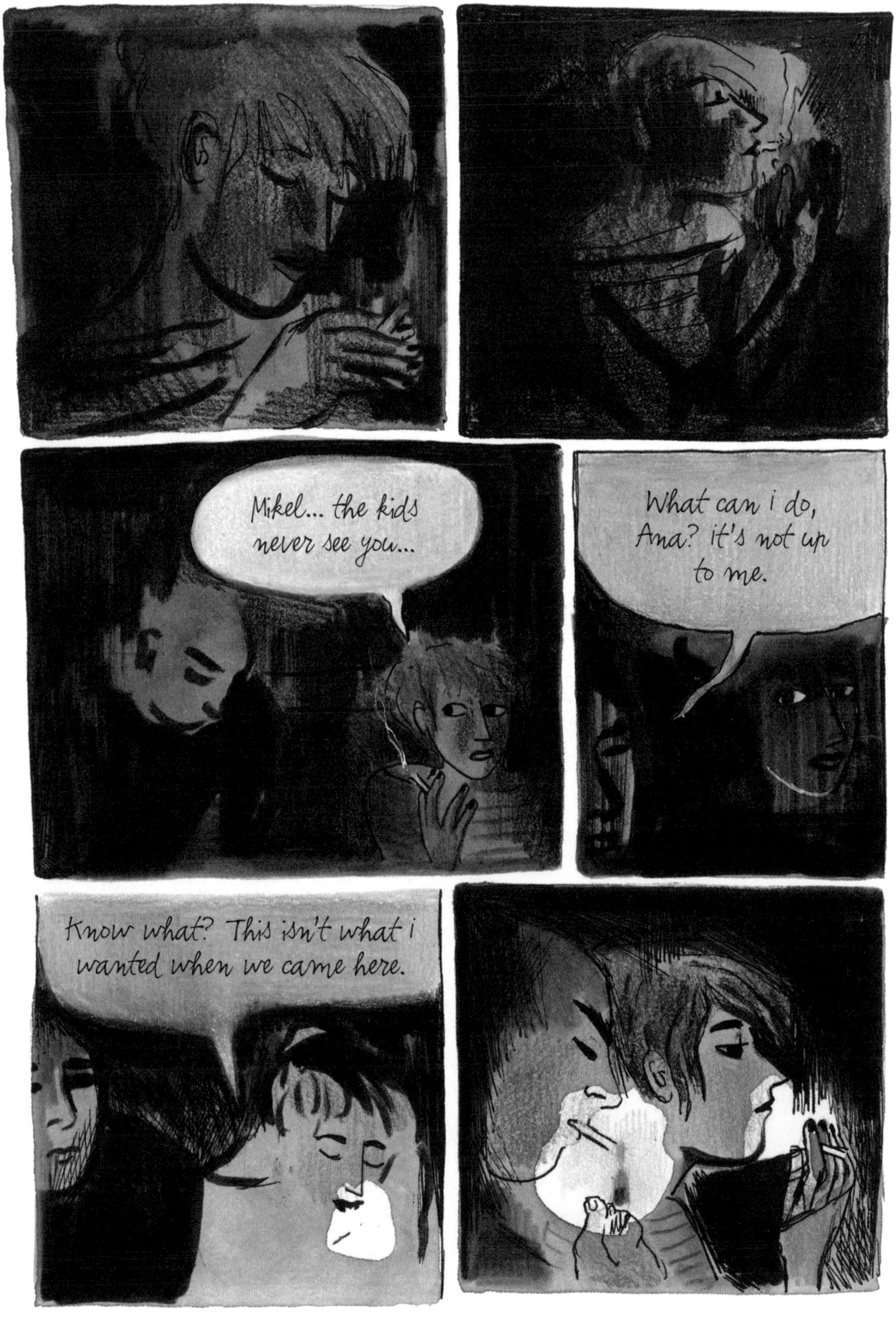
Mikel... the kids never see you...
What can i do, Ana? it's not up to me.
Know what? This isn't what i wanted when we came here.

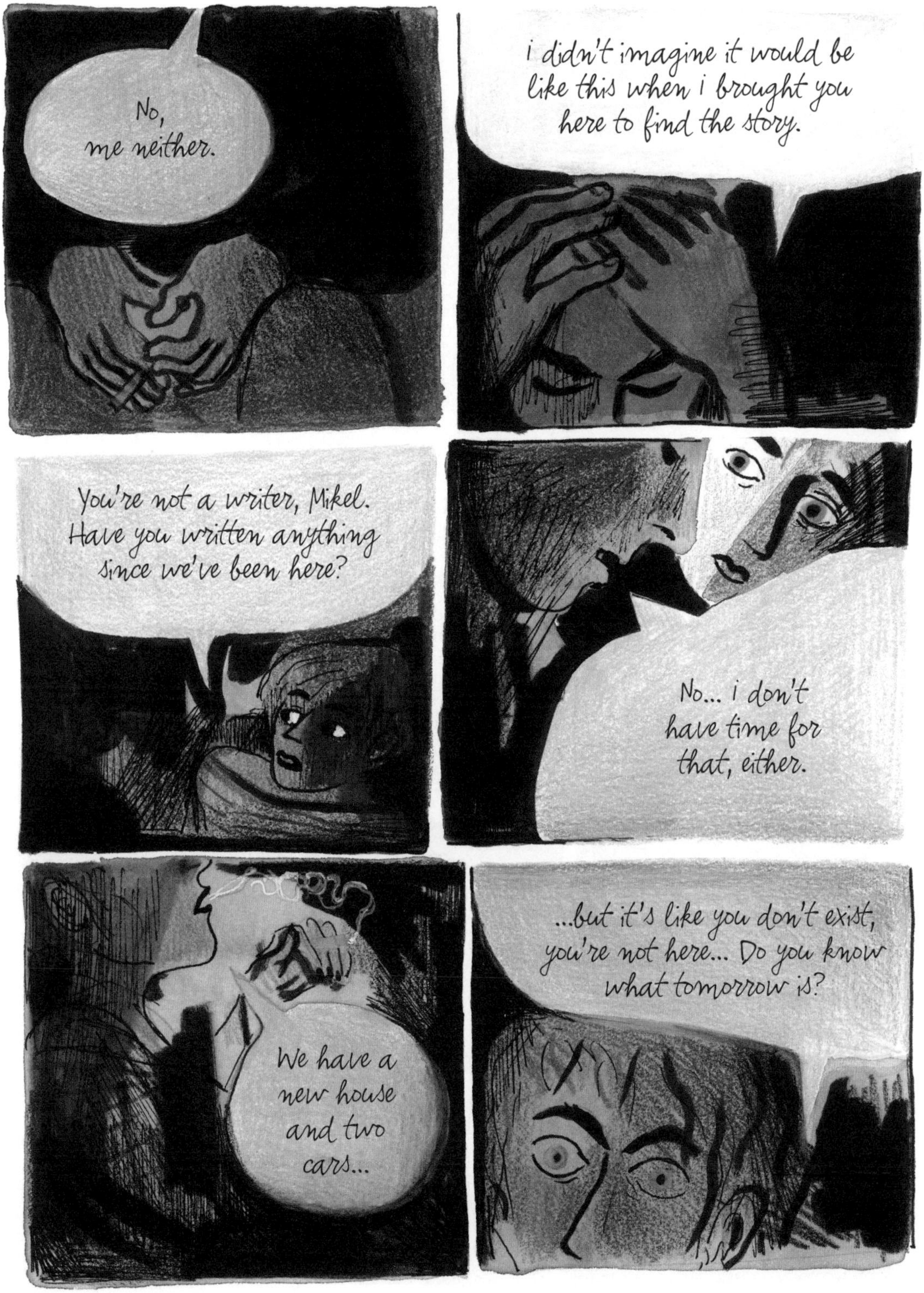
No, me neither.
i didn't imagine it would be like this when i brought you here to find the story.
You're not a writer, Mikel. Have you written anything since we've been here?
No... i don't have time for that, either.
We have a new house and two cars...
...but it's like you don't exist, you're not here... Do you know what tomorrow is?

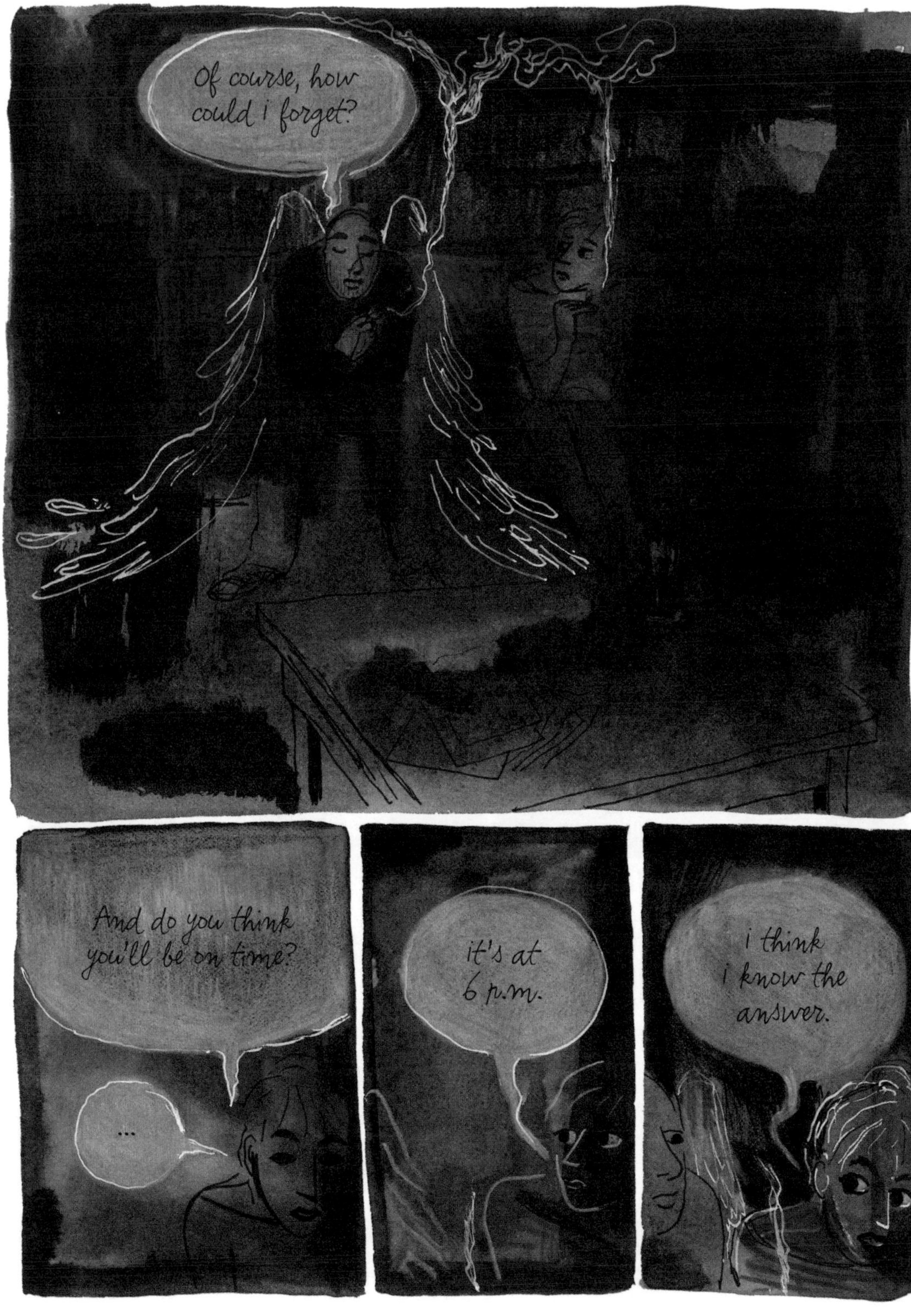
Of course, how could i forget?
And do you think you'll be on time?
...
it's at 6 p.m.
i think i know the answer.

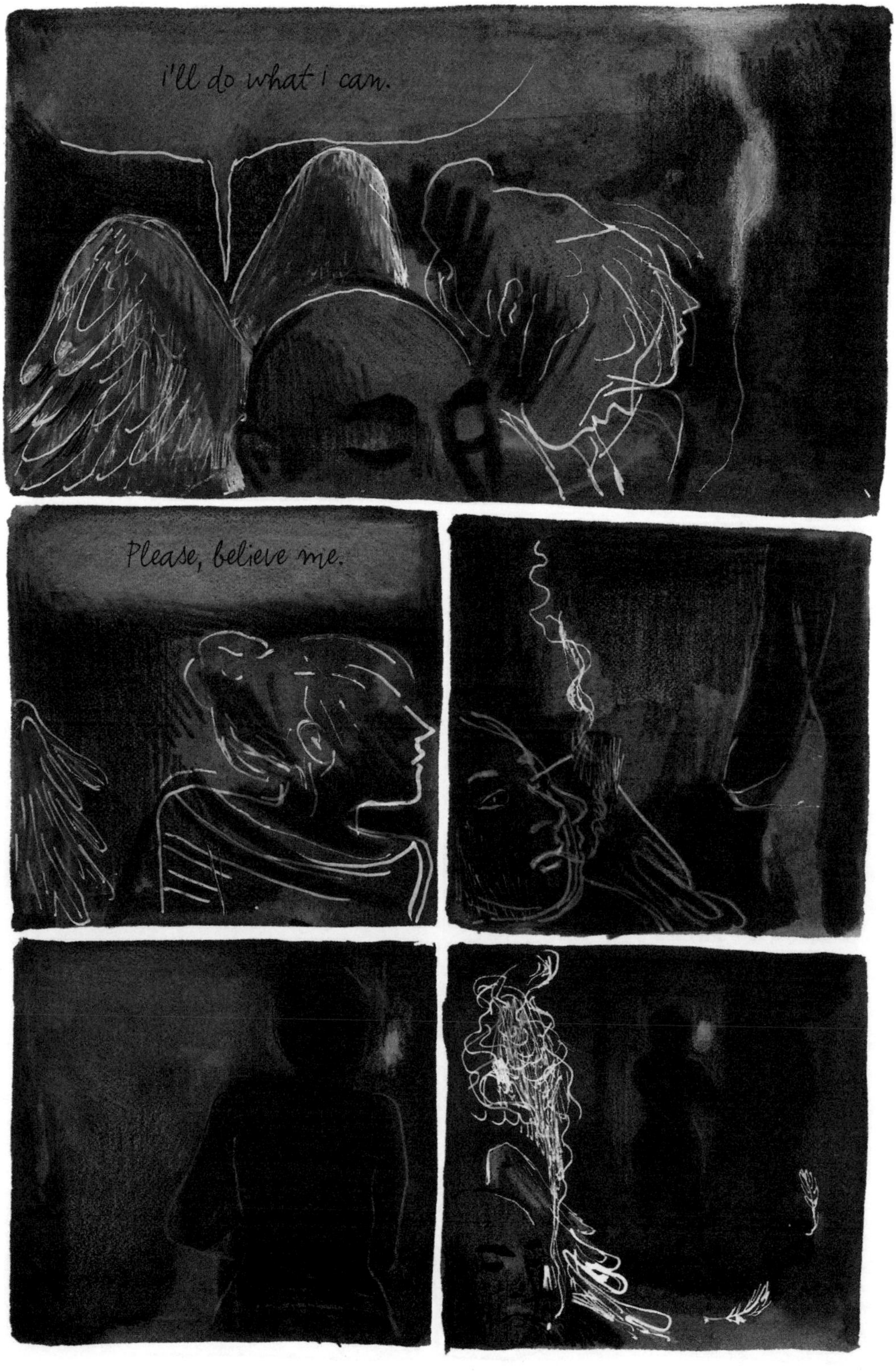
i'll do what i can.
Please, believe me.

24 January 2008. Julito's birthday.

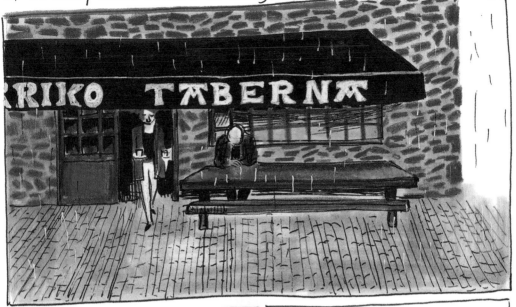

Problems
at home?

it's julito's birthday. i don't
want to miss it.

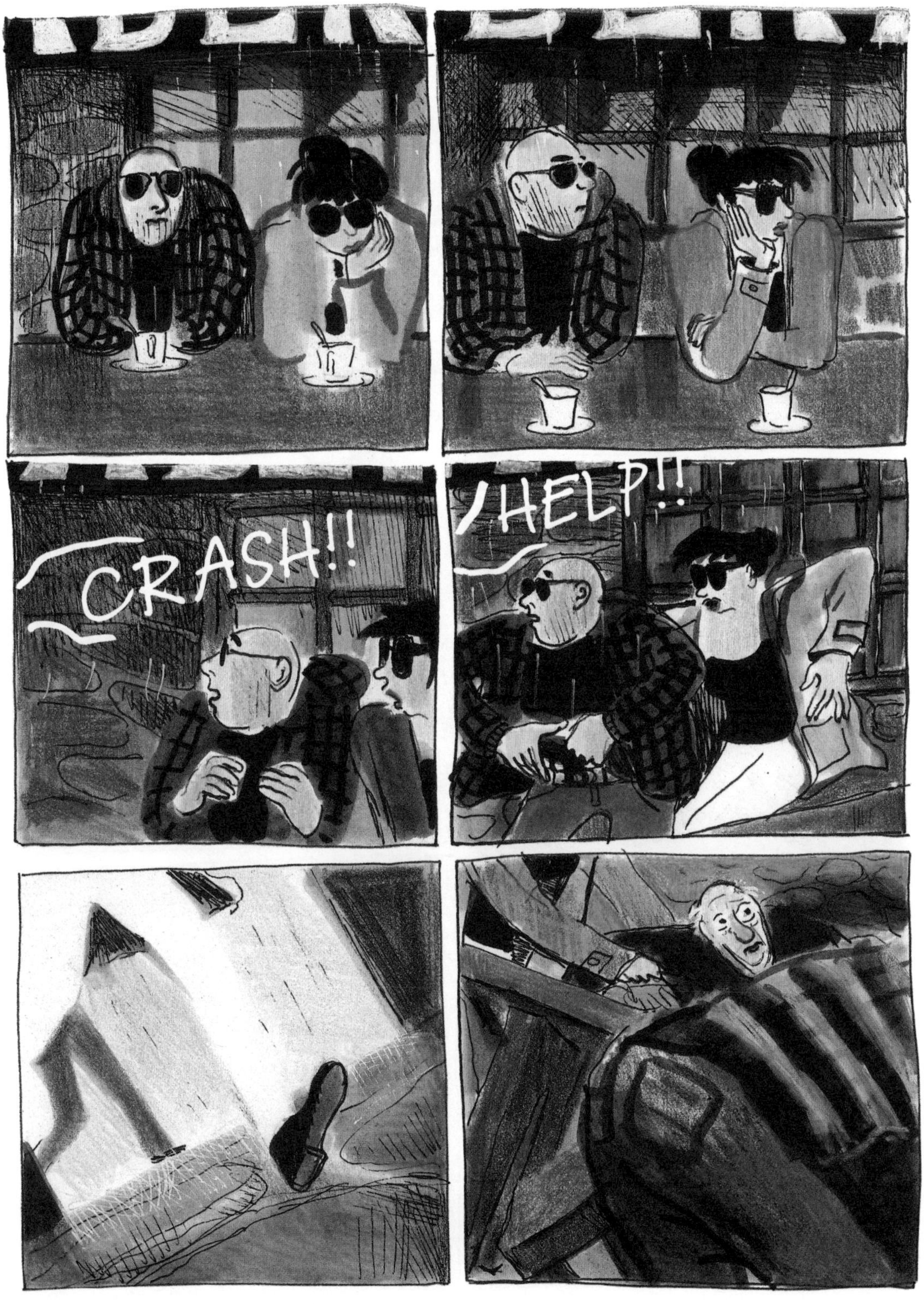
CRASH!!
HELP!!

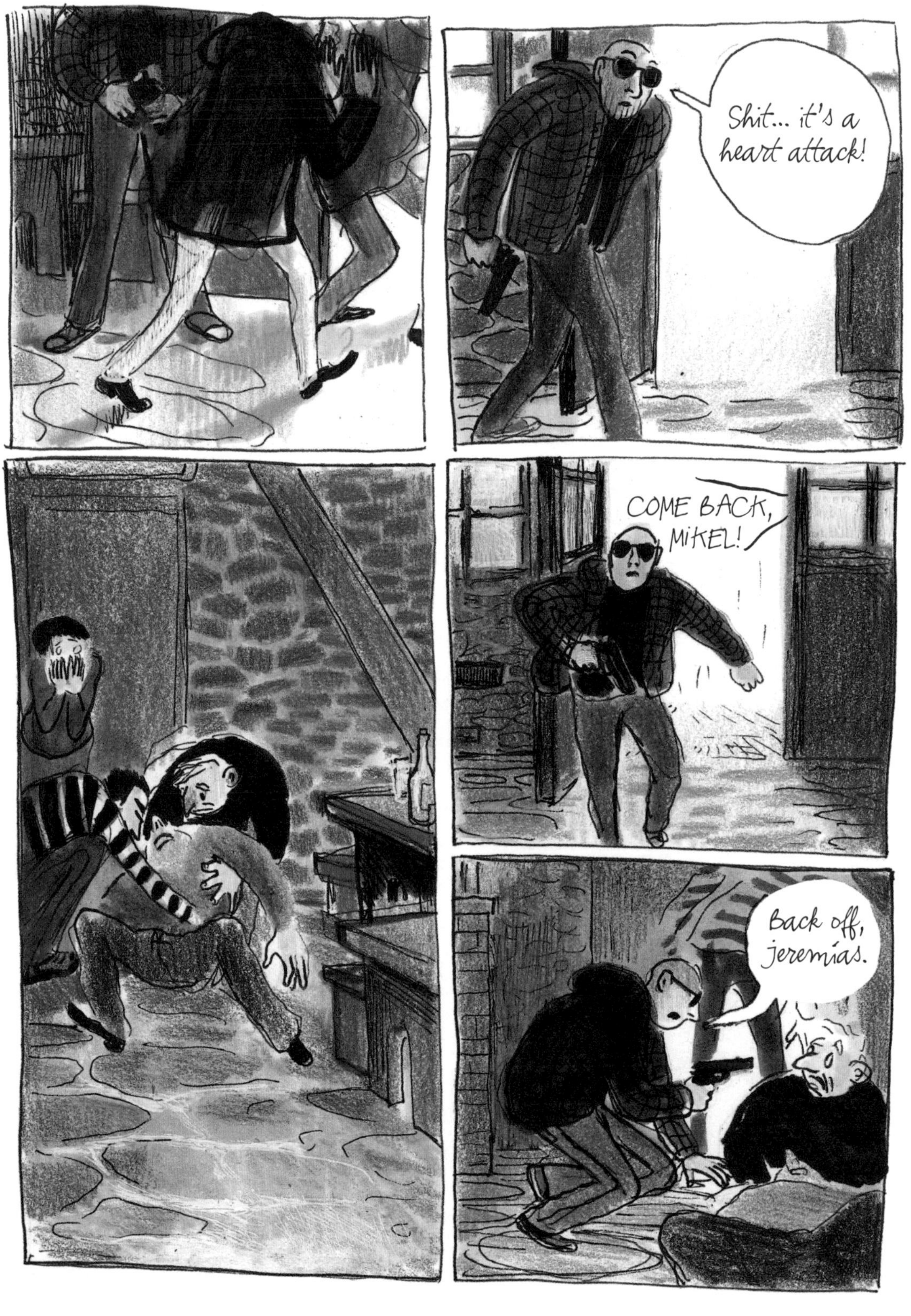
Shit... it's a heart attack!
COME BACK, MIKEL!
Back off, jeremias.

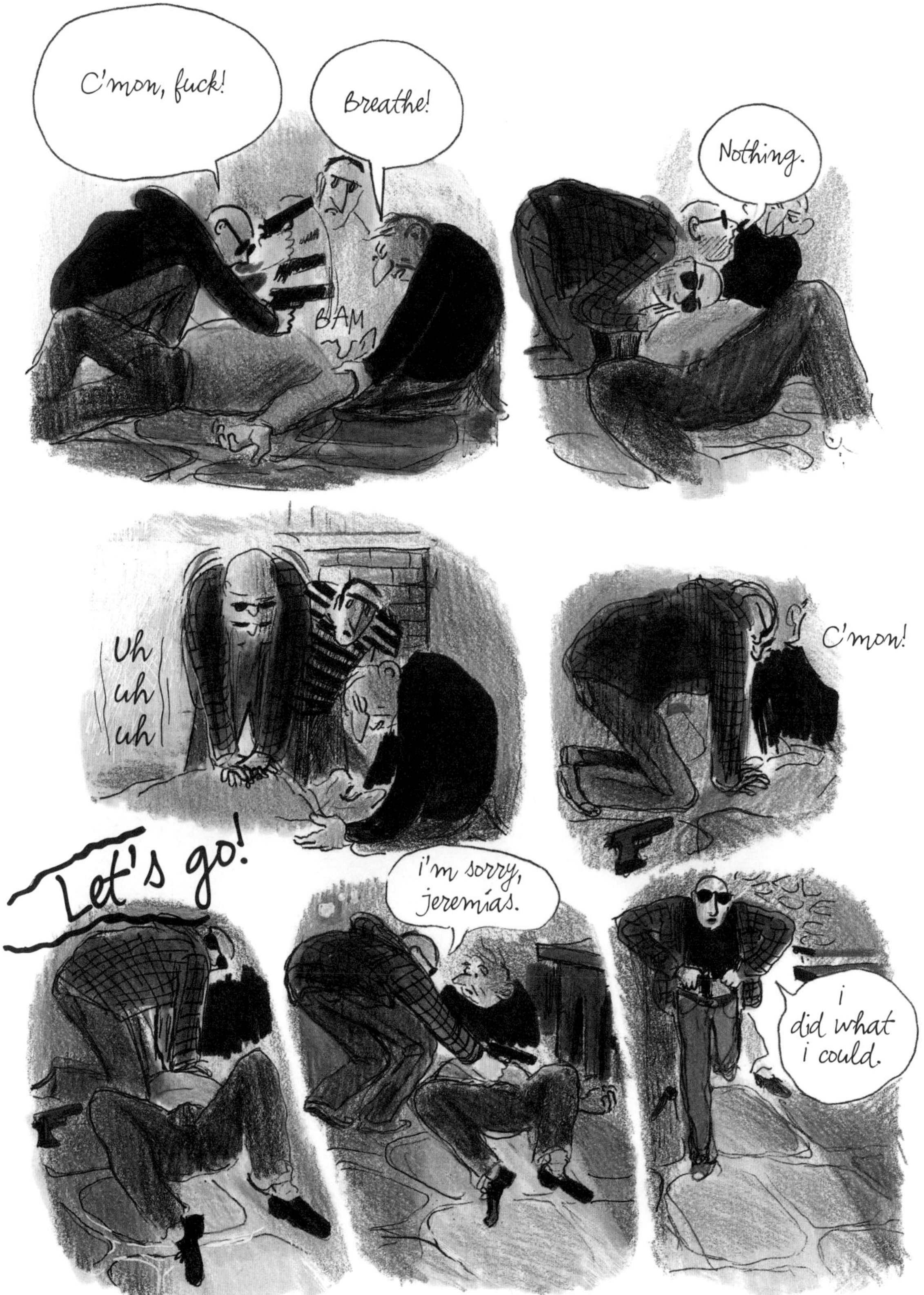
C'mon, fuck!
Breathe!
BAM
Nothing.
Uh
uh
uh
C'mon!
Let's go!
i'm sorry, jeremias.
i did what i could.

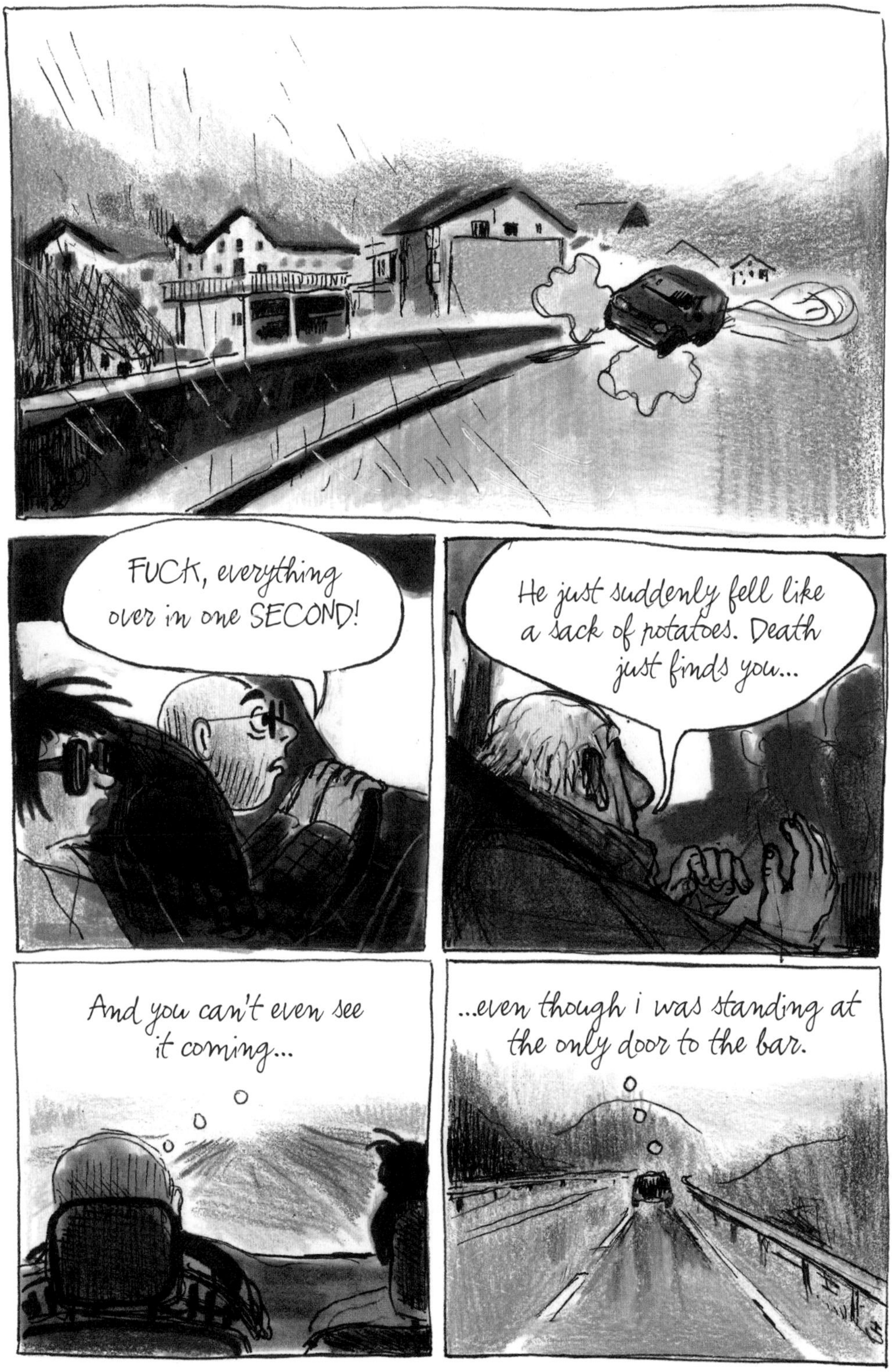
FUCK, everything over in one SECOND!
He just suddenly fell like a sack of potatoes. Death just finds you...
And you can't even see it coming...
...even though i was standing at the only door to the bar.

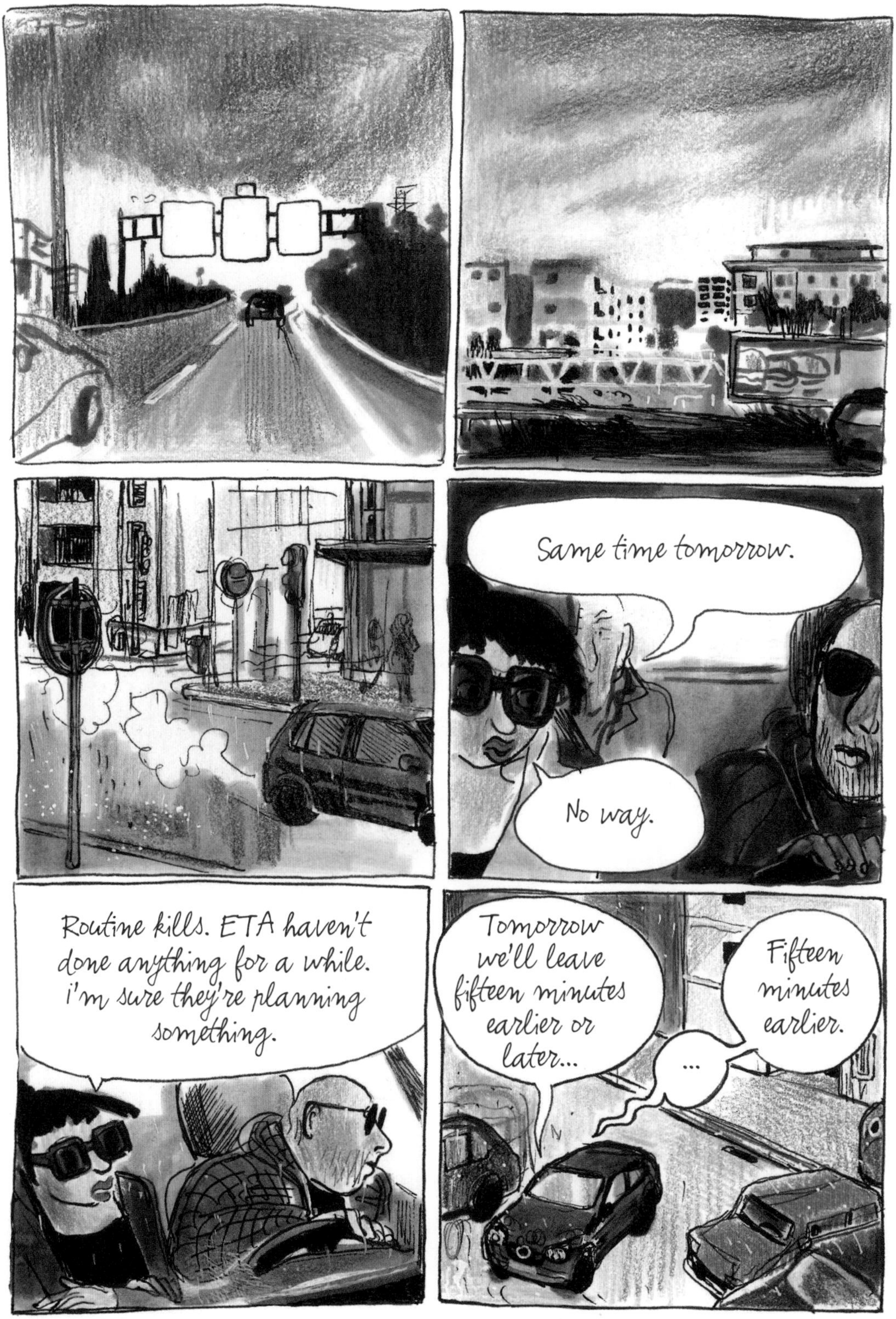
Same time tomorrow.
No way.
Routine kills. ETA haven't done anything for a while. i'm sure they're planning something.
Tomorrow we'll leave fifteen minutes earlier or later...
...
Fifteen minutes earlier.

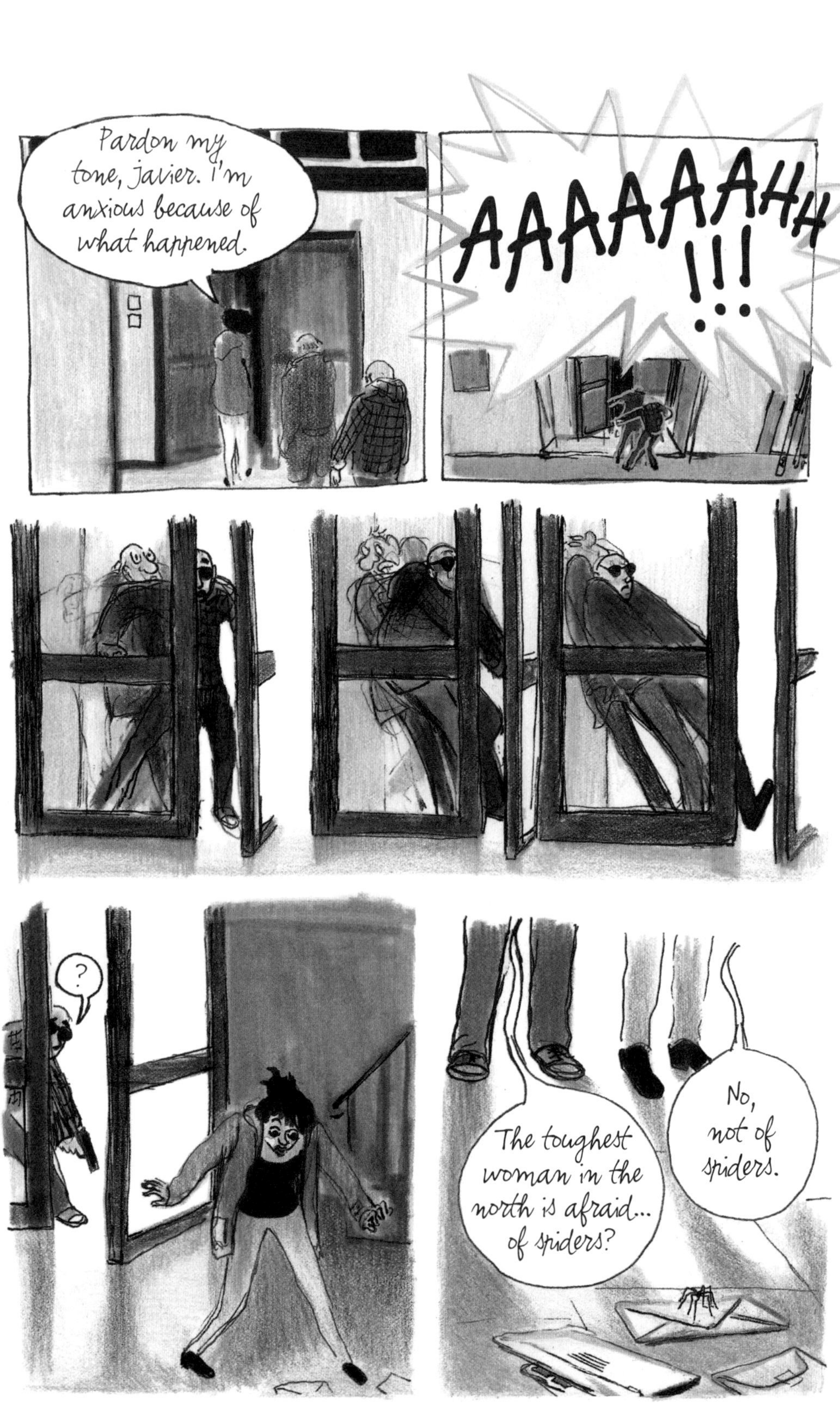
Pardon my tone, Javier. I'm anxious because of what happened.
AAAAAAHH!!!
?
The toughest woman in the north is afraid... of spiders?
No, not of spiders.

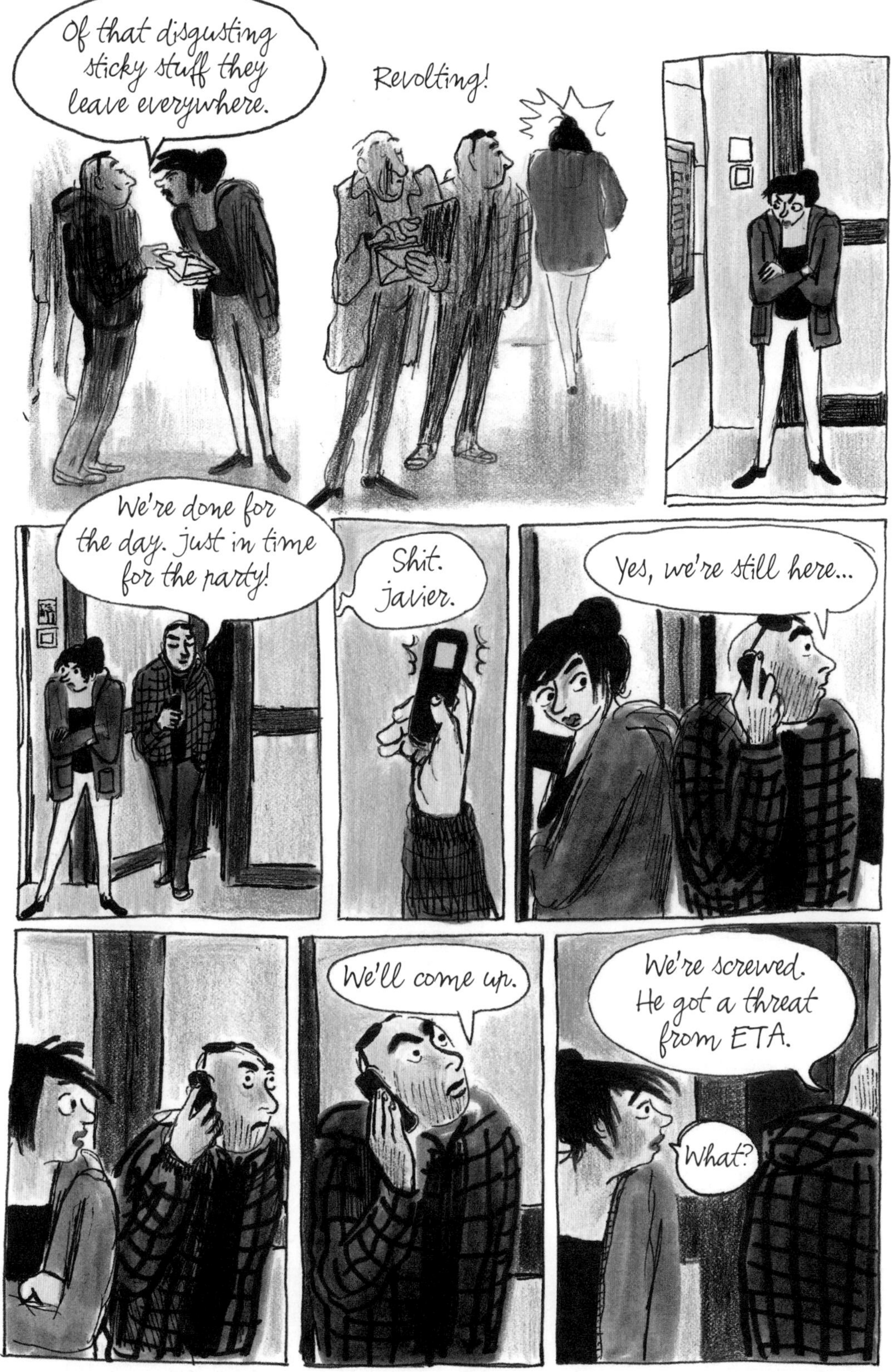
Of that disgusting sticky stuff they leave everywhere.
Revolting!
We're done for the day. Just in time for the party!
Shit. Javier.
Yes, we're still here...
We'll come up.
We're screwed. He got a threat from ETA.
What?

National Police Headquarters, Pamplona.

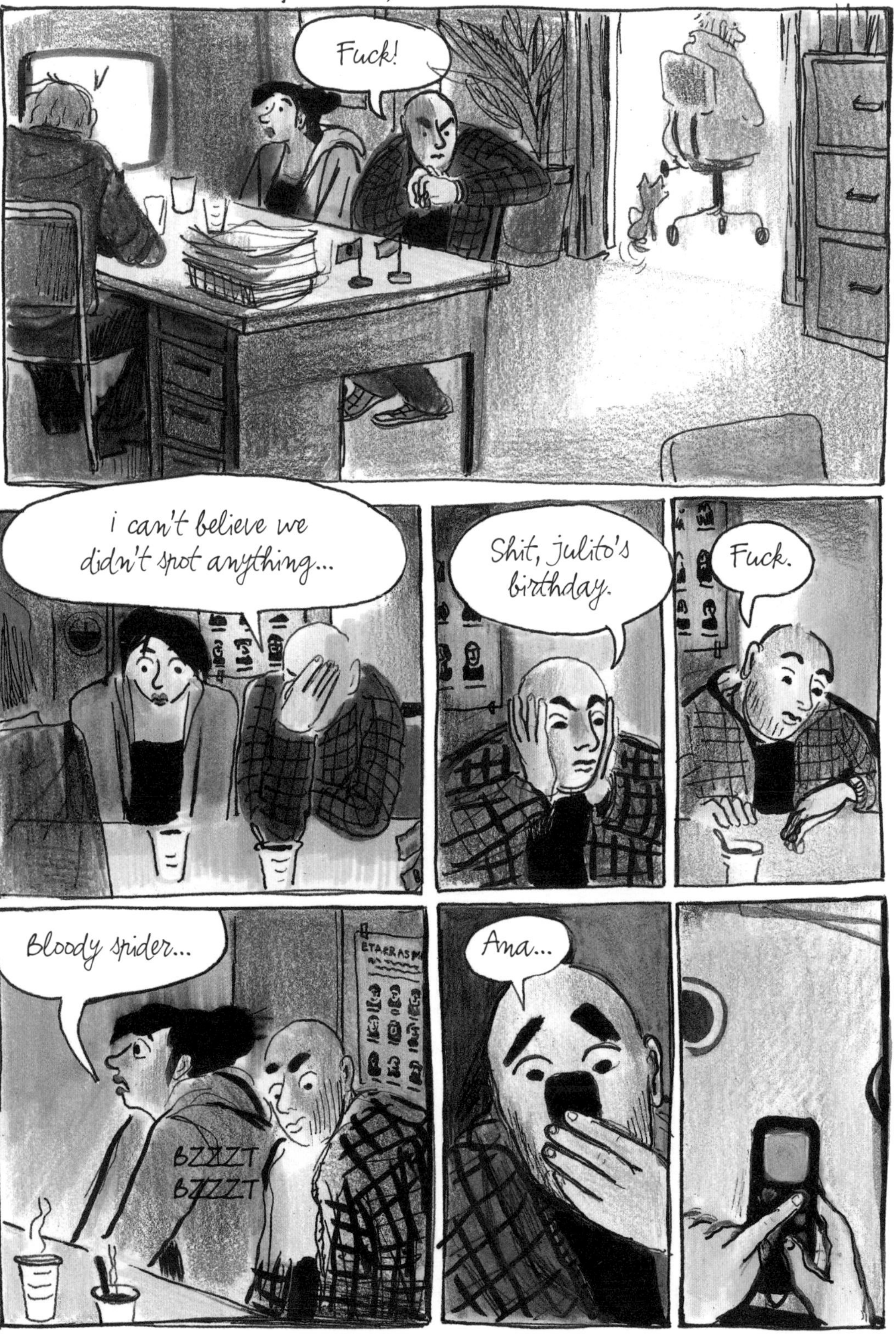

Fuck!
i can't believe we didn't spot anything...
Shit, julito's birthday.
Fuck.
Bloody spider...
ETARRAS
BZZZT
BZZZT
Ana...

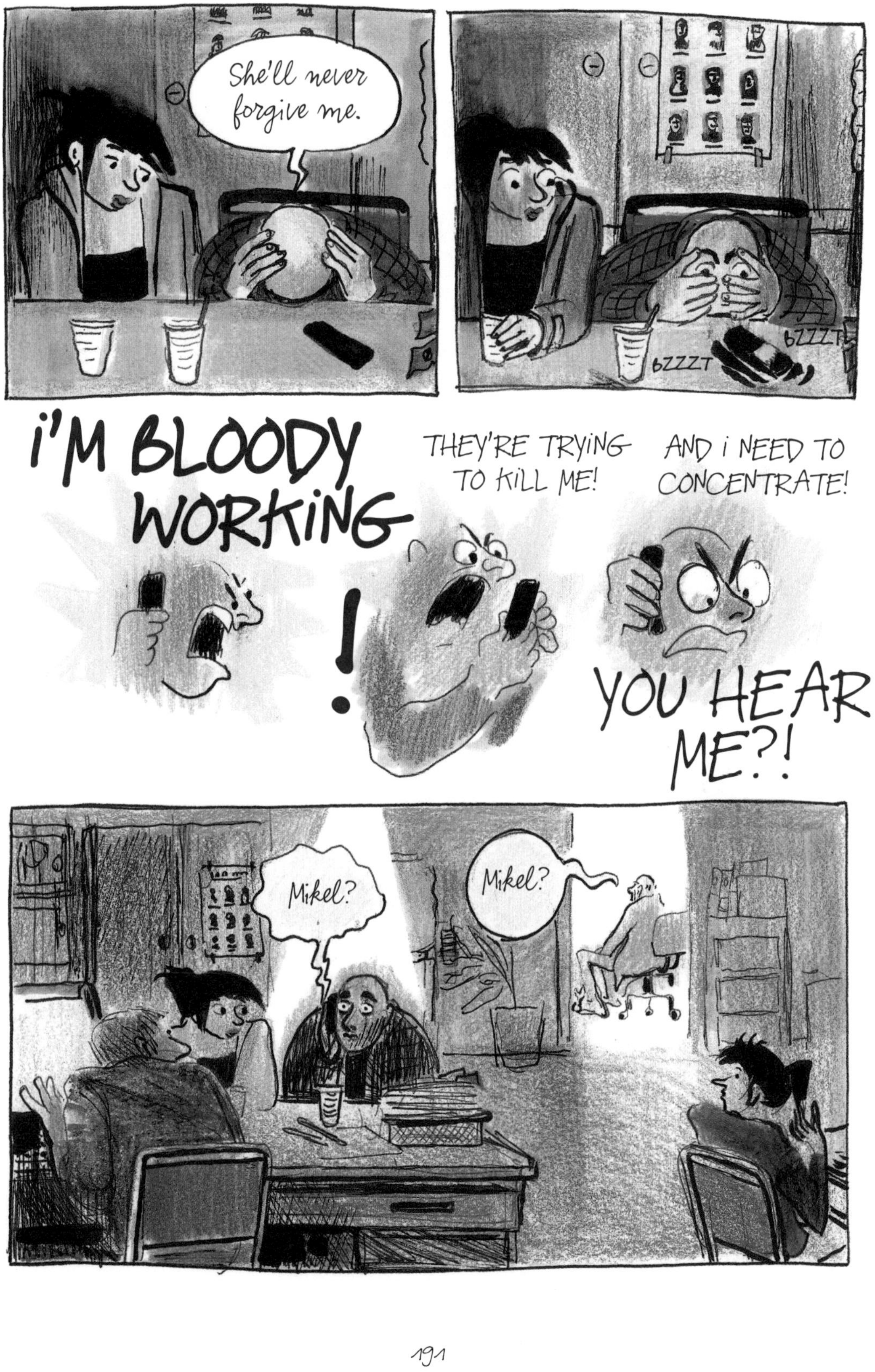
She'll never forgive me.
BZZZT
BZZZT
I'M BLOODY WORKING
!
THEY'RE TRYING TO KILL ME!
AND I NEED TO CONCENTRATE!
YOU HEAR ME?!
Mikel?
Mikel?

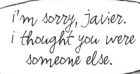
i'm sorry, Javier. i thought you were someone else.

Well, i wouldn't want to be in his shoes!

No.

No.

i just wanted to say that when we're done here, we'll go to josetxo's wake.

The one who died this afternoon. i have to make an appearance, as mayor and as a good Christian.

Fine.

Whenever you want.

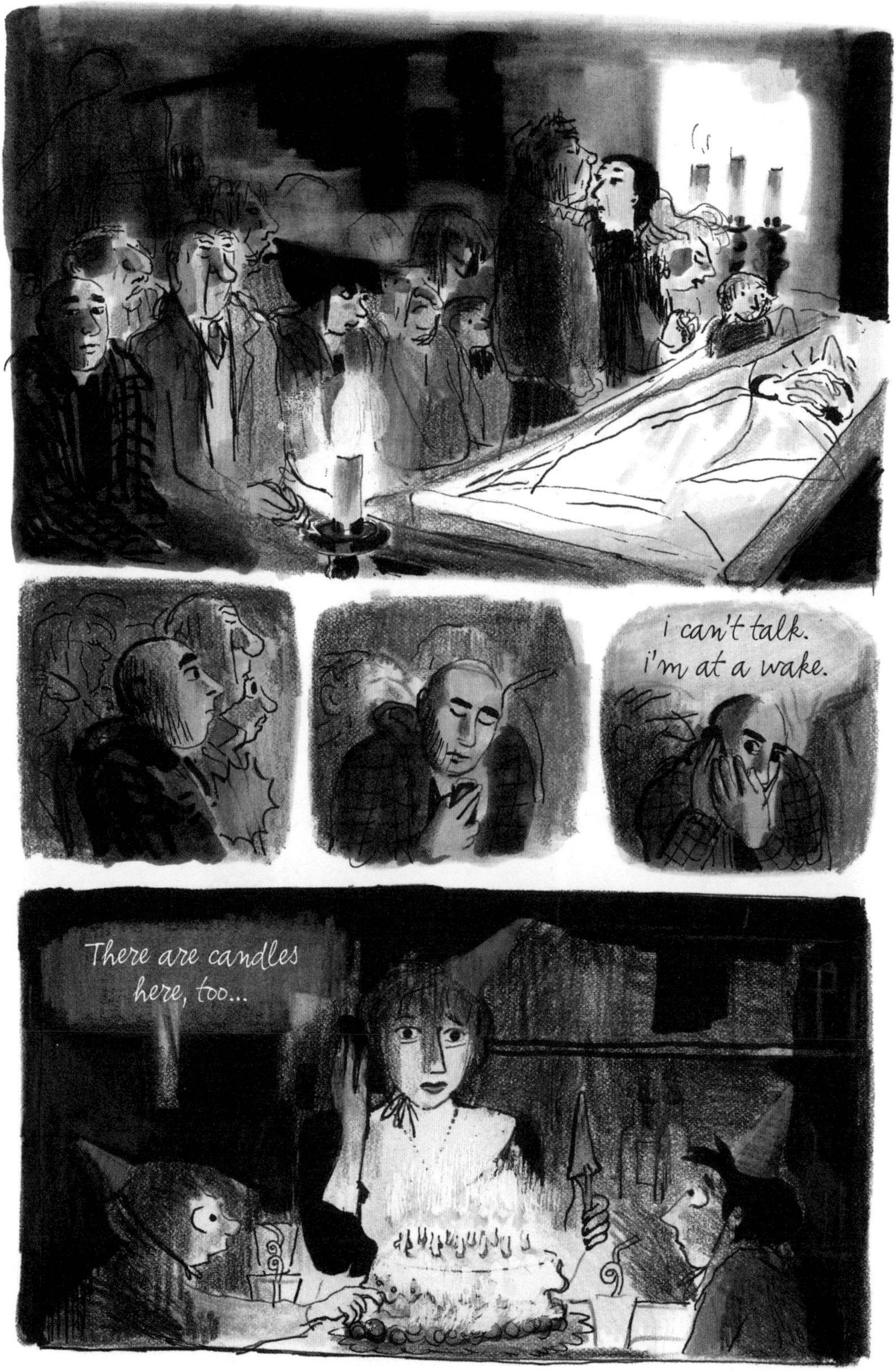
i can't talk.
i'm at a wake.
There are candles
here, too...

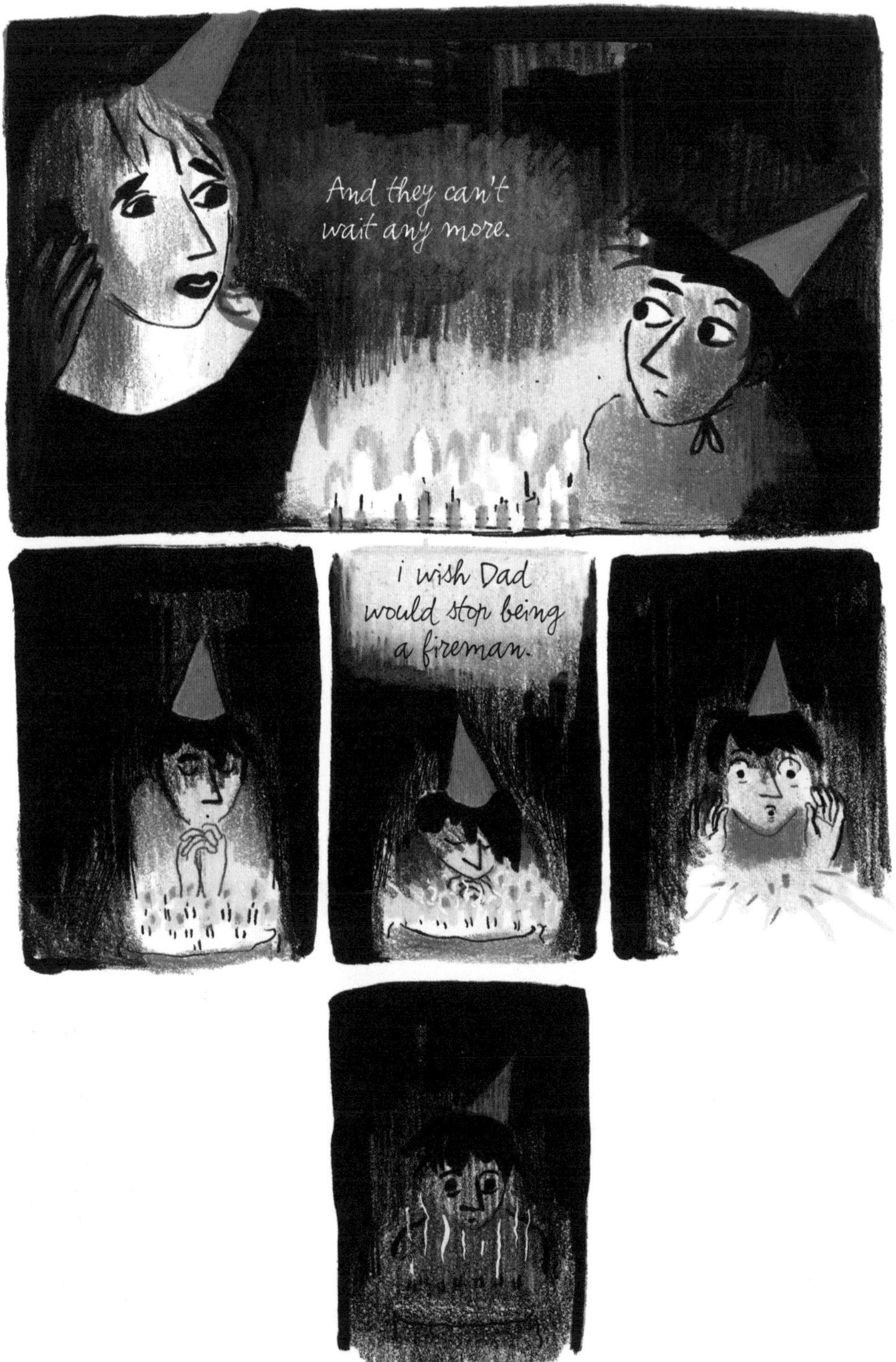
And they can't wait any more.
i wish Dad would stop being a fireman.

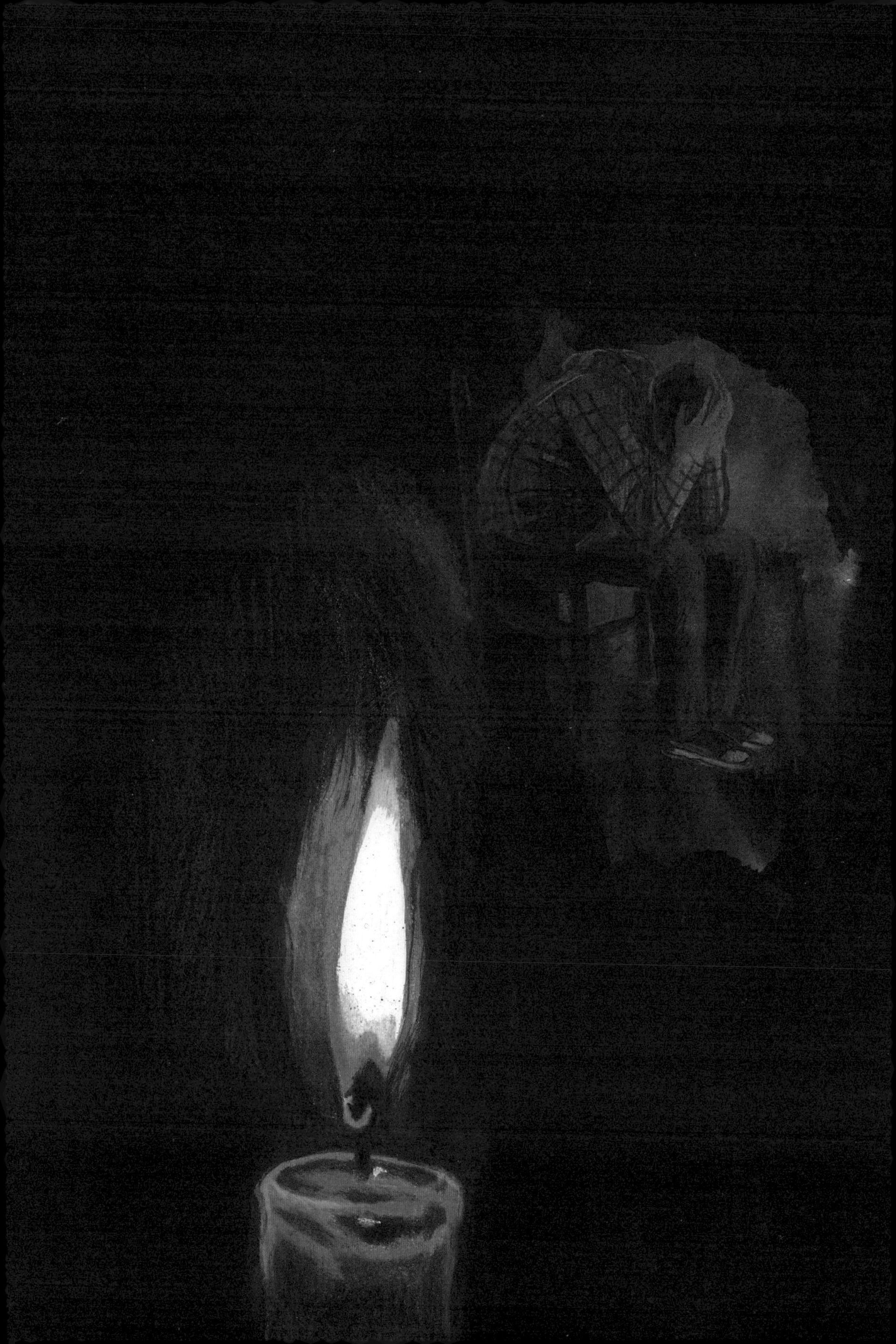

30 October 2008, 9.15 a.m.

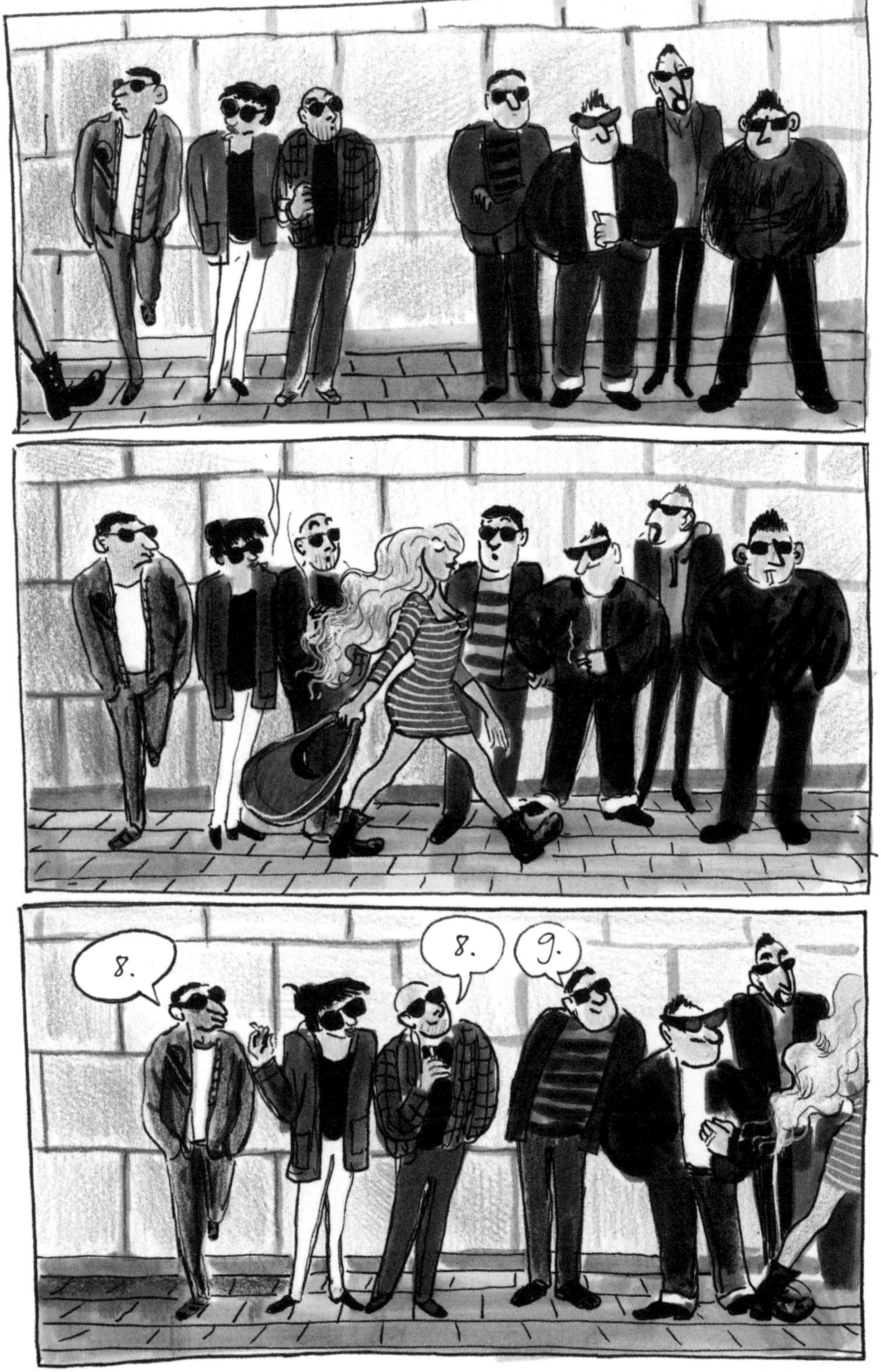
8.
8.
9.

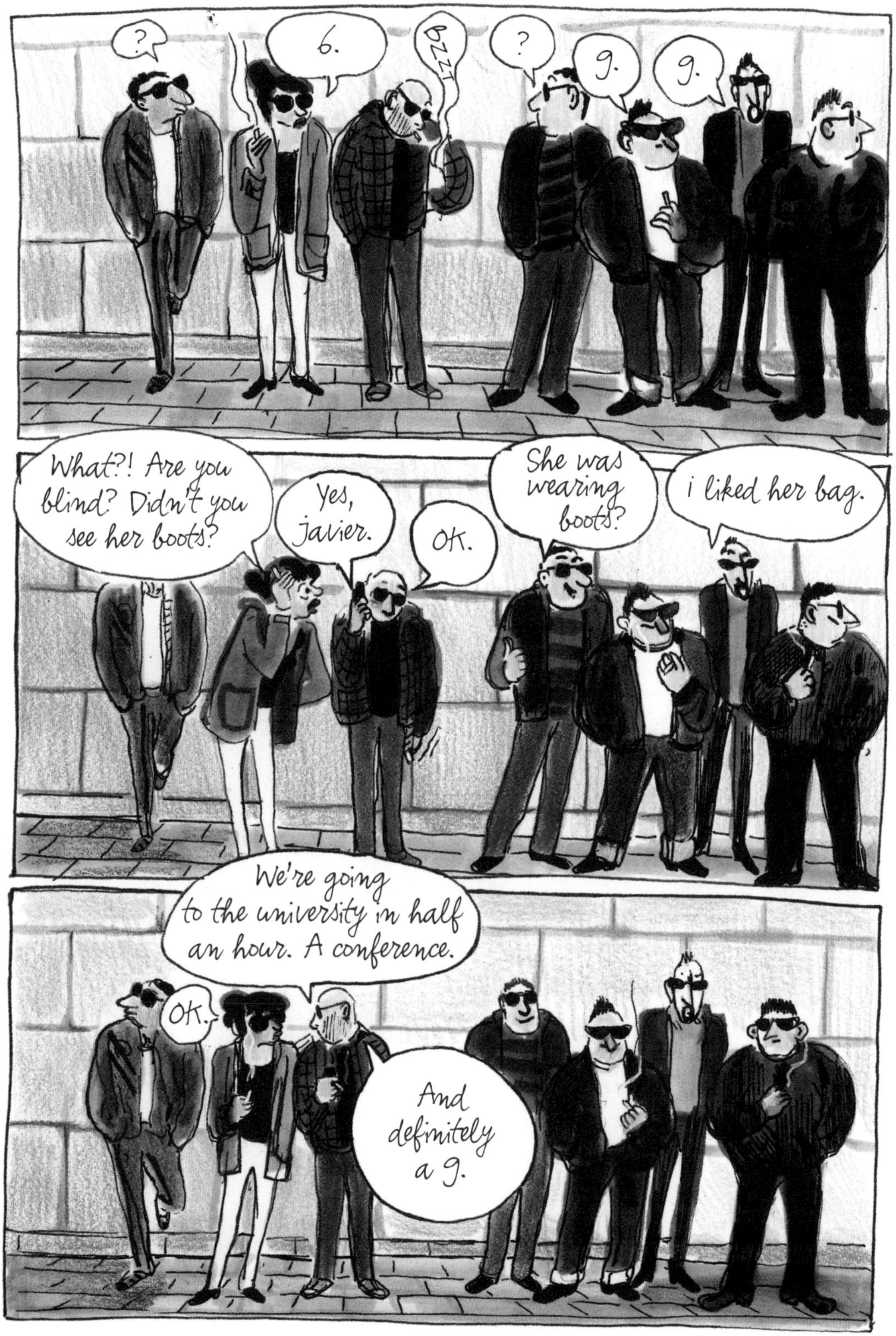
?
6.
BZZT
?
9.
9.
What?! Are you blind? Didn't you see her boots?
Yes, Javier.
OK.
She was wearing boots?
i liked her bag.
We're going to the university in half an hour. A conference.
OK.
And definitely a 9.

University of Navarra, 10.35 a.m.

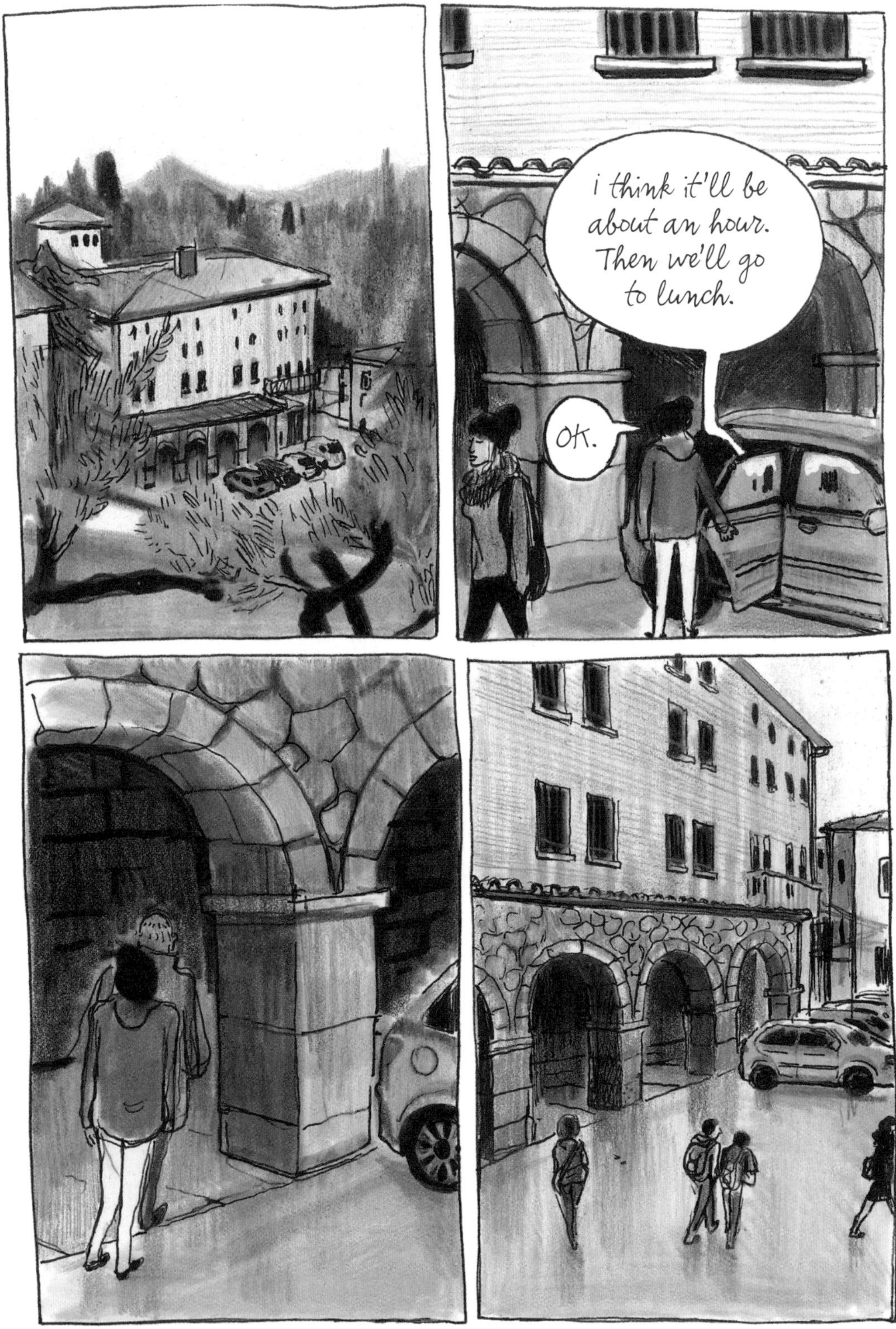
i think it'll be about an hour. Then we'll go to lunch.
OK.

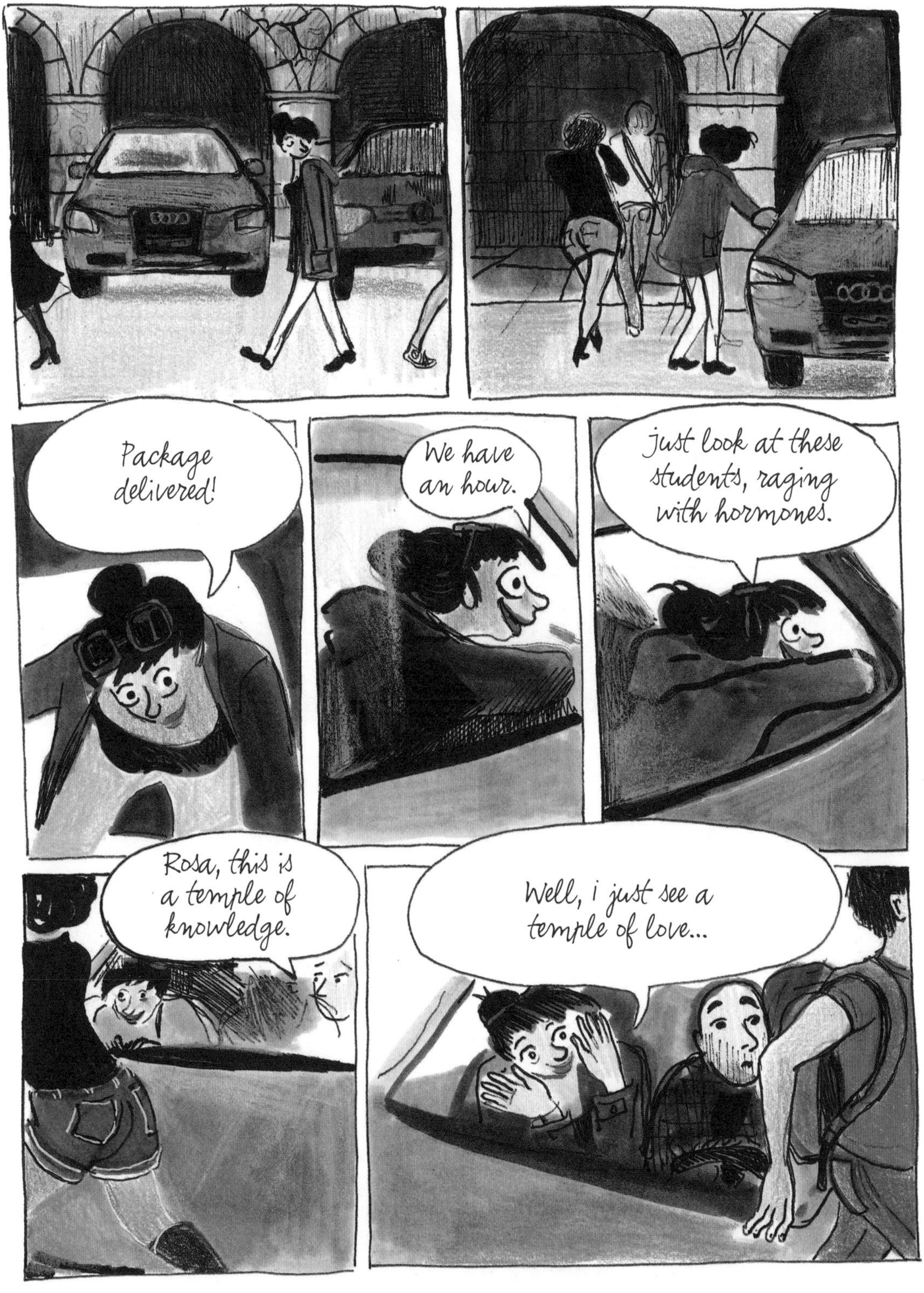
Package delivered!
We have an hour.
Just look at these students, raging with hormones.
Rosa, this is a temple of knowledge.
Well, i just see a temple of love...

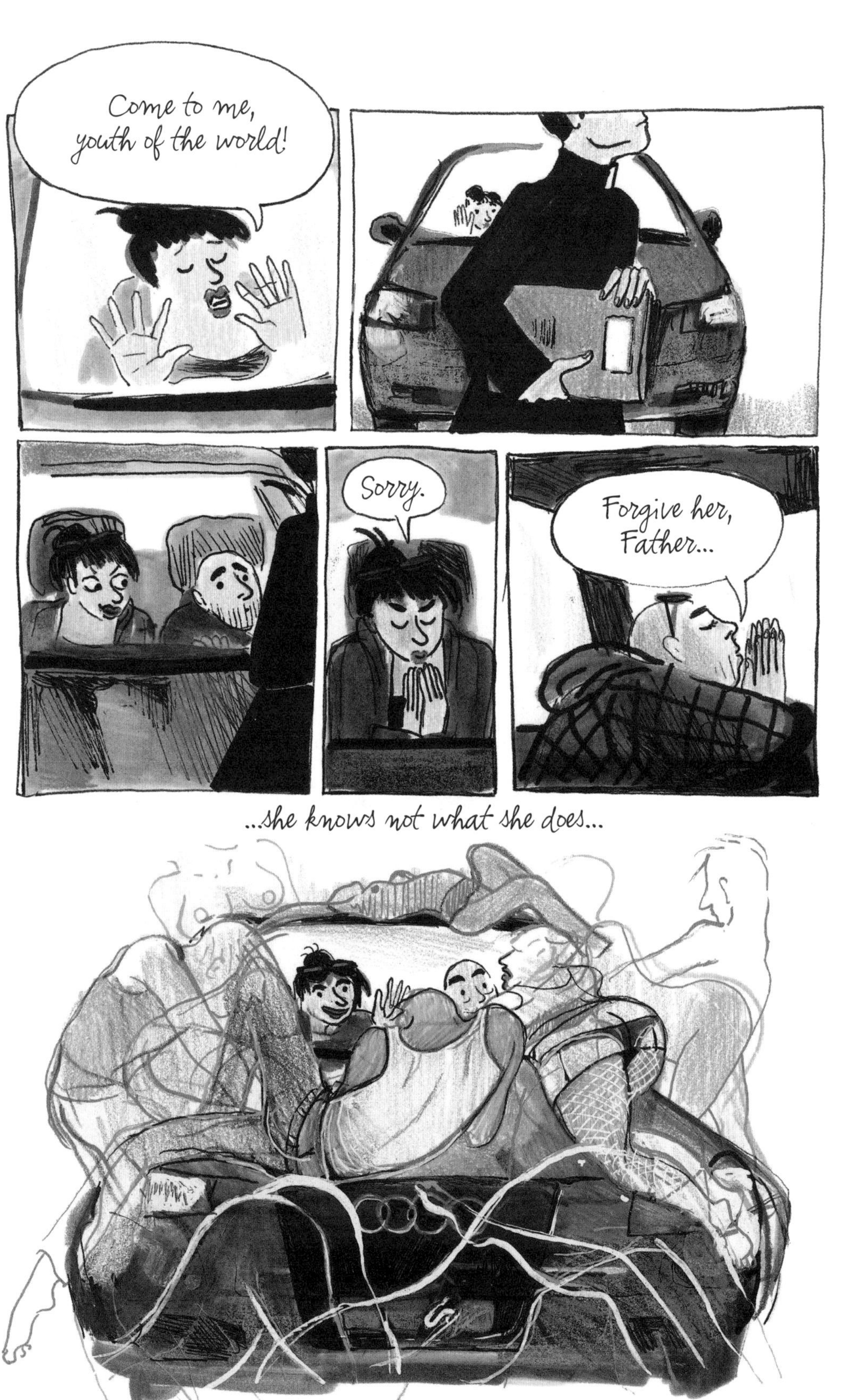
Come to me, youth of the world!
Sorry.
Forgive her, Father...
...she knows not what she does...

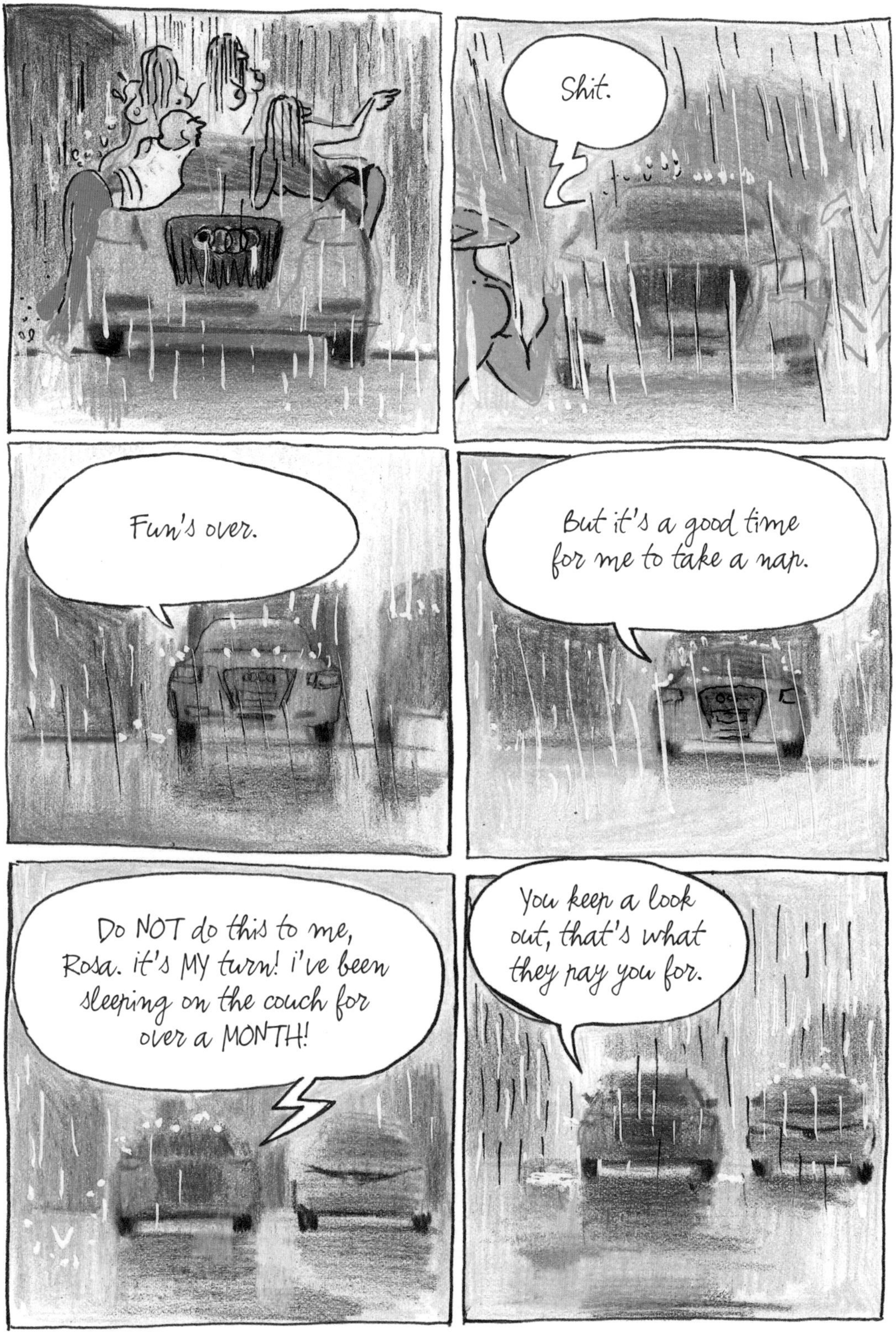
Shit.
Fun's over.
But it's a good time for me to take a nap.
Do NOT do this to me, Rosa. it's MY turn! i've been sleeping on the couch for over a MONTH!
You keep a look out, that's what they pay you for.

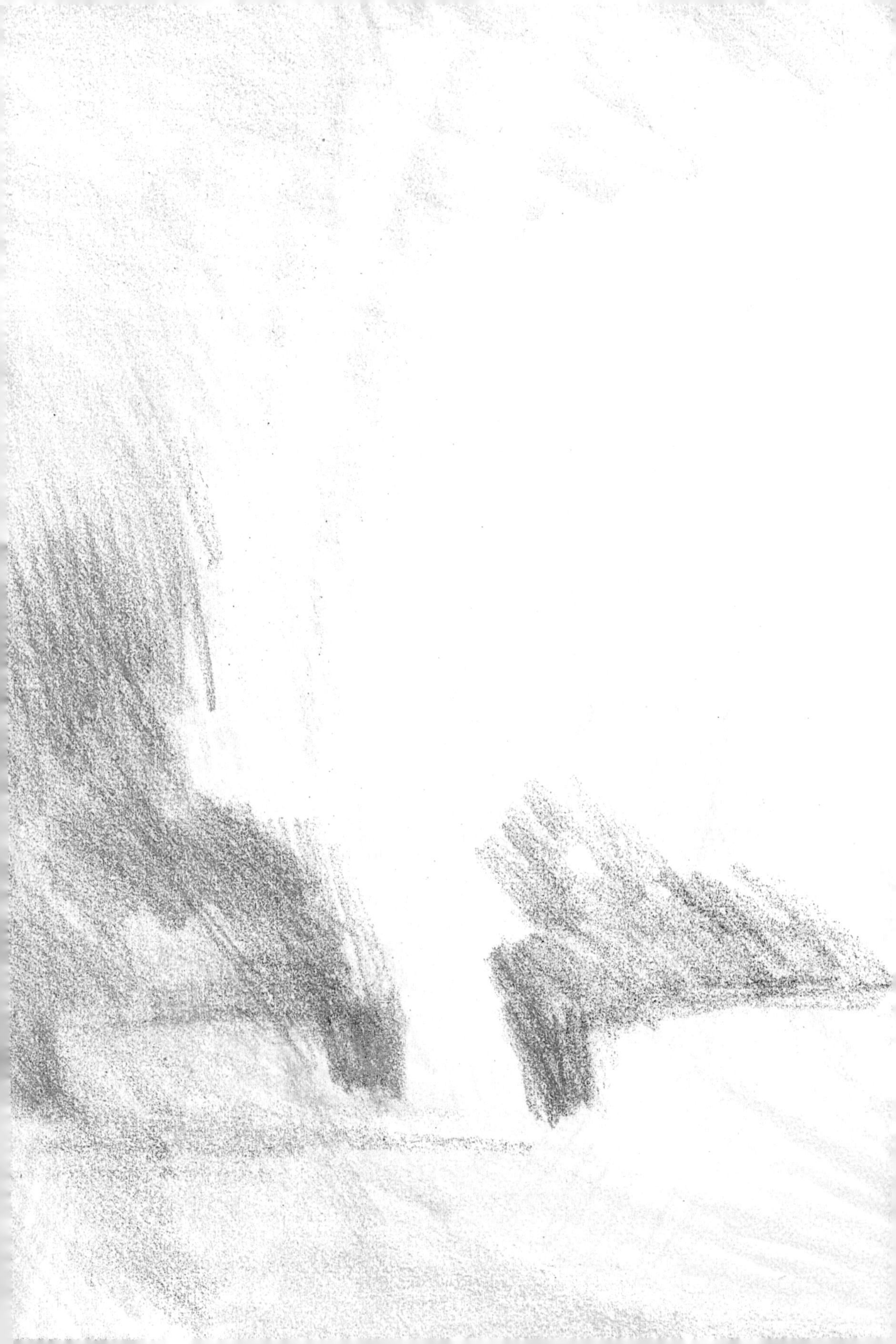

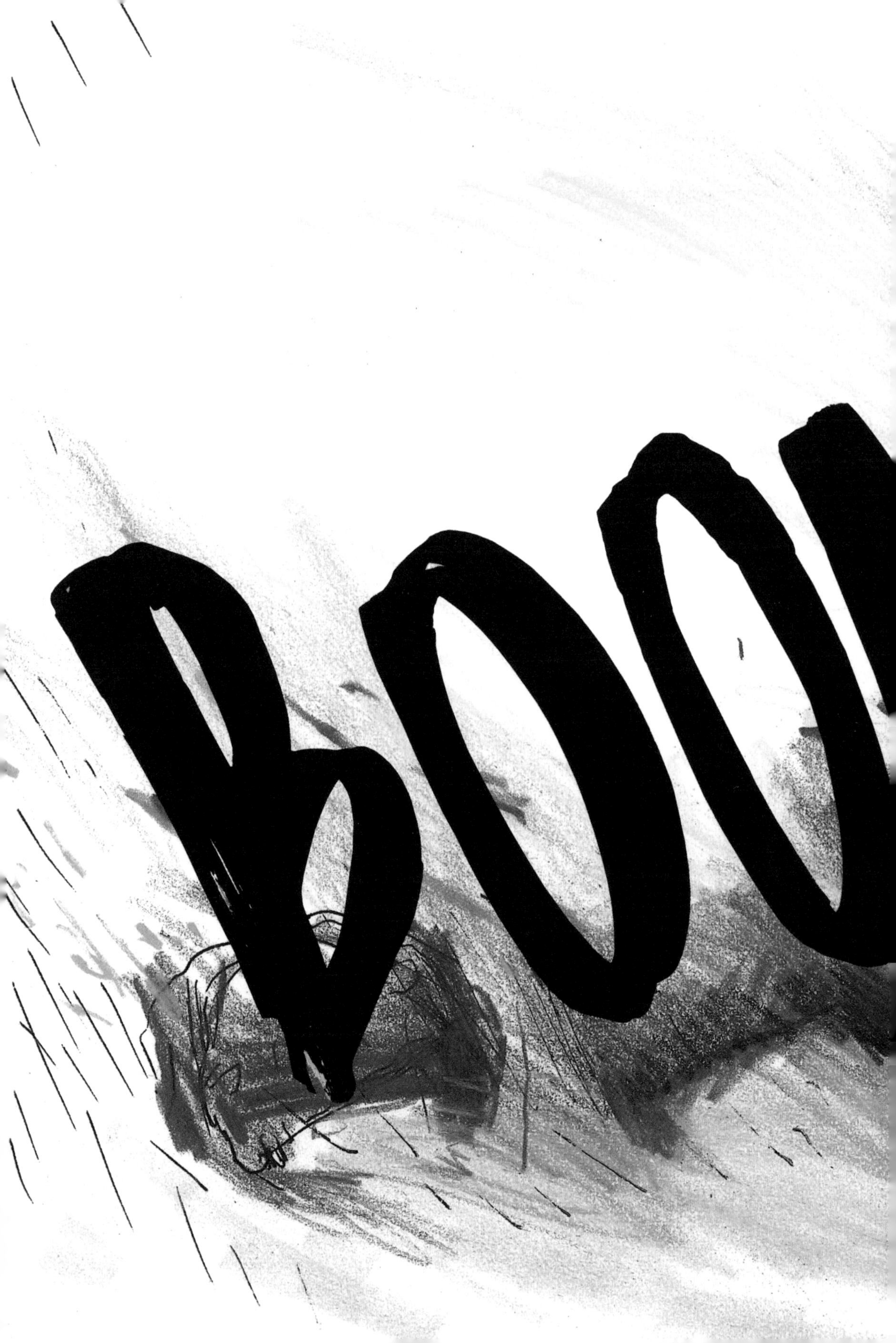
BOO

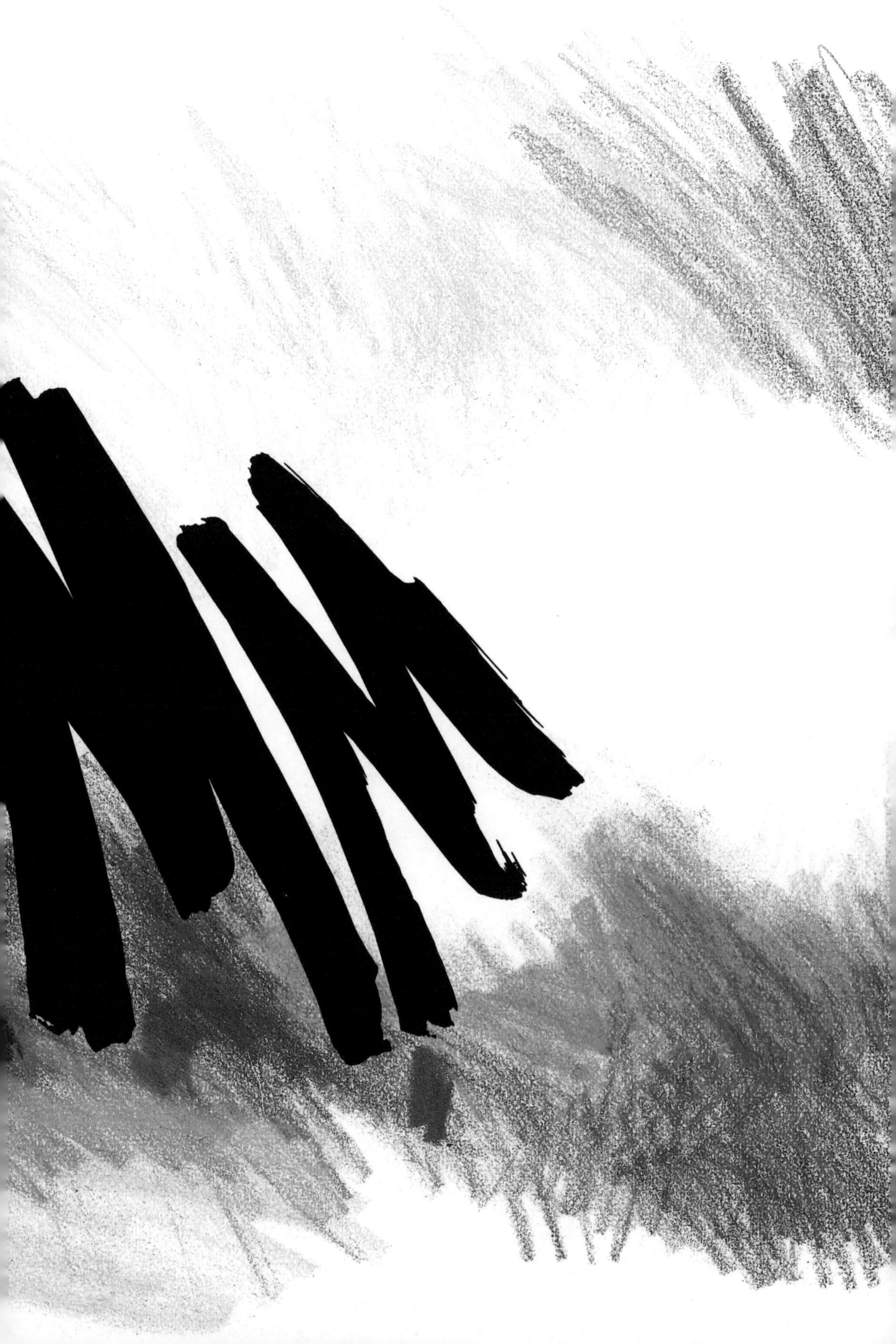

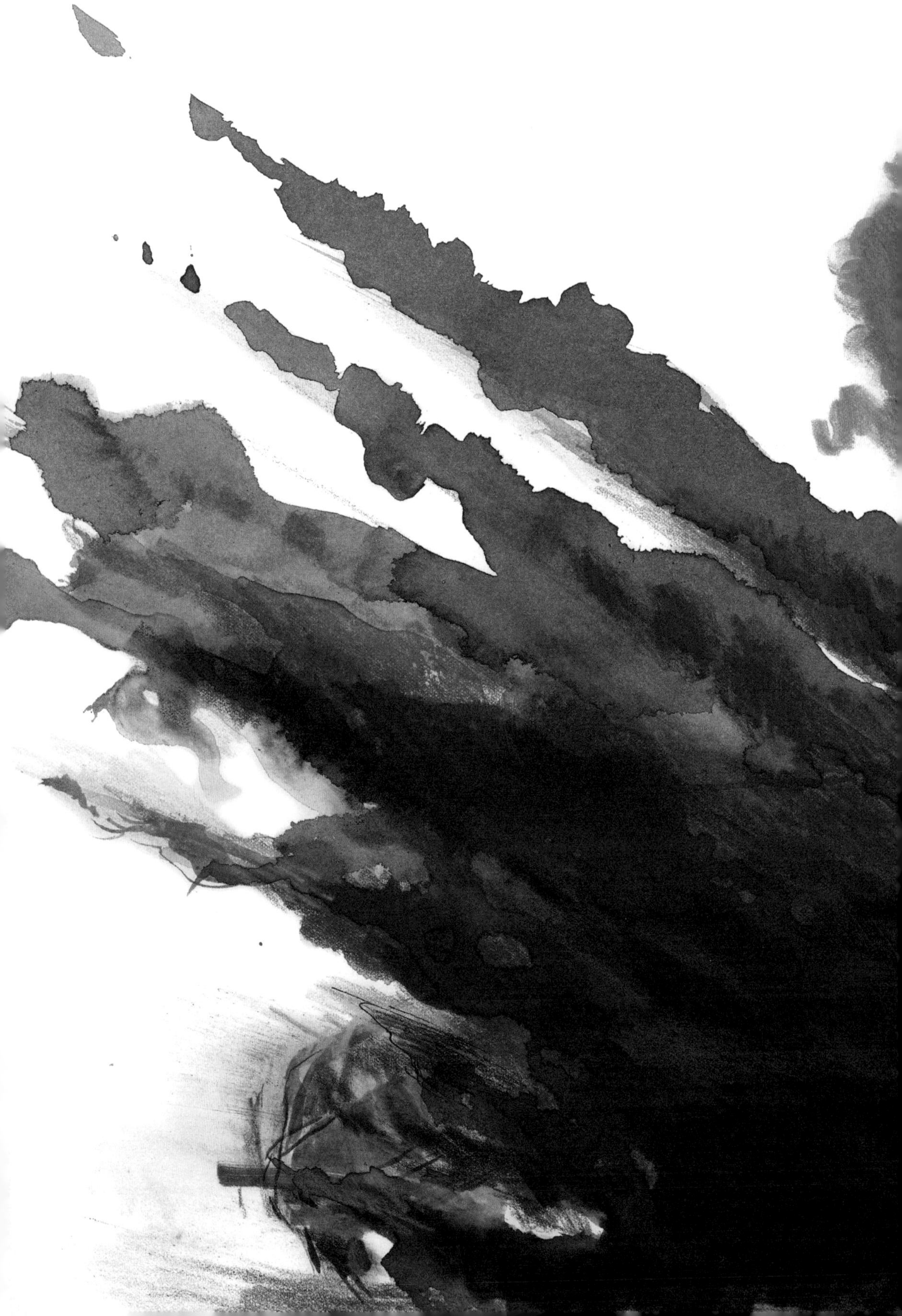

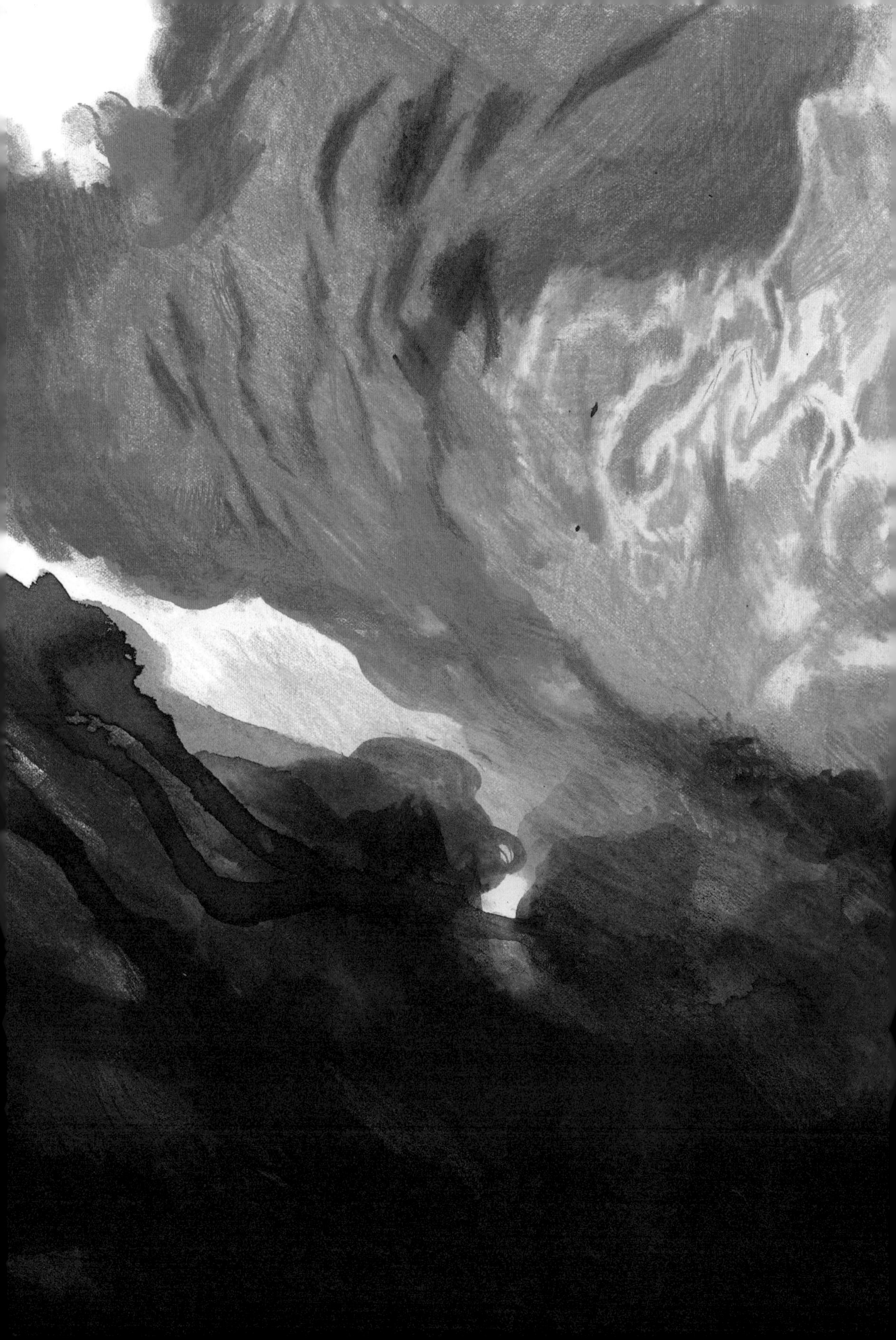

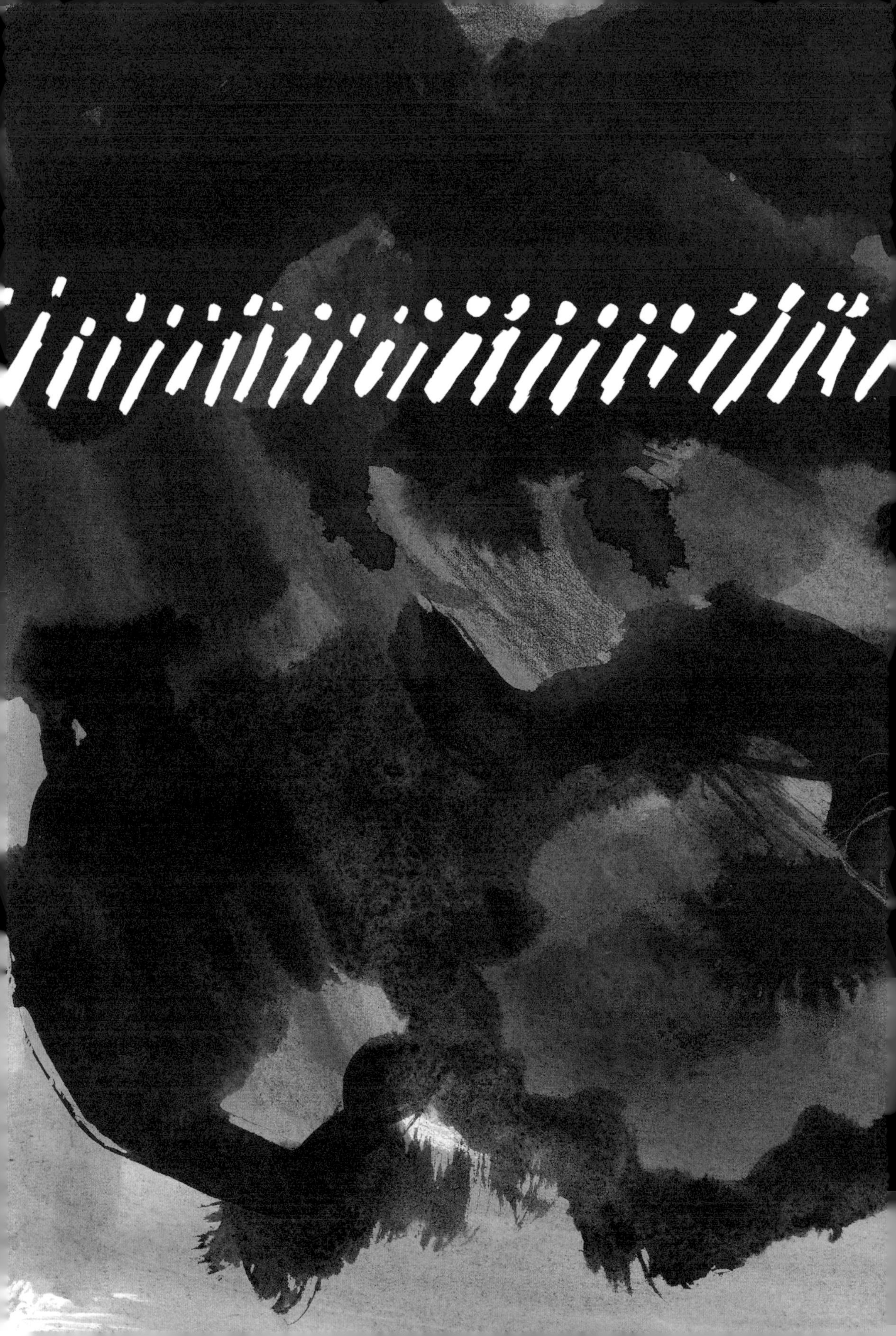

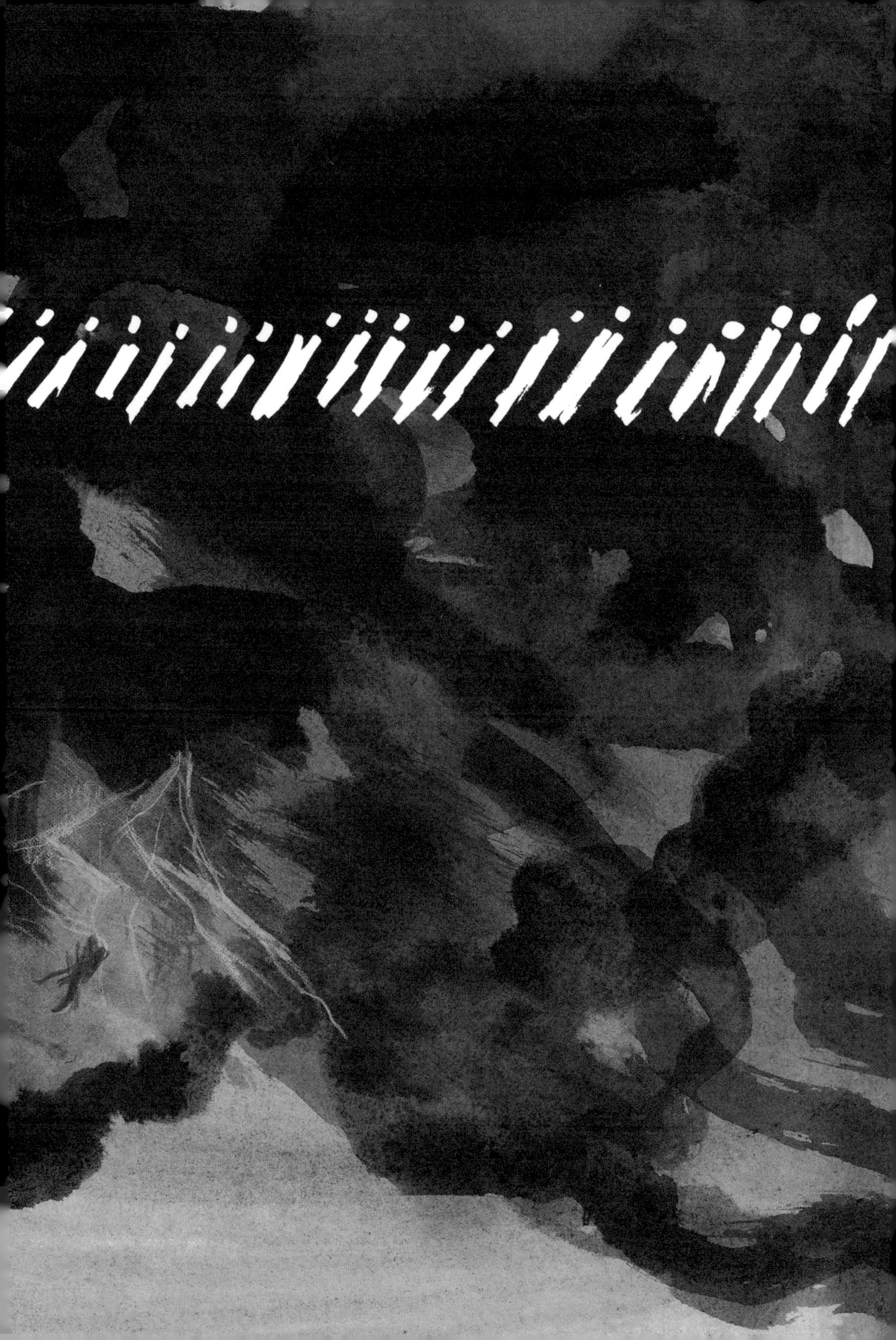

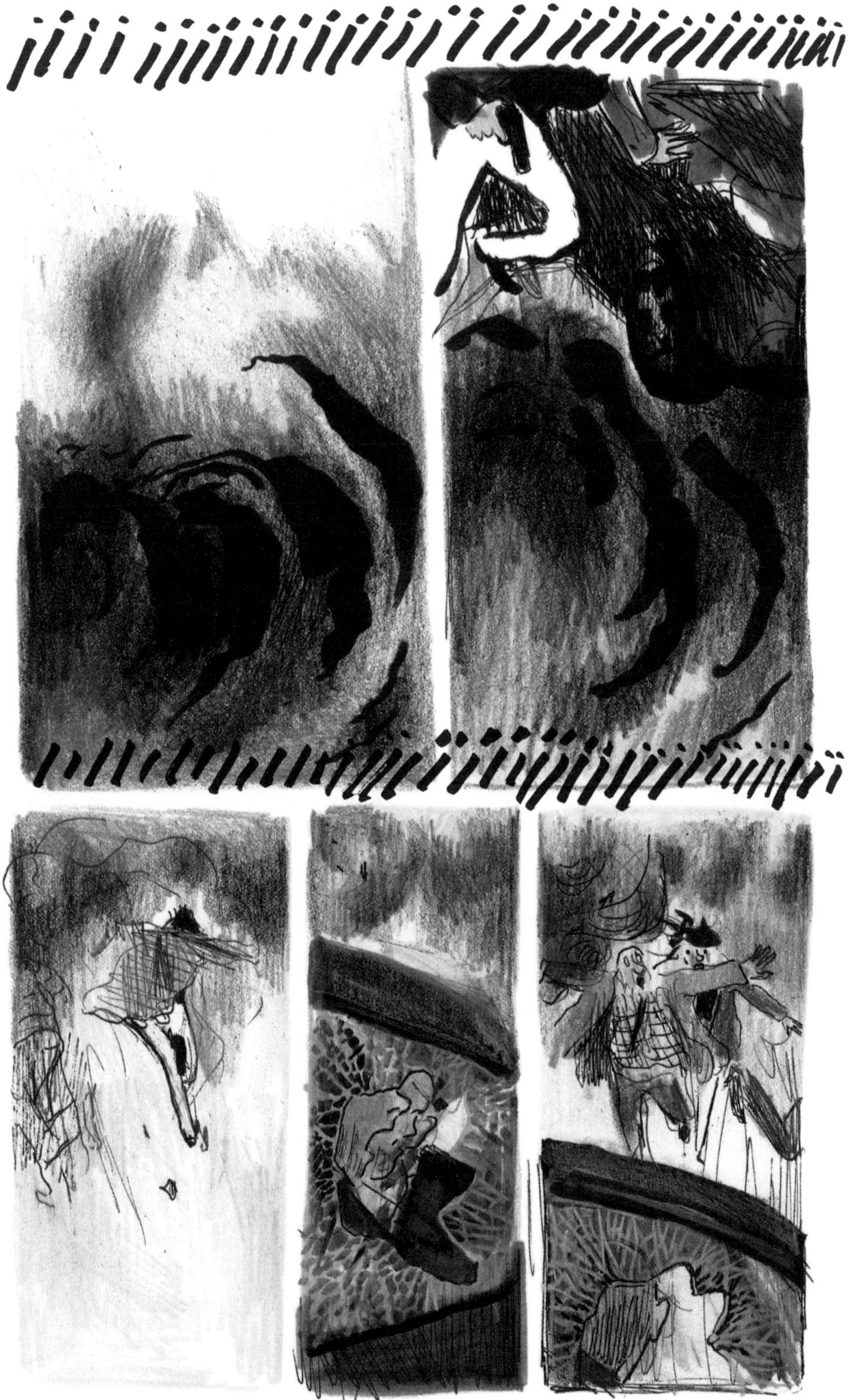

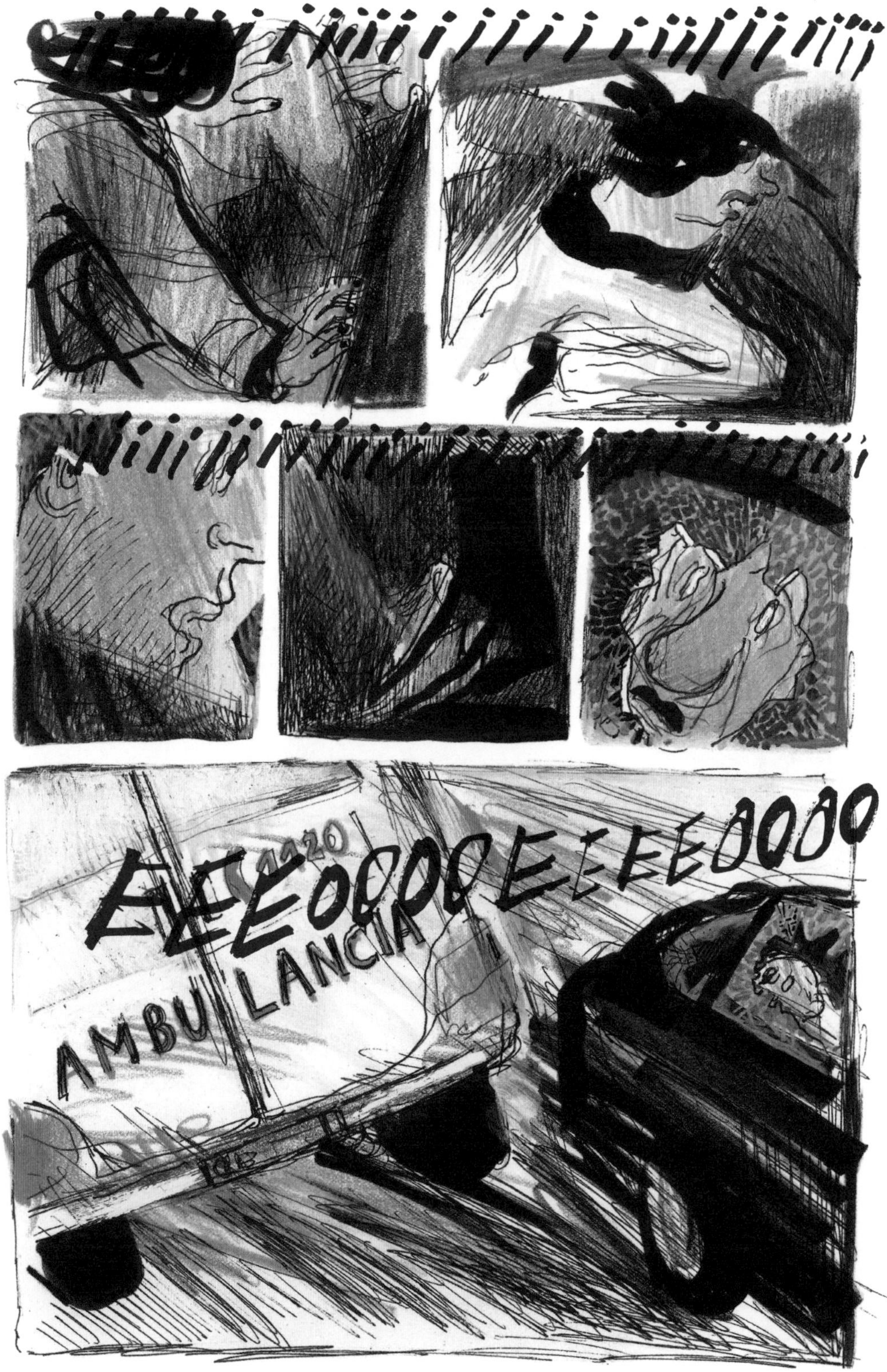
EEEOOOO EEEEOOOO
AMBULANCIA

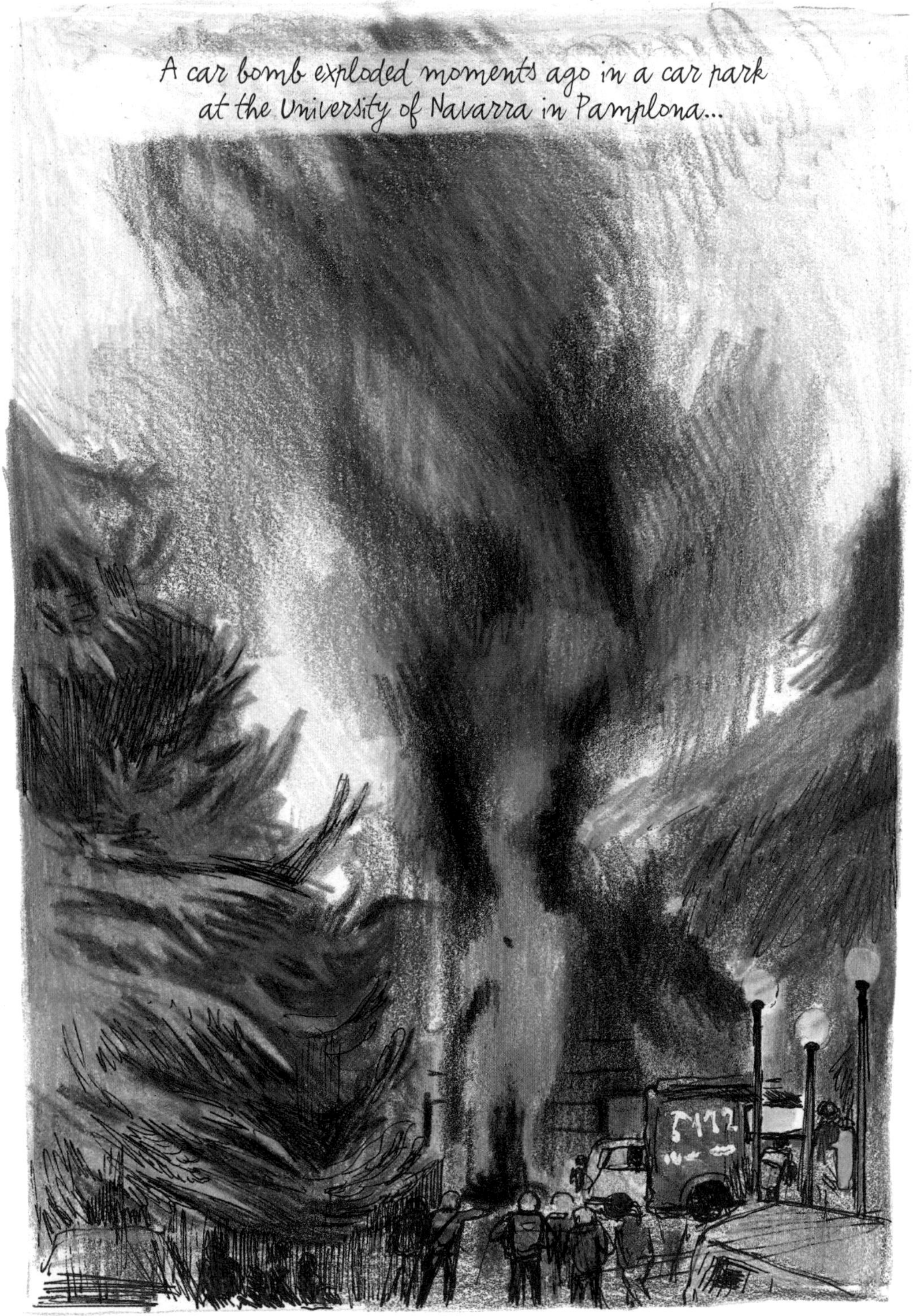
A car bomb exploded moments ago in a car park
at the University of Navarra in Pamplona...

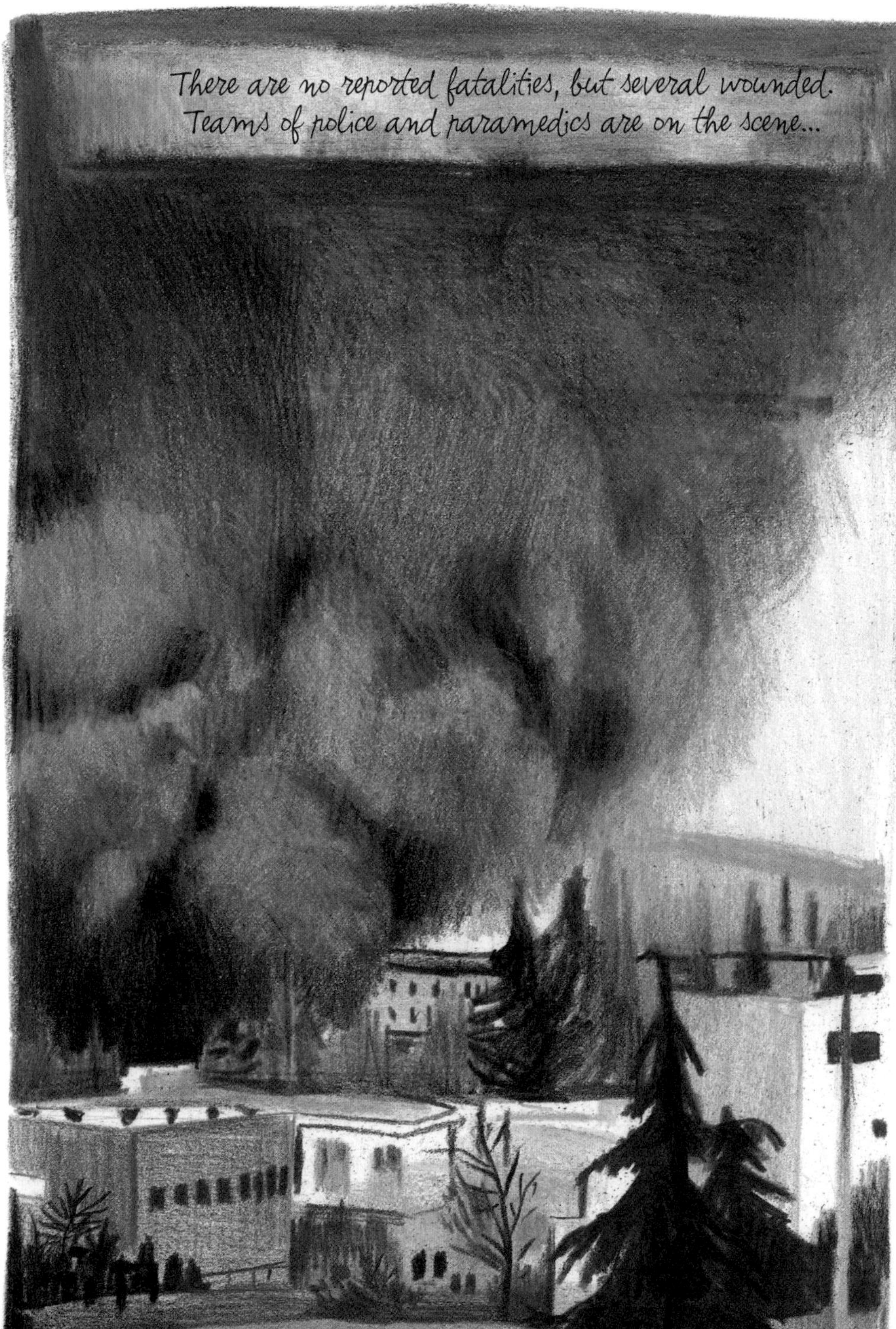
There are no reported fatalities, but several wounded. Teams of police and paramedics are on the scene...

But that bomb didn't only explode at the university.

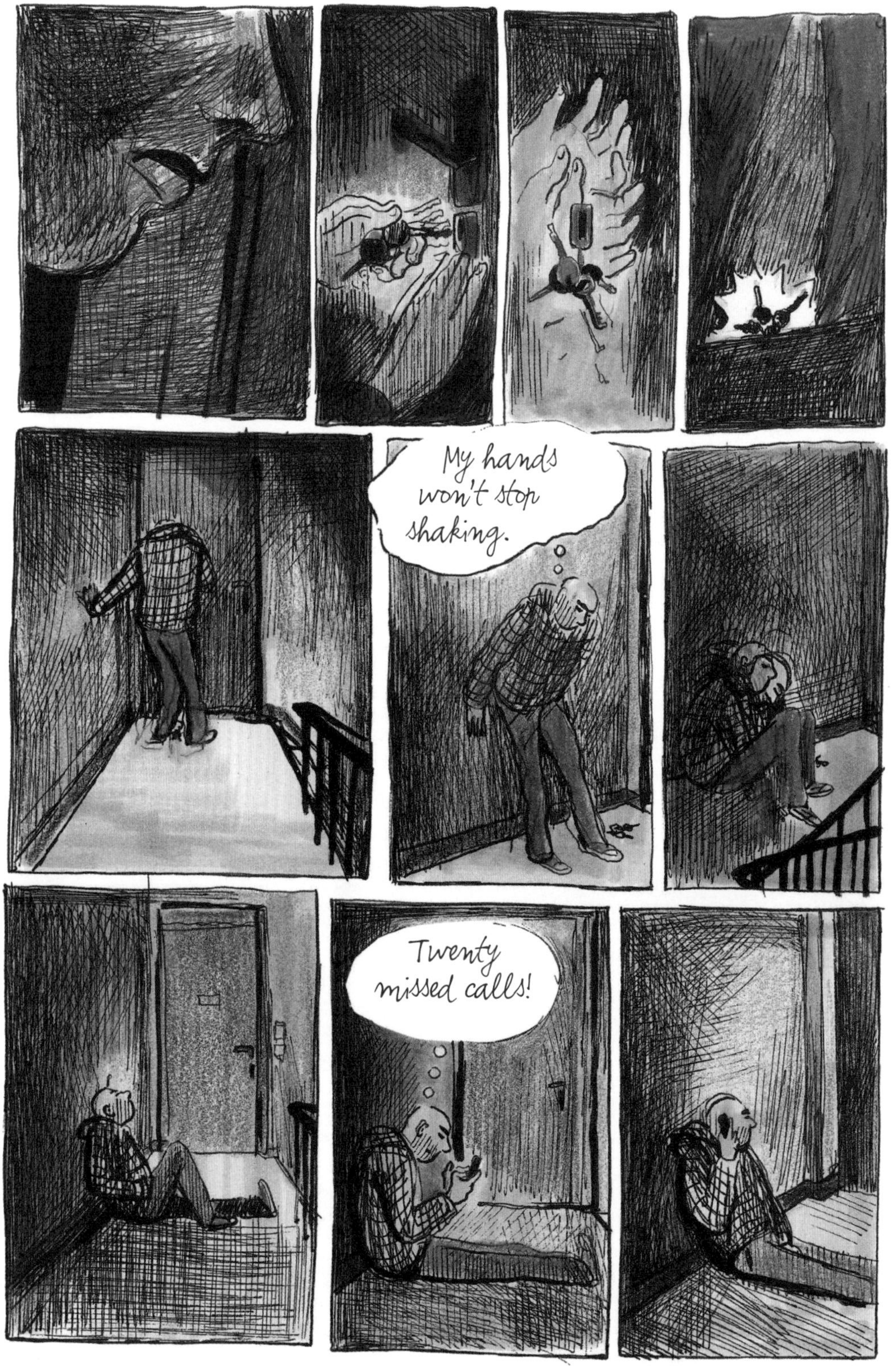
My hands won't stop shaking.
Twenty missed calls!

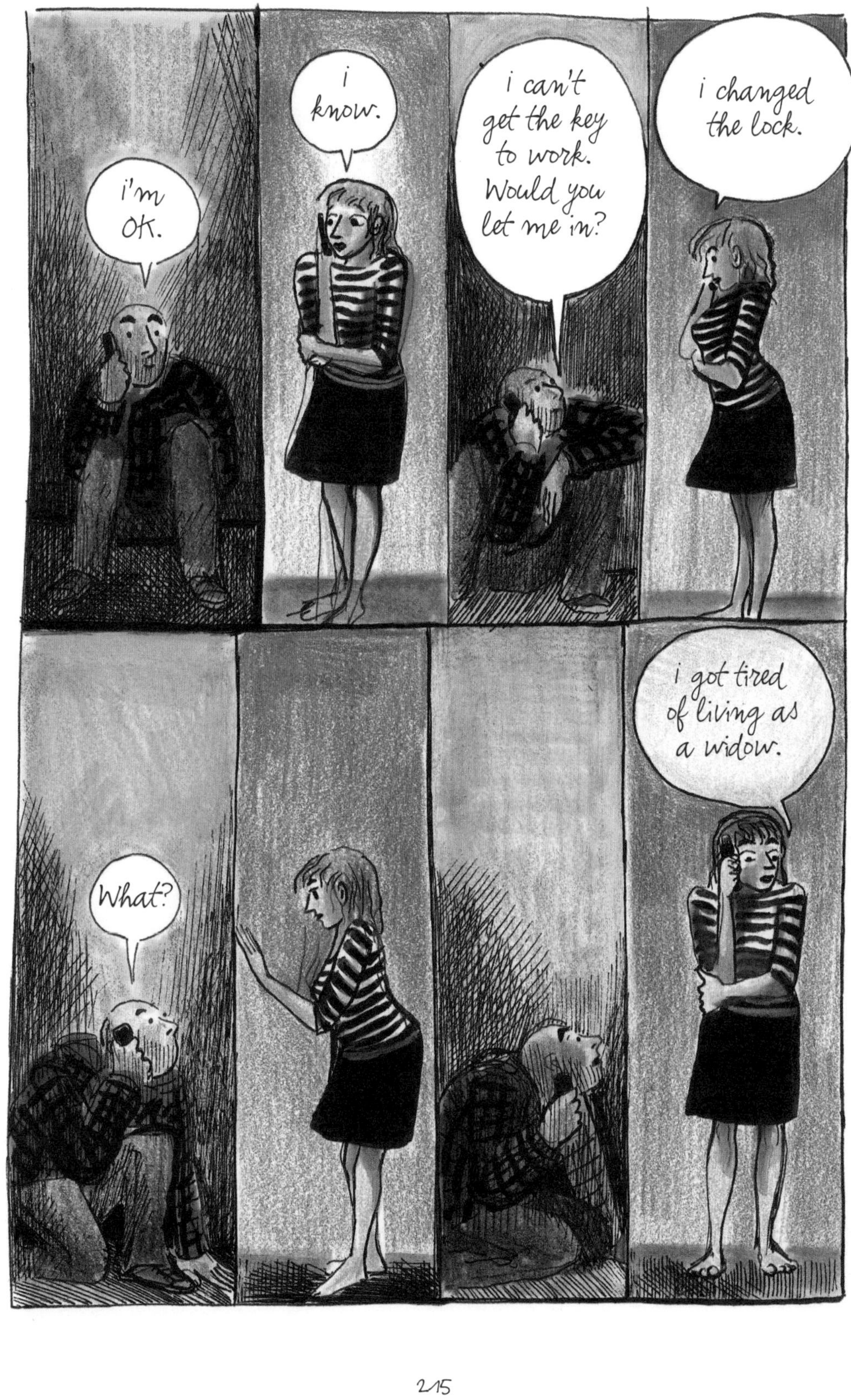
i'm OK.
i know.
i can't get the key to work. Would you let me in?
i changed the lock.
What?
i got tired of living as a widow.

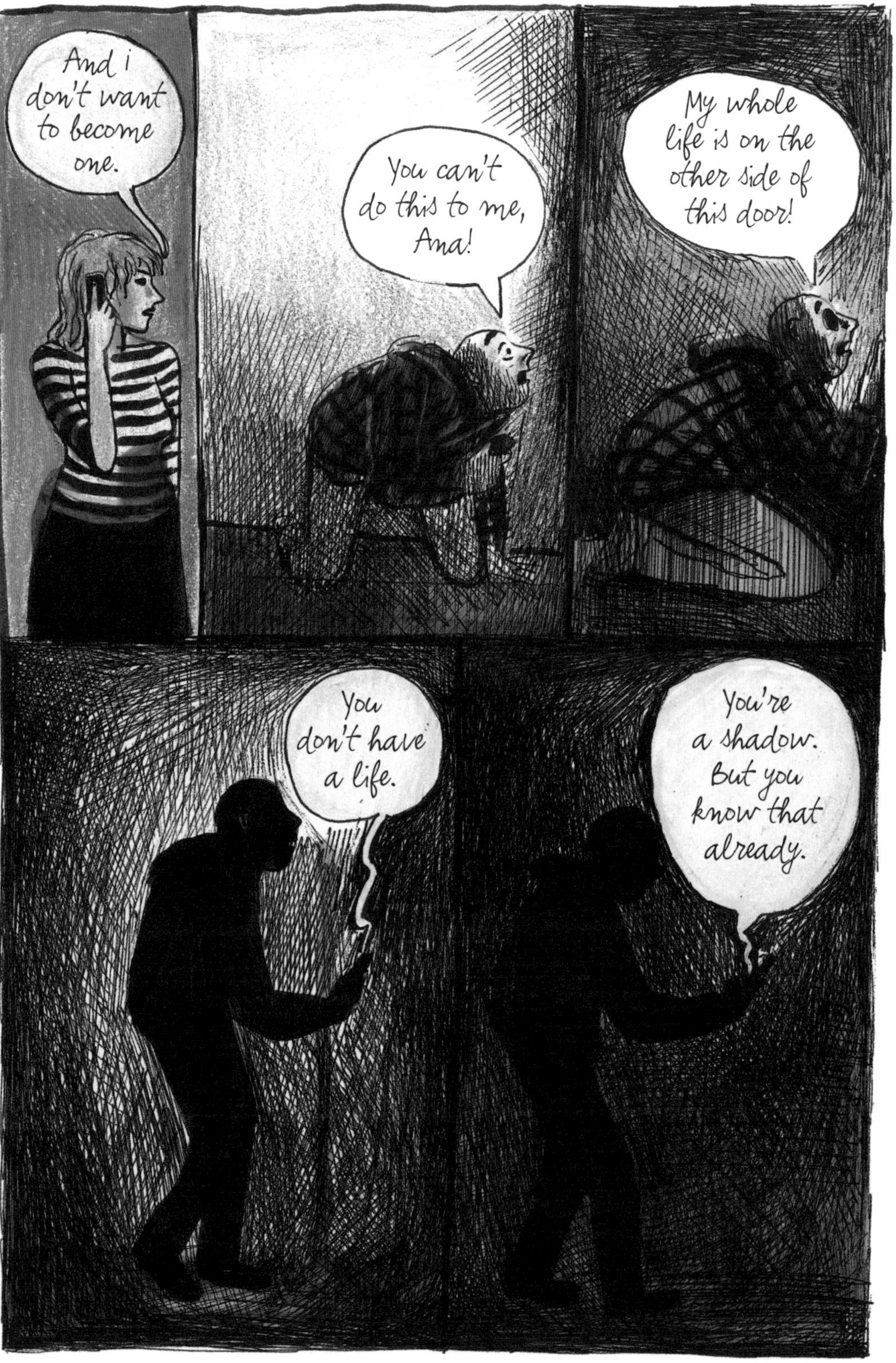
And i don't want to become one.
You can't do this to me, Ana!
My whole life is on the other side of this door!
You don't have a life.
You're a shadow. But you know that already.

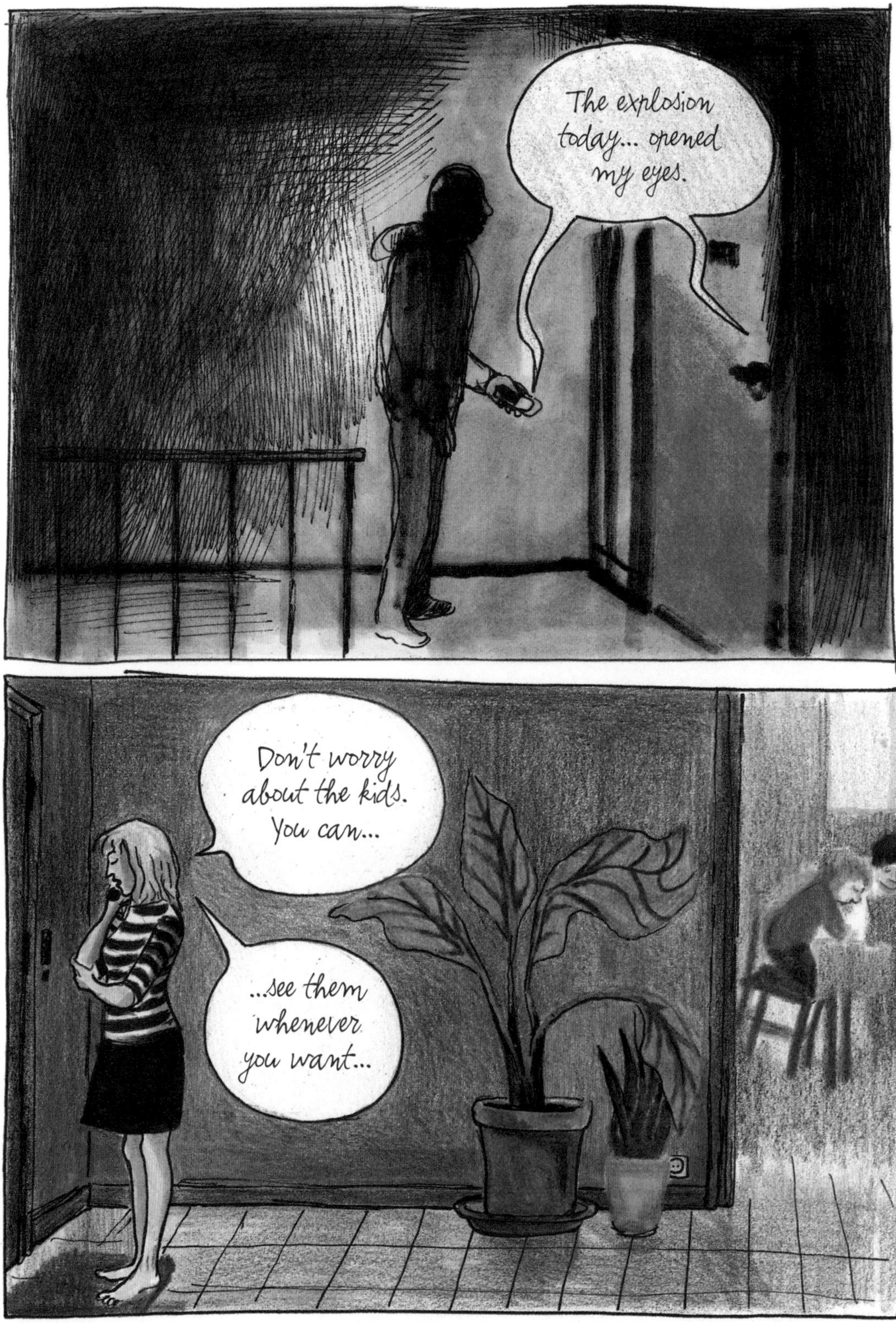
The explosion today... opened my eyes.
Don't worry about the kids. You can...
...see them whenever you want...

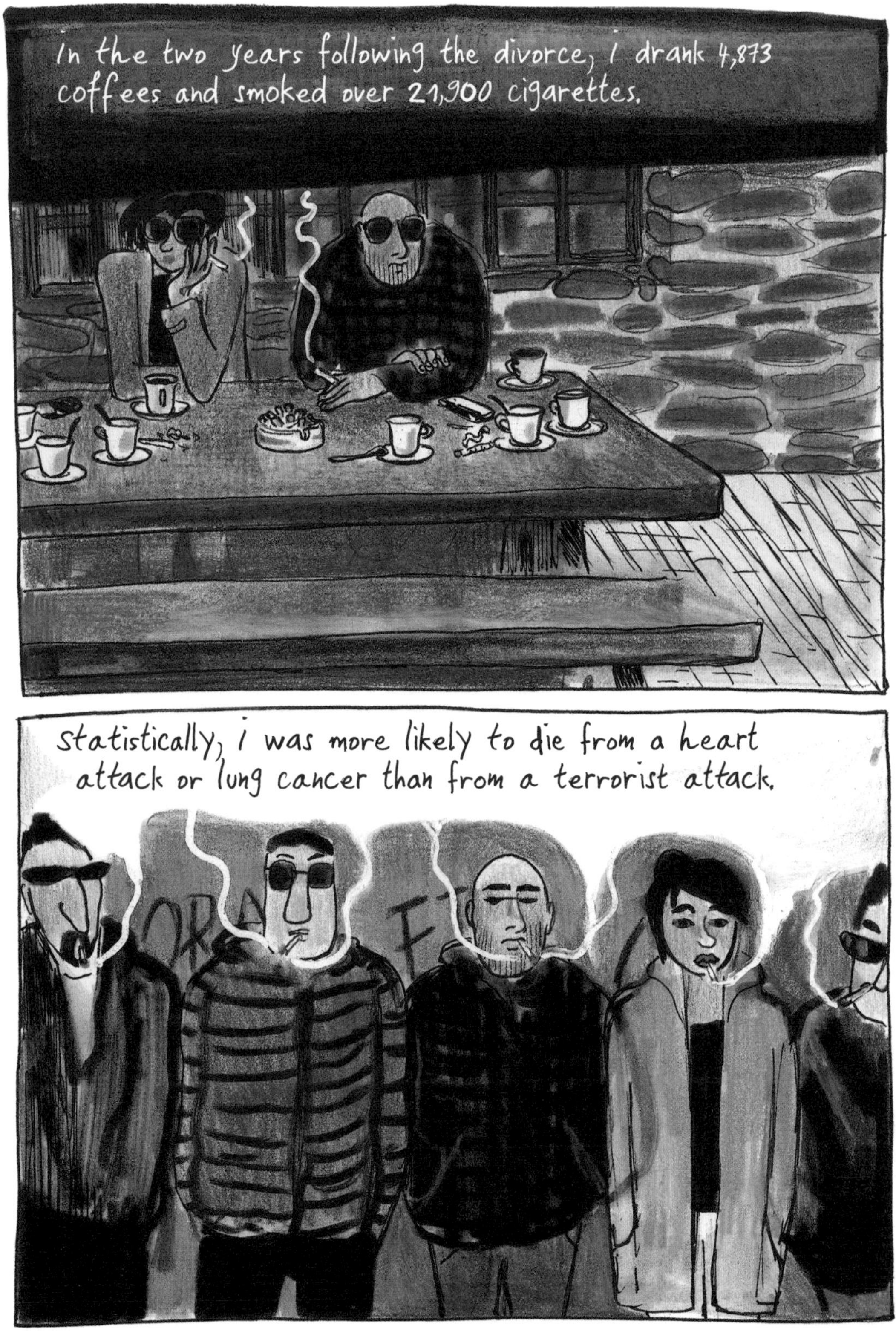
In the two years following the divorce, I drank 4,873 coffees and smoked over 21,900 cigarettes.
Statistically, I was more likely to die from a heart attack or lung cancer than from a terrorist attack.

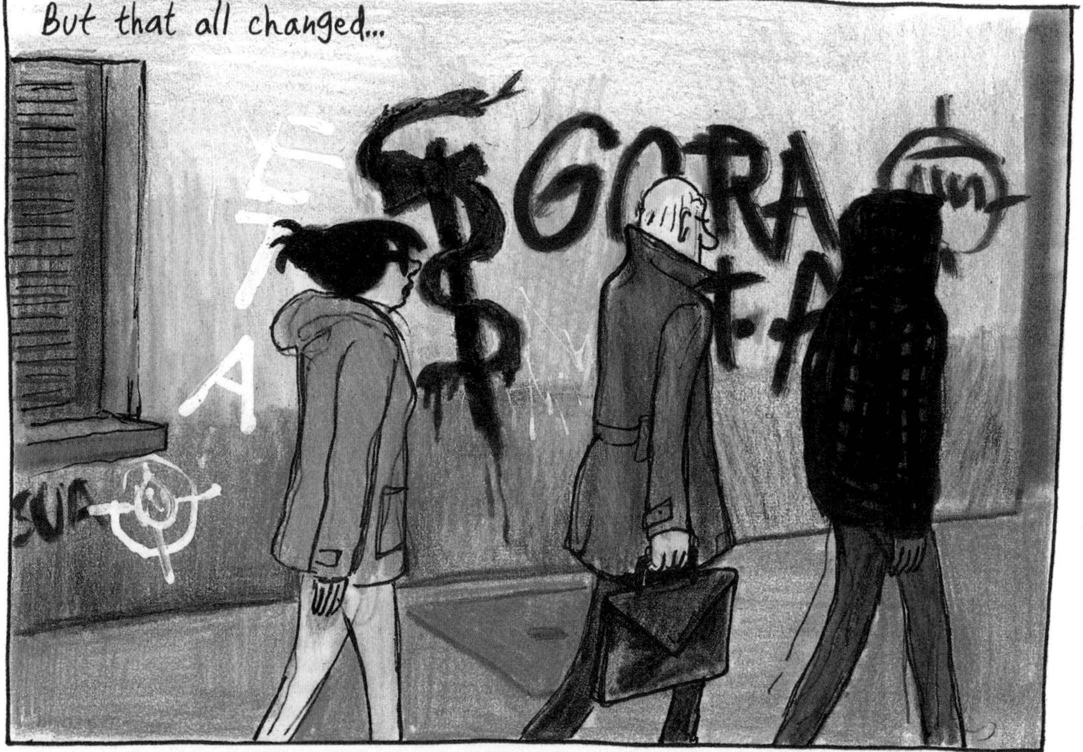
But that all changed...

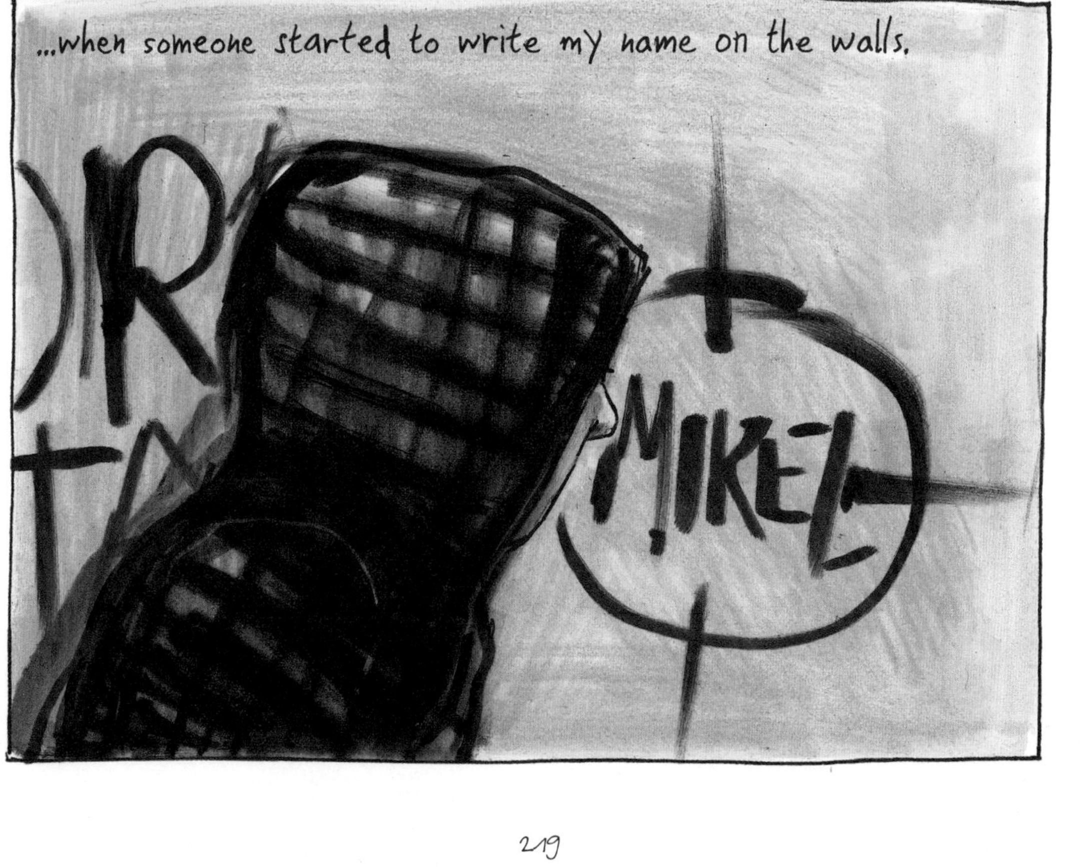
...when someone started to write my name on the walls.
MIKEL

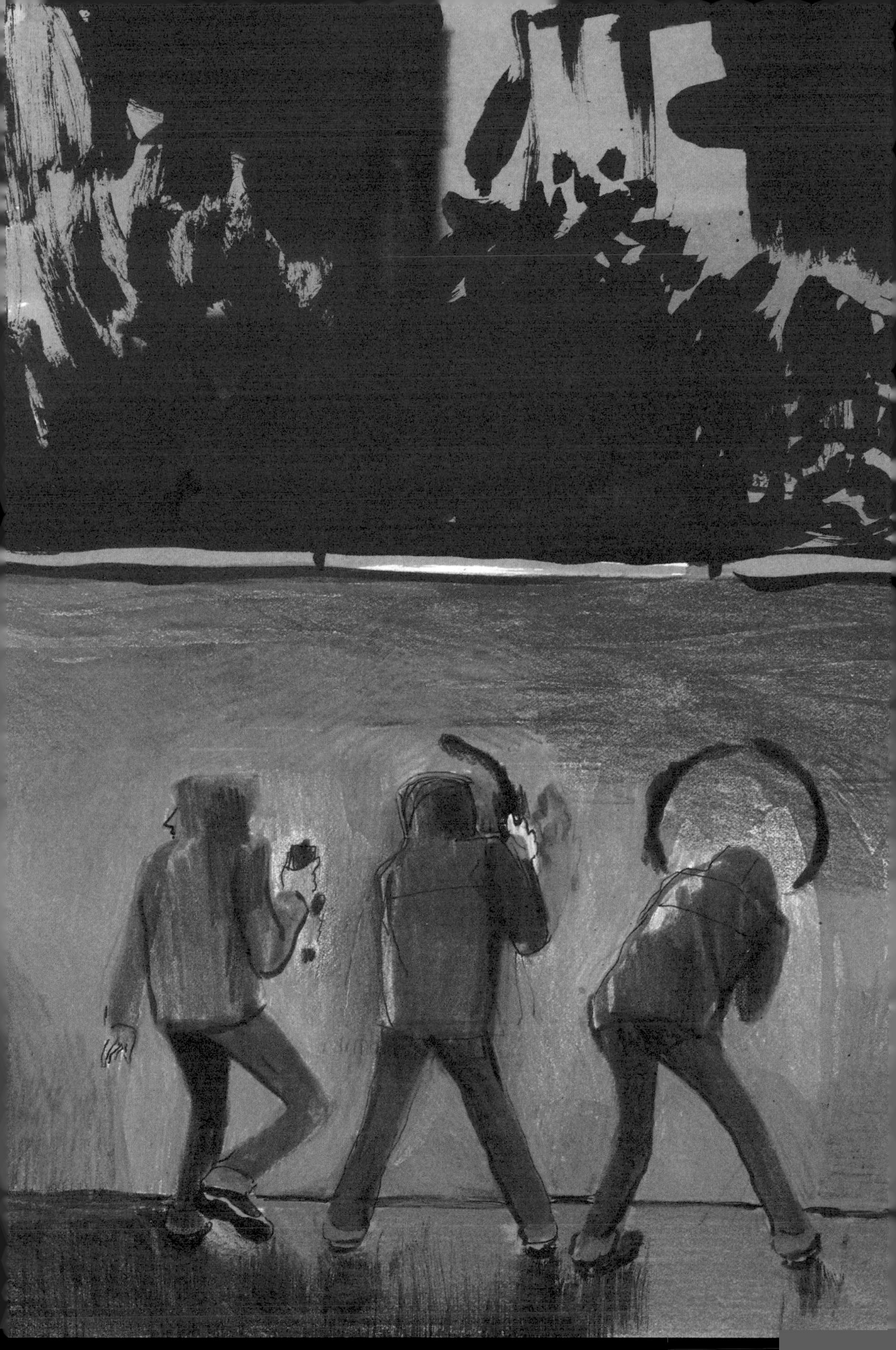

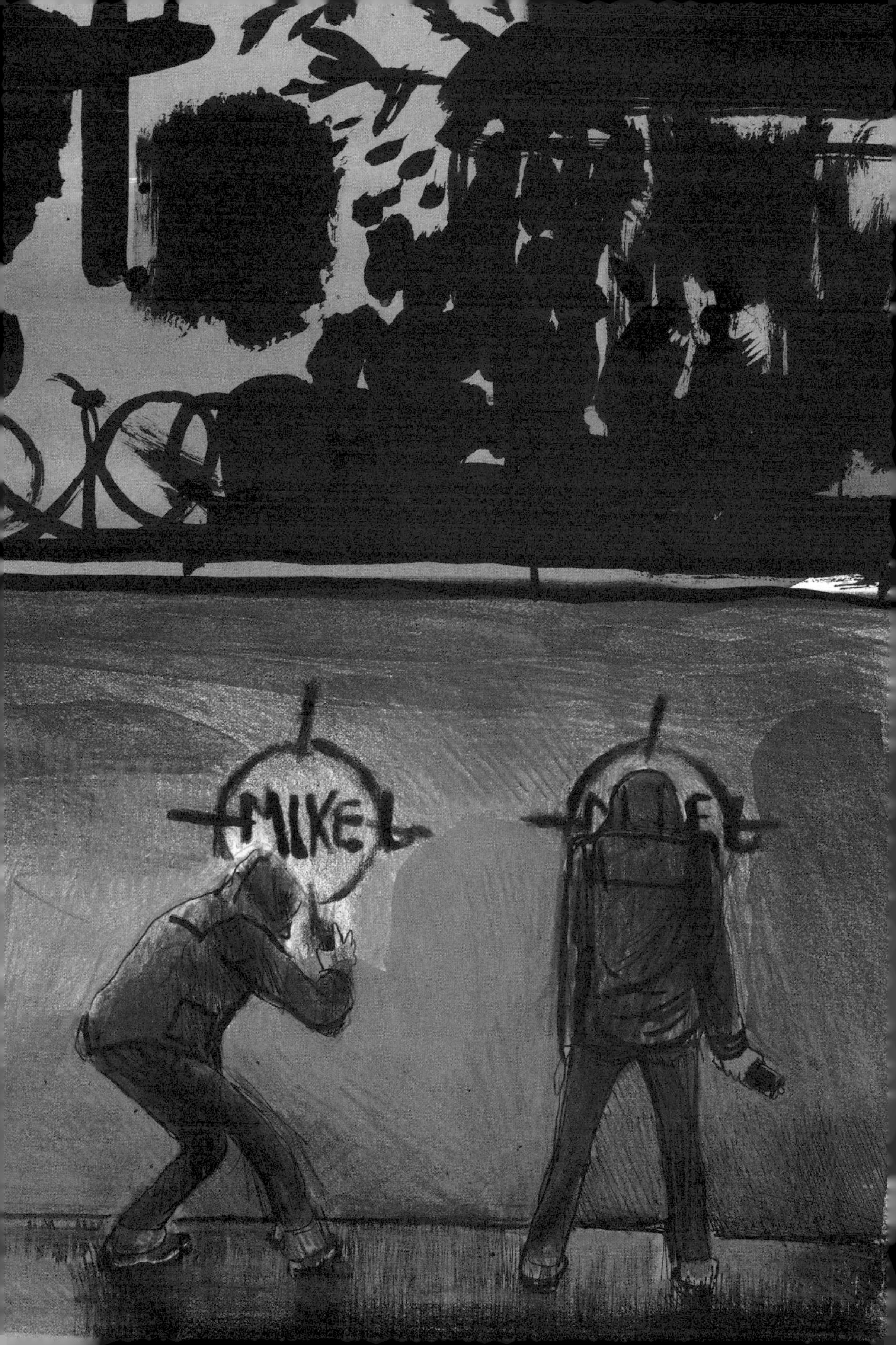
MIKE

That was the fourth time i had to move.

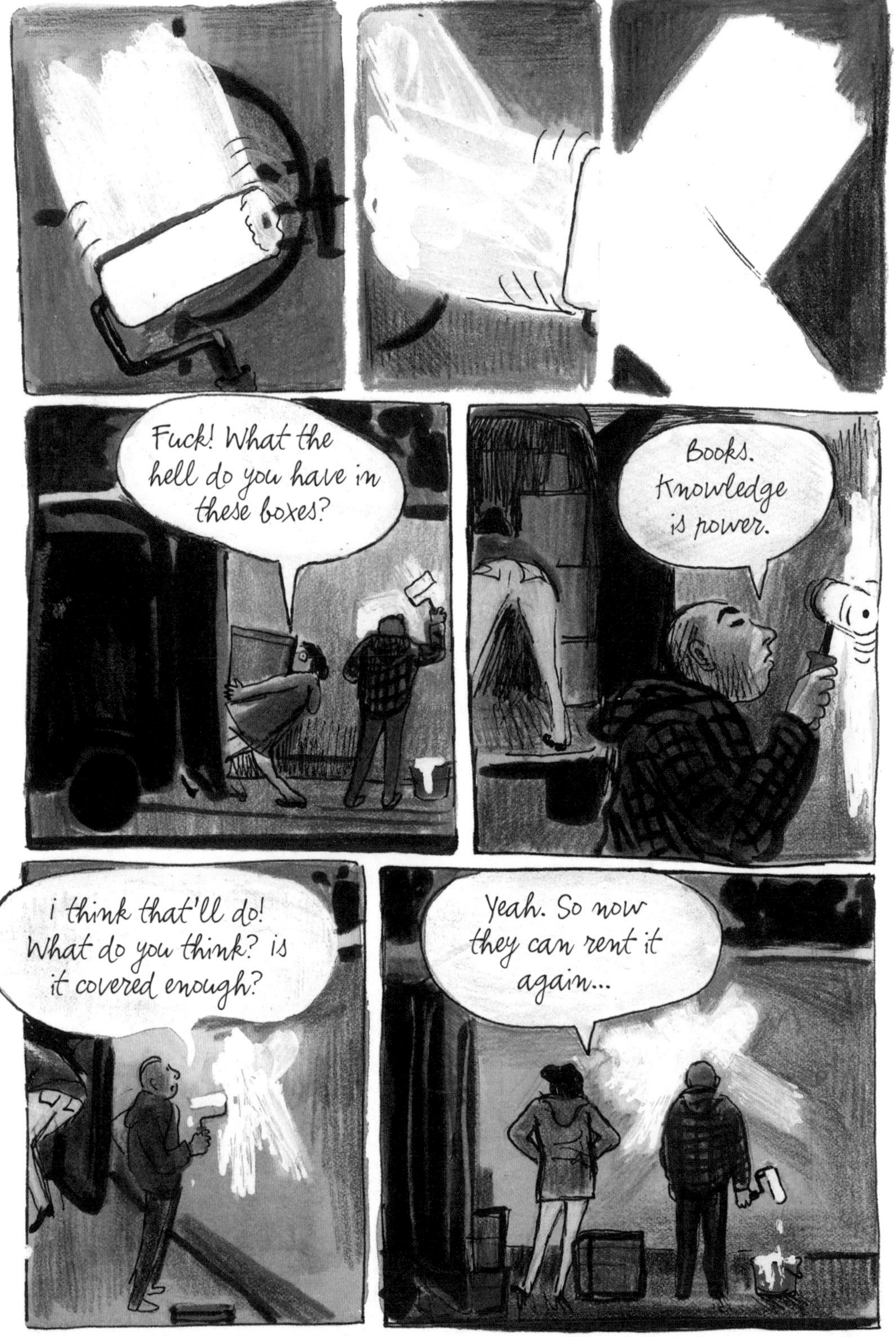
Fuck! What the hell do you have in these boxes?
Books. Knowledge is power.
i think that'll do! What do you think? is it covered enough?
Yeah. So now they can rent it again...

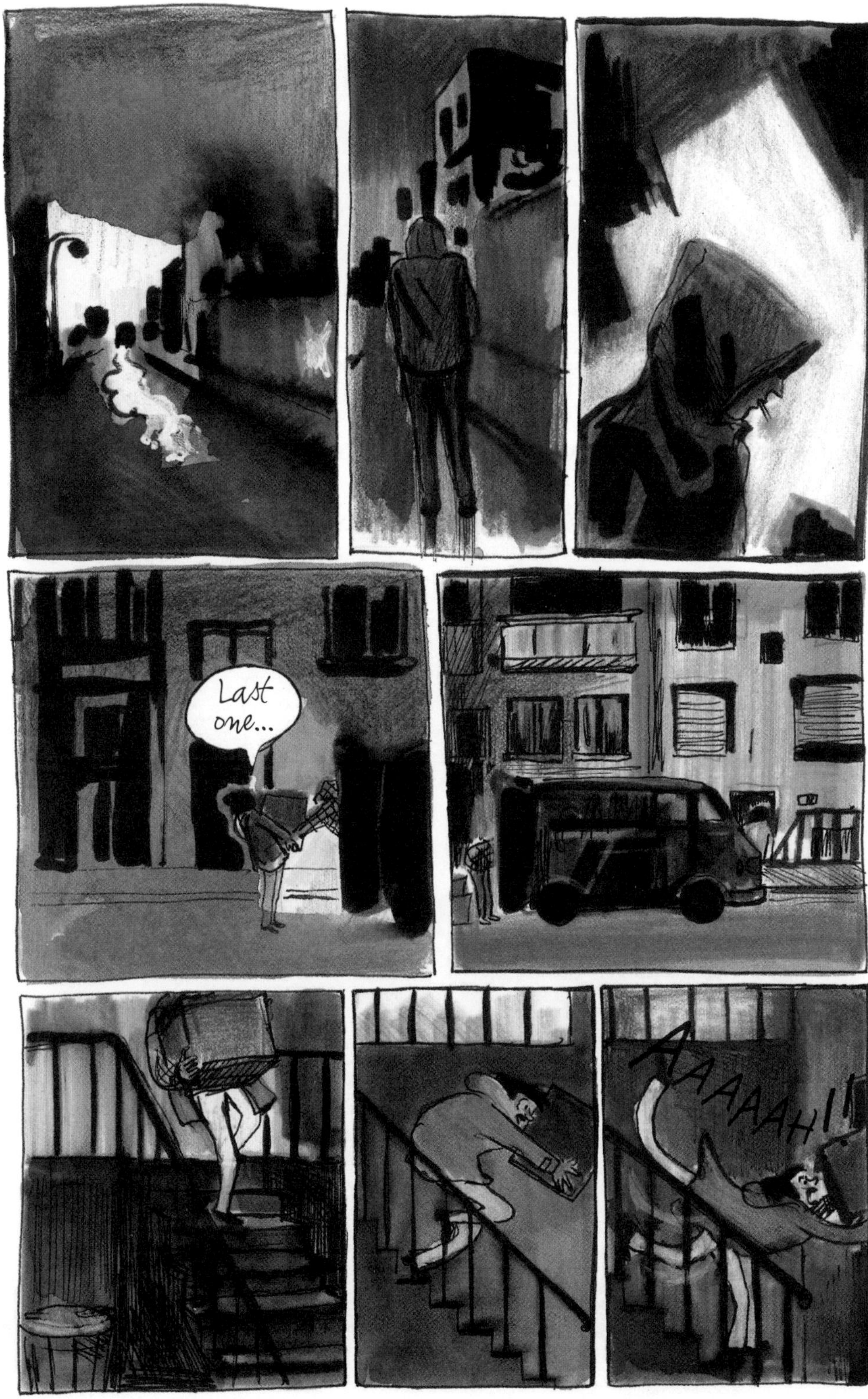
Last one...
AAAAAH!!

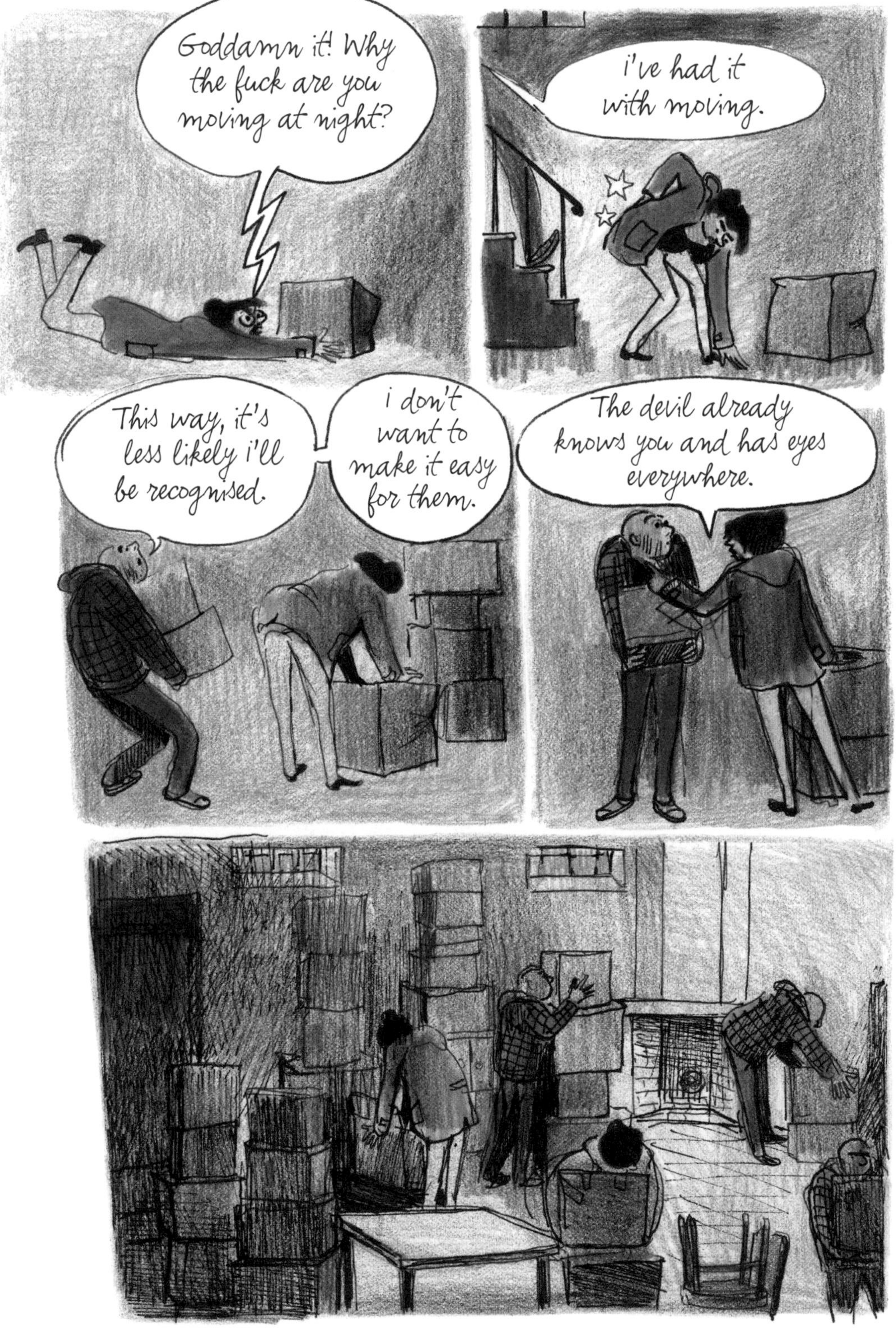
Goddamn it! Why the fuck are you moving at night?
i've had it with moving.
This way, it's less likely i'll be recognised.
i don't want to make it easy for them.
The devil already knows you and has eyes everywhere.

Well, i don't get it. When something bad happens, no one sees anything.
How about we order pizza?
No, i have plans.
i have a favour to return...
i have a date with a secret service agent.
Uh-huh...
Can i meet this brave man?
No, no...
i already told you, it's secret.
But pizza...
No, no and no!

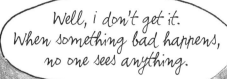

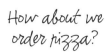

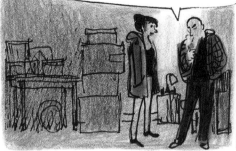

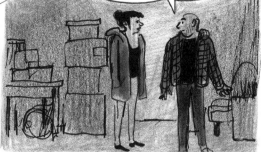

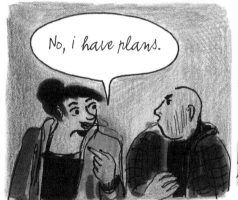

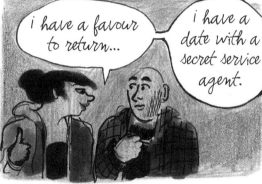

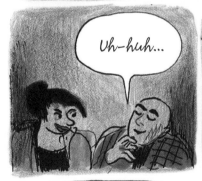

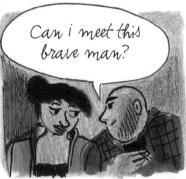

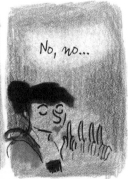

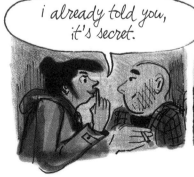

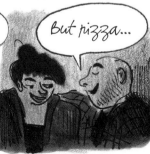

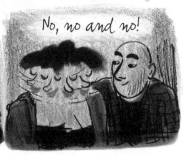

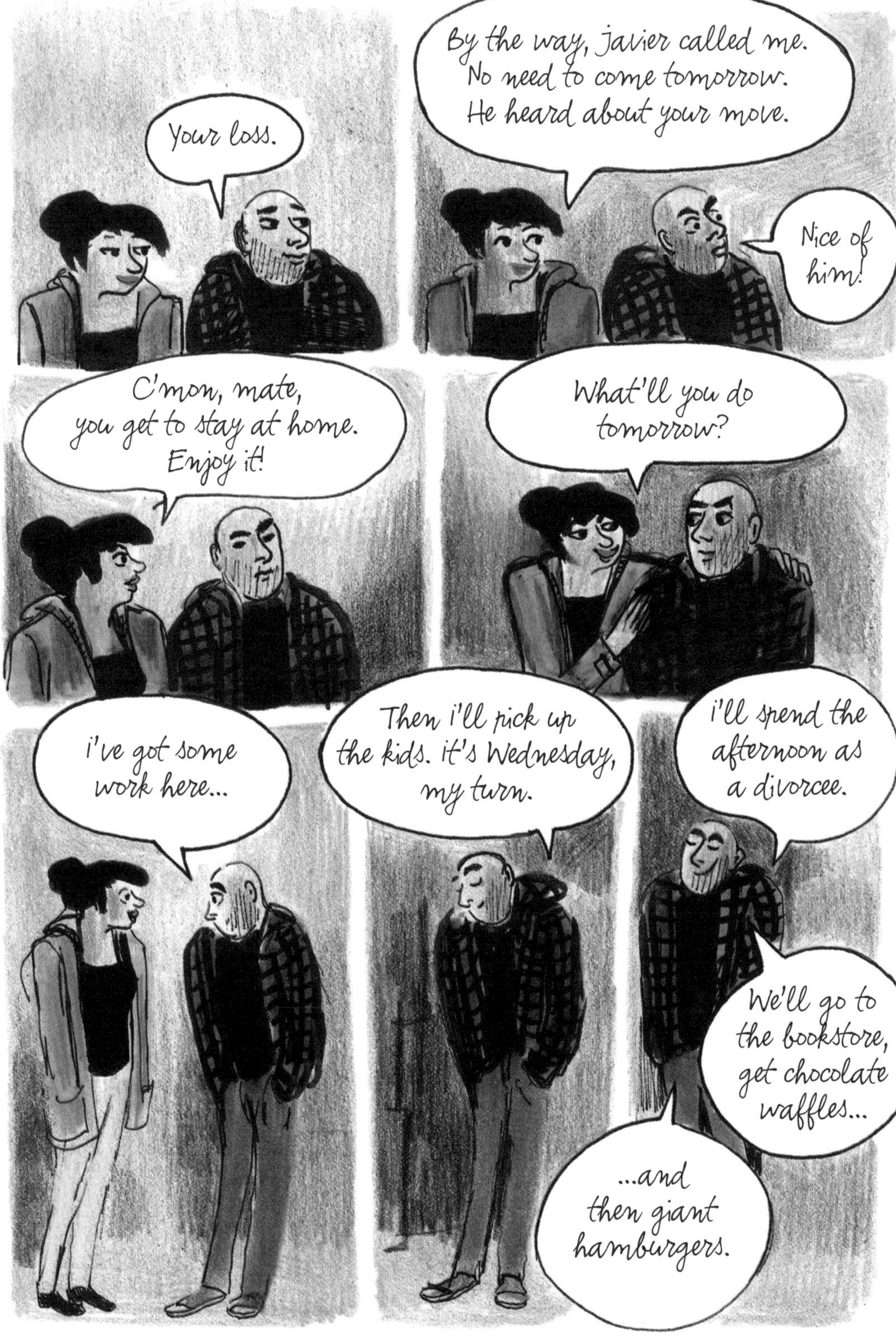
Your loss.
By the way, javier called me. No need to come tomorrow. He heard about your move.
Nice of him!
C'mon, mate, you get to stay at home. Enjoy it!
What'll you do tomorrow?
i've got some work here...
Then i'll pick up the kids. it's Wednesday, my turn.
i'll spend the afternoon as a divorcee.
We'll go to the bookstore, get chocolate waffles...
...and then giant hamburgers.

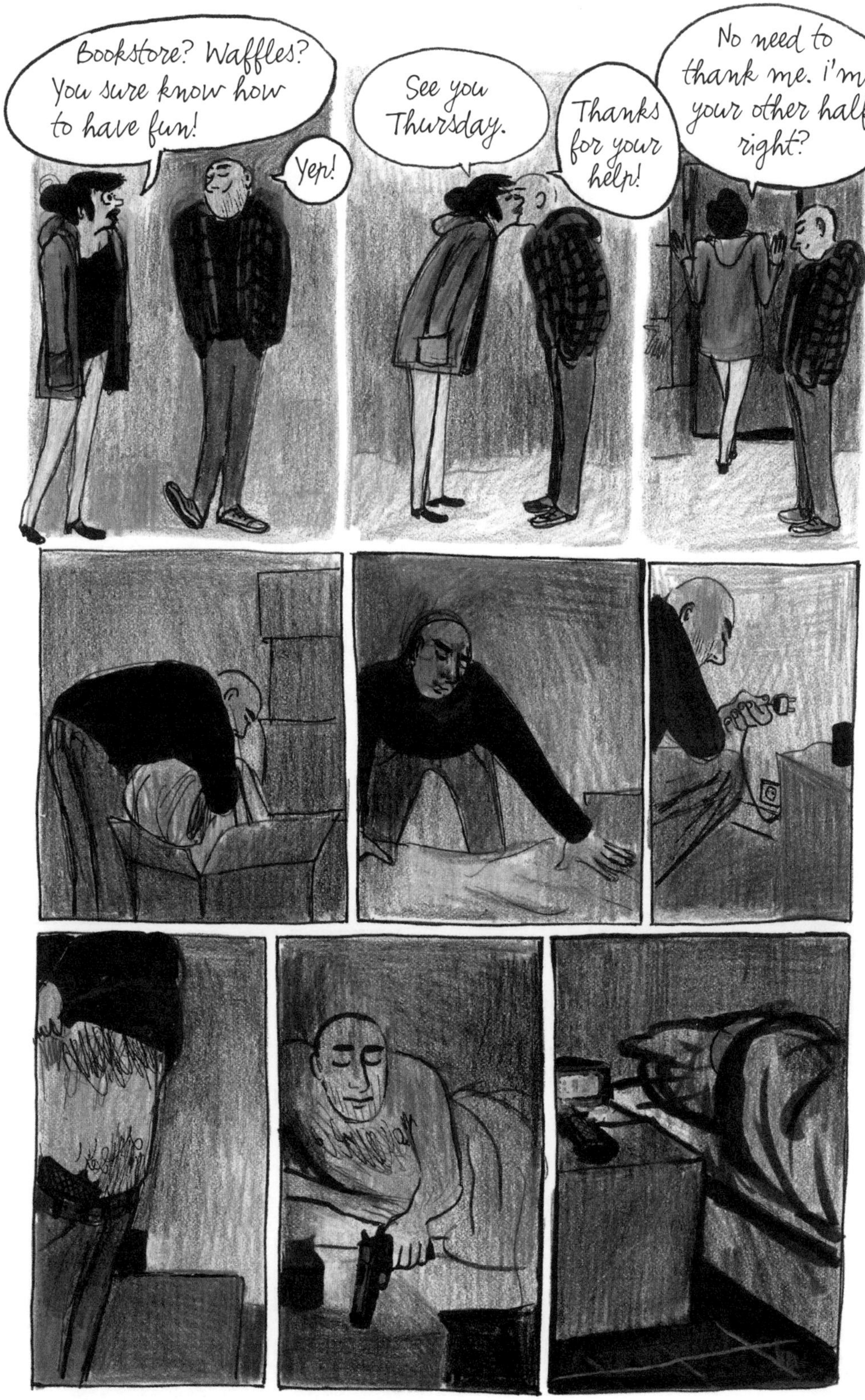
Bookstore? Waffles? You sure know how to have fun!
Yep!
See you Thursday.
Thanks for your help!
No need to thank me. i'm your other half, right?

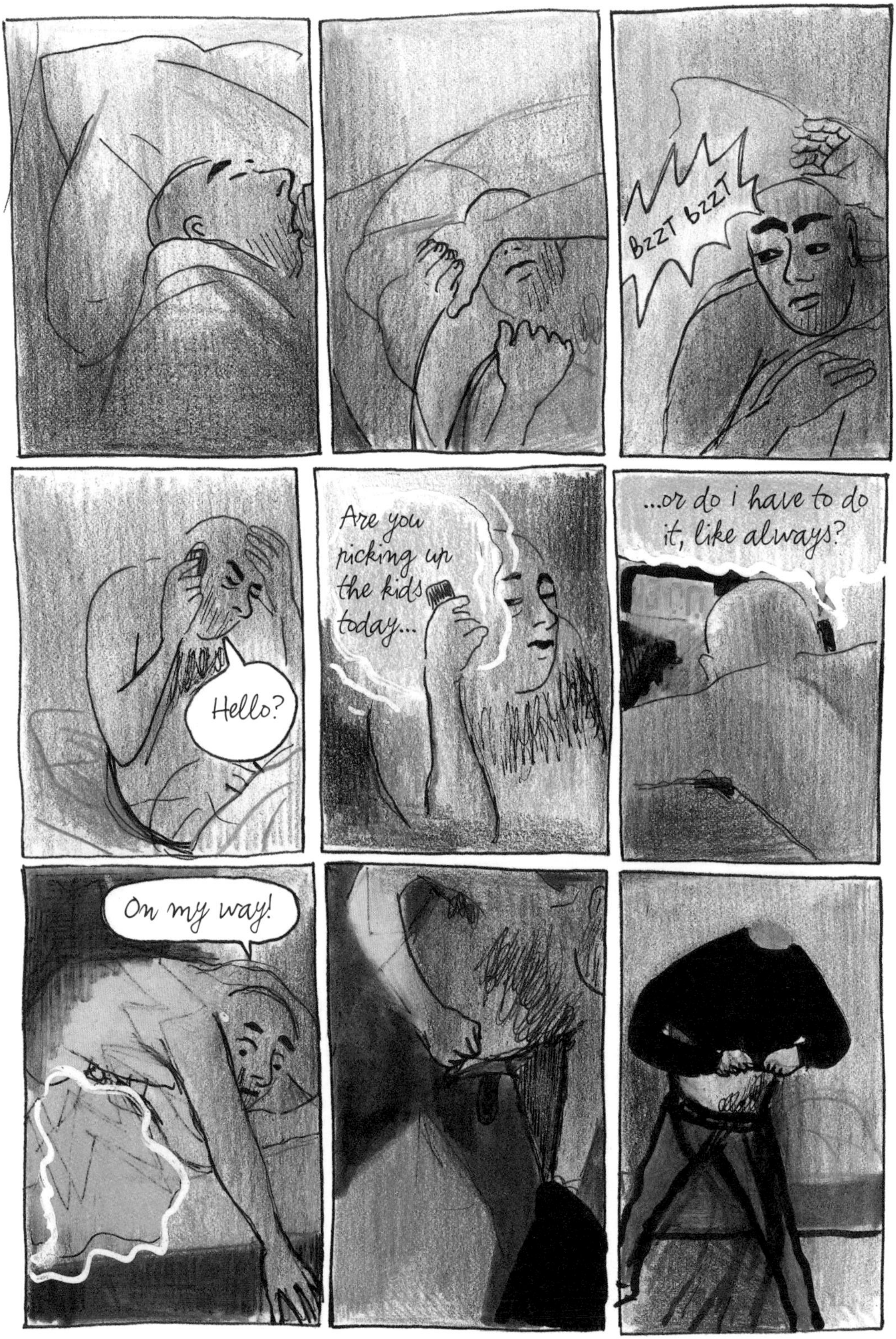
BzzT bzzT
Hello?
Are you picking up the kids today...
...or do i have to do it, like always?
On my way!

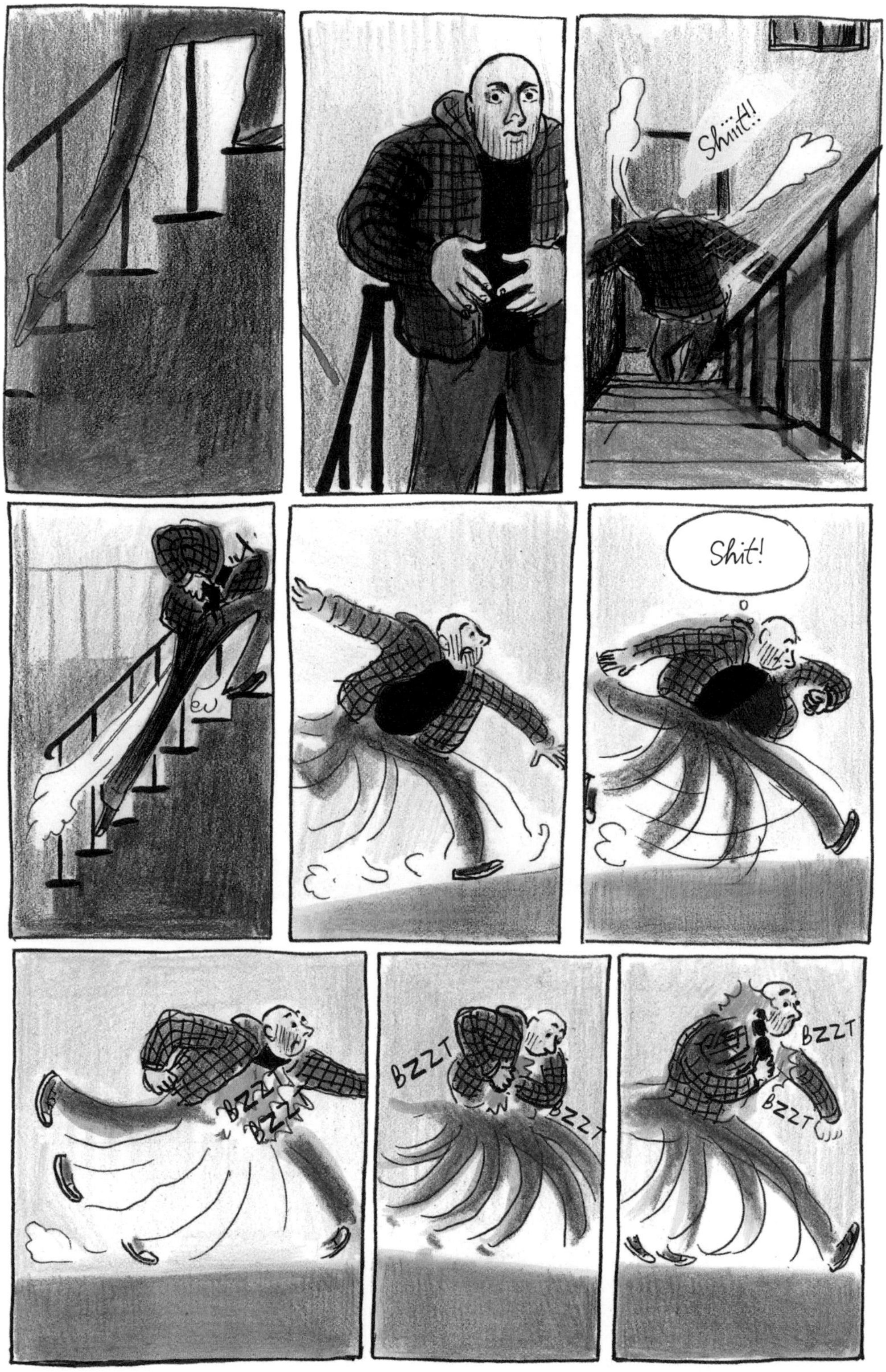
Shiiit!!
Shit!
BZZT
BZZT
BZZT
BZZT
BZZT
BZZT

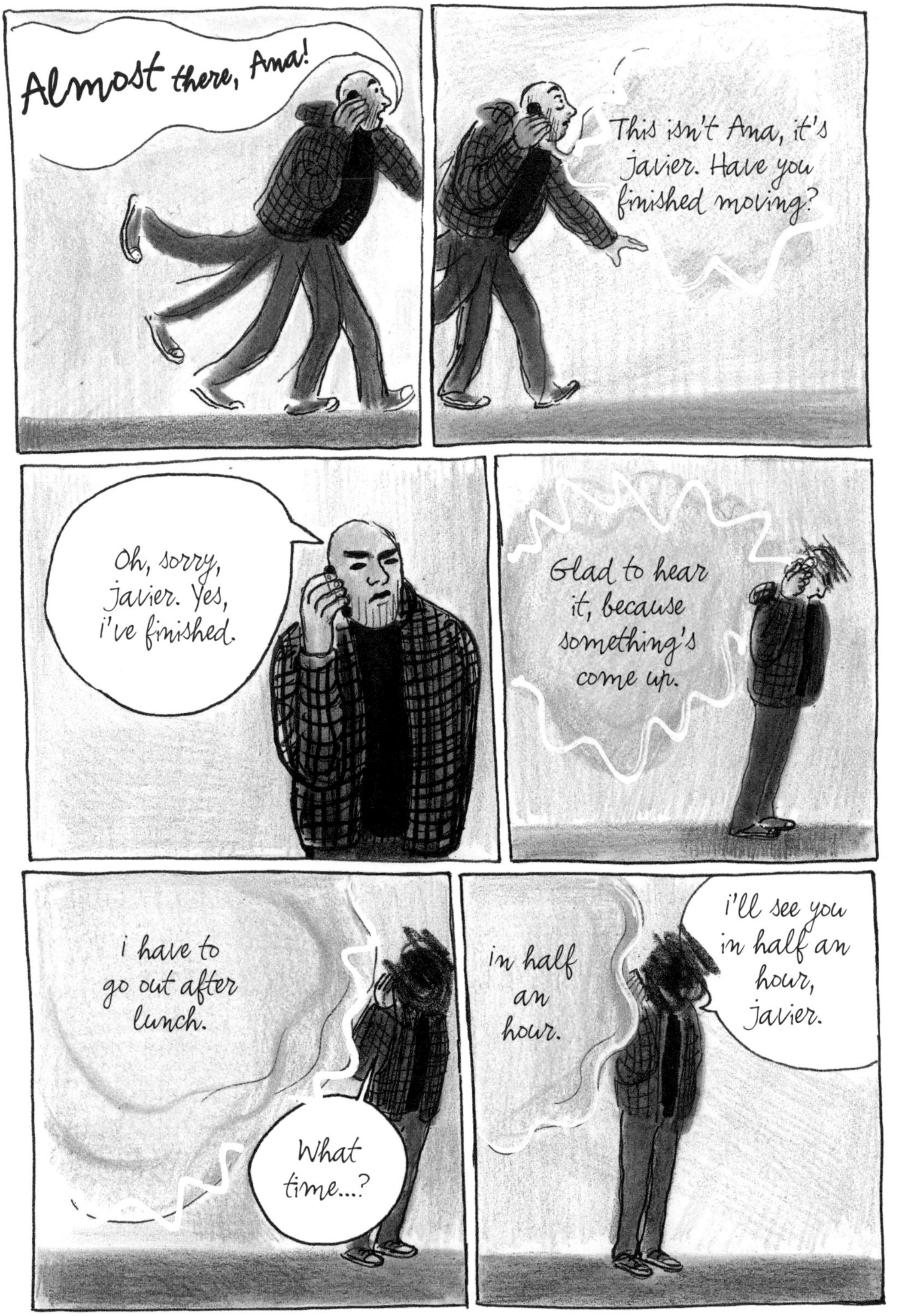
Almost there, Ana!
This isn't Ana, it's Javier. Have you finished moving?
Oh, sorry, Javier. Yes, i've finished.
Glad to hear it, because something's come up.
i have to go out after lunch.
What time...?
in half an hour.
i'll see you in half an hour, Javier.

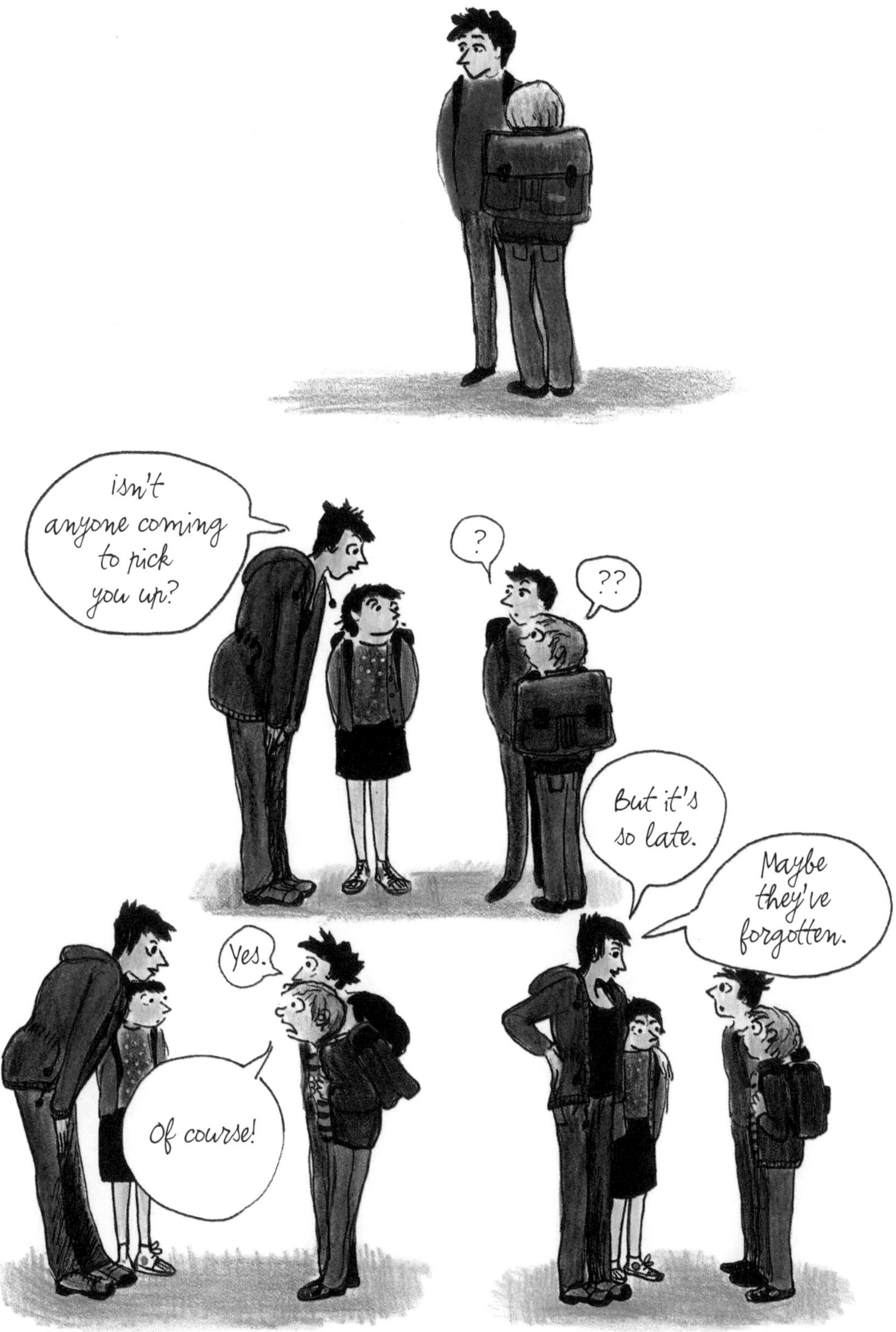
isn't anyone coming to pick you up?
?
??
Yes.
Of course!
But it's so late.
Maybe they've forgotten.

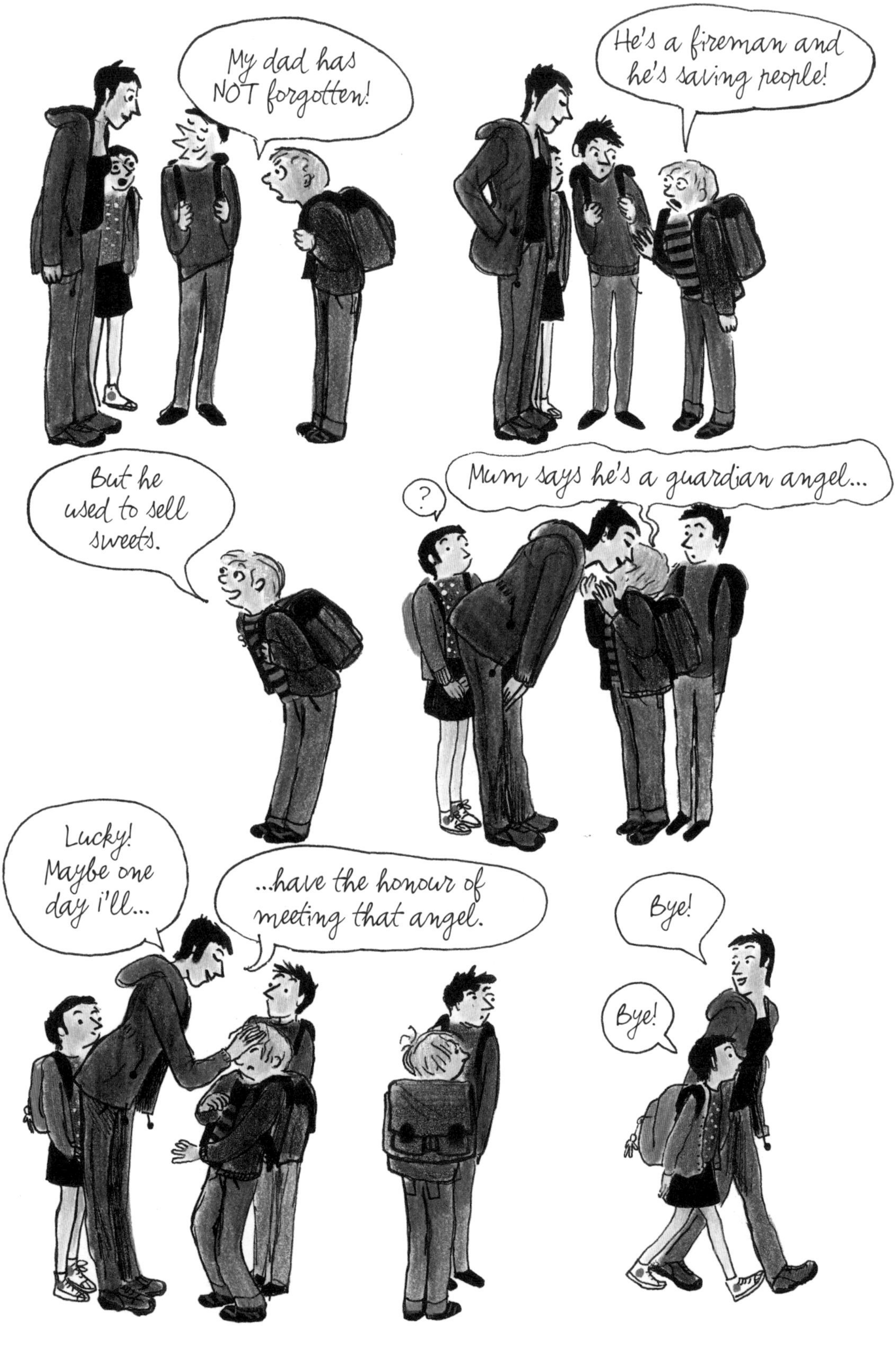
My dad has NOT forgotten!
He's a fireman and he's saving people!
But he used to sell sweets.
?
Mum says he's a guardian angel...
Lucky! Maybe one day i'll...
...have the honour of meeting that angel.
Bye!
Bye!

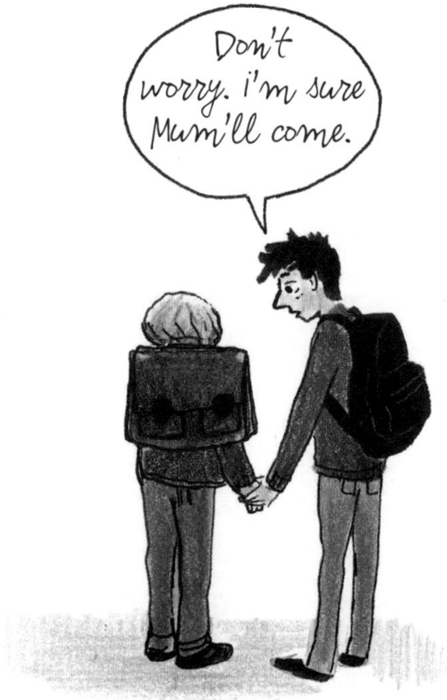
Don't worry. i'm sure Mum'll come.

Plaza del Castillo, Pamplona. November 2010.

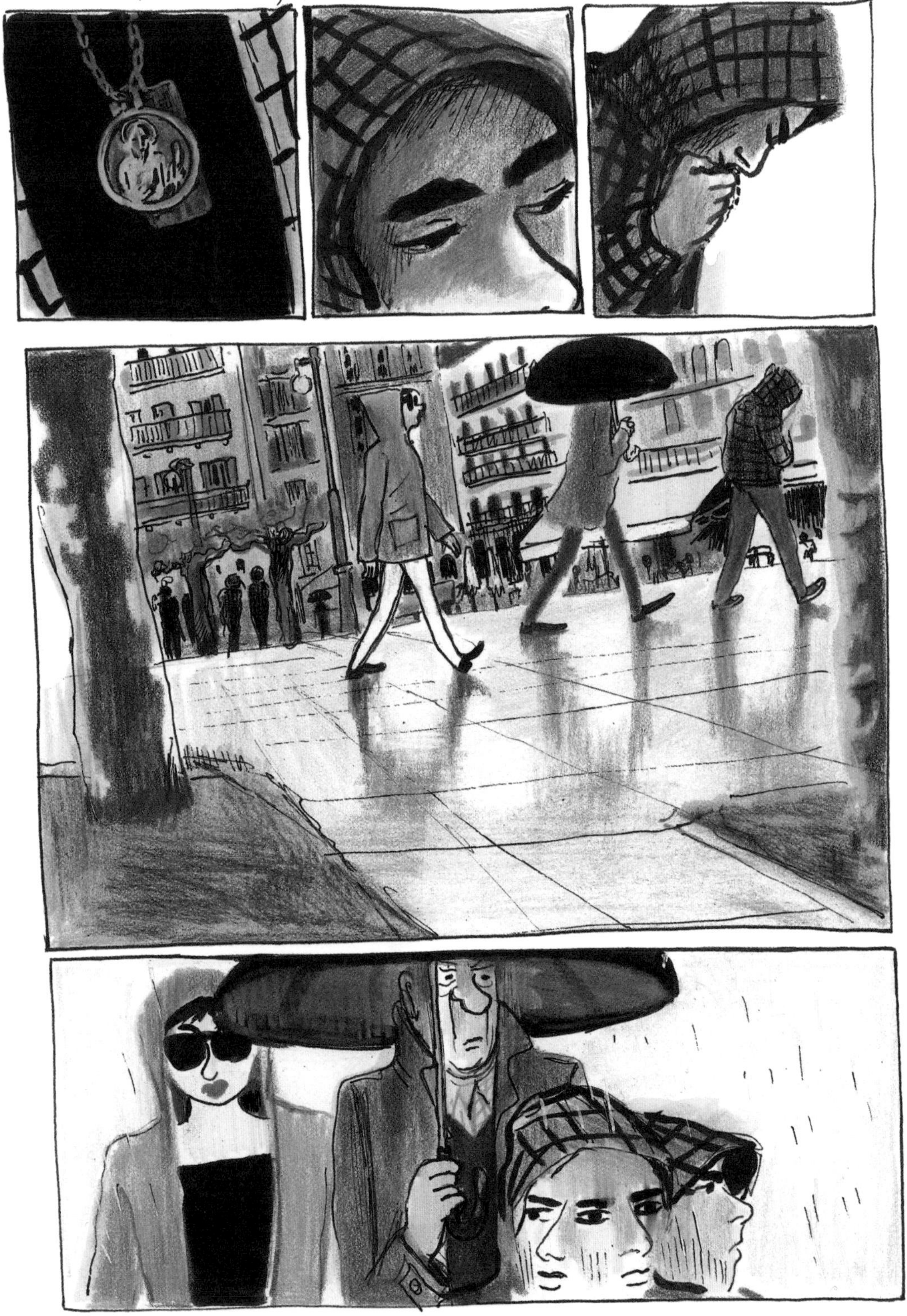

EUSKAL PRES
EUSKAL

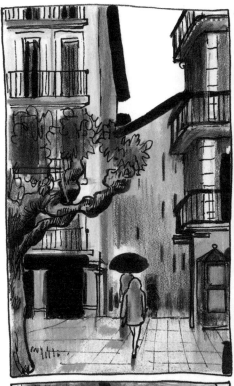

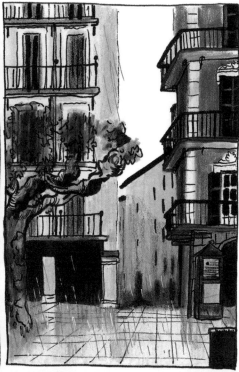

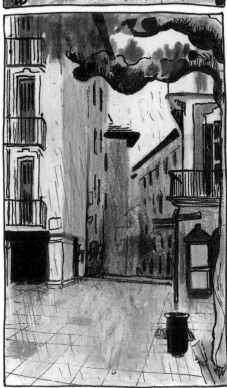

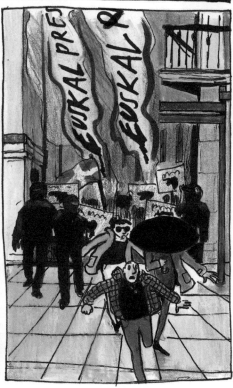

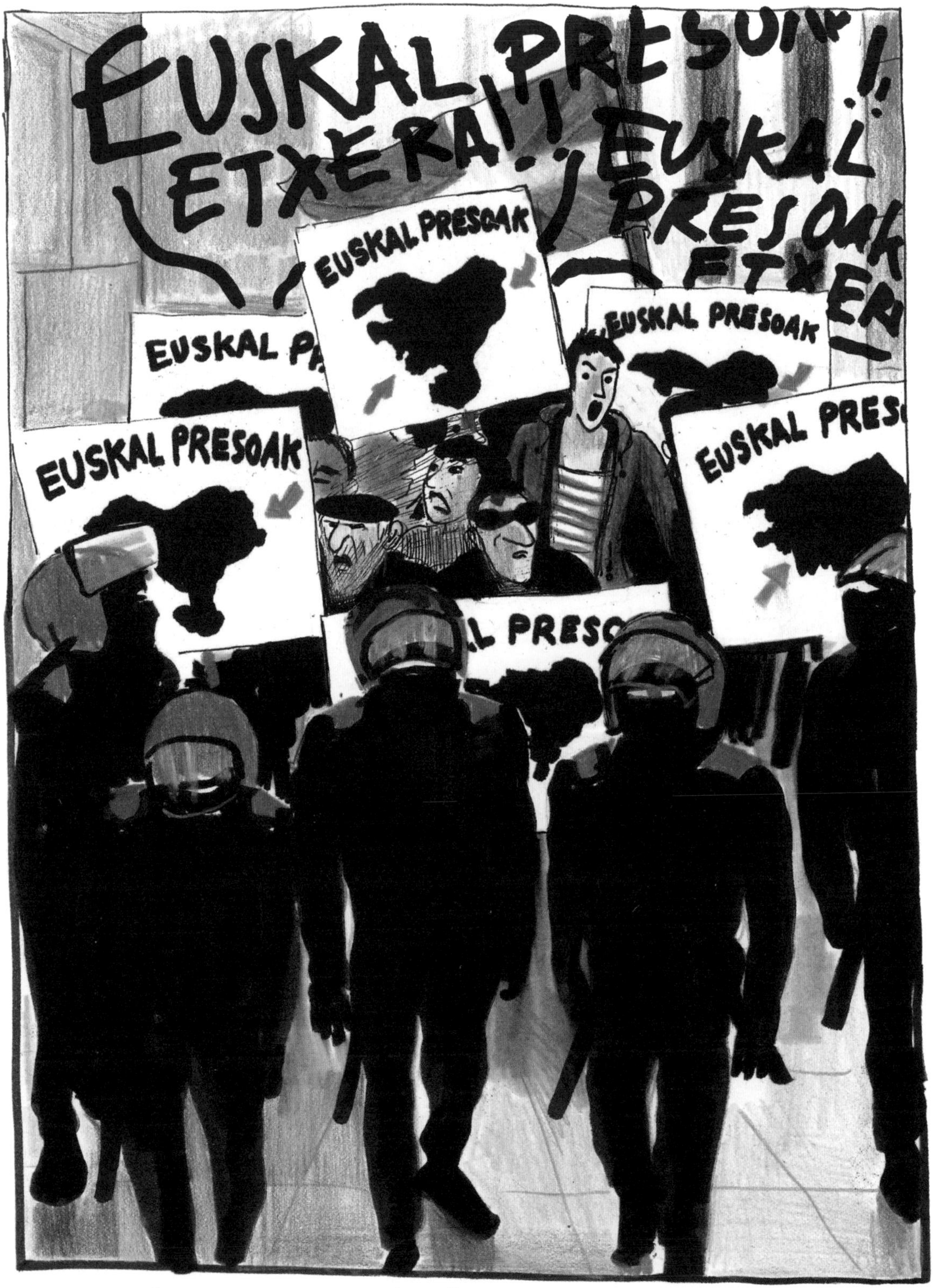
EUSKAL PRESOAK ETXERA!!
¡EUSKAL PRESOAK ETXERA!
EUSKAL PRESOAK
EUSKAL PRESOAK
EUSKAL PRESOAK

in Basque: "Bring Basque prisoners home!"

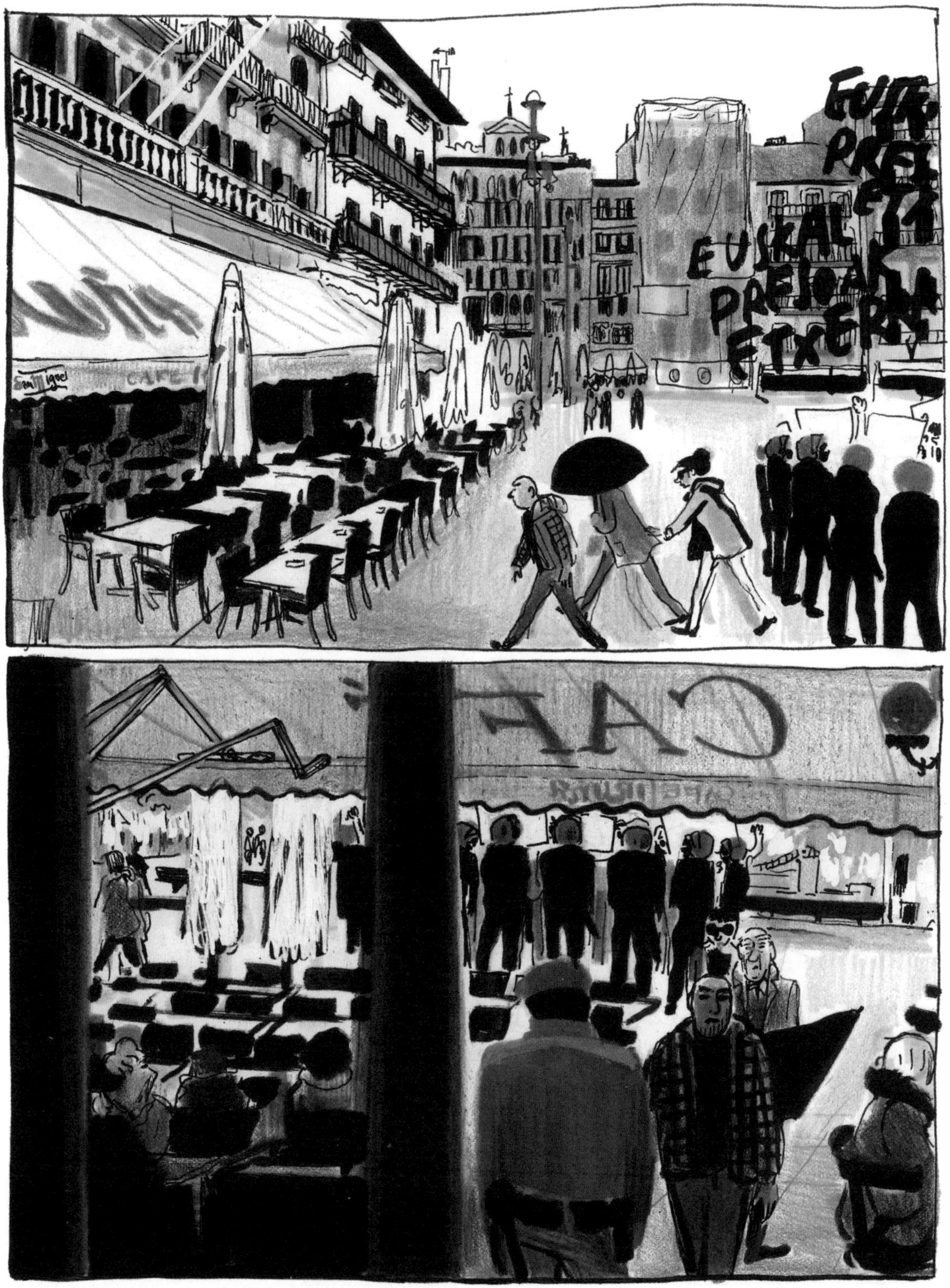
San Miguel
CAFE
EUSKAL
PRESOAK
ETXERA
CAF

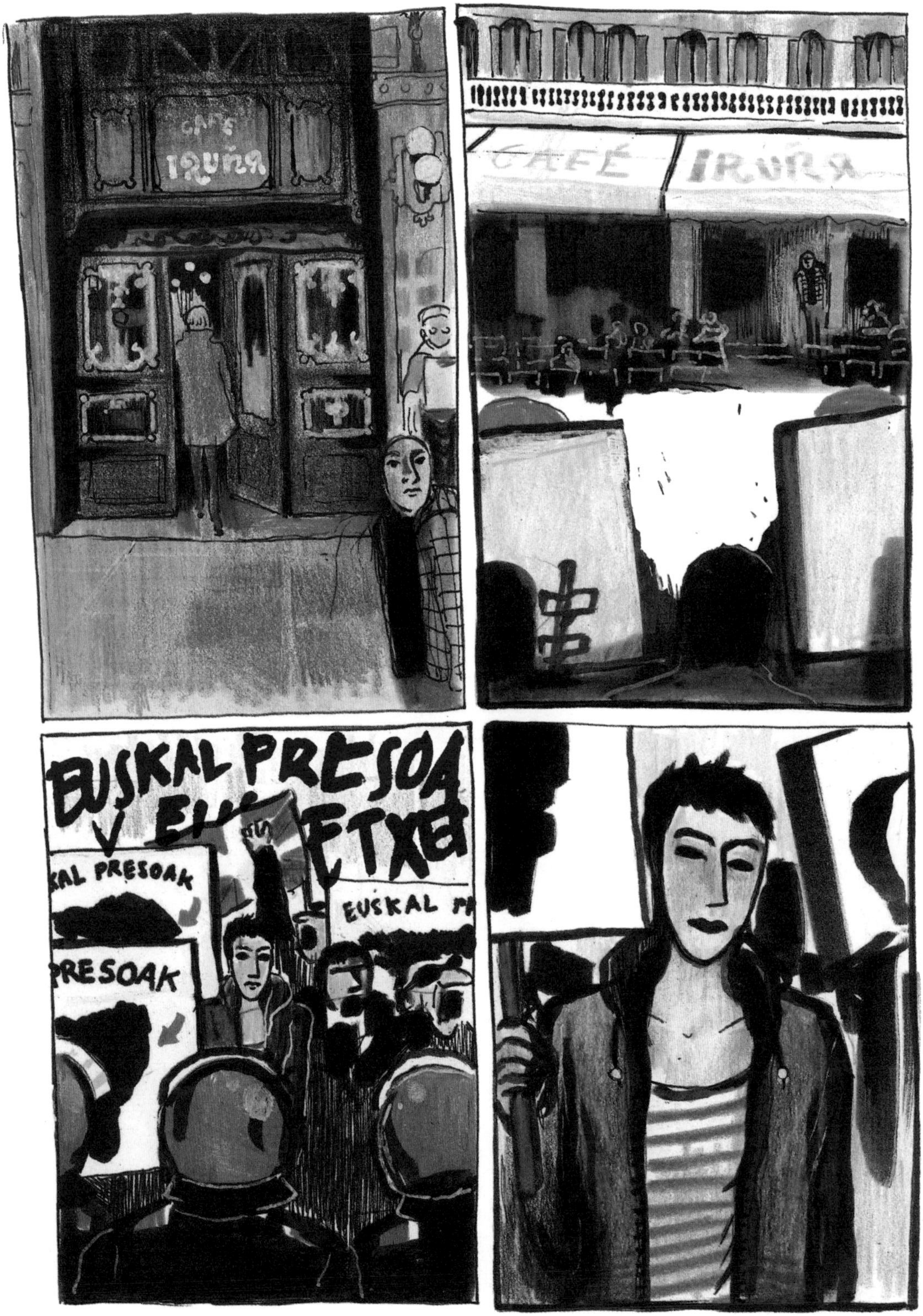

CAFÉ
IRUÑA
CAFÉ
IRUÑA
EUSKAL PRESOA
ETXE
KAL PRESOAK
EUSKAL P
PRESOAK

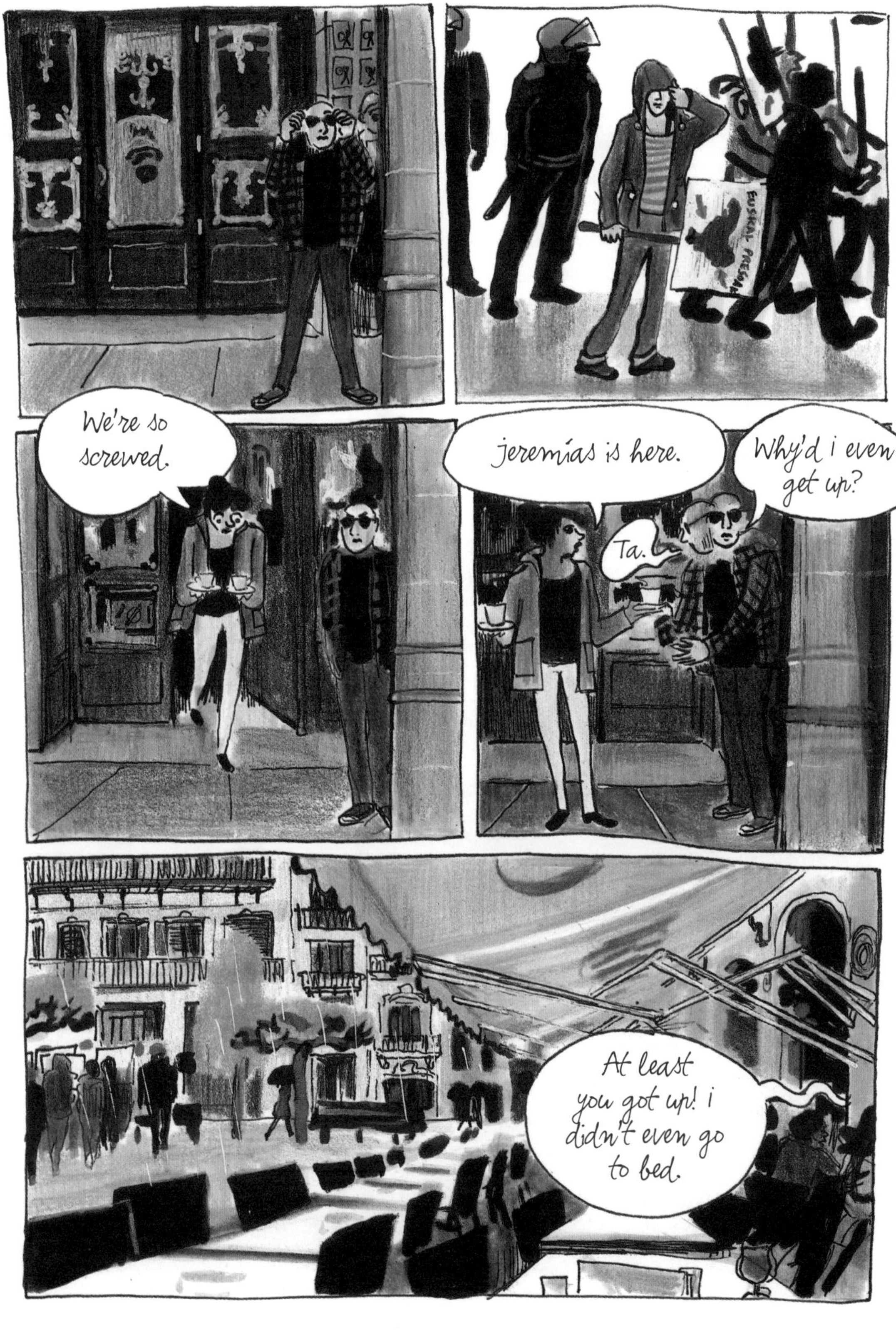
EUSKAL PRESOAK
We're so screwed.
jeremias is here.
Why'd i even get up?
Ta.
At least you got up! i didn't even go to bed.

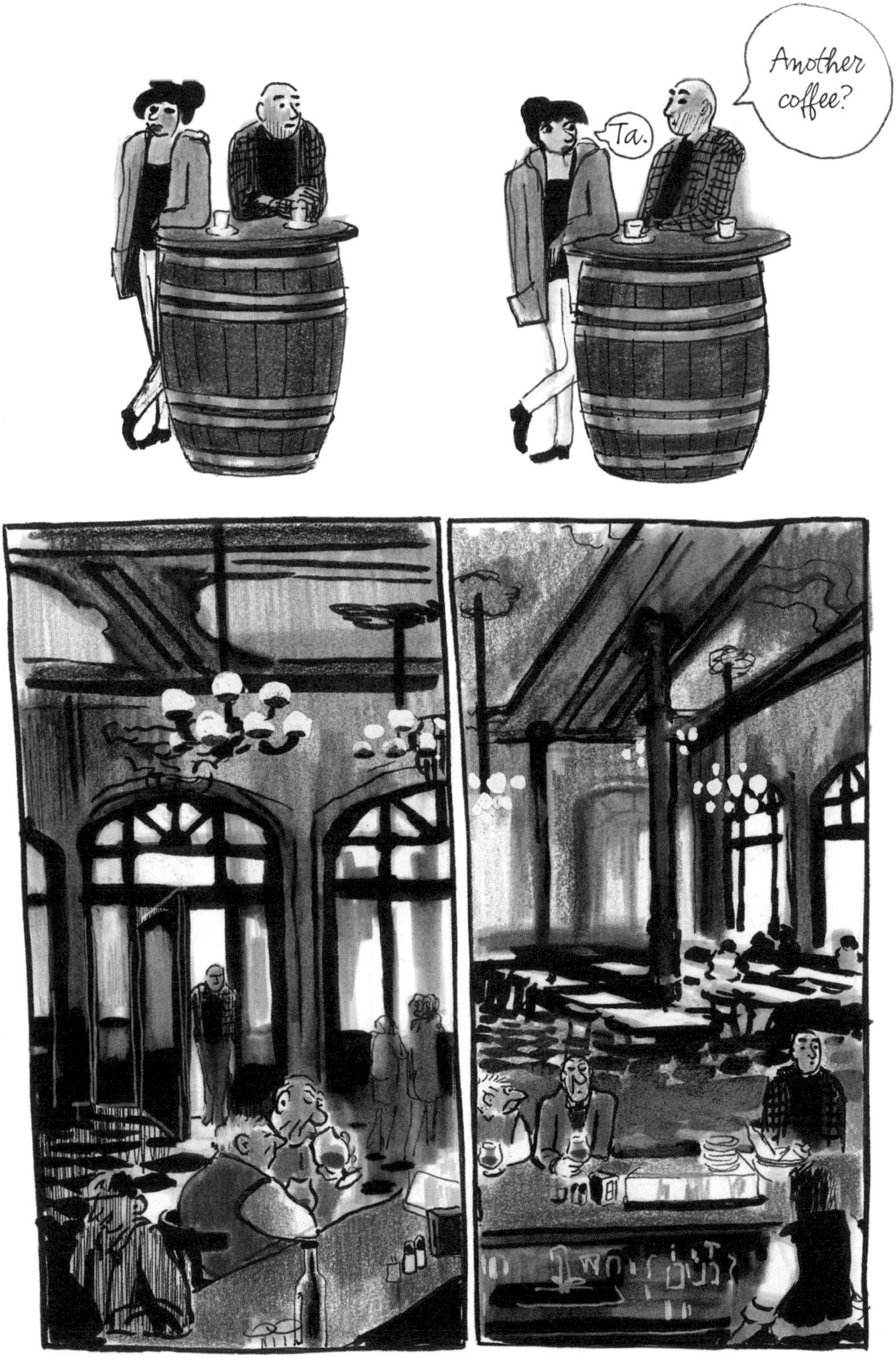
Another coffee?
Ta.

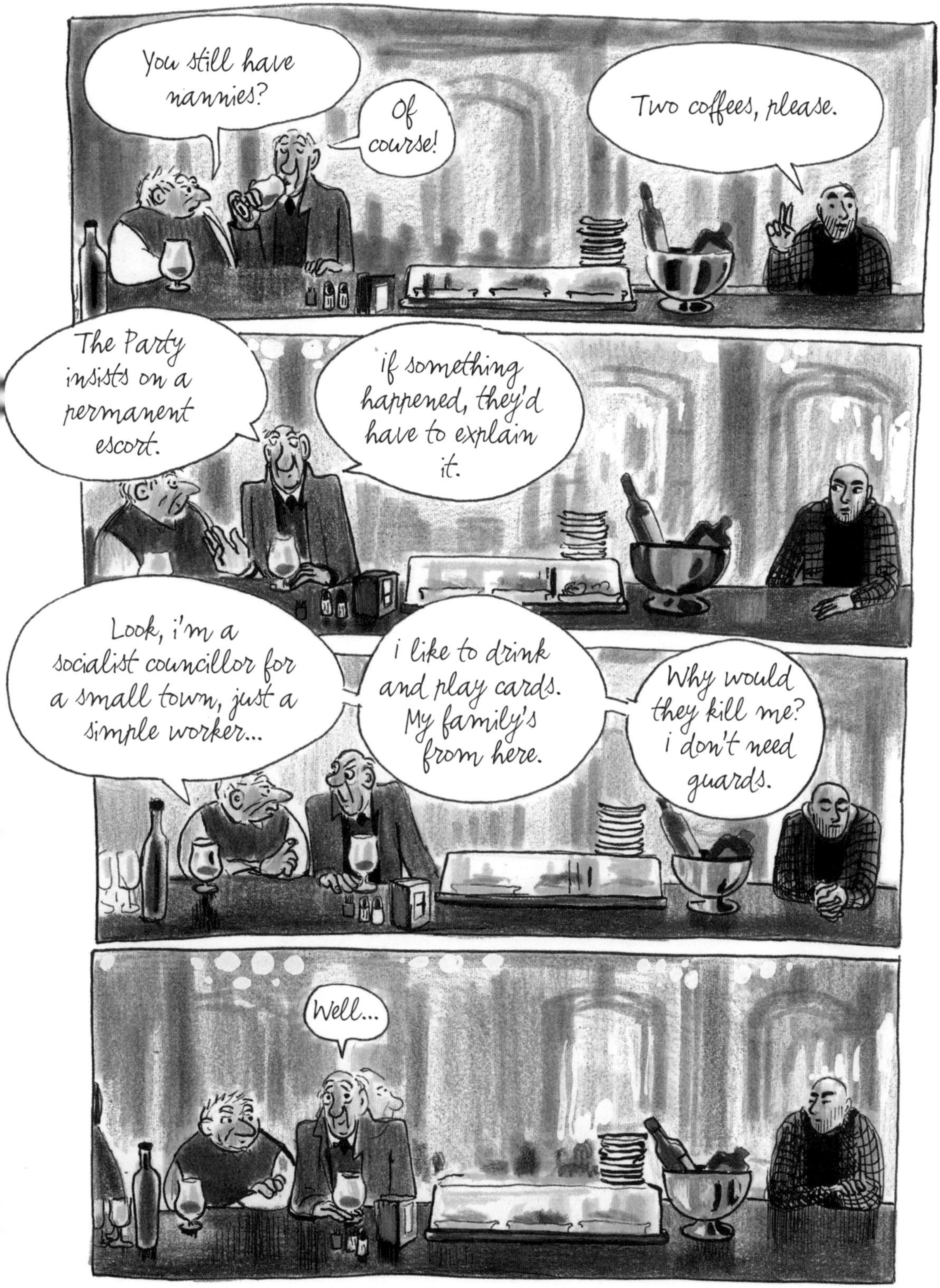
You still have nannies?
Of course!
Two coffees, please.
The Party insists on a permanent escort.
if something happened, they'd have to explain it.
Look, i'm a socialist councillor for a small town, just a simple worker...
i like to drink and play cards. My family's from here.
Why would they kill me? i don't need guards.
Well...

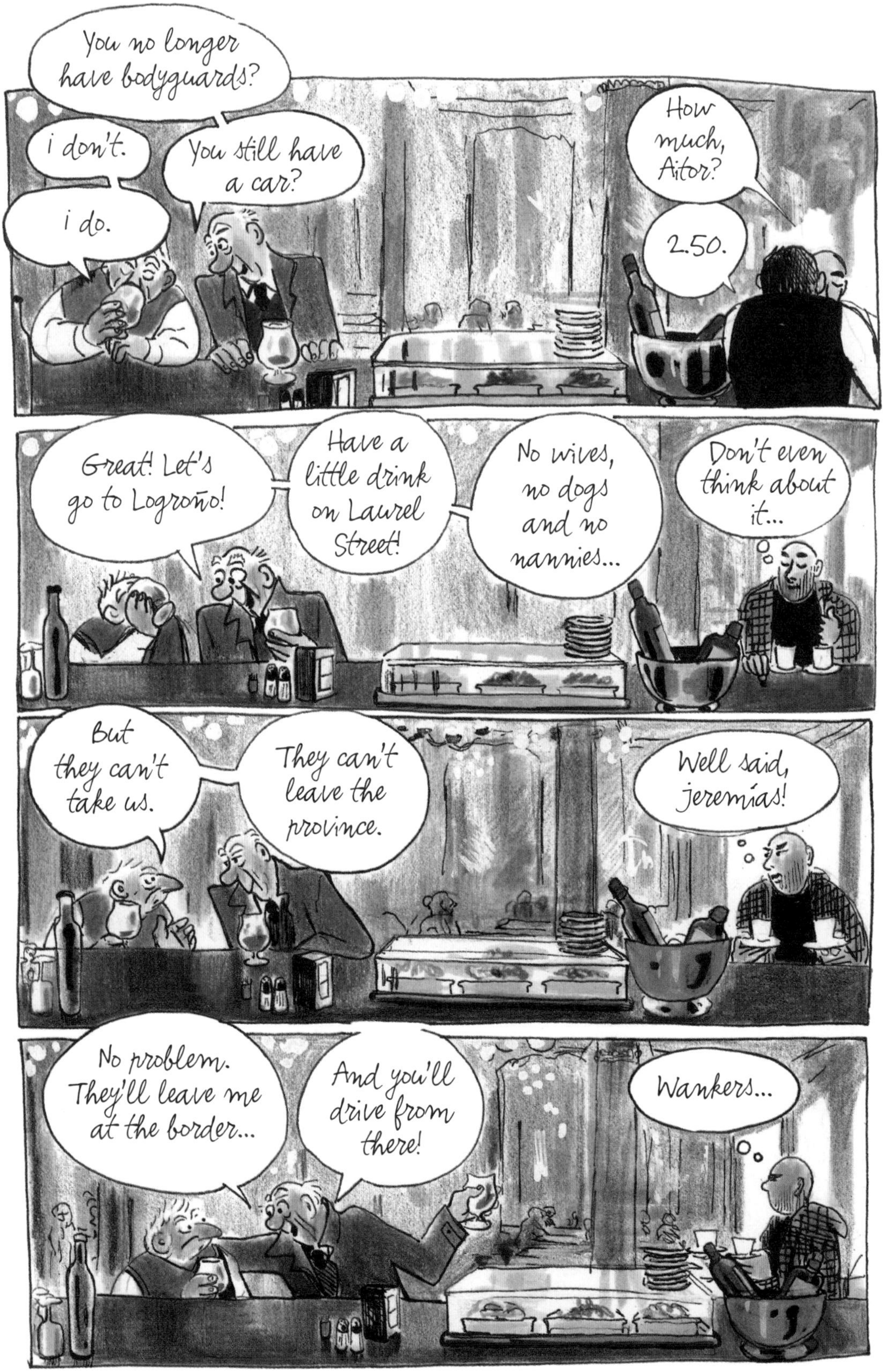
You no longer have bodyguards?
i don't.
You still have a car?
i do.
How much, Aitor?
2.50.
Great! Let's go to Logroño!
Have a little drink on Laurel Street!
No wives, no dogs and no nannies...
Don't even think about it...
But they can't take us.
They can't leave the province.
Well said, Jeremías!
No problem. They'll leave me at the border...
And you'll drive from there!
Wankers...

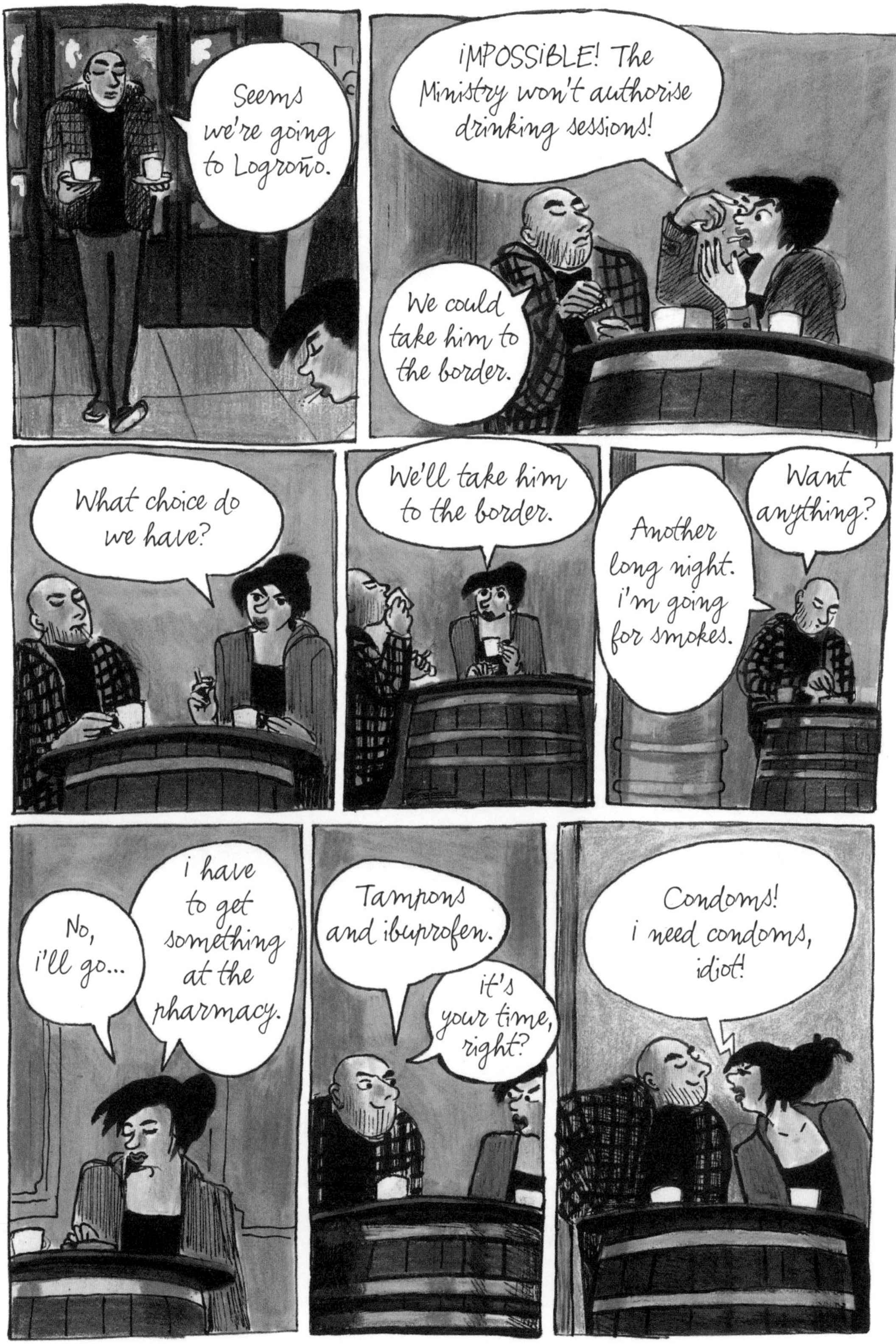
Seems we're going to Logroño.
¡IMPOSSIBLE! The Ministry won't authorise drinking sessions!
We could take him to the border.
What choice do we have?
We'll take him to the border.
Want anything?
Another long night. i'm going for smokes.
i have to get something at the pharmacy.
No, i'll go...
Tampons and ibuprofen.
it's your time, right?
Condoms! i need condoms, idiot!

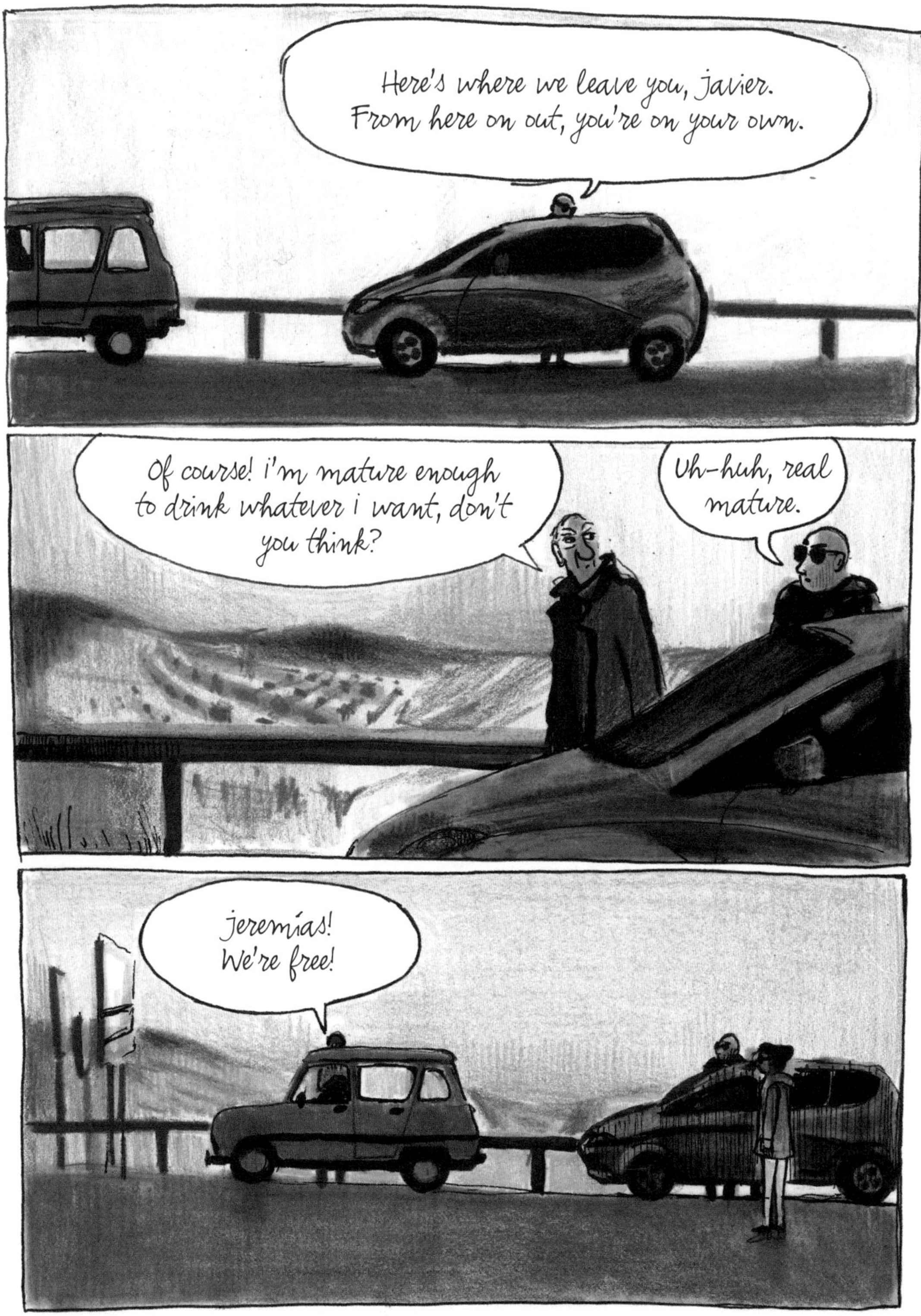
Here's where we leave you, Javier. From here on out, you're on your own.
Of course! i'm mature enough to drink whatever i want, don't you think?
Uh-huh, real mature.
Jeremías! We're free!

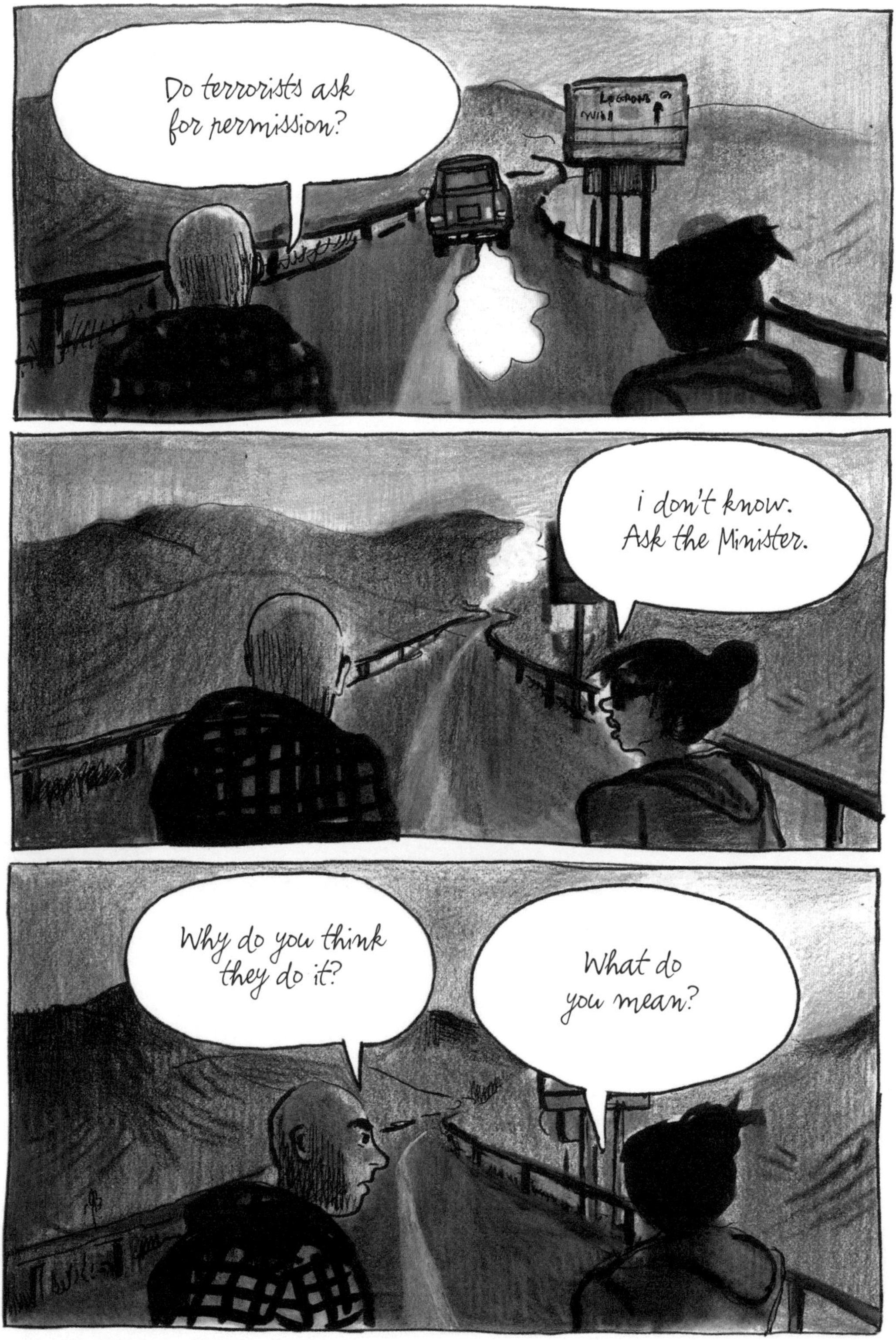
Do terrorists ask for permission?
i don't know. Ask the Minister.
Why do you think they do it?
What do you mean?

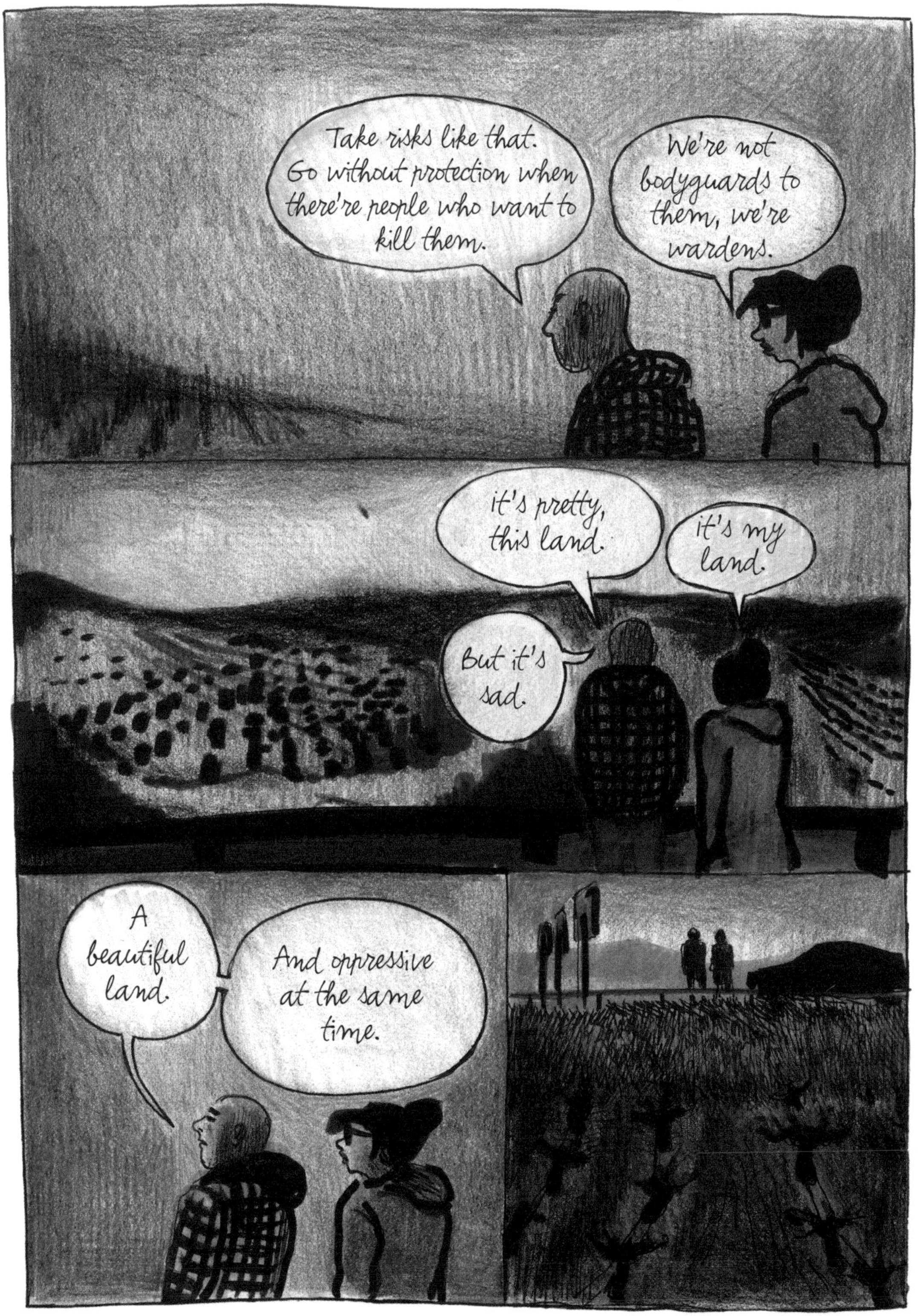
Take risks like that. Go without protection when there're people who want to kill them.
We're not bodyguards to them, we're wardens.
It's pretty, this land.
It's my land.
But it's sad.
A beautiful land.
And oppressive at the same time.

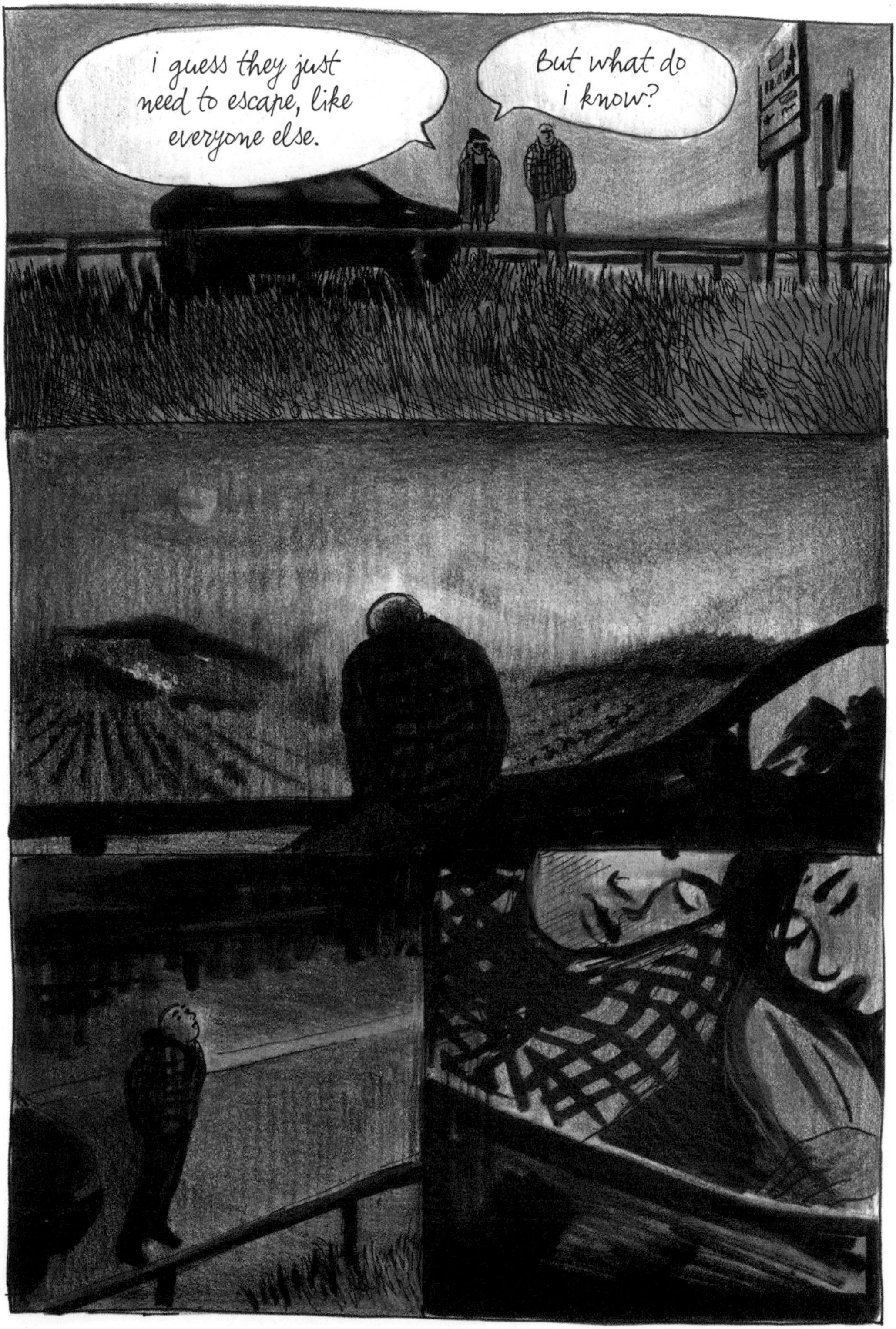
i guess they just need to escape, like everyone else.
But what do i know?

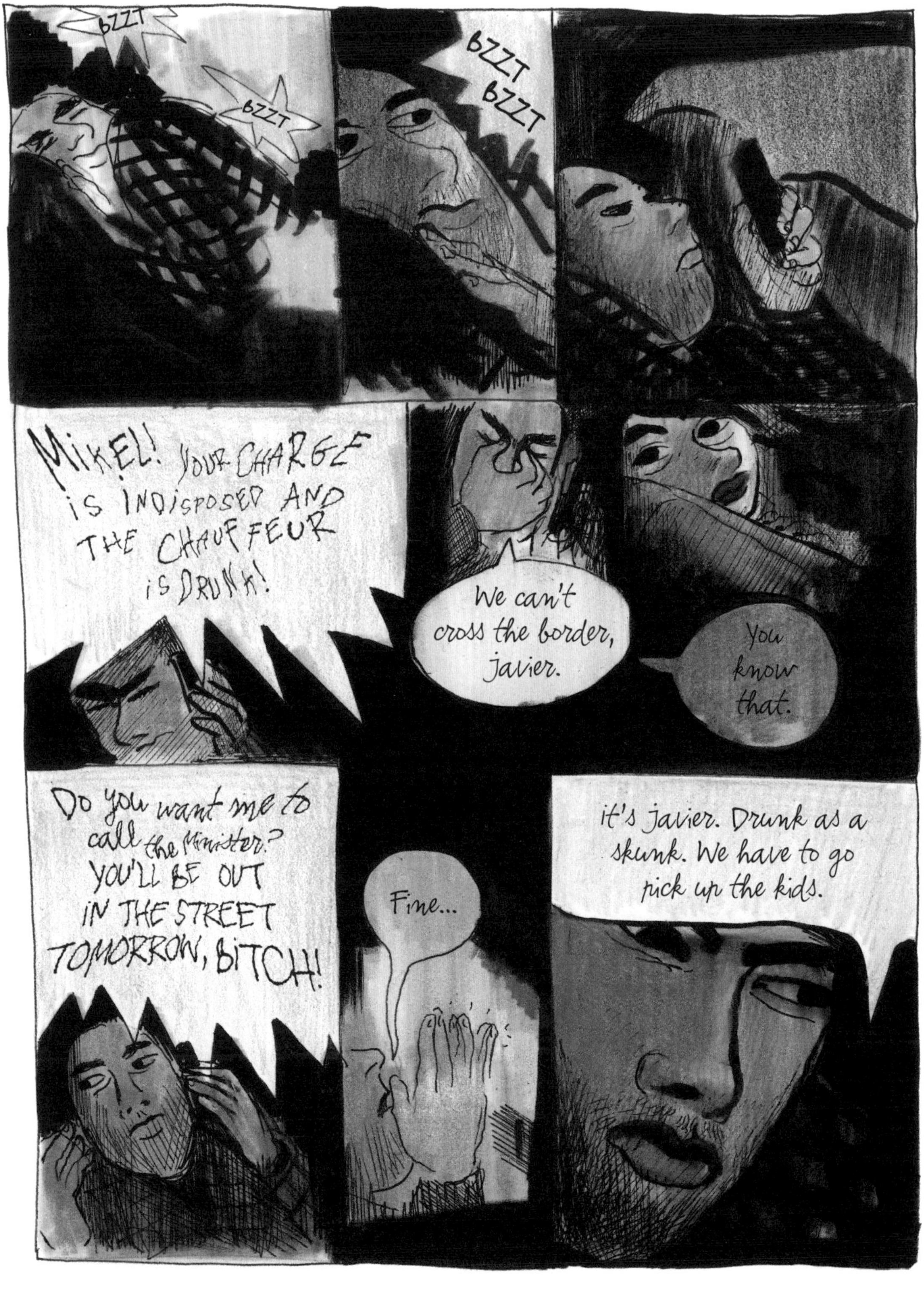
BZZT
BZZT
BZZT
BZZT
MIKEL! YOUR CHARGE IS INDISPOSED AND THE CHAUFFEUR IS DRUNK!
We can't cross the border, javier.
You know that.
Do you want me to call the Minister? YOU'LL BE OUT IN THE STREET TOMORROW, BITCH!
Fine...
it's javier. Drunk as a skunk. We have to go pick up the kids.

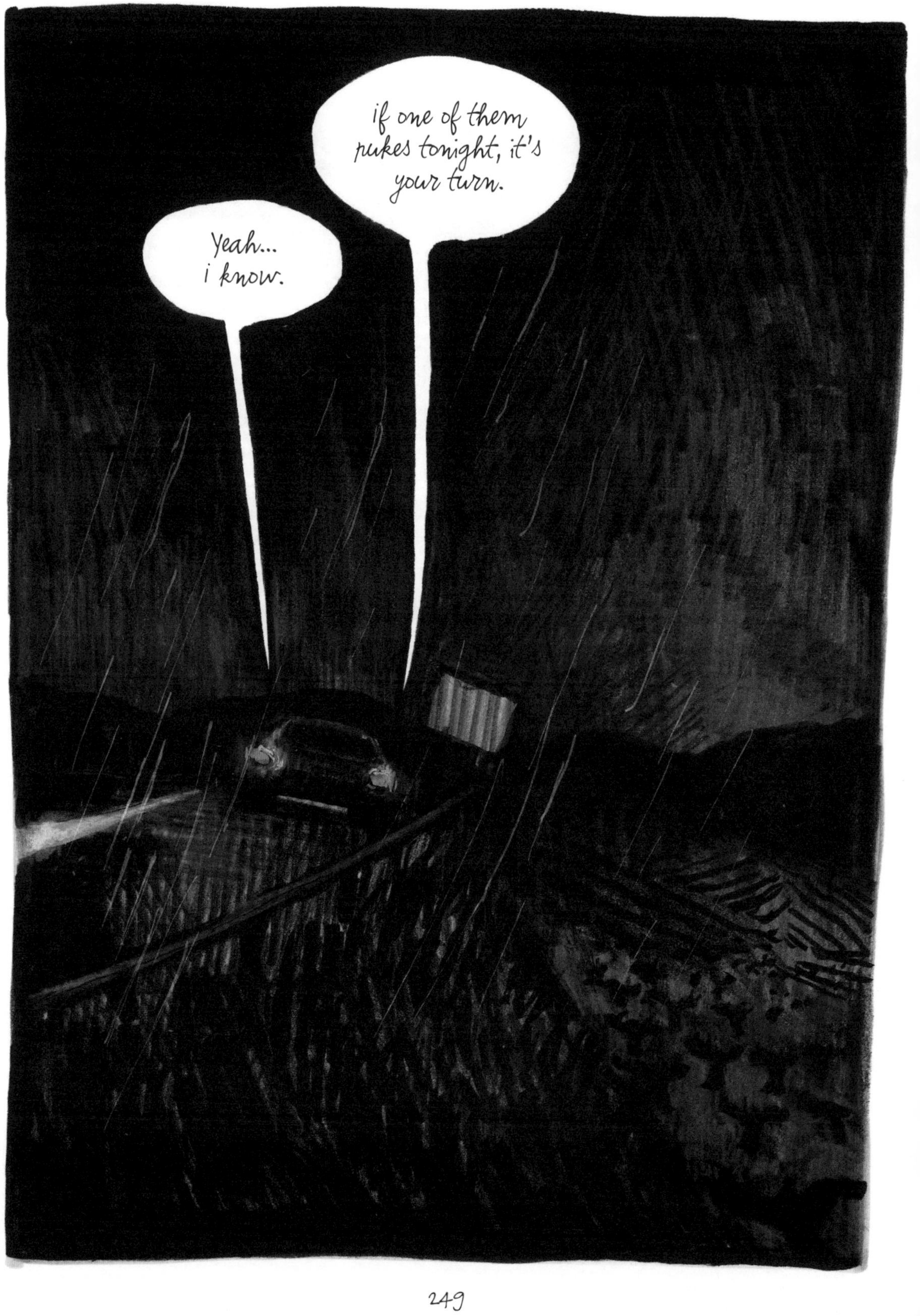
Yeah...
i know.
if one of them pukes tonight, it's your turn.

security firm offices, Pamplona.

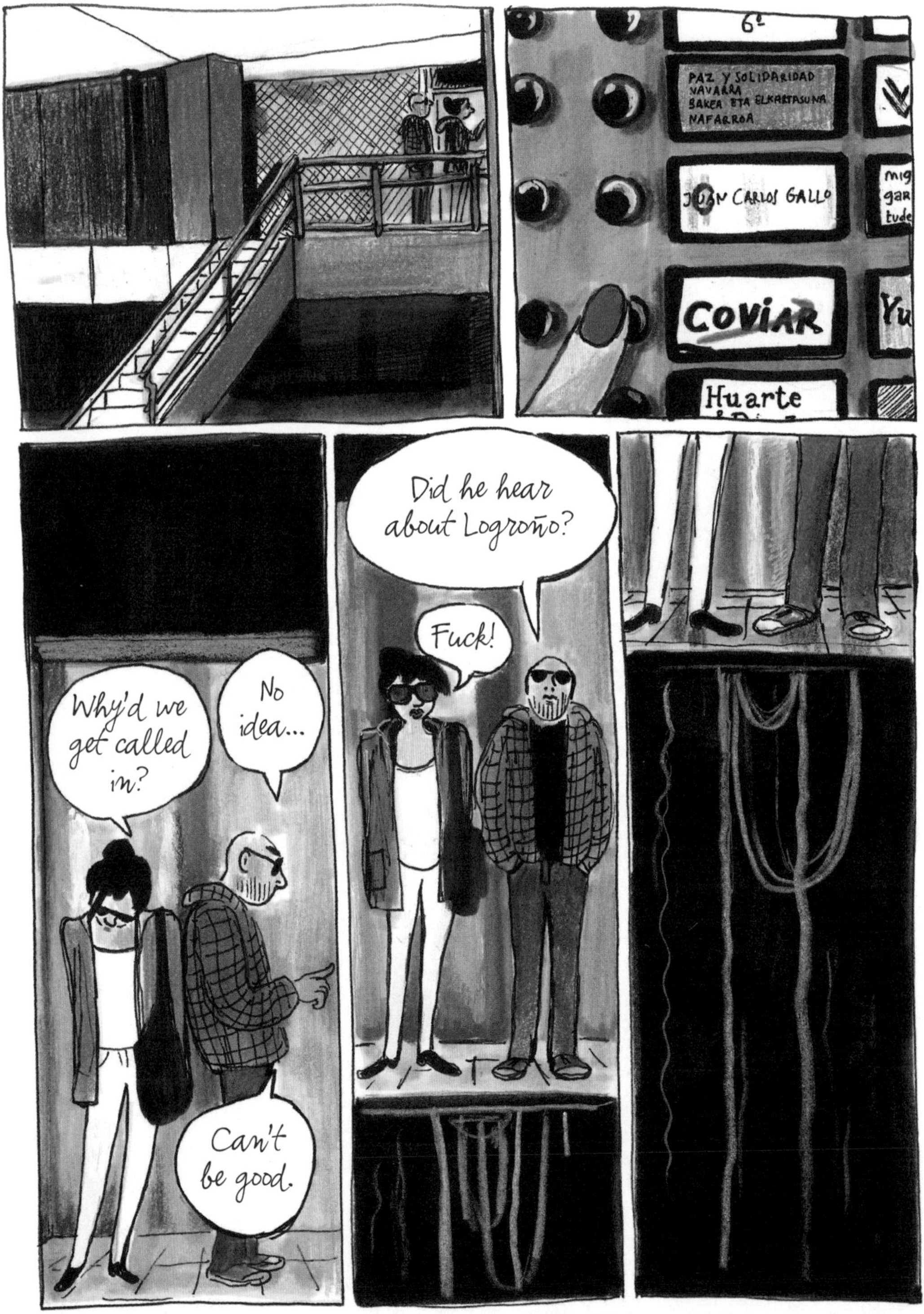
PAZ Y SOLIDARIDAD NAVARRA BAKEA ETA ELKARTASUNA NAFARROA
CARLOS GALLO
COVIAR
Huarte
Why'd we get called in?
No idea...
Can't be good.
Did he hear about Logroño?
Fuck!

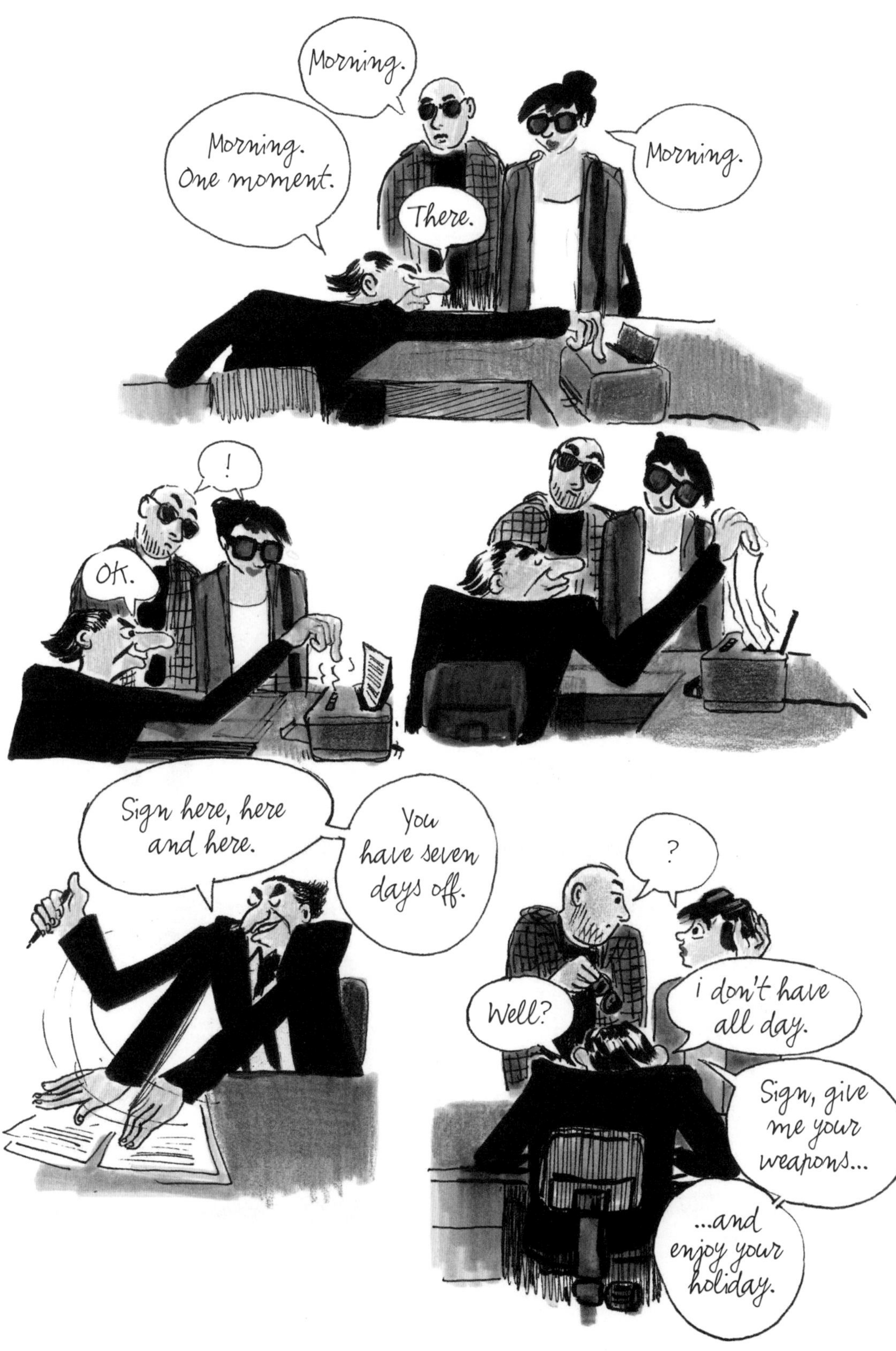
Morning.
Morning. One moment.
Morning.
There.
!
OK.
Sign here, here and here.
You have seven days off.
?
Well?
i don't have all day.
Sign, give me your weapons...
...and enjoy your holiday.

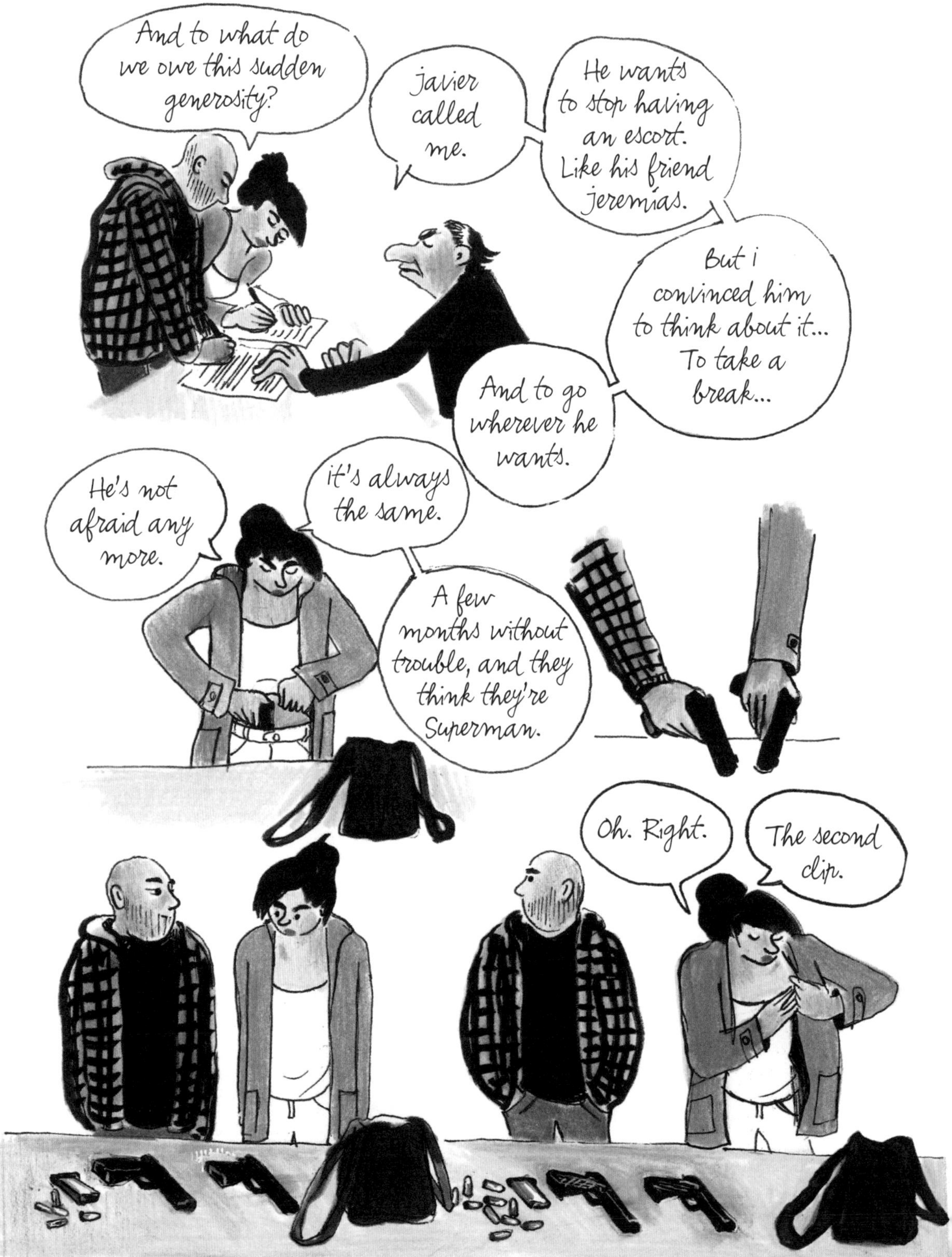
And to what do we owe this sudden generosity?
javier called me.
He wants to stop having an escort. Like his friend jeremias.
But i convinced him to think about it... To take a break...
And to go wherever he wants.
He's not afraid any more.
it's always the same.
A few months without trouble, and they think they're Superman.
Oh. Right.
The second clip.

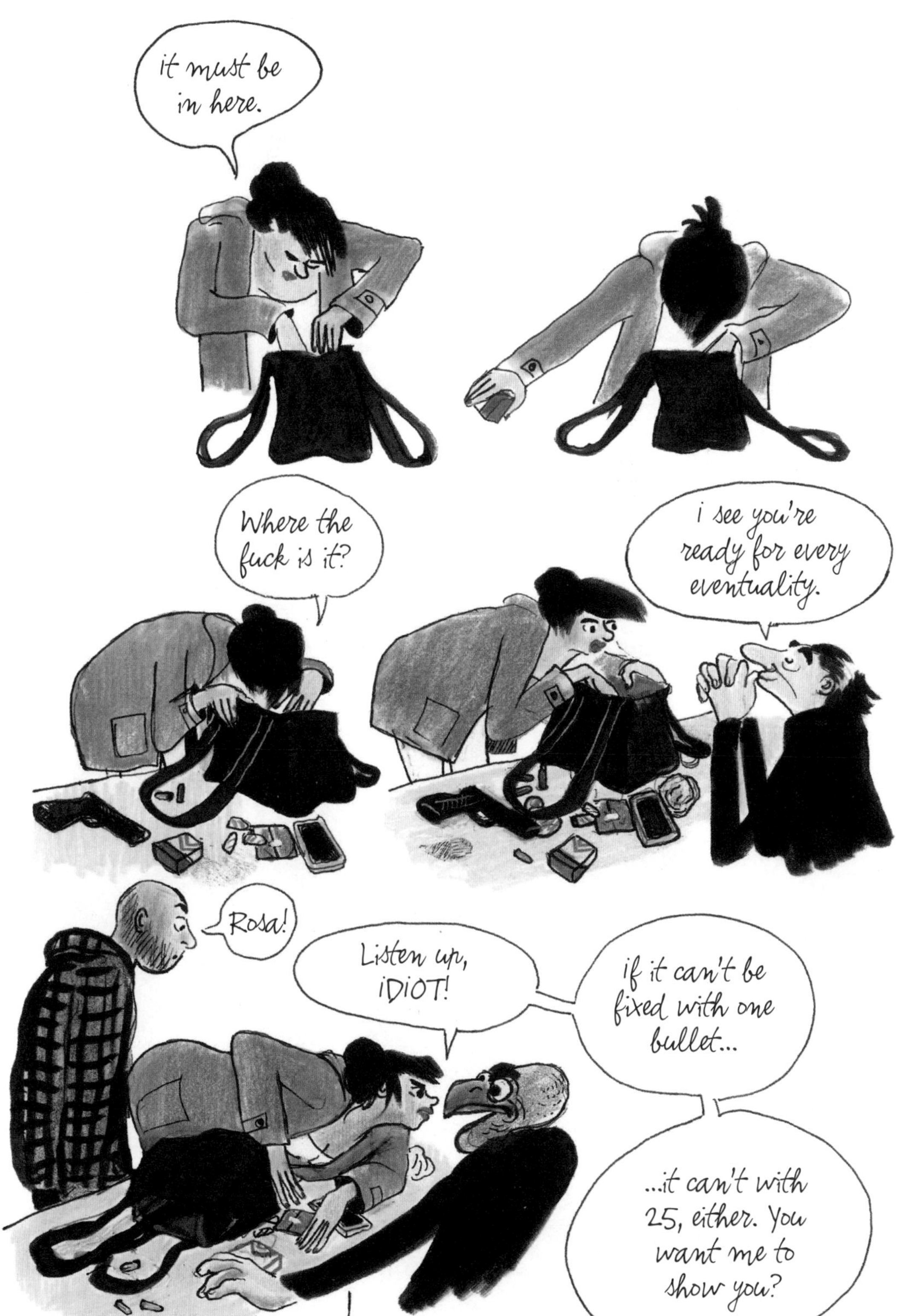
it must be in here.
Where the fuck is it?
i see you're ready for every eventuality.
Rosa!
Listen up, iDiOT!
if it can't be fixed with one bullet...
...it can't with 25, either. You want me to show you?

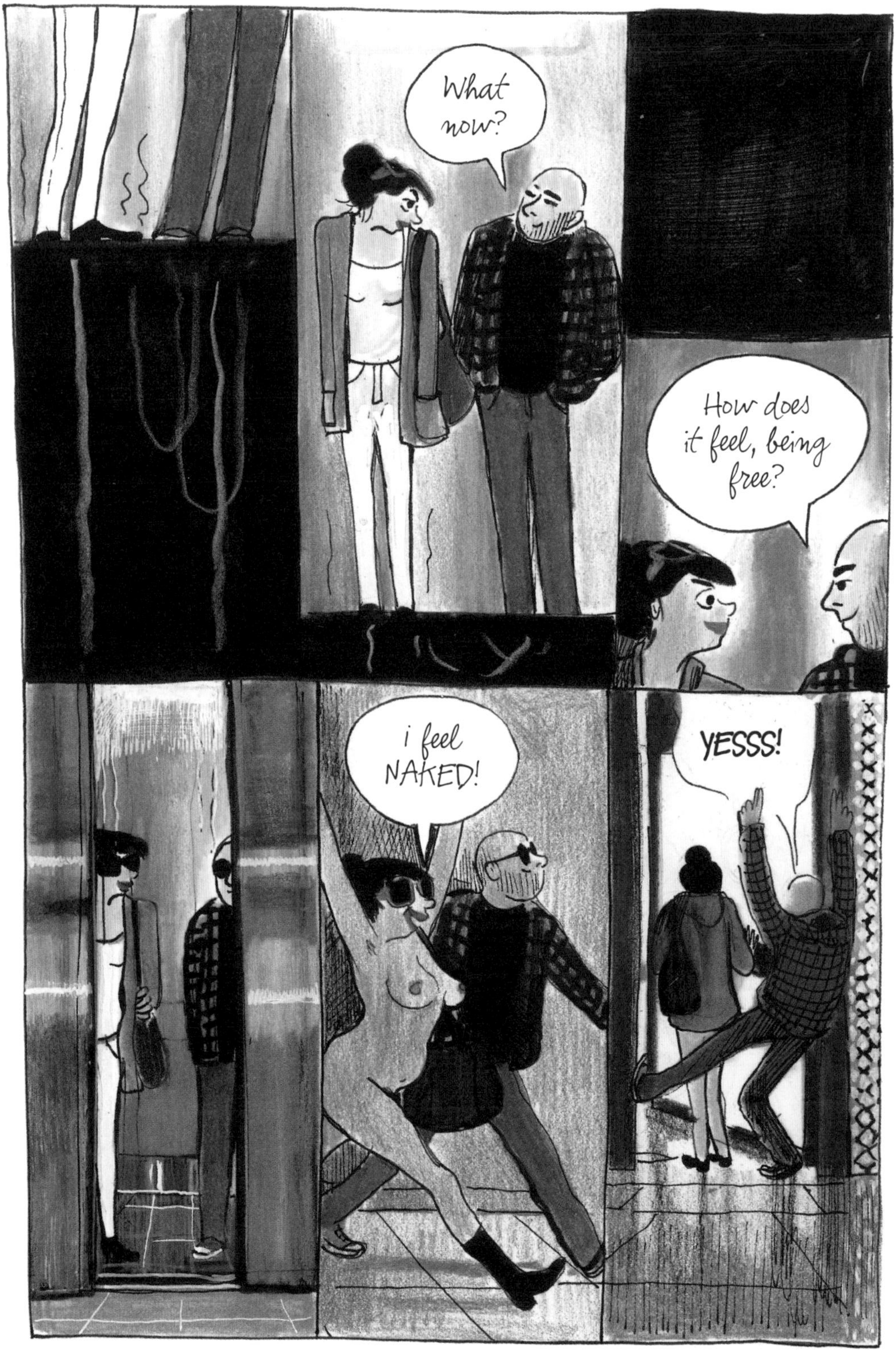
What now?
How does it feel, being free?
i feel NAKED!
YESSS!

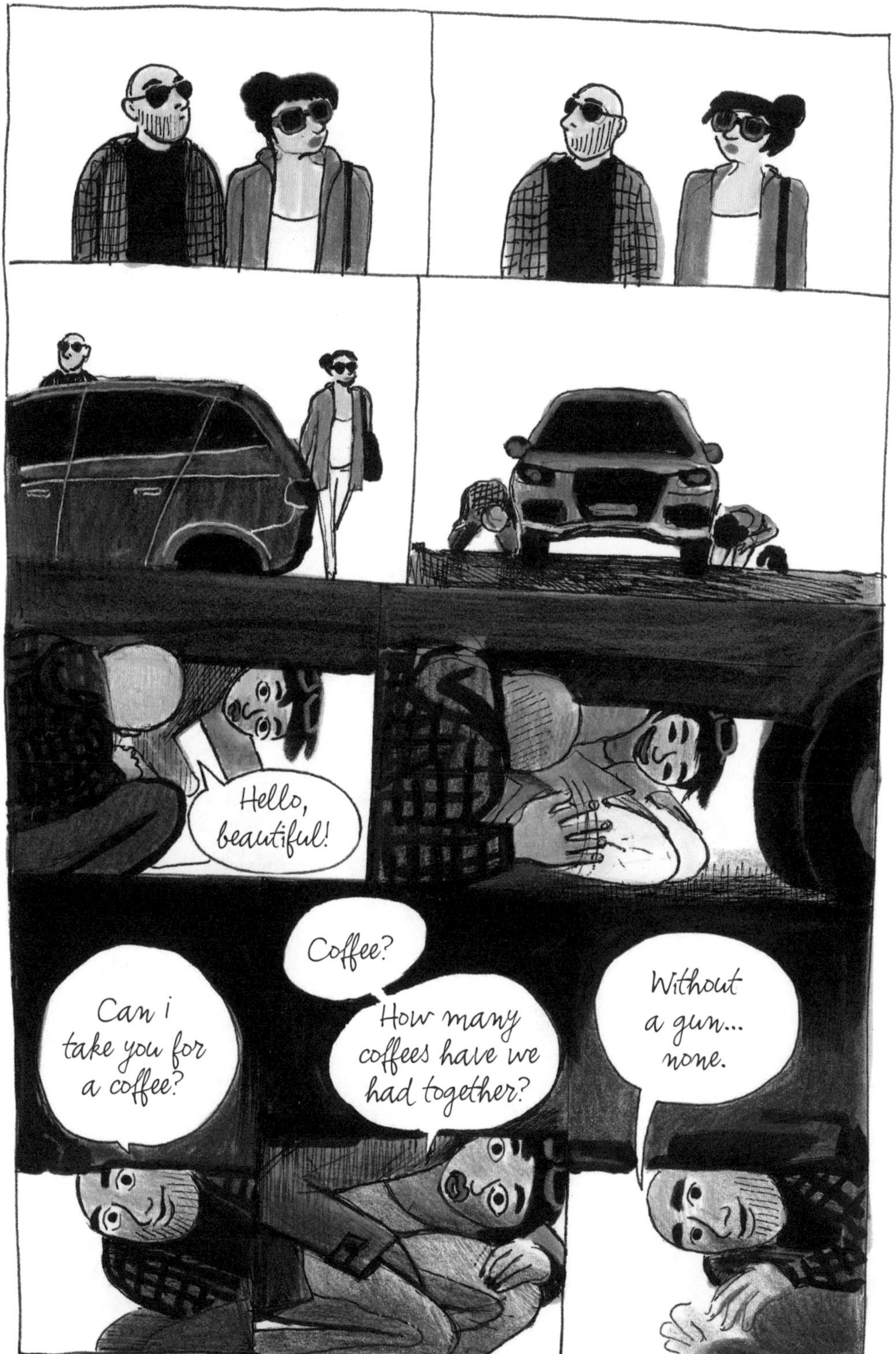
Hello, beautiful!
Can i take you for a coffee?
Coffee?
How many coffees have we had together?
Without a gun... none.

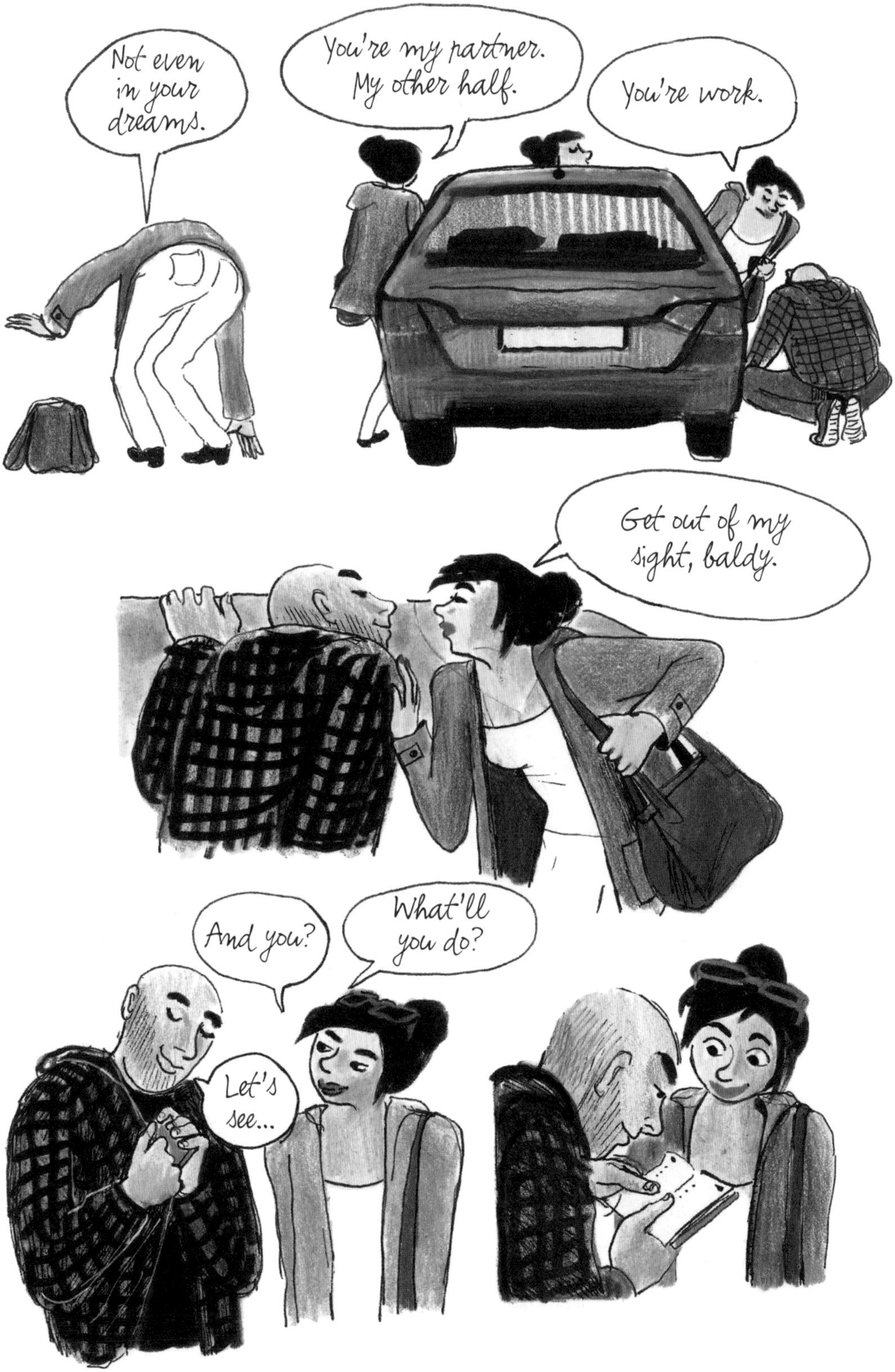
Not even in your dreams.
You're my partner. My other half.
You're work.
Get out of my sight, baldy.
And you?
What'll you do?
Let's see...

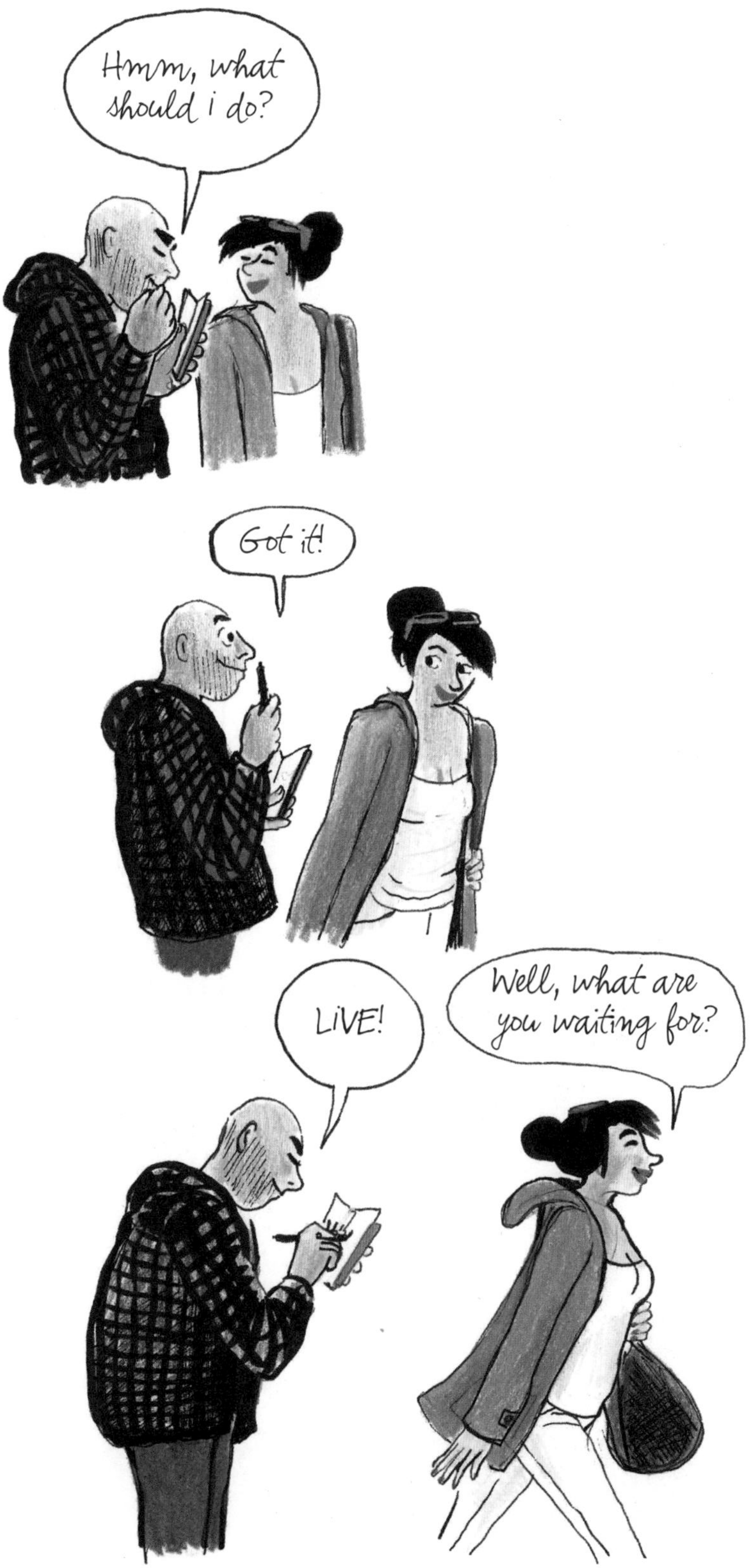
Hmm, what should i do?
Got it!
LiVE!
Well, what are you waiting for?

Holiday. Day 1: sightseeing.

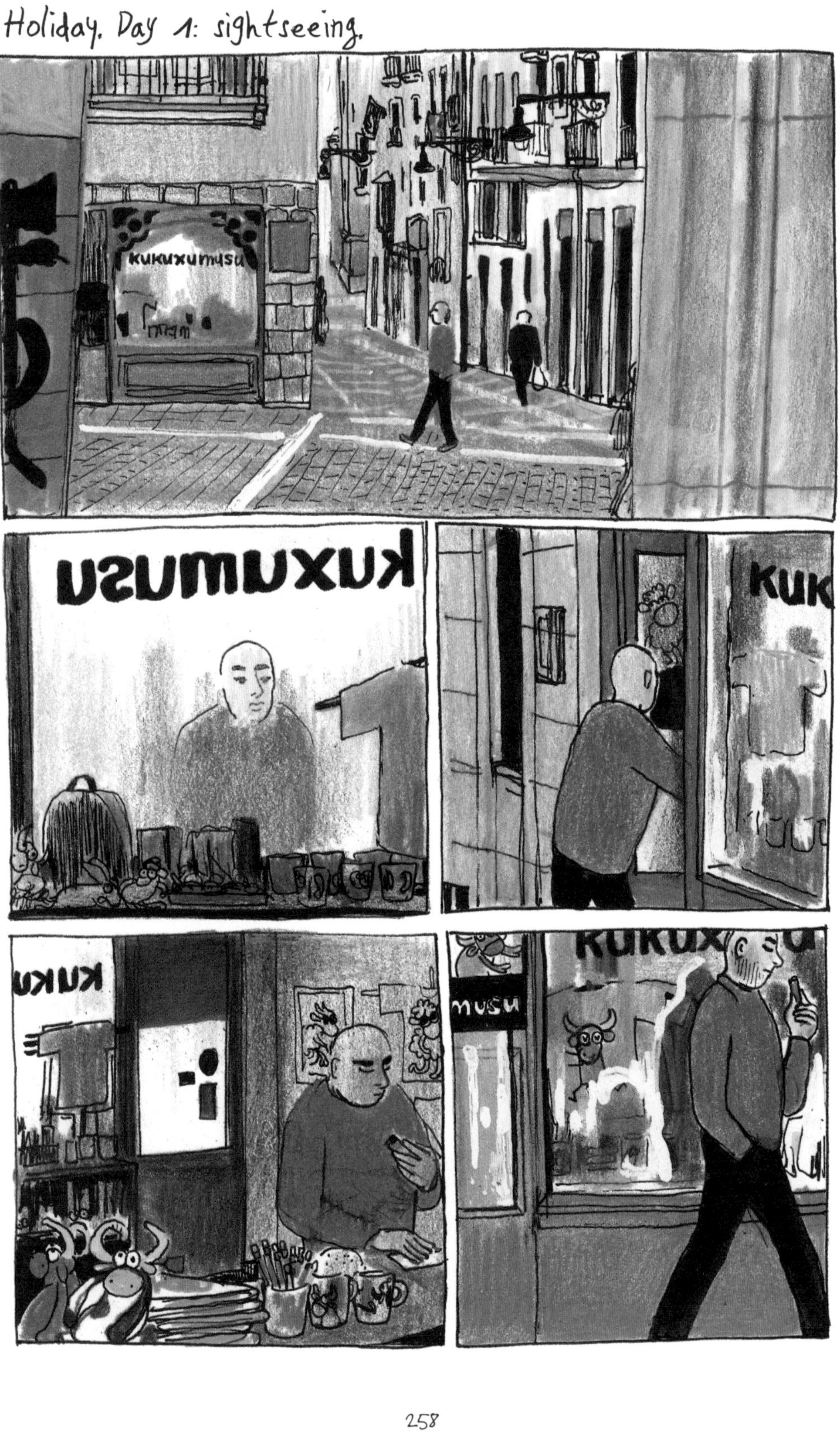
kukuxumusu

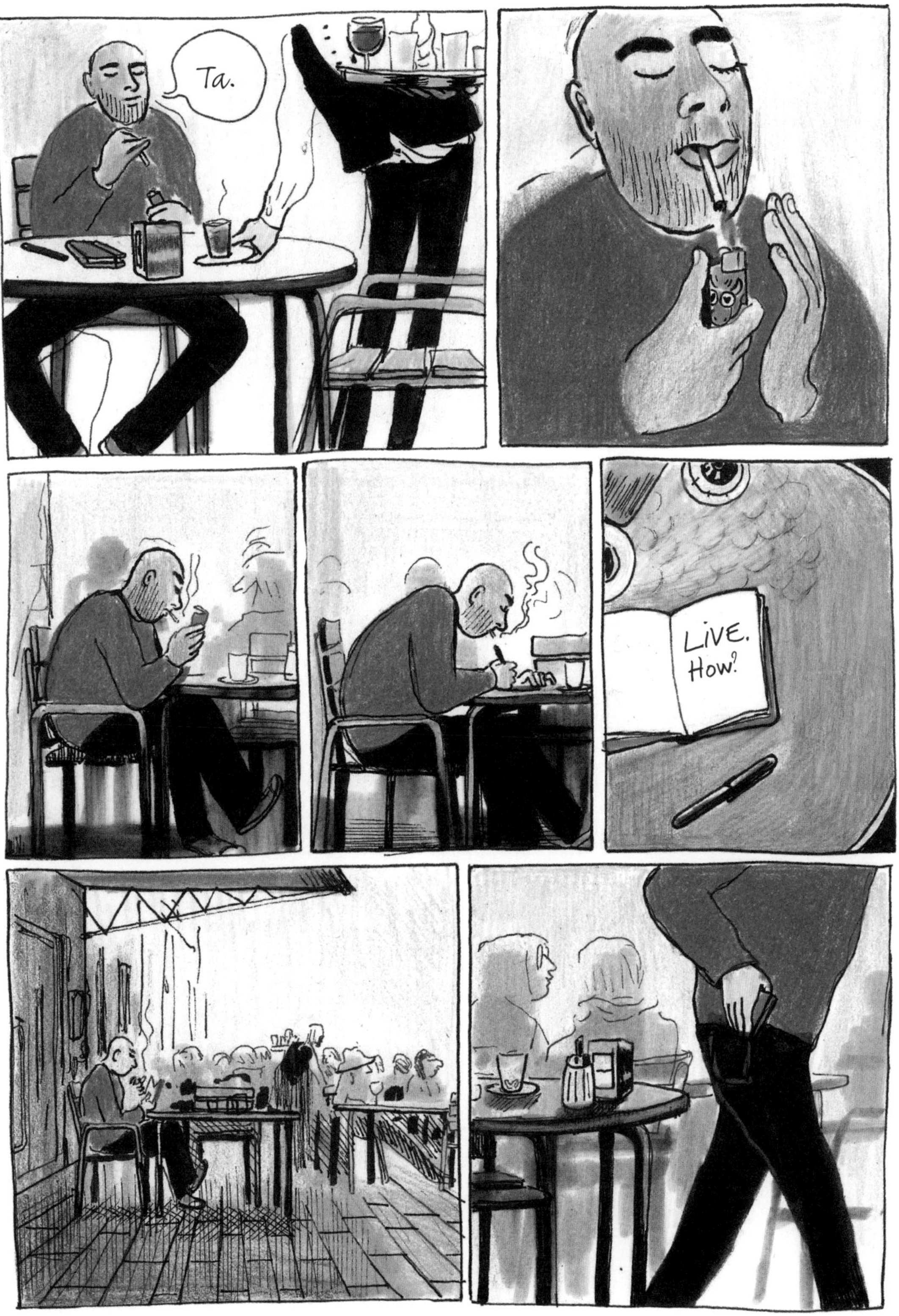
Ta.
LIVE.
How?

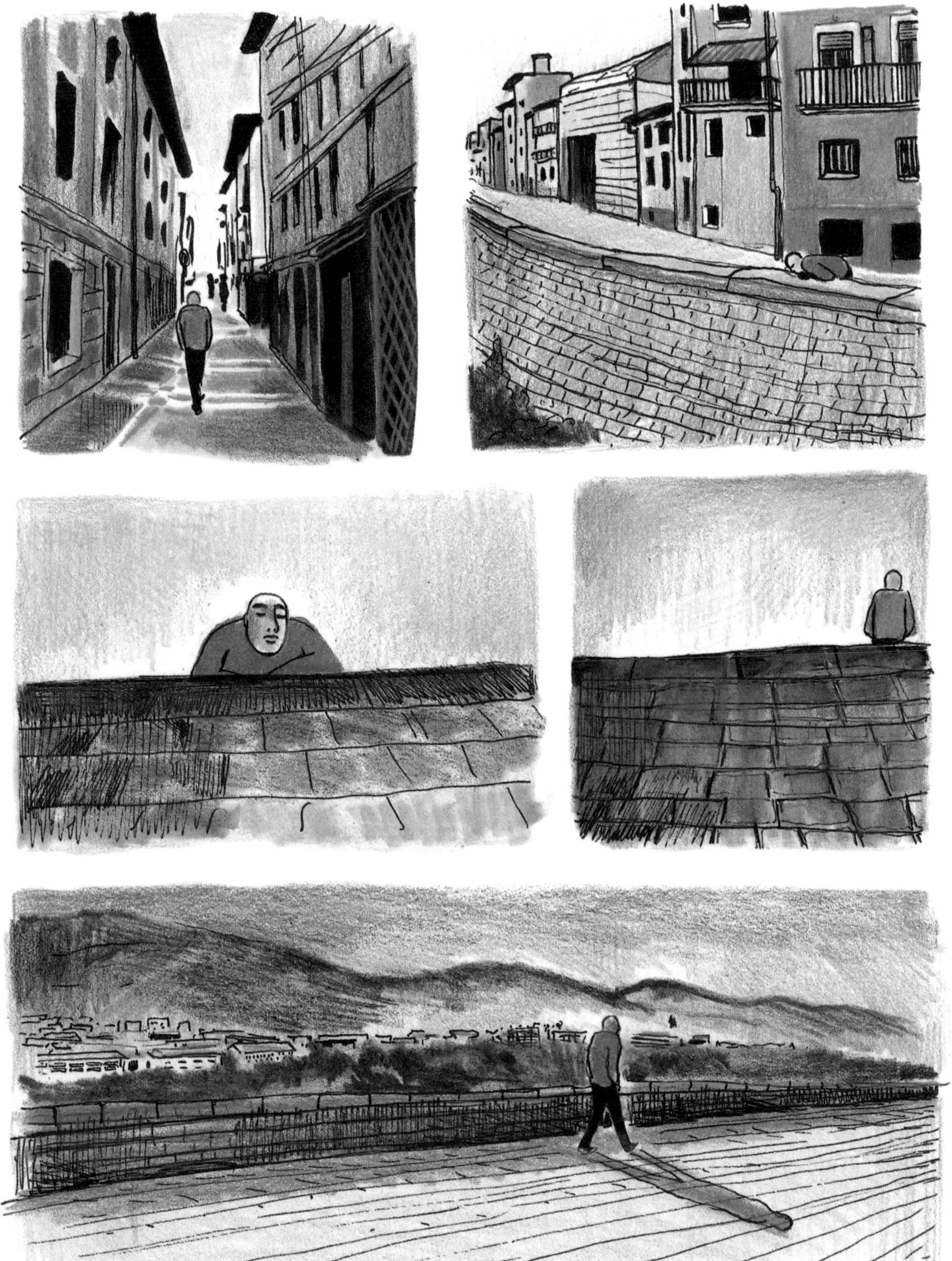

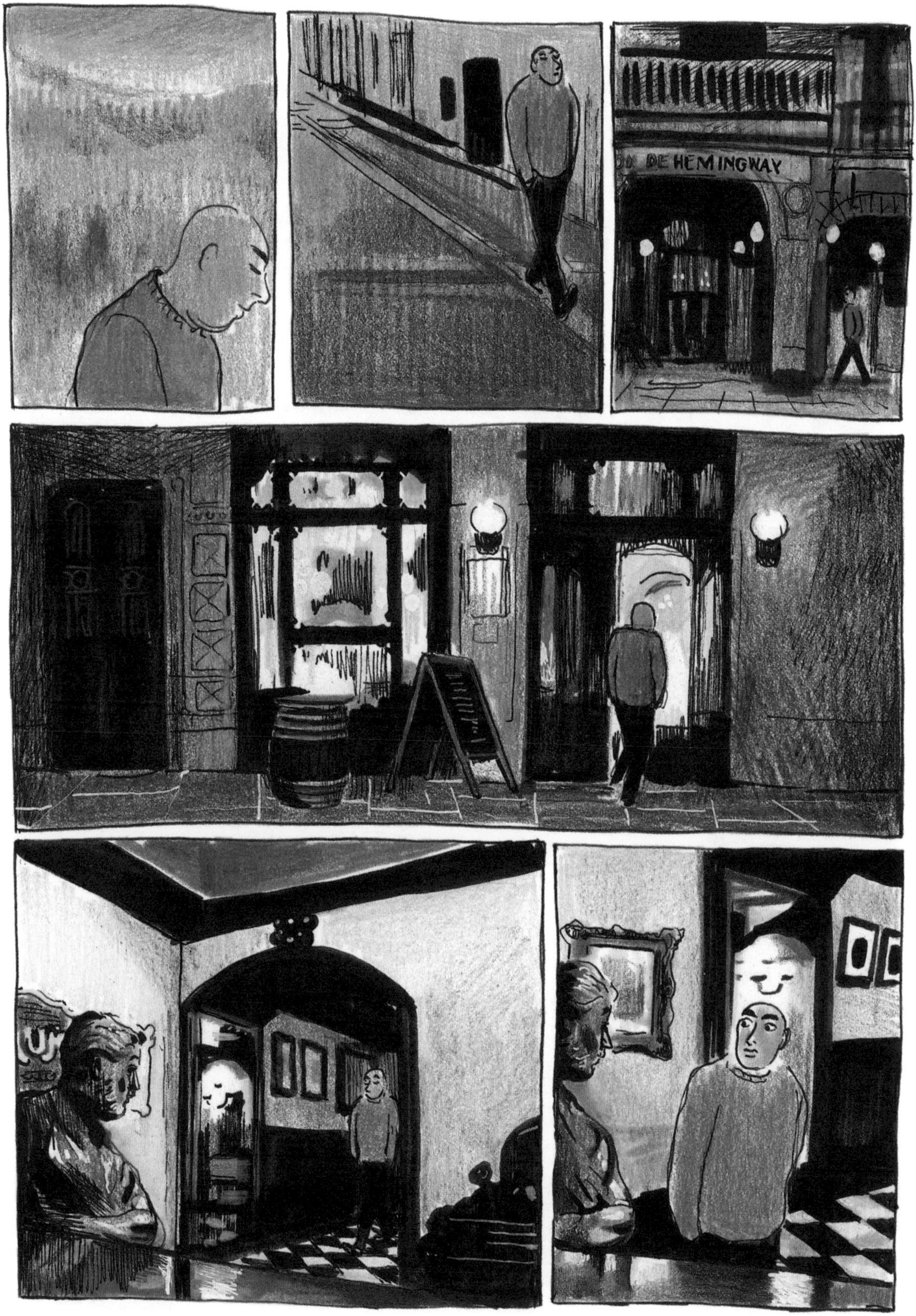
DE HEMINGWAY

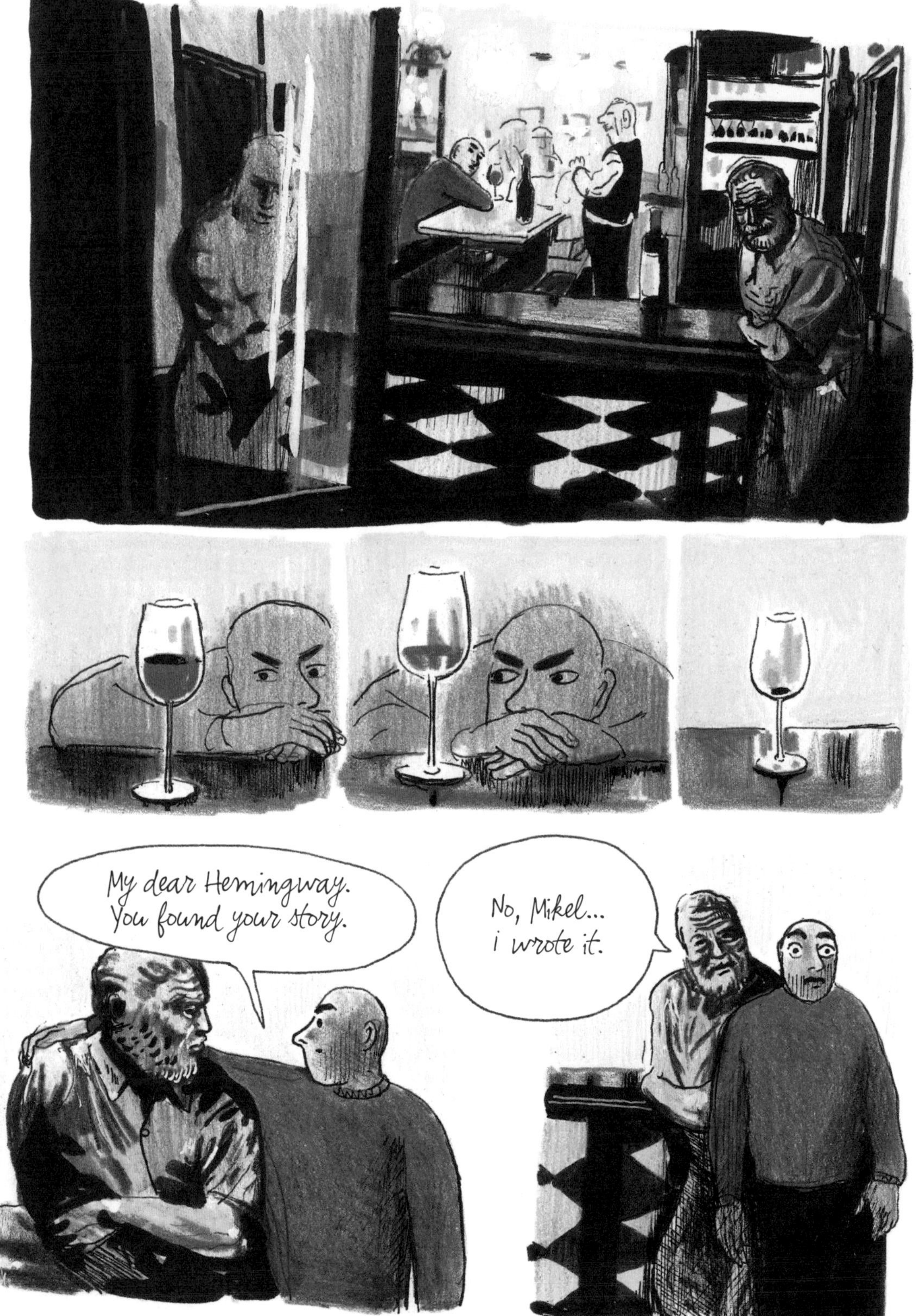
My dear Hemingway. You found your story.
No, Mikel... i wrote it.

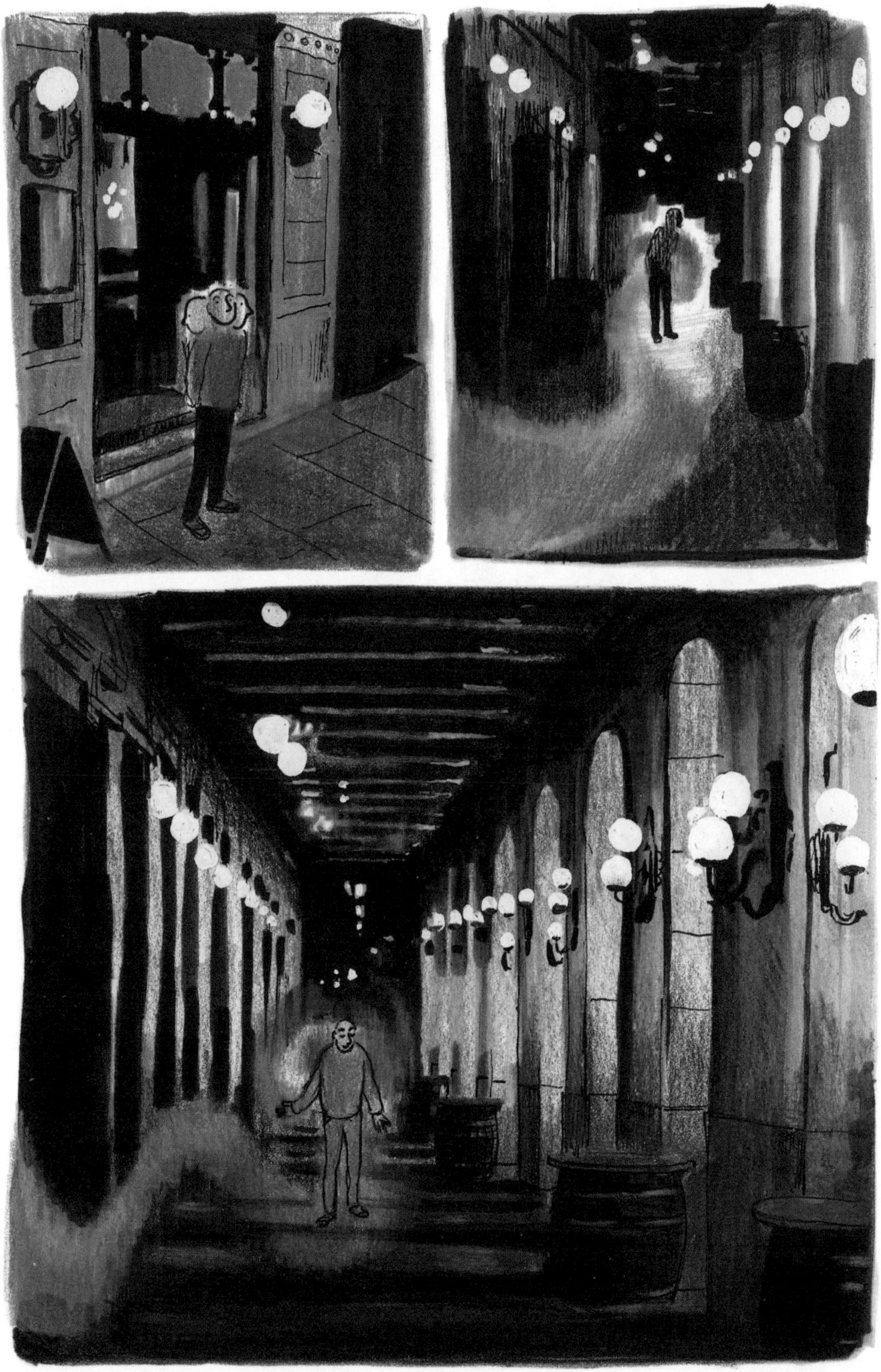

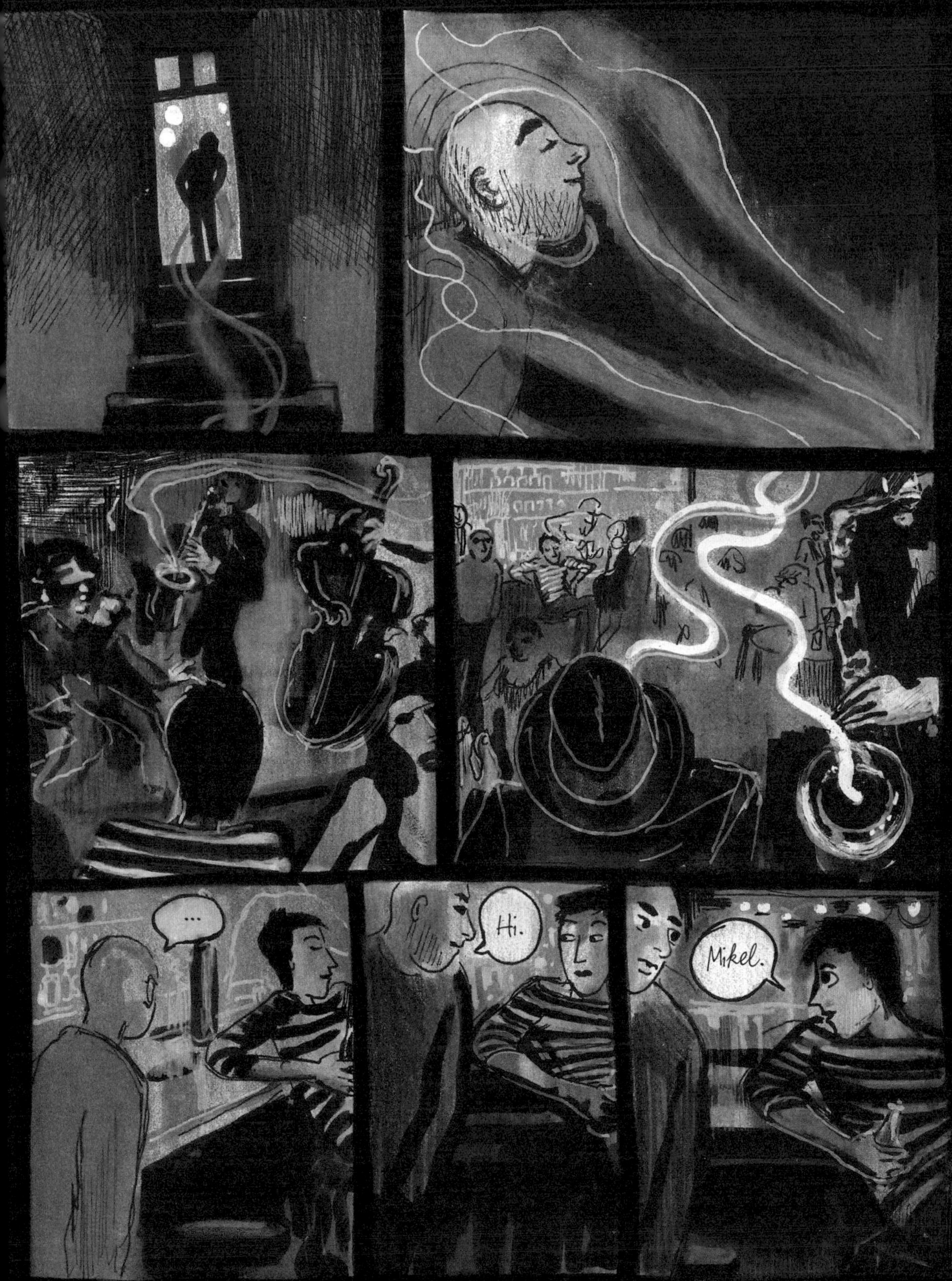
...
Hi.
Mikel.

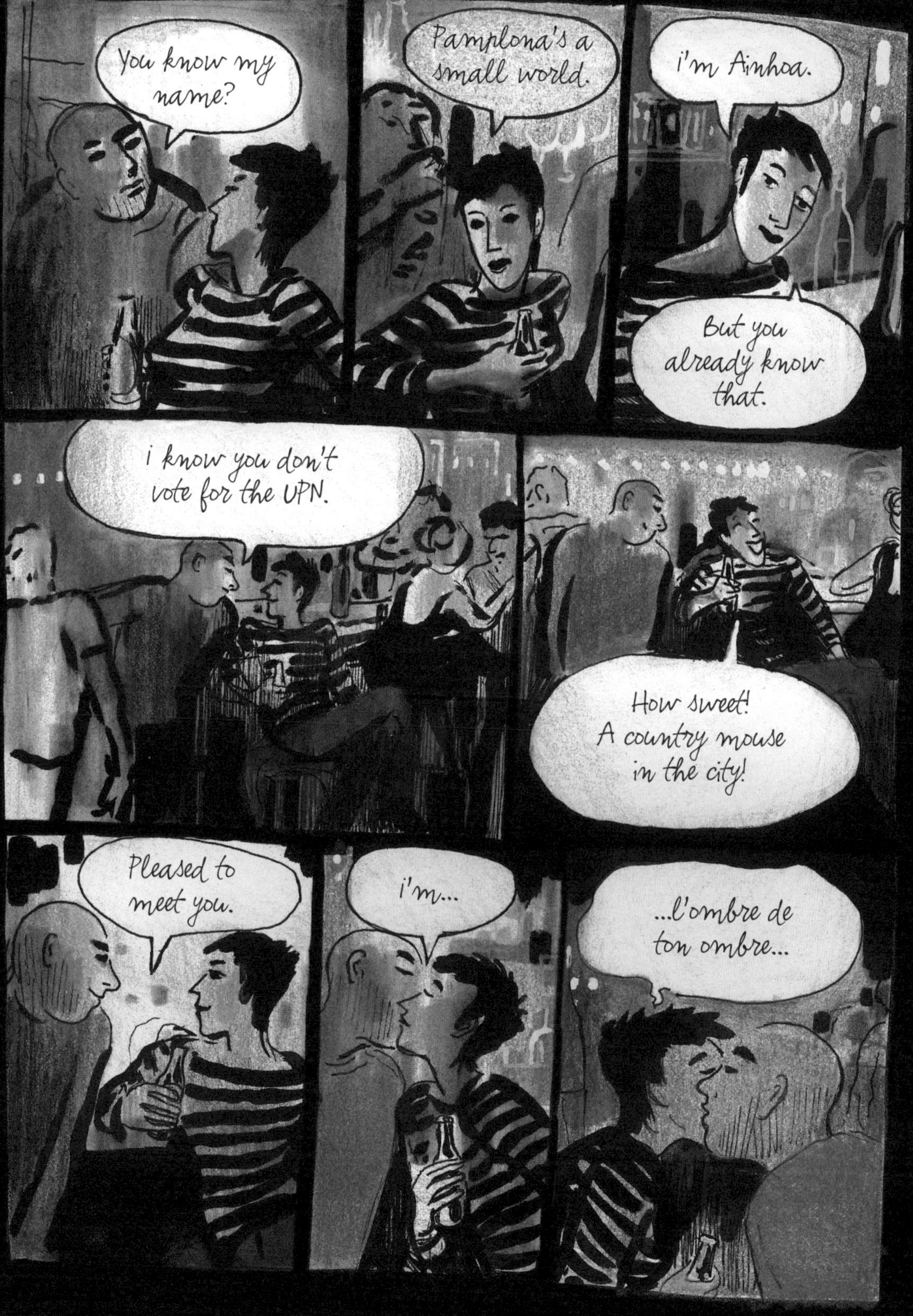
You know my name?
Pamplona's a small world.
i'm Ainhoa.
But you already know that.
i know you don't vote for the UPN.
How sweet! A country mouse in the city!
Pleased to meet you.
i'm...
...l'ombre de ton ombre...

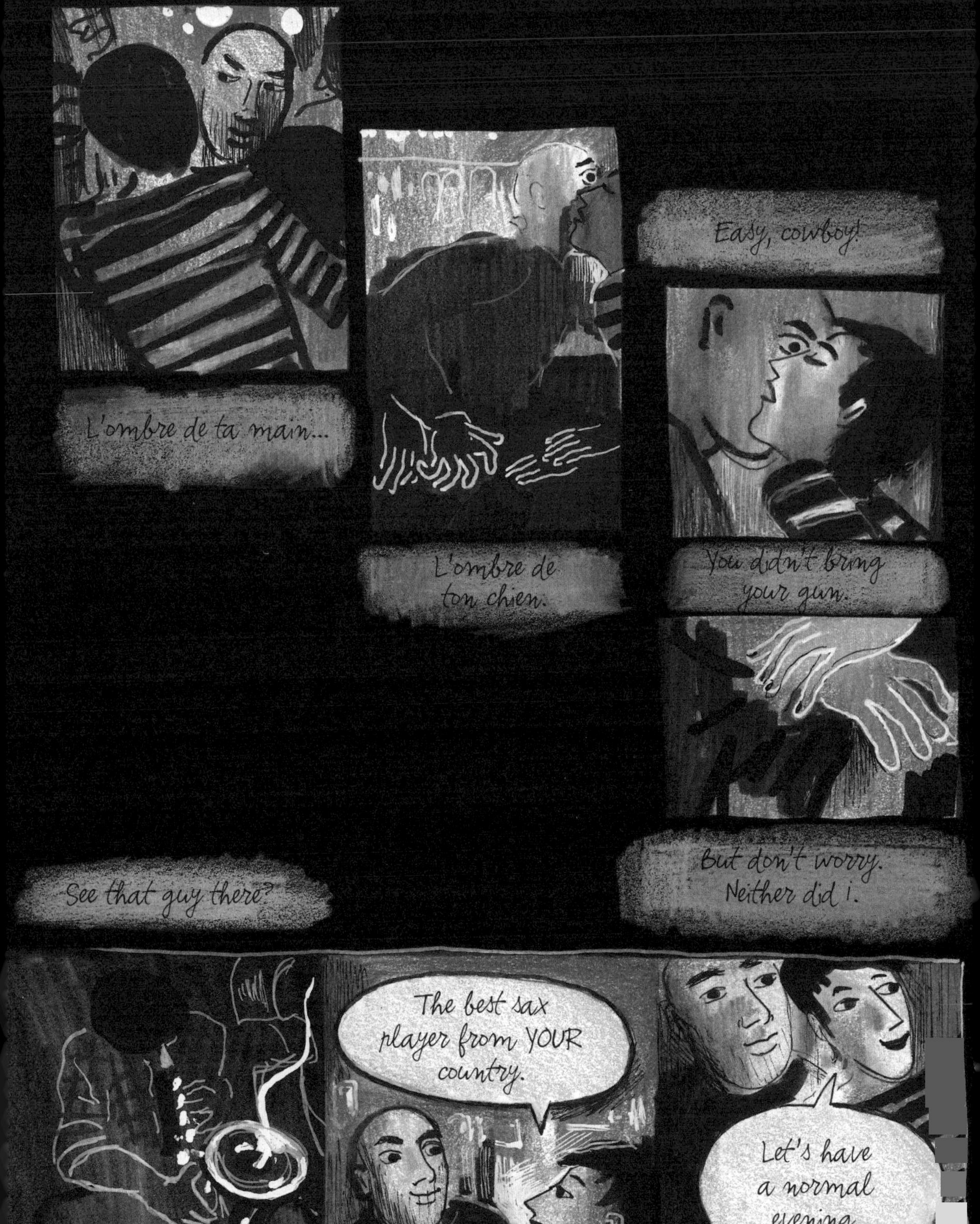
L'ombre de ta main...
L'ombre de ton chien.
Easy, cowboy!
You didn't bring your gun.
But don't worry. Neither did I.
See that guy there?
The best sax player from YOUR country.
Let's have a normal evening.

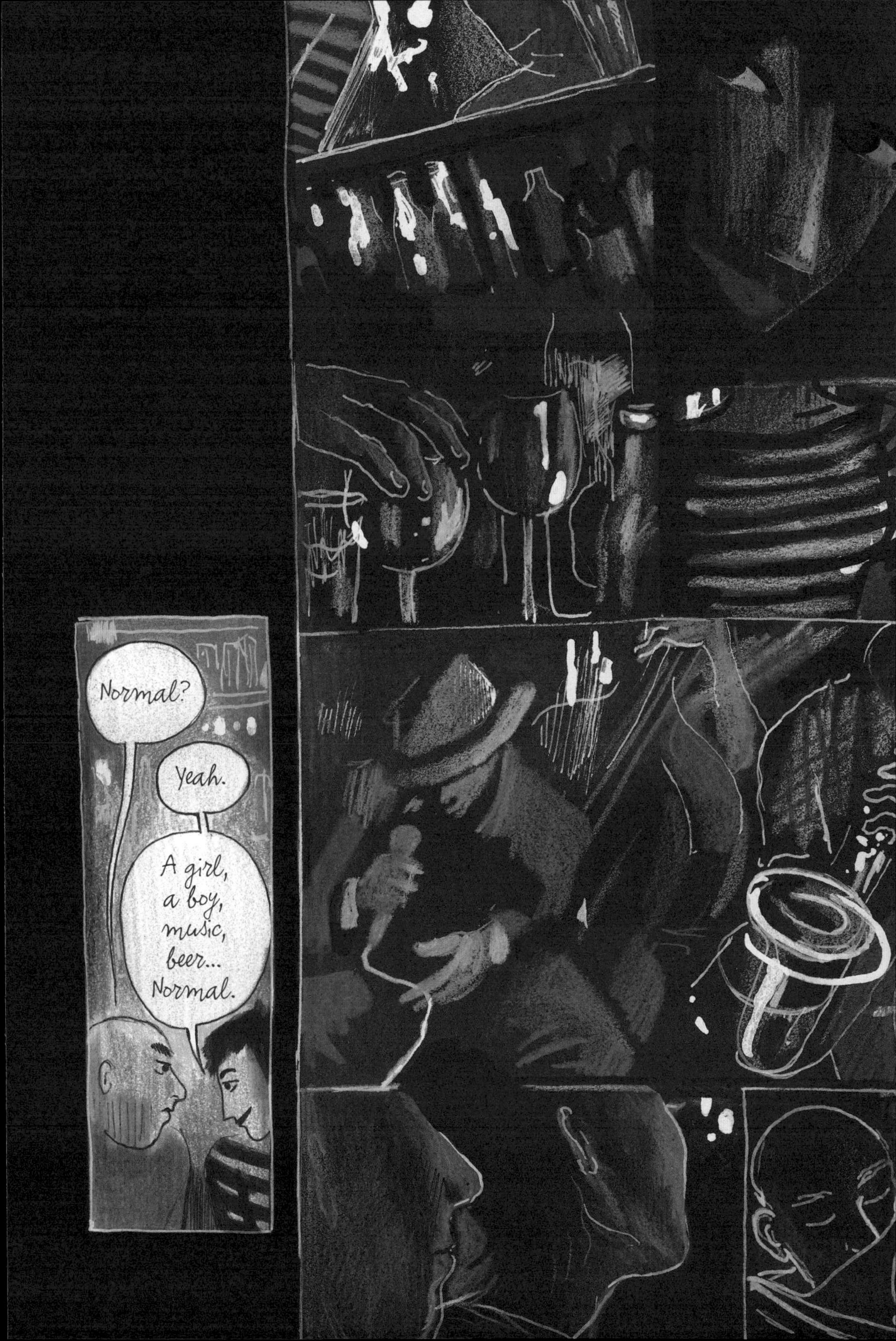
Normal?
Yeah.
A girl, a boy, music, beer... Normal.

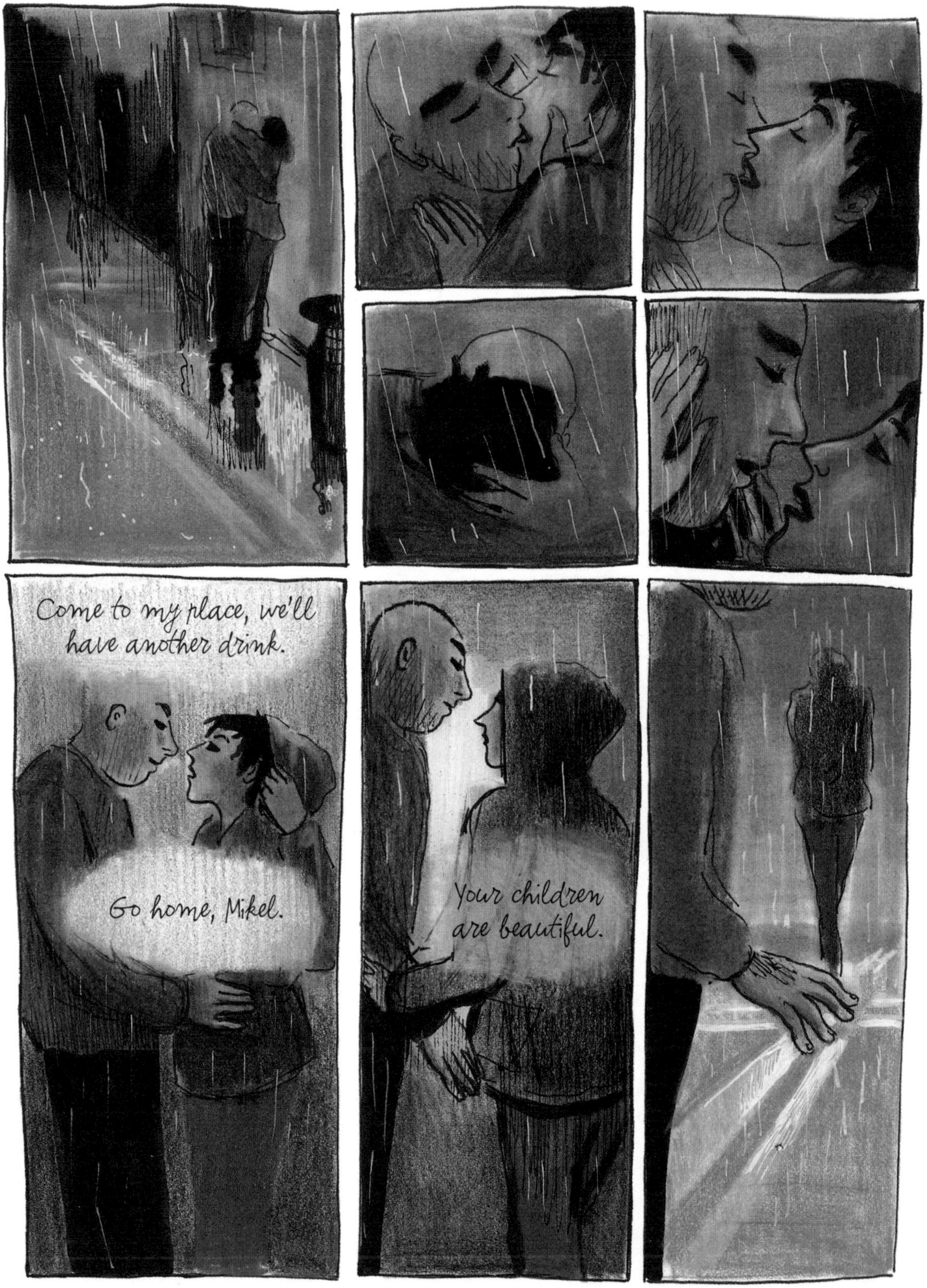
Come to my place, we'll have another drink.
Go home, Mikel.
Your children are beautiful.

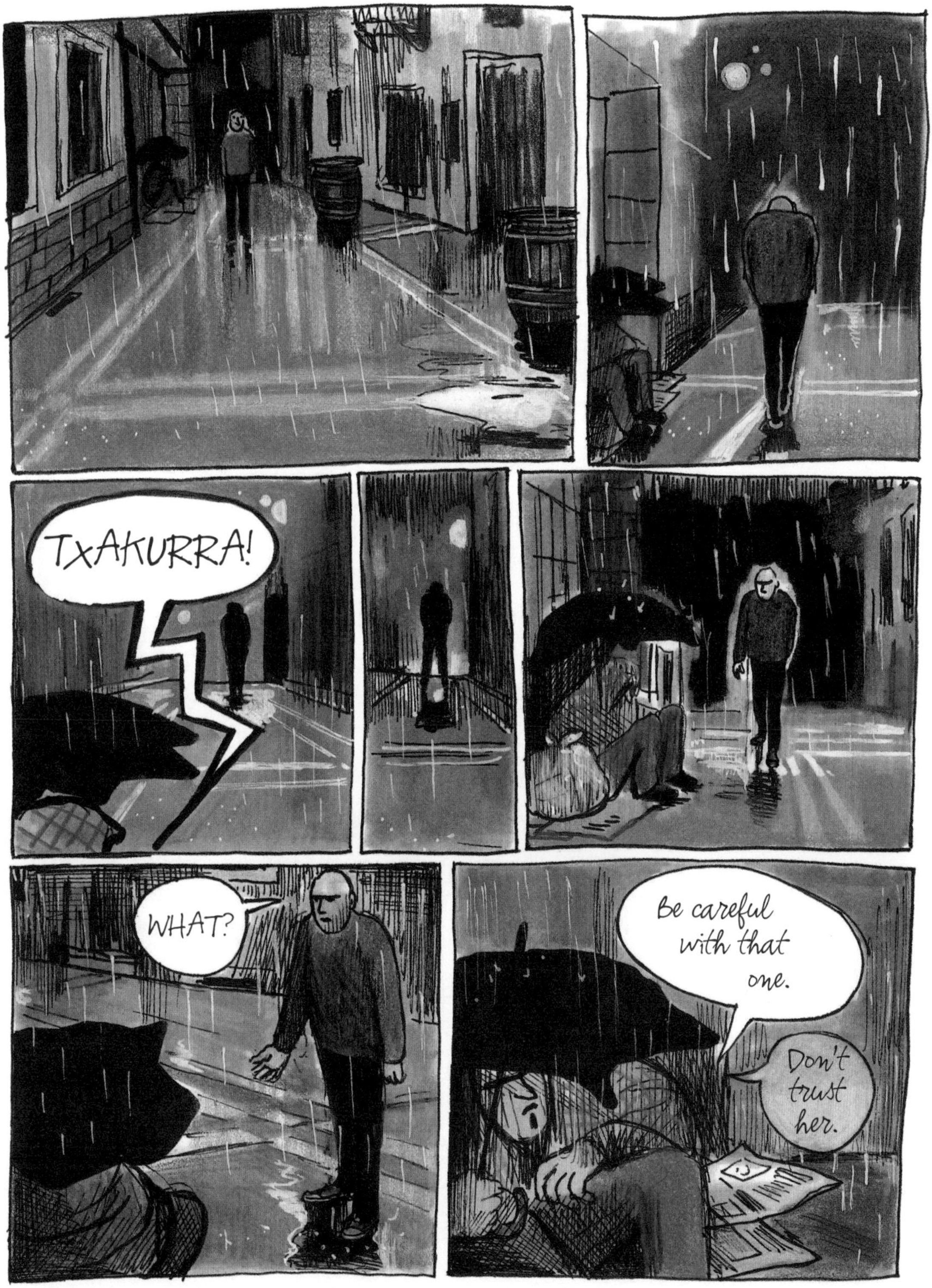
TXAKURRA!
WHAT?
Be careful with that one.
Don't trust her.

Holiday. Day 2: take Hemingway's advice.

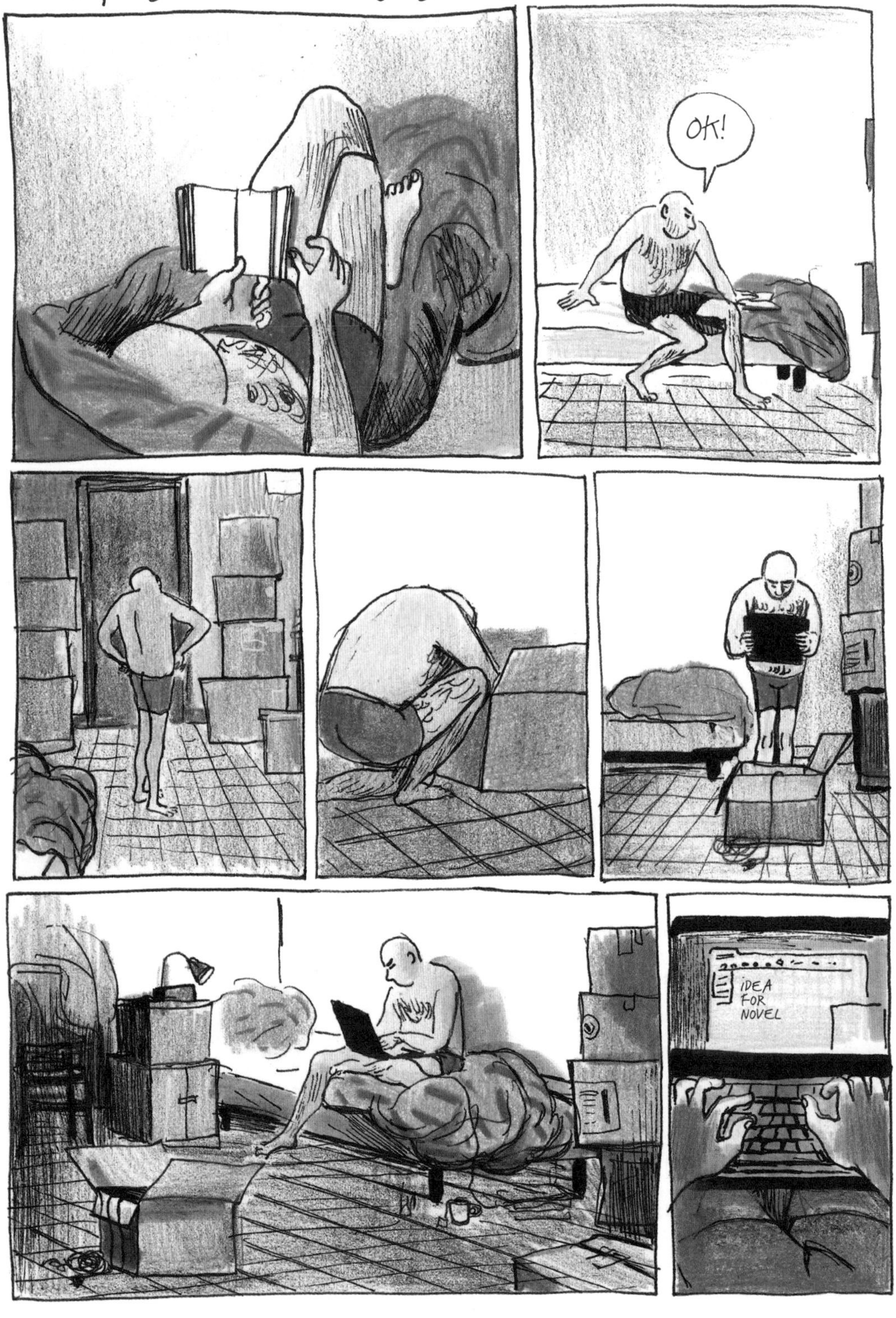
OK!
IDEA
FOR
NOVEL

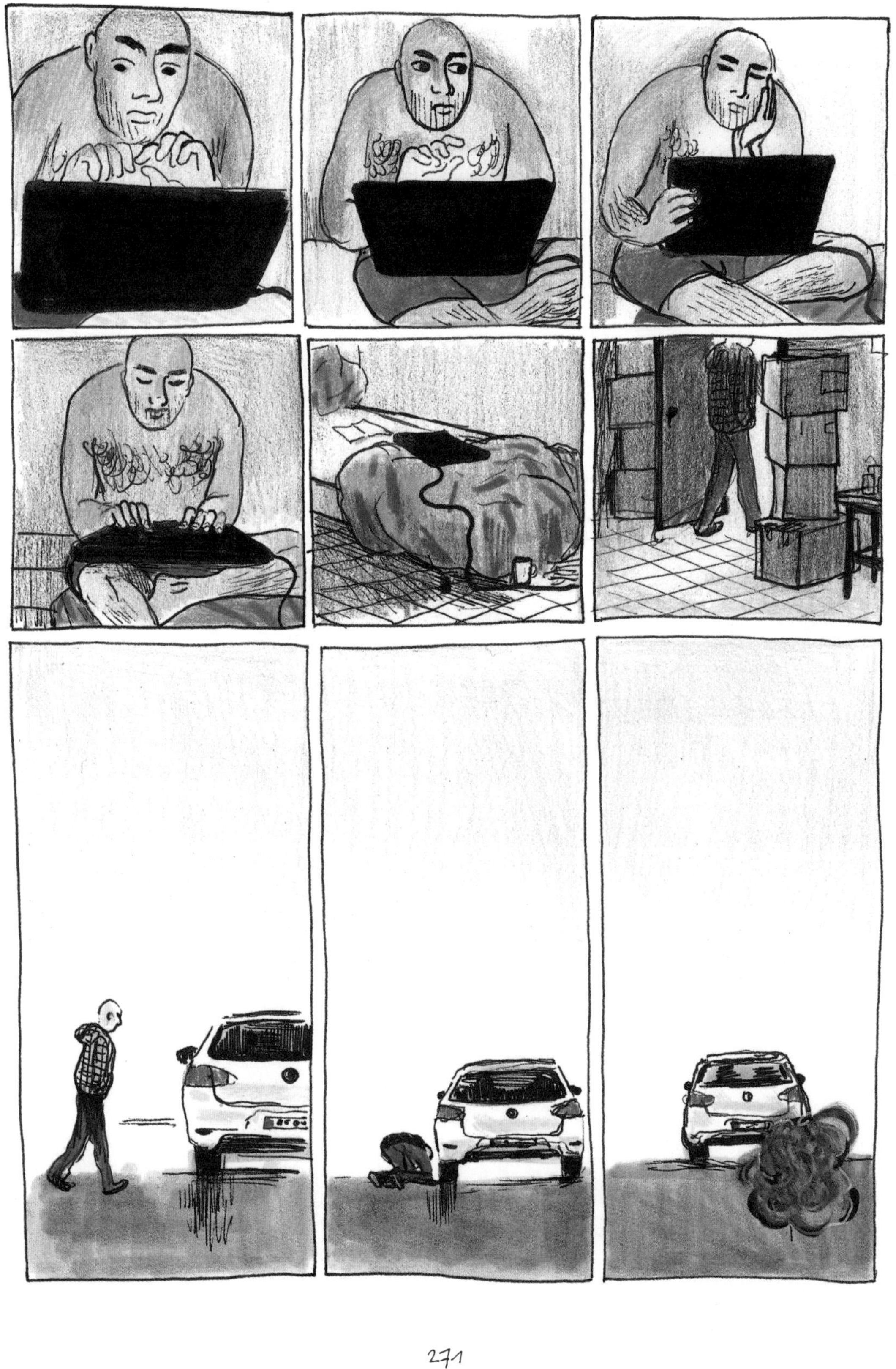

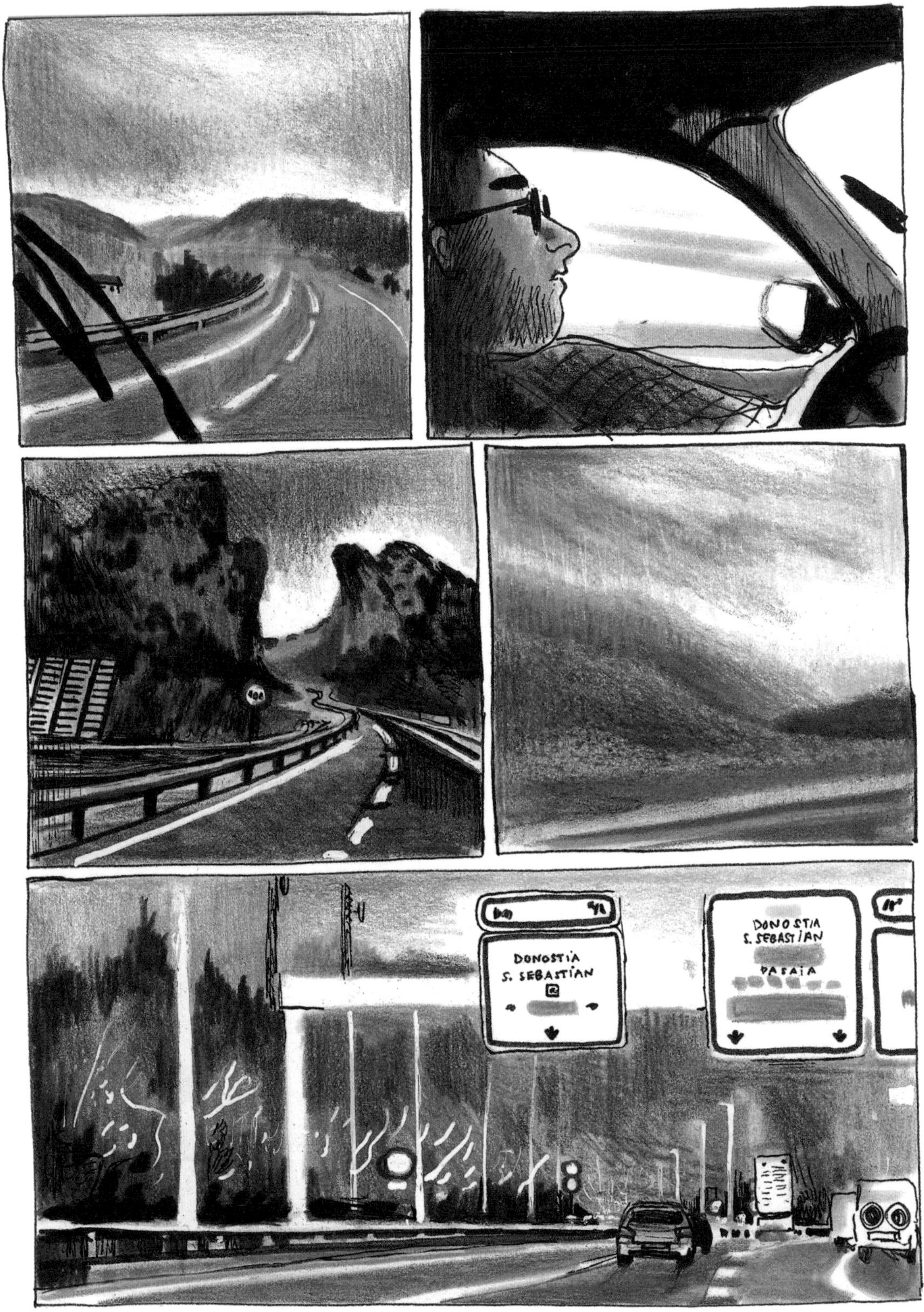
DONOSTIA
S. SEBASTIAN
DONOSTIA
S. SEBASTIAN
PASAIA

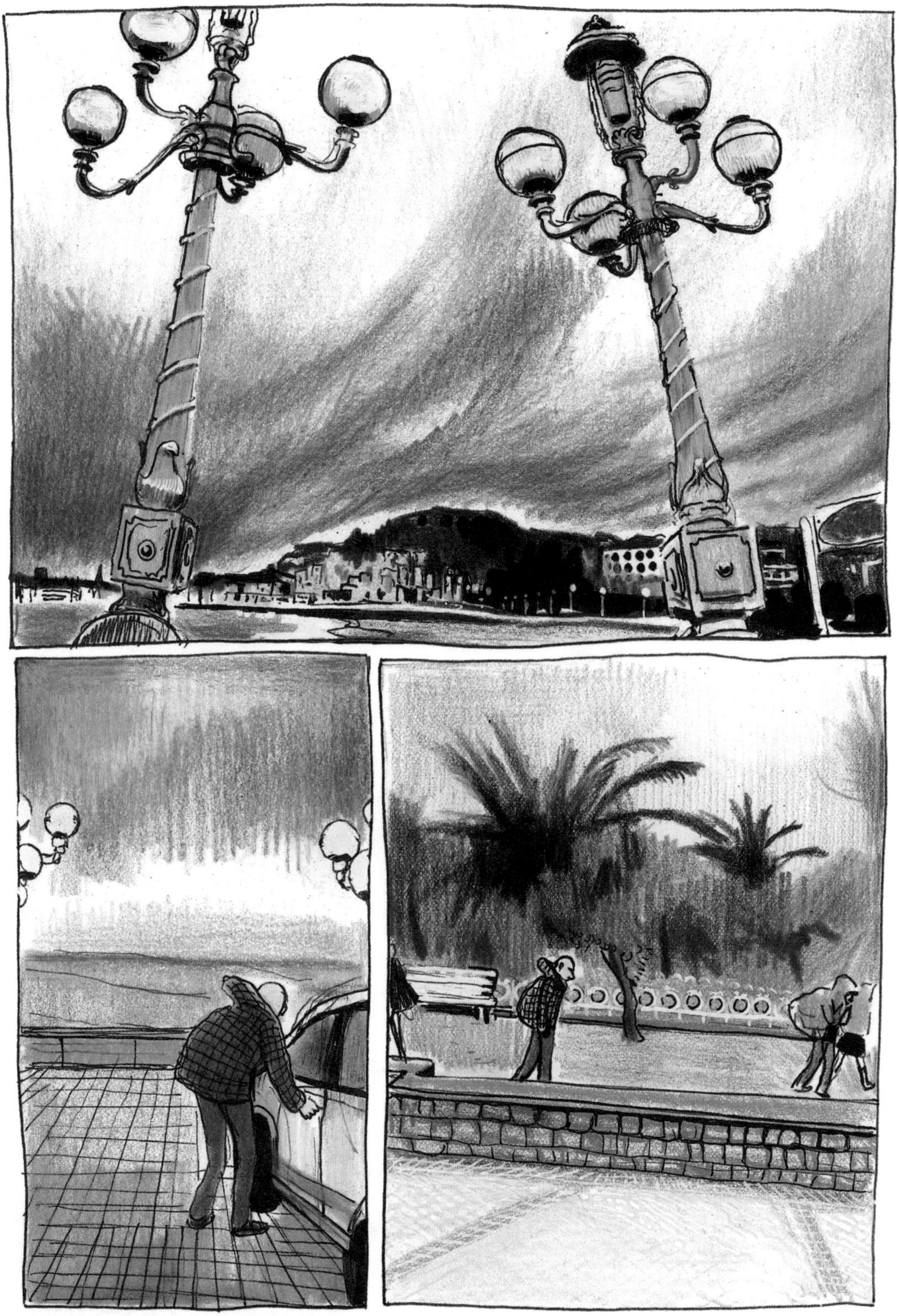

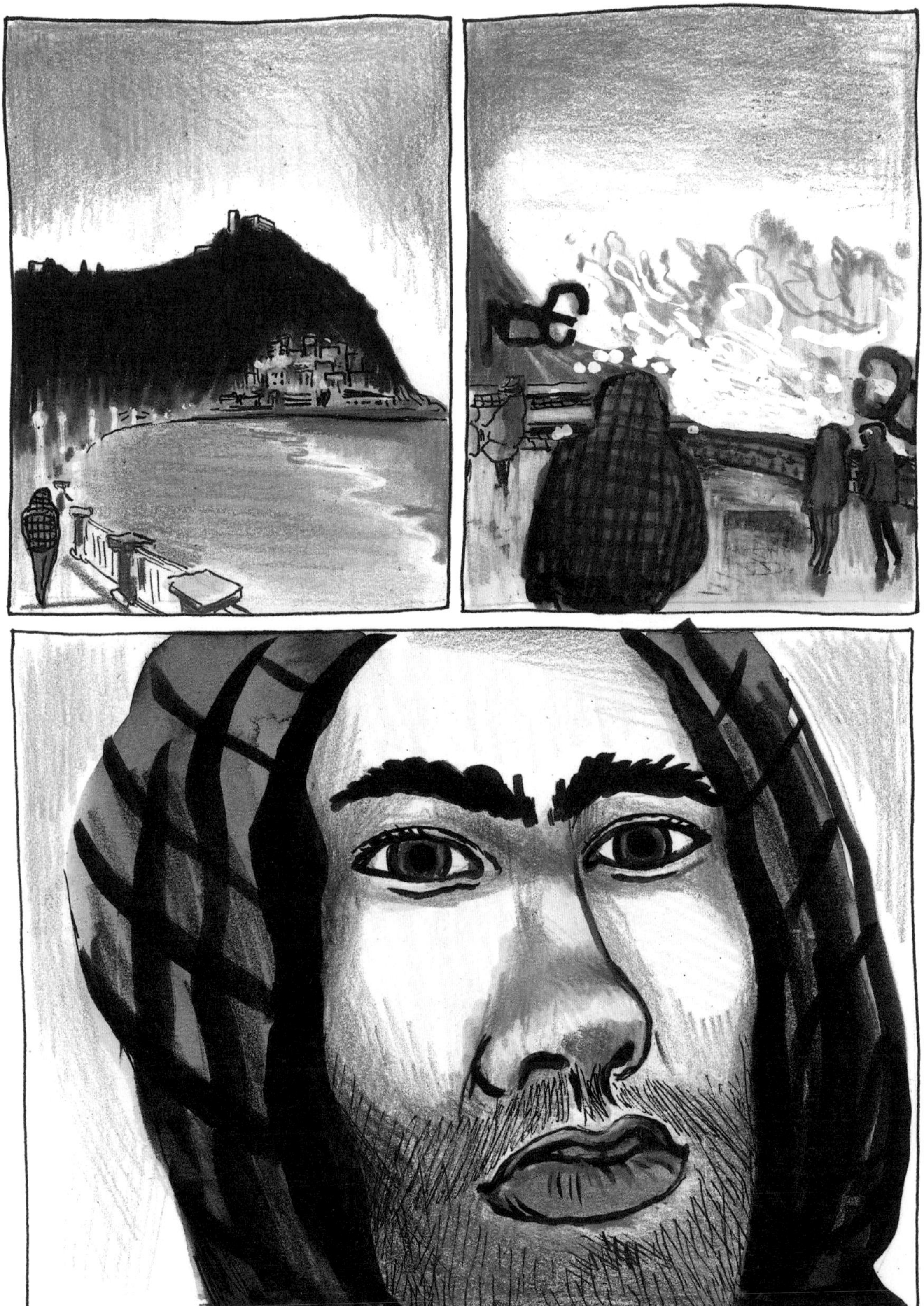

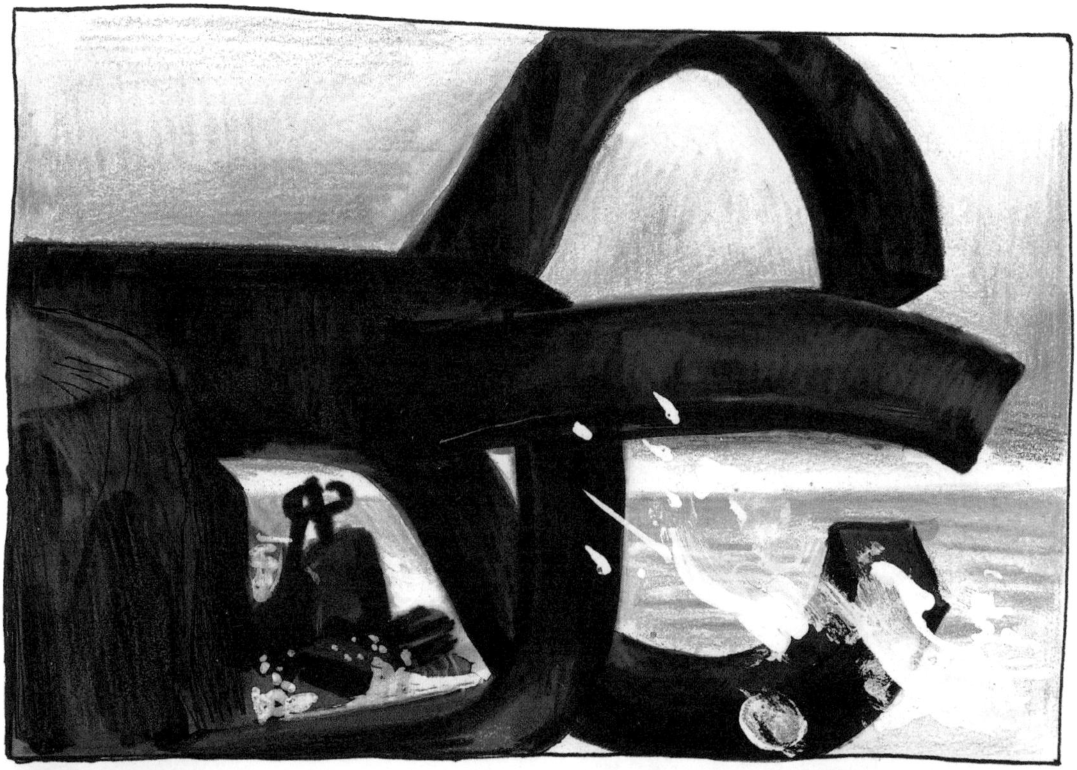

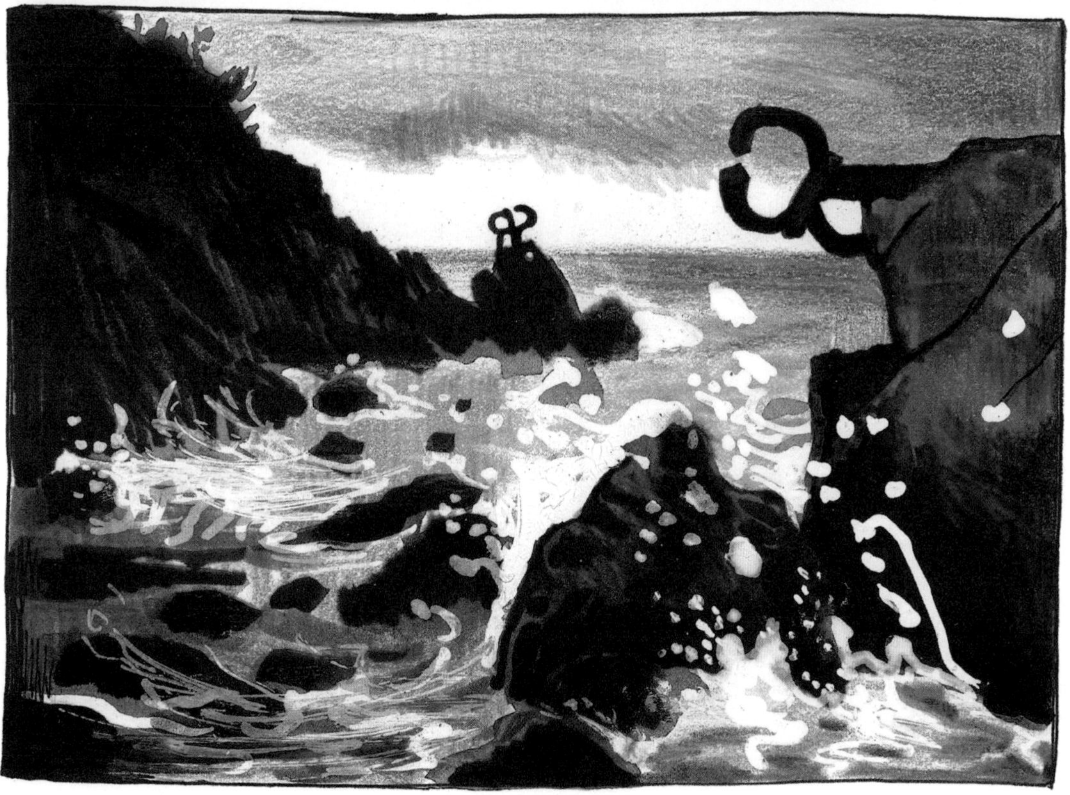

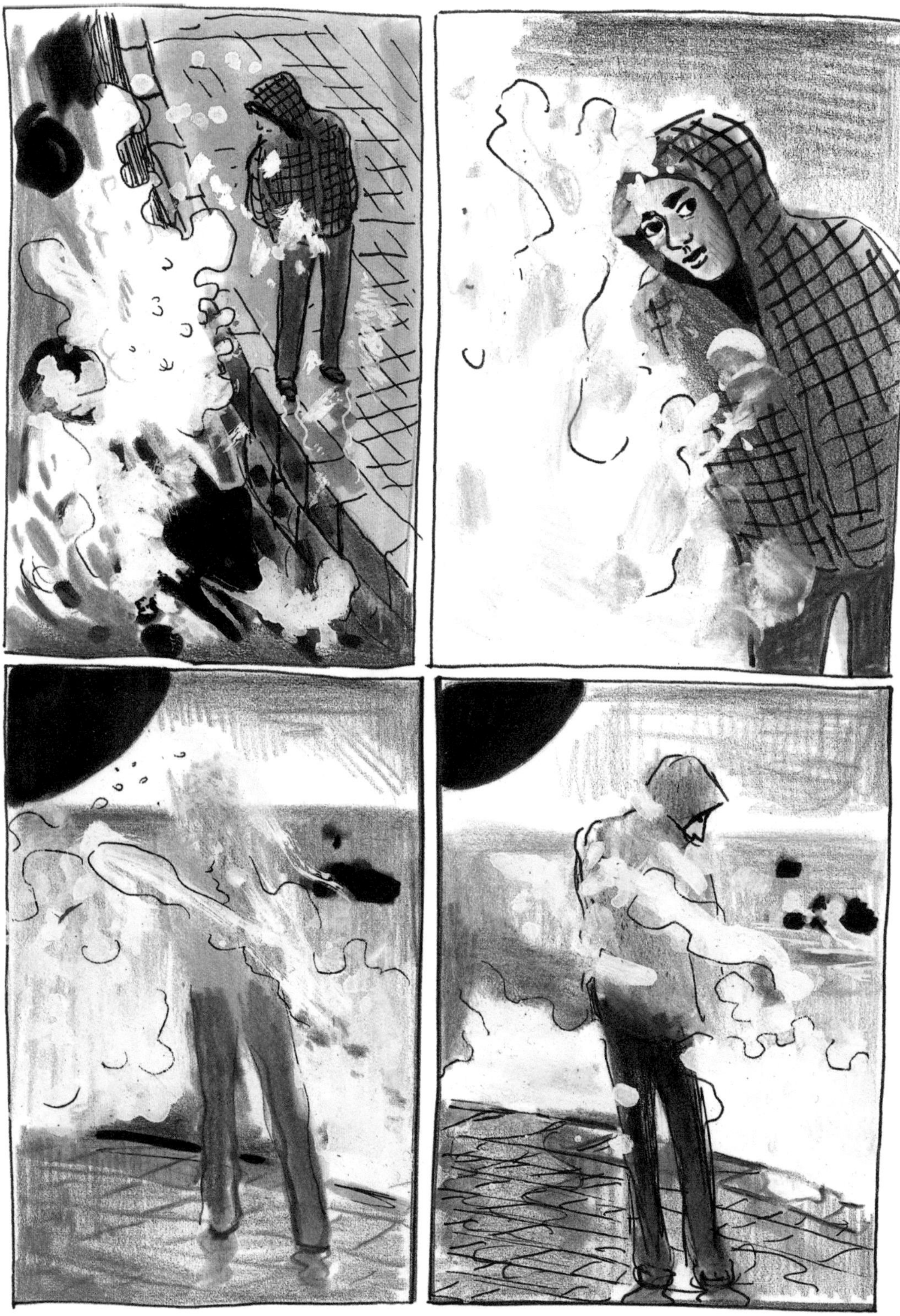

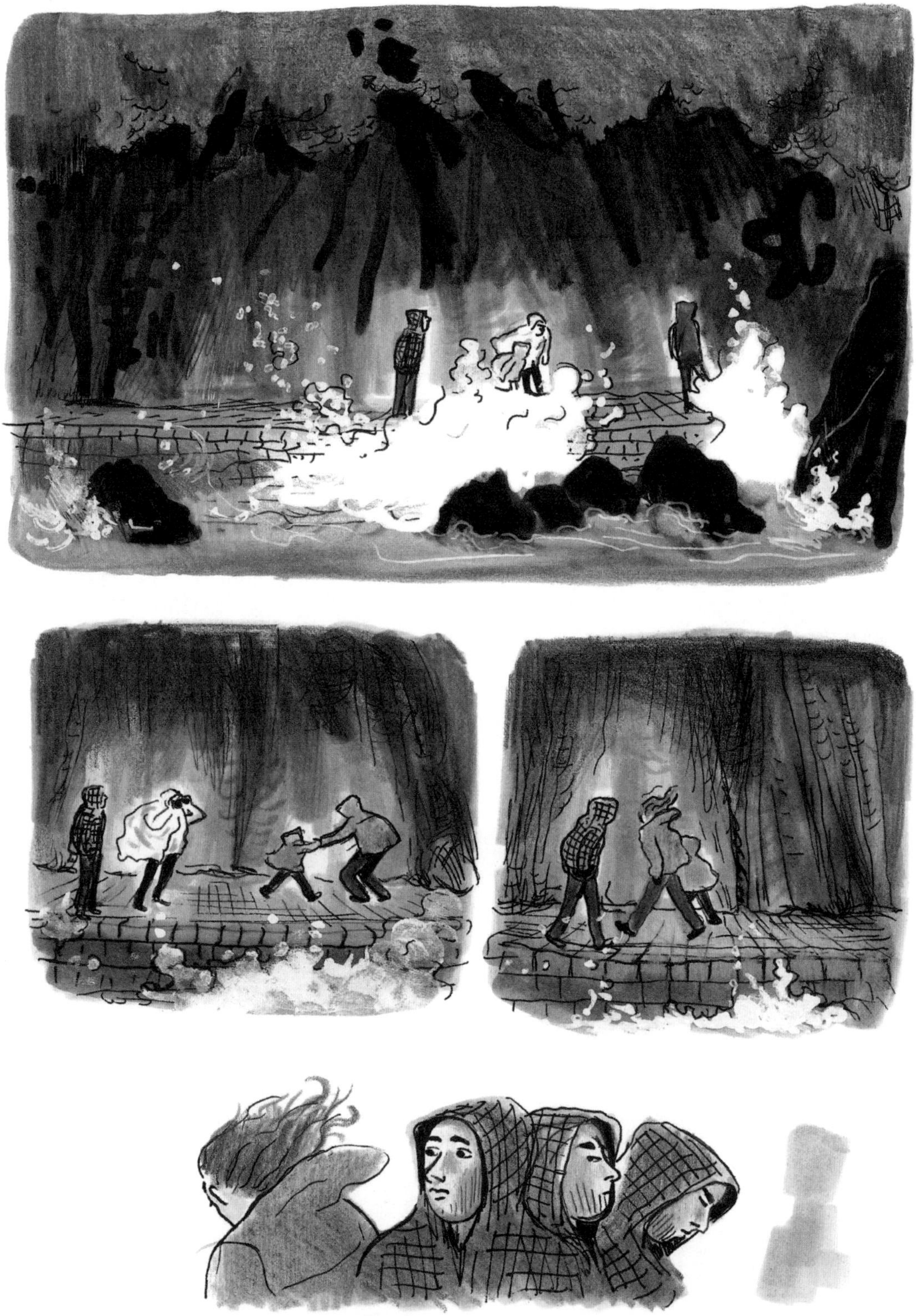

Holiday. Day 3: look for inspiration.

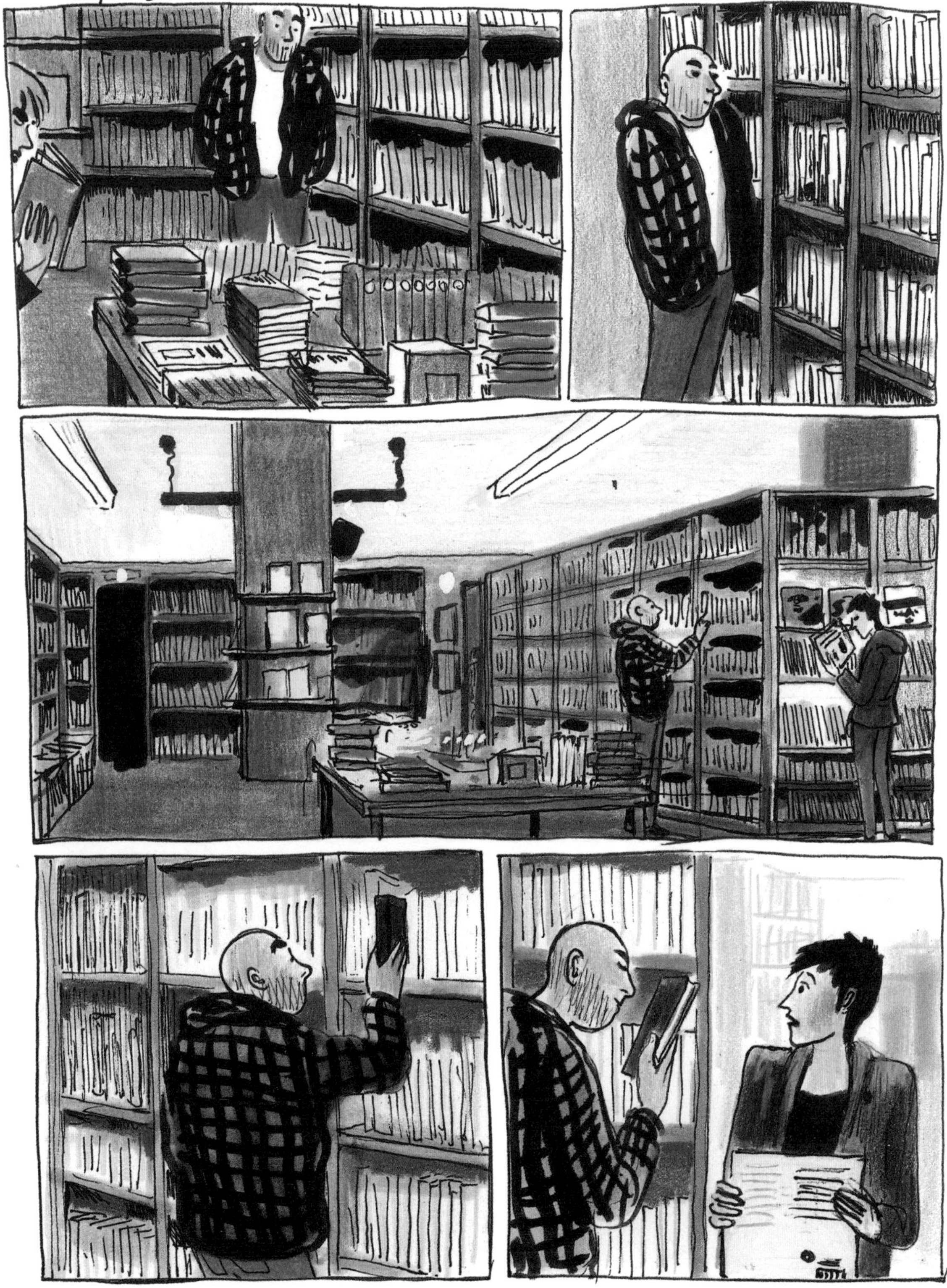

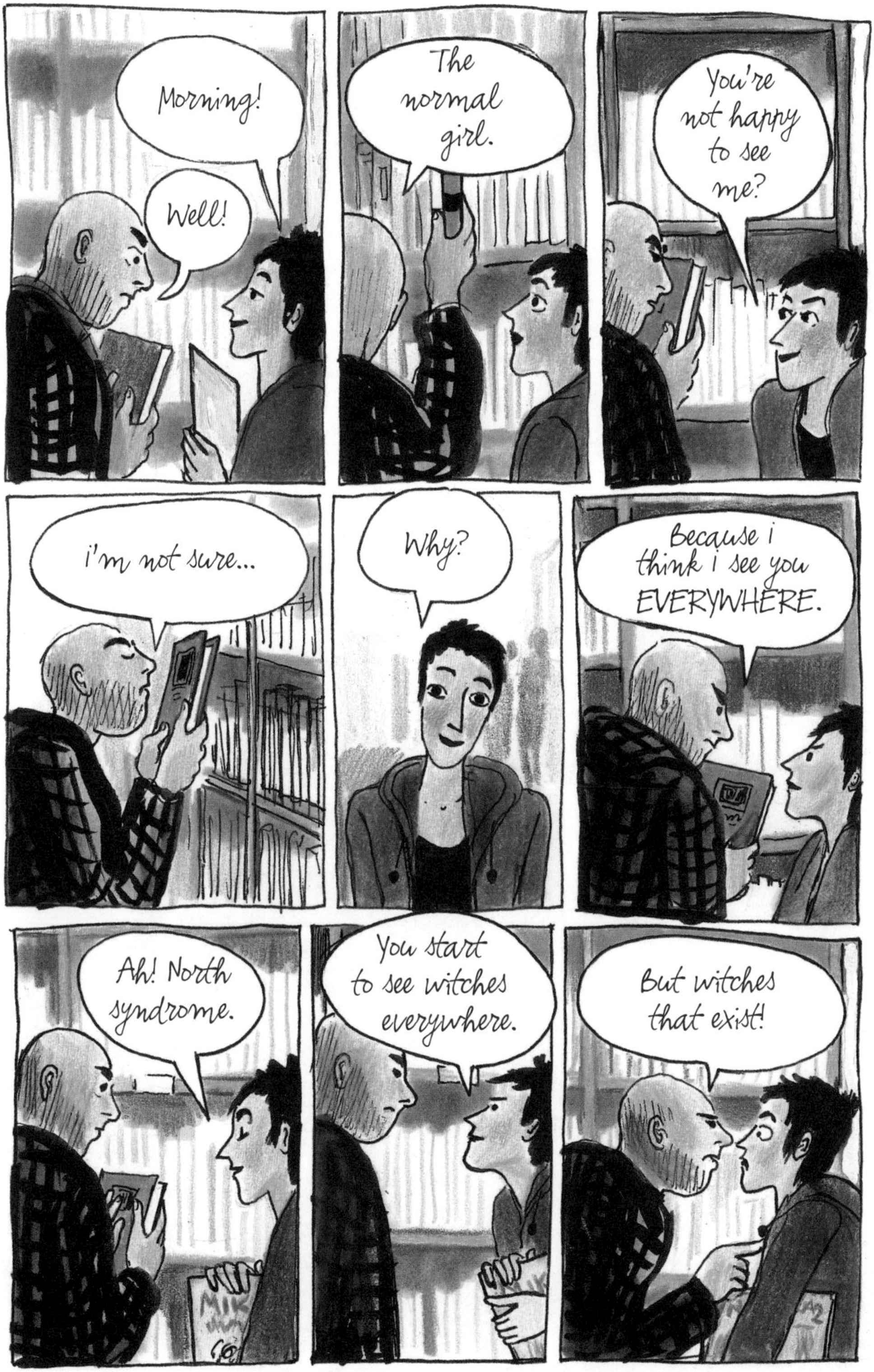
Morning!
Well!
The normal girl.
You're not happy to see me?
i'm not sure...
Why?
Because i think i see you EVERYWHERE.
Ah! North syndrome.
You start to see witches everywhere.
But witches that exist!

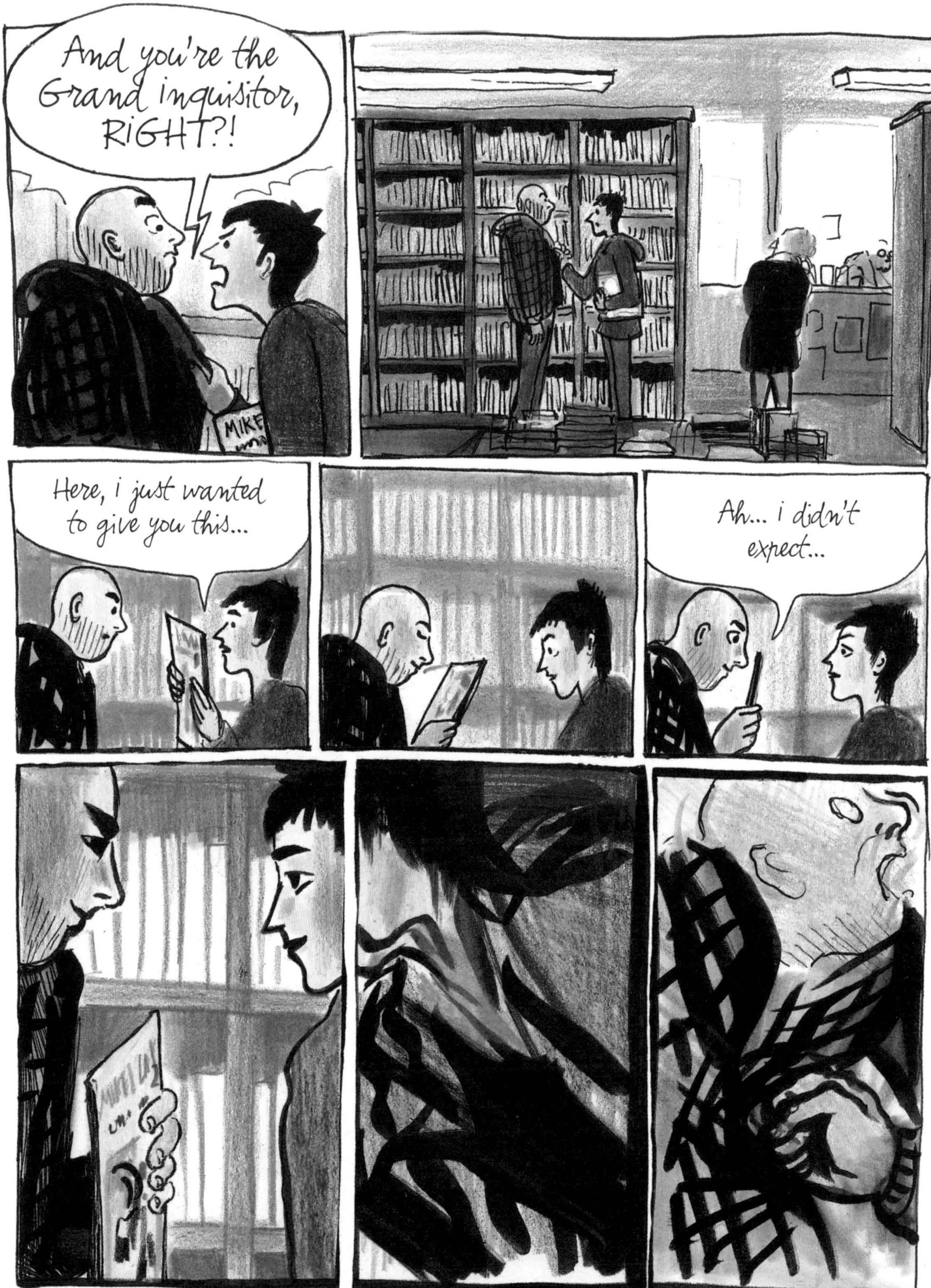
And you're the Grand inquisitor, RIGHT?!
MIKE
Here, i just wanted to give you this...
Ah... i didn't expect...

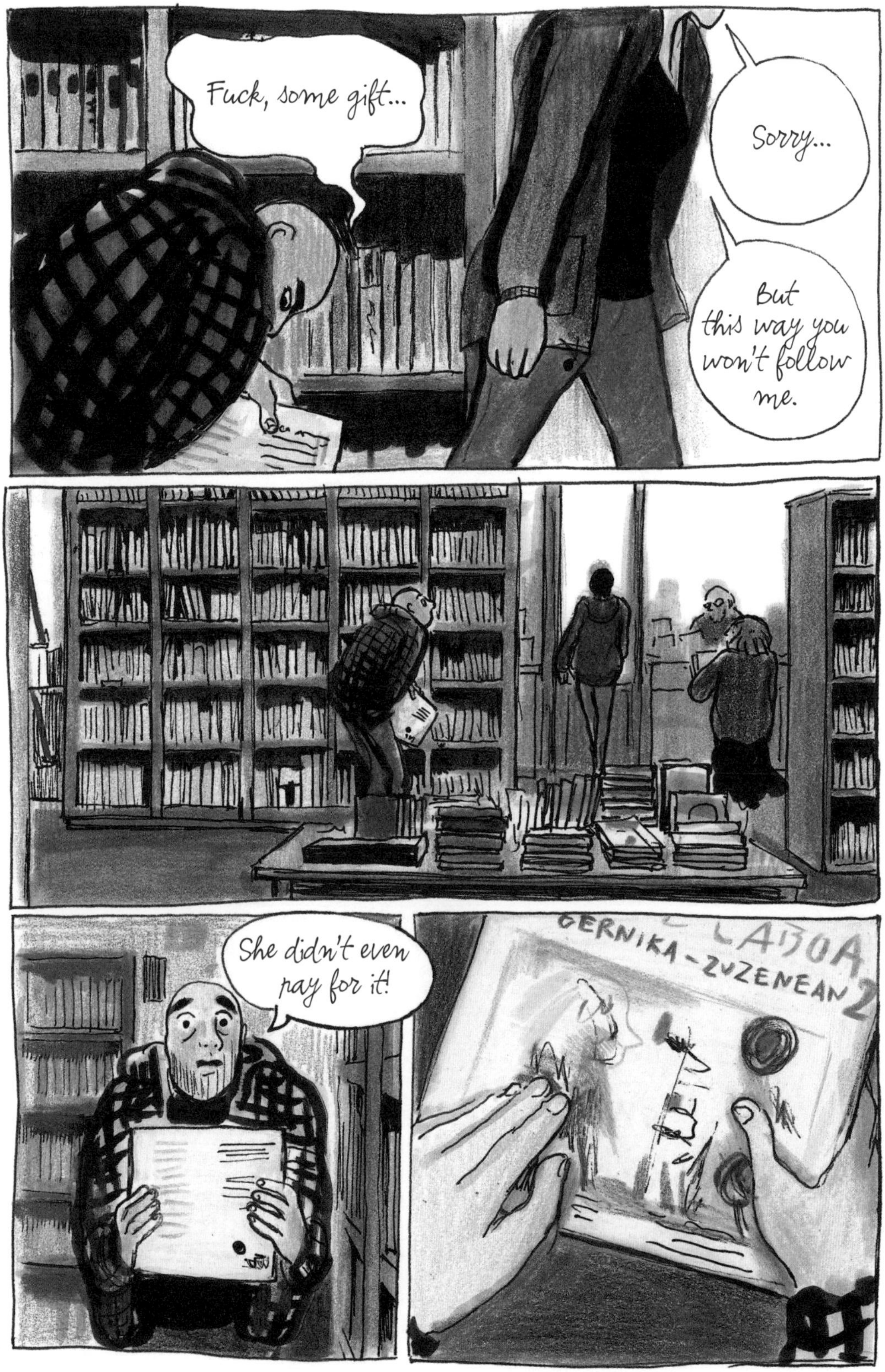
Fuck, some gift...
Sorry...
But this way you won't follow me.
She didn't even pay for it!
LABOA
GERNIKA-ZUZENEAN 2

Holiday. Day 4: shopping.

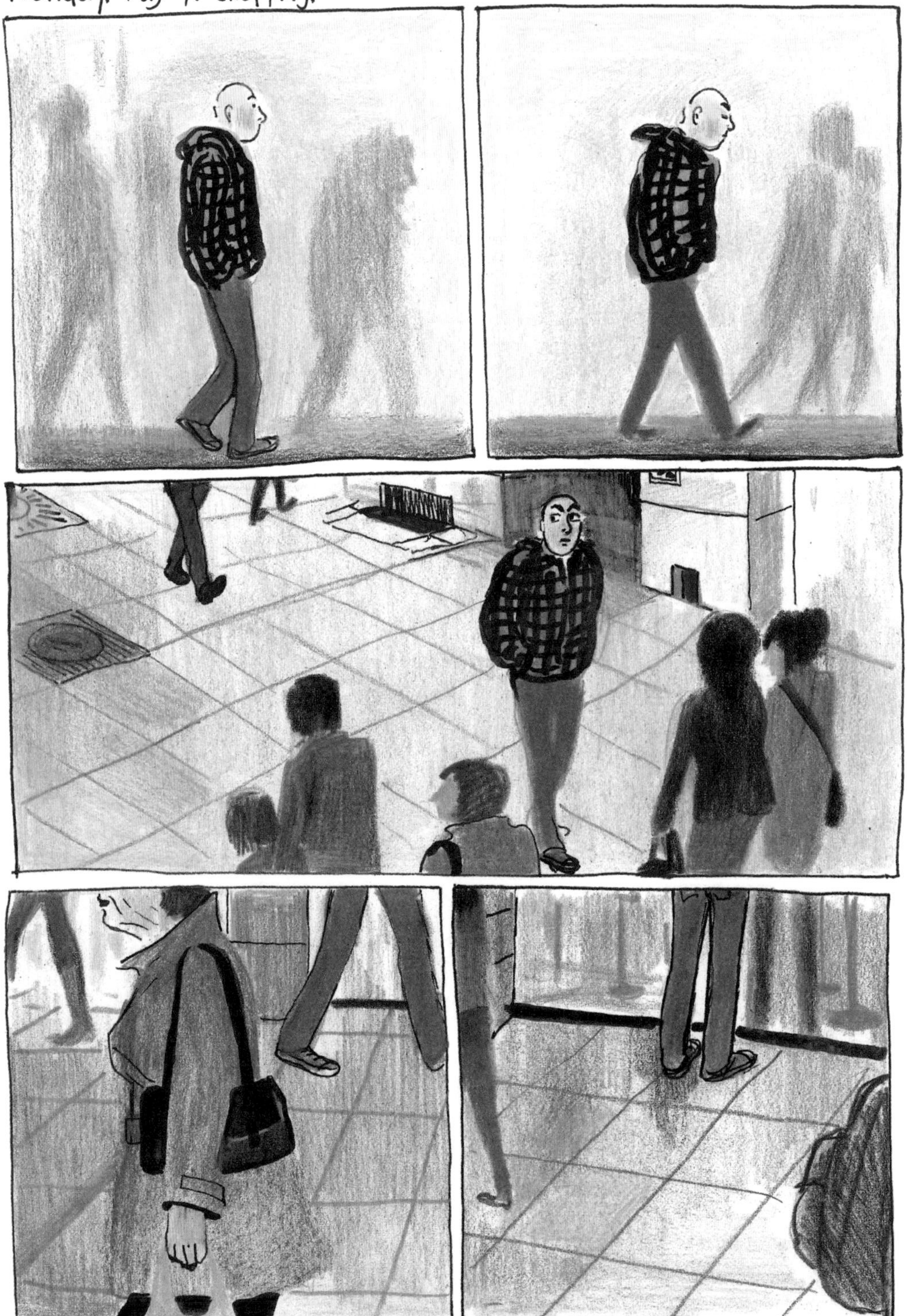

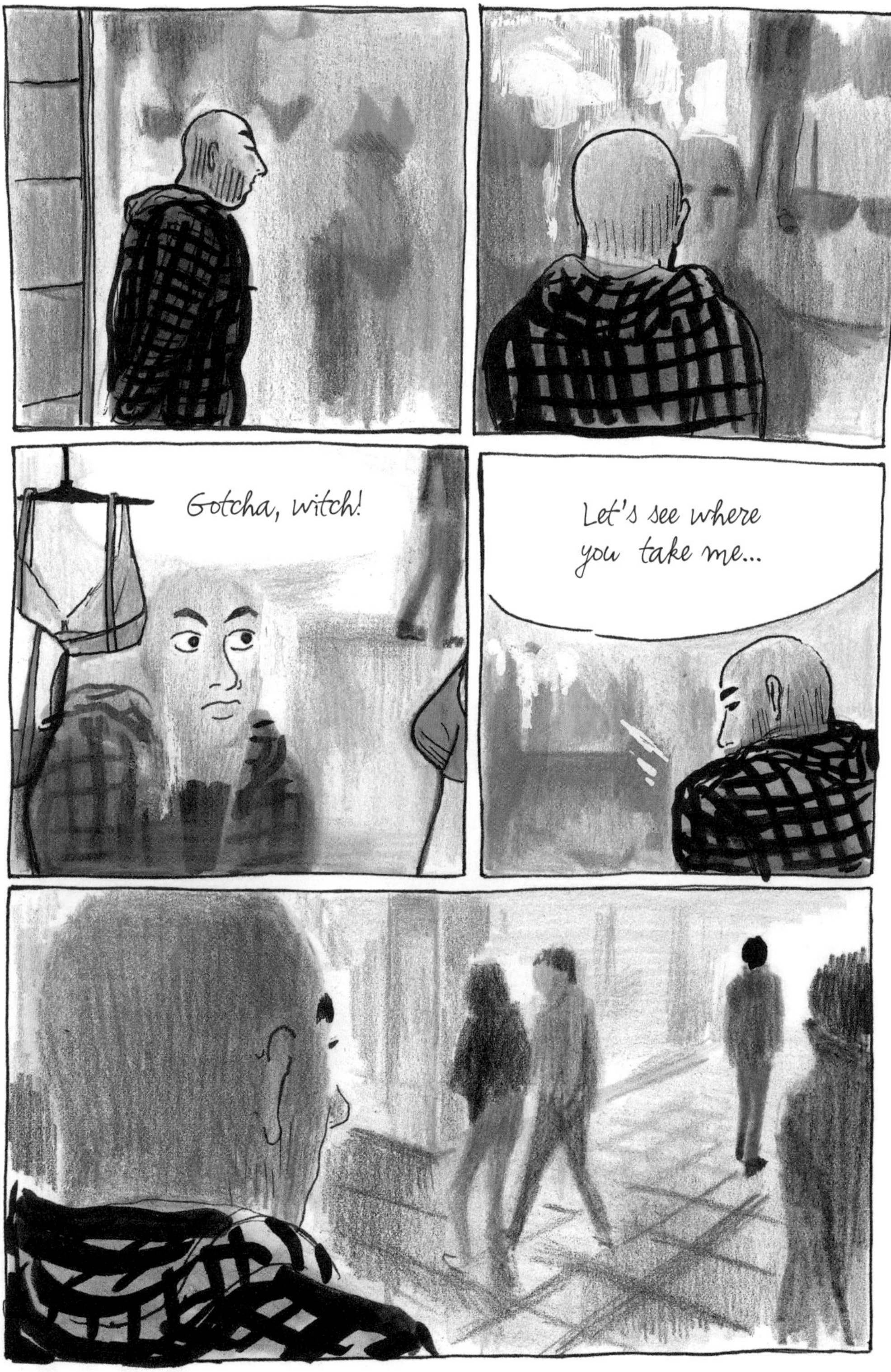
Gotcha, witch!
Let's see where you take me...

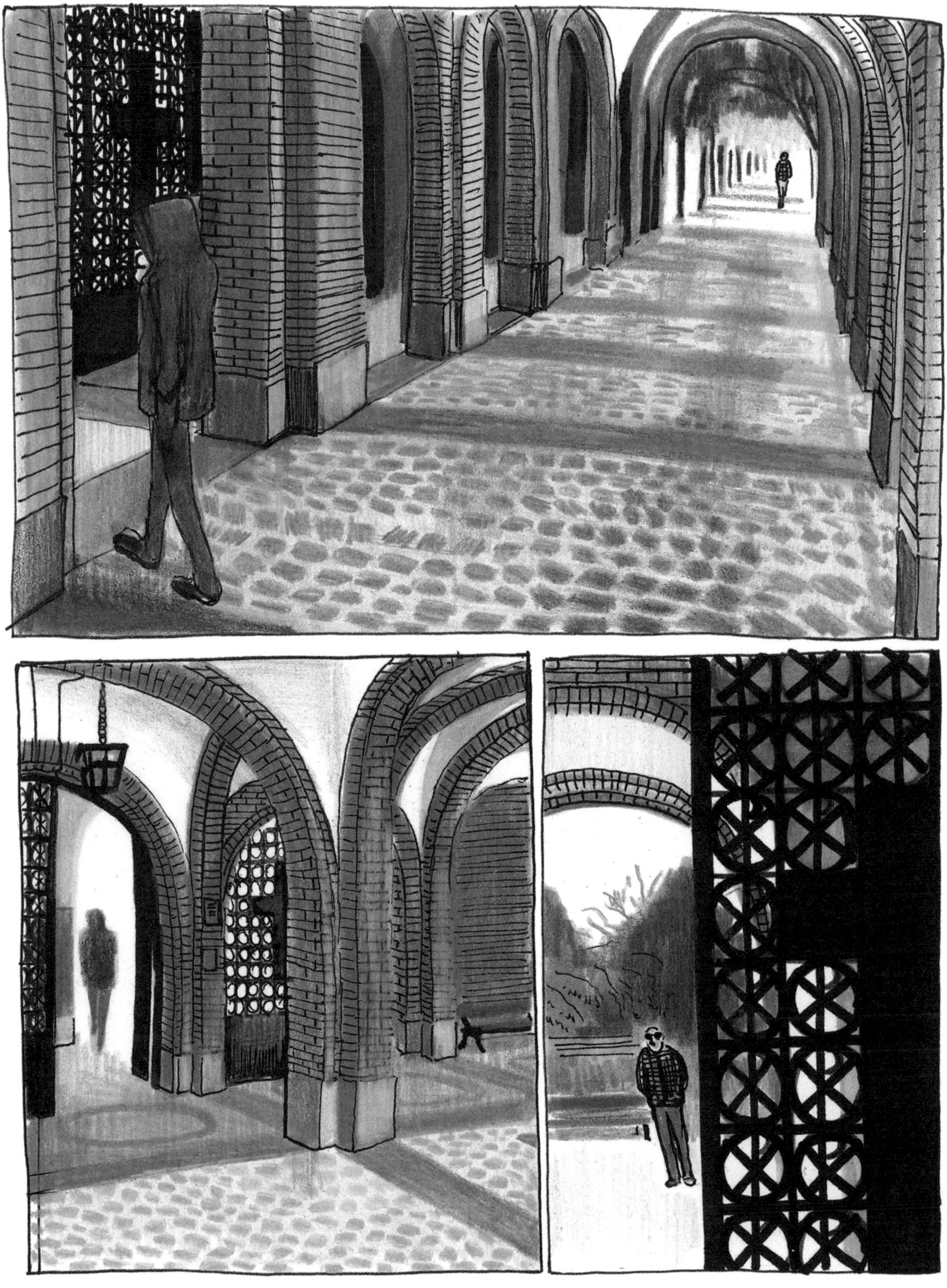

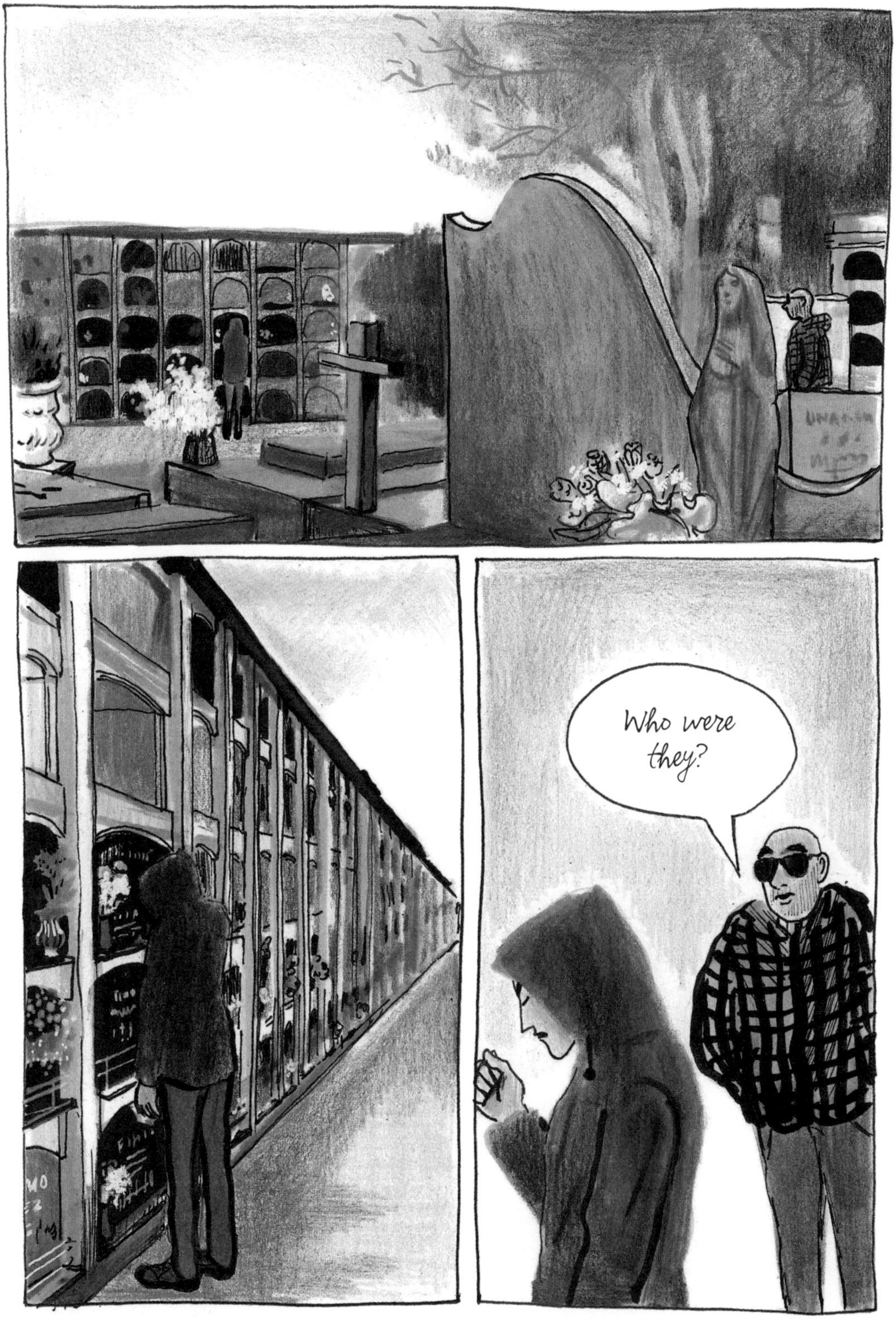
Who were they?

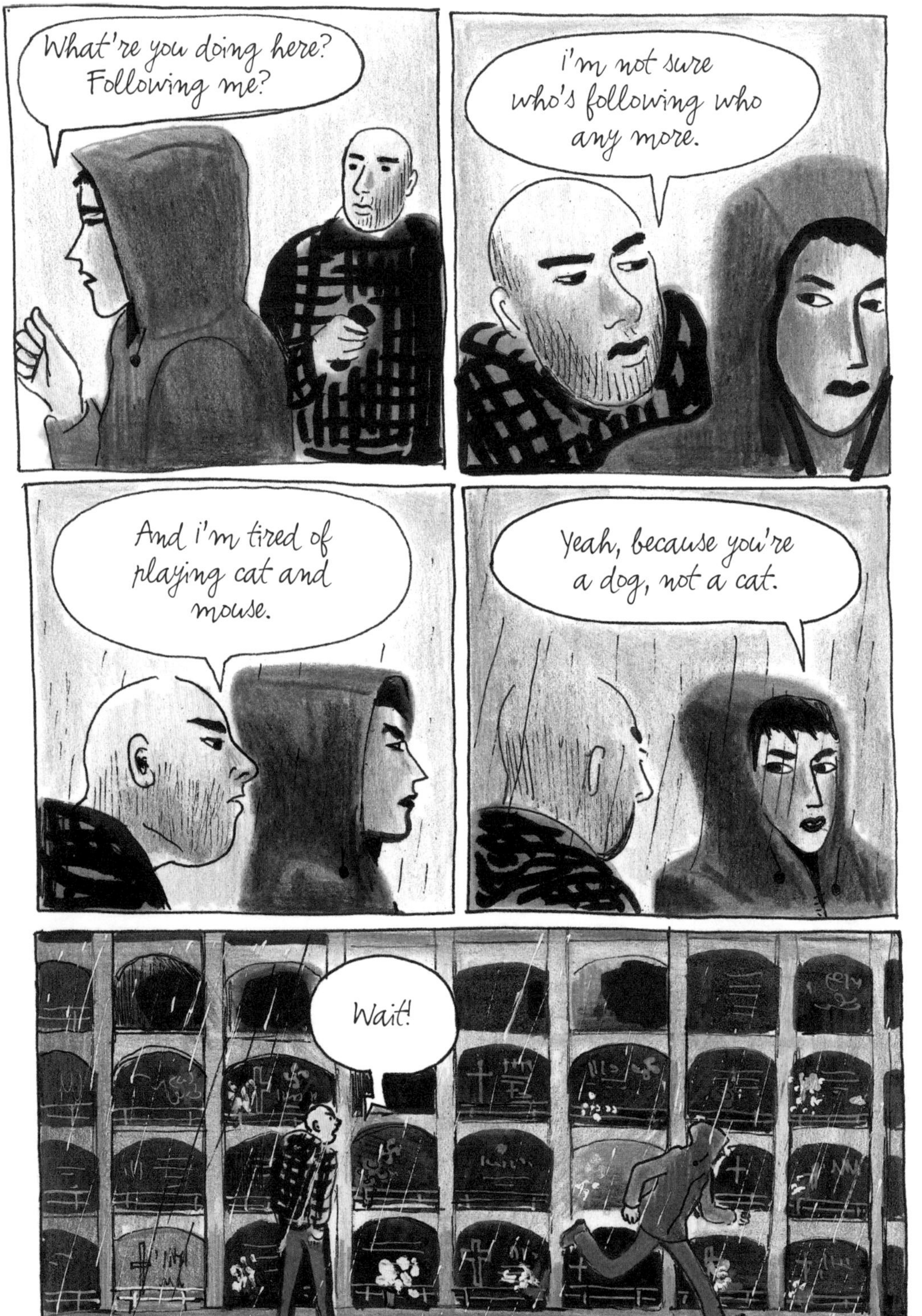
What're you doing here? Following me?
i'm not sure who's following who any more.
And i'm tired of playing cat and mouse.
Yeah, because you're a dog, not a cat.
Wait!

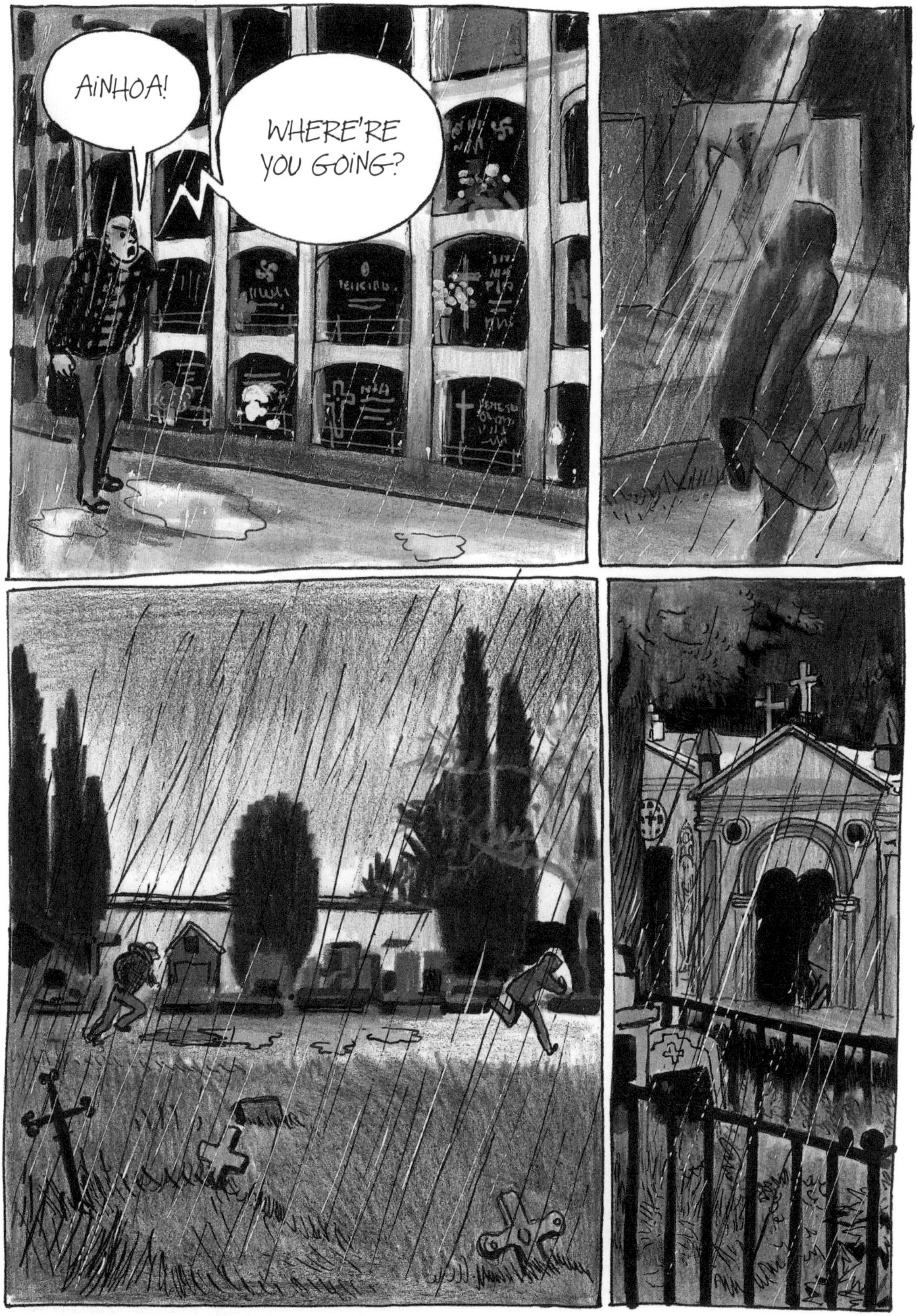
AINHOA!
WHERE'RE YOU GOING?

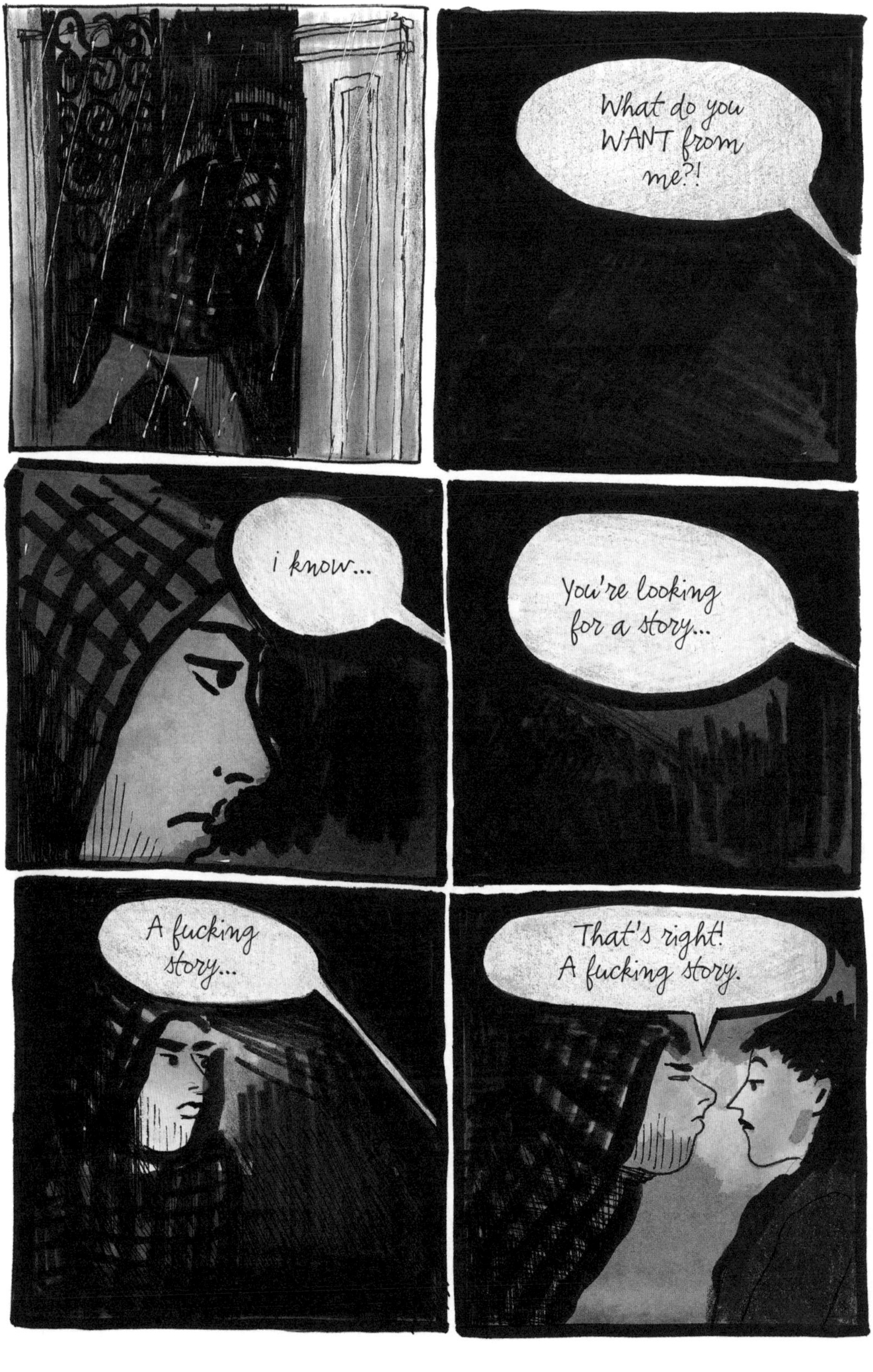
What do you WANT from me?!
i know...
You're looking for a story...
A fucking story...
That's right! A fucking story.

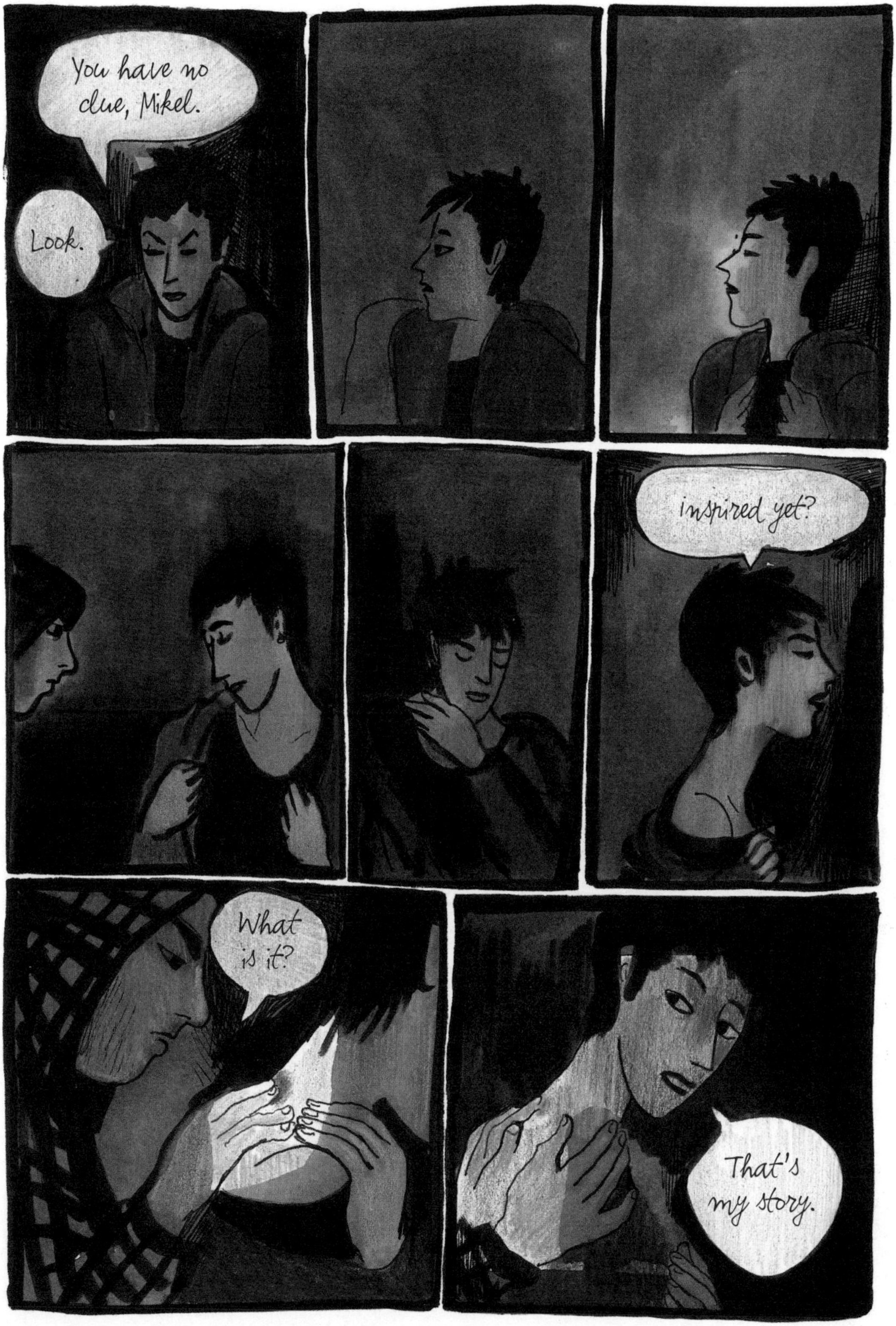

You have no clue, Mikel.
Look.
inspired yet?
What is it?
That's my story.

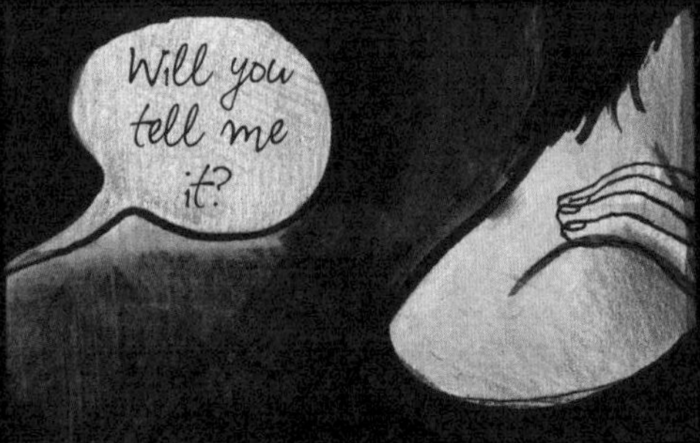
Will you tell me it?

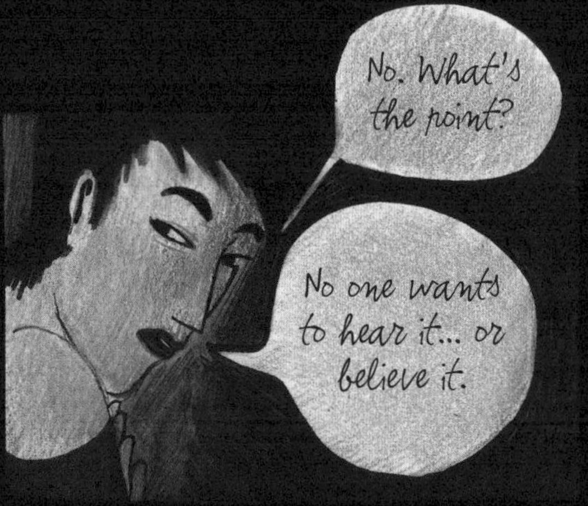
No. What's the point?
No one wants to hear it... or believe it.

Holiday. Day 5: looking for Ainhoa's story.

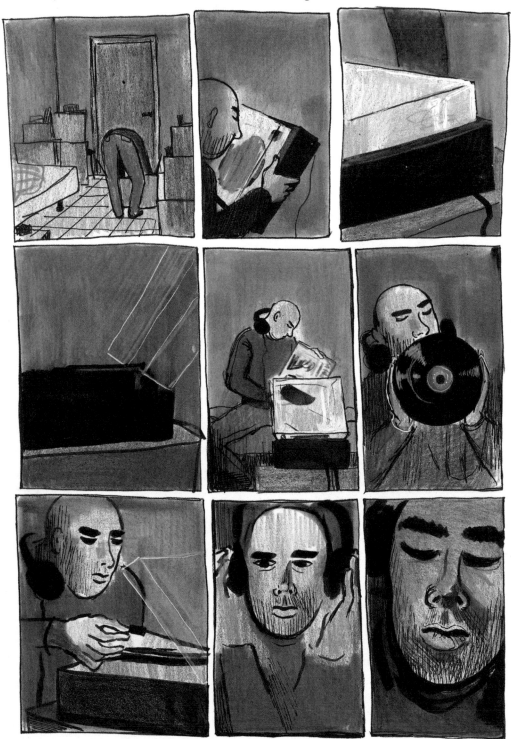

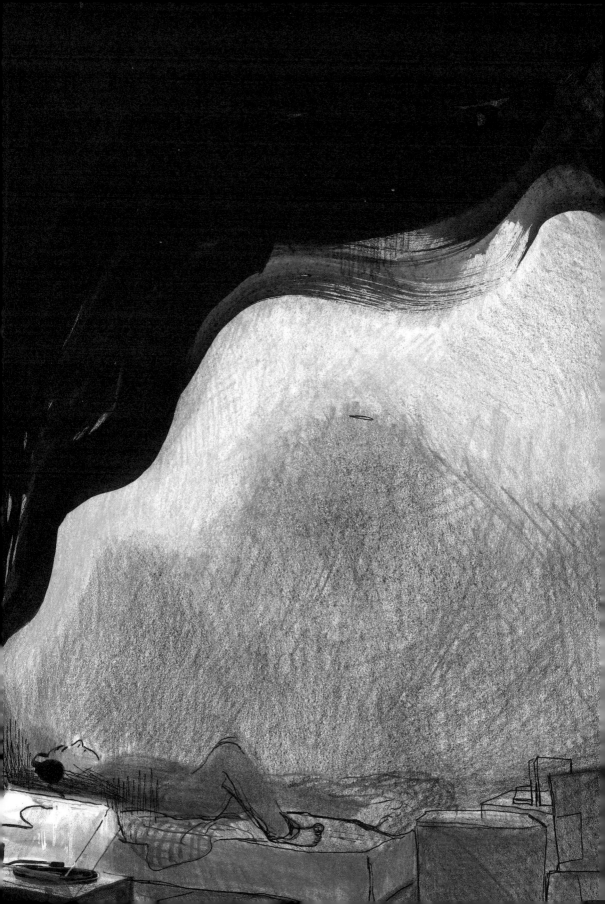

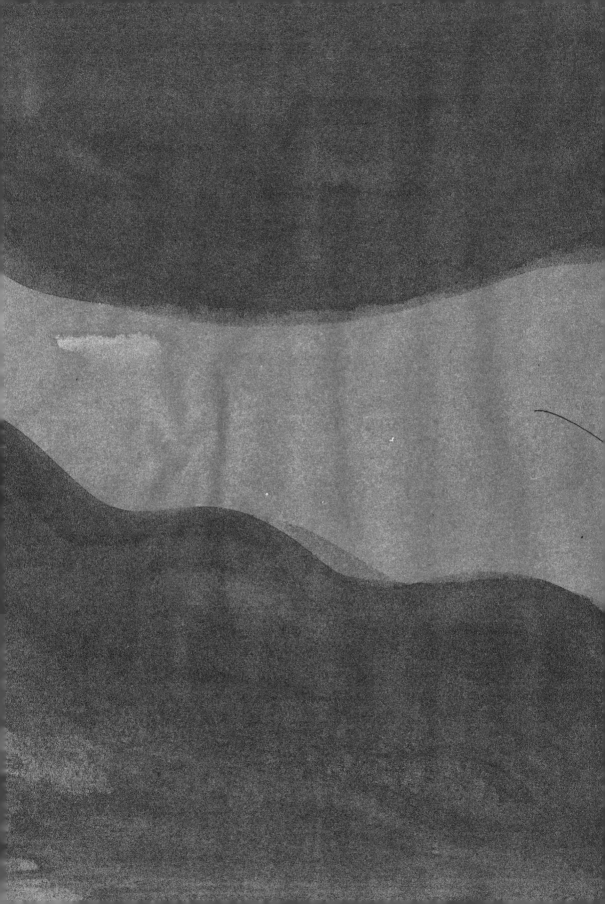

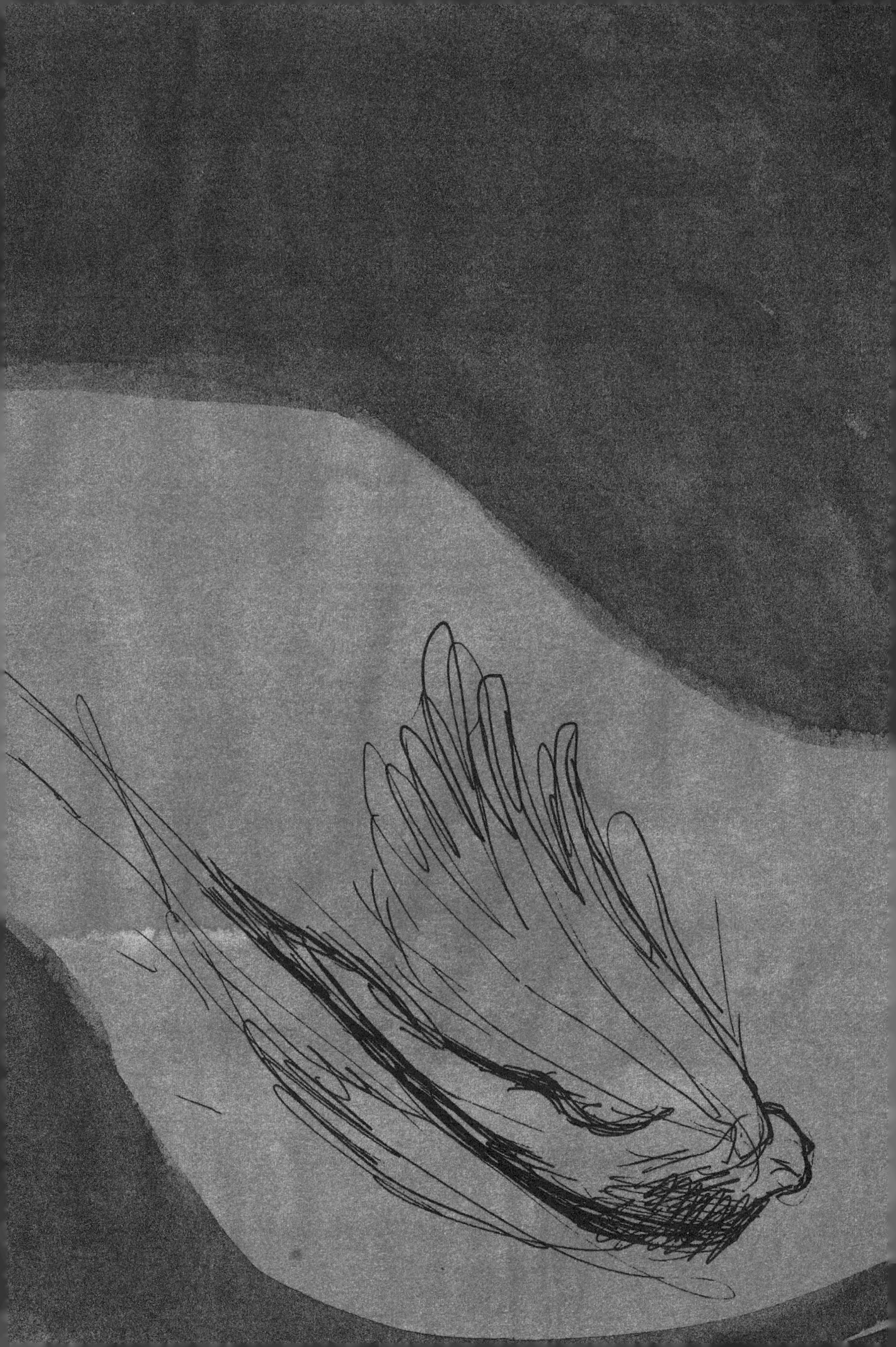

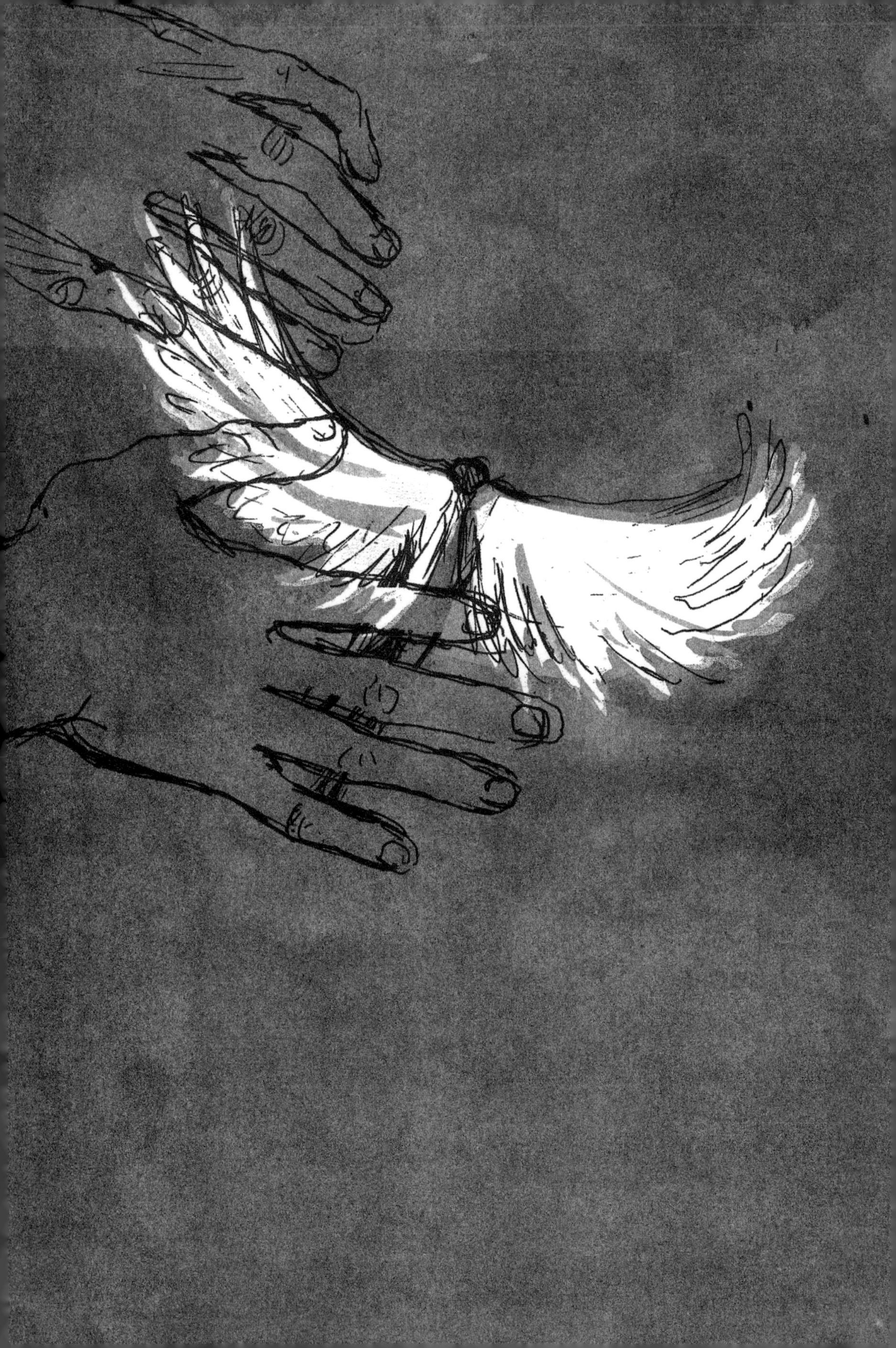

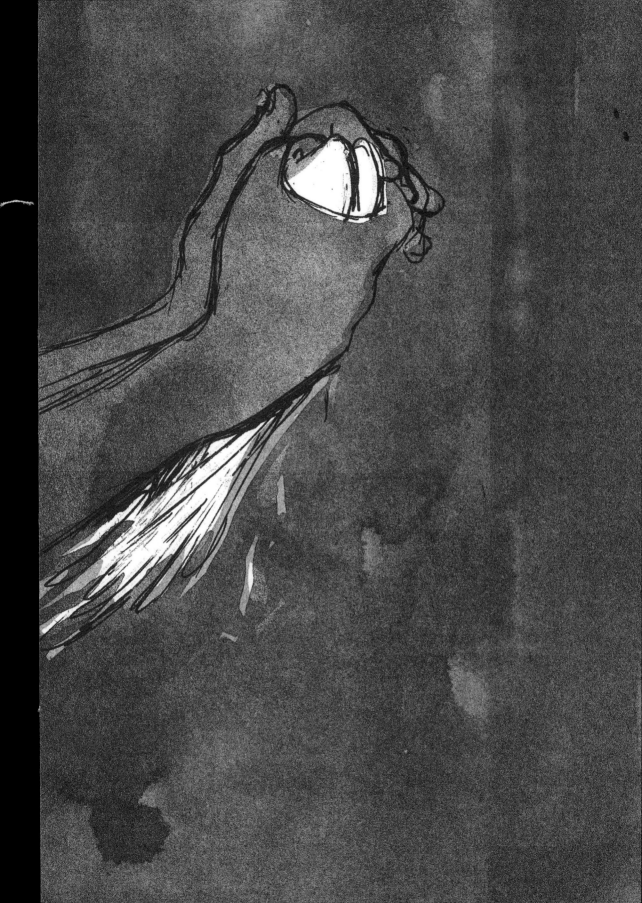

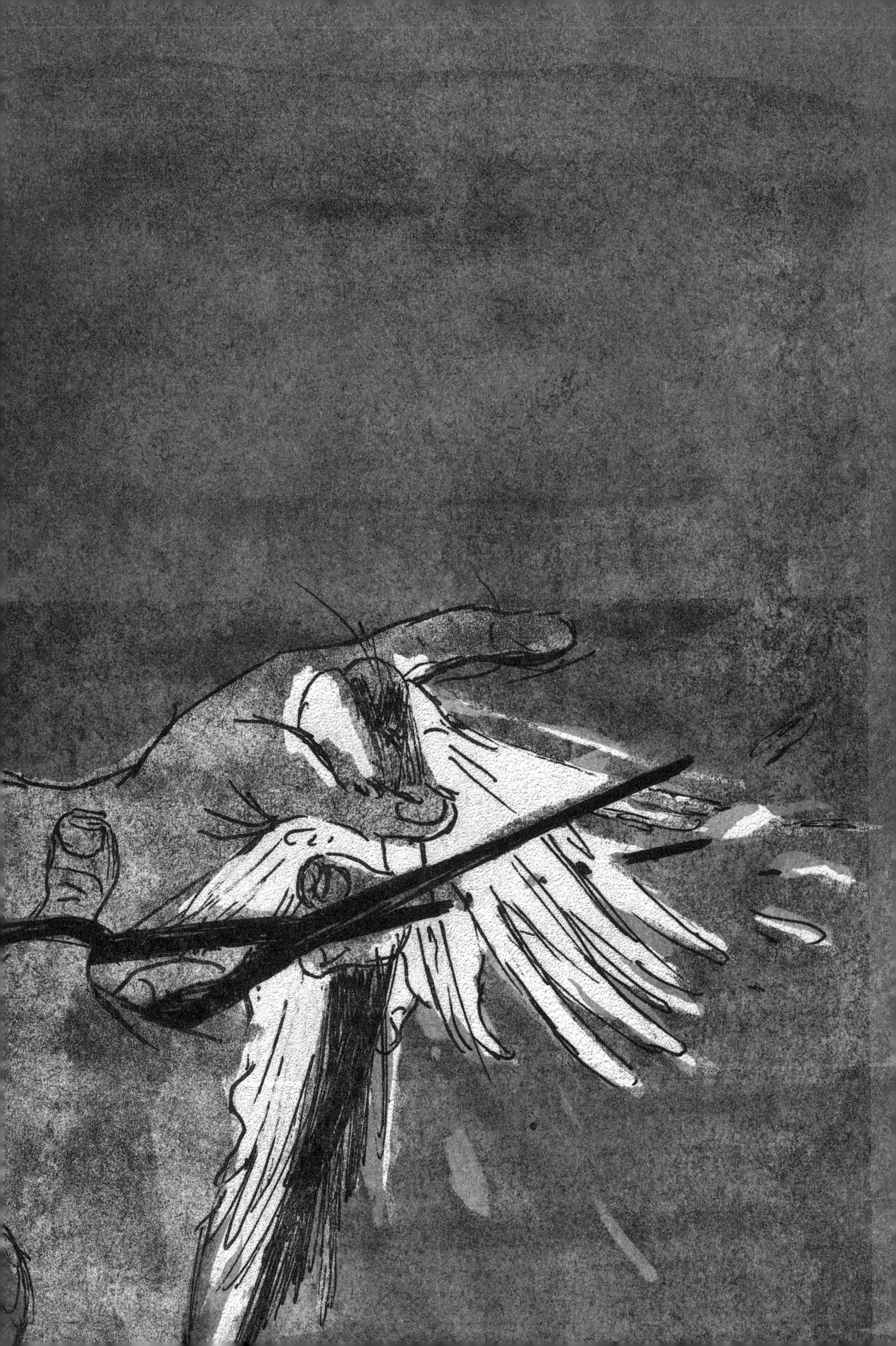

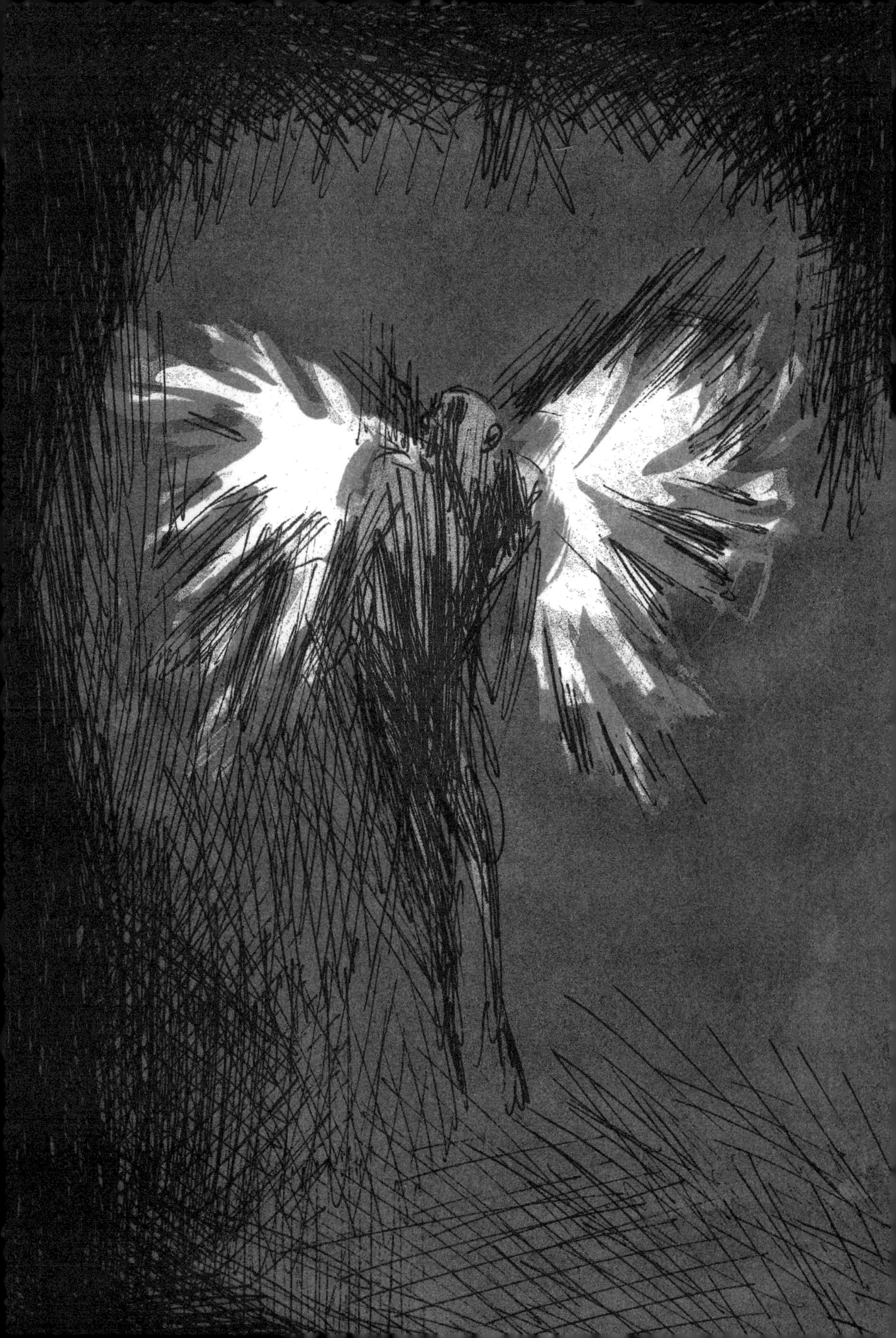

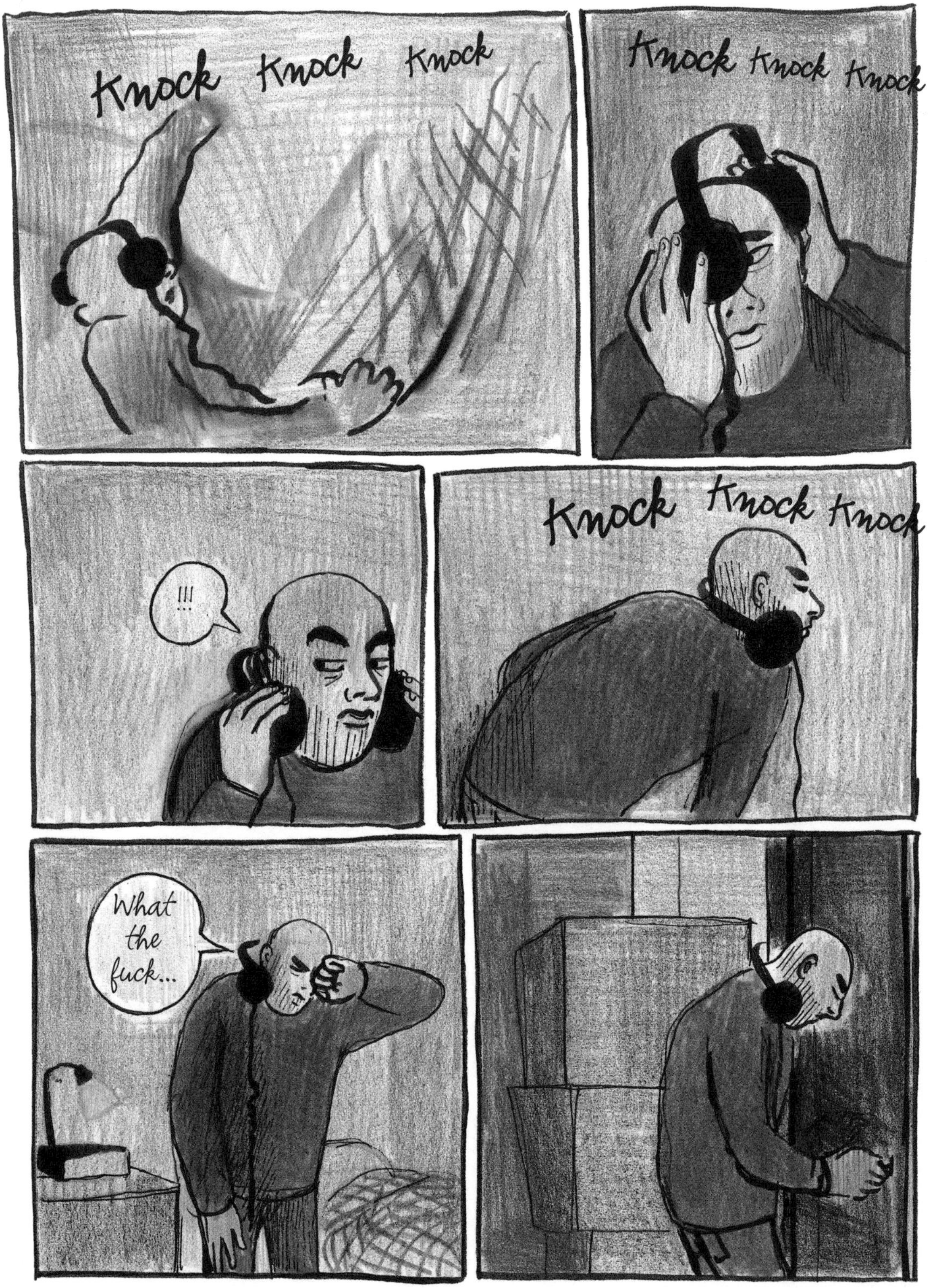
Knock Knock Knock
Knock Knock Knock
!!!
Knock Knock Knock
What the fuck...

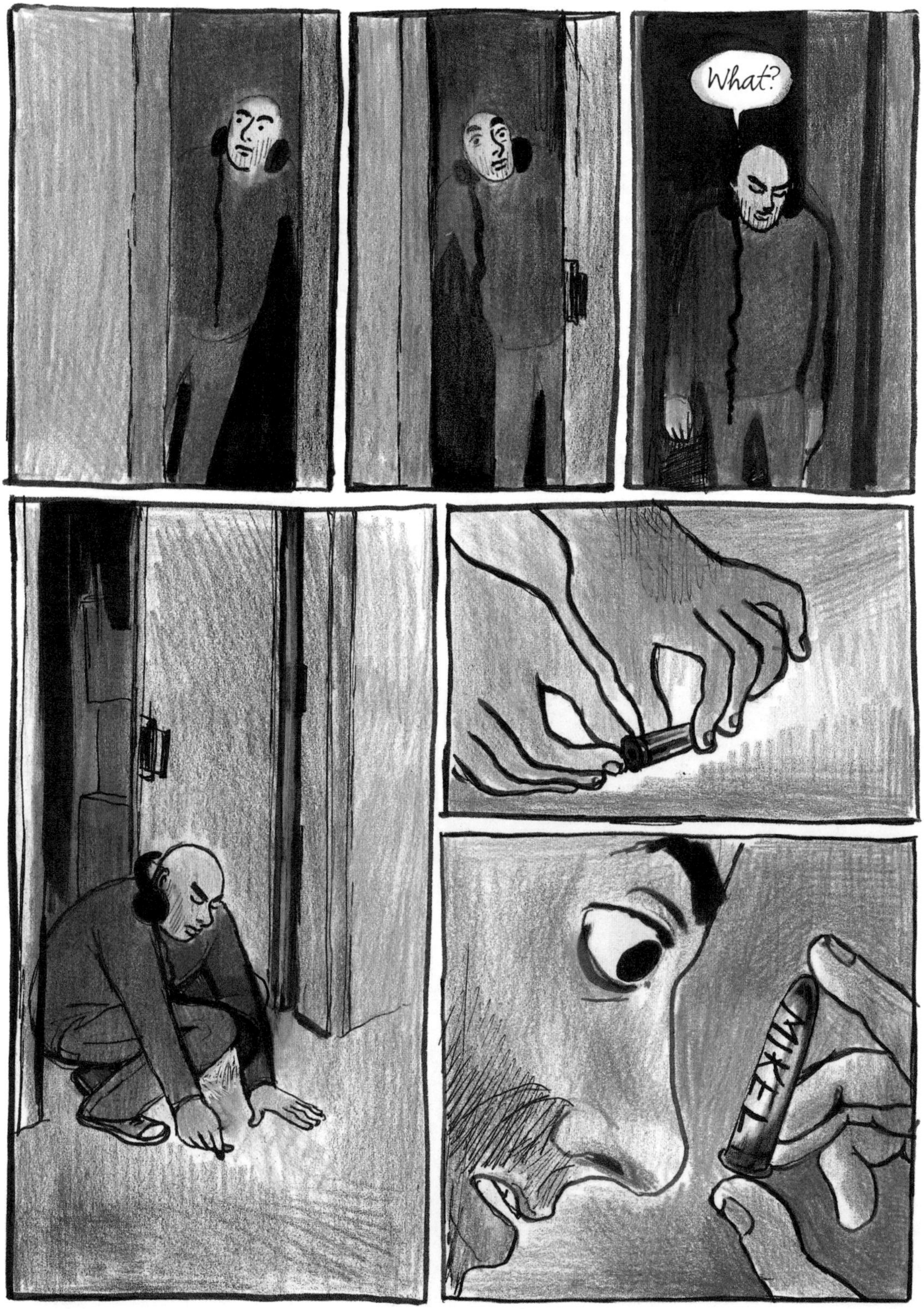
What?
MIKEL

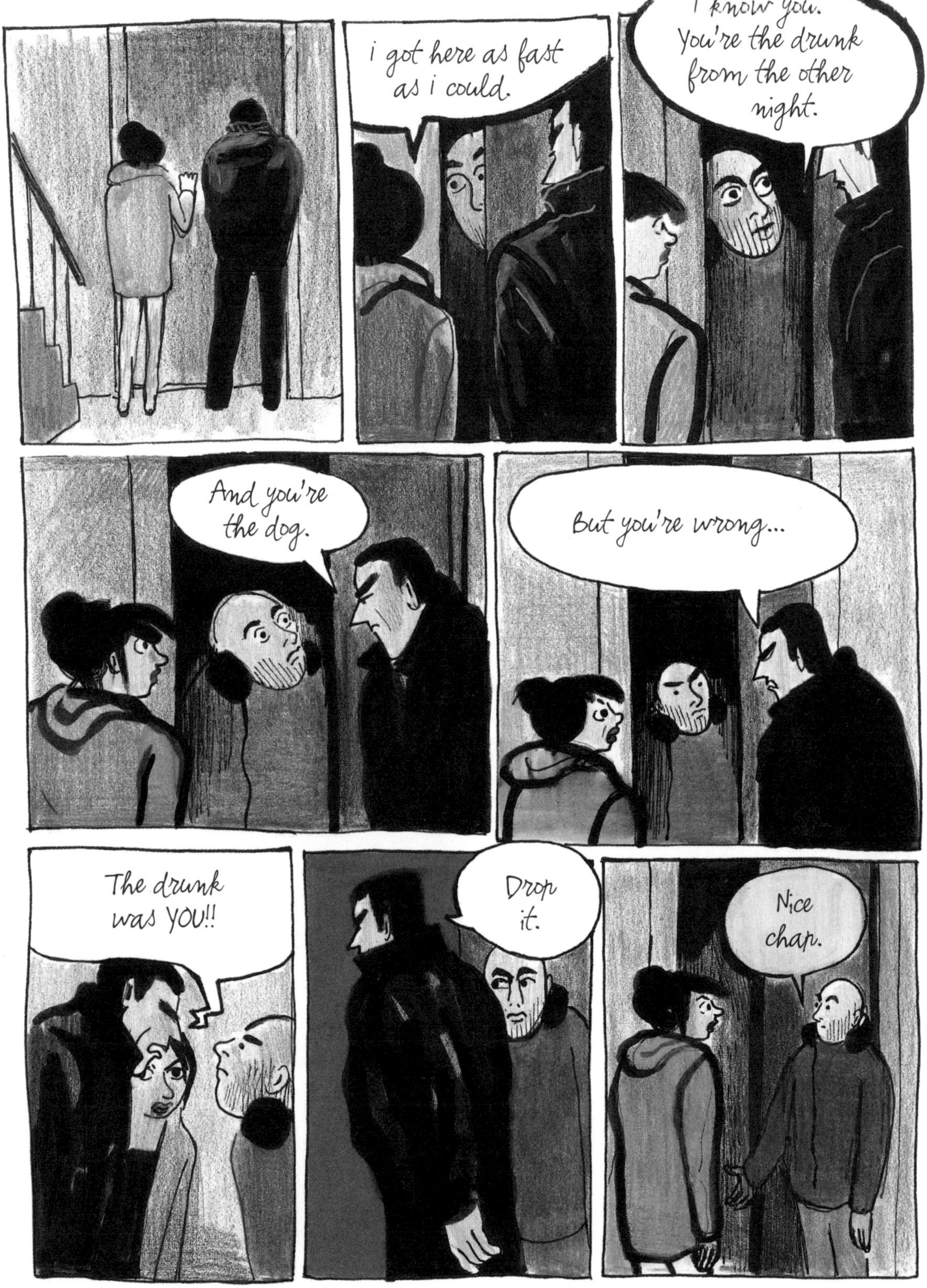
i got here as fast as i could.
i know you. You're the drunk from the other night.
And you're the dog.
But you're wrong...
The drunk was YOU!!
Drop it.
Nice chap.

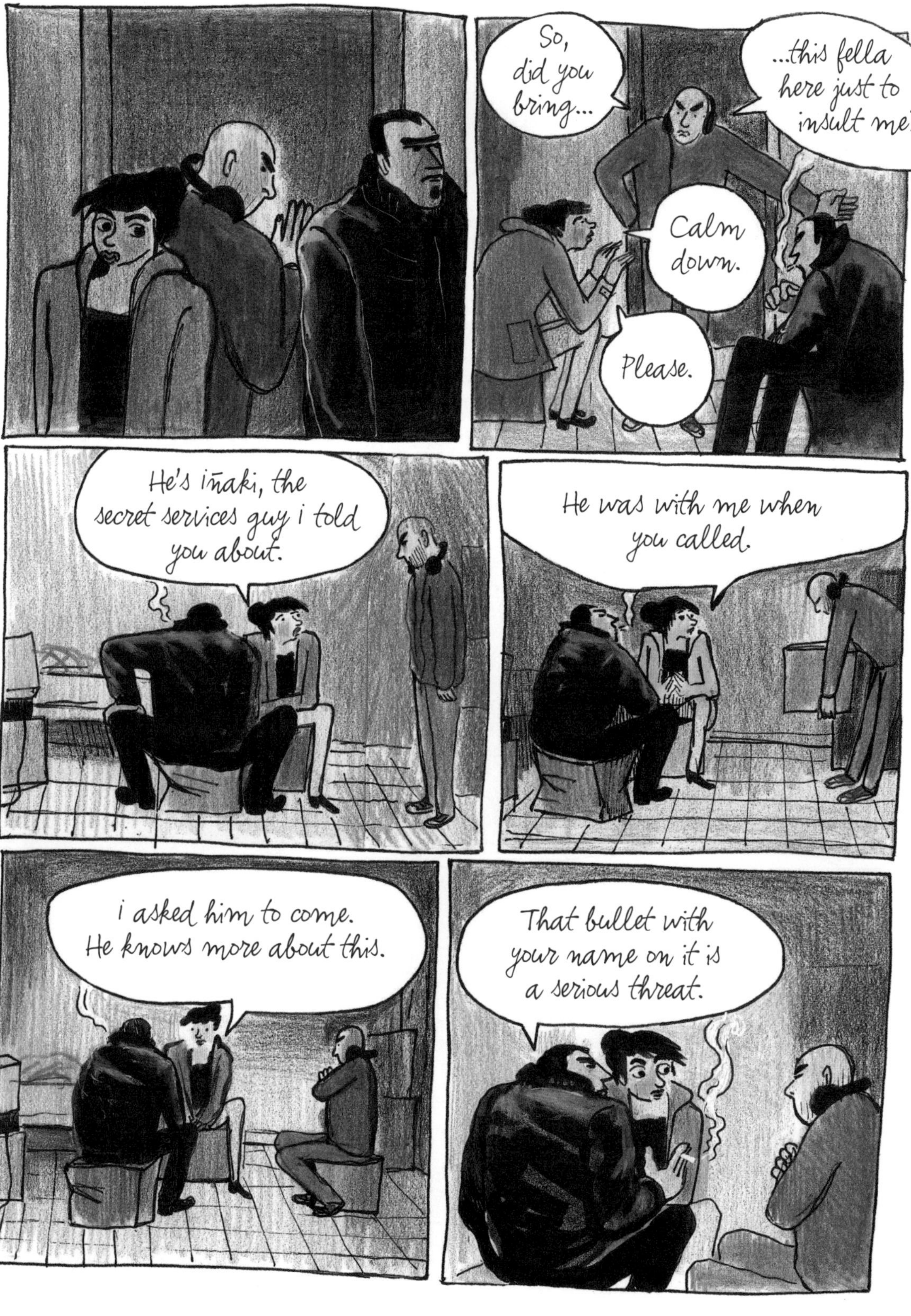
So, did you bring...
...this fella here just to insult me?
Calm down.
Please.
He's iñaki, the secret services guy i told you about.
He was with me when you called.
i asked him to come. He knows more about this.
That bullet with your name on it is a serious threat.

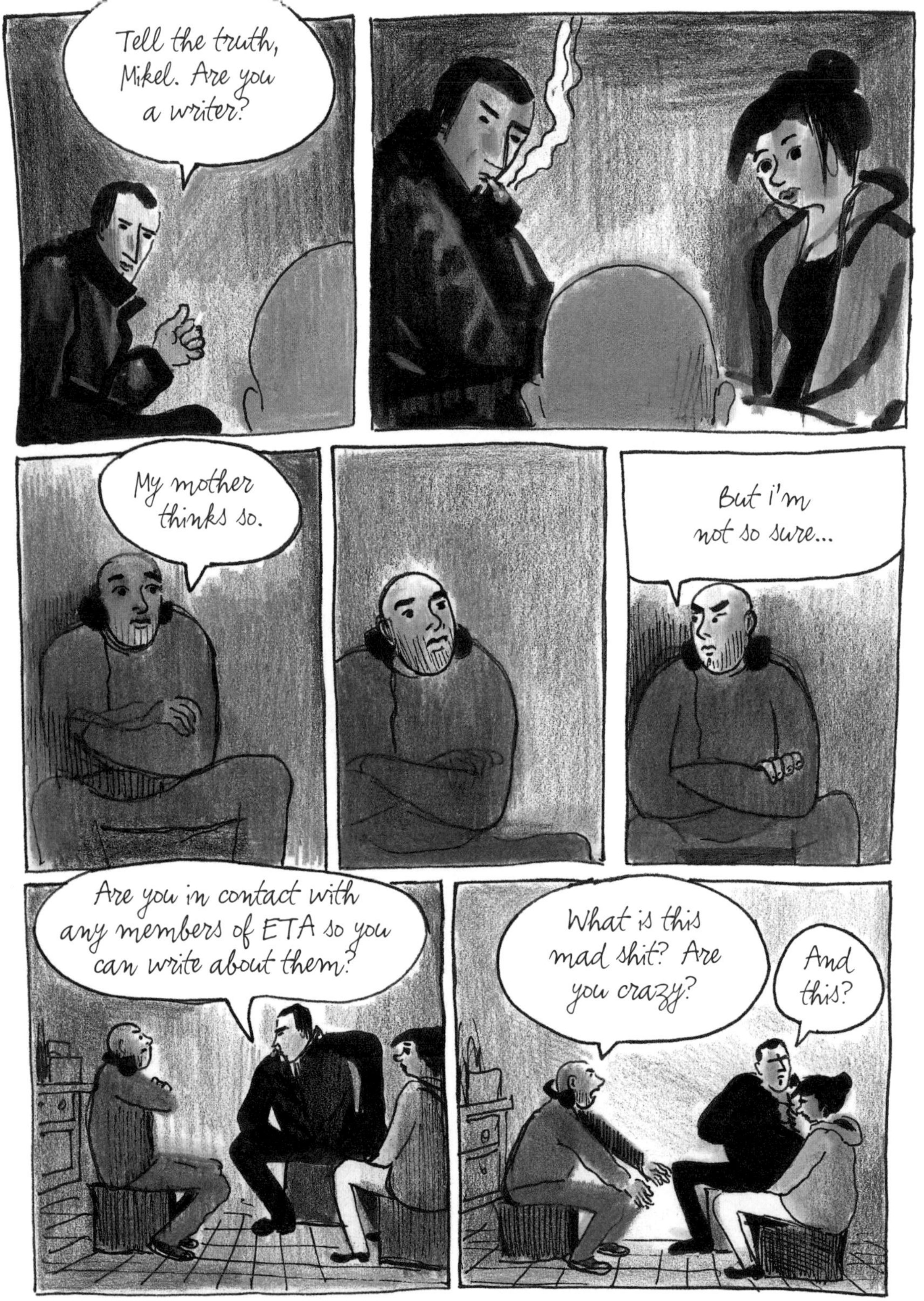

Tell the truth, Mikel. Are you a writer?
My mother thinks so.
But i'm not so sure...
Are you in contact with any members of ETA so you can write about them?
What is this mad shit? Are you crazy?
And this?

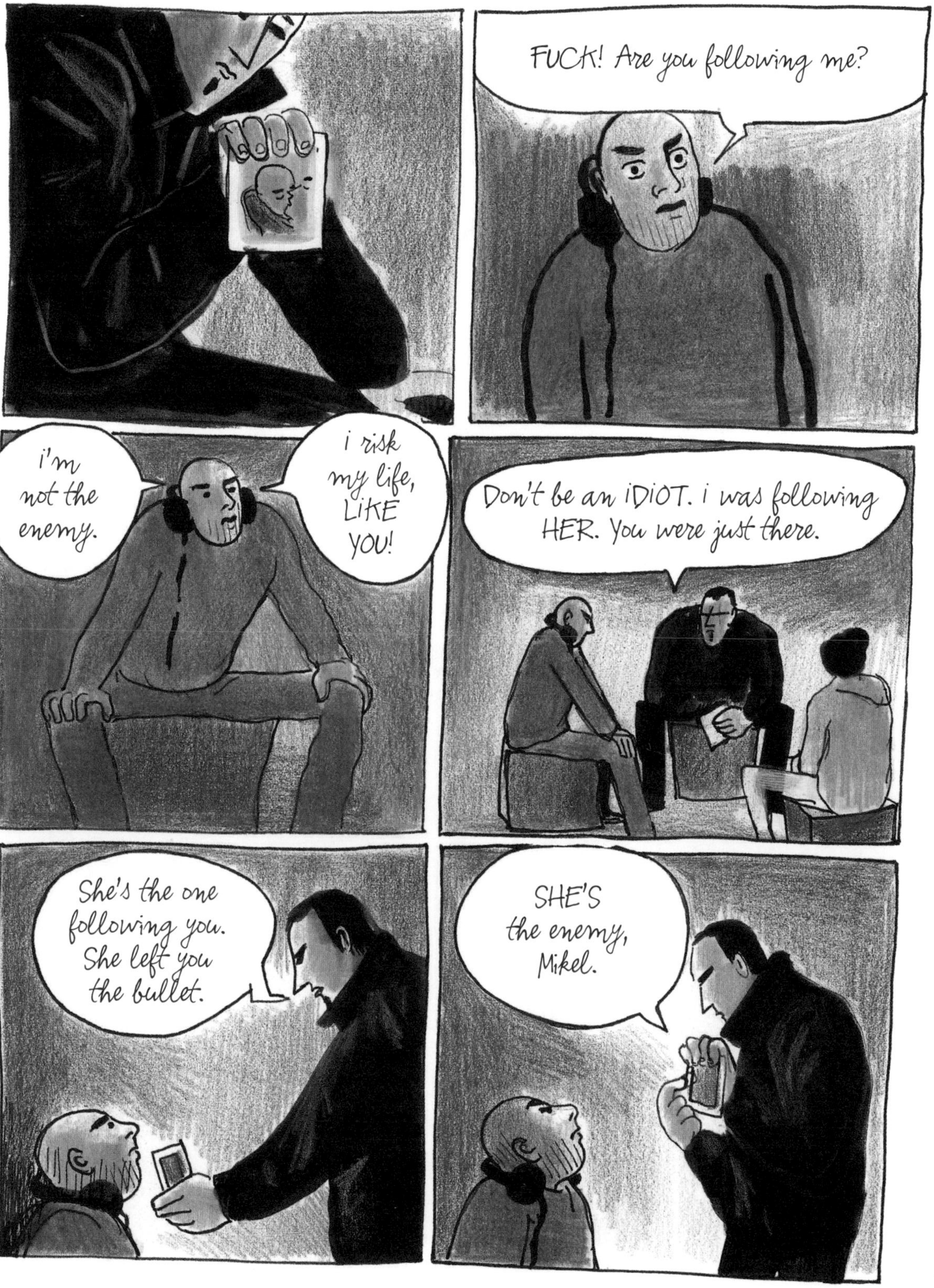
FUCK! Are you following me?
i'm not the enemy.
i risk my life, LIKE YOU!
Don't be an iDIOT. i was following HER. You were just there.
She's the one following you. She left you the bullet.
SHE'S the enemy, Mikel.

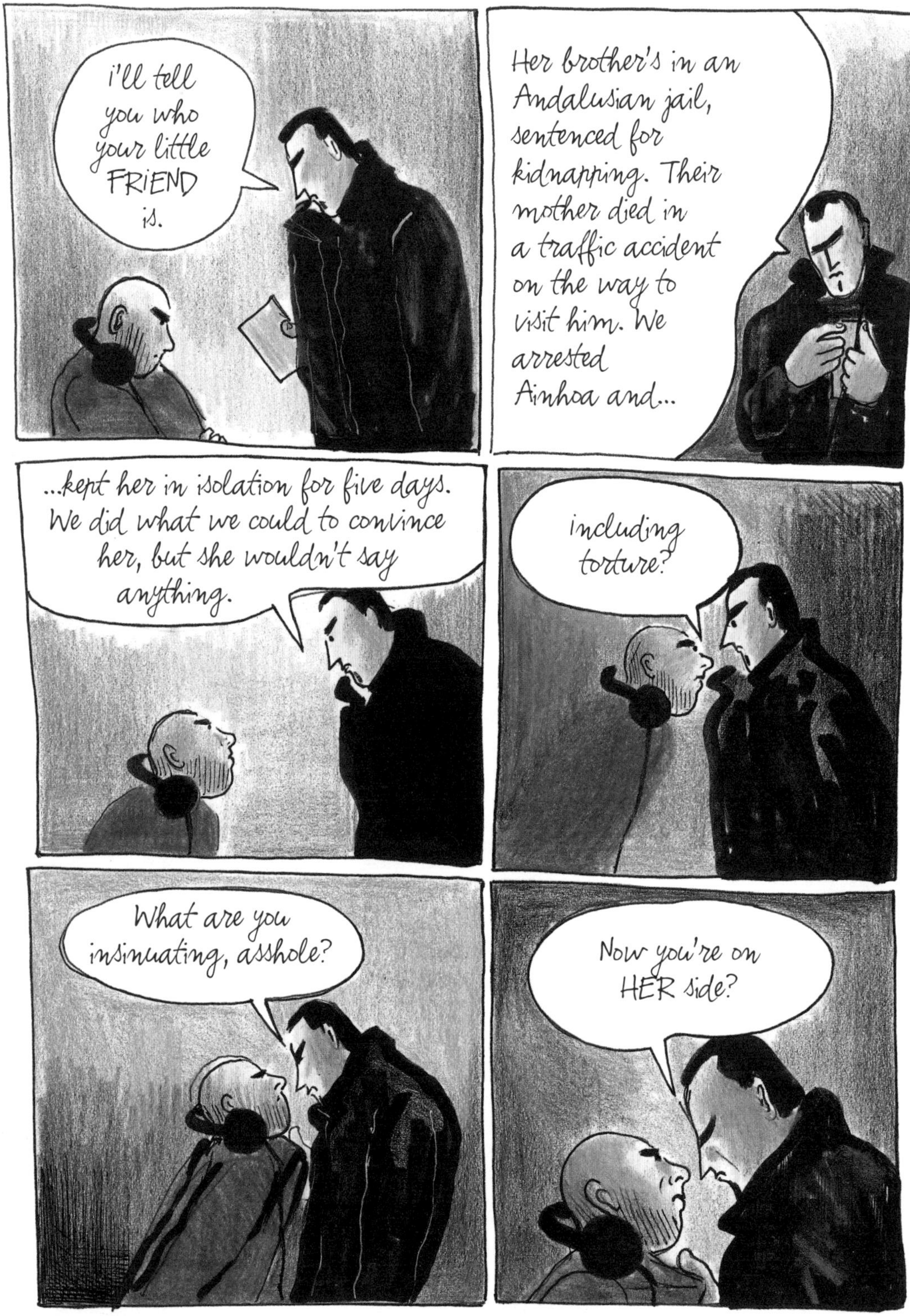
i'll tell you who your little FRIEND is.
Her brother's in an Andalusian jail, sentenced for kidnapping. Their mother died in a traffic accident on the way to visit him. We arrested Ainhoa and...
...kept her in isolation for five days. We did what we could to convince her, but she wouldn't say anything.
including torture?
What are you insinuating, asshole?
Now you're on HER side?

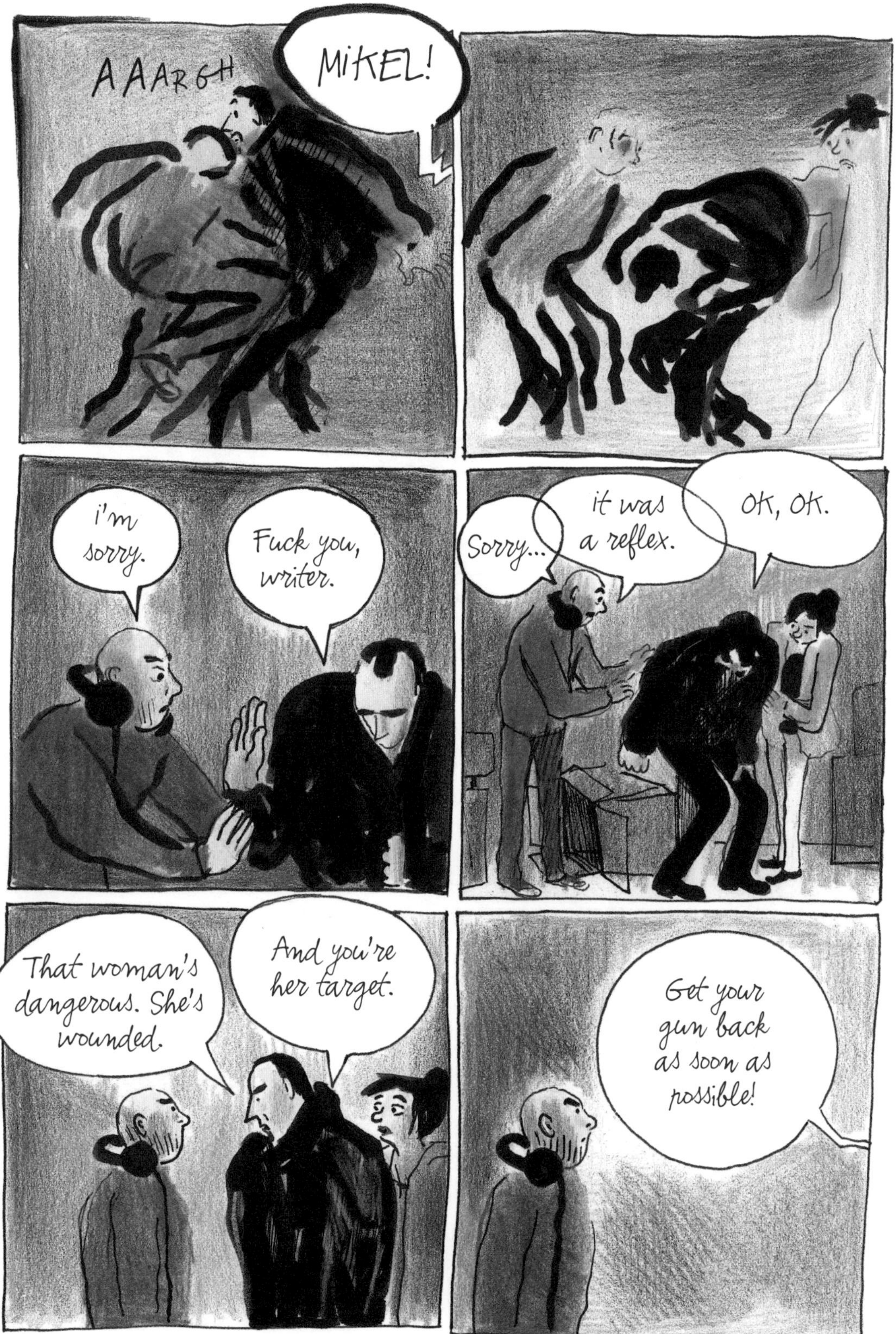
AAARGH
MIKEL!
I'm sorry.
Fuck you, writer.
Sorry...
It was a reflex.
OK, OK.
That woman's dangerous. She's wounded.
And you're her target.
Get your gun back as soon as possible!

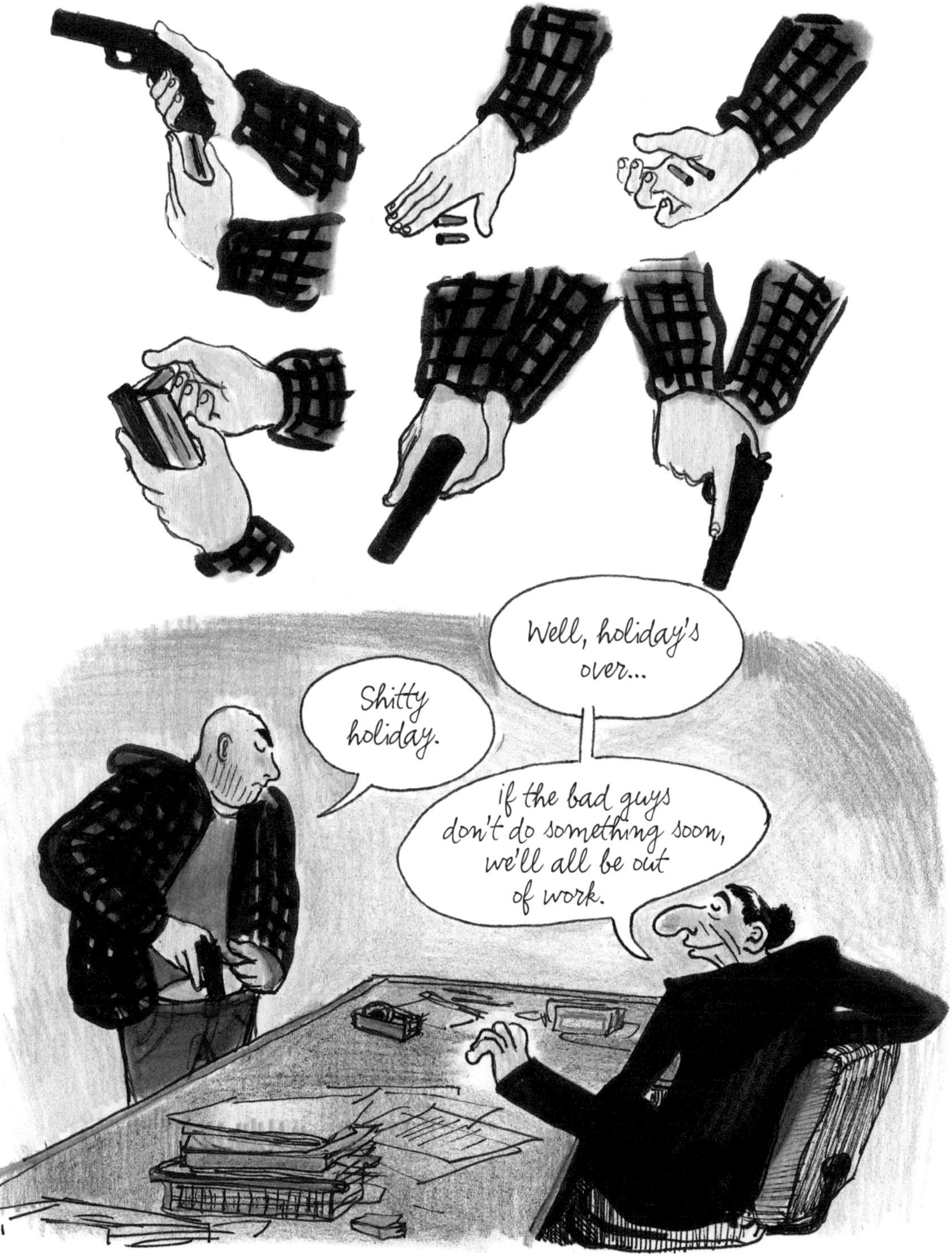
Shitty holiday.
Well, holiday's over...
if the bad guys don't do something soon, we'll all be out of work.

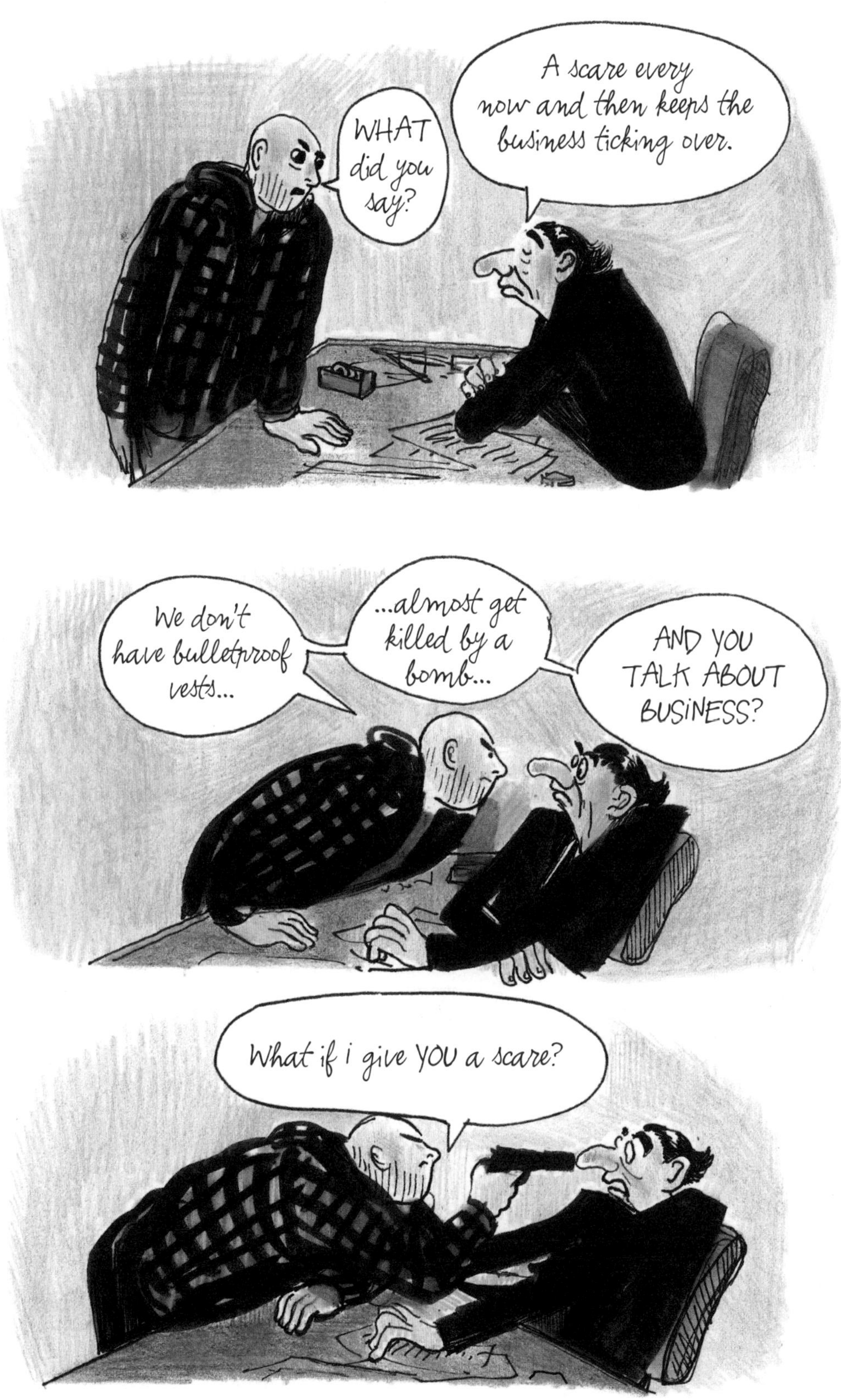
WHAT did you say?
A scare every now and then keeps the business ticking over.
We don't have bulletproof vests...
...almost get killed by a bomb...
AND YOU TALK ABOUT BUSINESS?
What if i give YOU a scare?

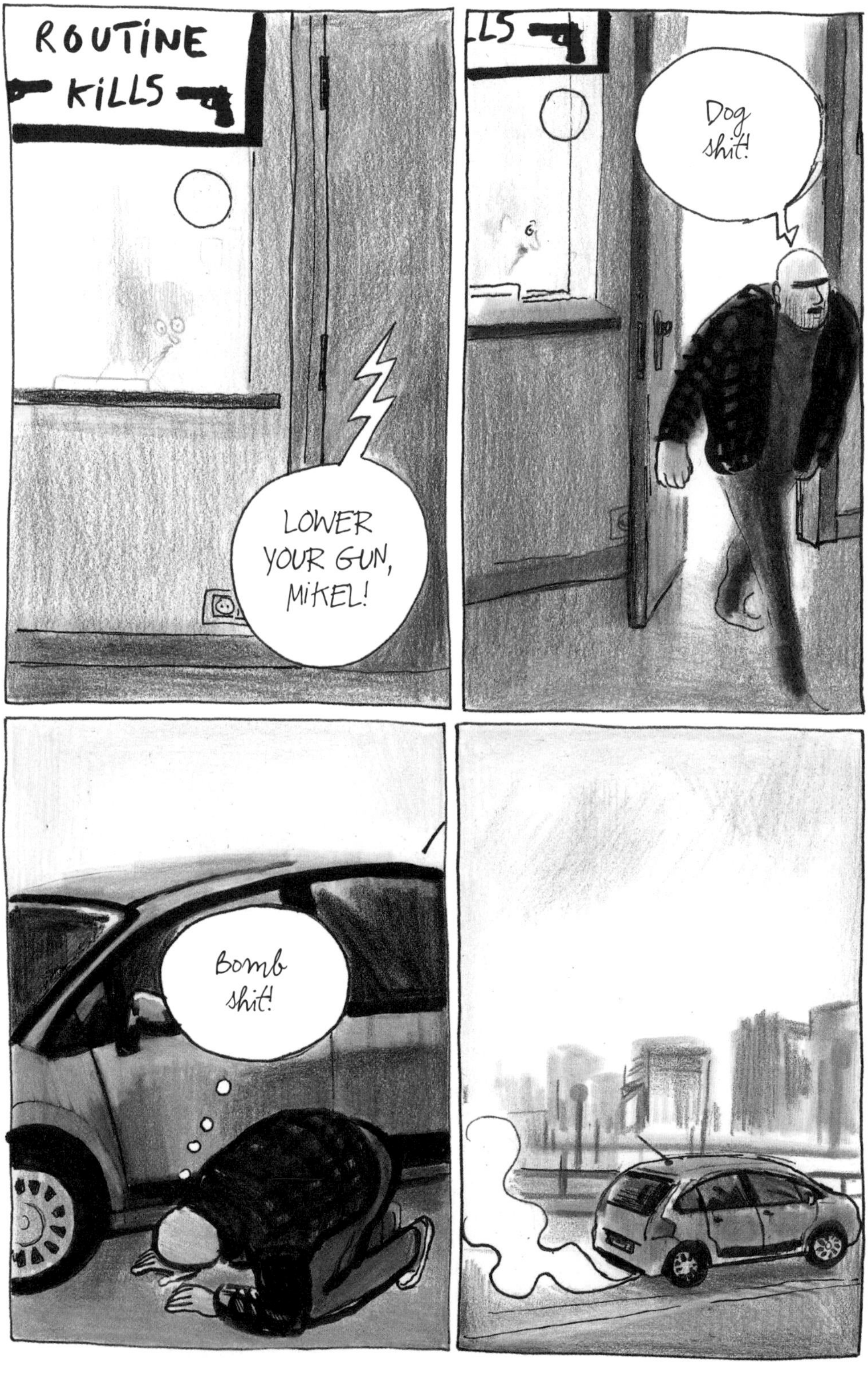
ROUTINE KILLS
LOWER YOUR GUN, MIKEL!
Dog shit!
Bomb shit!

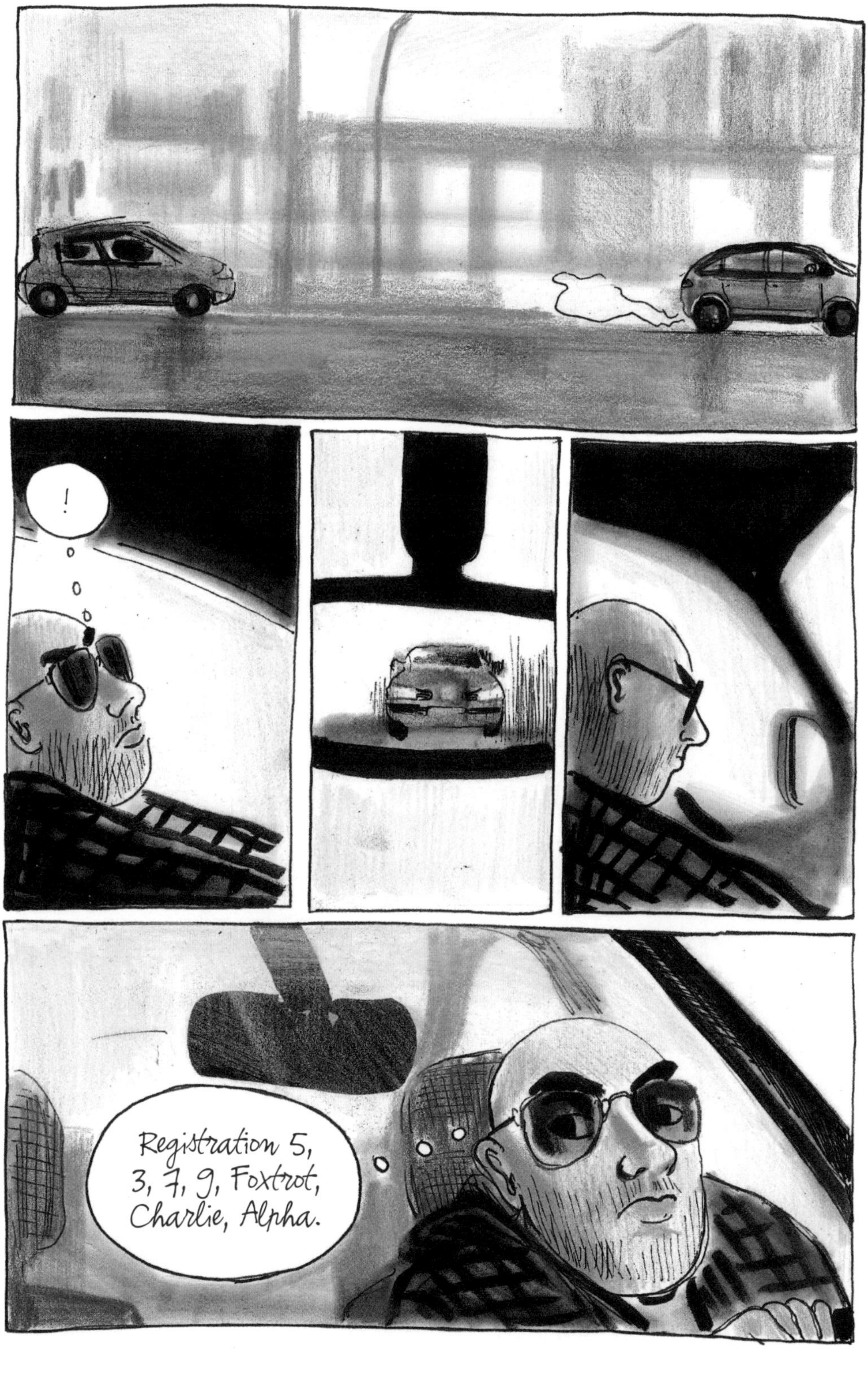
!
Registration 5, 3, 7, 9, Foxtrot, Charlie, Alpha.

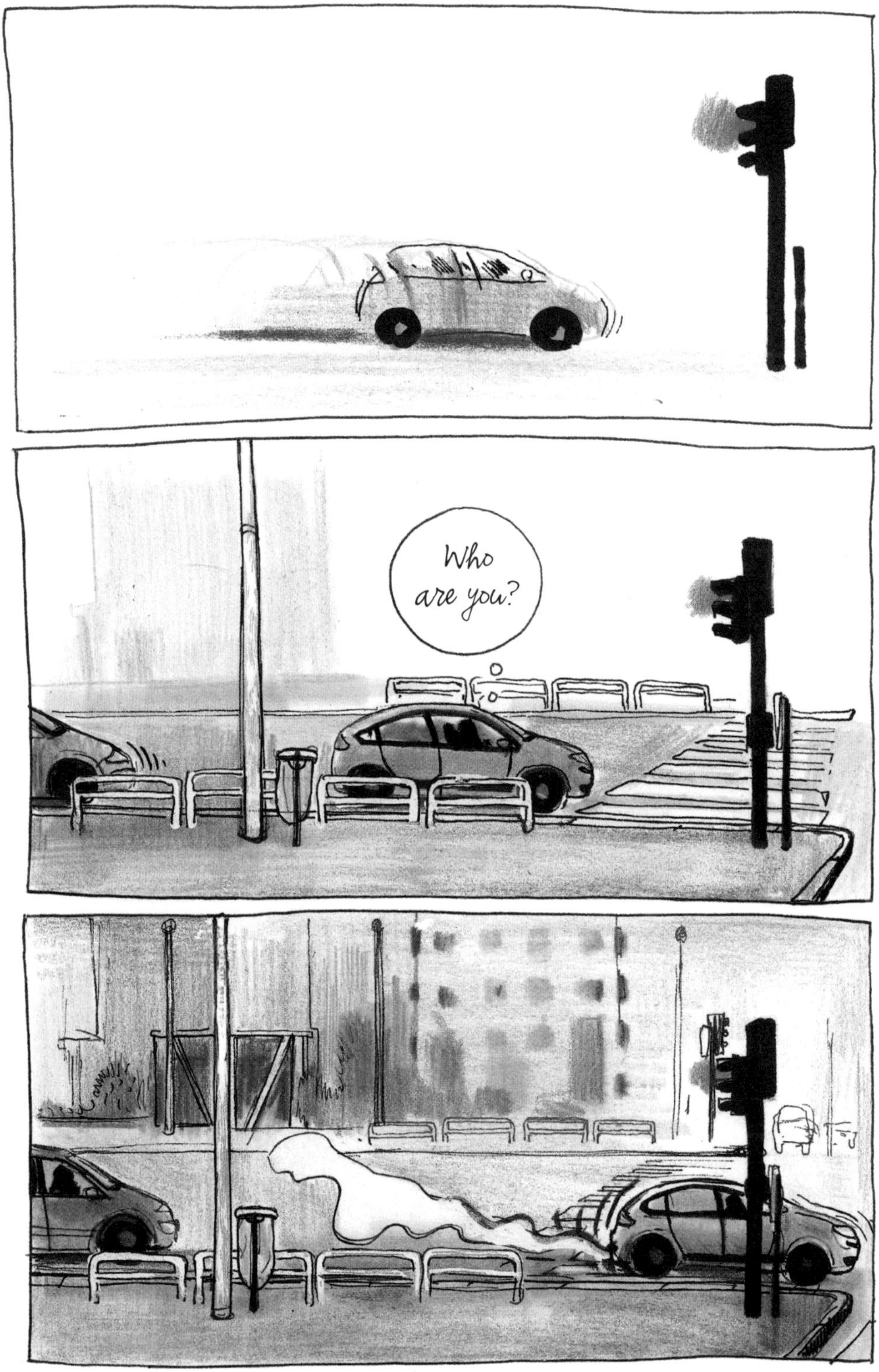
Who are you?

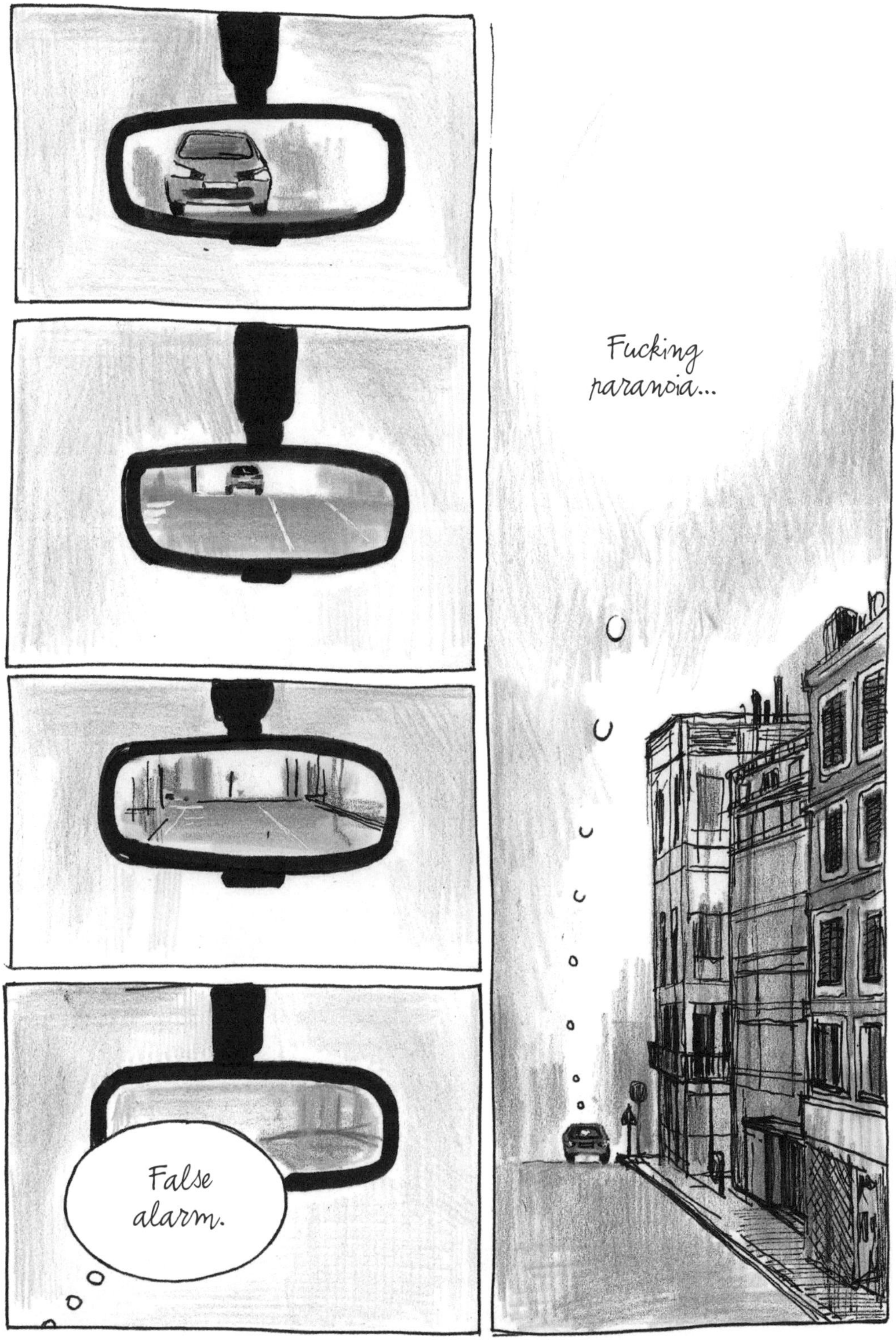
False alarm.
Fucking paranoia...

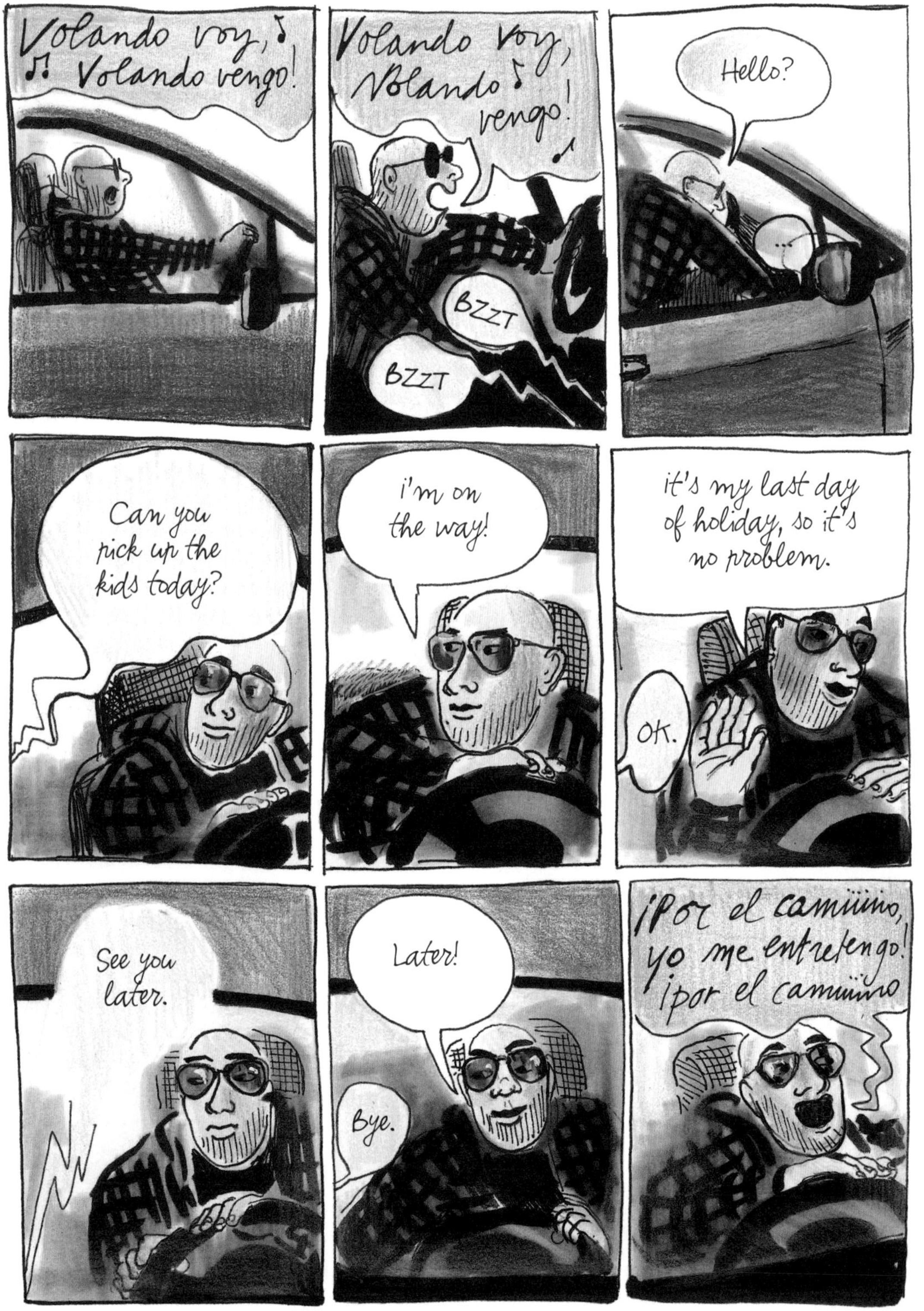
Volando voy, Volando vengo!
Volando voy, Volando vengo!
BZZT
BZZT
Hello?
Can you pick up the kids today?
i'm on the way!
it's my last day of holiday, so it's no problem.
OK.
See you later.
Later!
Bye.
¡Por el camiiino, yo me entretengo! ¡por el camiiino

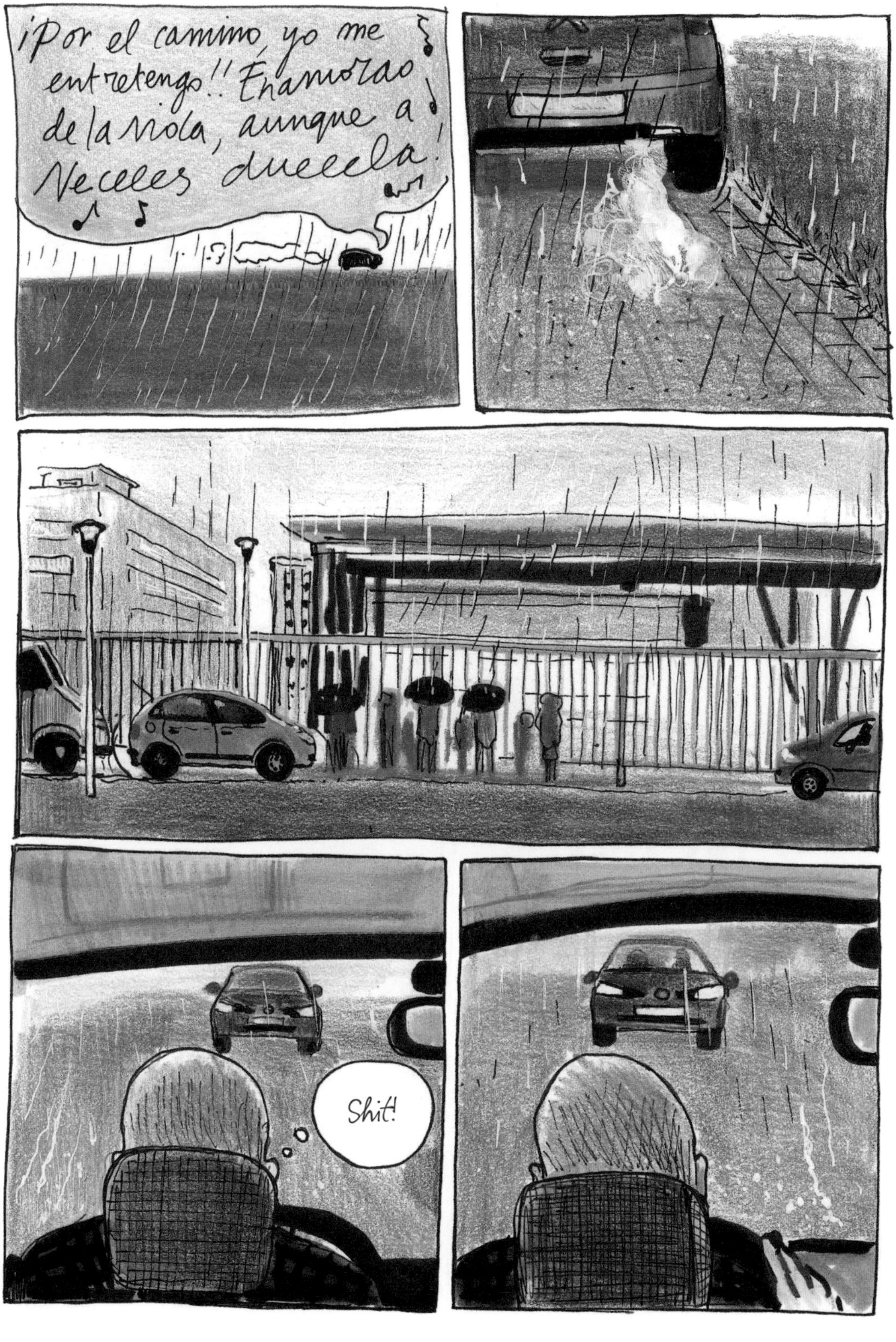
¡Por el camino, yo me entretengo!! Enamorao de la viola, aunque a Neceles dueeela!
Shit!

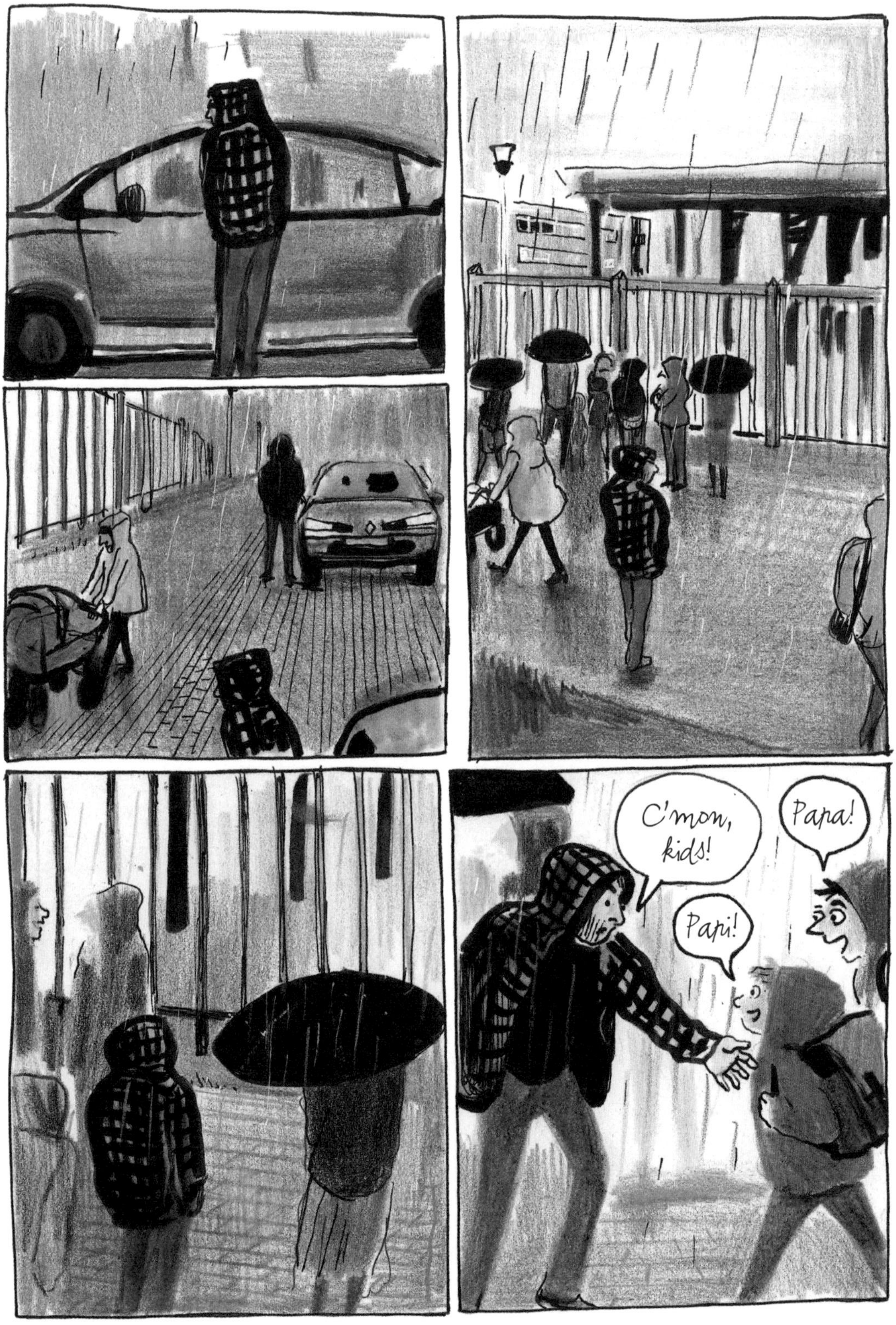
C'mon, kids!
Papa!
Papi!

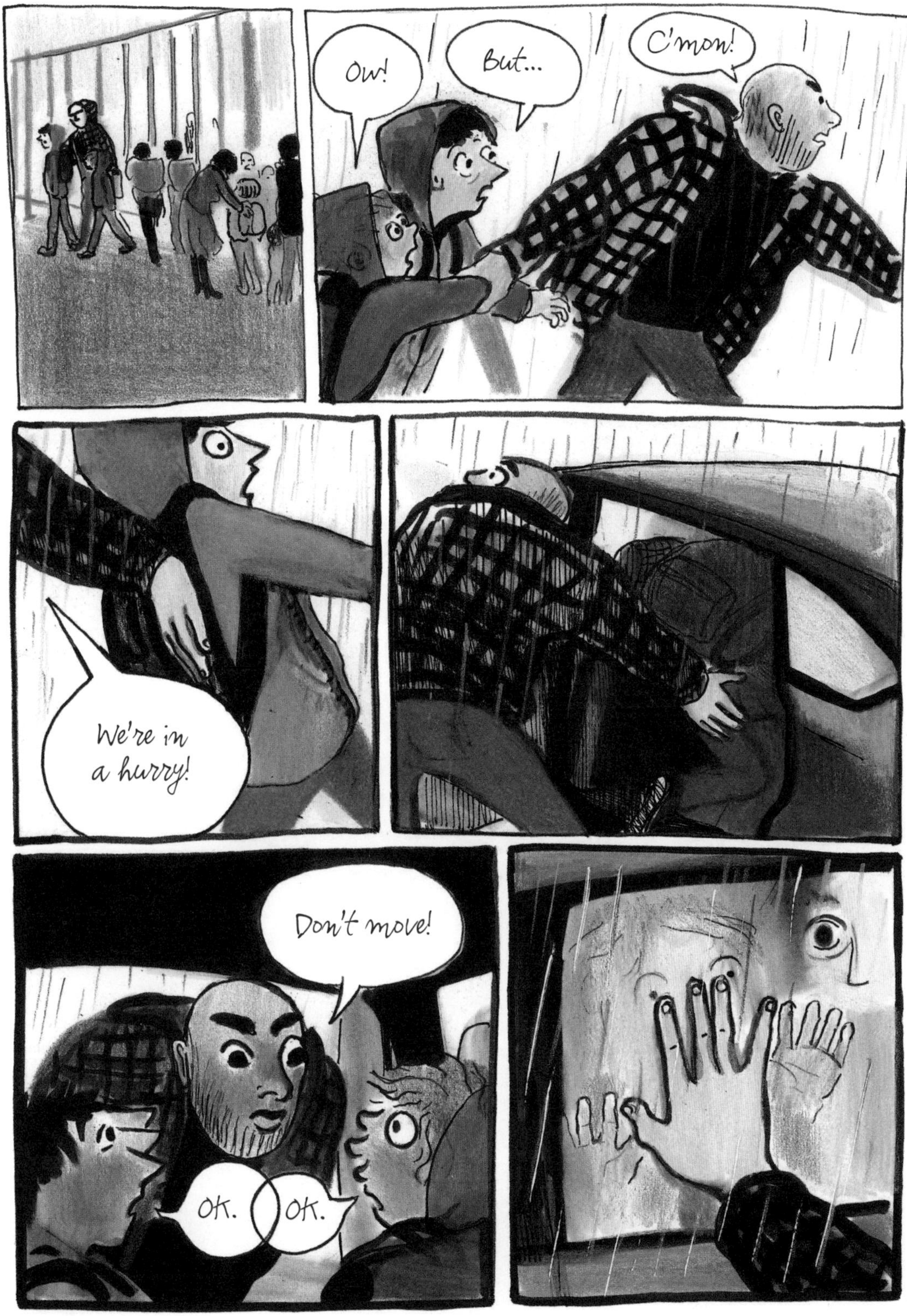
Ow!
But...
C'mon!
We're in a hurry!
Don't move!
OK.
OK.

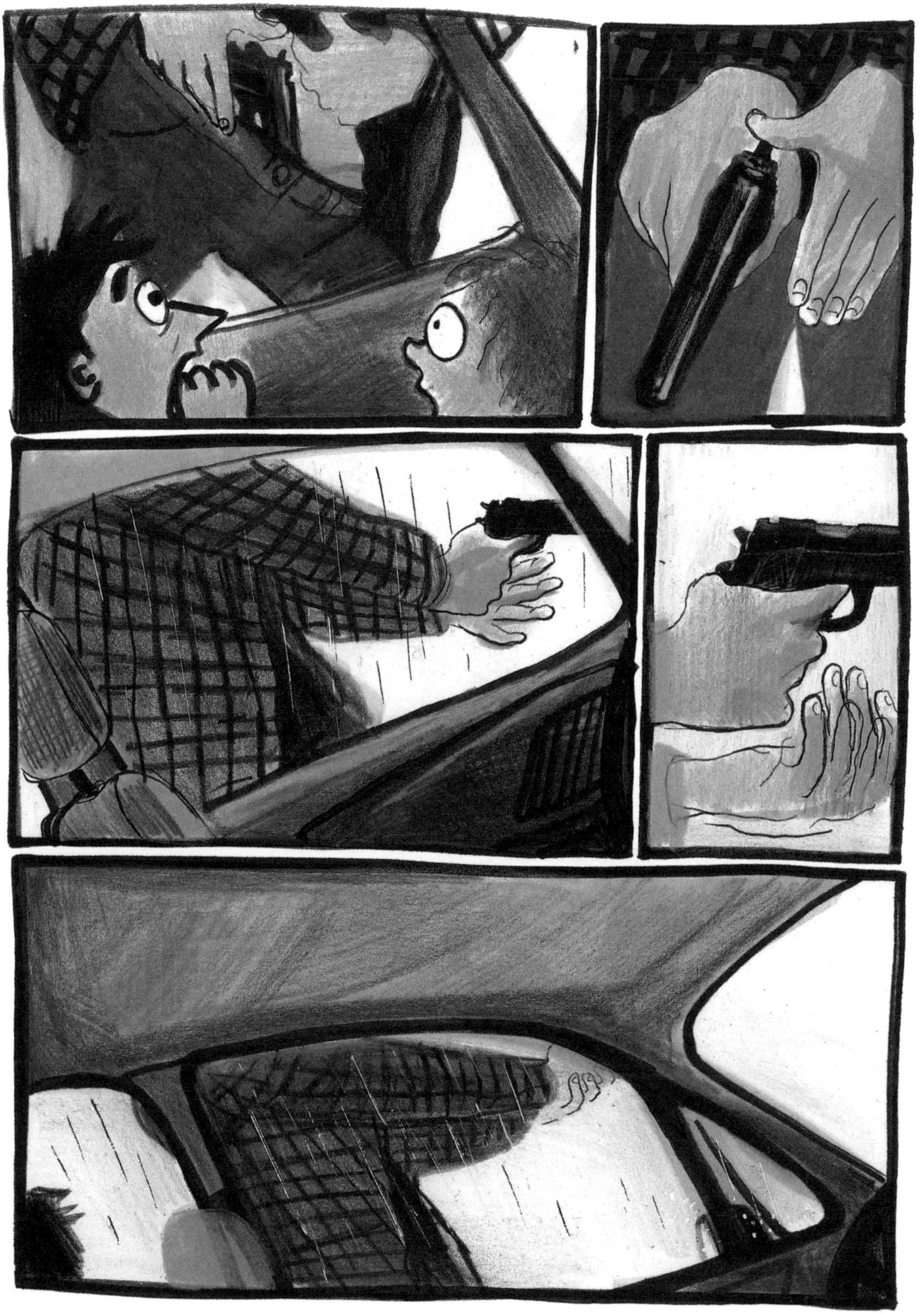

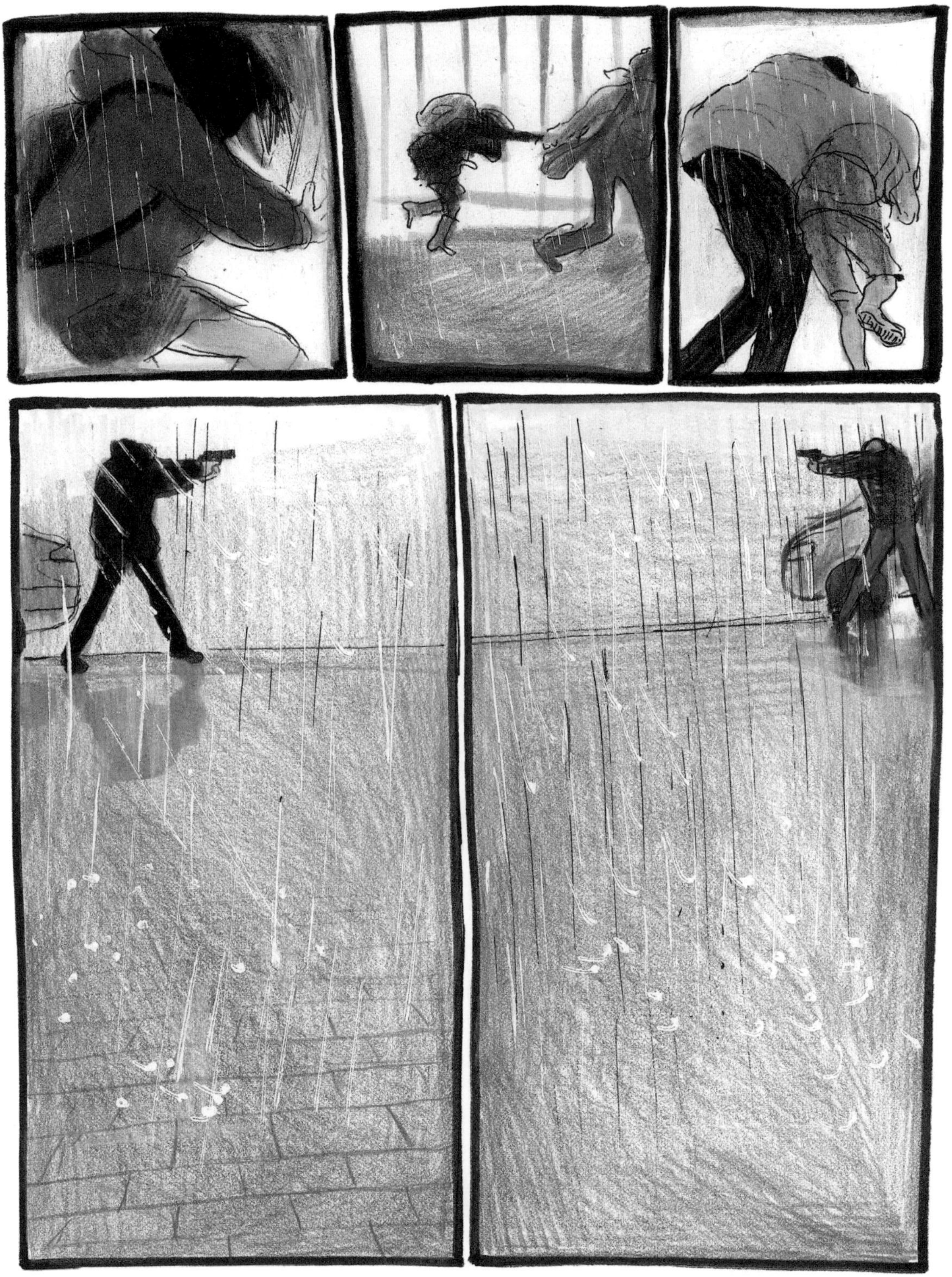

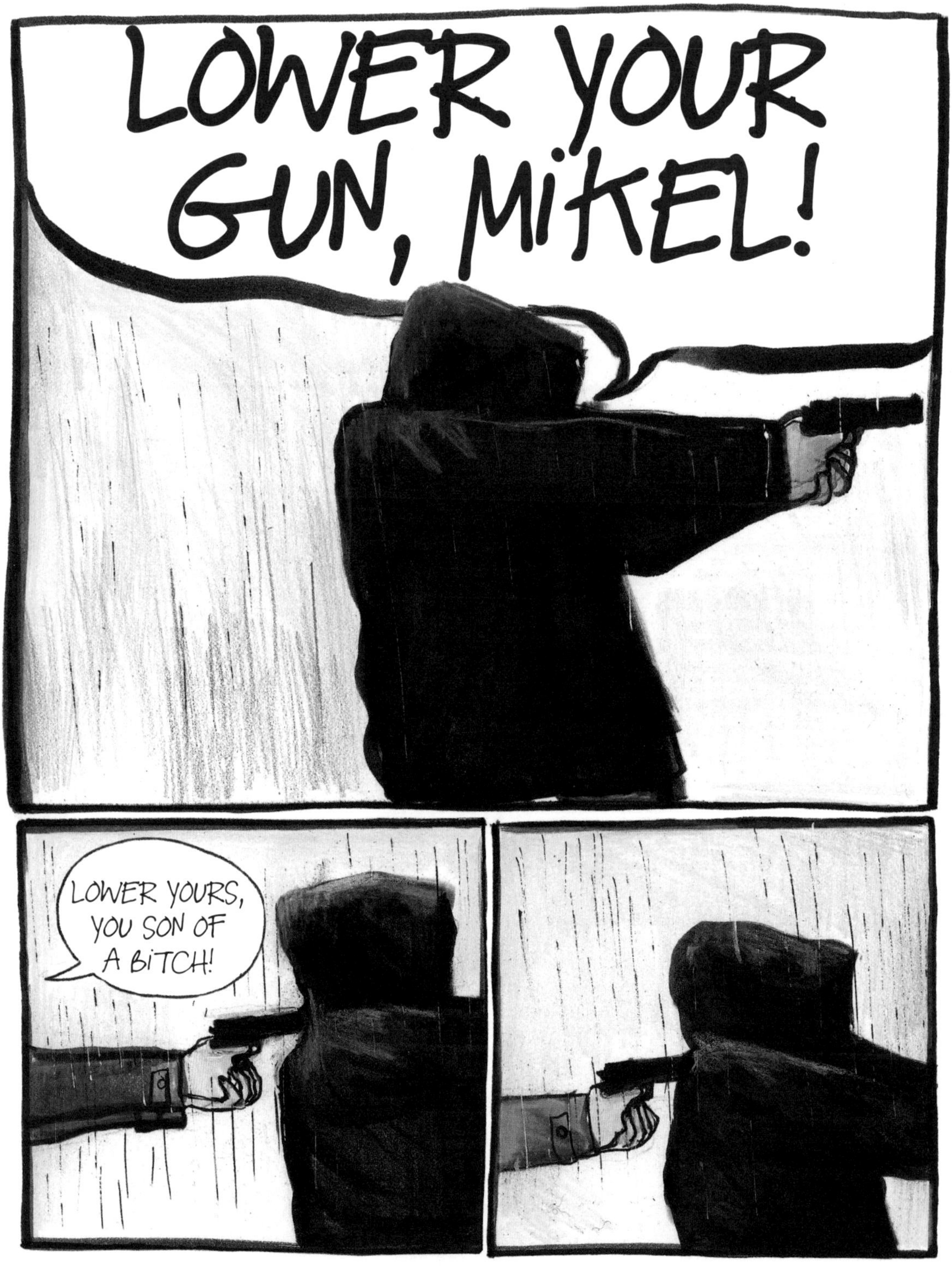
LOWER YOUR GUN, MIKEL!
LOWER YOURS, YOU SON OF A BITCH!

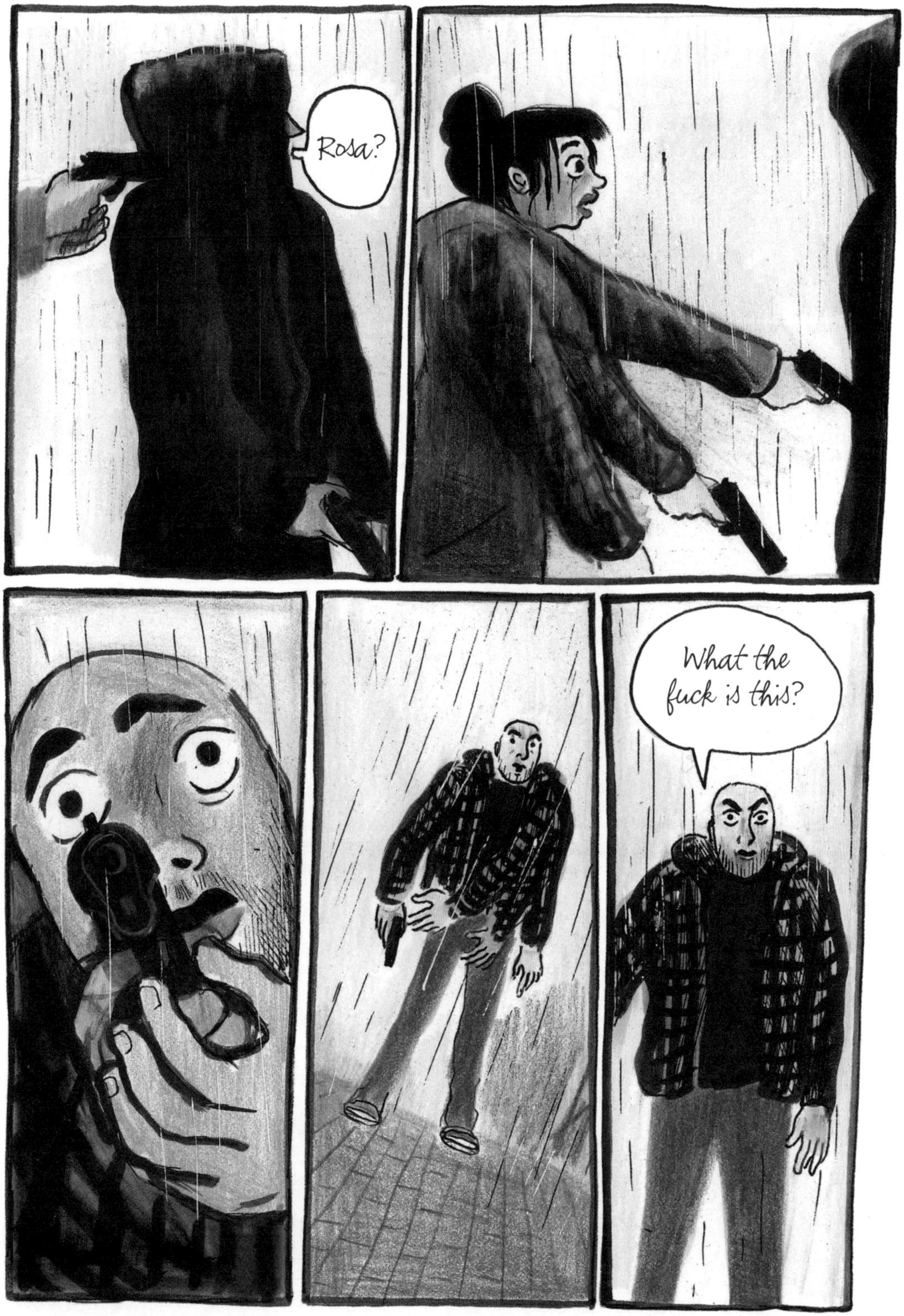
Rosa?
What the fuck is this?

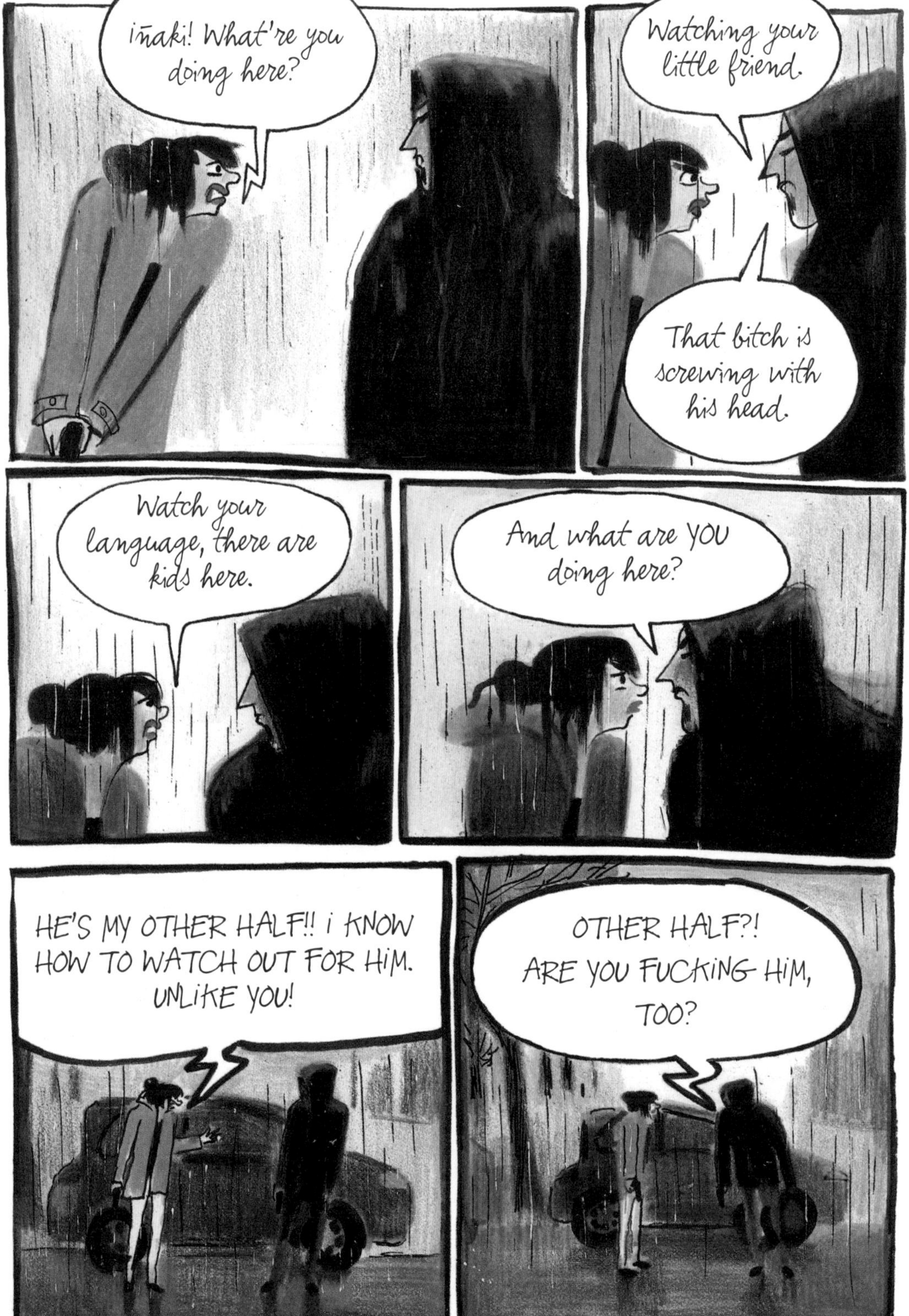

iñaki! What're you doing here?
Watching your little friend.
That bitch is screwing with his head.
Watch your language, there are kids here.
And what are YOU doing here?
HE'S MY OTHER HALF!! i KNOW HOW TO WATCH OUT FOR HiM. UNLiKE YOU!
OTHER HALF?! ARE YOU FUCKiNG HiM, TOO?

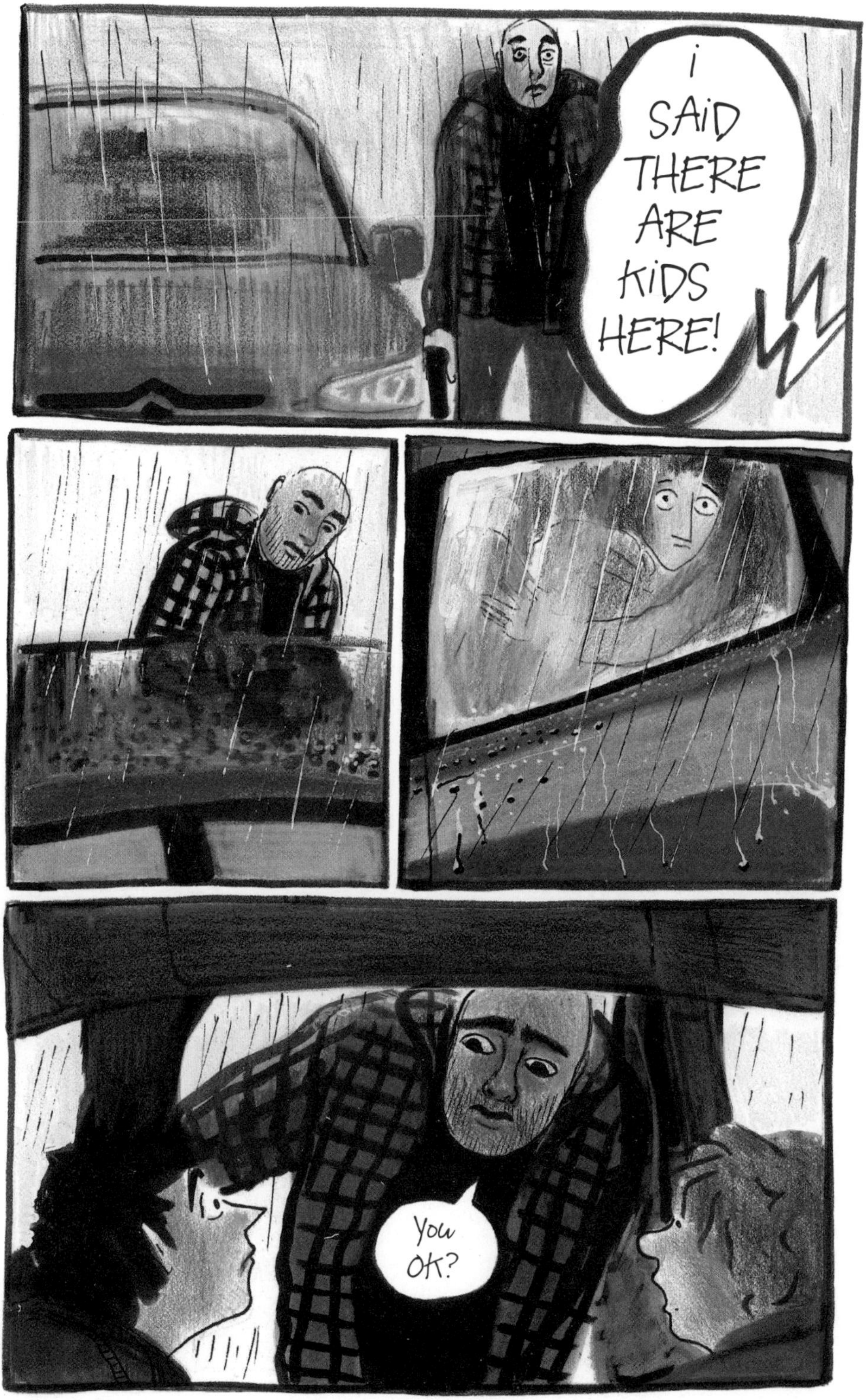
I SAID THERE ARE KIDS HERE!
YOU OK?

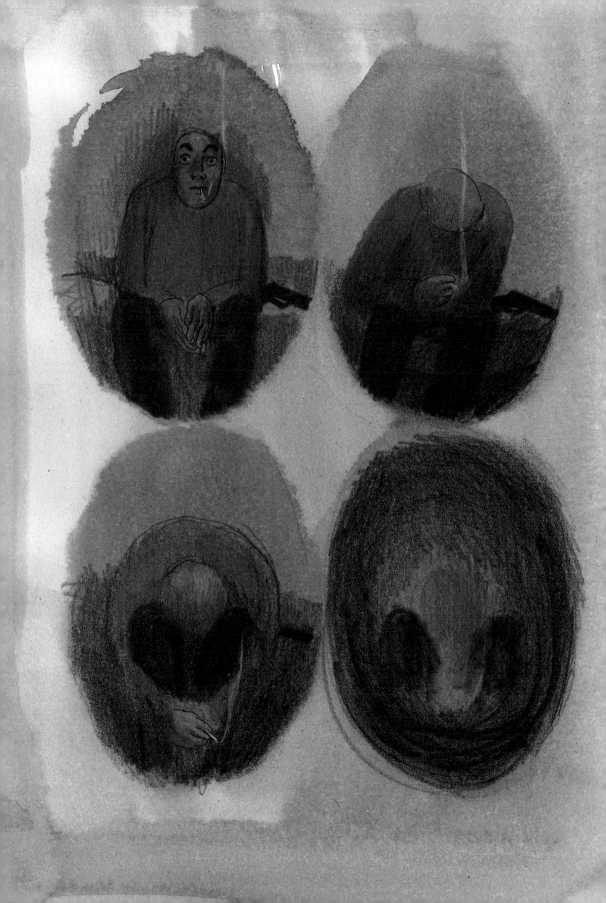

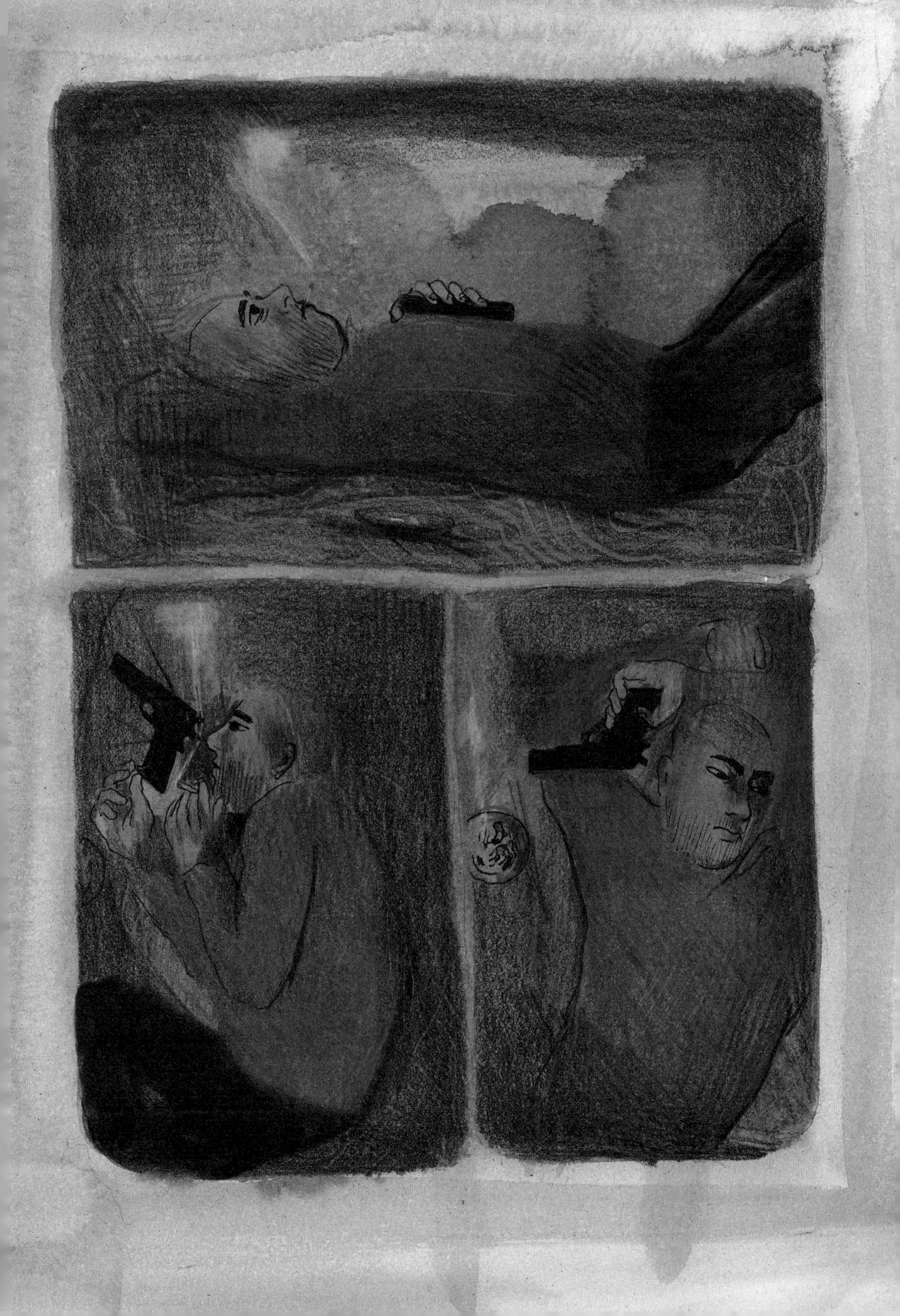

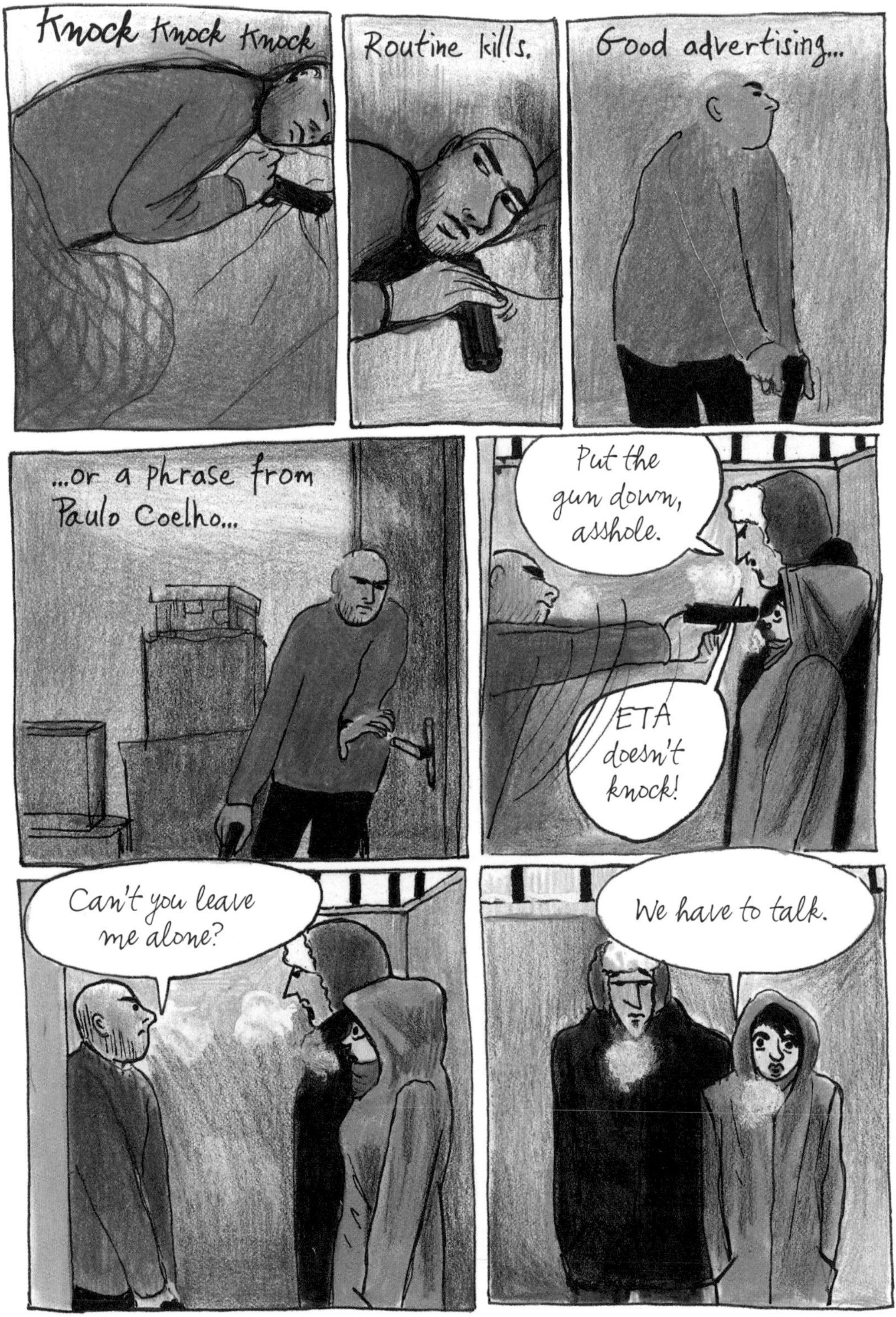
Knock Knock Knock
Routine kills.
Good advertising...
...or a phrase from Paulo Coelho...
Put the gun down, asshole.
ETA doesn't knock!
Can't you leave me alone?
We have to talk.

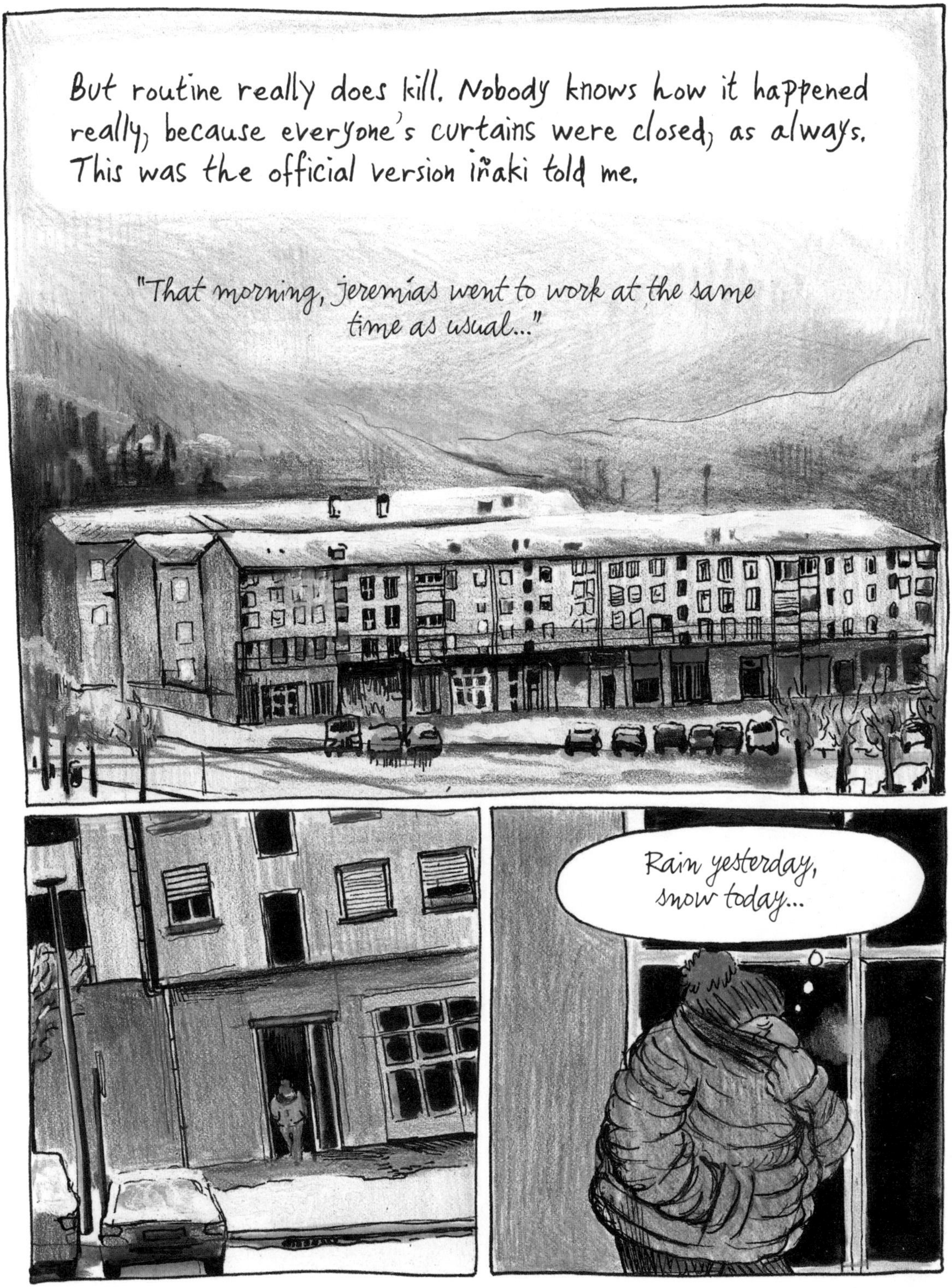
But routine really does kill. Nobody knows how it happened really, because everyone's curtains were closed, as always. This was the official version iñaki told me.
"That morning, jeremias went to work at the same time as usual..."
Rain yesterday, snow today...

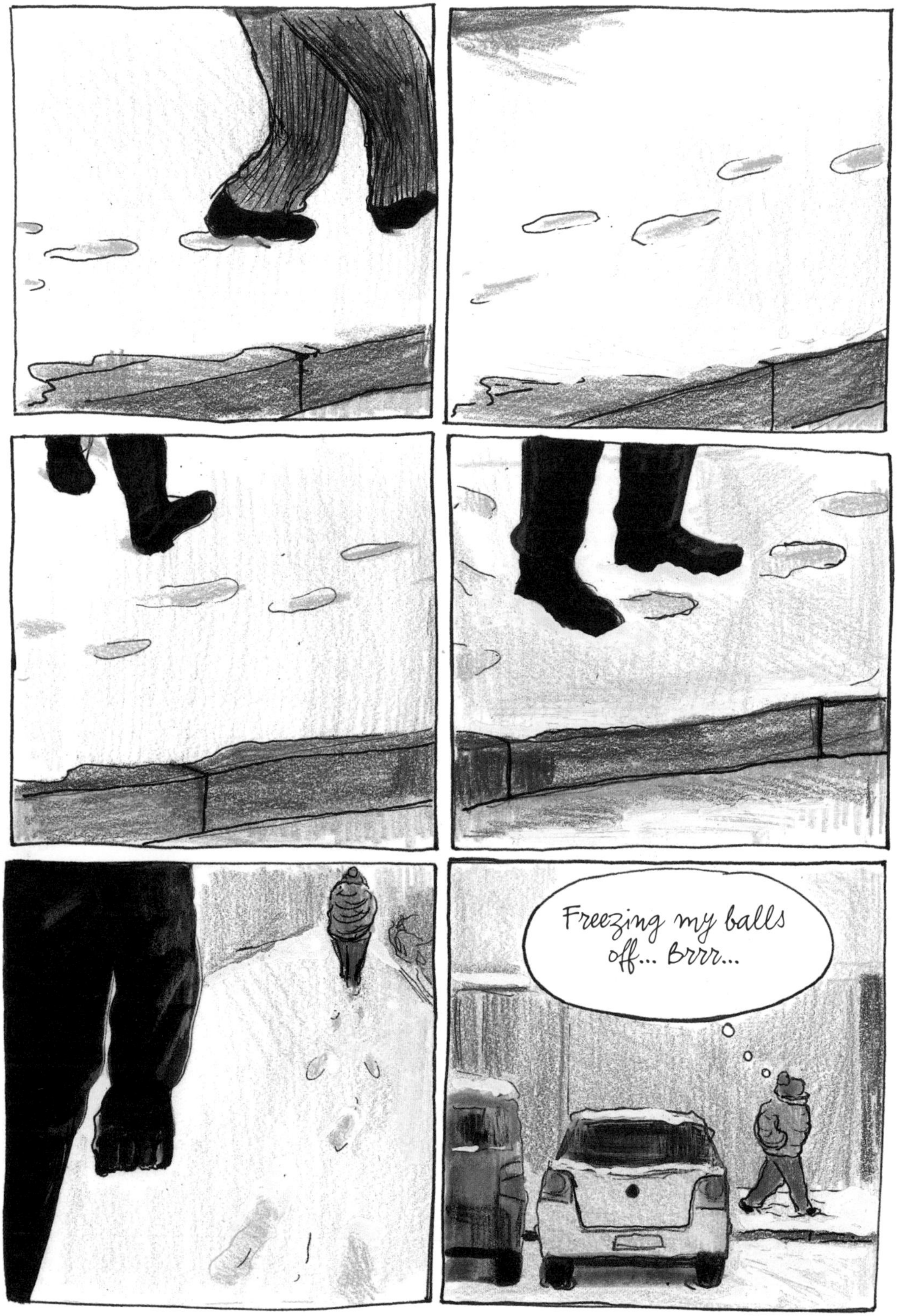
Freezing my balls off... Brrr...

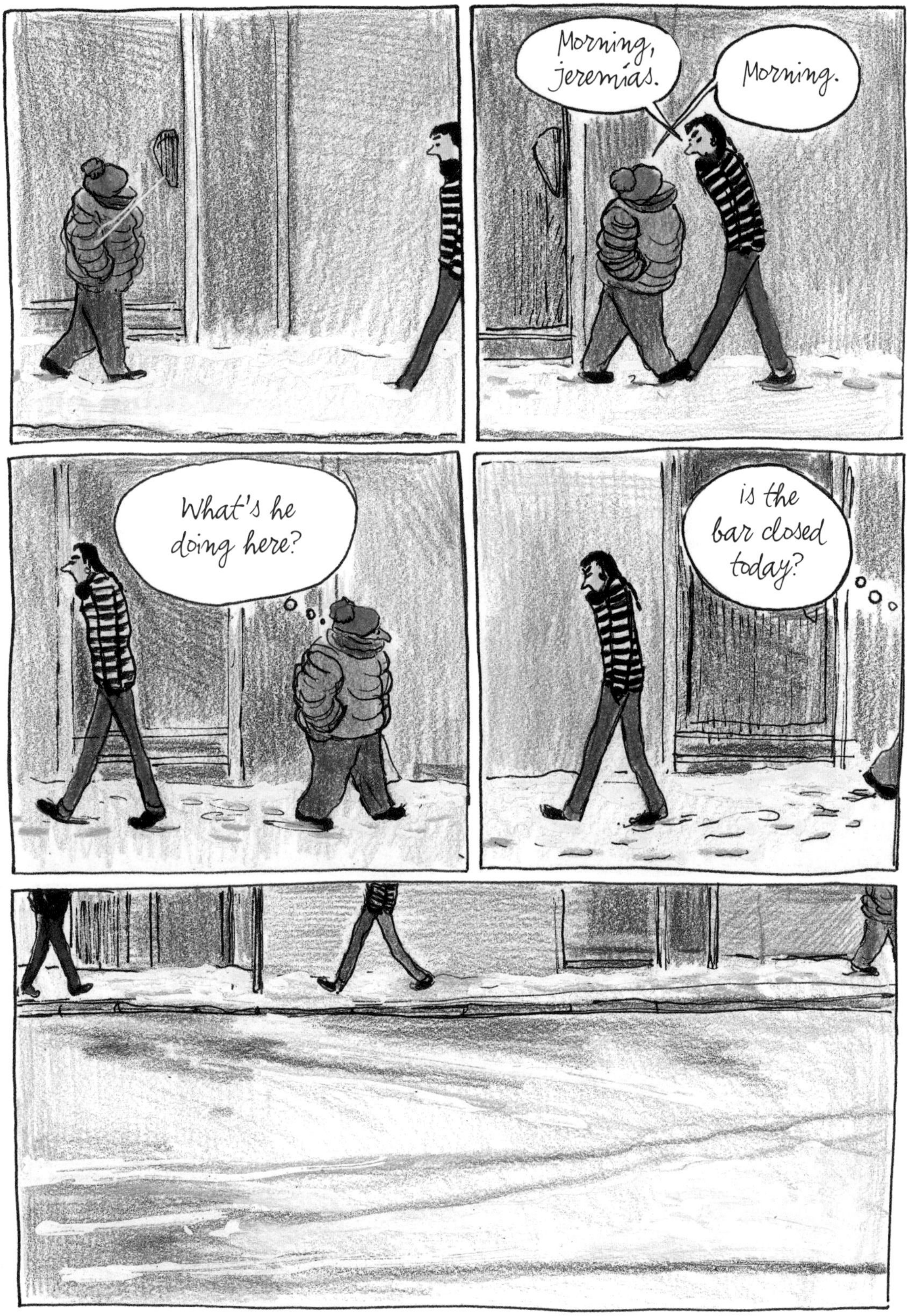
Morning, jeremías.
Morning.
What's he doing here?
is the bar closed today?

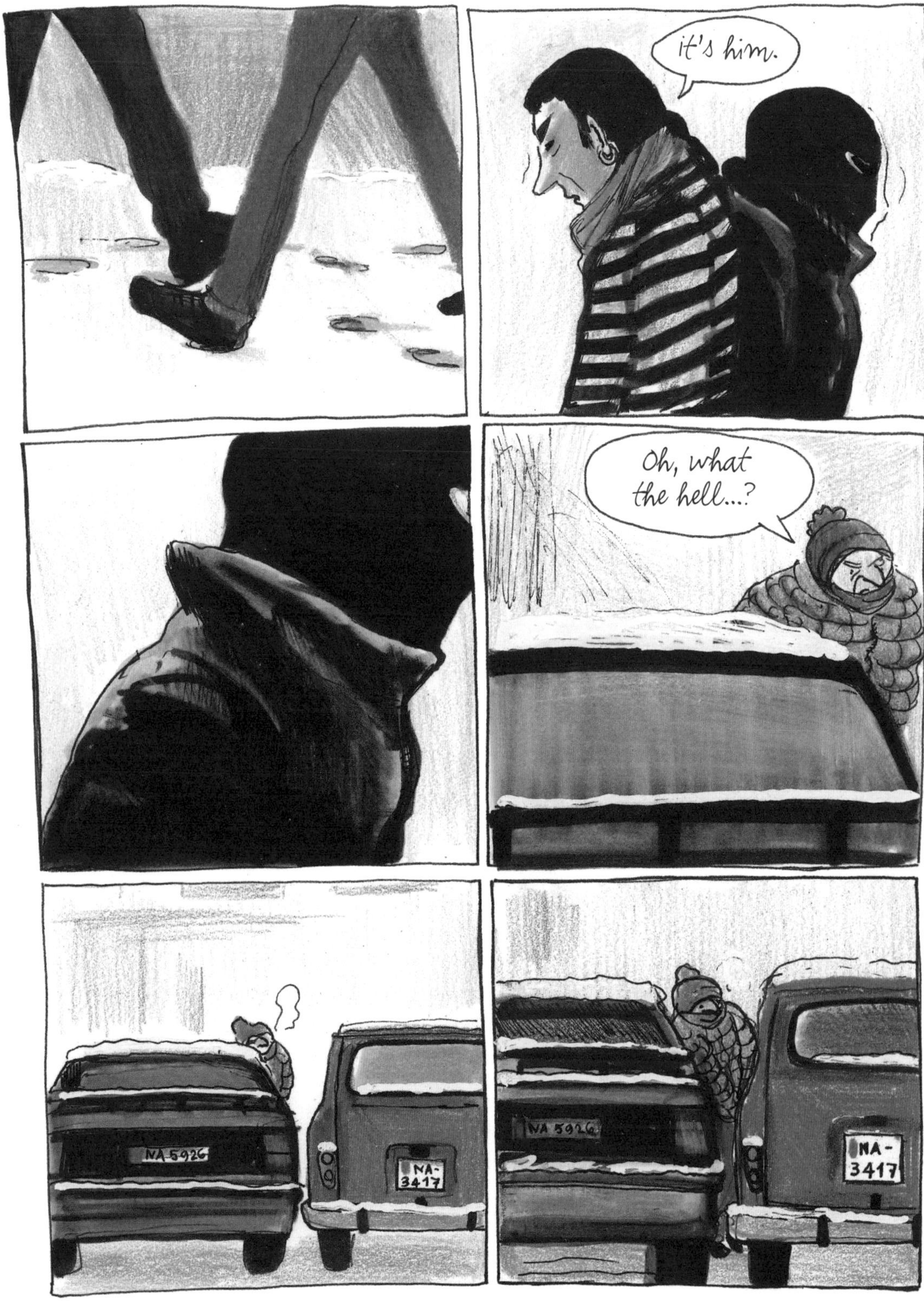
it's him.
Oh, what the hell...?
NA-5926
NA-3417
NA-5926
NA-3417

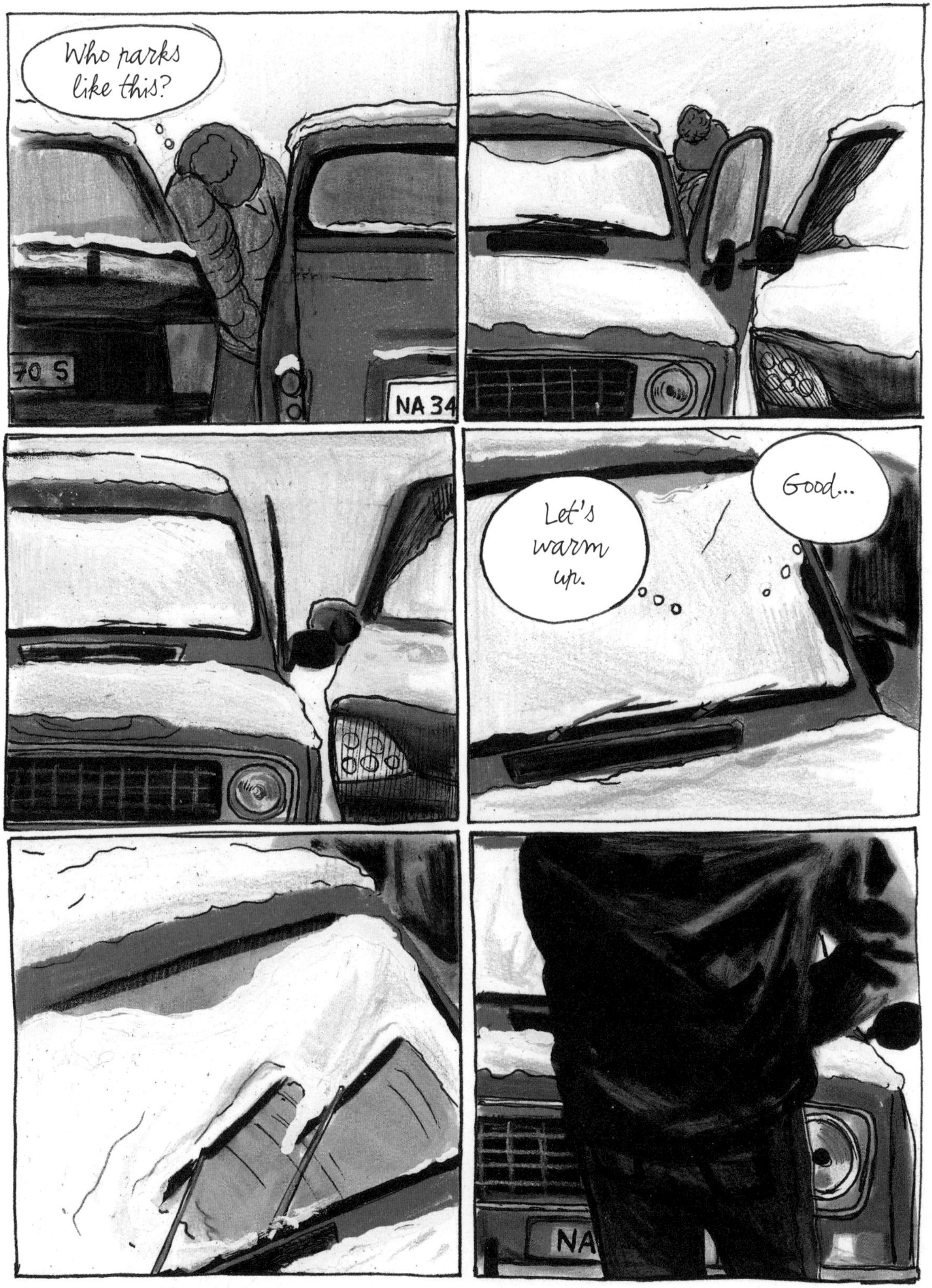
Who parks like this?
70 S
NA 34
Let's warm up.
Good...
NA

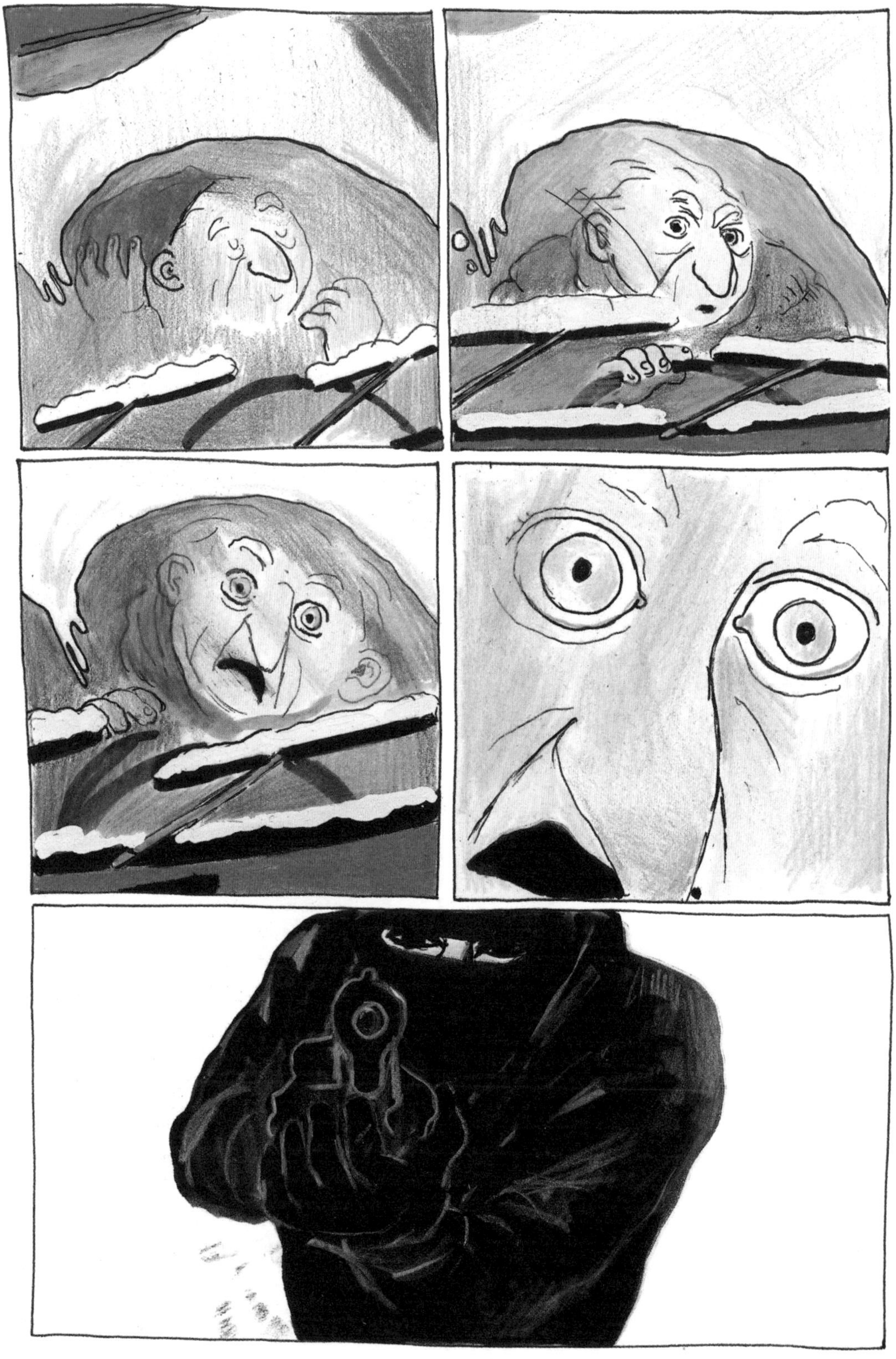

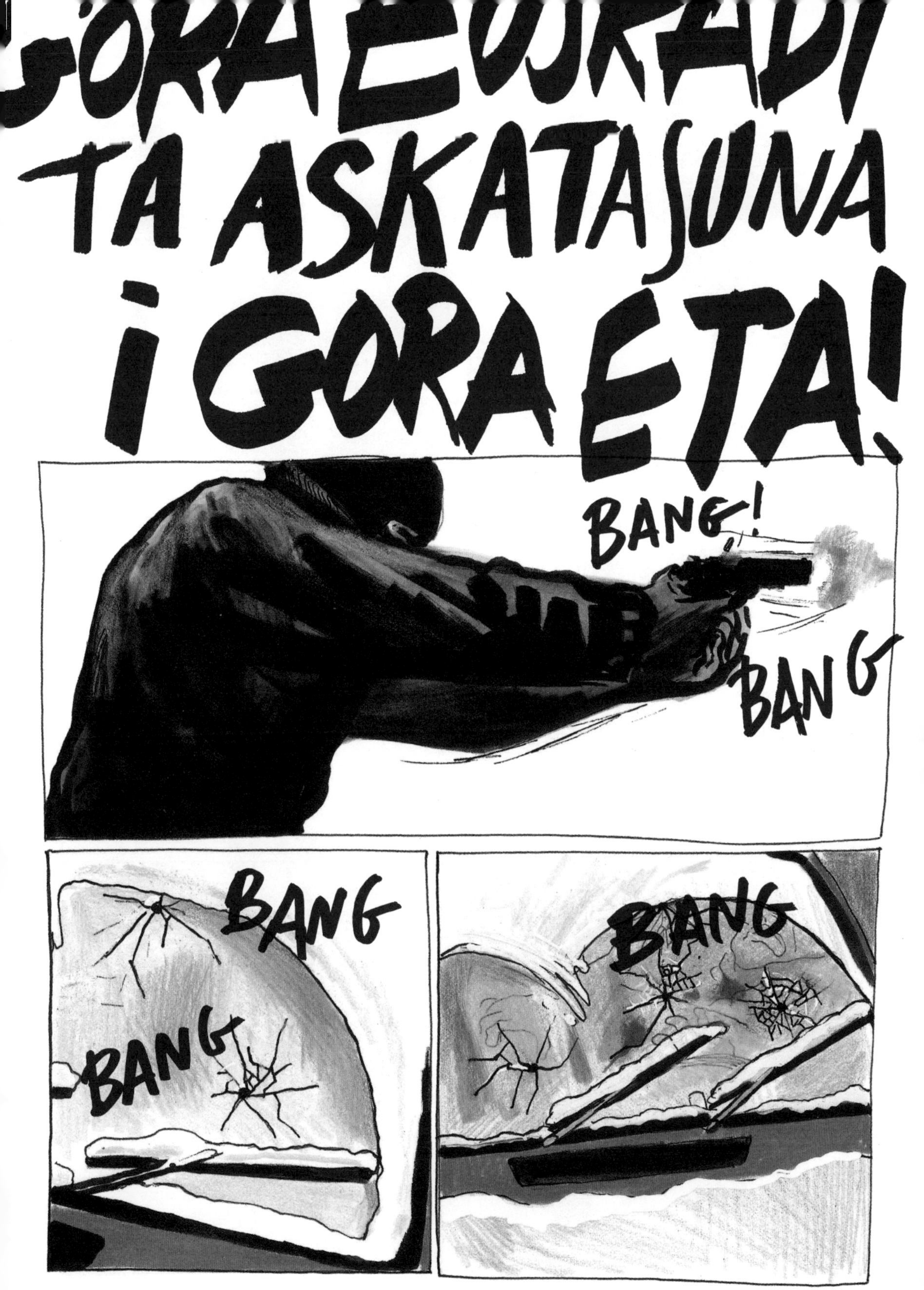
GORA EUSKADI
TA ASKATASUNA
¡GORA ETA!
BANG!
BANG
BANG
BANG
BANG

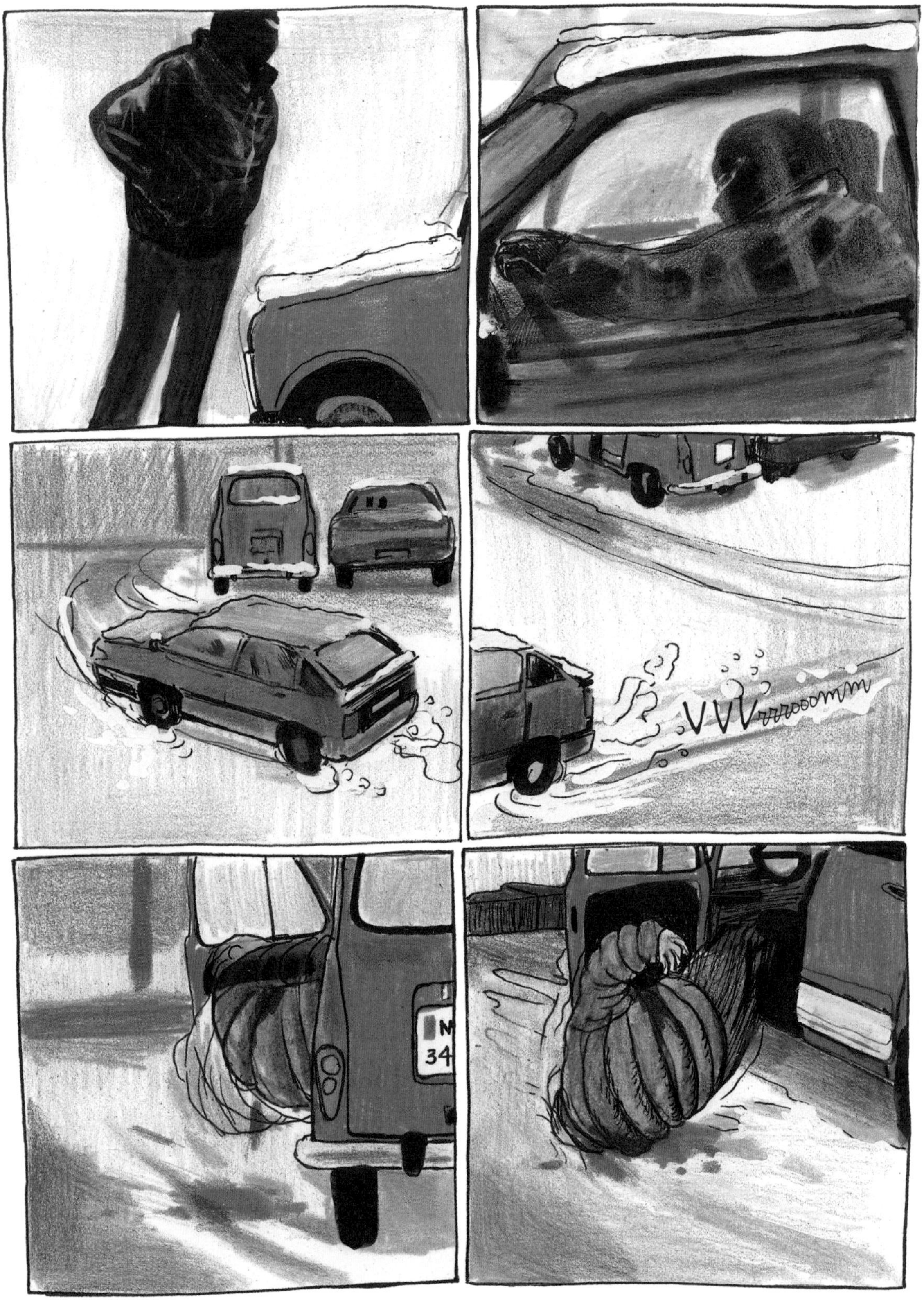
VVVrrrooommm

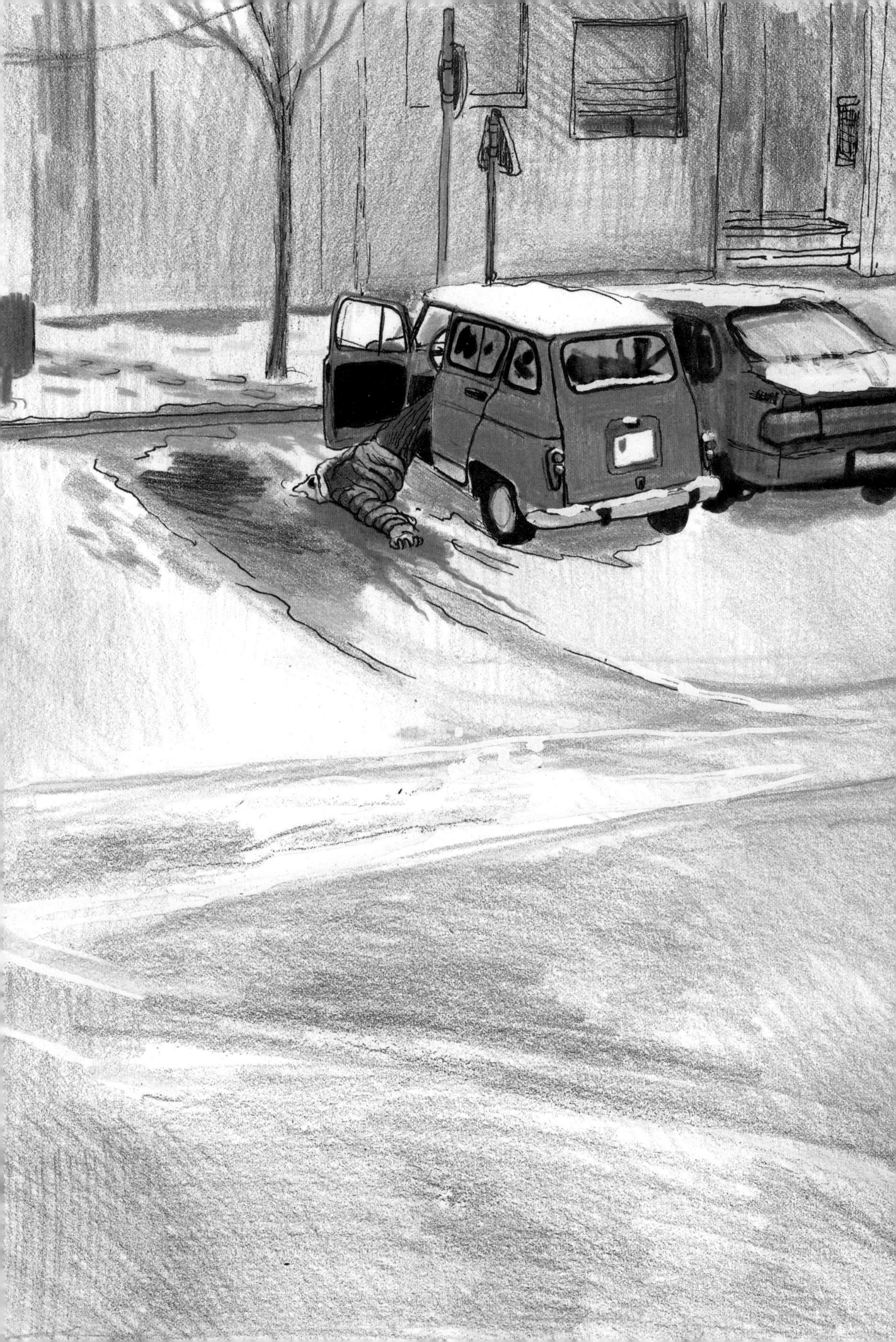

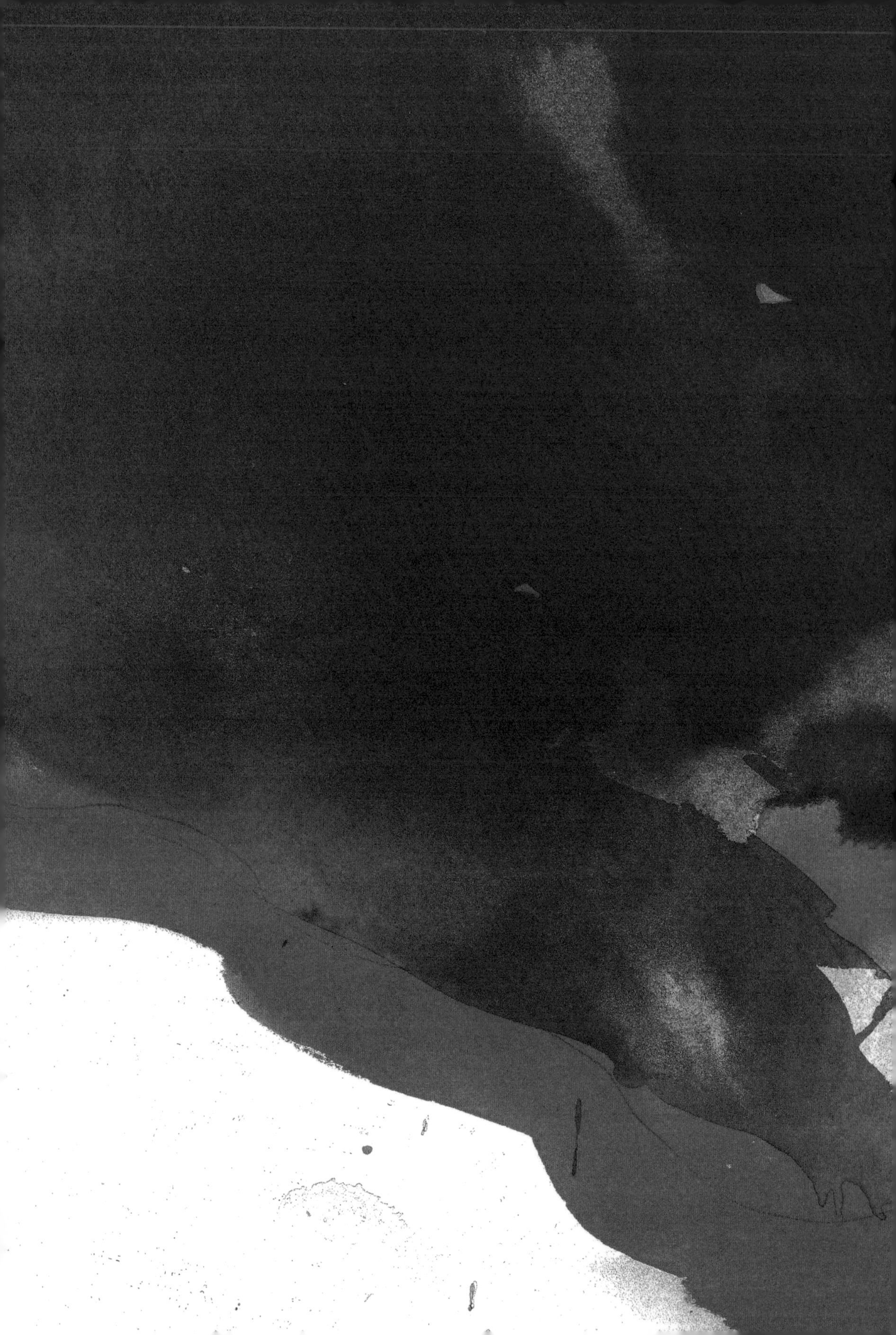

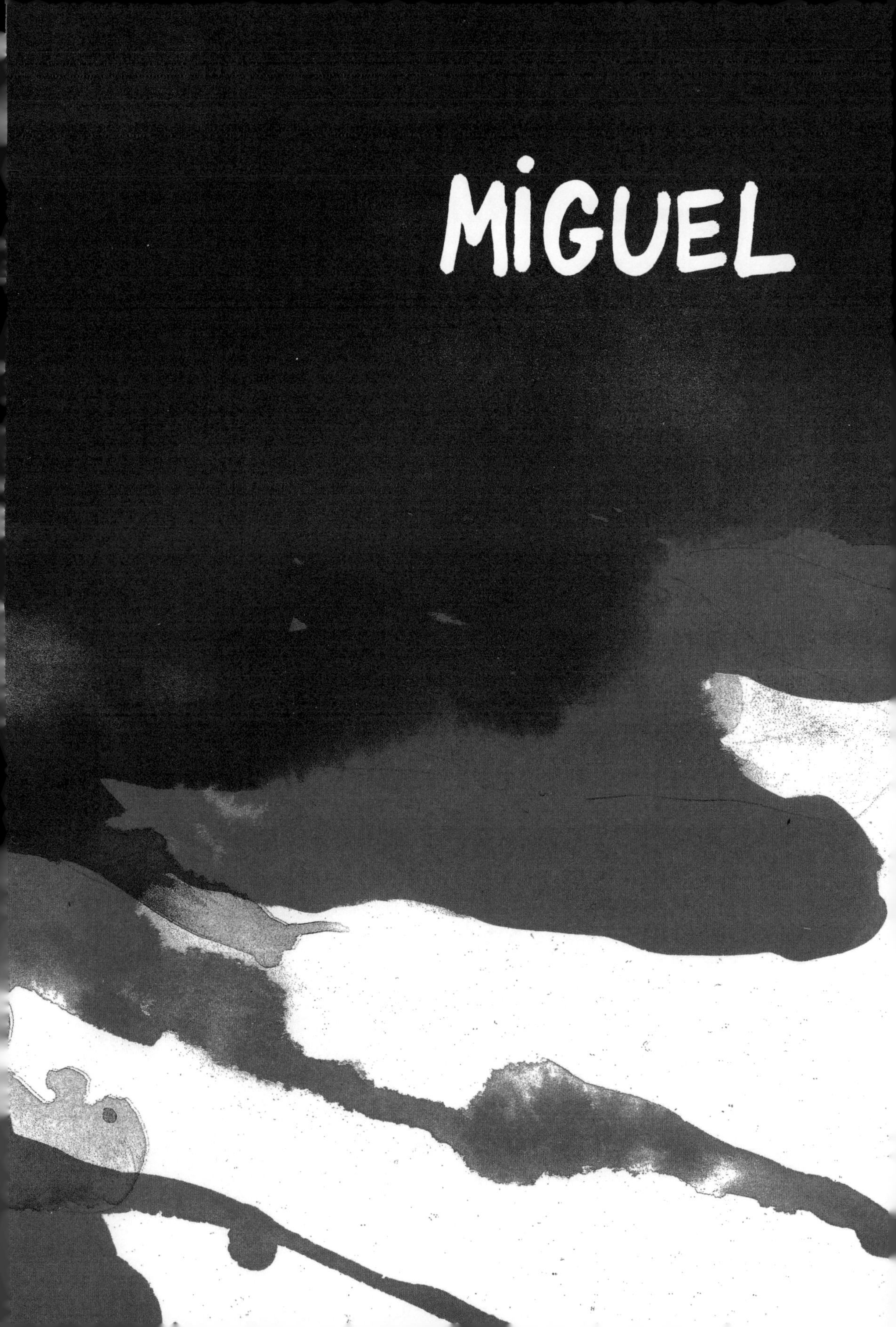
MIGUEL

Today, 8 December 2010, Pamplona.

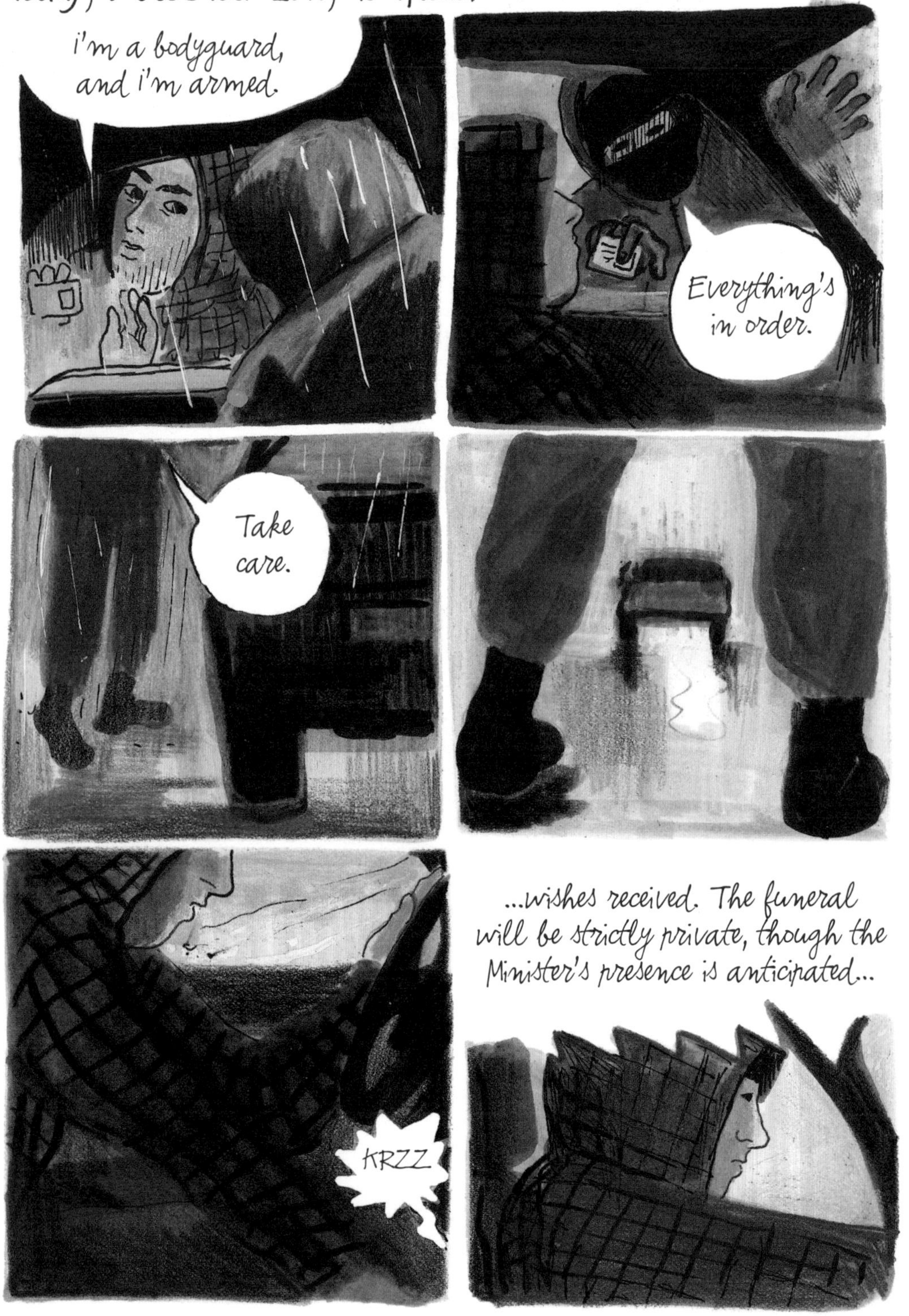
i'm a bodyguard, and i'm armed.
Everything's in order.
Take care.
KRZZ
...wishes received. The funeral will be strictly private, though the Minister's presence is anticipated...

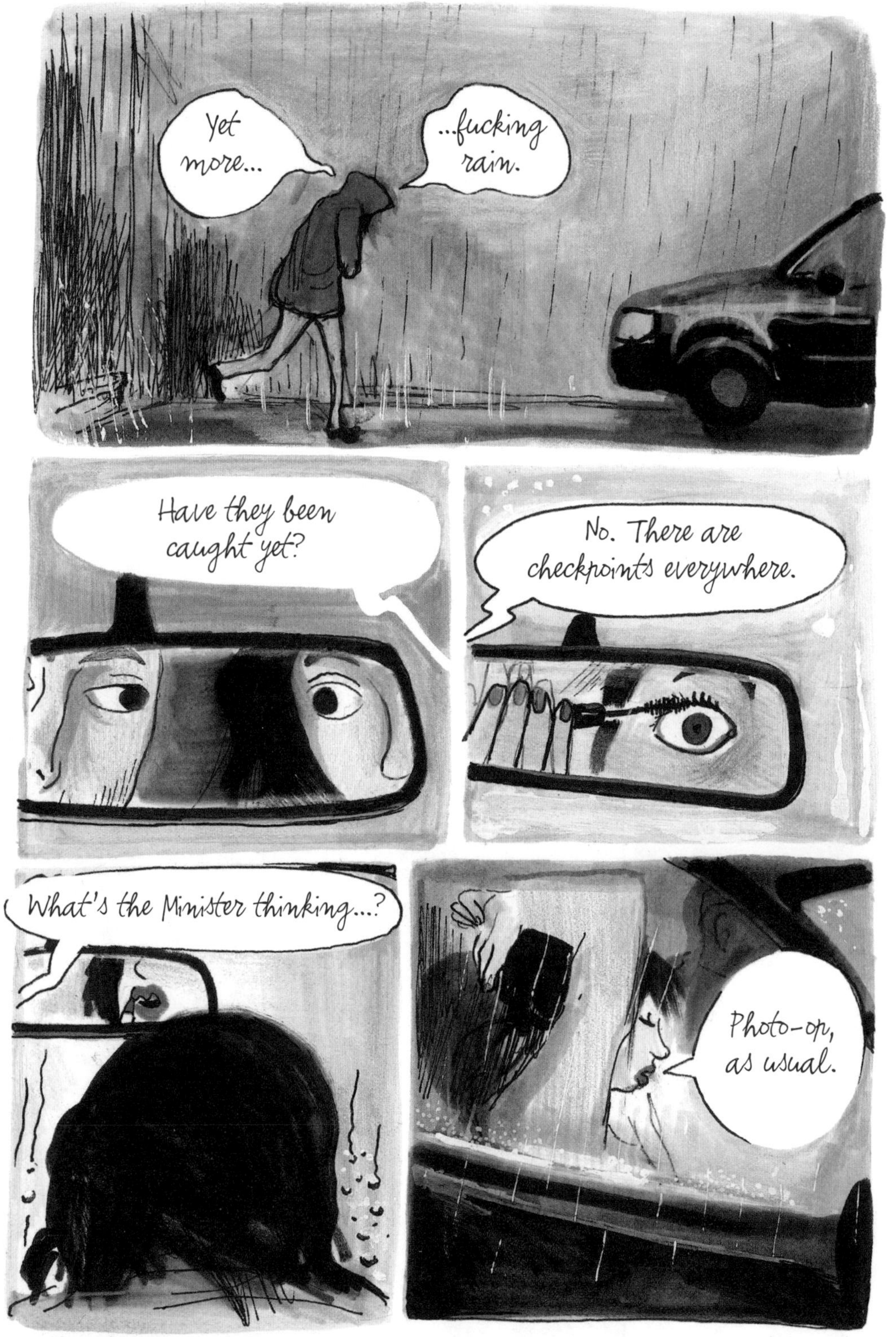
Yet more...
...fucking rain.
Have they been caught yet?
No. There are checkpoints everywhere.
What's the Minister thinking...?
Photo-op, as usual.

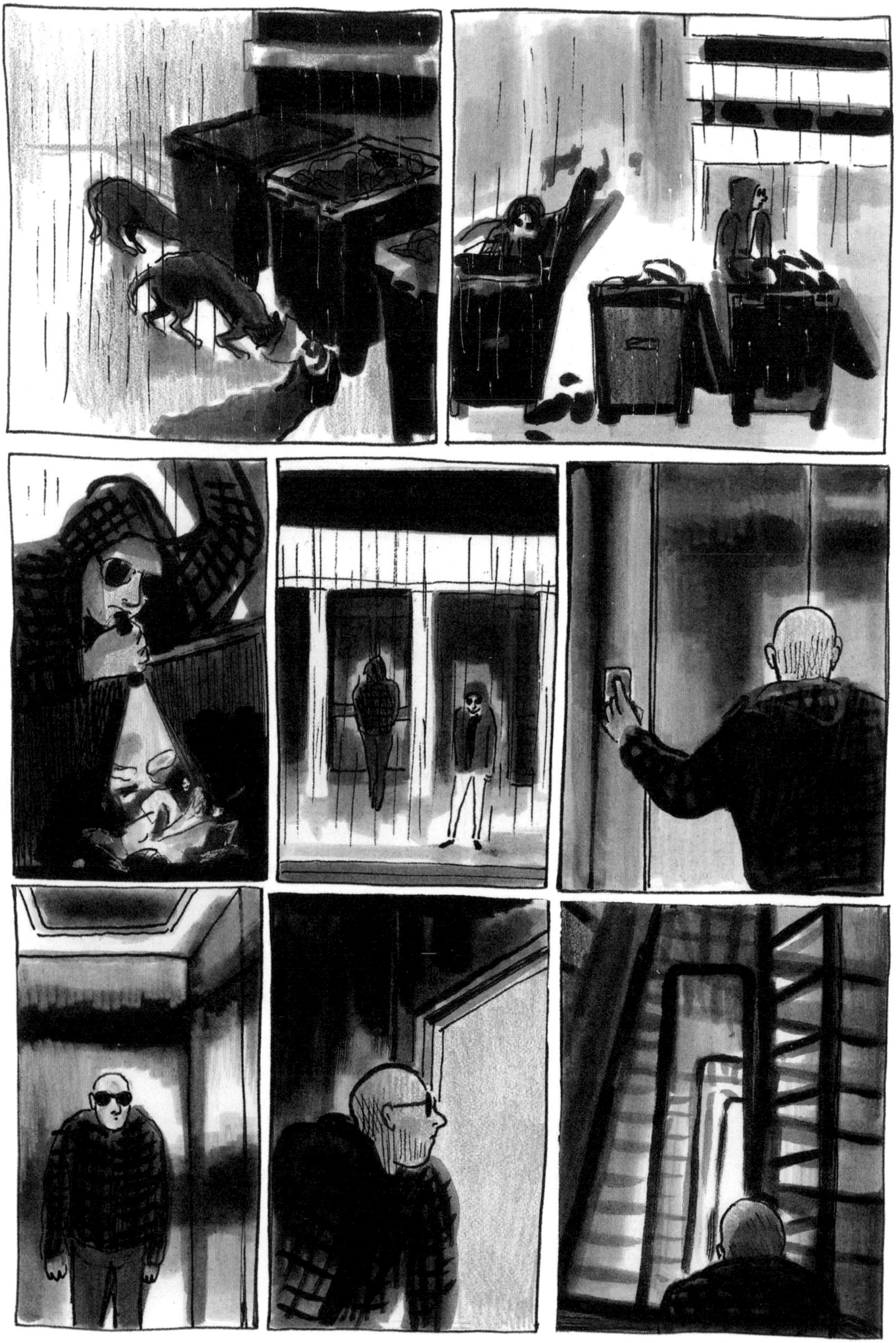

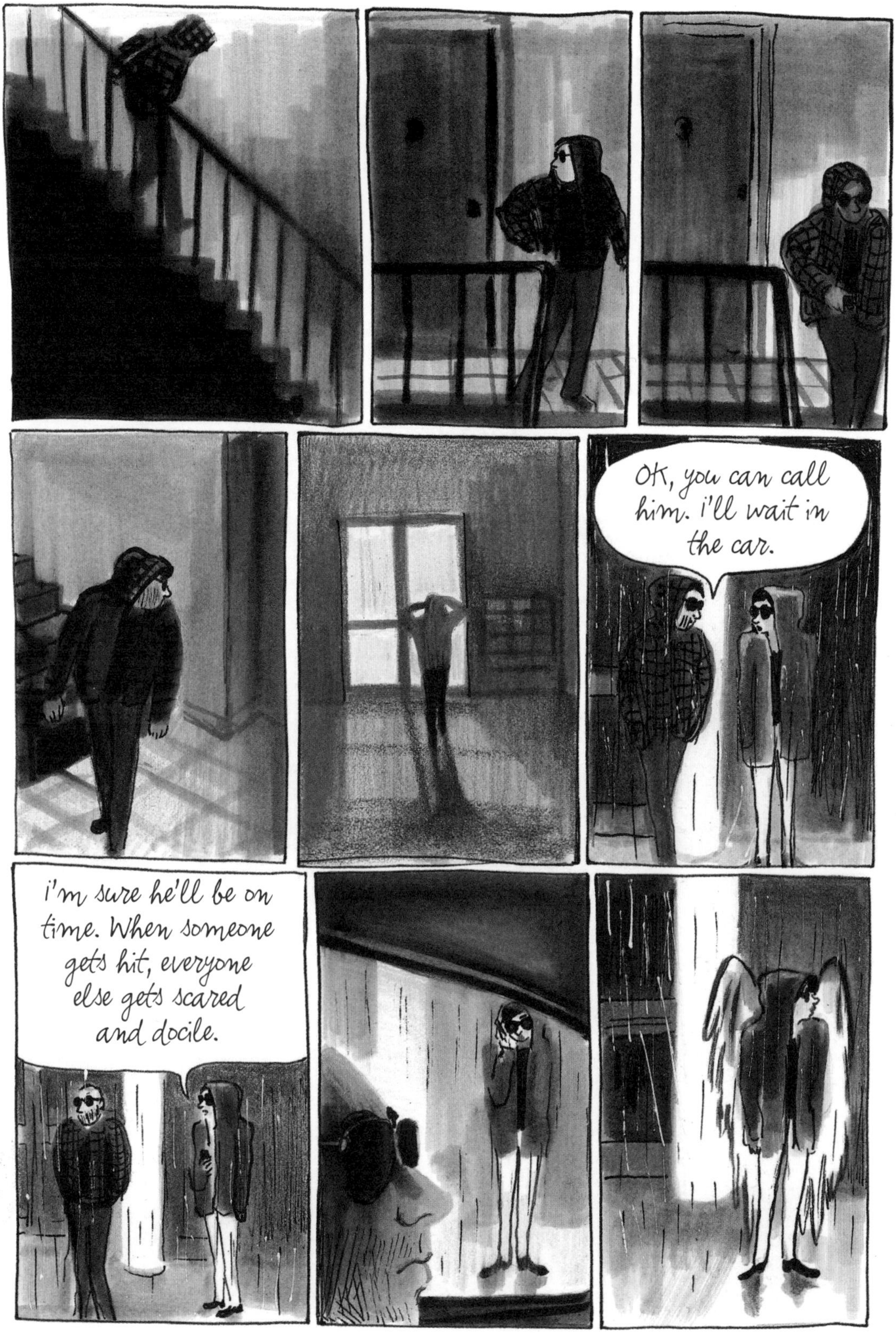
OK, you can call him. i'll wait in the car.
i'm sure he'll be on time. When someone gets hit, everyone else gets scared and docile.

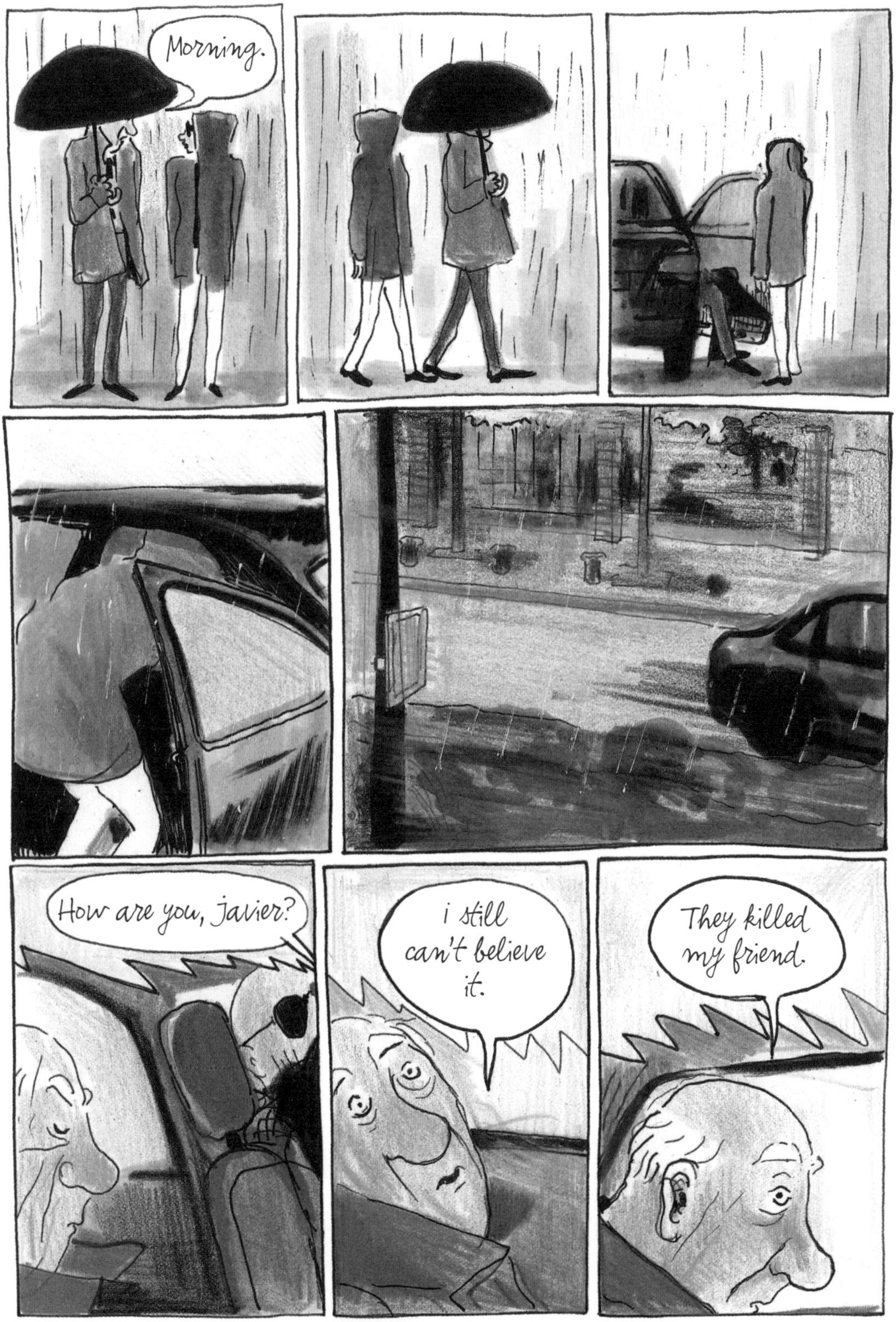
Morning.
How are you, Javier?
i still can't believe it.
They killed my friend.

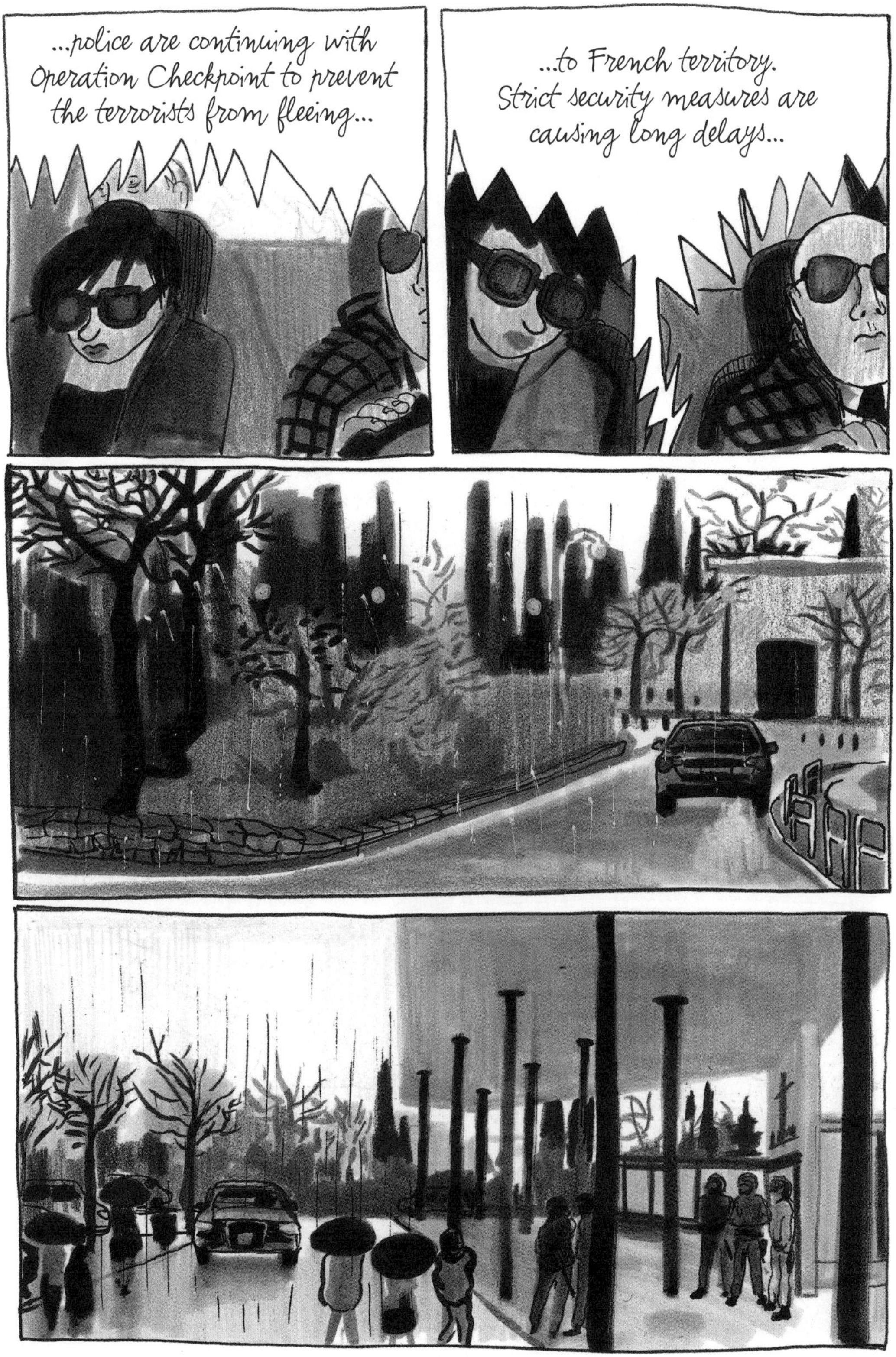
...police are continuing with Operation Checkpoint to prevent the terrorists from fleeing...
...to French territory. Strict security measures are causing long delays...

Today, Pamplona cemetery.

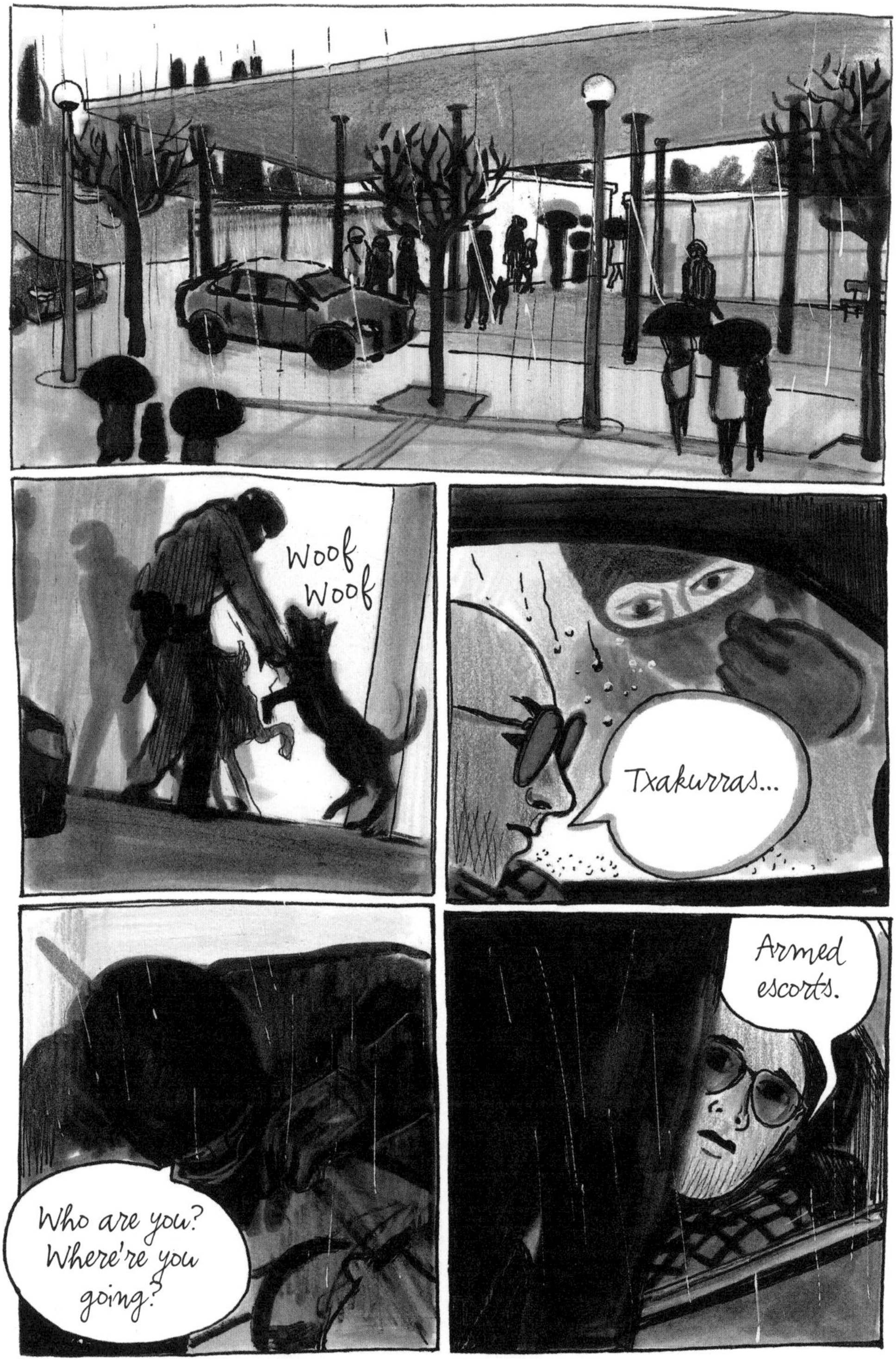
Woof Woof
Txakurras...
Who are you? Where're you going?
Armed escorts.

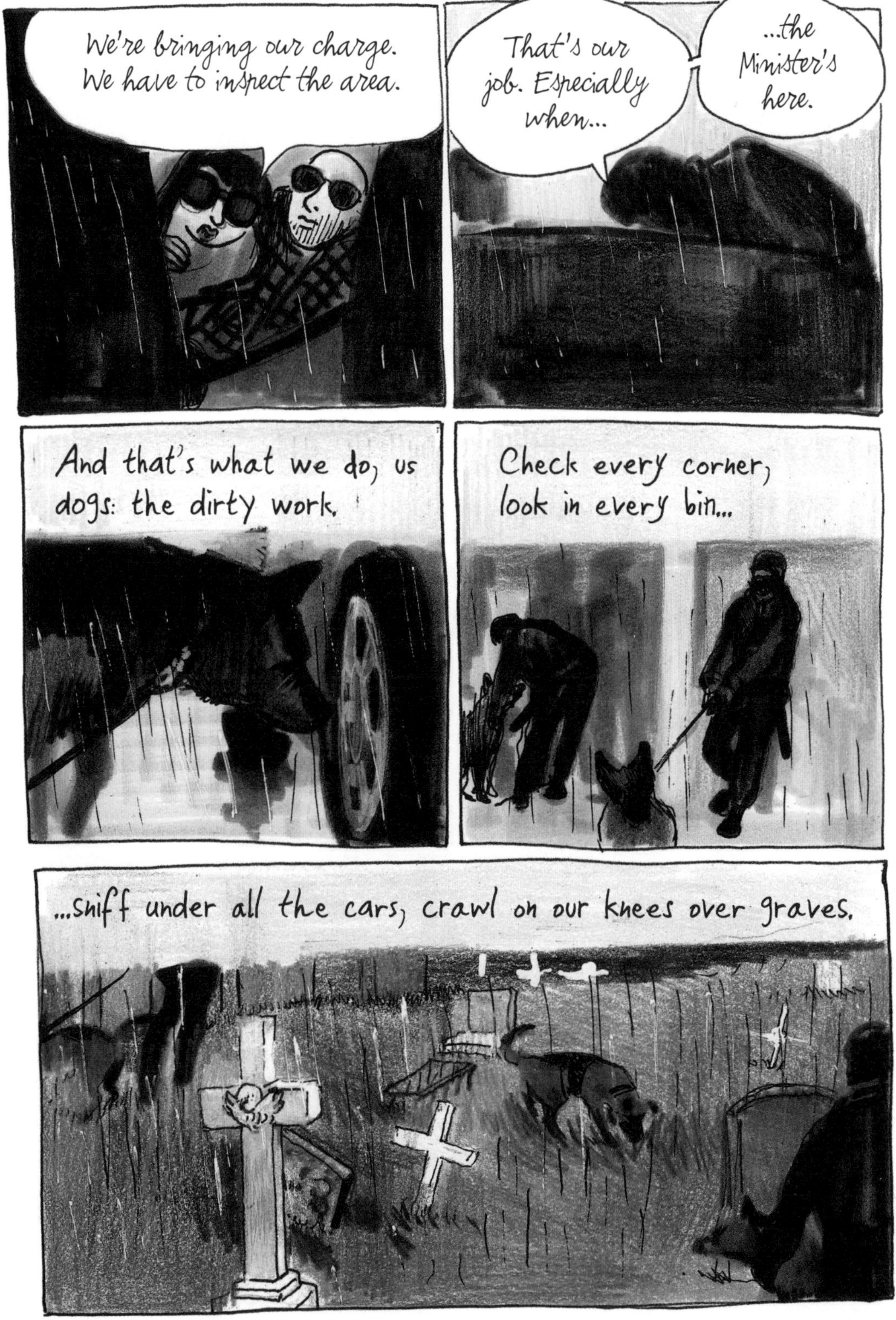
We're bringing our charge. We have to inspect the area.
That's our job. Especially when...
...the Minister's here.
And that's what we do, us dogs: the dirty work.
Check every corner, look in every bin...
...sniff under all the cars, crawl on our knees over graves.

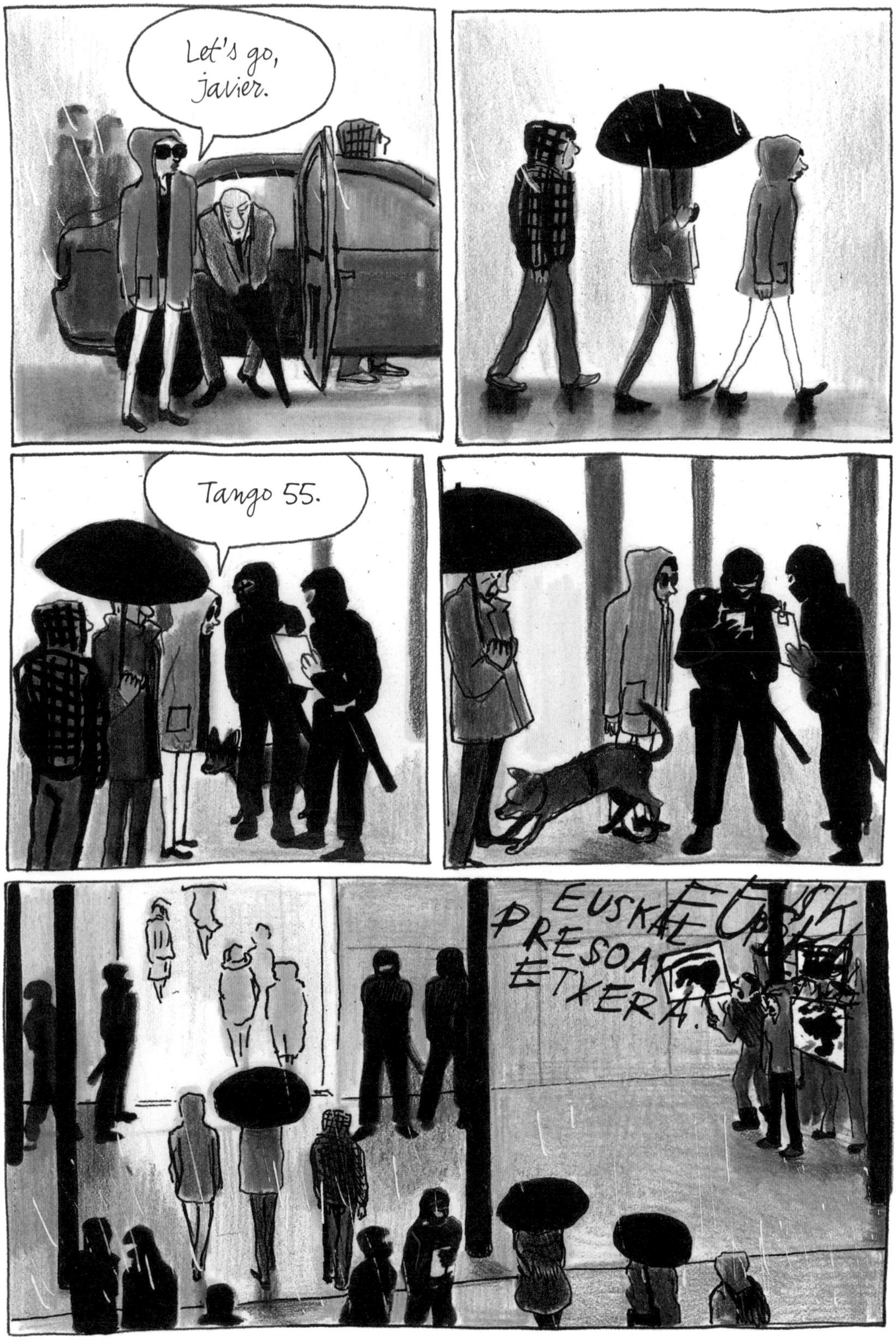
Let's go, Javier.
Tango 55.
EUSKAL
PRESOAK
ETXERA.

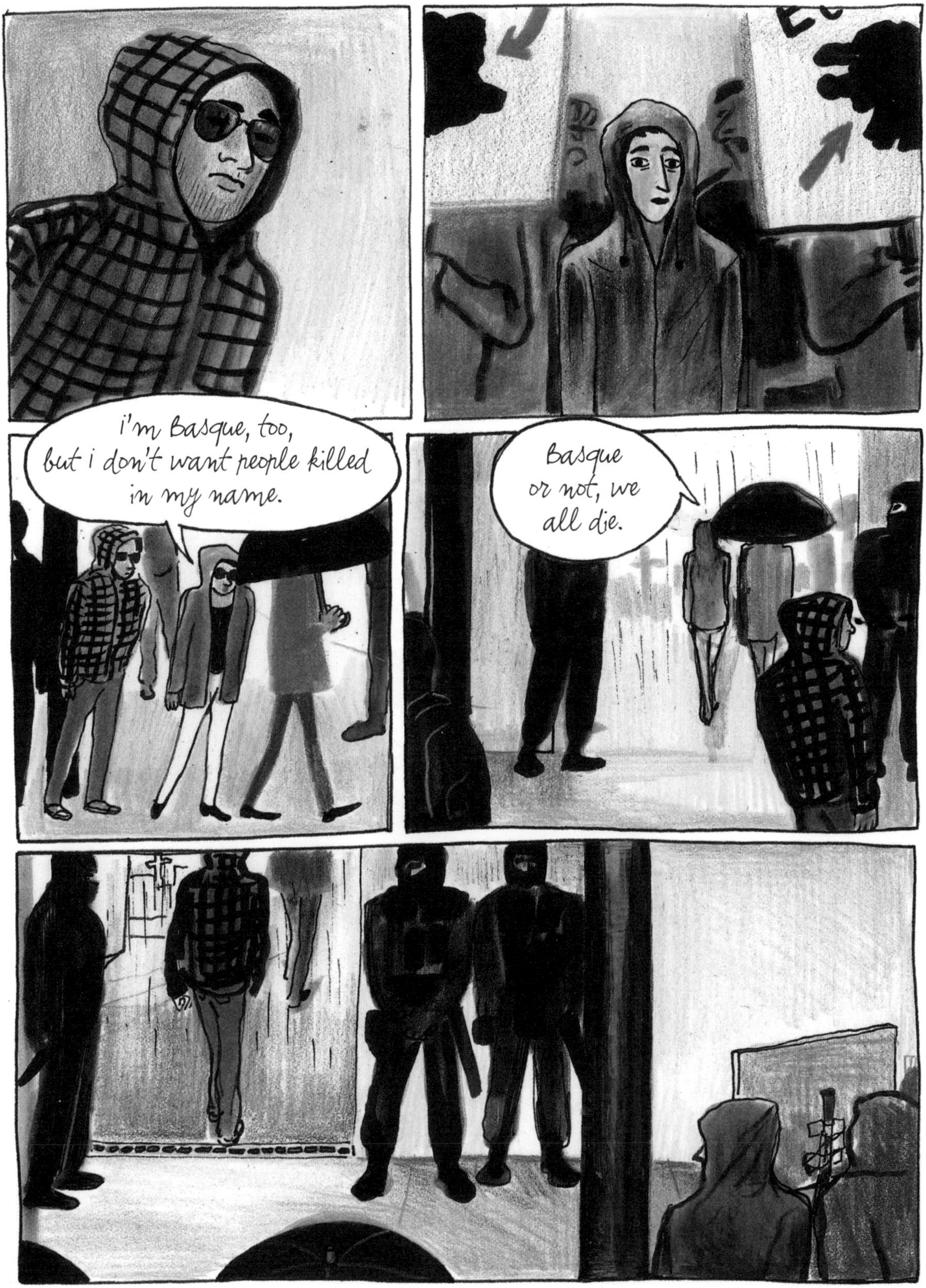
i'm Basque, too, but i don't want people killed in my name.
Basque or not, we all die.

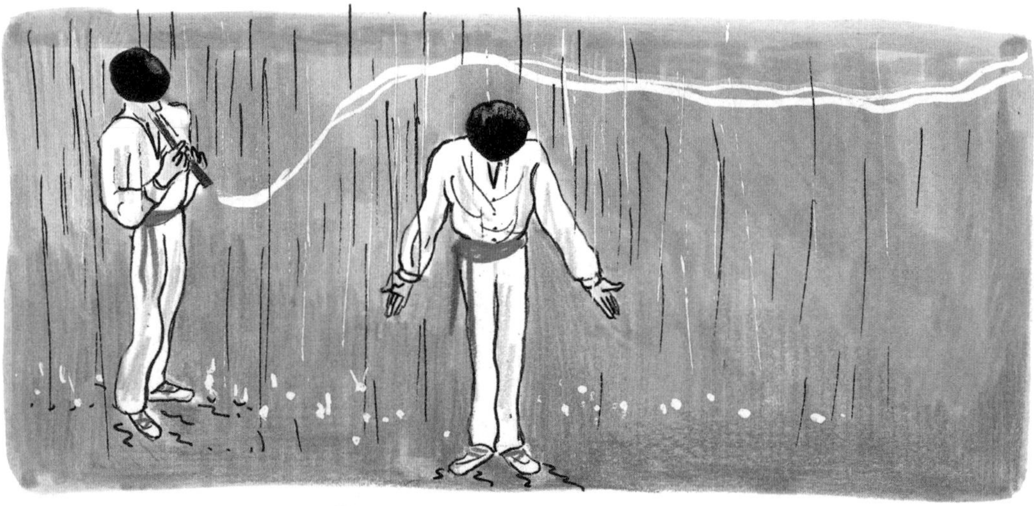

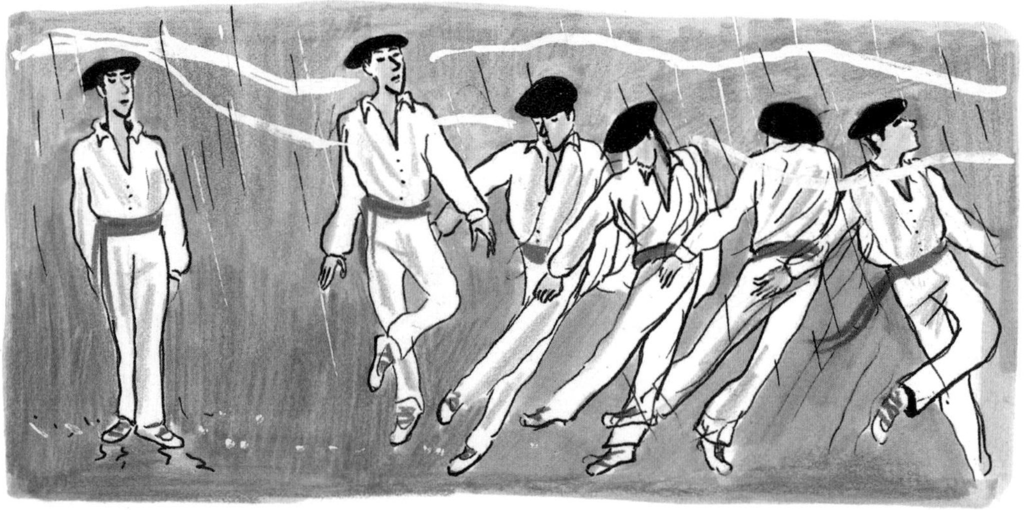

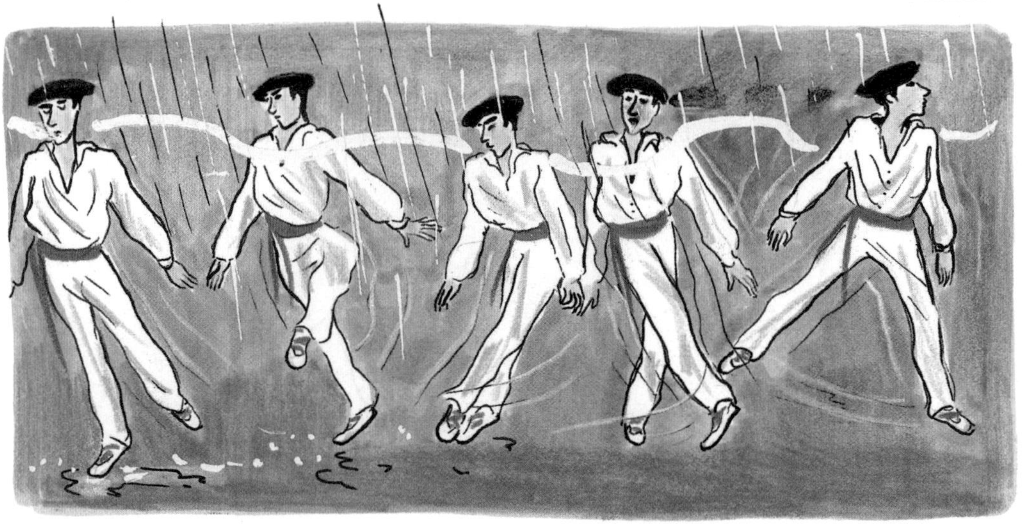

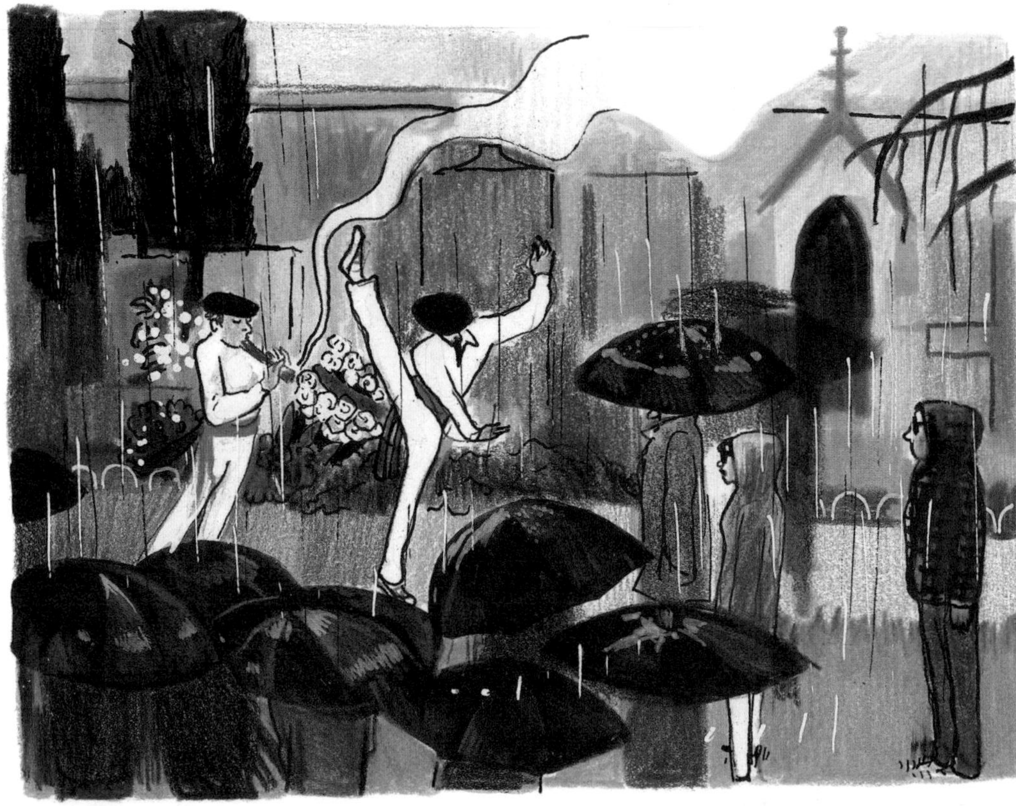

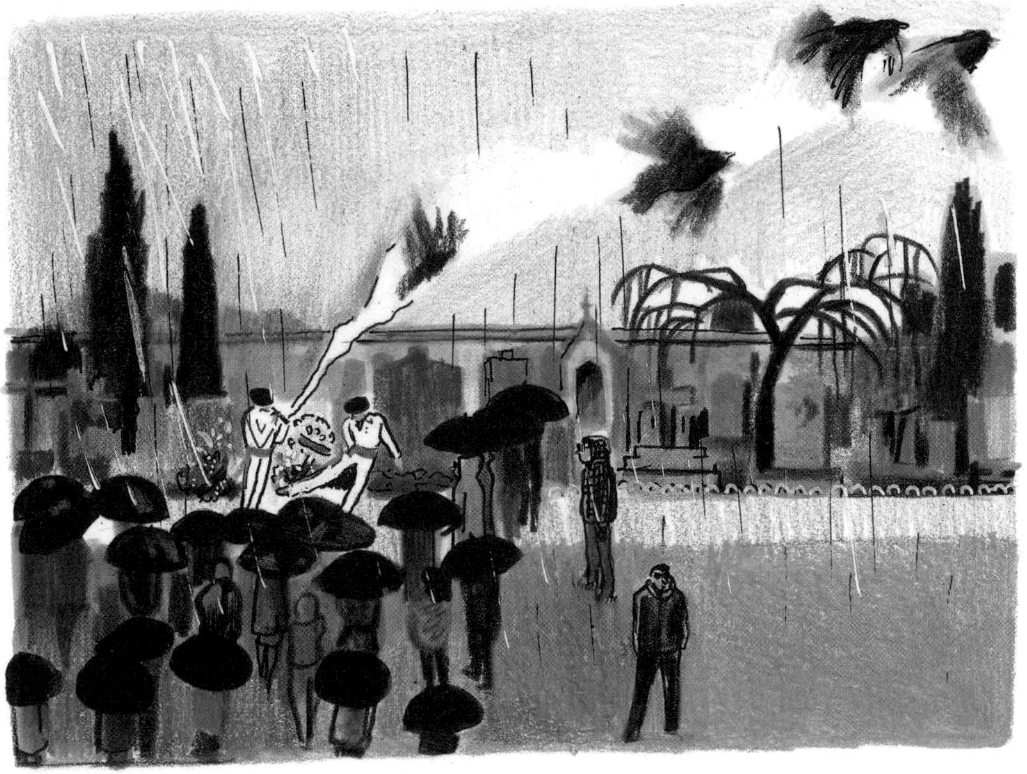

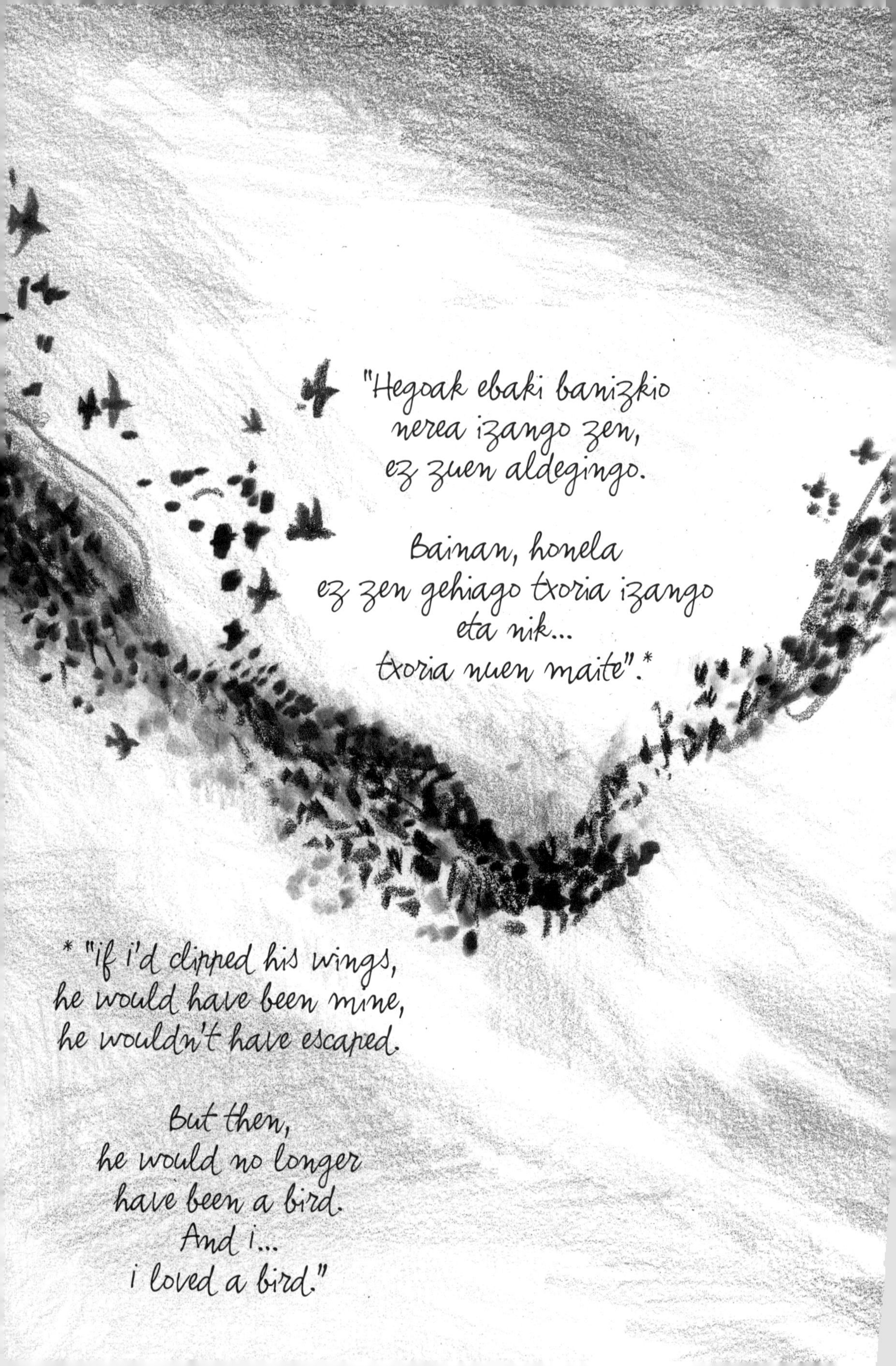
"Hegoak ebaki banizkio
nerea izango zen,
ez zuen aldegingo.
Bainan, honela
ez zen gehiago txoria izango
eta nik...
txoria nuen maite".*
* "if i'd clipped his wings,
he would have been mine,
he wouldn't have escaped.
But then,
he would no longer
have been a bird.
And i...
i loved a bird."

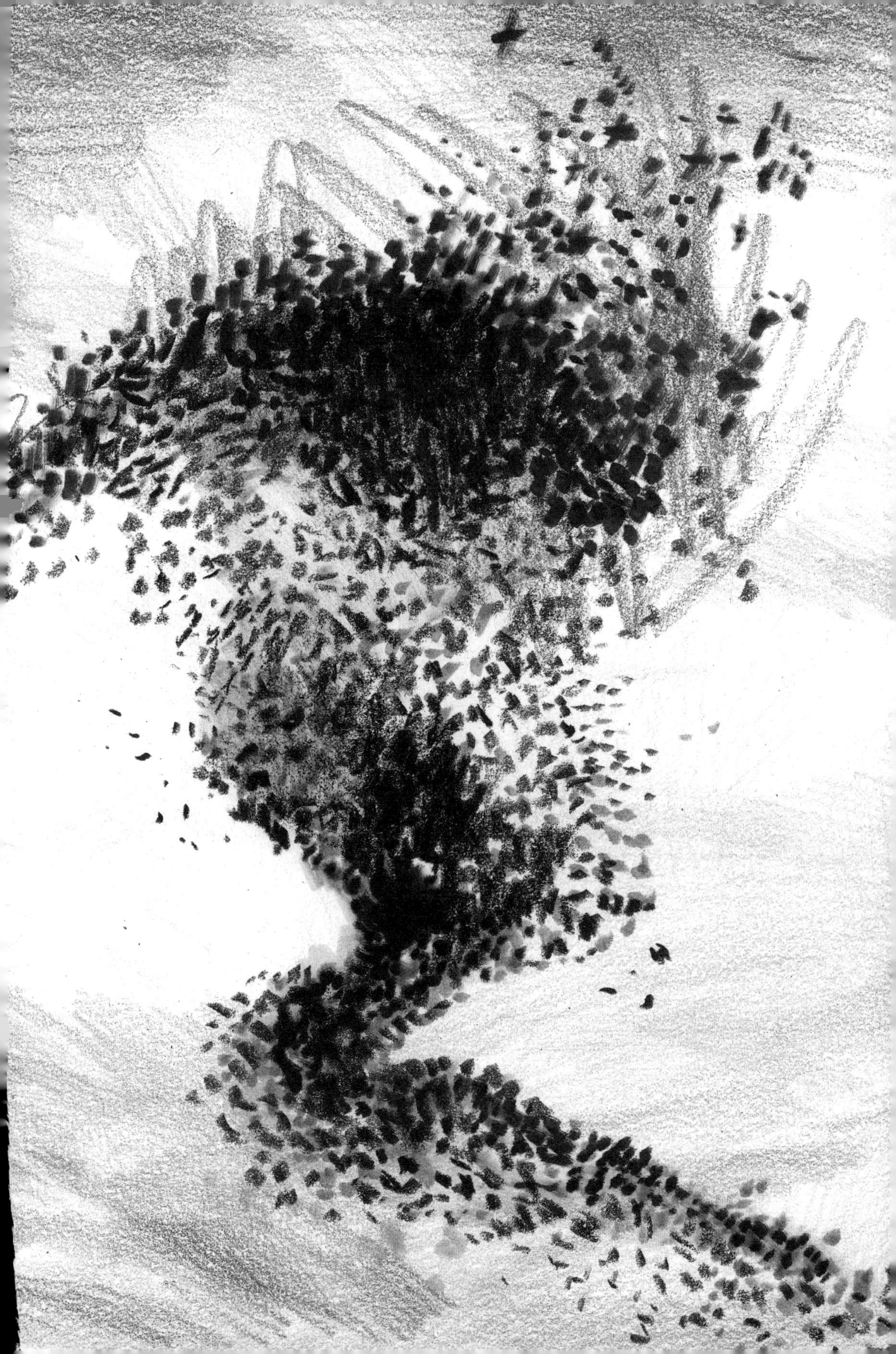

Jeremías was killed for loving a bird, for not allowing his wings to be clipped by two dogs. He was killed for wanting to live without fear.

Fear, like this drizzle, is always present, so fine that you forget it. Until it ends up soaking you, and like a sponge you breathe it in, you carry it inside... and it rots everything away.

The same terrorists who killed Jeremías sentenced me to death, but I'll be quicker. I'll shoot first.

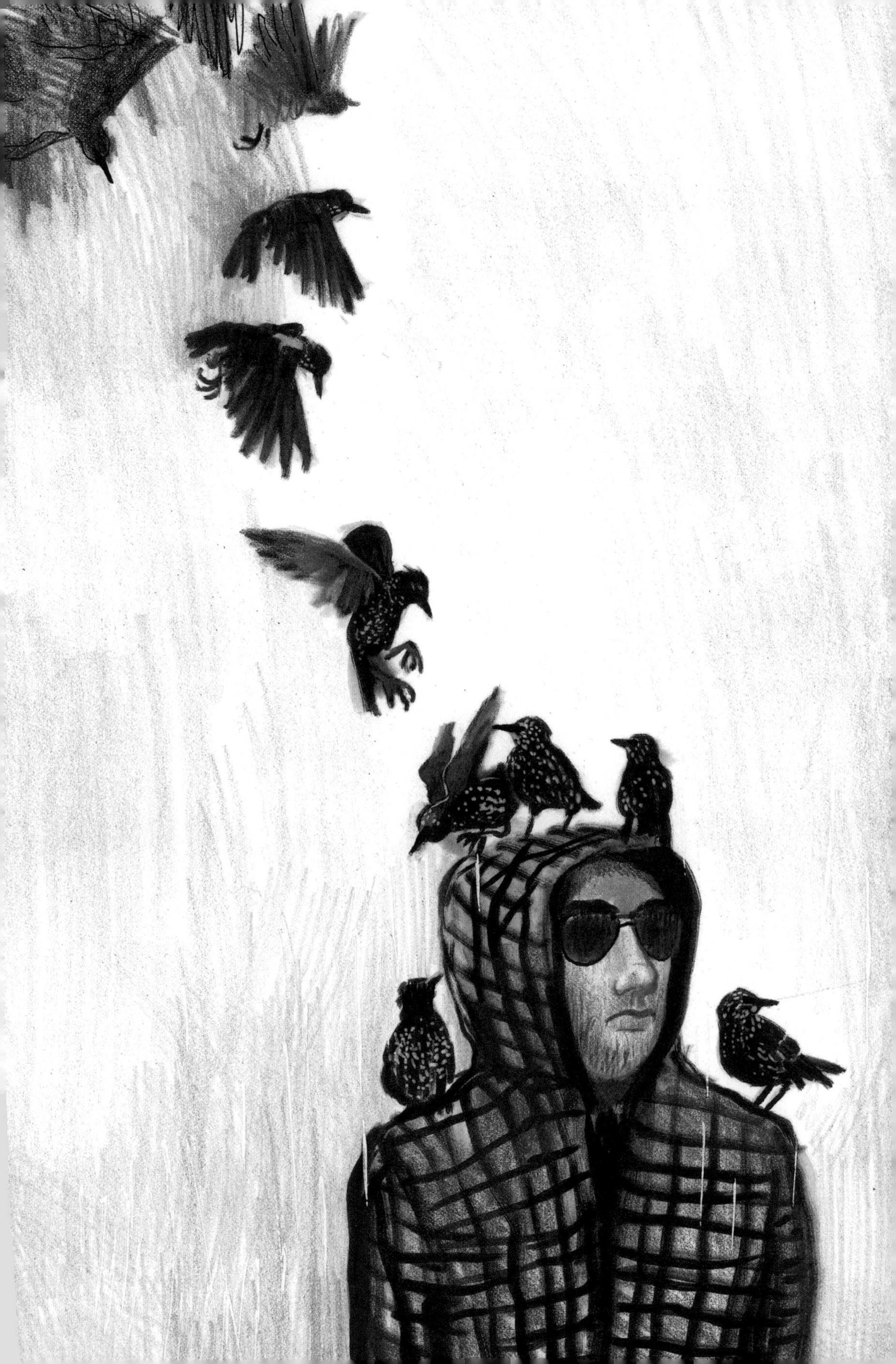

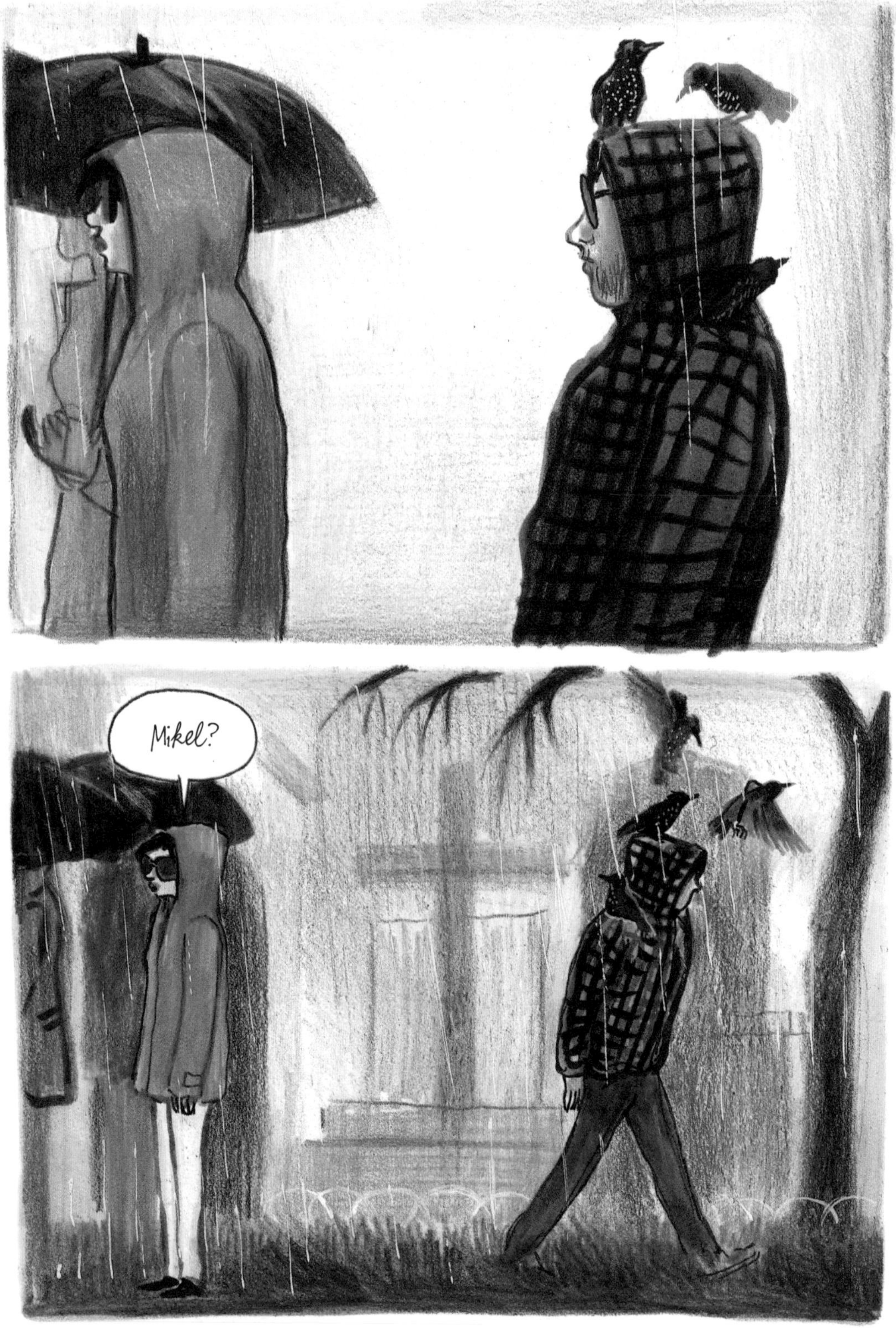
Mikel?

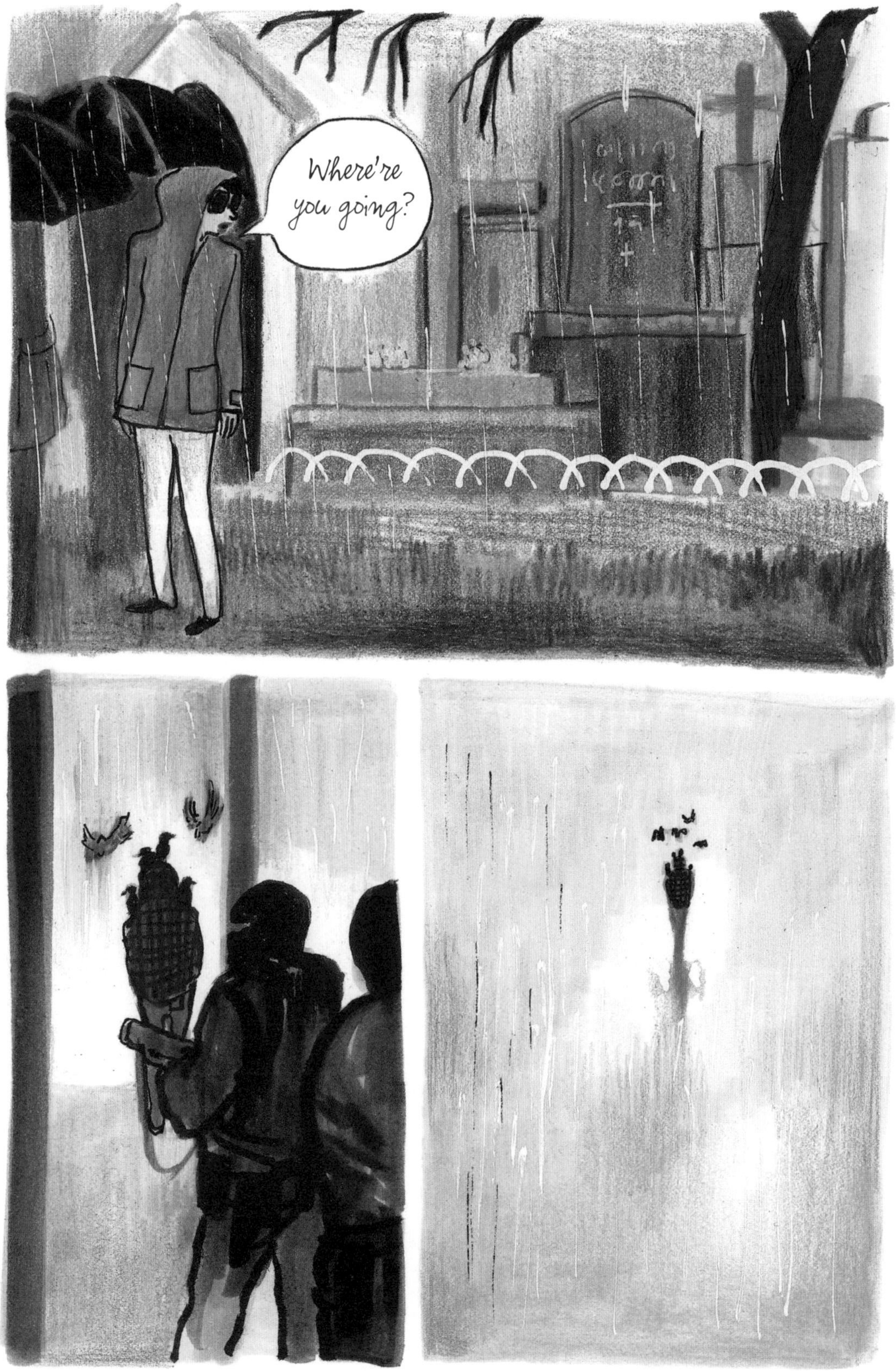
Where're you going?

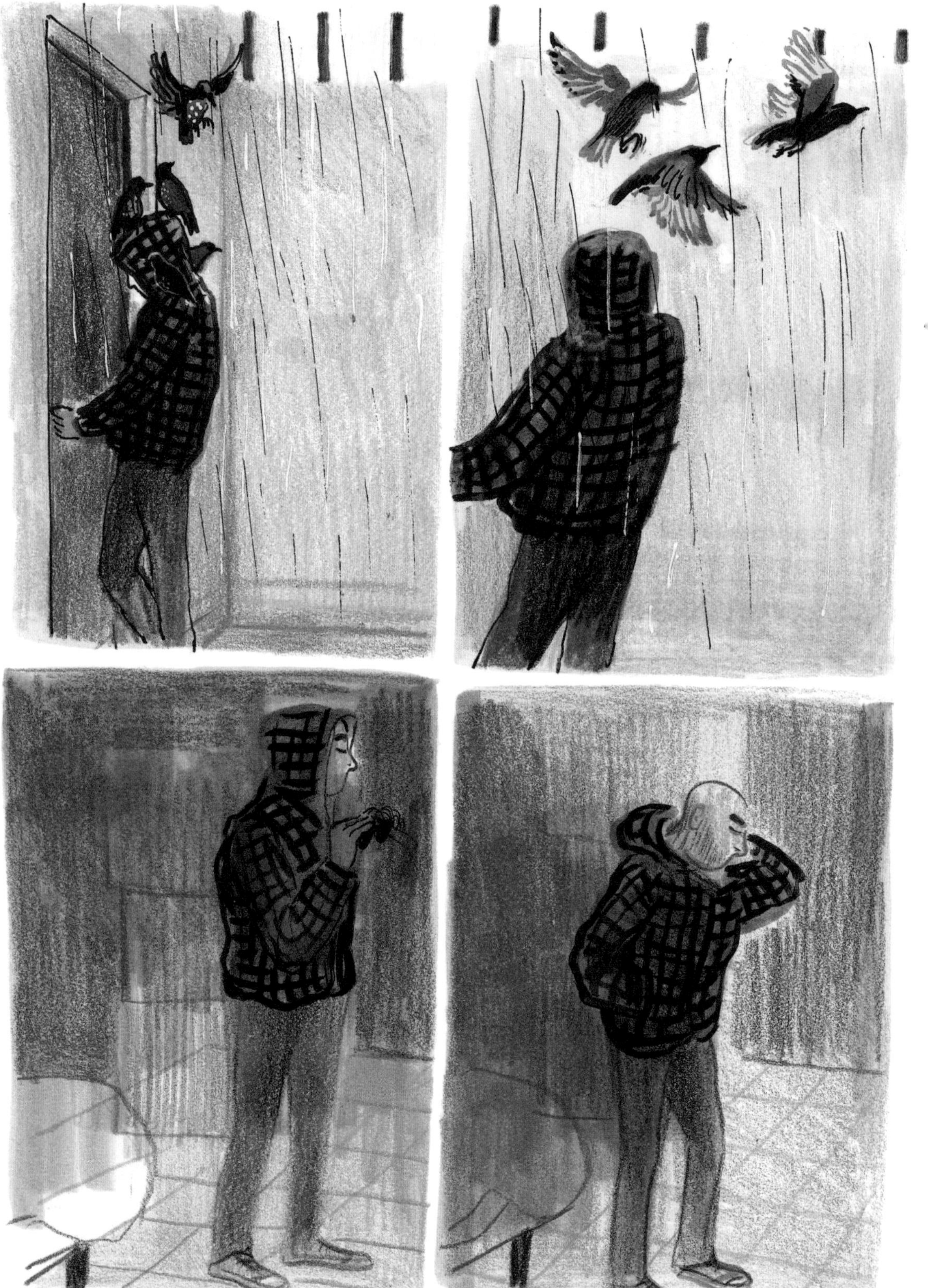

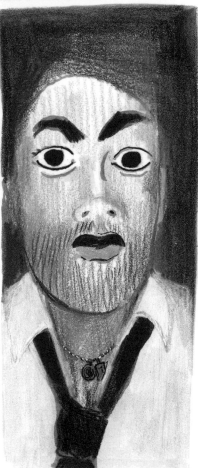

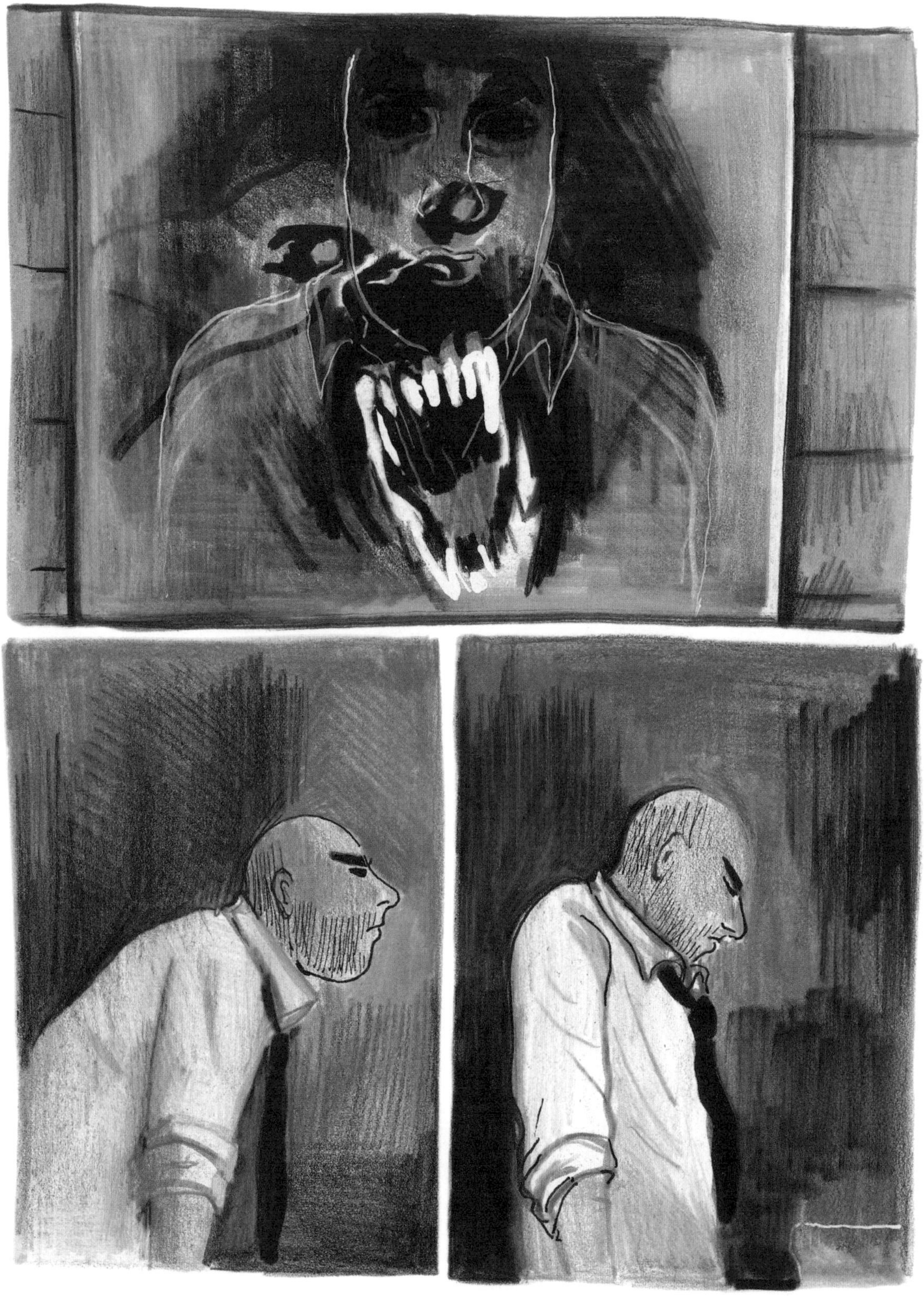

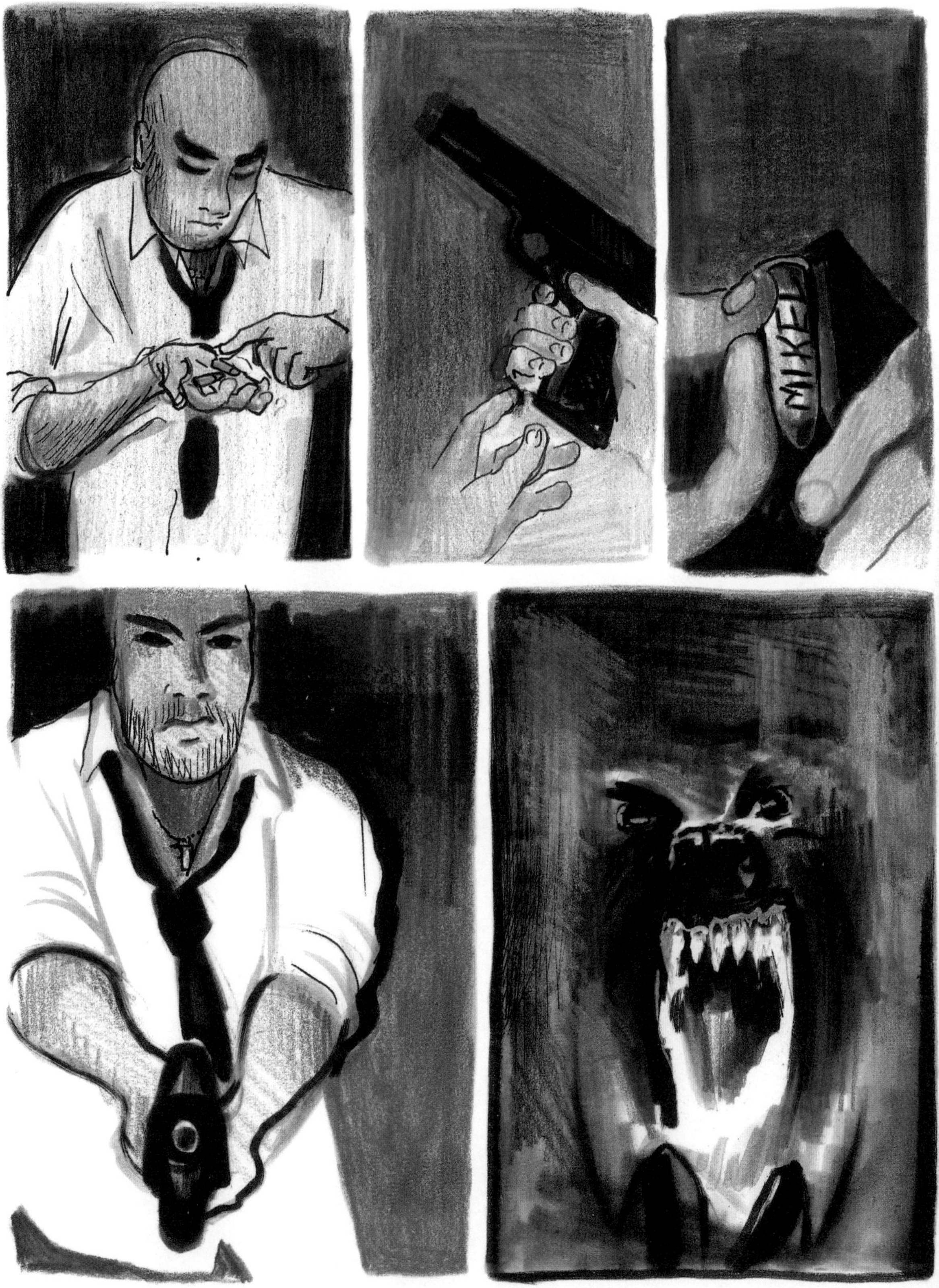
MIKEL

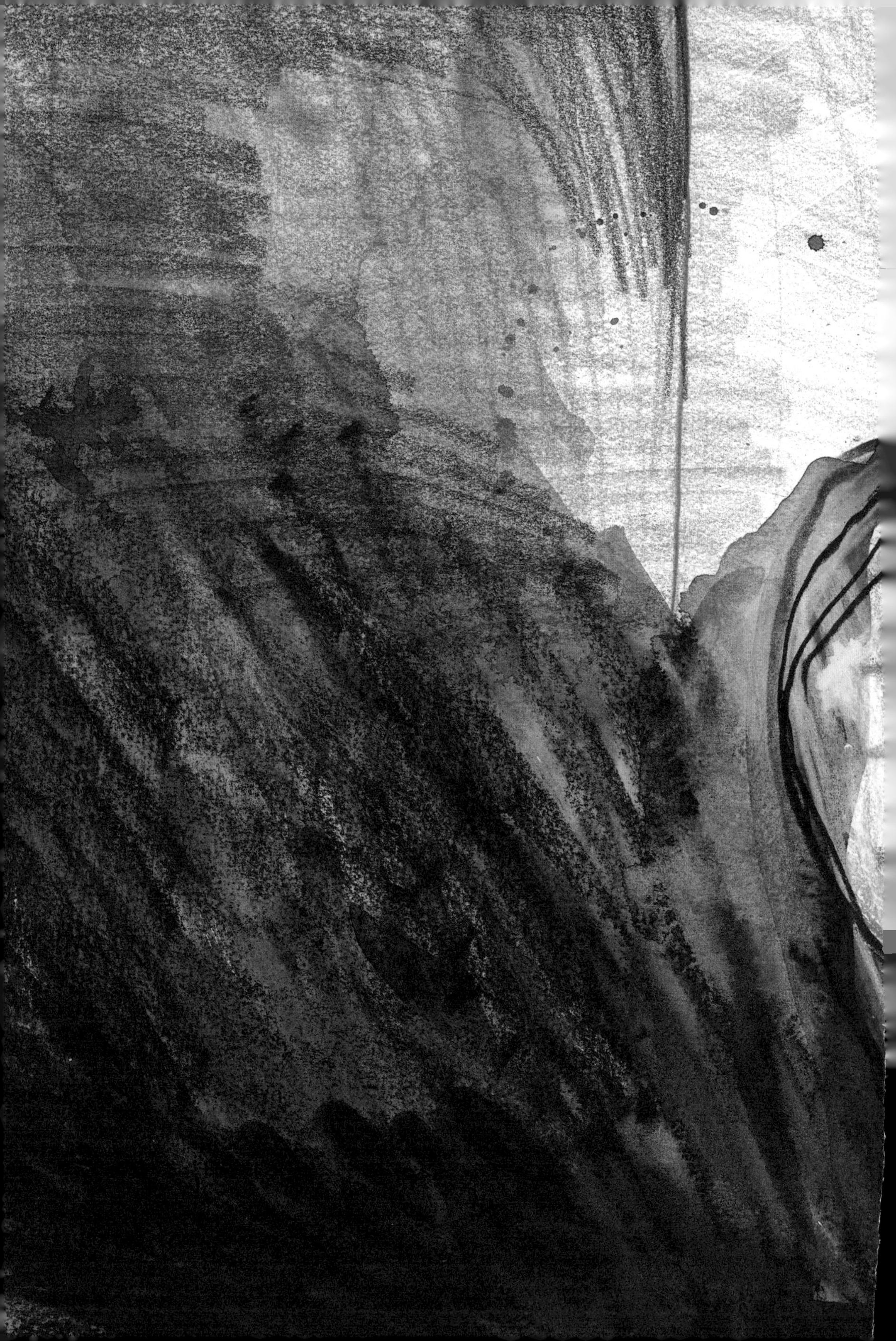

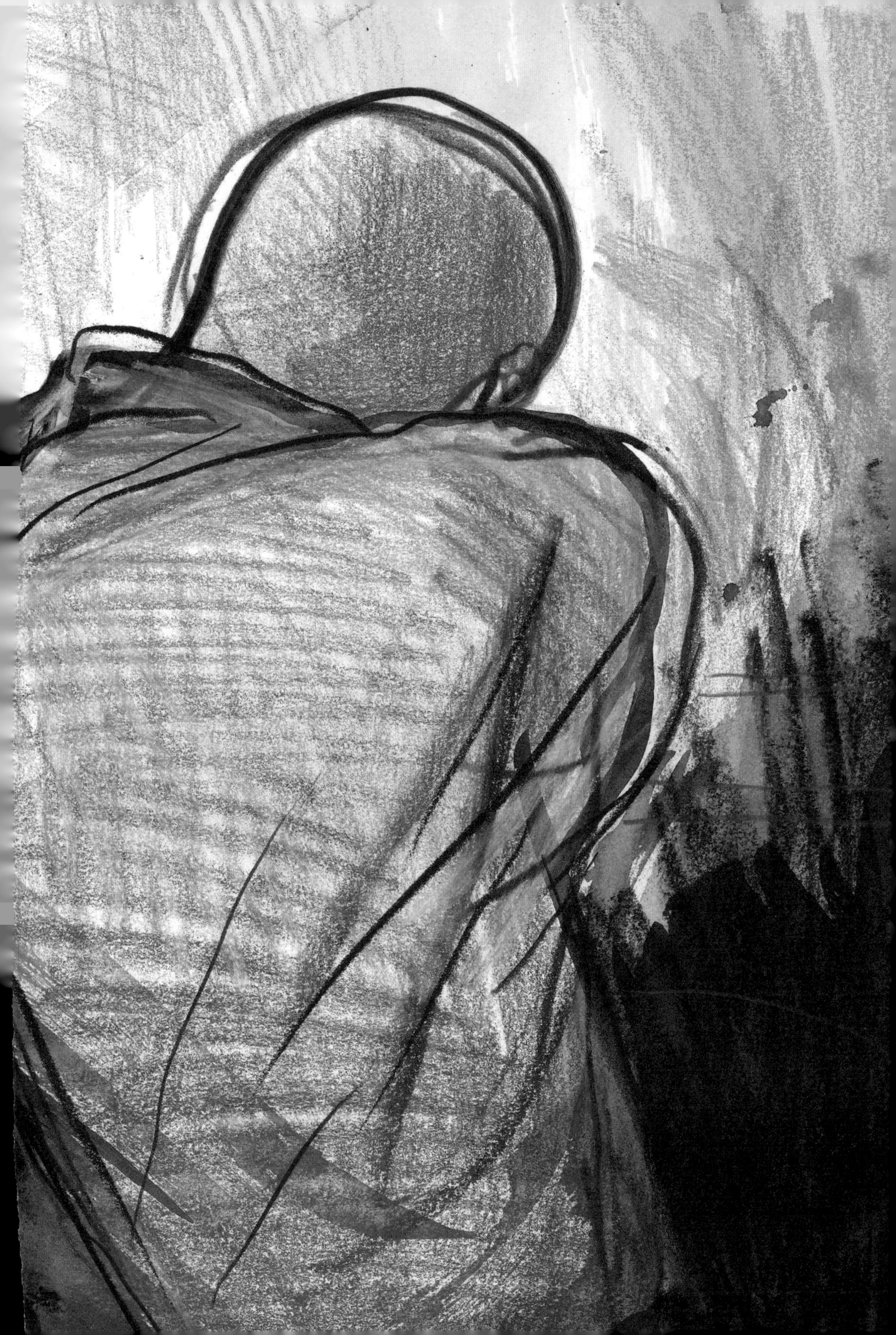

My name is Miguel,
and I'm a writer.

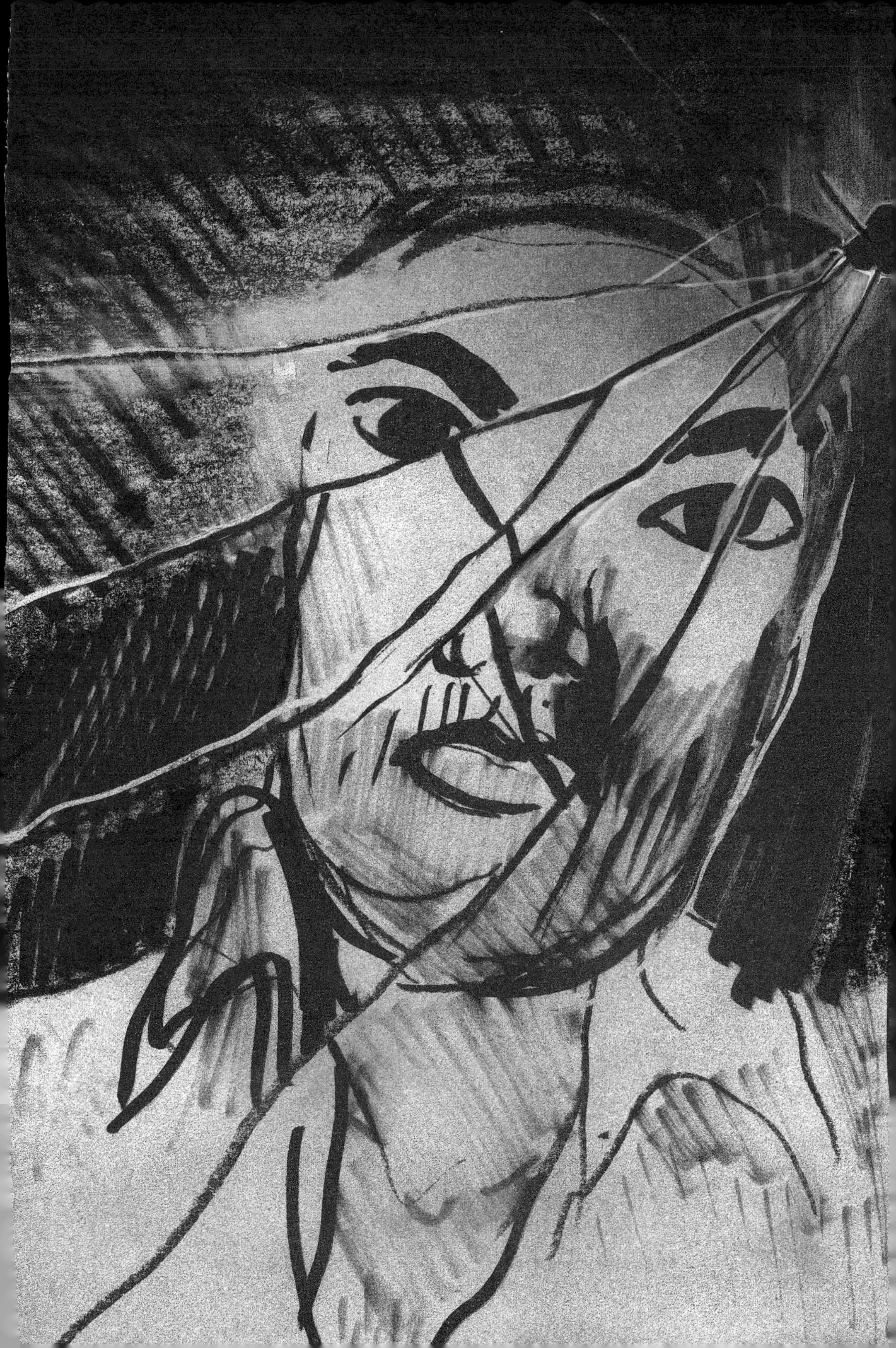

THE AUTHORS

# JUDITH VANISTENDAEL

Born in 1974, Judith Vanistendael is a Belgian comics author and illustrator. She studied at the Hochschule der Kunste in Berlin and at the University of Ghent, before focusing on Latin America as a postgraduate. She is also a graduate of the comic strip course at the Sint Lukas art school in Brussels. Her graphic novels include the Eisner Award-nominated When David Lost His Voice (SelfMadeHero, 2012) and the semi-autobiographical Dance by the Light of the Moon (SelfMadeHero, 2010), which was nominated twice for the prestigious Angoulême Grand Prize and has been translated into several languages. She lives in Brussels, Belgium.

# THANKS

it hasn't been easy making this book. i had to draw things i have no interest in: cars, guns, explosions and lots of sunglasses. And then there were all these pages, too many... and its six possible endings, all different. But here's the book. And i'd like to thank all the people without whom this long adventure would have been much less enjoyable...

Thanks to Frank, for standing by my side – with a smile, with small, thoughtful gifts, sometimes with a firm voice and a determined stance, but above all with a lot of love and tenderness.

Thanks to Hanna, for your wonderful and joyful ability to share a different perspective.

Thanks to Simon, for being so beautifully disarming.

And thanks to Gloria, for being so happy.

You are the suns without whom i wouldn't be creative.

To my parents, Chris, Geert and Lies, because you're steadfast and here for me with love and warmth. To my brother Kor, and Tjorven, and your newborn, Marie.

Peter and Axel: my dear friends, thank you for making room for me, for the laughs we share, for your generosity, for your eyes cast over my shoulder, for pastéis de nata... You are one of the most beautiful friendships i've had in recent years.

Eva, Barbara, Sara, Christine, Fran, Katrien, Ann, Laure, Tina, Nathalie and Nathalie, Elise, Bjoke, jeroen and Stephan and Bart, Lidia, Nando, Alex, Marcos, Armin, Ruth, Miriam, Eliora, Hélène...
You are my pillars.

Mara, i especially thank you because you are very dear to me.

Eva and inge: you, too!
How could it be otherwise?

Greg, my physiotherapist, who came to the rescue of my shoulders, strained from tireless drawing.

The dream pages were made using a risograph, in collaboration with Axel Claes. i will be eternally grateful to him for having opened new paths to me, and for teaching me to work differently, with blocks and stains.

judith

# MARK BELLIDO

Mark Bellido was born in Seville in the spring of 1975, during the agony of Franco's dictatorship. He studied fine arts, followed by nursing, psychology, oceanography and industrial design. He also has a master's degree in security and investigation. Some will know him as a war photojournalist; for the Spanish authorities, he is a political activist; but in reality, he is just a teller of lies, using images and words. In search of stories, and armed with a camera, he has been through wars and a few nights in prison. His past work includes Venus Vestida de Azul (Opera Prima, 1998) and El Mesías (Blloan, 2015). For four years, he protected Basque politicians threatened by ETA. He lives everything he writes. His name is Mark Bellido, but that is also a lie...

# THANKS


That I managed to finish this book is due to a lot of people. Thank you to all those who have given their time and talents in the creation of this work.

"Eskerrik Asko, Henskal Herria", because even though it's said that she never existed, from now on she lives inside me.

Thanks to Beatriz for being such a welcoming mother earth.

Thanks to Judith for looking in my direction.

Thanks to Wauter for opening doors.

Thanks to Mara Joustra for her blind faith.

Thanks to Lucia Montes, for reminding me who I want to be.

And thank you very much to Brussels, this bastard city, for taking in the mongrel dog that I am.

Mark


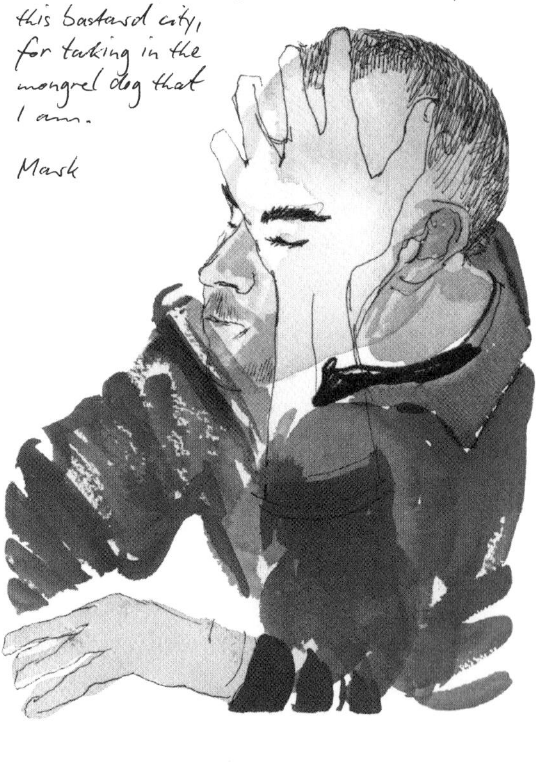